Great Britain. India Office

East India, Chinchona Plant

SALZWASSER
VERLAG

Great Britain. India Office

East India, Chinchona Plant

Reprint of the original, first published in 1863.

1st Edition 2022 | ISBN: 978-3-37500-651-8

Verlag (Publisher): Salzwasser Verlag GmbH, Zeilweg 44, 60439 Frankfurt, Deutschland
Vertretungsberechtigt (Authorized to represent): E. Roepke, Zeilweg 44, 60439 Frankfurt, Deutschland
Druck (Print): Books on Demand GmbH, In de Tarpen 42, 22848 Norderstedt, Deutschland

EAST INDIA (CHINCHONA PLANT).

RETURN to an Address of the Honourable The House of Commons, dated 9 March 1863;—*for*,

" COPY of CORRESPONDENCE relating to the Introduction of the CHINCHONA PLANT into *India*, and to Proceedings connected with its Cultivation, from March 1852 to March 1863."

India Office, 18 March 1863.

E. D. BOURDILLON,
Secretary, Public Department.

Ordered, by The House of Commons, *to be Printed*,
20 *March* 1863.

CONTENTS.

COPY of CORRESPONDENCE relating to the Introduction of the CHINCHONA PLANT into *India*, and to Proceedings connected with its Cultivation, from March 1852 to March 1863.

— No. 1. —

From the Governor General of India to the Court of Directors of the East India Company.

Honourable Sirs, Fort William, 27 March 1852.

WE have the honour to submit the accompanying letter from the Government of Bengal, with its enclosures, and to recommend for the early consideration of your honourable Court the proposal therein made for deputing a qualified gardening collector from England to South America, to procure an ample supply of seeds and young plants of the best species of the quinine-yielding cinchonas, with a view to their introduction into India.

We have, &c.
(signed) *Dalhousie.*
F. Currie.
J. Lowe.

— No. 2. —

MINUTE recorded at a Revenue, Judicial, and Legislative Committee of the Directors of the East India Company, 16 June 1852.

THE Committee having had before them a letter from the Government of India in the Public Department, dated the 27th March (No. 18) 1852, with its enclosures, recommending compliance with the proposal of the Governor of Bengal for deputing a gardening collector from England to South America for the purpose of procuring a supply of seeds and plants of the best specimens of the quinine-yielding cinchonas, with a view to their introduction into India, —Ordered, that the above papers be referred for the consideration of Dr. Royle, with a request that he will furnish this Committee with his sentiments as to the measure therein recommended, together with his opinion as to the probable expense of carrying it into execution.

— No. 3. —

REPORT on the Introduction into *India* of the Quinine-yielding Cinchonas, or Peruvian Bark Trees, by Dr. *Royle*.

India House, 27 June 1852.

AMONG the vast variety of medicinal drugs produced in various parts of the world, there is not one, with probably the single exception of opium, which is more valuable to man than the quinine-yielding cinchonas. The great value of Peruvian bark as a medicinal agent was universally acknowledged very shortly after it became first known in Europe. Its utility and employment have been greatly increased ever since its active principle has been separated in the form of quinine. So great indeed has the consumption increased, and so little care has been bestowed upon the preservation of the natural forests, that great fears have been entertained that the supply might altogether cease, or be obtainable only at a price which would place it beyond the reach of the mass of the community.

The Bolivian Government seem of late to have become more sensible of the value of their bark, but the measures adopted seem directed rather to the enhancement of its price than to the continued preservation of its supply. For a national bank of bark has been established since January 1850, "with sufficient funds to give regularity to the bark trade," "purchasing it in the interior of the country at a fixed price," and "selling it abroad at the value due to an article of exclusive production in the woods of Bolivia, and of the first necessity and great demand in the trade of the world." "The free export of bark," it is stated, "would be fatal to our commerce," as "bringing down the price." "Consequently the bank maintains the monopoly, and with it the high value and price of bark."

Such measures, if unaccompanied by any attempts to preserve the forests, will certainly enhance the price to all, without any assurance of an increased supply being obtainable for the continually increasing demand. The bark collectors, who are usually employed by contractors, search out for new localities as the old ones become exhausted; cut down the trees and remove the bark, but take no care of planting or sowing seeds for future supplies, and the cinchona forests, like the teak forests of India, have become exhausted in many places, and will be so unless timely measures are adopted.

The introduction into other countries having suitable localities and climate for so valuable a tribe of plants, could not fail to be of advantage to such countries, not only for home consumption, but also for export commerce. To the Indian Government a home supply of a drug which already costs about 7,000 *l.* a year, would be advantageous in an economical point of view, and invaluable as affording increased means of employing a drug which is indispensable in the treatment of Indian fevers, and a deficient supply of which, in consequence of the probably much increased expenditure, is so much apprehended by the Medical Board of Bengal as to form "a real and cogent reason for regulating, by all justifiable means, the expenditure of this valuable drug, and this irrespective of the high price of the article."

The probability of entire success in the cultivation of the cinchona trees in India seems to admit of hardly any doubt, if ordinary care is adopted in the selection of suitable localities. I myself recommended this measure many years ago, when treating of the family of plants to which the cinchonas belong. I inferred from a comparison of soil and climate with the geographical distribution of cinchonaceous plants, that the quinine-yielding cinchonas might be cultivated on the slopes of the Neilgherries, and of the Southern Himalayas, in the same way that I had inferred that Chinese tea plants might be cultivated in the Northern Himalayas. It is to the above opinion that Dr. Falconer alludes, and with which he coincides.

The probability of success being great, and the introduction of the quinine-yielding cinchonas having been strongly recommended by the several authorities in Bengal, I have no hesitation in stating that after the Chinese teas, no more important plants could be introduced into India. The measures to be adopted for this purpose would, however, require great care and consideration. For though cinchona, or, as it is commonly called, Peruvian bark, has been so long esteemed as a medicine, the plant yielding the most valuable kind of yellow bark has only been discovered within the last two or three years. This in consequence of the investigations of Mr. Weddell, an English surgeon, who accompanied the French scientific expedition of M. de Castelnau into the interior of Brazil and Peru. From him we have the most accurate information respecting the extent and localities, the destruction and gradual disappearance of the nearer forests, as well as his opinion that the most valuable kind of cinchona will probably altogether disappear as an article of commerce.

Useful and quinine-yielding cinchonas are, however, found in the neighbourhood of Santa Fe de Bagota. The pale barks in forests near Loxa, the most valuable, or yellow bark tree (*Cinchona Calisaya*) in the interior of Bolivia, about the latitude of La Paz; and the red bark from near Lima, or from 11 degrees of north, to about 20 degrees of south latitude, is the extent of distribution of these valuable plants along the Andes; but the useful species do not

not extend much to the eastward. The operations of a collector would therefore require to be turned chiefly to the western coast of South America, from whence he could make incursions into the interior to collect seeds or plants, and convey them to the coast for shipment to Europe or India.

It is evident that such measures could not be adopted, without exciting considerable attention, and I believe jealousy, if we consider the late proceedings of the Bolivian Government. But an agent who had some other objects in view, might safely carry on his operations along the whole coast, and have his time fully occupied. I am happy to be able to suggest a measure which will, I have every confidence, be effective, at the same time that it is economical.

The Horticultural Society of London have for some time had it under consideration to send a gardening collector to the west coast of South America for the purpose of visiting the mountain ranges which run along the coast, and collecting such seeds and plants as are likely to be of value in this country. It was only at the last meeting of the council that directions were given to make inquiries respecting the most suitable person. I would recommend that the person employed by the Horticultural Society should be engaged also to collect seeds and plants of the quinine-yielding cinchonas in the different localities which I have indicated, not as a secondary measure, but as one of his principal objects, which I believe would be best effected while he was ostensibly employed in making more general collections. The expenses of such a collector has been from 400 *l.* to 500 *l.* a year, and they need not exceed the latter sum on the present occasion. If one half of such expenses were paid by the Honourable Court, I feel no doubt that the objects in view might be as successfully attained as by employing a separate collector. If authorised, I should be happy to make the necessary arrangements.

(signed) *J. Forbes Royle*, M.D.

— No. 4. —

From the Secretary at the India House to the Secretary, Board of Control.

Sir, East India House, 7 October 1852.

1. I AM commanded by the Court of Directors to forward to you the accompanying copy of a public letter from the Government of India, dated the 27th March last, No. 18, and of its enclosures, on the subject of obtaining a supply of seeds and young plants of the quinine-yielding cinchonas of South America, with a view to the cultivation of the tree in India.

2. The accompanying papers set forth at length the grounds of the proposal submitted by the Government of India; and the Court, being of opinion with reference to the augmented demand for quinine in India, and to the large and increasing amount (7,000 *l.*) annually paid for that drug for consumption there, that the introduction of the proper genus of the cinchona into India, several localities of which are stated to be well suited for its cultivation, is a highly desirable measure, are prepared to take immediate steps for the accomplishment of the object.

3. It appears to the Court that the most simple mode of proceeding will be to obtain the necessary supply of seeds and plants through the instrumentality of Her Majesty's Consular Agents; and I am directed to request that, if the Board concur in this opinion, they will take measures for ascertaining from the Earl of Malmesbury, in the first place, whether his Lordship is aware of any peculiar difficulties likely to impede the attempt to procure specimens of the plants in question; and secondly, if no such impediments are believed to exist, whether his Lordship will be willing to empower Her Majesty's Consuls in Bolivia, and the other South American States, to take measures for procuring the seeds and plants required.

4. In the event of a favourable reply being returned by Lord Malmesbury on these points, the Court will be prepared, if his Lordship thinks it desirable, to supply, for transmission to the various Consuls, copies of Dr. Falconer's memorandum

memorandum on the subject, that document containing all the requisite information as to the plants to be sought for, and as to the best means of transmitting to India such specimens as may be procured.

I have, &c.,
(signed) *James C. Melvill*,
Secretary.

C. L. Cumming Bruce, Esq., M. P.
&c. &c. &c.
India Board.

— No. 5. —

From Dr. *Forbes Royle* to *J. C. Melvill*, Esq., Secretary to the Court of Directors of the East India Company.

Sir, East India House, 14 December 1852.

THE Indian Government having recommended the introduction of the true cinchona plant for cultivation in suitable localities in India, and measures being in progress for forwarding this important object, I have thought it desirable to endeavour to obtain some plants from the different botanic gardens, which I knew had been raised from seed collected by Dr. Weddell, the discoverer of the true cinchona plant, as that yielding the best yellow bark.

I am happy to say that Dr. Balfour, of the Edinburgh Botanic Gardens, informs me that he has some plants ready for despatch, and which will arrive here in a few days; also that the Horticultural Society, and the Royal Botanic Gardens at Kew, may be able to add a few additional plants.

As it is very desirable to send these valuable plants under safe and careful custody, I beg to suggest that advantage be taken of Mr. Fortune's departure for China by the next mail; and that he be authorised to take charge of the box containing plants as far as he proceeds on the course to India. Freight will probably be charged upon the box, as it will not probably be included as a part of Mr. Fortune's baggage; but all the expenses will necessarily be trifling in amount.

I have, &c.,
(signed) *J. Forbes Royle*, M. D.

— No. 6. —

MINUTE.

At a Revenue, Judicial, and Legislative Committee of the Court of Directors, 15 December 1852.

THE Committee having before them a letter from Dr. Royle, dated the 14th inst., reporting that he has succeeded in procuring from the Horticultural and Botanical Gardens in this country, a few plants of the true cinchonas, which it is desired to introduce into India, and that Mr. Fortune is willing to take charge of the same, as far as he can, on his way to China.

Ordered, that Mr. Fortune be authorised to take charge of the plants in question, and to incur such charges for freight, and other incidental expenses, as he may find to be necessary, on account of them.

— No. 7. —

From Dr. *Royle* to Sir *James Melvill*, K.C.B., Secretary to the Court of Directors of the East India Company.

Sir, East India House, 3 January 1854.

Mr. Cope forwarding cinchona plants.

I HAVE the honour to report the arrival of some cinchona plants and seeds sent through the Foreign Office by Her Majesty's Consul in the State of Equator. Mr. Cope writes on the 31st of October 1853, that he had transmitted to the Earl of Clarendon a box containing plants of the yellow cinchona bark of of Cuenca, and also plants, flowers, and seeds of the Crown cinchona bark of Loxa. These arrived at the India House on the 22d of December. On opening the box, I found that the plants and seeds had all been packed up in damp moss, which, though useful in preserving the former, is almost sure to destroy the vegetative power of seeds. I therefore immediately sent them down to the Horticultural Society's garden, at Chiswick, as the only likely place where I could be sure of their being carefully managed, so as to preserve them if possible, and saw them myself carefully unpacked on the 23d. Some of the upper layer of plants were dry and quite dead; those lower down damp, and apparently alive; the seeds all damp, indeed soaking in wet, but being contained within their capsules, it is possible some may vegetate, as their native climate is damp, and they must often lie for some time before they vegetate. I saw the plants again yesterday, but though alive, it is impossible at present to say whether any will survive, or any of the seeds vegetate.

On arrival sent to Chiswick garden.

Though Mr. Cope mentions the yellow bark, I doubt if this can be anything more than one of the substitutes for that most valuable of the barks. But the grey cinchona is one of the valuable kinds, and would probably yield returns four or five years after it is established in the mountains of India.

Yellow? of Cuenca. Crown bark of Loxa.

Mr. Sullivan, Her Majesty's Chargé d'Affaires in Peru, writes from Lima, that having no means there of procuring seeds of cinchona plants he had addressed himself to Mr. Crompton, Her Majesty's Vice-consul, at Islay and Arica.

Mr. Sullivan writes to Mr. Crompton, who promises seeds of yellow bark.

Mr. Crompton writes from Islay, 18th October, that having proceeded to Arequipa, he there found that the only means of accomplishing the object in view would be through one of the bark collectors employed in the interior, by the house of Gibbs & Co., "as it would be impossible from the jealousy of these people to accomplish a successful result, if they conceived the British to be interested." He however states, that Mr. Stubbs, managing partner of Messrs. Gibbs' house, at Arequipa, had agreed to send a person into the Montana to endeavour to get some seeds, and from a private communication to that gentleman from his agent, there appear hopes of getting some of the seeds in about April and May.

Of the seeds of the true yellow bark which, through the kindness of Mr. Pentland, I was enabled to send to the Calcutta Botanic Gardens, I am sorry to say that none have vegetated; but of the six plants contributed by the Royal Botanic Gardens at Kew and Edinburgh, and by the Horticultural Society, four, I am happy to say, that Dr. Falconer writes that they are doing well, as well as four cuttings which Mr. Scott, the gardener, has obtained from them.

Cinchona plants in Calcutta.—*B. G.*

As the present reliance for seeds of the calisaya, or true yellow bark, is upon the private firm at present engaged in the very traffic which may be interfered with, though certainly not for some time with regard to the thick yellow bark, I would beg leave to suggest that I may be authorised to endeavour to get seeds through other sources also. For instance, I am acquainted with a gentleman (Mr. Bollaert), who is well known to some of my friends, and who was formerly assistant in Dr. Faraday's laboratory, and who has been recently deputed to Peru to inquire into some of its mineral products. I have no doubt that if he was authorised to incur some moderate expense in procuring the seeds of these calisaya plants (of which we could not have too many), he would be able to do so, and without exciting any suspicion while engaged in other pursuits. I would therefore request to be authorised to enter into a correspondence with him on the subject, guaranteeing him any expenses he may incur in procuring these seeds, if he should be in the neighbourhood of where the best plants grow. The expense would not be greater than that to be incurred through the foreign consuls, and the object is of great importance to secure so important a culture for India, save great expense in the supply of so expensive a drug for the Indian Government, besides being for the general benefit that such valuable drugs as the cinchona barks, and their alkalis, quinine and cinchonene, should not be confined to one or two localities where no care is taken in preserving the forests.

Application for leave to authorise Mr. Bollaert, now in Peru, to collect cinchona seeds.

I have, &c.
(signed) *J. Forbes Royle*, M.D.

— No. 8. —

From Mr. *Melvill* to Sir *T. Redington.*

Sir, East India House, 5 January 1854.

I AM commanded to forward copy of a resolution passed by the Court of Directors of the East India Company on the 4th instant, proposing to authorise Dr. Royle to communicate with Mr. Bollaert, who has recently been deputed to Peru, upon the subject of a supply of seeds of the calisaya, from which quinine is obtained, and to guarantee to him the repayment of any expenses he may incur in collecting the seeds to the extent of fifty pounds (50 *l.*), and I am desired to request that you will submit the said Resolution for the approval of the Board of Commissioners for the affairs of India.

I have, &c.
(signed) *James C. Melvill,* Secretary.

— No. 9. —

From *Thomas Thomson,* Esq., M.D., Superintendent H. C. Botanic Garden, to *W. Grey,* Esq., Secretary to the Government of Bengal; dated 14 May 1855.

Sir,

IN obedience to the instructions contained in your office memorandum, dated the 21st ultimo, calling for a report on the seeds and plants of the quinine-yielding cinchonas sent out by the Honourable Court in 1852, I have the honour to forward a copy of a letter addressed by my predecessor, Dr. Falconer, to the Secretary of the Medical Board, embodying all the information which exists in this office regarding the cinchona trees.

2. I regret to say that I have just been informed by Dr. Campbell, superintendent of Darjeeling, that the three cinchona trees there were killed by the cold of last winter. I have the honour to forward a copy of Dr. Campbell's communication to that effect in reply to a letter which I addressed to him on receipt of your memorandum.

3. I fully concur with Dr. Royle and Dr. Falconer in believing that the climate of the Eastern Himalaya will be found well suited to the growth of cinchona, and I do not think that the failure of the first attempt to introduce this valuable plant ought in the least to deter us from further trial.

4. I shall communicate the loss of the cinchona plants at Darjeeling by the first mail to Dr. Royle, for the information of the Honourable Court, in the hope that a further supply of young plants will be sent out as soon as possible to renew the experiment.

I have, &c.
(signed) *Thomas Thomson,* Superintendent.

Enclosure to No. 9.

From *H. Falconer,* Esq., M.D., Superintendent H. C. Botanic Garden, to *J. Macpherson,* Esq., Secretary, Medical Board, dated 9 April 1855.

Sir,

I HAVE the honour to acknowledge the receipt of your letter, dated the 19th ultimo, soliciting information for the Medical Board, regarding cinchona plants which were received in the Botanic Garden from England; I shall reply to the Board's questions in the order in which they have been put.

1. The plants were brought to India overland, in a Ward's glazed case, under charge of Mr. Robert Fortune, who was then *en route* to China. The cases were transported across the desert without damage of any kind, although hurried along with the passengers.

2. Seeds

2. Seeds of the Cinchona Calisaya of Dr. Weddell, who gathered them in South America, were procured by Dr. Royle, and transmitted to the Botanical Garden here, but although watched with the utmost care by the European head gardener, none of them showed the slightest disposition to germinate.

3. Only six plants were despatched, of which five were alive. They were retained in the Botanic Garden through the hot weather and rains in conservatory cases, with the object of propagating from them. They bear pruning of all kinds very ill, and were in consequence but very sparingly wounded. The buds survived for a very long time, but never struck root, and finally perished. The original plants did not thrive well in the Botanic Garden, the climate of which is much too hot for cinchona caleseya.

4. The original surviving plants were sent to Darjeeling, where three of them arrived alive. But the period of trial has been too short, and the plants were too unfavourably placed to admit of any decided opinion. The experiment ought to be tried with more materials, and a wider range of elevation than was practicable in this case.

5. I submitted an opinion to Government about four years ago, that it was feasible to grow cinchona successfully in India for medical purposes, and I have seen no reason since to alter that opinion. But the experiment must be conducted upon a sufficiently large scale to admit of a full trial, and with a wide range of the different species; cinchona condamonia is one of the species that promises most favourably.

6. The best information on the subject is contained on a monograph on the genus cinchona, by Dr. Weddell, who was deputed by the French Government to South America for the express object.

7. I enclose an extract from Dr. Royle's Materia Medica, second edition, which contains a good epitome of what is known up to the present moment.

I have, &c.
(signed) *H. Falconer*, M.D., Superintendent.

— No. 10. —

From the Government of India to the Honourable the Court of Directors of the East India Company.

Honourable Sirs, Fort William, 2 June 1855.

WITH reference to the 39th paragraph of your Honourable Court's Despatch, No. 44, of 1853, dated the 6th July, we have the honour to transmit the accompanying correspondence regarding the result of the experiment for the introduction of the cinchona plant into India. The seeds are reported to have failed and the plants to have died.

To Government of Bengal, dated 17 April 1855. From ditto, No. 602, dated 17 May; and enclosures.

2. Both Dr. Falconer and Dr. Thomson, the late and present superintendents of the Botanic Garden, consider that the failure of the first experiment, which was on a very small scale, should not deter the Government from a second and more extensive trial, and they hold to the opinion that the climate of the Eastern Himalayas is well suited to the growth of the plant. Under these circumstances, and referring to the interest attaching to the successful introduction of the plant into India, we beg to recommend the trial of a further experiment, and on a larger scale than the last.

We have, &c.
(signed) *J. A. Dorin.*
J. Low.
J. P. Grant.
B. Peacock.

— No. 11. —

EXTRACT, from Dr. *Royle* to Sir *J. C. Melvill*, K.C.B., Secretary to the Court of Directors of the East India Company.

Sir, 9 August 1855.

Cinchona plants for India.

IN the first place, E. W. Mark, Esq., H. B. M. Vice-Consul at Bagota, having written to me respecting his readiness to assist again in the attempt to introduce into India the different species of cinchona, yielding what are commonly called

called Peruvian barks, I have written him the enclosed, and forwarded a note from Dr. Weddell, the highest authority we have on this subject. As it is seldom that any seeds or plants are obtained through the aid of consular agents, I think it the more desirable to take advantage of Mr. Mark's offer of his services, as all that is usually required of an individual on the spot is, that he should take a personal interest in the matter, and see that the instructions sent are carefully attended to. As some expense may be incurred, though not more than originally contemplated, I have thought it proper to forward the correspondence through you. I still continue to think that the successful introduction into India of the cinchonas will be of great benefit, not only to that country, but to the world in general, as there is great fear that the supply from the original sources may become so much diminished as to be beyond the reach of the mass of those who require the aid of quinine. The Dutch Government continue to pursue active measures for establishing the culture of the Cinchona Calisaya (the best species), and Dr. De Vry, the Dutch Commissioner here, has been directed to inquire of me the result of the experiments making in India.

2. By a remarkable coincidence, to which I trust I may refer, I had written thus far when a note from Dr. Thomson, Superintendent of the Botanic Garden at Calcutta, reached me, by which I regret much to learn that the Cinchona Calisaya sent out by the Court two years ago all died on their removal to Darjeeling. The loss is, I fear, irremediable, as Dr. Weddell informs me that, without a special agent, he does not believe it possible to procure fresh seeds or plants. It is the more desirable, therefore, that the consuls at Bagota and at Guayaquil should be requested to repeat their efforts to send living plants and carefully dried seeds of the best plants near those localities.

— No. 12. —

MEMORANDUM by Dr. *Royle.*

East India House, 31 March 1856.

THE accompanying letter from the Government of Bengal, dated 2d June, 1855, reports the failure both of the seeds and of the plants of the quinine-yielding cinchona, which had been sent out to Calcutta in consequence of the former application. It further states that both Dr. Falconer and Dr. Thomson, the late and the present superintendents of the Calcutta Botanic Gardens, consider that the failure of the small experiment should not deter from a second and more extensive trial, and they hold to the opinion that the climate of the Eastern Himalayas is well suited to the growth of the plant. I myself continue of the same opinion as I have been for many years; indeed, recommended the culture of these cinchonas in the above locality more than 20 years ago.

But I would beg to observe that the experiment which has failed was never intended to be the sole, or, indeed, principal one, but rather auxiliary to it.

When the original proposal arrived for the introduction of the true quinine-yielding cinchona into the Eastern Himalayas, I wrote a memorandum, recommending, in consequence of the difficulties of the undertaking and the jealousy of the local governments, that a person who had other objects of a similar kind in view should be employed, and as the Horticultural Society of London proposed sending a plant collector to the American mountains, I suggested that he might be well employed in introducing the seeds and plants of the desired cinchonas at the same time. As the proposal was not approved of, it was not proceeded with. The Horticultural Society's plant collector, Mr. Bottari, is now on his return from the mountains of Mexico, and I know of no suitable person at present who could be recommended for employment.

In order to endeavour to get some seeds and plants of these cinchonas through Her Majesty's Consuls, I wrote the second of the accompanying papers; and the results which had been obtained were reported in my letter dated 4th January 1854, which amounted only to Mr. Mark having been unable to bring with him alive the cinchona plants, which he had collected at Bagota, while Mr. Cope from Guayaquil sent some young plants and seeds in wet

wet moss, and packed up in a box. These, as might be expected, did not vegetate. On this occasion I applied for 50 *l.*, to be advanced to Mr. Bollaert, who was being dispatched from this country to the American coast, in order that he might, if possible, get some cinchona seeds; but he left the country before I had an opportunity of making arrangements with him.

The experiment which was made was a small one; it consisted of a few plants which I was able to obtain from the Botanic Gardens of Kew, of Edinburgh, and of the Horticultural Society at Chiswick; and the seeds were some old ones which had been collected by Dr. Weddell, in one of his trips to South America, and from whom the first seeds had been obtained from which the above plants had been grown in the Botanic Garden, proving that the seeds, if carefully gathered and dried, would retain their vegetative properties sufficiently long to grow when sown in this country, perhaps also even when sent to India.

Though I do not know at present of any method which is likely to succeed in getting the best kind of yellow bark, that is, the calisaya, from Bolivia, there are two or three species which are very valuable for medicinal purposes, in the neighbourhood of Quito and Loxa; and I have lately learnt that there is a gentleman at present in Quito (Dr. Jamieson) who employs himself at his leisure in collecting seeds and dried plants for his scientific friends in Europe. I believe his services might be obtained; and if I was authorised to write to him, to enable him to incur some expense, say about 50 *l.*, and say that an equal sum shall be given to him on the successful execution of the Commission with which he should be charged, I shall be disposed to think that considerable quantities of the seeds of the species of cinchona common in that part of America might be certainly secured.

(signed) *J. F. Royle*, M. D.

— No. 13. —

EXTRACT.

From the Governor of India to the Honourable the Court of Directors of the East India Company.

Honourable Sirs, 10 November 1856.

IN continuation of our Letter, No. 40 of 1855, dated the 2d June, respecting the experimental introduction of the quinine-yielding cinchona tree of South America into India, we have the honour to transmit for your Honourable Court's consideration the accompanying copy of a Minute by the Governor General, dated the 20th ultimo.

2. We earnestly recommend this subject to your Honourable Court's early and careful attention; and we hope to be made acquainted with the views of your Honourable Court on the proposals made in the Minute, and with the measures it may be determined to take in consequence, in order that timely inquiries may be completed in India, as to the sites on which the plants, when received, may best be cultivated.

Enclosure to No. 13.

MINUTE by the Governor General, concurred in by the Members of Government; dated 20 October 1856.

Introduction of the cinchona tree of South America into India.

THIS important subject engaged the attention of the Government of India, on the representation of the Agricultural Society, made to the Government of Bengal in 1852; and in consequence of a communication made to the Honourable Court of Directors, some seed and plants were procured, and sent out to India.

The experiment unfortunately failed, the seeds having in no instance germinated, and only five plants having reached Calcutta alive. These last, after having been kept at the Botanical Gardens during a rainy season, were sent to Darjeeling, where they were killed by the cold of the following winter.

In 1855 the Medical Board took up the question again; but their report by some accident not having been received, a duplicate has been called for, and at the same time the Agricultural Society have again addressed the Government.

The proposals of the Medical Board and of the Agricultural Society are, first, that the experiment of introducing cinchona plants should be tried upon an extensive scale, with several species of the plants, and in many parts of the country, especially in the Neilgherries, in the range to the east of Sylhet, at Chittagong, in the Tenasserim Provinces, and in the neighbourhood of Darjeeling.

That an establishment under the orders of a person properly qualified be deputed to collect cinchona plants of the best species (the seeds being too delicate to survive the voyage), and to despatch them in "Ward's cases" from Trinidad or Demerara direct to Calcutta and Madras, so as to arrive in India not later than November.

That officers possessing the requisite botanical and geological knowledge should be deputed to inquire as to the sites best calculated to receive the plants; that these officers, duly supplied with all aids and appliances, should receive the plants upon arrival, and convey them to the selected spots.

That considerable reward should be offered to native gardeners employed under these officers, to encourage them to attend to the plants with the necessary assiduity.

I submit that the substance of these proposals should be recommended to the favourable consideration of the Honourable Court. The supply of South American cinchona is actually threatened with extinction; the consequences of the loss of this most valuable febrifuge would be most lamentable, and the experiment, if successful, would introduce into India an article which would be largely exported, and would be the source of a considerable revenue.

The experiment already tried affords no sort of criterion as to the possibility of a successful introduction of the cinchona into India.

The plants appear to have received precisely that treatment which would make their growth impossible, having first been subjected to the heat and moisture of Bengal, and then transferred to the cold climate of Darjeeling, without, as it would seem, having been placed at the latter place under competent care.

The experiment, carried out in the manner proposed, will be costly; but it is shown in these papers that in five years the Government of India has expended nearly 54,000*l.* in quinine and cinchona bark, and therefore I believe that success will be well worth the cost; and looking to the political condition of the countries in which the plants are to be found, I doubt whether they can be surely procured in any other way.

There is good reason to hope that the cinchona may thrive in India. The reasons of this are fully set forth in the letters of the Medical Board and of the Agricultural and Horticultural Society; moreover, the opinions of all the gentlemen who have given their attention to the subject are the same, not only as to the desirableness of introducing the cinchona, but as to the possibility of so doing.

Under these circumstances, and considering the incalculable benefits to be derived from having a native supply of this most valuable medicine at hand, I am of opinion that the experiment as proposed should be fairly tried, and that the Honourable Court should be moved at once to send a properly qualified collector to South America, to collect and bring to India the best species of cinchona.

It is probable that the person so employed might conveniently take advantage of emigrant vessels returning from Demerara and Trinidad to Madras and Calcutta. As the mission to South America will occupy some time, I do not propose that any steps should be taken towards ascertaining the sites in this country best suited to the plants, until the Honourable Court shall have expressed their views upon the present proposal.

It is some incentive to the measure that the Dutch Government have already adopted it in Java, where after a considerable loss in plants it is reported to promise success.

The plants were received in Java in 1854; and I propose that the Resident at Singapore be directed to address the Governor General of Batavia, with the view of obtaining from his Excellency any information or suggestions which the recent experience of the authorities in that island may enable them to offer, both as to the parts in South America where the best plants should be sought, and as to their culture in the East.

20 October 1856. (signed) *Canning.*

We quite agree.

23 October 1856.	(signed)	*J. A. Dorin.*
2 November 1856.		*J. P. Grant.*
5 November 1856.		*B. Peacock.*

— No. 14. —

From *H. Piddington*, Esq., to *C. Beadon*, Esq., Secretary to the Government of India.

Sir, 24 November 1856.

LEARNING from the public papers that the Government is desirous of introducing the cinchona bark tree into India, I beg respectfully to submit in aid of its efforts the accompanying memorandum, from the which his Lordship will perceive that there are important considerations to be kept in view besides the mere obtaining of plants or seeds, and that the neglect of one of these may have been the cause of the failure of the plants brought out by Mr. Fortune, and sent to Darjeeling. A glance at the accompanying memorandum in aid of the introduction of the Carolina rice will satisfy his Lordship that these subjects are not unfamiliar to me.

2. It would seem also that the Government is not aware that the extract of the "golunchee," a common hedge and forest plant all over India and the Eastern Islands, is, for natives, if not a complete substitute for quinine, something very near to it, and for Europeans it is certainly a very powerful adjunct, so that I have no hesitation in saying, and this on the authority of many medical friends, that at least one-half of all the quinine now expended in India either by the Government or by private individuals, might be economised at a very moderate charge.

3. It is not here the place to enter further into the merits of this invaluable extract, which is well known to scientific members of the profession; but I may mention that, about two years ago, it was brought to the notice of Government and of the public as a discovery by a medical officer and a superintending surgeon in the North West Provinces, who were evidently ignorant of my previous researches of 1826 to 1828. I shall willingly furnish further details and references regarding this valuable medicine, which has been so strangely neglected of late years, if desired.

4. It will be, perhaps, some excuse to his Lordship for intruding my views on this matter to say that I have long taken a deep interest in it. I procured seed of the best cinchona from Cuba as far back as 1828, which unfortunately did not germinate. I have constantly kept the object in view, and I should probably have obtained plants through the Admiralty had Lord Auckland lived. I have given more chemical research than I like to speak of, and, perhaps, more expense than my poor means justified, for 30 years, to this one great question of humanity for India, the placing of a bottle of a cheap febrifuge of some kind within the reach of the means of the poorest ryot; and that, finally, I have now in my hands a new preparation from a common Indian plant which can be prepared at a very cheap rate, and may I hope fulfil this great object, as a medical friend speaks favourably of it so far.

I beg to place at his Lordship's disposal a small specimen of the rocky soil of the cinchona alluded to in my memorandum, as also for his satisfaction a small bottle of my new bitter vegetable salt, "Indianine."

I have, &c.

Calcutta, 24 November 1856. (signed) *H. Piddington.*

Enclosure to No. 14.

MEMORANDUM to aid in the Introduction and successful Cultivation of the Quiniferous Cinchona Plants in India, by Henry Piddington.

Calcutta, 24 November 1856.

1. IT is quite unnecessary to dissert here at length upon the imperative necessity of attention to the three great requisites for the successful acclimation and profitable product of every vegetable production; every forester, nurseryman, and herbalist knows that, from the oaks of Sussex, and the pines of Araucaria and the Jura, to the tobacco of Virginia and Cuba, and the mint and lavender of the Surrey druggists' gardens, soil, climate, and situation so govern growth and produce that deficiency or failure, in any of these three requisites entails deficiency or failure in the growth or production of the plant.

 2. But

2. But I have seen with regret by the papers now published, that when the precious cinchona plants brought by Mr. Fortune were received they were all sent to Darjeeling; climate alone, and perhaps situation as to drainage, &c. being apparently considered, but the question of soil utterly neglected.

3. For we perfectly well know here (better, perhaps, even than in Europe where the labours of the Asiatic Society are little known) what the soil in which the cinchona of one part of Peru grows is composed of; for in 1831 I published the following short paper, which I copy here; it will be found in the "Gleanings in Science," vol. iii. p. 28, as part of the researches of the Physical Class of the Asiatic Society.

On the Soil in which the Cinchona thrives.—By *H. Piddington*, Esq.

(Read before the Physical Class of the Asiatic Society.)

In examining a collection of minerals from Peru, which had been sent to our worthy Vice-President, I found the following label to one of the specimens:—

"No. 76. Piedra que se encuentra en las margenes de Gualláza, Cerro de San Cristoval, legua y media N. al S. de altura considerable. La falda del este no tiene un solo arbol de quina y la opuesta esta cubierta; se cria en esta classe de piedra que esta cubierta con hojas del mismo arbol con un espesura de ¾."

TRANSLATION.

"Rock found in the neighbourhood of Guallaza, Sierra of San Cristoval, a league and a-half from N. to S., and of considerable altitude. The western slope has not a single bark tree (cinchona), and the opposite side is covered with them. They grow in this sort of rock, which is covered with their leaves to the depth of three-quarters of a yard."

Looking to the probability that this valuable tree may one day become an article of culture both in India and Australia, perhaps even in Europe, it appeared probable that an analysis of the rock might, with propriety, occupy a space in the Society's records.

It proved to be, upon examination, a decomposing granular dolomite, the exterior of which was friable, while the interior was perfectly compact.

100 Grains were found to consist of water	2·06
Siliceous matter, with some trace of vegetable matter (from the outside)	0·62
Carbonate of lime	46·00
Carbonate of magnesia	51·00
Loss	0·32
	100·00

REMARKS.

In a mineralogical point of view it is remarkable that the proportion of carbonate of magnesia far exceeds that found in those analysed in Europe, which are published in Jameson; but it is a singular physical fact that the cinchona, the most valuable medical product of the vegetable kingdom, is found to flourish on a soil so utterly destructive to every other useful product that we are acquainted with; a beautiful instance added to those which science is hourly disclosing of the beneficent economy of the universe.

I send a small specimen of the rock, the disintegration of which, we can see, would easily form a soil in which, as described on the label, small trees like the cinchona could grow. Geologically, nothing is easier than to explain how the soil in one side of a hill or mountain may be quite different from that on the other.

4. We do not, it is true, learn from this analysis whether it be the lime or the magnesia, or both, which are essential to the growth of the tree, or to the quantity of quinine produced. It may be that it simply requires lime, when any calcareous soil would suit it, but it may also require both; at all events, the soil of Darjeeling, where limestone is unknown (except a very small concretionary deposit of which I examined a specimen in 1842) does not seem to me to have been that which would have best suited the plant, while the calcareous hills of Sylhet and Cachar would at least afford it plenty of lime.

5. All that is clearly shown then is, I submit, that we want accurate information on this most essential question, to guide us; and from all one can glean from books, and from what I have learned from South American Spaniards, I should say too that the apparently capricious growths of the cinchona groves and forests, seem to be much like our own tea tracts in Assum and Cachar. Soil may be the essential element for its successful thriving;* climate cannot differ to the extent of making an abundant growth in one place and a total absence of the trees at a few miles of distance from it, while soil may do this everywhere.

* *See* also the positive words of the label.

6. I submit

6. I submit then respectfully, for the consideration of Government, whether the agent whom it is proposed to send should not be instructed as follows:—

(*a.*) To collect with the plants specimens of the soils in which the trees grow (taken at a foot deep, near their roots) as also of all the rocks and even loose stones about them.

(*b.*) To obtain all the information he possibly can regarding climate.

(*c.*) To note with care the situations of the groves of the trees, as their aspects, and whether on the sides of hills or in level places, and if in dry or moist localities; for as the barks differ so much it may be that some of the varieties prefer a moist soil to a dry one.

(*d.*) That, if possible, a few mule-loads of the soil should be brought down with the plants, so as to fill the Ward's cases with it. If these are used, and if a few seeds are sown between the plants, there is a chance of their germinating also on the voyage, which would at least supply the place of the plants which die.

(signed) *H. Piddington.*

— No. 15. —

om the Medical Board to the Hon. *J. A. Dorin*, Esq., President in Council; dated Fort William, 9 June 1855.

Honourable Sir,

THE entire correspondence being now before us, and the subject being one of very high importance, we beg leave to submit to your Honor's attention a brief report upon an attempt which has recently been made to introduce the cultivation of the cinchona tree into this Presidency.

2. It was long since held by Dr. Forbes Royle, that the introduction of the cinchonas into this country was highly desirable, and that the experiment would doubtless succeed in the Neilgherries. In his work on the productive resources of India.

3. In September 1850, Mr. John Grant, then holding the appointment of apothecary, Honourable East India Company, addressed a communication to this Board, in which, after insisting very strongly upon the danger of a failure of the cinchona supply in America, under the annually increasing demands for the medicinal bark from nearly all parts of the world, the writer suggested, that to obviate such risk it would be expedient to introduce varieties of the cinchonaceæ into India, where the steep declivities of the spurs of the Himalaya, &c. form promising localities, where they would in all probability thrive well. No. 97 of 13 September 1850.

4. In 1852, the secretary to the Agri-horticultural Society addressed a letter to the Government of Bengal, forwarding a copy of a valuable paper upon the introduction into India of the quinine-yielding cinchonas of South America, with the Society's respectful request that the most Noble the Governor of Bengal would be pleased to give the suggestions which it embodied the consideration which, they submitted, the importance of the subject deserved. In his subsequent communication upon the subject with the Home Department, his Lordship strongly supported the proposals of Dr. Falconer, and pointed to the attention of the Government of India the Medical Board's lately printed report on the treatment of fever, as showing the deficiency in the market of the supply of quinine, and the increased consumption of it which may be expected, at least in India. 23 February 1852. No. 447 of the 9th March 1852.

5. The result of this correspondence was a communication from the Home Department to the address of the Secretary to the Government of Bengal, announcing that the proposal of deputing a qualified person from England to South America to procure seeds and young plants of the best species would be submitted to the Honourable the Court of Directors with the favourable recommendation of the Governor General in Council. No. 289 of the 27th March 1852.

6. Early in the present year a valuable essay on the introduction of the cinchona trees into India was forwarded to us by Assistant Surgeon Thomas Anderson, M.D., F.R.S.E. It will be found that the views entertained on this subject by Dr. Anderson mainly agree with those held by Dr. Royle, Mr. Grant, and Dr. Falconer.

No. 1696 of 19 March 1855. No. 802, 7 April 1855.

7. Previous to the departure of the last-named officer for England, we communicated with him, requesting that he would furnish us with information respecting a supply of cinchona plant which we understood had been received at the Botanical Gardens some time previously. In his reply we were informed that the plants were brought to India overland in a Ward's glazed case, under charge of Mr. Robert Fortune. They were transported across the desert without damage of any kind.

8. The seeds of the *Cinchona Calisaya*, a highly valuable species of yellow bark, containing a large proportion of quinine, although gathered by Dr. Weddell,* and forwarded by Dr. Royle, and therefore obtained under the most favourable circumstances, showed not the slightest disposition to germinate, although watched with the utmost care by the European head gardener.

* Dr. Weddell was deputed by the French Government to South America with the express object of obtaining information relative to the cinchonaceæ.

9. Only six plants were dispatched, of which five were alive, they were retained in the Botanical Garden through the hot weather and rains in conservatory cases. They bore pruning very ill, and were in consequence but very sparingly wounded. The cutting survived for a very long time, but never struck root, and finally perished. The original plants did not thrive well in the Botanical Garden, the climate of which Dr. Falconer considered to be too hot for *Cinchona Calisaya*.

10. The original surviving plants were sent to Darjeeling, where three of them arrived alive.

No. 248, of 30 April 1855.

11. Upon receipt of the above information, we requested that the Superintendent of Darjeeling would furnish us with information regarding the condition of the three cinchona trees which reached that station in safety. In his reply, Dr. A. Campbell states that all the cinchona trees were killed by the cold of last winter, and suggests that in any future trial at Darjeeling, the trees should not, he thinks, be planted at an elevation of more than 2,000 feet.

12. Unsuccessful as this experiment has proved, we would venture to submit that, considering the very limited scale upon which it was tried, and the now perfectly obvious causes of the failure which attended it, its result has by no means lessened our faith in the possibility of introducing the cinchona tree into India.

13. When it is recollected that Dr. Weddell discovered the *Cinchona Calisaya*, yielding the invaluable yellow bark of English commerce, flourishing abundantly in the cinchona regions of Bolivia and a part of Peru between 19° and 13° of south latitude, and that the corresponding parallels of the Eastern hemisphere include the Neilgherries and that great chain of hills which extends from Muneepore to Cape Negruis, many of whose rocky peaks and platforms rise to an elevation of at least 5,000 feet. When, further, it is borne in mind that the coffee, a plant nearly allied to the cinchona, is apparently indigenous to a portion of the latter range; that, as shown by Dr. Falconer two trees, very nearly allied to the true barks, the *Hymenodictyon excelsum* and the *Lucalia gratissima*, are native in India, the latter growing abundantly in Sylhet, at the foot of the Kasia Hills. And also when it is recollected that the rocky nature of the soils and the hygrometric condition of the atmosphere in many of those situations appear very closely to approach those of the tracts in which the cinchonaceæ thrive best, it can scarcely be doubted that the experiment under consideration might be tried again with every prospect of success.

Wild coffee grows abundantly in the Chittagong Hills; this fact was noticed by Sir W. Jones not many years after the establishment of the English Factory there. It may have been introduced by the Portugnese, but we have no evidence of the fact. It is, however, sufficiently evident that the shrub is capable of reaching its highest perfection in that soil. The cultivated coffee of Chittagong is, we believe, of excellent quality.

14. We would especially beg leave to insist upon the fact that when introduced into this country the plants were kept in Bengal during the hot season, and the rains, and that although doubtless carefully tended at Darjeeling, they do not appear to have remained under the care of a professed botanist, at that place, where, weakened by cutting and by previous detention in a hot and close climate, in which all plants of their species must necessarily deteriorate, they were almost inevitably destroyed by the cold.

Note.—Dr. Falconer, in his remarks upon the climates in which the cinchonaceæ thrive, observe, that "the same species of cinchona is said to be so much affected by situation and increase of temperature, as to alter the habit of the tree, and produce an entirely different quality of bark; low and hot valleys deteriorating its virtues so greatly, that it is rejected by the merchants as unfit for commerce."

15. The

15 The steps which we would now venture tosuggest for adoption by the Government, are the following:—

1st. That the experiment of introducing the cinchonaceæ into India should be tried upon an extensive scale, with several species of the plant, and in many parts of the country, but especially in the Neilgherries, in the range to the east of Sylhet, Chittagong, and the Tenasserim Provinces, and in various localities around Darjeeling.

That an establishment under the orders of a person properly qualified be deputed to collect cinchona plants of the best species (the seeds appearing to be too delicate to survive the voyage), and to despatch them in Ward's cases, duly tended; not as was done in the first experiment *viâ* Europe and the overland route, but as was originally recommended by Dr. Falconer, from Trinidad or Demerara direct to Calcutta and Madras, care being taken that they should not arrive in India later than the month of November.

2nd. That officers possessing the requisite botanical and geological knowledge should be deputed to inquire into those sites in the above localities which appear to be best calculated to receive the plants. That these officers being liberally furnished with the necessary aid and appliances, should receive the plants upon their arrival in India, and convey them forthwith to the spots prepared for their reception.

That considerable rewards should be offered to the native gardeners employed under these officers, with a view to encourage them to attend to the plants with the necessary assiduity.

16. At the present stage of this inquiry, it is almost needless that we should insist upon the advantages which would result from the success of such an experiment. The fact that in the five years 1849-53, nearly 54,000 *l.* were expended by the Honourable East India Company upon quinine and cinchona bark in the three Presidencies of India is, we would urge, of far less imperative import than the well-established certainty that the failure, and possibly the extinction of the South America cinchona supply is actually threatened, and that India is the only other country in the world which appears to afford a fitting habitat for the cinchonaceæ.

We have, &c.

(signed) *G. G. Spilsbury*, Physician General.
C. Renny, Surgeon General.
J. B. Clapperton, Inspector General.

(True copy.)
(signed) *Norman Chevers*,
Secretary Medical Board.

— No. 16. —

Report by Dr. *Royle* on the Introduction into India of the Quinine-yielding Cinchonas, and of the means which have hitherto been adopted for the purpose.

East India House, March 1857.

The almost inappreciable value of the cinchona, commonly called Peruvian bark, especially since the separation from them of the health and strength-restoring quinine and other alkalis is universally acknowledged. Hence it becomes a duty to humanity, not only to keep up but even to increase the supply of the cinchona trees which yield such valuable barks. The great difficulty is to find a suitable climate in a mountainous region for their healthy growth. Two Governors General, and the Government of Bengal, and the Medical Board on two occasions, the Agri-horticultural Society, and several medical officers, have recommended the introduction of cinchonas into suitable situations in India. Successive superintendents of the Honourable Company's Botanic Gardens in India have been of opinion that there is every probability of their successful cultivation in the Eastern Himalayas, that is, in the mountainous regions about Assam, and to the eastward of Silhet, also on the sides of the Neilgherries; probably also in parts of the Malabar coast.

 I was

I was myself, I believe, the first person to recommend the introduction of the true cinchona into India, and this, as long since as the year 1835, in my work on Himalayan botany. Thus, when treating of the family of plants to which the cinchonas belong, I inferred, from a comparison of the soil and climate with the geographical distribution of cinchonaceous plants, that the quinine-yielding cinchonas might be cultivated on the slopes of the Neilgherries and of the Southern Himalayas, in the same way that I had inferred that the China tea plant might be successfully cultivated in the Northern Himalayas.

Again, in the year 1847, when Mr. Blackwood, of Lima, offered through the Foreign Office to introduce the true cochineal insect and plant into India, I recommended that he should at the same time endeavour to introduce some of the cinchonas. This year he has again offered to introduce the cochineal insect into India, and has given some information about the cinchonas, but much more is known about them than Mr. B. seems to be aware of.

In the year 1852, Dr. Falconer, superintendent of the Honourable Company's Botanic Garden at Calcutta, wrote a paper which was read before the Agri-horticultural Society of Calcutta, and which was subsequently brought by them to the notice of the Most Noble the Governor of Bengal. In that paper Dr. Falconer strongly advocated the introduction of the cinchonas, and stated: " Dr. Royle has entertained the subject already, and I entirely concur in the opinion expressed by him, that the best situations for a trial are presented by the Khasya Hills, the mountains behind Chittagong and hilly parts of Upper Assam. The experiment, he continues, might also be extended to the hilly tracts around Darjeeling. The Neilgherries and the higher elevations of the Western Ghats appear to offer the most promising situations for Southern India. From the difficulties of the undertaking, and the little success that had attended the various endeavours to introduce cinchona plants into Europe, he recommended that an intelligent and qualified gardening collector should be deputed for a couple of years to the mountains of South America, for the purpose of exploring the cinchona forests, and for procuring an ample stock of young plants and seeds of all the best species.

When these papers were referred to me, as I coincided in opinion, and thought the measure proposed the best that could be devised, I recommended that it should be adopted, but with a slight variation. This, because the Bolivian Government, within whose territories had been found the best kind of cinchona, or that called Calisaya, had, as I explained, displayed considerable disinclination to the extension of the commerce of bark, except at greatly enhanced prices. I therefore thought that the gardening collector, deputed for the collection of cinchona plants and seeds, should also and ostensibly be employed in collecting other plants and seeds for the Horticultural or any other society, and thus divert attention from what would be his principal object; also that he should extend his investigation from 10° N. to 20° of S. latitude, as useful and quinine-yielding cinchonas are found about Santa Fé de Bagota, pale, and probably other barks in the mountains near Loxa, with one of the red barks from the mountains near Lima, and the best yellow or Calisaya bark from Bolivia.

As the proposal for sending a gardening collector was not approved of, and it was suggested that endeavours should be made to obtain seeds and plants of the several useful cinchonas by means of Her Majesty's Consuls, in the countries where these are known to grow, I therefore drew up detailed instructions on the subject, as it was hopeless to obtain any useful results, unless the directions to each Consul were of a specific nature. I therefore pointed out the plants to which Her Majesty's Consuls in New Granada, Equador, Peru, and Bolivia, should respectively attend; exports taking place from the ports of Carthagena, Guayaquil, Payta, Lima, and Arica. Having corrected the nomenclature of the species, according to the most recent investigation, as of Dr. Weddell, in Paris, and of Mr. Howard in this country, and pointed out the exact localities in the several Consulates, where such particular species was found, I added the English and the provincial names of the several barks which they produced, and by which they were known in commerce.

As I was at that time engaged in publishing the second edition of my Manual of Materia Medica, I had copies of the sheets referring to the cinchona barks struck off, and sent copies for each of the consuls.

Though not in the regular course of events it will probably be preferable to relate

relate in this place the results of these applications, though I have already done so in a great measure in my report, dated 3d January 1854.

Mr. E. Marks, who had been acting British Consul General at Santa Fé de Bagota, and who had been obliged to visit this country on account of his health, endeavoured to bring with him plants of two distinct species of cinchona (probably *C. Lancifolia*, and *C. Cordifolia*), which were obtainable in that neighbourhood. He wrote that he had had the plants for two months in his house at Bagota, and had considerable trouble in trying to bring them down the mountains, and along the Magdalena River, and on board of the steamers. He also wrote, " I believe that unless some experienced gardener, or botanical collector, be sent out to the countries producing the bark, there is but very little chance of getting any live plants from those countries."

Mr. Cope, Her Majesty's Consul in the State of Equator, wrote on the 31st October 1853, that he had transmitted to the Earl of Clarendon a box, containing plants of the yellow cinchona bark of Cuenca, and also plants, flowers, and seeds of the grey cinchona bark of Loxa (*C. Condaminea*). The plants and seeds had unfortunately been packed up in damp moss, which though it might possibly have been useful to the former, was the worst kind of packing for the latter. I sent the box and its contents to the gardens of the Horticultural Society on the 23d January 1854, and was sorry to observe that the plants seemed dead, and the seeds so damp, that there was little hope of their being alive. Mr. Gordon, the head gardener, in the Society's Gardens, reported that "the seeds were unripe when gathered, and dead when received, the seedlings sent along with the seeds were dead, being quite dried up and very badly packed; no skill could restore them."

Mr. Sullivan, Her Majesty's Chargé d'Affaires in Peru, wrote from Lima, that having no means there of procuring seeds of cinchona plants, he had addressed himself to Mr. Crompton, Her Majesty's Vice-Consul at Islay and Arica.

Mr. Crompton wrote from Islay, 18th October 1853, that having proceeded to Arequipa, he there found that " it would be impossible from the jealousy of these people to accomplish a successful result, if they conceived the British to be interested," except through the bark collectors employed in the interior, by the house of Gibbs & Co. He further wrote, that Mr. Stubbs, managing partner of that house, had agreed to send a person into the Montana to endeavour to get some seeds, but none have yet been received.

In reference to these experiments, it may be observed, that judging from the experience of all others, who have hitherto attempted to get rare seeds and plants by the same agency, as much was done as could have been expected, though the result has been nil.

But preceding these events, I was enabled to institute a small experiment with living cinchona plants, which I had hoped would have had a successful issue. Knowing that Dr. Weddell, who has explored the southern cinchona regions, discovered the calisaya, or that species which yields the best yellow bark, and that he had brought home seeds of this valuable species, which had germinated and produced young plants, both in France and in this country, I applied to, and obtained from the Botanic Gardens of Kew and Edinburgh, as well as from the Horticultural Society six plants of the true cinchona calisaya. As Mr. Fortune was at that time proceeding by the overland route on his mission to China to obtain tea seeds and plants as well as manufactures, he was requested to take charge of these plants, which he himself packed into a small Ward's case. These were conveyed by him along with the passengers of the mail of January 1854 across the desert, and five of the plants safely reached the Calcutta Botanic Garden, which was then under the superintendence of Dr. Falconer. Dr. Falconer, in his report dated 9th April 1855, states that the plants were retained in the Botanic Garden, throughout the hot weather and rains, in conservatory cases with the object of propagating from them. "It was however discovered there, as in the Horticultural Society's Garden here, that the plants bear pruning or cutting of any kind very ill, and were therefore no doubt injured by it. 'The buds,' Dr. F. continues, "survived for a very long time, but never struck root, and finally perished. The original plants did not thrive well in the Botanic Gardens,' they were sent to Darjeeling where three of them arrived alive." Dr. Campbell reported from that place on the 30th September 1855, "that all the plants were killed by the cold of last

last winter." He therefore recommends that in every future trial, "the plants should not be taken to a higher elevation than 2,000 feet." But the eligibility of a situation depends in a great measure upon the degree of warmth and moisture of climate, as well as in protection from other trees; and no doubt something also upon the soil.

About the same time that these plants were sent to India, I obtained through Mr. Pentland some of the calisaya seed which Dr. Weddell had collected either in his first journey or in some subsequent occasion, but which I know he had had for some time in his possession. These seeds I sent to Dr. Falconer, by whom they were sown in the Botanical Garden of Calcutta, but he wrote that "although watched with the utmost care by the European head gardener, none of them showed the slightest disposition to germinate." From this it has been inferred in the present correspondence that it is useless to obtain seeds of these cinchonas, and that reliance should be placed on plants only. These are no doubt the most important, and should be obtained; but it is a very erroneous inference to come to (from seeds of which nothing could have been known), that the seeds of the cinchonas are of no value. For the plants of *C. Calisaya*, which were at one time very numerous in hothouses in Europe, were all obtained from seeds brought home, by Dr. Weddell. What is required, is that the seeds should be collected by a competent person when ripe, then carefully dried and sent off in small parcels by successive mails. Some should be sown on arrival in the West Indies, others in hothouses in this country, and the remainder sent on to India. The great advantage would be that as they vegetated, a forest of cinchonas might be raised from them in a comparatively short time.

Moreover, as I have already referred in my letter of the 29th March 1856, to the efforts of the Dutch Government to introduce cinchona plants into the mountains of Java, it may be mentioned, as quoted from the Pharmaceutical Journal, for 1 April 1856, "A qualified careful person was sent to Peru, in order to import thence into Java, by way of the Pacific Ocean, a whole ship-load of plants and seeds. M. Hasskarl was charged with the expedition, and before one year had elapsed arrived safely with his cargo in Java, where he found the seeds sent out by him *viâ* Holland already in luxuriant growth."

Again, on the receipt of the despatch from the Government, dated 2d June, 1855, respecting the unsuccessful result of the experiment made in the year 1854, for the introduction of the quinine yielding cinchona plants into India, I recommended that a small sum should be expended in employing Dr. Jamieson, who is resident at Quito, in obtaining seeds of some valuable species, which are to be met with in the neighbourhood of Quito and Loxa. A sum of 50 *l.* was in consequence authorised for this purpose, with a promise of a further sum in case of success. I have not yet obtained any seeds from Dr. Jamieson, nor, indeed, have I heard from him in reply, but as the seeds are ripe in April and May, it is probable that some will shortly be sent, as he has written to the council of the Horticultural Society, who wrote to him for a more general supply, that he was going to send seeds to this country. I have no doubt, therefore, that I shall soon receive some, as Dr. J. is in the habit of supplying others with seeds and dried plants.

In addition to this source, I hope to obtain seeds of some of the useful species of cinchona through other channels, that is, through some of the large consumers of bark; of these, Mr. Howard, who is the largest manufacturer of quinine in this country, and the person who is probably better acquainted than any one else with all the different kinds of bark known in European commerce, has entered warmly into the project, and has written to his managing agent in South America to obtain seeds of the best kinds in his neighbourhood. Another consumer of bark has engaged, though not directly with me, to use his best efforts in obtaining seeds of the species common in the district where his agents are employed. In both cases as in that of Dr. Jamieson, I have offered to pay the expenses that are incurred in obtaining such seeds, which will probably not amount to any large sum.

The foregoing arrangements for obtaining seeds of the quinine yielding cinchonas, all depend upon the exertions of agents who may or may not second the proposals of their principals, and with all it must occupy a very subordinate place. Besides that they themselves would have to employ other agents to collect

collect the seeds, as they seldom if ever proceed into the bark forests. We cannot, therefore, rely upon getting any large quantities of good seed, though I consider it probable that we shall obtain some. The subject is yet of such great importance, both in an economical and philanthropic point of view, that every exertion should be made to ensure its accomplishment. I, therefore, consider that it is essential to employ a special agent or gardening collector as recommended by the Government of India; and I think that his ostensible object should be, that of making a general collection either for the gardens of India or of this country, while his special directions should be to keep as much as possible in the vicinity of the mountain tracts, along which the valuable cinchonas are known to grow. For instance, he might take what is comparatively an easy course, that is, by the steamer up the Magdalena, and first collect seeds and plants of the cinchonas near St. Fé de Bagota, and then proceed back or across to Payta, Quito, and the neighbourhood of Loxa, near all which several valuable kinds of cinchona are produced. The greater the number of species obtained, as well as the greater the extent of country over which the seeds are collected, the greater is the probability of success in finding soils and climates in the mountainous regions of India for the successful culture of some at least, if not of all, the species of useful cinchonas. The most valuable species of all, that is the cinchona calisaya, is unfortunately not only the most inaccessible, but also that which appears to have a more limited range of distribution, and to require a more peculiar climate. The attempts to obtain it by the special agent might be deferred to the second season, as there would be ample occupation for any one in obtaining seeds and plants of the other useful species in the first season. I do not more particularly refer to all these, or the localities where they are to be found, as they are detailed in the memorandum which I drew up for the use of the several consuls; but further instructions will require to be prepared in case of a special agent being appointed.

The kind of person best suited to accomplish successfully the object in view, is a gardening collector, that is, a gardener who has been sufficiently accustomed to plants to be able to distinguish those he is in search of, and who has also had sufficient experience in the collecting and drying of seeds, as well as in the transplanting of young plants, as to insure their safe carriage; say, in the first instance, to the Government Botanic Garden in the West Indies, until he himself could bring the last supplies to this country, or if thought desirable, take them to India and see them planted in the very mountains where they are to grow. Such a person, and well qualified for the purpose, may be obtained for 200*l.* or 250*l.* a year, and the travelling and other expenses would probably require as much more; the total of the whole being only about a fourth of the sum now spent yearly in the purchase of quinine by the Indian Government; but the quantity of which, as well as of the other cinchona alkalis, might very beneficially be increased in consumption, as nothing is so safe and has so powerful a control over all Indian fevers. If, on the other hand, we contemplate the possibility, nay probability of diminishing supplies of cinchona bark, when the more remote forests have been cleared, as the easily accessible forests have already been, every feeling of policy as well as of humanity prompts the adoption of measures, which may extend the basis of supply of one of the most valuable, indeed indispensable, means of cure for a vast number, not only of dangerous cases of otherwise fatal fevers, but also of still more numerous cases of the most painful neuralgic affections.

J. Forbes Royle, M. D.

— No. 17. —

EXTRACT DESPATCH from the Court of Directors to the Government of India; dated 3 March (No. 35), 1858.

Para. 41. WE did not fail to take immediate measures for carrying out the recommendations of your Government on this important subject. We regret, however, that these measures have not yet been attended with the desired success. We hope that we may be

Letter from India, 10 November (No. 131) 1856.
Letter from India, 15 December (No. 142) 1856.

be able, at no distant period, to obtain a collection of both plants and seeds of the quinine-yielding cinchonas; and we will give you early intimation of the same, in order that the necessary preparation may be given for disposing of them to the best advantage on their arrival in India.

—No. 18.—

From Sir *J. Emerson Tennent* to *J. C. Melvill*, Esq.

Office of Committee of Privy Council for Trade,
Sir, Whitehall, 27 October 1858.

UNDERSTANDING that some years ago an experiment was made by the East India Company to introduce the cultivation of cinchona (Peruvian bark), into their territories, the Lords of the Committee of Privy Council for Trade direct me to request that you will convey to the Secretary of State for India their desire to be furnished with any documents illustrative of the nature of the attempt, the districts in which the experiment was instituted, the degree of success which attended it, and the nature of the causes (if any) which proved unfavourable. My Lords would be glad to know the opinion formed as to its ultimate practicability, and to be furnished with particulars of soil, climate, and temperature which seem to be most suitable.

I have, &c.
(signed) *J. Emerson Tennent.*

—No. 19.—

From Sir *George Clerk* to Sir *J. Emerson Tennent.*

Sir, East India House, 2 December 1858.

IN reply to your letter of the 27th October, relative to the experiments made by the East India Company on the cultivation of cinchona (Peruvian bark) in India, I am desired by the Secretary of State for India in Council to transmit, for the information of the Lords of the Committee of Privy Council for Trade, a copy of the documents noted in the margin,* showing the measures taken for obtaining seeds and plants of the quinine-yielding cinchonas from South America, and the failure of the attempt to procure the growth and germination in India of the few plants and seeds which it has as yet been found practicable to obtain.

On a consideration of Dr. Forbes Royle's memorandum, in April 1857, the Court of Directors authorised that officer to despatch a botanical collector to the cinchona districts in South America, with such instructions as he might deem most applicable to the occasion, for the purpose of collecting plants and seeds of the quinine-yielding cinchona. Dr. Royle is understood to have taken steps to find an eligible person for this duty, but his death prevented the necessary arrangements from being completed. A successor has just been appointed to Dr. Royle's post, who will be directed to carry out the instructions above alluded to without any further delay.

I have, &c.
(signed) *G. Clerk.*

---

* Letter from T. Thomson, esq., Superintendent Botanic Garden, dated 14 May 1855.
Letter from H. Falconer, esq., M. D., dated 9 April 1855.
Letter from A. Campbell, esq., M. D., dated 30 April 1855.
Letter from Dr. J. F. Royle, M. D., dated East India House, March 1857.
Memorandum by Dr. Royle, regarding the introduction into India of the quinine-yielding cinchonas, dated March 1857.

— No. 20. —

From Mr. *Clements Markham* to Sir *George Clerk*, K.C.B.

Sir, India Office, 5 April 1859.

UNDERSTANDING that it is the intention of the Secretary of State to take measures for the introduction of the cinchona plant into India, on a large scale, I venture to offer my services for that purpose.

It will be well, in the first place, to recapitulate the arguments proving the urgent necessity of the measure, and the best means for effecting it; and secondly, the qualifications which I possess in order to bring it to a successful conclusion.

"Among the vast variety of medical drugs," says Dr. Royle in 1852, "there is not one, with probably the single exception of opium, which is more valuable to man than quinine-yielding cinchona." In 1853 he says, "The successful introduction into India of the cinchona will be of great benefit not only to that country, but to the world in general, as there is great fear that the supply from the original sources may become so much diminished as to be beyond the reach of the mass of those who require the aid of quinine. To the Indian Government a home supply of a drug which already costs about 7,000 *l.* a year, would be advantageous in an economical point of view, and invaluable as affording means of employing a drug which is indispensable in the treatment of Indian fevers."

"The probability of entire success in the cultivation of the cinchona trees in India seems to admit of hardly any doubt, if ordinary care is adopted in the selection of suitable localities on the slopes of the Neilgherries, and the Southern Himalayas."

It has been proved, by fruitless experiments, that it is useless to attempt to procure either the plants or the seeds, through the instrumentality of Her Majesty's consuls; or through agents, having no interest in the success of their labours, and who probably employ other agents to deal with the actual *cascarillero* or collector.

Great care and attention are necessary in collecting seeds or plants, the latter especially. The seeds must be ripe when gathered, they must then be dried in the sun, and kept dry, as well as occasionally exposed to the air. Much personal attention is necessary, to ensure the seeds being gathered from the right trees. Plants require still more care. Considerable tact also is required in order to avoid exciting jealousy in the minds of Government officials.

These facts are pointed out, in order to show how fruitless it will be to trust to agents and consuls, and how necessary it is to employ some person whose heart is really in the business.

I now venture to refer to the qualifications which I possess for this service.

I am well acquainted with several of the forests in Peru, and on the frontiers of Bolivia, containing the cinchona tree. I already know three of the more useful species by sight, and should be able to acquire a thorough knowledge of the others before leaving England. I know not only the Spanish language, but also the Quichua, or language spoken by the Indians of those districts; and I am intimate with many of the public men, and the landowners on the eastern slopes of the Cordillera. I trust I may add that I am most anxious to perform this service well, which I feel to be of such great importance.

I have, &c.

Sir George Clerk, (signed) *Clements R. Markham.*
&c., &c., &c.

— No. 21. —

RESOLUTION of the Revenue, Judicial, and Legislative Committee approved by the Secretary of State for India in Council, 8 April 1859.

THE Committee have had under their consideration a letter from Mr. J. Gerstenberg, "Chairman of the Ecuador Land Company (Limited)," dated 29th ultimo, respecting the measures proposed to be taken by the Company for developing the resources of the territory made over by the State of Ecuador for the benefit of its British creditors, and submitting a proposal that the Indian Government should take part in a scientific mission, which it is proposed to attach to the commercial enterprise, and in which it is designed that the French Government should also take part, the special object proposed in the arrangement being the collection of seeds and plants of the quinine yielding cinchonas for despatch, on the one hand to Algeria, and on the other to the East Indies.

The Committee, bearing in mind the extreme importance of quinine as a medical agent in India, and the expense to which the Government has annually been put in procuring a supply, and which expense must, under present circumstances, be largely increased, have given their careful consideration to the proposal before them. But in the first case they find that there is no evidence that the most valuable species of the cinchona are to be found in the territory granted by the Ecuador Government, and further, they are of opinion that a mission conducted by a commercial association, whose principal object must be to develope resources which will prove a permanent source of income, is not the most likely means of attaining the object to be aimed at, the full success of which would in effect render India independent, as regards the supply of quinine, of those provinces of South America, where the more valuable cinchona trees abound. The Committee are therefore unable to recommend to the Secretary of State the acceptance of the proposals contained in the letter of Mr. Gerstenberg.

The Committee, however, have had under their consideration a plan for obtaining the requisite supply of seeds and plants of the cinchona, which is in accordance with the measures formerly approved by the Court of Directors, and which appears to them well fitted to attain the object.

On the failure of the attempt made to provide a supply of plants and seeds through the instrumentality of Her Majesty's Consuls in the South American States, where the quinine-yielding cinchonas are known to exist, the court sanctioned a proposal for the deputation of a special agent for the purpose, and the late Dr. Forbes Royle was engaged for two or three years before his death in seeking for a properly qualified collector to undertake the duty. He did not succeed in his attempt; and, though the subject has since, with special reference to a renewed representation from the Government of India on the subject, been under reference to Dr. Forbes Watson, the present reporter on the products of India, no fit person has hitherto been met with.

A proposal to undertake the mission, which seems to the Committee to be well worthy of acceptance, has now been made to them by Mr. Clements Markham, a clerk in the department of India correspondence. The letter of Mr. Markham offering his services in this behalf, is submitted for the information of the Secretary of State in Council, and from that it will be seen that his qualifications for the duty consist of a knowledge of the best cinchona districts, acquired during a residence in Peru and Bolivia; a general knowledge of various species of the cinchona tree; an acquaintance with the Spanish language and with the Quichua or language of the Indians of the districts in question, and an intimacy with many of the public men and landowners on the eastern slopes of the Cordilleras where the cinchonas abound.

It appears to the Committee that having regard to the urgent importance in both a medical and an economical point of view, of introducing the plant into India without further loss of time, and to the failure of the attempts hitherto made to procure the services of a suitable collector, it is advisable to take advantage of the offer of Mr. Markham, and to entrust to him the proposed commission.

It will probably not be necessary for Mr. Markham to start much before the close of the present year, in order to procure the first available supply of seeds and young plants; and he will, therefore, have ample time to make himself more thoroughly acquainted with the varieties of the cinchona plants which he is especially to seek for, and with all the details with regard to the packing and despatch of his collections, the knowledge of which may be requisite to the satisfactory performance of the duty he proposes to undertake.

It will be observed that Mr. Markham does not ask for more than his present salary, and the payment of all his expenses; but if the Secretary of State in Council should give his general assent to the proposal, the Committee would suggest that they may be empowered, subject to his Lordship's final approval, to to settle all necessary details with Mr. Markham, both as regards the terms on which he would proceed on his mission, and the arrangements for his journey, and for the collection and despatch to India of the seeds and plants which he may collect.

It will of course be necessary, if Mr. Markham is deputed on this service, that some arrangement should be made for the temporary discharge of his duties in the Revenue Department to which he is attached.

— No. 22. —

(No. 59.)

From Lord *Stanley* to the Governor General of India.

My Lord, India Office, London, 9 June 1859.

Having again taken into consideration the subject of introducing seeds and plants of the quinine-yielding cinchona into India, I have resolved, in Council, to depute a confidential officer to South America during the ensuing season, to make a collection of the seeds and plants, and to convey them to Calcutta, Madras, and Ceylon.

2. I therefore have to request that you will call upon the superintendent of the Botanical Gardens at Calcutta, to furnish you with his opinion respecting the best locality for planting the cinchona in your Presidency, and with any other observations which he may deem useful, respecting the cultivation of those plants in India.

I have, &c.
(signed) *Stanley.*

— No. 23. —

From the Government of India to the Right Honourable Sir *Charles Wood*, Bart., G.C.B., Secretary of State for India.

Sir, Fort William, 9 January 1860.

In continuation of our Despatch No. 102 of 1859, dated the 24th of September, we have the honour to forward to you copies of the reports that we have procured, in pursuance of the Despatches noted on the margin, from the Agricultural and Horticultural Society; from Dr. Thomson, the Superintendent of the Calcutta Botanical Gardens; and from Dr. Jamieson, the Superintendent of the Botanical Gardens in the North-Western Provinces, regarding the measures to be taken preparatory to the arrival of the cinchonas in India, and the localities to be selected in this Presidency for their cultivation.

No. 59 of 1859, dated 9 June.
No. 99 of 1859, dated 7 October.

2. We have, however, since received your Despatch No. 119, dated the 24th November, 1859, and its enclosure, from which we learn that the experiment is to be confined, in the first instance, to the Neilgherry Hills, in the Madras Presidency, and that it is not therefore necessary that we should take, at present, any further steps in this Presidency, in accordance with the previous Despatches of the 9th June and 7th October, 1859. A communication to this effect has been made to his Excellency the Governor General, and to the Governments of Bengal, the North-Western Provinces, and Bombay.

3. We forward an interesting memorandum, furnished to us by Dr. Brandis, the Superintendent of Forests in Pegu and Tenasserim, on the suitability of the mountain tracts of those provinces for the cultivation of the quinine-yielding cinchonas.

We have, &c.,
(signed) *J. Outram,*
H. B. E. Frere.

Enclosure 1, in No 23.

From *A. H. Blechynden*, Esq., Secretary, Agricultural and Horticultural Society, to *W. Grey*, Esq., Secretary to the Government of India, dated Calcutta, the 24th August 1859.

I AM directed by the Agricultural and Horticultural Society to acknowledge the receipt of your letter of the 23rd ultimo, intimating that Her Majesty's Government have determined on deputing a confidential officer to South America, to make a collection of seeds and plants of quinine-yielding cinchonas, and conveying them to Calcutta, Madras, and Ceylon, and requesting information from the society as to the best locality for planting the trees in this Presidency, with any other observations that they may deem useful respecting the cultivation of those species of cinchonas in India.

2. In reply I am directed to state that the requisites for the successful cultivation of these valuable plants appear to be a moist and equally temperate climate. Frost and snow, and dry heat are to be avoided. For this reason, the localities in this Presidency best adapted for attempting their culture, appear to be those already enumerated in the fourth paragraph of my letter of the 28th August 1856, namely, the Hills near Darjeeling or say Sikhim, the Khasyah Hills, the mountains beyond Chittagong, the hilly parts of Upper Assam, the Tenasserim Provinces; and, in Southern India, the Neilgheries and the high elevation of the Western Ghauts.

3. The society, I am directed to observe, are scarcely in a position to offer any practical observations in regard to the second point adverted to in your letter under acknowledgment. They would, however, venture to submit the few following remarks, which, if acted on, may, they conceive, lead to the successful introduction and cultivation of the plant in India :—

First. It would be very desirable so to time the despatch of the plants and seeds from their native country as to reach India at the commencement of the cold season. The recommendations contained in Dr. Falconer's paper (Journal of the Agricultural and Horticultural Society, vol. VIII., p. 16) in respect to the mode of despatch of seeds and plant are, the society think, well worthy of adoption.

Second. It would be further desirable, the society conceive, to act on the suggestions of the late Mr. Piddington, as detailed in his memorandum, published in the Society's Journal (vol. X., p. 140), more especially those parts which relate to soil and climate, as enumerated under Sections A. to D. of the memorandum in question.

Third. The proposal in the Minute of the Right Honourable the Governor General (vol. X., page 144), namely, " that officers possessing the requisite botanical and geological knowledge should be deputed to inquire as to the sites best calculated to receive the plants; that these officers, duly supplied with all aids and appliances, should receive the plants upon arrival, and convey them to the selected spots," appear to the society also worthy of adoption, with the view of giving the interesting and important experiment a full and fair trial.

4. The best and most reliable information as respects the cultivation of these trees in their native climate is to be found, the society believe, in Weddell's " Histoire Naturelle des Quinquinas." This information, modified according to circumstances, will doubtless prove very useful to those officers who may hereafter be entrusted with the superintendence of cinchona plantations in various parts of India.

Enclosure 2, in No. 23.

From *Thomas Thomson*, Esq., M.D., Superintendent of Botanic Garden, Calcutta, to the Secretary to the Government of Bengal—(No. 193, dated the 6th September, 1859).

Sir,

I HAVE the honour to acknowledge the receipt of your lettter of 2d August, calling for my opinion on the best locality for planting the cinchona, and for any other observations I may deem useful respecting the cultivation of that tree in India.

2. The various species of cinchona differ widely in physical qualities, and grow in very different climates; but the attention of the officer deputed to America will doubtless be specially directed to the best kinds, and in particular to *Cinchona Calisaya*, which is believed to yield the finest quality of bark. This species is a native of tropical South America, between 13 and 16 south latitude, at elevations of 5,000 and 6,000 feet. It delights in a very humid, temperate climate, in which there is but little variation of temperature throughout the year, so that the tree is never subject either to a powerful sun or to severe frost.

3. As

3. As regards the best locality for the cultivation of cinchona, I can add little to what has been stated by Royle, Falconer, and others. It is of course desirable that the places selected for the experiment should possess as nearly as possible the climate in which the plant is indigenous. As the cultivation must be directed by qualified officers, the number of spots selected cannot be numerous, but they should not, I think, be less than two.

4. If two be the number fixed on, one should be (as was long ago stated by Dr. Royle towards the southern extremity of the Madras peninsula, where the mountains afford the requisite elevation and humidity, in a latitude not very different from that in which the plant is indigenous. The selection of the exact spot must be left to local experience. Thence, after the cultivation is established, it may be extended to Ceylon, and perhaps to the Malayan peninsula.

5. The other site should, I think, be on the Khasia Hills, where the climate is very well suited to the growth of cinchona, notwithstanding a little difference of latitude, and where elevations of 5,000 to 6,000 feet are easily obtained.

6. Thence the cultivation will probably hereafter be extended to the Sikhim Himalaya, which is abundantly humid, but which from the occasional excess of winter cold, caused by the proximity of the snowy mountains, is on the whole less suited for a first experiment.

7. The cinchona plants and seeds will of course be forwarded by the most expeditious route from the west coast of South America. They should arrive in India early in December, and not sooner. This will give ample time for transport to a cool climate before the hot season.

8. As the successful conduct of the experiment will require great care, I consider that it is important to avoid everything which can possibly cause delay. It is, therefore, essential that the exact sites should be selected, the ground cleared, and every minor arrangement made before the plants arrive in India.

Enclosure 3, in No. 23.

From *W. Grey*, Esq., Secretary to the Government of India, to *T. Thomson*, Esq., M.D., Superintendent Botanical Garden, Calcutta—(No. 2,312, dated the 24th November, 1859).

With reference to your communication to the Bengal Government, No. 193, dated 6th September, I am directed to forward to you a copy of a pamphlet drawn up by Mr. Markham, the gentleman who has been employed by the Home Government to proceed to South America for the purpose of procuring cinchona plants and seeds, and to request that you will be good enough to submit any further suggestions regarding the best locality for the cinchonas, as well as regarding any other practical points connected with the experiment about to be made, which may occur to you from a perusal of Mr. Markham's pamphlet.

2. The seeds and plants which will be received in Calcutta are intended to be disposed of in Bengal and its dependencies. Separate consignments are to be made to Madras and Ceylon.

Enclosure 4, in No. 23.

From *W. Jameson*, Esq., Superintendent Botanical Gardens, North Western Provinces, to *F. B. Outram*, Esq., Officiating under Secretary to the Government of the North Western Provinces, No. 439, dated Camp Kowlaglier, Dehra Dhoon, the 11th September 1859.

I have the honour to acknowledge the receipt of your letter No. 1416, dated 7th ultimo, enclosing two letters regarding the cultivation of the cinchona plant in India, and calling for a report on the best localities for cultivating it in North-West Provinces.

2. The number of species of cinchona known amounts to upwards of 20, which are found occupying a belt extending over nearly 30 degrees of latitude, or from 10 degrees north to 20 degrees south.

3. The true cinchonas are chiefly confined to the Andes of Peru, Columbia and Bolivia, and occur at altitudes varying from 1,200 to 10,000 feet above the level of the sea. They are thus met with in different kinds of climates, varying from tropical to temperate, which abound in the Himalayas in Kumaon, and Gurhwal and Kohistan, of the Punjaub.

4. By most travellers who have visited the districts where the cinchona plants are found, the rock formations are described as belonging to the primary series, consisting of mica and clay slates, gniess, granite, &c,

5. Some species of cinchona grow in dense forests in warm valleys, ranging from 1,200 to 2,000 feet in altitude. Others are met with on the declivities of mountains, and at altitudes varying from 6,000 to 10,000 feet, or the former in a tropical, and the latter in temperate climates. To meet these extremes, it will therefore be necessary to select several localities.

6. For the species met with in hot valleys, I would recommend Chegouri at the southern base of the Tyne Range in Western Gurhwal.

7. For the species met with in more temperate regions, and at higher altitudes, or from 4,000, to 6,000 feet, I would recommend Kote, on the northern side of the Tyne Range.

8. And for species formed in the highest altitudes, or from 7,000 to 10,000, I would recommend Danoulti, east of Landour.

9. All these localities are in primary districts, and similar in formation to the districts where the plants now occur, and from this we may infer, that the soil is of a similar nature, the primary rocks of the Andes being nearly identical with those of the Himalayas.

10. Until, however, the report of the officer deputed to collect the plants be submitted, stating the localities where the plants have been collected, it would be premature to assign localities at present, unless in a general manner, as has been done.

11. But the receiving officer in Calcutta ought to be careful not to mix the species, as the locality that suits one species may be quite unfitted for another.

12. The localities recommended by me are of easy access, and all situated in the late Teeree Rajah's country. I brought this to the notice of Major Ramsay, Commissioner, Kumaon, before the country was made over to the late Rajah's illegitimate son, and he stated that there would be no difficulty whatever in procuring from the rajah a grant of the lands on very easy terms.

13. There are other localities where the cinchona plants might be advantageously tried, as in the Cherra Poonjee and Neilgherie Hills. But as I have not visited them, and as the former have been examined by Dr. Thomson, of Calcutta, and to the latter the labours of Dr. Cleghorn, of Madras, extend, these gentlemen will be better prepared to give opinions as to the localities on these mountains to be selected for the purpose.

No. 1732, dated Allahabad, the 23rd September 1859.

Order.—Ordered that copy of the foregoing be forwarded to the Secretary to the Government of India, Home Department, in reply to No. 1499, dated the 23rd July last.

(signed) *A. M. Monteith,*
Offg. Asst. Sec., Govt., N. W. P.

Enclosure 5, in No. 23.

From *T. Thomson*, Esq., M.D., Superintendent Botanic Garden, Calcutta, to *W. Grey*, Esq., Secretary to the Government of India, No. 202, dated the 6th December 1859.

I HAVE the honour to acknowledge the receipt of your letter No. 2312, dated 24th ultimo, forwarding a copy of Mr. Markham's pamphlet on cinchonas, and calling on me to submit any further remarks on the subject, which its perusal may suggest.

2. The information contained in it confirms me in my opinion, that the cinchona will succeed well in the Khasya hills. No other place in the Bengal Presidency appears to me equally suitable for a first experiment. Suitable elevation and climate may perhaps be found in Tennasserim, but the interior of that province is too little known to make this certain.

3. The exact site should be selected by a practical botanist, after careful comparison of the vegetation and climate of the Khasya hills with that of the Cinchona forests, as described by Weddell and others.

4. The officer deputed for this purpose should pass the whole of next rainy season in the hills, so as to become familiar with the physical features and climate of the range. He should visit the most promising places repeatedly during the season, and make the final selection

selection about the beginning of November, before which time the active preparations for the reception of the plants need not be begun.

5. An intelligent English gardener should, I think, be engaged for the practical supervision of the cultivation, and especially for the raising of the seeds and preparation of cuttings, two very delicate operations, upon which the rapid extension of the plant will mainly depend. The gardener need not be here till the plants arrive, and if Mr. Markham is accompanied to South America by a gardener, he will probably be glad to remain. After a time, the services of the gardener will be required for the extension of the cultivation to new districts, which, after a year or two's residence in the country, he will be quite qualified to superintend.

6. A supply of bell glasses should be indented for from England, and kept in readiness here, to be forwarded with the plants to their destination.

Enclosure 6, in No. 23.

From Dr. *D. Brandis*, Superintendent of Forests, Pegu, Tennasserim and Martaban Provinces, to *W. Grey*, Esq., Secretary to the Government of India, dated Calcutta, the 29th December 1859.

In compliance with your verbal request, I have now the honour to submit a memorandum of remarks concerning the localities suitable for the cultivation of the Peru bark tree in the Pegu, Tenasserim and Martaban Provinces. I have been obliged to enter into some detail regarding the general configuration of the country, as the ideas generally entertained, of the situation of the mountainous parts of those provinces are not very clear, and a partial description might have led to misunderstanding, and this has led me to add some notes on the establishment of a sanatarium there.

2. As I have not the means here of keeping copies, I would solicit the favour of your directing them to be sent to the Commissioner of Pegu. If such should appear unobjectionable, I should be glad to be permitted to publish the memorandum with additional notes, lists of plants, the detail of my meteorological observations, and extracts from my journals—in the Journal of the Asiatic Society or elsewhere.

Enclosure 7, in No. 23.

Memorandum by Dr. *Brandis*, on the Prospects of an Experimental Cultivation of the Quinine-yielding Cinchonas on the Mountain Tracts of the Pegu, Tenasserim, and Martaban Provinces, with notes on the establishment of a Sanatarium there by Dr. *Brandis*, Superintendent of Forests, Pegu and Tenasserim.

Points to be observed in selecting localities for cinchona cultivation.

The quinine-yielding cinchonas are found within the tropics of South America, in the vallies of the Andes, range at an elevation of from 3,000 to 6,000 feet, in the immediate neighbourhood of mountain masses, which rise up to 18,000 feet, and are partly covered with eternal snow.

This indicates, in a general way, the requirements of the plant; but although in the first instance such places should be selected for the experiment as are particularly suitable, it must not be lost sight of, that the cultivation of the Peru bark tree may also succeed in localities not appearing to offer exactly the same conditions regarding climate and the general character of the country, which are peculiar to their native place.

Localities available in India.

There is no lack in India of situations apparently well suited for the experiment, and as several of them, viz. the Neilgherries, Darjeeling, and the Khasya Hills, offer particular facilities for making the trial; it would appear that at first a further extension of the projected cinchona plantations is not called for, unless indeed the mountains of the Pegu, Tenasserim, and Martaban Provinces should offer superior advantages. The following remarks will show that this is not the case, and that it appears preferable to delay the introduction of the tree into the eastern provinces, until its cultivation shall have proved successful in other parts, when it can be managed with greater facility.

Hereafter, when plants can be obtained from the older plantations, it may well be worth while to extend the cultivation of the tree, and indeed it is not impossible that some of the tracts described below, will be found to possess peculiar advantages for the production of the quinine-yielding bark.

To avoid misunderstanding, it appears necessary to review the general configuration of Pegu, the Tenasserim, and Martaban provinces.

 2. Four

General structure of the mountain masses of the provinces.

2. Four great mountain ranges, running more or less parallel to the sea coast, from north-west to south-east, form as it were the skeleton of these provinces. They separate from each other the valleys of the principal rivers of the country, and intervene between them and the coast. Geologically they are composed of rocks widely differing in character, but the strike of the strata, whenever there is stratification, and the direction of the main spurs and ridges, pursues, as far as is known, with due deviations, but upon the whole with remarkable regularity, a line running from 15° to 45° west of north.

Arracan Yomah.

Proceeding from west to east, the first range is the Arracan Yomah, which divides the province of Arracan from Pegu and Burmah Proper, not attaining within Pegu an elevation exceeding 4,000 feet; this range cannot be selected for the first cultivation of the Peru bark tree. Its northern part, which divides Arracan from the Burmese empire and Munipoor, and which forms a connexion with the Khasya and other mountains east of Bengal, is said to be higher; but of this portion I cannot speak.

Pegu Yomah.

The second range is the Pegu Yomah, which separates the valley of the Irawaddee and Sitang rivers. Its highest point is the Kambalootoun, near the source of the Pegu river, nearly in the latitude of Akontoun on the Irawaddee, below Prome. The height of this hill has not been measured, but by comparing it with others in its immediate vicinity, I have estimated it at about 3,000 feet. The mean elevation of the range is not above 2,000 feet. Hence these hills also, which are the principal seat of the Pegu teak forests, are not suited for an experimental cultivation of the cinchonas.

Sitang range and Tenasserim coast range.

The third range consists of two parts, of which the northern may be designated the Sitang and Martaban range, the southern the Tenasserim coast range. It commences north-east of Toungoo, where it separates the tributaries of the Sitang river from the different branches of the Thonkyeghat, and further south from the Yoonzaleen river. North-east of Shoaegyeen it divides into two great branches, the western running down between the Sitang and Beeling rivers, the eastern between the Beeling and Salween. The eastern branch which maintains the general direction of the range, ceases near Martaban, but recommences immediately south of Moulmein, and thence skirts the coast of the Tenasserim Provinces down to Mergui, and beyond it.

Like all the others, this range is not one interrupted ridge, but a system of numerous longitudinal spurs, some shorter, others longer, and joined by transverse ridges, frequently lower than the longitudinal spurs.

Many parts of this range are entirely unexplored; but it does not appear to exceed a height of 5,000 feet, and this is not a sufficient elevation to warrant an attempt in the first instance.

Salween range.

3. The fourth or easternmost range is the only one which appears to offer sufficient inducement for an experimental cultivation of the Peru bark tree. It is the main out-runner or projection of the great Karenee and Shan plateau, which extends from the Salween to the Irawaddee valley. South of this plateau, this range forms the water-shed between the Sitang and Salween rivers.

Yoonzaleen mountain mass.

South-east of Toungoo it attains a considerable elevation, and at the same time extends into a large and compact mountain mass, separated from the third or Sitang range by a remarkable longitudinal valley, through which two rivers run in opposite directions, separated at their head waters only by a low and narrow saddle. These streams are the Myitgnam, a tributary of the Thonkyeghat, running from south to north, and the western branch of the Yoonzaleen from north to south. This mountain mass, which appears to me the fittest place, both for the establishment of a sanatarium and the experimental cultivation of cinchonas, is drained on the east and north-east of the Salween side, by the feeders of the Karenee Choung (Pounloung), the Kaymapjoo or Tin Choung, and the Pah Choung, fixed by Major Allan as the northern boundary of the Martaban Province. The drainage to the west and north-west goes into the Sitang river, principally through two great feeders of the Thonkyeghat, the Rjay Choung and Myitgnan Choung. To the south the drainage runs almost entirely into the two great branches of the Yoonzaleen, the Braillo or western, and the Llaillo or eastern branch. The different peaks and spurs of this mountain mass have numerous Karen names, but no designation has as yet been adopted for the whole of it. It may fitly be called the Yoonzaleen mountain mass, but for the entire range, of which it forms a part, I would propose the name of the Salween range for the northern portion, and Thoungyeen range for the southern part.

The highest points here visited by me were the Tapio Ridge, on the west side, one of the lower spurs between the Myitgnan and Rjay Choung, 5,850 feet high, and two passes on the road from the Kaymapjoo Choung to Toungoo, one on the north-east side, 5,000 feet, and one on the north-west side, 5,237 feet high. But numerous spurs of great extent, and considerably higher, were observed from these points, and by taking the angle of elevation, and estimating the distances, I came to the conclusion that numerous points seen by me could not be less than 7,000 feet high, and probably considerably above this.

Major Allan, in his report on the northern frontier of the Martaban Province, arrives, I believe, at a similar conclusion with regard to one of the southermost peaks of this mountain mass, the Tsotseeko, and Mr. O'Riley estimates another, the Nat-toung at 8,000 feet.

The highest spurs, which themselves cover a considerable space, are surrounded by masses of mountains with an average elevation of 4,000 feet; the area of the whole may be estimated at 100 square miles. Nearly the whole of this Yoonzaleen mountain mass is situated north of of the imaginary line laid down by Major Allan as the north boundary of the Martaban Province, and belongs, therefore, to the Toungoo division of the Province of Pegu, as far as it may be claimed by the British Government.

We now proceed to trace the further course of the Salween mountain range to the south. In the latitude of Kolodo, 25 miles to the south of the north end of the mountain mass here described, the range begins to contract, and its elevation is considerably diminished. In crossing the range on the road from Kolodo to Shoaegyeen, the elevation of the water-shed is only 3,264 feet (Hottalo Sakan) and the mean elevation of the Yoonzaleen table-land, which skirts the south-west side of the mountain mass above described, is from 2,600 to 3,200 feet. South of Kolodo (1,973 feet elevation) the Salween range assumes the shape of a narrow range between the Yoonzaleen and Salween, falling off more gradually towards the latter river. From here down to the mouth of the Yoonzaleen, it is called the Bithoko range. As there are Teak localities on both flanks, I had to cross it at four different places, viz.:—

South of Kolodo at an elevation of - - - - - -	3,393 feet.
Near Papoon - - - - - - - - - - -	3,137 „
„ Pagotivill - - - - - - - - - -	3,967 „
„ the great Salween rapids - - - - - -	3,910 „

It is clear that these elevations are not sufficiently high to admit of their being selected for the cultivation of cinchonas.

4. The Salween range ceases at the junction of the Salween and Yoonzaleen, but its continuation, the Thoungyeen range, commences in the fork formed by the latter river and the Salween, and, pursuing the same south-easterly direction, it extends along the Thoungyeen, separating the valley of this river from that of the Hlimbong and Houndrow. In this range two points of considerable elevation are known, the Mooleyit and the Daunat Pass. The former, which is near the Siamese boundary, is described by Major Tickell as an isolated peak, 7,171 feet high, and the latter was measured by me in April last, and found to be 5,474 feet. But as far as is yet known, the Thoungyeen range is much more irregular and broken than the Salween range, and has not any extent of mountain land to be compared to that north of the Yoonzaleen. From the height of the Daunat Pass a number of isolated peaks are seen, but few of them are higher than the Pass, and the difference in elevation does not appear to be considerable. There are several entire breaks in the Thoungyeen mountain range; the main road from Moulmein to Zimmay, in Siam, leads through one of these breaks (the Yimbine road.) This more irregular and less compact character of these mountains may be connected with the prevalence of limestone masses here, which in the Salween mountains are found on the outskirts only, and in the valleys of the neighbouring streams. Thoungyeen range.

The country round the Mooleyit peak, which I have not visited myself, may possibly offer sites advantageous for cinchona cultivation, and in case the establishment of a sanatarium at that place should be decided upon, it would be comparatively easy to form an experimental cinchona plantation there; but for the present my remarks will be limited to the Yoonzaleen mountain mass, and I will now proceed to add a few remarks regarding the climate, rocks, vegetation, and inhabitants of those mountains, the extent and elevation of which has above been discussed.

5. No regular series of observations of temperature, humidity, and rainfall on these hills at an elevation exceeding 4,000 feet, is available. I had only two opportunities of visiting them, once in February 1859, when coming from Toungoo to the Salween Forests, and once in May of the same year, when returning from Toungoo. On both occasions I was obliged to hurry on, the observations therefore were taken only during a few days. Further remarks regarding the Yoonzaleen mountain mass. Climate.

But the following facts seem to be established by the observations available, and the testimony of the natives:—

1st.—The rainfall is considerably greater than in the neighbouring plains, and the rains commence earlier and cease later.

2nd.—The temperature throughout the year is lower, and of a more uniform character. That is, although the daily changes are occasionally very great, the difference between the seasons is less considerable.

From the 13th to the 22nd February, the daily minimum about sunrise was found to vary from 42 to 69 degrees at elevations between 2,600 and 3,500 feet. The daily maximum varied between 82 and 85.5 degrees.

From the 16th to 19th May, at elevations of 3,100 and 4,300 feet, the thermometer ranged as follows: minimum from 66 degrees to 69.5 degrees, maximum from 74 to 76 degrees.

At an elevation of 5,850 feet, the thermometer stood at 67 degrees at noon of the 14th February, and at 5,237 feet, on the 19th May, at 2. 45 P.M. it was 73·75 degrees.

The temperature of the two branches of the Yoonzaleen river, at the points where they the higher mountains was found:—

West branch, 17th February, at noon, 59 degrees, temperature of air 70 degrees.
18th „ at 9 A.M., 56 degrees, „ 60 degrees.

On the Yoonzaleen plateau, a wide extent of country south-west of the main mountain mass,

mass, from 2,600 to 3,200 feet high, frost is said to cover the ground nearly every morning in December and January, and this is given as the reason why the Betel palm will not thrive here, although it is cultivated to a great extent in the valleys round about.

Rocks.

6. The rocks observed on the mountains here described are granite, gneiss, and quartz. Limestone is only found much lower down in the valleys of the Salween, Sitang, and Yoonzaleen rivers and their tributaries. The tin washings near the head waters of the Kaymapjoo Choung are on the ridges of several of the outer spurs on the east side of these mountains, at an elevation of from 3,000 to 4,000 feet. They are worked by the Karen inhabitants of Khilo village (3,107 feet elevation) who barter the tin to the Red Karens for cattle, which they do not keep, but slaughter for their own consumption.

Vegetation.

7. The vegetation has an entirely tropical character up to an elevation of 3,000 feet, when teak entirely disappears, and the pine forests begin. These pine forests (of *Pinus Khasyana Royle*) do not rise above 5,000 feet, and are always on dry, gravelly soil. With them occur several species of oak, vaccinium, gordonia, and *Rubus moluccanus* with *Clematis acuminata*. The higher spurs and the moist valleys and slopes within the pine region are covered with dense evergreen forest, except where it has been cleared away for the toungyas or hill clearings of the Karens, which do not occupy any considerable space above 4,000 feet elevation. Thus the entire surface of the higher mountains, with the exception perhaps of isolated peaks, is clothed with uninterrupted dense evergreen forest. The trees composing this forest are as yet little known; but the absence of many tropical forms, and the prevalence of species of quercus and castanea indicates an approach to the vegetation of a more temperate climate.

The cultivation of quinine-yielding cinchonas, if anywhere in these provinces, might be attempted here on ground rendered fertile by the undisturbed occupancy of these dense primeval forests, and kept moist by their retaining rain and dew, and collecting the atmospheric moisture. The dense vegetation which covers the highest spurs has also this advantageous effect, that even at considerable elevations there is an abundance of small mountain streams, with running water of low temperature throughout the year. This is an advantage which may possibly not be found in the same degree in many other localities available in British India for the cultivation of the Peruvian bark tree.

Inhabitants.

8. The whole of the mountains between the Sitang and Salween inhabited by various tribes of Sgan Karens, who cultivate paddy on their hill clearings or toungyas, the large bamboo round their villages, and the betel pepper, betel palms, and an indigo-yielding acanthaceous plant (*Goldfussia sp.*) in the moist valleys.

The population in some of the lower parts, particularly near the Myitgnan valley, is comparatively dense; so much so, that instead of shifting their habitations and clearings annually to another locality, they have been obliged to adopt a system of rotation in their hill clearings, their fields remaining fallow for three years only, after which the grass and bushes which grow up during that time are cut down and burnt, to obtain a new crop.

The number of villages on elevations exceeding 3,000 feet is small, and two or three only are located higher than 4,000 feet. Yet deserted toungyas are occasionally met with as high as 5,000 feet. The number of villages in the immediate vicinity of the mountains here described amounts to about 15, with a population of from 1,000 to 1,500 souls. One-third of these acknowledge the authority of the Deputy Commissioner of Toungoo, one-third (those on the east side) pay tribute to the Karenee chiefs, and one-third are in a state of savage wildness. A number of these villages are Christian, connected with the American Baptist Mission; and the possibility of obtaining the assistance of these people would be an advantage in forming an establishment on these hills.

Facilities for communication, and general remarks.

9. The distance of the mountains here described from Toungoo is 40 miles as the crow flies. From Shoaegyeen the distance in a straight line is 56 miles, but the access from this place would be far more difficult. From Toungoo a road might be cleared practicable for ponies and elephants, leading in two or three marches to the foot of the range. One march would then bring the traveller to the water shed between the Sitang and Salween, the average height of which is 5,000 feet. It would, however, scarcely be advisable to select this spot either as a sanatarium or for the cultivation of cinchonas. It would be preferable to go one march further to the south, and to select a higher elevation.

But it is clear that the want of villages in the neighbourhood, and the great distance from the nearest station, would render the establishment there of a European superintendent of cinchona plantations a matter of great difficulty. He would not easily succeed in inducing a sufficient number of natives to settle in a locality where the Karens themselves have never settled before; and if he succeeded in obtaining labourers, he would run the risk of finding himself deserted whenever sickness broke out, or the weather became too cold. Another difficulty would be the expense of maintaining an establishment in a place like this. The carriage of provisions and stores alone from Toungoo, where a coolie employed in town cannot be hired for less than 12 annas a day, would be excessive. To this must be added, that the journey up the Sitang river from Rangoon to Toungoo occupies from 15 to 20 days.

Under these circumstances it does not appear justifiable to select the mountains between the Sitang and the Salween, in the first instance, for the establishment of a cinchona plantation.

If

If hereafter the mountains here described should be found to offer sufficient inducement for the formation of a sanatarium, greater facilities would be given for the establishment of cinchona plantations on these mountains, and it is not impossible that they will prove successful.

28 December 1859. (signed) *D. Brandis.*

Enclosure 8, in No. 23.

(No. 38.)

From *W. Grey*, Esq., Secretary to the Government of India, to *C. Beadon*, Esq., Secretary to the Government of India, with his Excellency the Governor General, dated Fort William, 9 January 1860.

Sir,

In the Despatches noted on the margin, the Secretary of State notified the intention of Her Majesty's Government to depute a confidential officer to South America, to collect a large supply of the best cinchonas, in order to try thoroughly the experiment of introducing the culture of this valuable product into India and Ceylon. The plants were expected to reach India in the early part of 1861, and this Government was directed to determine what measures should be taken preparatory to their arrival, and what localities should be selected in this Presidency* for the experiment.

Home department. Public No. 59 of 1859, dated 9 June. Public No. 00 of 1859, dated 7 October.

2. Reports on the subject were accordingly called for from the Agricultural and Horticultural Society, from Dr. Thomson, the Superintendent of the Calcutta Botanical Garden, and from Dr. Jamieson, the Superintendent of the Botanical Gardens in the North-Western Provinces.

3. The society suggested Darjeeling, or Sikhim, the Khasya Hills, the Hills in Chittagong and Upper Assam and the Tenasserim provinces, as best adapted for the experiment, and they recommended that proper officers should be appointed to be in readiness to receive the plants, and to convey them to their destination.

4. Dr. Thomson advocated the restriction of the experiment in the first instance to the Khasya Hills; and he suggested that a practical botanist should be appointed at once to go and reside in those hills, in order that he might select, after a full experience of the climate, the exact localities which should appear suitable.

5. Dr. Jamieson expressed an opinion that the locality to be selected must depend upon the species of the plants which might be brought to this country, some species of the cinchona requiring a more temperate climate than others.

6. While these reports were under consideration, the President in Council has received the accompanying Despatch, No. 119, dated 24th November 1859, and its enclosure, from the Secretary of State, from which it would appear that the experiment of the introduction of the cinchona tree into India is intended to be confined for the present to the Neilgherry Hills, in the Madras Presidency.

7. His Honour in Council therefore considers that it is not necessary to take, at present, any further steps in accordance with the previous Despatches of the Secretary of State, dated respectively the 9th June and 7th October 1859. The correspondence which has already passed will be reported home, and a copy of the Despatch of the 24th November, and of its enclosure, will be communicated to the Governments of Bengal, the North-Western Provinces, and Bombay, for information.

8. An interesting memorandum, furnished by Dr. Brandis while recently on a visit to Calcutta, on the suitability of Pegu, Tenasserim, and Martaban, for the growth of the quinine-yielding cinchonas, is submitted herewith for his Excellency's information.

I have, &c.,
W. Grey,
Secretary to the Government of India.

---

* The Government of Fort St. George, and, it is presumed, the Government of Ceylon, were addressed direct by Her Majesty's Government.

— No. 24. —

From Mr. *Clements Markham* to Mr. *T. G. Baring*.

Sir, India Office, 20 July 1859.

THE question of introducing plants and seeds of the quinine-yielding cinchona trees of South America into India has become very important since the immense consumption of quinine has increased the demand, and the rapid destruction of the trees has rendered the supply exceedingly precarious. During the years 1857–58, the supply of quinine cost the Indian Government upwards of 53,000 *l.*

Lord William Bentinck suggested the advisability of this measure, more than 20 years ago, and it has been discussed, at intervals, ever since, without any attempt, worthy of the name, being made to procure the plants and seeds from South America.

Last April, Lord Stanley, in Council, determined to send me to Peru, to procure seeds and plants of the cinchonas, and to convey them to India. It is absolutely necessary that this should be done in one season; but I should, of course, only be able to proceed to one particular region, and to procure one species, while there are at least eight of the more valuable species scattered over a space of more than 1,400 miles, along the eastern slopes of the Andes.

If the thing is worth doing at all, it is worth doing well; all these eight species ought to be procured, they are all valuable, and it is impossible to say which might thrive best in India; while the chances of final success are much increased by trying all the more valuable species.

I venture to address you, as to the way in which this important enterprise ought to be undertaken, in the hope that you may support a plan of operations on a more extensive scale than is at present in contemplation, and which, by giving a better prospect of success, will prove more economical.

It is now merely intended to send me to Peru, with a gardening assistant, to procure plants and seeds, and to convey them to India in the best way I can. The dangers, accidents and hindrances which might thwart me at every turn, decrease the chances of success, because the whole thing would depend entirely upon the luck of one individual. In my opinion four separate expeditions should be sent in four different directions, their collections should be received on board one vessel, and taken direct to India; and thus all the eight more valuable species of cinchonas would be obtained. I will briefly touch upon each of these four expeditions, and state my views as to the best way in which they might be undertaken.

I. Beginning from the south, the most valuable species of cinchona, containing the largest per-centage of sulphate of quinine, is the *C. Calisaya*, found in the forests of Bolivia, and the Peruvian province of Caravaya, where the *C. micrantha*, which is also valuable, is likewise met with. I propose to undertake this region myself, and, landing in the Peruvian port of Islay, to proceed to these forests. There will be many difficulties, amongst which may be mentioned the jealousy of the native governments, the difficulties in penetrating into the dense virgin forests, in finding the trees, and in conveying the plants and seeds along the dangerous route to the coast. I trust, however, through my knowledge of the country, the people, and the languages, to surmount these difficulties, and to procure a supply of the *C. Calisaya* and *C. micrantha*, conveying them to the port of Islay.

II. The forests of Huanuco and Huamalies, 250 miles from Lima, abound in two species of cinchonas, the *C. nitida* and *C. glandulifera*, which yield a valuable alkaloid, fetching a very high price in the European markets, and much used in intermittent fevers. I would suggest that I should be empowerd to secure the services of some competent person, should I succeed in finding one either in England or at Lima, to proceed to the forests near Huanuco, and procure seeds and plants of these cinchonas, to be delivered to me on my arrival at Callao, from Islay.

III. The forests near Cuença and Loxa in the Republic of Ecuador, produce barks,

To face page 32.

RETURN.—EAST INDIA (CHINCHONA PLANT).

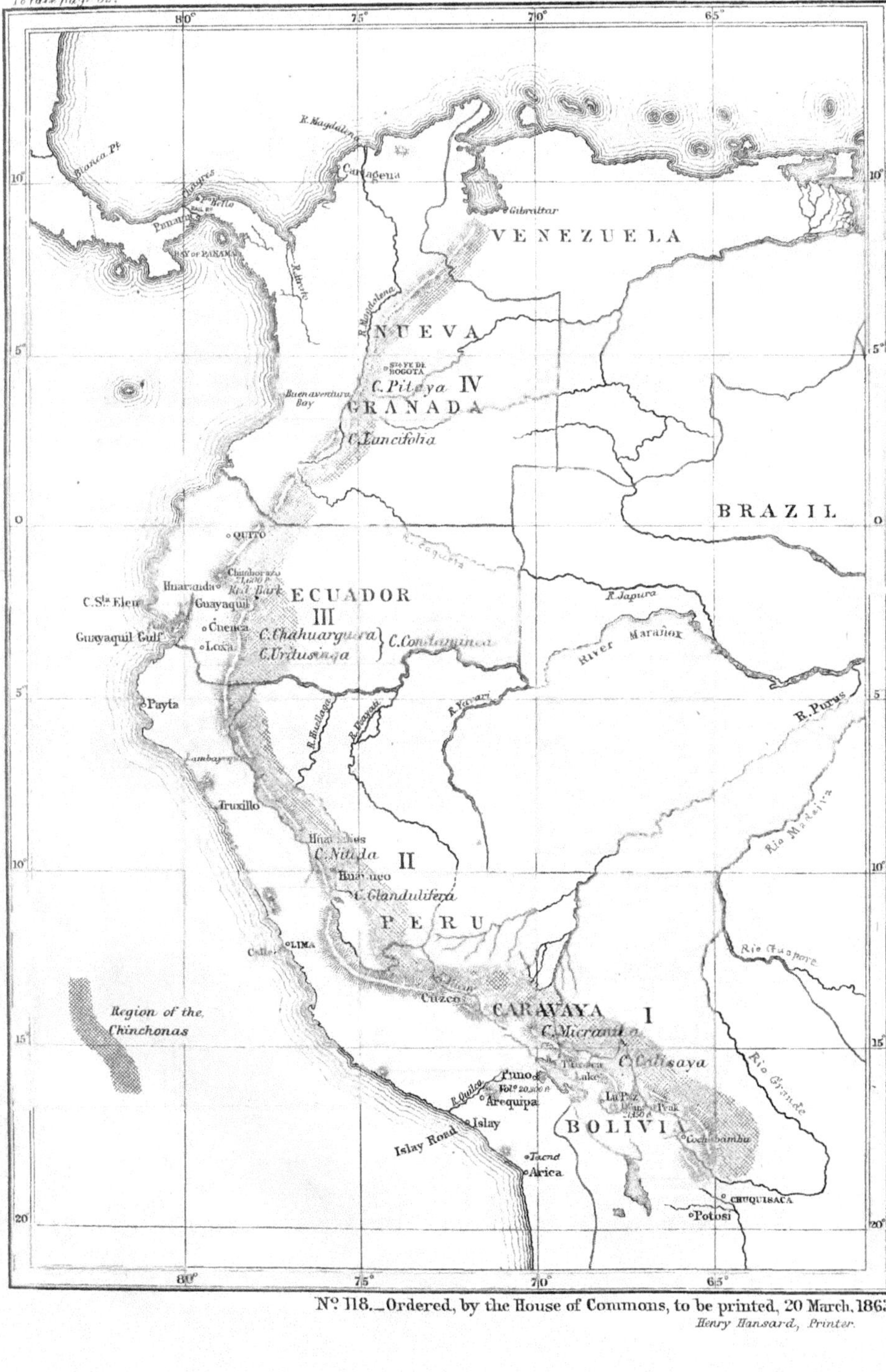

No. 118.—Ordered, by the House of Commons, to be printed, 20 March, 1863.

Henry Hansard, Printer.

barks, second only to the *C. Calisaya* of Bolivia, called *C. Chahuarguera* and *C. Uritusinga*, varieties of the *C. Condaminea*; while the valuable red bark is found at Huaranda, on the road between Quito and Guayaquil. A Company formed in London, for the purpose of developing the resources of land allotted by the Government of Ecuador for the discharge of its debt, and called the "Ecuador Land Company," has made an offer to this office to procure seeds and plants of the above cinchonas, to be delivered at the port of Guayaquil; but should no arrangement be made with this company, I trust that a botanist, now in the country, will be employed to perform this service; and I should receive the seeds and plants from him at Guayaquil.

IV. In the forests of Nueva Granada there are two valuable species of bark trees, the *C. Pitaya* and *C. lancifolia*, which have lately been imported into Europe in great quantities, especially between the years 1849 and 1855. A person has offered to procure these species for Government, who is well acquainted with the bark collectors, and with the principal men in Nueva Granada. He should be directed to deliver them to me, at Buenaventura, a port in the Pacific.

If these four enterprises were sanctioned, I should, after safely depositing my own collection on board a vessel at Islay, go up the coast to receive the collections from the Huanuco forests, at Callao; from the Ecuador forests, at Guayaquil; and from Nueva Granada, at Buenaventura; then sailing direct to India.

No arrangement has yet been made for supplying me with a suitable vessel to convey the collections of seeds and plants from South America to India; yet this is the most important part of the whole enterprise; its success depends entirely on the rapidity with which the plants and seeds, which are very perishable, can be taken to their destination. There are upwards of 10 Government vessels on the Pacific station; two are stationed at Vancouver's Island, and another bears the admiral's flag, but all the rest are doing nothing particular; and I would suggest that, when the time comes, a requisition might be made to the Admiralty for the use of one to convey the collections across the Pacific to India. At all events, if this is refused I ought to be empowered to charter a vessel for the purpose; but the use of one of Her Majesty's vessels, especially a steamer, would be the best and cheapest way of bringing the objects of the enterprise to a successful result.

I believe that the Neilgherry Hills will be found to be the best locality for planting the cinchonas; and if this is reported to be the case, the vessel would go direct to Calicut, and the Ward's cases containing the plants might be conveyed to their destination in the hills within three days. The celerity of their removal and the shortness of the journey are very important points. The superintendents of botanical gardens in India have been called upon to report their opinion on the best localities for the growth of the cinchonas; and both Darjeeling and Ceylon will probably be tried as well as the Neilgherries.

I am sent out single handed; I may succeed, and assuredly no efforts of my own will be wanting; but the chances of success will be greatly increased, and the undertaking will be far more complete if the measures which I have indicated in this letter, are adopted.

I intend to leave England in December next, so as to be in the forests by April and May, when the seeds are ripe.

I have, &c.
(signed) *Clements R. Markham.*

— No. 25. —

MEMORANDUM, by Mr. *Markham*, on the means of conveying the Cinchona Plants from South America to India.

15 September 1859.

WITH reference to the question of supplying a vessel for conveying the collections of seeds and plants of the quinine-yielding cinchona trees to India, which I have been commissioned to procure in South America, I beg to submit the following remarks in obedience to Mr. Baring's desire.

 The

The best and surest plan would, of course, be to induce the Admiralty to place one of their vessels on the Pacific station, at the disposal of the India Office, for this service. Besides the flag ship, there are, I believe, six or seven of Her Majesty's vessels on the west coast of South America, three of which are steamers, and one of them, the little "Vixen," would be peculiarly well adapted for the service in question. In going direct from Callao to India, with a fair trade wind most of the way, she need not be absent from her station for more than eight months, and the India Office might engage to pay for the wear and tear, coaling, &c. This would be by far the simplest, cheapest, and best way of conveying the plants; and the Admiralty are scarcely likely to raise any objection. The vessel would be required in the Autumn of 1860.

Should the Admiralty refuse to give any assistance, one of the steamers of the Indian Government, either from Bombay or Calcutta, might be sent over to South America to receive the plants; and this was, I believe, the plan adopted by the Netherlands government when they undertook the introduction of cinchonas into Java.

In case both these plans should fail, and no Government vessel should be supplied to perform this service, I ought to be empowered to freight a sailing vessel at Callao. There would be no difficulty in doing so, but of course the voyage would be much longer, and the expense much greater. I am afraid that the freight of a suitable vessel would certainly not be less than 700*l.*; but even this sum is insignificant in comparison to the benefits and advantages which may be expected from the introduction of cinchonas into our Indian possessions.

Finally, if every means of conveying the plants direct to India is withdrawn, I should take a passage in the mail steamer from Callao to Panama, thence in the American line of steamers to San Francisco, thence in a sailing vessel to Hong Kong, and so to India. This would involve voyages of doubtful, but certainly of many months duration; and, as I have before stated, there would be but little chance of any of the plants arriving alive. The seeds would stand a better chance.

I cannot, however, doubt that when the importance of the undertaking is considered, either a Government or an Indian steamer will be supplied, or that, at least, I shall be authorised to freight a vessel at Callao.

The undertaking has already been determined upon. I have been diligently engaged for several months in collecting all the information that can be procured in Europe, and in making necessary preparations, and the Ward's cases, which will be required (worth nearly 50 *l.*), are on the point of being shipped off round the Horn to meet me on my arrival at Callao. Mr. Spruce, also a botanist of some eminence, now in the Ecuador, has been induced to accept an offer from this office of employment on a similar service in that region; and I presume, therefore, that there can now be no idea of abandoning the enterprise on account of any apparent difficulty in conveying the plants and seeds to India.

— No. 26. —

Memorandum by Mr. *C. R. Markham*, India Office, 13 May 1859.

With reference to the statement contained in Mr. Gerstenberg's (the managing Director of the "Ecuador Land Company") letter to Lord Stanley, that the company had already appointed Mr. Spruce, an eminent botanist now in the country, to be their agent for transplanting cinchonas; it appears that Mr. Spruce has received no communication from the company, and that he is not inclined to accept their offer if it should be made. Mr. Spruce is, therefore, free to accept any other offer that may be made to him.

In sending expeditions to procure seeds and plants of the cinchona in South America for introduction into India, much may be learnt, both from the mistakes and the final success of the Dutch undertaking in 1852–54.

Mr. Hasskarl, a gentleman of scientific acquirements, but unacquainted either with the country or the language, was sent out by the Dutch government; but he proceeded to the wrong point in the forests, and arrived too late in the year. Thus a whole season was lost. The following season, however, found him in the

the forests of Caravaya, and he succeeded in collecting a great number of plants of the most valuable kind, but no seeds. He proceeded with his collection direct from Callao to Java, where the plantation is reported to be in a flourishing state; indeed the Netherlands government boast that they have done good service to, and may reckon on the approbation of, the whole civilised world.

They, however, only procured one of the valuable species of cinchonas, and at an enormous expense.

By the employment of Mr. Spruce, as well as of myself, the British Government will be able to procure at least three of the more valuable species, and perhaps more at a moderate outlay. Mr. Spruce would be employed to collect the *C. Condaminea* in the forests of Ecuador, while I should direct my labours either towards the Province of Huanuco, or towards that of Caravaya. The whole collection of plants and seeds would be united at Callao, and I should personally superintend their conveyance to India.

If my proposal should be adopted, I would suggest that Mr. Spruce should be addressed directly from this office, or through Mr. Cope, Her Majesty's Consul General in Ecuador, in a letter offering to employ him for the purpose of making a collection of cinchona plants and seeds, in the forests of Ecuador, to be delivered at the port of Guayaquil, for a reasonable remuneration. The details as to time, &c. should be left for arrangement between myself and Mr. Spruce. It will also be advisable to address a letter to Dr. Thomson, of the Calcutta gardens, Dr. Cleghorn, of the Madras forest conservancy, and Mr. M'Ivor, superintendent of the gardens on the hills (Neilgherry), instructing them to report upon the localities in India best suited to the growth of the plants; and to obtain all possible information of the state of the cinchona plantations of the Dutch in Java up to the most recent time.

— No. 27. —

MEMORANDUM by Mr. *Markham*, India Office, 8 September 1859.

WITH reference to the permission I received from the Revenue Committee, on the 13th of last May, to put myself in communication with Mr. Spruce, a botanist now in the Republic of Ecuador, in order to ascertain upon what terms he would be willing to procure seeds and plants of the more valuable species of cinchonas, which are found in that territory, for the Indian Government; I have now to report that I have received Mr. Spruce's reply to my letter.

Mr. Spruce says, "My services are at the command of the India Office, for the object of procuring young plants and seeds of the most valuable kinds of cinchonas for transportation to India. My present occupation yields me about 20 *l.* a month, and as the one proposed to me is of uncertain duration, I think 30 *l.* a month is as low as I could rate my services, besides the expenses incurred in collecting and transmitting the plants to Guayaquil."

The offer made by Mr. Spruce, with respect to his salary, is very moderate. Mr. Fortune, a man of less knowledge and education, received 500 *l.* a year for his services in the transportation of the tea plants from China to India, a much less onerous duty than the one under consideration. Sir William Hooker says, that "the terms offered by Mr. Spruce are particularly liberal, and it is a great saving to Government that he is already in the field of his labours, and thus the expense of the voyage is saved."

Sir William Hooker, in his letter to me, speaks very strongly upon the necessity of a thoroughly good practical gardener accompanying each scientific collector, and he considers this to be an imperative requirement.

Through Mr. Spruce a supply will be obtained of the *C. Condaminea*, one of the most important species, and of the *Cascarilla roja*, the bark of which is exceedingly rich in valuable alkaloids. He will undertake to have a good supply of young plants and seeds at the port of Guayaquil by the time that I shall have completed my collection. The expenses of transmitting the plants and seeds from the forest to the port cannot be exactly estimated, but Mr. Spruce will endeavour to perform this service as economically as possible, and Sir William Hooker speaks of him as a first-rate botanist, a well-educated and most honourable man.

I would, therefore, suggest to the Committee that I should be authorised to close with Mr. Spruce's offer, and to make all necessary arrangements with him. I would also request, that I should be permitted to send him out a few things with which it is essential he should be provided, such as Weddell's and Howard's works on the quinology of the Ecuador, and instruments for ascertaining the position, elevation, and temperature of the localities where the cinchonas grow. The Wardian cases which will be required for his collection, will go out with mine, round the Horn.

It is of very great importance for the success of the enterprise, which has now been undertaken by the Secretary of State in Council, that as many of the valuable species of cinchonas as possible should be introduced into India. This is the opinion of Mr. Howard, the largest quinine manufacturer in England; of Dr. Weddell, the highest European authority on all questions respecting these plants; and of Sir William Hooker. Of the four regions which it is necessary to explore, in order to complete the undertaking satisfactorily, and to procure all the more important species of cinchonas, two will thus be provided for. I shall myself endeavour to collect plants and seeds of the *Calisaya*, the most highly prized bark of all, and of two other valuable species, the *micrantha* and *Zamba morada*, in the forests of Caravaya; and Mr. Spruce will obtain a supply of the *Condaminea* and *Cascarilla roja*, in Ecuador.

It is necessary, however, for the complete success of the enterprise, that the more important species of cinchonas in New Granada and in the forests of Huamalies and Huanuco, in Peru, should also be procured.

I have received an offer to procure these cinchonas, from Mr. Bollaert, a gentleman who was mentioned by Dr. Royle as well qualified to perform such a service. He has been many years in South America, knows the language, has had much experience in travelling in those countries, and is personally acquainted with several of the cascarilleros or bark collectors of New Granada. I trust that the Committee will authorise me to put myself in communication with this gentleman, with a view to ascertain the terms on which he would be willing to undertake this portion of the enterprise. This would still leave the forests of Huanuco and Huamalies unprovided for.

With regard to the conveyance of the collections from the west coast of South America to India, I would venture to remind the Committee that there is very little chance of succeeding, unless a vessel is specially provided for the purpose.

— No. 28.—

RESOLUTION of a Revenue, Judicial, and Legislative Committee, India Office, 22 September 1859.

APPROVED by the Secretary of State in Council.

THE Committee having had before them a memorandum by Mr. Markham, reporting that, in pursuance of an order received by him on the 13th May last, to ascertain upon what terms Mr. Spruce, a botanist, now in the Ecuador, would be willing to procure seeds and plants of the more valuable species of cinchonas which are found in that territory, for the Indian Government; he wrote to him, and has received a reply from Mr. Spruce, stating that he is willing to undertake that service for 30 *l.* a month, besides the expenses incurred in collecting and transmitting the plants and seeds to the port of Guayaquil.

The Committee having further considered that part of Mr. Markham's memorandum referring to the great importance of introducing as many of the valuable species of cinchonas into India as possible; and representing the necessity of providing a vessel for conveying the collections of plants and seeds from the West coast of South America to India:—

Ordered, that Mr. Markham be instructed to close with Mr. Spruce's offer, on the part of the Secretary of State for India, in Council; that he be authorised to expend sums not exceeding 500 *l.* for each region, in procuring plants or seeds of the more valuable species of cinchonas, which grow in New Granada, and in the provinces of Huamalies and Huanuco in Peru, if opportunities of doing so should offer themselves; and to charter a vessel on the west coast of South America, for the voyage to India.

— No. 29.—

Clements R. Markham, Esq., to Dr. *Forbes Watson*.

My dear Sir, Lima, 8 February 1860.

I WRITE by this mail a short report of my proceedings thus far, which you will perhaps kindly show to Mr. Bourdillon.

On January 19, I arrived at the port of Guayaquil, in the Republic of Ecuador, and made arrangements with regard to Mr. Spruce's part of the undertaking. We found the President of Peru, with a large fleet and army in hostile possession of the river and a part of the town, and the country in a complete state of anarchy. I had some conversation with Castilla, the President of Peru, with our Minister, Mr. Cope, and with the Vice-consul Mr. Mocatta. The latter has got passports, so as to prevent any of Mr. Spruce's mules from being seized, and will make all necessary arrangements about sending Cross up the river with the Wardian cases when he arrives. Cross should, therefore, be told to go to him on his arrival at Guayaquil; and I think he should also be provided with a letter to Her Majesty's Acting-consul at Panama, Mr. Bidwell, as he has never travelled before.

I think there is every prospect of Mr. Spruce's undertaking being successful; and I have told him to send the plants and seeds in charge of Cross, by the first steamers to Southampton, and thence, without delay, to India. He will collect chiefly, I believe, in the forests where the "red bark" is found.

On January 26th I arrived at Lima, where I remain for a short time, to collect information, make some necessary arrangements, and obtain letters of introduction.

I have met several persons connected with the forests on the eastern slopes of the Cordilleras, such as Don José Maria Costas, Don Modesto Basadre, and others; and they all tell me that good cinchona trees have become exceedingly scarce, both in the forests of Caravaya and Bolivia; that 10 years ago, when Dr. Weddell was out here, it would have been comparatively easy to make a large collection, but that now it will be an enterprise of very great difficulty. The natives, both in Peru and Bolivia, have lately become extremely jealous of strangers, and there is almost the certainty of a war between those two Republics in a few months. The obstacles in the way of success are of no small magnitude; but at the same time every year of delay would most undoubtedly greatly increase them.

John Weir (the gardener) is now at Islay, putting together 15 of the Wardian cases in a court-yard which has been provided for the purpose; the other 15 will be sent to Guayaquil for Mr. Spruce, by the first opportunity. The freight from Callao to Islay, and custom-house charges were exorbitant; but I keep a regular account of all expenses.

On my arrival here, a long complimentary article appeared in the "Lima" newspaper, announcing my second visit, and reviewing my former works. This has, I think, thrown the people off the scent as to my real object, although it must necessarily be known to several. The extreme scarceness of the trees has made me doubtful whether to go to Caravaya, or to alter my plans, and enter some of the Bolivian forests, the objection to the latter course being the lawless and unscrupulous character of the Bolivians; the position of whose country on the other side of the Andes, enables them to defy European governments. I shall probably be unable to decide finally until I am much nearer the theatre of action.

With regard to conveying the plants from here to India, I have consulted several people, consuls, merchants, and captains of vessels; and have come to the conclusion, if no steamer is provided in the Pacific, that the best route will be by steamers to Southampton, and thence by the ordinary line to India. There is the certainty of having steam all the way, the Wardian cases would be safer, and there would be no necessity of engaging freight beforehand: while to obtain freight in a vessel from Callao would be ten times as expensive, with greater risks. Another advantage would be, that in case I am knocked over by fever and ague, or any accident, there will be no difficulty in Weir taking charge of the cases to India; as Cross will do with Mr. Spruce's collection.

The secretary of the Royal West India Mail Steam Company (55, Moorgate-street,

street (E.C.), should be requested to give directions to the captains of the company's steamers to render every assistance in their power, and to give accommodation for the cases aft, on the upper deck, and that their agents on the Isthmus should take charge of their conveyance from the Pacific to the Atlantic. Mr. Just, the secretary of the Pacific Steam Navigation Company (Liverpool), and the Peninsular and Oriental Company should also be written to, for the same object. I think the Peninsular and Oriental boat sails four days after the arrival of the West Indian mail at Southampton.

I am now about to proceed to Arequipa, and shall continue my journey to the forests, as soon as the roads are practicable. Whatever the result of my enterprise may be, be assured that I shall do my best and spare no labour, neglect no chance, for the attainment of the important object in view.

Ever yours, &c.
(signed) *Clements R. Markham.*

P.S.—I shall write next from Arequipa.

— No. 30. —

From *C. R. Markham*, Esq., to Dr. *Forbes Watson.*

Port of Islay (Coast of Peru),
5 March 1860.

Dear Dr. Watson,

I HAVE got the 15 Wardian cases* here, all put together, ready to receive the plants, without further accident than the breaking of one of the panes of glass. They will remain here, under a corridor, until my return from the interior. While here, waiting the arrival of beasts from Arequipa, I have been examining the ravines in search of good soil for the Wardian cases.

* I have sent the other 15 Wardian cases to Guayaquil to await the arrival of Cross, or further orders from Mr. Spruce.

Islay is a little sea-port, surrounded by a sandy desert, which extends inland as far as Arequipa, a distance of 90 miles, and the soil of the latter place is poor, and, therefore, not likely to be suitable for the cinchonæ. A range of mountains, however, averaging a height of 1,500 to 2,000 feet, runs along the coast, at a distance of about a league or two from the sea, called the Lomas. From June to December they are green, and covered with wild flowers, but dried up during the remainder of the year. They are broken by several ravines which descend towards the coast, where small springs are met with, causing vegetation, and giving live to a few olive, fig, pomegranate, and acacia trees; those near Islay are called Mataranes, Yuta, Guerreros, through which the road to Arequipa passes, Tintayale, and Catarindo.† From the little springs of Mataranes, a pipe is laid down, which supplies Islay with water,; and, amongst the roots of the olive trees, in this ravine I found soil, apparently rich, and suitable for the Wardian cases. Owing to the extraordinary rains, a number of plants were still in flower; so that I found, in the soil of the Mataranes ravine, olives, figs, acacia, an amaranth, verbena (two kinds), heliotrope, salvia, several compositæ, a little grass, a poppy, tobacco, castor oil, a rumex, a convolvolus, solanum (two kinds), an umbellifer, aloe, and oxalis. In July there are great quantities of amancaes, a liliaceous plant.

† *See* accompanying map.

By this post, I forward to your address, a small bag, containing a sample of the soil of Mataranes, for analysis, together with specimens of the rock, apparently gneiss, of which the ravine is formed. I also enclose a sketch map of the locality. I shall be obliged, if you would forward me the result of the analysis of this soil,‡ and if it contains nothing pernicious, its proximity to Islay (less

‡ Amongst the papers on cinchona, in the office, you will find an analysis of soil, where a cinchona grew, by Mr. Piddington, with this result:

100 grains of water	2·06
Siliceous matter	0·62
Carbonate of lime	46·00
Carbonate of magnesia	51·00
Loss	0·32
	100·00

Memorandum, dated 21 November 1856.

(less than a league), will enable me to obtain it quite fresh, when the plants arrive on the coast. Meanwhile, I have made arrangements for a sufficient quantity to be ready for the Wardian cases; and I shall find your answer to this letter when I pass through Arequipa in time, if the analysis is unfavourable, to procure soil elsewhere. I shall bring down specimens of the soil in which the cinchonæ grow (at a foot deep, near the roots) together with bits of the rock, and loose stones near them. I shall also be obliged, if you would let me know what the fine white powder is composed of, which is scattered over the desert, and a specimen of which I have also forwarded in the bag.

I have examined these ravines, and traversed the sandy desert on foot (as they have no beasts here), and frequently under a burning sun.

War is about to commence between Peru and Bolivia, and it will be right in my line of march; they also tell me, that the cascarilleros will try to prevent my procuring plants and seed, but I will overcome these difficulties if it is possible.

I leave this to-morrow morning for Arequipa, whence I will write again.

Ever yours, &c.
(signed) *Clements R. Markham*

— No. 31. —

C. R. Markham, Esq., to *E. D. Bourdillon*, Esq.

Dear Sir, Arequipa (Peru), 20 March 1860.

In acknowledging the receipt of your letter dated January 24th, I take the opportunity of reporting my proceedings, in continuation of my letter dated from Islay, in answer to that addressed to me by Dr. Forbes Watson, on December 31st, 1859.

With my letter from Islay I forwarded some soil for analysis, which, after some search, I had found in the neighbourhood of that port, hoping that it would be found suitable for establishing the cinchona in the Wardian cases. I have since examined the soil in the valley of Arequipa,* and find that it is poorer, and that in most parts, especially where maize crops are raised, a great deal of guano is used. This makes me more anxious that the soil of the "*Lomas*" of Islay may contain nothing pernicious.

* Most of the wild flowers of the *Lomas* of Islay, however, are also found in the valley of Arequipa.

Mr. Wilthew, Her Majesty's Consul at Islay, has kindly made arrangements to have the soil ready when I arrive from the interior, and the Wardian cases conveniently placed for the reception of the plants.

I arrived at Arequipa, after a two days' ride over the desert, on the 8th of this month, and find that this is the rainiest season that has ever been known in Peru since the year 1819, and that the roads over the Andes are said to be impassable. Nevertheless, as the rains must necessarily be drawing to a close, and as I am anxious not to lose any time, I intend to leave Arequipa for the interior on the day after to-morrow, March 22d.

During my stay here, I have been carefully collecting information respecting the bark trade; chiefly from Mr. Renny, the agent of the house of Gibbs, Don José Maria Peña, an exporter of Bolivian bark, and Don Agustin Aragon, one of the principal men of the Caravaya province. All commercial men combine in saying that the bark of Caravaya is of little value, and the house of Gibbs has forbidden its agents to purchase it; and they assure me that all calisaya bark comes from Bolivia, either through the port of Arica, or smuggled across the frontiers of Arequipa and Islay. On the other hand, Dr. Weddell, Dr. Junghuhn, and other botanists, whose statements are confirmed by Don Agustin Aragon, assert that the shrub calisaya (var. *B. Josephiana*) is the same plant as the tree calisaya, only growing under different circumstances; and this variety abounds in Caravaya, though little sought after, on account of the small quantity of bark it yields.† Moreover, Dr. Weddell, in a letter to me, dated September 20th 1859, assured me that small plants of the tree calisaya were common in the forests of Caravaya; and this assertion is also confirmed by Aragon. Other valuable species of cinchona, such as the *Zamba morada, C. Boliviana*, and *C. micrantha*, are known to abound in Caravaya.

† Dr. Weddell, in a letter to me, dated 10 August 1859, advised me by all means to collect the *C. Josephina*.

I am

I am thus left in the difficult and very responsible position of having to select the region in which to work, and on the correctness of my decision will depend the success of the undertaking, at least for this season.

The case as between Bolivia and the Peruvian province of Caravaya, so far as I am now informed, stands thus: In the Bolivian forests there is undoubtedly the greatest quantity of *C. Calisaya* trees, but the difficulties of procuring plants and seeds is very great. The Bolivians are the most ignorant, barbarous, and jealous of all the South American republicans, and they have an intense hatred and suspicion of foreigners. Both the authorities and the bark collectors, when my object was known, would throw every obstacle in my way, and not improbably imprison me. Besides all this, a war between Peru and Bolivia appears to be certain as soon as the dry season comes on, which would render the conveyance of the plants across the frontier in safety almost impossible.

In Caravaya it is true that the tree Calisaya is rare; "that is large ones, for the small ones are common;"* and the shrubby variety, together with other valuable species can, I am told, be easily procured. The road from the forests of Caravaya to the coast is shorter than from any point of the Bolivian forests; the Peruvian authorities would give me every assistance in their power in the way of supplying me with mules, collecting provisions, and obtaining experienced guides; at the present moment, the Peruvian Government having quarrels with France, and the United States, is particularly anxious to keep on good terms with Great Britain during its war with Bolivia; and my route to the coast will probably be beyond the actual scene of the approaching campaign.

* Weddell to me, 20 Sept. 1859.

Having carefully weighed these considerations, it is my present intention to proceed in the first place to La Paz, the principal city of Bolivia, where Mr. Jerningham has supplied me with a letter to the Minister of Foreign Affairs; and then to continue my journey along the verge of the Bolivian forests, until I again reach the eastern banks of the Titicaca, on the frontier between Peru and Bolivia. I should, during this journey, collect information, and form my judgment by personal observation, and if I came to the conclusion that the risk of personally attempting to make my collection in Bolivia would be so great as to render success improbable, I should abandon the idea, and endeavour to make some such arrangement with the agents of Don José Maria Peña, as Mr. Hasskarl made so successfully with some Bolivian cascarilleros.

Having thus done all in my power with regard to Bolivia, I shall proceed to the forests of Caravaya in May, in time to see the cinchona in flower, and commence at once to work at making as large a collection as possible in the southern division, and as near as possible to the Bolivian frontier. The *C. Boliviana*, which Dr. Weddell believes to be hardly more than a variety of the *C. Calisaya*,† is found in abundance in Ayapata, the northern district of Caravaya, where Don Agustin Aragon has a large estate, and I shall endeavour to make an arrangement with him to supply me with plants of that species.

† Weddell to me, 20 Sept. 1859.

Don Pablo Pimentel, the present Sub-Prefect of Caravaya, will be directed to give me every assistance; and the cura of the frontier village is my personal friend, so that I anticipate no difficulty in procuring guides and a sufficient stock of provisions to enable me to proceed into the forests. I hope to complete the collection by September, and to reach the coast during the same month.

With regard to the conveyance of the plants and seeds to India, I am still of opinion that by far the safest and cheapest way would be by sending a Government steamer direct from the coast of Peru to India, as was done by the Dutch; and that every other way involves numerous risks and chances of failure. Of the two other ways that are left, namely, by steamers to Southampton, and thence by the overland route, or by a sailing vessel across the Pacific; I am convinced that the former, with all its risks, is preferable for many reasons. In obtaining a vessel there would be many delays, a necessity of waiting for the Ecuador collection, the chance of calms on the Line, much more expensive, and under the most favourable circumstances a longer voyage. I should not therefore think of taking any steps respecting the "Kittiwake." By the former way there would be the great advantage, that the collections from Southern Peru, and from Ecuador could be sent away at once, without waiting for each other. It is true that there would be more risk from the numerous trans-shipments; but by having proper directions given to the various captains, and with ordinary care, I have no doubt that the Wardian cases might be conveyed without accident to India by this route.

I would

I would repeat, however, what I have already said in a former letter to Dr. Forbes Watson, that the secretaries of the Pacific,* West Indian,† and Peninsular and Oriental Steam Navigation Companies should be written to, requesting that the captains of their steamers be directed to give every assistance and good stowage room on the upper decks. With regard to the passage across the Isthmus of Panama, it would be well to request, that the agent of the West Indian Steam Navigation Company at Panama be directed to see the cases safely conveyed across the isthmus. Mr. Spruce's collections can be sent away (without waiting for mine) in charge of the gardener, Cross.

* Mr. Just (Liverpool).

† Mr. Reep (55, Moorgate-street, E.C.)

I have now, I think, informed you of all that is settled respecting my future movements; which may, of course, be modified by further information that I may receive at Puno,‡ or when nearer the cinchona forests.

‡ I hope to reach Puno on Sunday, 25 March.

In justice to myself, I cannot conclude this letter, which is probably the last that I shall have an opportunity of writing, until my return from the interior, without expressing a hope that the Secretary of State in Council is aware of the difficulty of the service upon which I am employed. The forests where the cinchonæ grow are almost inaccessible, without roads or habitations. There is great risk of being disabled by fevers in the humid forests, by "sorochi," (an illness brought on by the great height) in crossing the Andes, and by dysentery and ague on the coast. The plants, after they are procured, will have to pass on mules' backs over the frozen plains of the Andes, and the hot arid deserts on the coast before reaching the Wardian cases; and then will follow several voyages in different steamers, which will last for three months. [It will be remembered that no human foresight could have prevented the loss of the priceless collections of La Condamine, Ruiz and Pavon, Humboldt, Stamford Raffles, Wallace, and others.] The roads from the forests, and across the Eastern Cordillera, pass along the edges of precipices, and over ridges, where one false step would cause the loss of mules and cargo.

Many of these obstacles may, of course, be overcome by energy and care, others are in the hands of Providence; but I take this opportunity of mentioning the many risks and dangers which must be encountered, in justice to myself; at the same time, assuring you that, humanly speaking, I feel some confidence in the success of the undertaking, and that no exertions will be spared on my part.

I have, &c.
(signed) *Clements R. Markham.*

— No. 32. —

T. G. Baring, Esq., M.P., to *Clements Markham*, Esq.

Sir, India Office, E.C., 31 March 1860.

Your letter, dated 8th February 1860, No. 1, addressed to Dr. Forbes Watson, has been laid before the Secretary of State for India in Council, and I am directed to inform you that your wishes with reference to the safe transport of such seeds and plants of the cinchona tree as your may be able to obtain; having been communicated to the Secretaries of the West India and Pacific Steam Navigation Companies, the directors have in each case expressed their willingness to issue the necessary instructions to the officers commanding the vessels on which the plants will be placed; on their arrival at Southampton they will be immediately forwarded to their destination in India. Mr. Cross, the gardener attached to Mr. Spruce's branch of the expedition, will proceed to Guyaquil by the steamer of the 17th proximo, as originally arranged; he will be furnished with a letter of recommendation to Her Majesty's consul at Panama, and be instructed to proceed up the river with the Wardian cases to join Mr. Spruce.

Sir Charles Wood notices with pleasure the zeal and intelligence with which you have entered on the duty entrusted to you, and feels satisfied that by the continued exercise of those qualities, you will be able to overcome the many difficulties inseparable from your undertaking. I am directed to convey to you his approval of your arrangements as far as they have already proceeded, and to add that the change in your plans, with regard to the transport of the seeds, *viâ* the Pacific, appears to be fully justified by the concurrent opinion of people who, from their position, are likely to be well informed upon this subject.

I am, &c.
(signed) *T. G. Baring.*

— No. 33. —

From *E. D. Bourdillon*, Esq., to *Clements R. Markham*, Esq.

Sir, India Office, London, 17 April 1860.

I HAVE to acknowledge the receipt of your letter, dated Port of Islay (coast of Peru), 5th March 1859 (1860), addressed to Dr. Watson, together with its enclosure and the specimens of earth which accompany it; when they have been analysed you shall be informed of the result of the investigations. The gardener Cross leaves for Arequipa, in accordance with the instruction conveyed in your last letter, by the present mail.

The enclosed letter from Mr. Cleghorn arrived by the last mail; you will see that that gentleman agrees in the Neilghery Hills being the most suitable locality for commencing the experiment for propagating the plants and seeds you may be able to transmit.

I am, &c.
(signed) *E. D. Bourdillon.*

Clements Markham, Esq.,
Port of Islay, Peru, South America.

Enclosure in No. 33.

H. Cleghorn, Esq., to *Clements Markham*, Esq.

My dear Sir, Utakamund, Nilgiris, 7 March 1860.

YOUR letter of November 17th reached me some time ago, whilst travelling to this sanatarium. I would have written sooner, but was much occupied during the stay of Sir Charles Trevelyan at this place. Your plan of operations, and the great object of your voyage is much in my thoughts, and has naturally been much discussed everywhere.

After careful perusal of the pamphlet drawn up by you, I have come to the conclusion that the best sites will be found in the Nilgiri range of mountains, and I concur with you that it will be best at first to concentrate all our efforts in this vicinity rather than to scatter the cases over different districts, as Salem, Tinnevelly, and Travancore, which may hereafter be supplied with seeds and cuttings.

The best efforts of Mr. McIvor and myself shall not be wanting to make the necessary preparations, and sites will be put in readiness immediately at the close of the monsoon (end of September), the rapid growth of vegetation during the rains renders any earlier attempt fruitless, except in a few sheltered localities.

So anxious do I feel to co-operate with you in the great work in which you are engaged, that I propose to modify my tour this season, so as to enable me to repair to Calicut as soon as the arrival of the cinchona ship may be telegraphed. Mr. P. Grant, Collector of Malabar, has received instructions from Government to afford you every assistance in facilitating transport up the Nilgiri ascent, and this will be attended with some difficulty, the short ghat road being very steep, whilst the cart road, *viâ* Polyat and Coimbatore, makes a detour through the low country, where the temperature is high. I think the short road will be the best.

It is well to remember that Mr. McIvor's conservatory is just being finished, and that he has a smaller glasshouse, which usually contains some of our indigenous *Melastomaceæ*, *Aristolochiaceæ*, &c.

The Wardian cases, which may be sent to Ceylon, and given in charge to Mr. Thwaites of the Royal Gardens, Peradinea, will be admirably cared for. I believe he is already prepared for your arrival, and writes with enthusiasm regarding the project.

Wishing you a pleasant and successful voyage from S. America to Calicut.

I remain, &c.
(signed) *H. Cleghorn.*

Clements Markham, Esq.,
India Office.
(To be forwarded.)

— No. 34. —

LETTER from *C. R. Markham*, Esq., to the Under Secretary of State for India.

British Consulate, Port of Islay, Peru,
9 June 1860.

Sir,

I HAVE the honour to report, for the information of the Secretary of State for India in Council, that, in performance of the service on which I am employed, I have arrived at this port with 529 of the more valuable species of cinchona plants, which are now in course of establishment in the Wardian cases, for conveyance to India.

2. I propose, in this report, to give a detailed account of my proceedings, from the time of my departure from the city of Arequipa (whence I addressed my last letter (No. 3) to Mr. Bourdillon), to my arrival, with the plants, at this port. Some of my observations in the cinchona region may prove useful to the gentlemen who will have charge of the cultivation in India, and should it be considered advisable to supply them with printed copies of this report, they should be in their hands one or two mails before the arrival of the plants.

JOURNEY ACROSS THE CORDILLERAS OF THE ANDES.

3. On March 22d, 1860, I left Arequipa, accompanied by John Weir, the gardener, and arrived at the city of Puno, on the banks of Lake Titicaca, on the 27th, a very painful journey, over snowy heights 15,500 feet above the level of the sea, in the worst season of the year, the rigours of which were increased by the debility brought on by an illness from which I had suffered at Arequipa, and by the *sorochi*, or violent headaches and sickness, occasioned by the great elevation of this region above the sea. The loftiest part of the road is several hundred feet above Mont Blanc.

4. At Puno, I was occupied for some days in collecting information, which induced me to alter the plans for executing this service that I had previously formed at Arequipa. I found that a war with Bolivia was imminent; that the state of that country, owing to the excessive rains, would render travelling exceedingly slow; and that the extreme jealousy of the Government and people, in preserving their present monopoly of the bark trade, would render it impossible for me to make a collection personally. I have a most complete distrust of all native agency; I therefore abandoned my intention of going into Bolivia, and it was very fortunate that I did so, for a decreee has since been issued by Dr. Linares, the President of that Republic, prohibiting all communication between Peru and Bolivia, and the passage of either travellers or goods across the frontier, this being, of course, the forerunner of war between the two countries.

5. There is no question that the calisaya tree, the most valuable species of cinchona, is found in greatest abundance in Bolivia; but, though scarcer and more difficult to collect, it is also to be met with in the Peruvian province of Caravaya. I finally resolved to proceed without delay to the cinchona forests of Caravaya, to make as large a collection as possible myself, without employing any native agent.

6. On the 7th of April I left Puno, and commenced my journey to Caravaya, travelling without a muleteer, and with the cheapest beasts, hired from one village to another, a way which entailed much trouble and annoyance, but which I adopted as being far more economical. There were four broad and very rapid rivers to cross on *balsas*, or long bundles of reed stitched together, while the mules swam. The plains and mountain ranges over which the way passed averaged a height of 12,000 to 13,000 feet above the level of the sea, and one snowy pass attained a height of nearly 17,000 feet. The season was one of violent storms, with hail and snow, and constant rains. The road passed through the towns of Lampa, Pucara, and Azangaro, to Crucero, the capital of the province of Caravaya, which I reached on the 16th of April, a distance of 160 miles from Puno.

7. Crucero is a mere collection of mud huts, built on a very elevated swampy plain, just on the western side of the snowy Caravaya range, whence roads branch off over the passes to the forest-covered valleys on the eastern slopes.

The Province of Caravaya.

8. The Peruvian province of Caravaya, in the department of Puno, consists of a snowy range of mountains, extending for 180 miles from the department of Cuzco to the frontier of Bolivia, from the eastern slopes of which long spurs run out to the north and east, until they gradually subside into the vast forest-covered plains which extend for thousands of miles to the shores of the Atlantic. These spurs or ridges enclose valleys the sides of which are generally covered with dense forest, while the summits of the ridges are clothed with rich pasture land, interspersed with small thickets in the ravines and gullies. These higher regions are called *pajonales*. The numerous streams and rivers which flow down the valleys of Caravaya, and which have long been famous for their gold washings, finally unite, in the plains, to form the river Ynambari, a tributary of the still unknown Purus, which is probably the largest secondary river in the world.

9. The most important of the Caravaya valleys, and that which I determined to examine first, is that of Sandia, which contains a population of 7,000 Indians, and annually yields 90,000 lbs. of coca, and 10,000 lbs. of most excellent coffee.

10. On April 18th I left Crucero, and crossing a lofty snow-covered ridge, commenced the descent from an arctic to a tropical climate, down the beautiful ravine of Sandia. The pass above Crucero is 13,600 feet, and the village of Sandia 6,667 feet above the sea, being a descent of 6,933 feet in 30 miles. Arriving at Sandia on the 20th, I began at once to collect provisions and make other necessary preparation for a further advance into the interior, intending first to examine the pajonales of the Sandia valley in search of the β *Josephiana* variety of the calisaya plant, which Dr. Weddell had informed me was to be met with in those localities, and then to cross a mountain ridge into the forests of Tambopata, where the tree calisaya and other valuable species of cinchonæ were said to abound.

Cinchona Calisaya, var. β Josephiana.

11. On the 24th of April I left Sandia, accompanied by the gardener, a native lad, and three Indians bearing a tent, provisions consisting of toasted stale bread, salted cheese, maize, and a few other necessaries, and proceeded down the valley, following the course of the river. The foaming torrent dashed through the centre of the valley, and the masses of verdure on either side were toned down by many flowers in large patches, purple melastomaceæ, orange cassiæ, and scarlet salviæ. At a distance of 15 miles below Sandia, the perpendicular cliffs rise up from the river on either side to a stupendous height, and the path winds up in zigzags, to creep along the edge of steep grassy slopes or pajonales, far above the tropical vegetation of the ravine.

12. It was at this spot that the *Calisaya* (*var.* β *Josephiana*) was first met with; a number of young plants growing by the road side, and older shrubs lower down the slope, with their exquisite roseate flowers and rich green leaves with crimson veins.

13. The rock appeared to be a hard schist, much discoloured with red oxide, quartz occurring here and there; the soil a stiff brown loam, with a little vegetable mould. A little above the road there was a small thicket of arbutus and purple melastomaceæ, in a shallow gully, surrounded by the long-bladed grass of the pajonal (*stipa ychu*). Here there was a *Cinchona caravayensis*, and another *Calisaya Josephiana*. The height of this spot above the sea was 5,422 feet, and the plants growing round the cinchonæ were purple melastomaceæ, arbutus, and blechnum and trichomanes ferns. The positions of a number of young plants, to be collected on our return, were noted down.

14. The scenery of this part of the valley is remarkably beautiful. Lofty mountains, with their cascades, rise up on either side, their summits crowned with

with rich grass, their gullies full of trees and flowers. Half way up, in many directions, terraces of coca rise, tier above tier, fringed with ferns and begonias. We have the shrub cinchonæ on the high pajonales, perhaps the finest coffee in the world in the ravine, and a little gilium, also of the cinchonal alliance, by the road sides.

15. On the 26th I travelled for a considerable distance along the skirts of mountains, at a great height, in the region of pajonales. No ravines or large cascades cut up the face of the mountains; all was exposed to the full glare of the sun; and though there was a profusion of melastomaceæ in the shallow gullies, there were no cinchonæ. The latter evidently dislike very exposed situations, at these heights.

16. On this day, also, I left the valley of Sandia, and, crossing a mountain range, went down from the grassy uplands to the banks of another river, the Huari-huari, flowing through a tropical forest full of palms and tree ferns. On the verge of the pajonal there were a number of *Calisayas* (β *Josephianæ*), which were also marked down, to be collected on our return.

17. From the banks of the Huari-huari, a very dangerous and tedious ascent led to the ridge which divides the valley of Sandia from that of Tambopata. The ridge consists of grassy slopes, with dense thickets of melastomaceæ, palms, tree ferns, bamboos, incense trees, and cinchonæ, in all the small ravines and gullies. The useless *Cinchona caravayensis*, with its large red capsules and coarse leaves, was common enough, but the *Calisaya Josephiana* very rare. One calisaya, whether it be the variety α or β of Weddell, was met with on this pajonal, 18 feet 6 inches in height, and 8½ inches in girth two feet above the ground; yet Dr. Weddell gives the height of the *C. Josephiana* as varying from 6½ to 10 feet.

18. I cannot but conclude that the *Josephianas* are not even a variety of the true calisaya, but exactly the same plants, stunted to the size of shrubs from their elevated or exposed situations. I have traced these calisayas from the shrub to the tree, without finding any difference in the flower or fruit to warrant even a variety. While still in the region of pajonales, I found four or five trees, 20 to 30 feet high, with flowers and fruit of Weddell's *Calisaya, var.* α *Vera.*

19. I had but slight opportunities of observing the temperatures of the pajonal region, about 5,000 feet above the sea, where the *C. Josephiana* is found. On April 25th to 27th the thermometer ranged between 7 A. M. and 9 P. M.; highest 67 degrees, lowest at night 56 degrees; and on May 12th to 14th, from 69 degrees to 53 degrees. The shrub calisayas were growing on the edges of the thicket, and not in deep shade.

20. The most common plants growing with the shrub calisayas were the melastomaceæ with purple flowers, and the *huaturu bajo*, or incense trees.

21. In returning from the forests, on May 13th and 14th, 20 plants of the shrub calisaya were collected in the Huari-huari ravine, and 55 on the pajonal where they were first seen, called *Paccay-samana*, most of them very promising young seedlings. Total 75.

Cinchona Calisaya, var. α *Vera.*

22. Having crossed the ridge of pajonales, I entered another of the Caravaya valleys, through which the river Tambopata flows, which rises in the mountains separating Peru from Bolivia. The Tambopata valley was visited by Dr. Weddell in 1847, and its forests were said to abound in cinchonæ. In the upper part of the valley I found a small clearing made by one Juan de la Cruz Gironda, who was obliging and willing to assist me, and I procured an excellent guide named Martinez, a native of the place, who was well acquainted with the forests.

23. With the exception of a few small clearings, the whole ravine is covered with one dense tropical forest, without road or path of any kind, and I resolved to penetrate in the performance of this service, where, as far as I could learn, no European had been before, and no human being for upwards of 12 years, when the bark trade of Caravaya came to an end. I knew the risks would

would be great, but that they would be fully justified by the importance of the object to be attained, and on the 1st of May I left Gironda's clearing, accompanied by the guide Martinez, the gardener, and four Indians, carrying a tent and provisions.

24. Beyond the river Challuma, a tributary of the Tambopata, and the extreme point reached by Dr. Weddell, there is no path of any kind, the trees are of great height, and the ground is entirely choked up with creepers, fallen masses of trees and bushes, and tangled bamboos. In many places the way led along the verge of a precipice overhanging the river, which boiled and surged many hundreds of feet below. Our encampments were made each night on any stony beach we could find where there was space to light a fire and pitch the tent, and all day we toiled and struggled through the closely-woven jungle.

25. On the 3rd of May I reached the confluence of the rivers Yana-mayu and Tambopata, where I formed an encampment, and resolved to make a thorough examination of the surrounding forests.

26. The forenoon of that day was devoted to the forest on the south-west side of the Yana-mayu ravine, a steep declivity, the lower part of which is covered with ferns, bamboos, palms, some spurious cascarillas,* and trees with buttressed roots of stupendous size, to a height of 400 to 600 feet, when the calisaya region commences. In this locality 25 plants of the *Calisaya, var. α Vera* of Weddell were collected, two of them seedlings, the remainder root shoots, but with good roots of their own. The search was exceedingly fatiguing and dangerous work, scrambling through matted undergrowth and up steep declivities, in drenching rain, with rotten vegetation and saturated moss under foot.

27. In the afternoon we examined the forest-covered heights on the north-east side of the Yana-mayu, and 21 more calisayas were collected. I concluded, from observations made on this day, that the calisaya avoids the banks of a river, never being found within several hundred feet of it, that it prefers the steepest declivities of the mountain sides, and a great deal, though not too much, shade. When in very shady places, it loses the purple hues on the petioles and mid-ribs. The plants were growing in moss, a few feet deep, which clung to the rocks.

28. On the 4th I made a toilsome and dangerous forest journey, along the most giddy precipices, overhanging the river, with no foot-hold but decaying leaves, nothing to grasp but rotten branches, every motion a drenching bath from the wet branches, every other step a painful and dangerous slip or fall. This tract of forest was remarkably bare of cinchonæ, without any apparent cause, and only ten calisayas were collected during the whole day. I also stripped the bark off a young tree to bring home as a specimen.

29. On the 6th, the whole day was devoted to the search of a forest-clad height, on the south-west side of the Yana-mayu, called the "Naregada de Yana-mayu;" and as this was a very successful day's work, and the locality seemed well adapted for the growth of the calisaya, I will describe it in some detail.

30. From 500 to 600 feet above the river, a ridge of rocks juts out from the forest-covered sides of the ravine, which is not nearly so densely covered with vegetation, where there are no palms, tree ferns, or plants requiring excessive humidity, and where young plants receive shade from taller trees, while they also enjoy plenty of sunshine through the spreading branches. The most common trees at this spot were the *Melastomaceæ*, a tall grass called *Huichu-huichu*, the *Huaturus*, the *Aceite de Maria*, and the *Campadre de Calisaya*.

31. These, with a few *Cascarilla carua* and *Cinchona* (*var. Huinapu*) form the upper shade of the ridge of rocks; below there is an undergrowth of ferns, colocasiæ, and moss. In different parts of this ridge of rocks 124 young Calisaya plants were collected, all growing out of the moss, which covered the rock to a thickness of from eight inches to a foot, in company with a few beautiful hymenophyllums

* Cascarilla carua. Lasionema cinchonoides. Gomphosia chlorantha.

hymenophyllums and other ferns. There was scarcely any soil, the roots spreading along the face of the rock, which is a clay slate, easily broken up into thin layers by the growth of the plants.

32. Having entirely exhausted the provisions, it became necessary to retreat upon Gironda's clearing, a distance of 30 miles, and the delicate operation of packing the plants, which had previously been deposited in damp moss under the trees, was commenced on May 6th. A Russia mat was cut in half, to form two bundles, and the plants, the longest of which was cut down to a length of 18 inches, were carefully packed in rows, on layers of rich damp moss, which was very abundant.

33. I had made two attempts to ford the river, which was much swollen, and rushing along with great violence; but both times, after wading in up to my middle, the fury of the stream obliged me to return.

34. On May 7th we started in pouring rain, being entirely without food, and devoted some time to the search for calisaya plants on the slippery sides of the magnificent precipice of "Ccasa-sani," where I collected 21.

35. I was on the banks of the Yana-mayu river from the 2d to the 7th of May, during which time the thermometer ranged between 75° and 70° at 3 p. m., and the coldest at night was 58°. It rained more or less every day, generally from a few hours after sunset until 10 a. m., when it cleared up; but on the 7th it rained all day.

36. Returning to Gironda's clearing, I formed a second encampment at a place called "Lenco-huayccu," on May 8th, intending to explore the forests in the neighbourhood.

37. Although in this ravine the calisayas seem to prefer very shallow poor soils, in rocky situations, they certainly could never attain to their largest growth without more and richer soil. If the experiment proves successful in India, it will probably be found advisable eventually to form the calisaya plantations on slopes where there is shade and moisture, but some rich soil, so as to enable the roots to increase to their fullest size, and the trees to attain their largest growth. Very humid or flat situations, especially near the banks of rivers, must always, however, be carefully avoided. The plants might first be placed under the shade of trees, which, when they began to interfere with the growth of the calisayas, could be destroyed. The calisayas which I saw seemed to propagate themselves to a great extent by throwing out numerous roots from the branches, in the same way as the vine.

Cinchona Calisaya, var. Morada (*Cinchona Boliviana of Weddell*).

38. This species is made distinct from the *Calisaya* (*var. a Vera*) by Dr. Weddell in his work, but in a letter to me, dated 20th September 1859, he says that, in his present opinion, it is hardly more than a variety of the calisaya, its bark being very generally collected and sold as that of the latter. He adds that it is not met with in Tambopata, but only in Bolivia, and in the valley of Ayapata, in Caravaya. I, however, found and collected it in great abundance in various parts of the valley of Tambopata. The bark collectors consider it equal to the other variety of calisaya.

39. On 8th May I searched the heights of Tambopata, and found a number of plants of the *Calisaya morada* growing out of moss amongst the rocks, with hardly any soil, and on the 9th I resolved to make a third attempt to cross the river and examine the forests on the right bank. The river was 40 yards broad, and rushing with great fury over the ford, but we succeeded in crossing it without accident. The day's work began by a very precipitous ascent through the dense forest for about 400 feet, when we reached a rocky ridge, and rapidly collected 109 good plants of the *Calisaya morada*. This variety appears to prefer a little more shade and a little more soil (or, rather, holding ground, for it is entirely composed of moss and decayed leaves), than the *Calisaya, var. a Vera* of Weddell. It grows in the same rocky situations, with the roots sometimes actually in the crevices of the rocks.

40. I should add, that the *Calisaya morada* has been chiefly met with in the

the upper part of the ravine, while the *Calisaya var. α Vera*, was almost entirely collected near the Yana-mayu, and several leagues lower down the course of the Tambopata river.

41. On the 11th I went to see a plant of the *Calisaya morada*, which had been planted in a small clearing, in order to obtain some particulars respecting its growth. I was told that it was planted in January 1859, from a root shoot less than a foot high. It is now 7 feet high, $6\frac{4}{10}$ths inches in circumference round the trunk near the ground, and 3 feet 3 inches across the longest branches, from one side of the stem to the other. It was growing on the side of a steep hill, open to the south and east, at the edge of a clearing, whilst forest-covered mountains rose up close behind it to a great height. The soil consisted of a yellowish brown loam, composed of the disintegration of the rock, mixed with decomposed vegetable matter.

42. These details respecting the transplantation of a calisaya were all that I was able to procure, beyond the statement of Dr. Weddell, that a calisaya planted as a specimen in Tambopata (now cut down) had a trunk two inches thick in 1847, when it was ten years old.*

43. When planted in a richer soil in India, however, the calisayas will doubtless rapidly attain a growth equal to the largest of those in the Bolivian forests.

Cinchona Calisaya, var. Verde.

44. The bark collectors and other natives assured me that there are three kinds of calisayas, namely, the *Calisaya amarilla* or *Fina* (*α Vera* of Weddell), the *Calisaya morada* (*C. Boliviana* of Weddell), and the *Calisaya verde*, or *alta*, or *blanca*, not mentioned, as far as I am aware, by any author. They say that the latter is a very large tree, generally growing very far down the valleys, and in much lower situations than the other varieties. The veins of the leaves are never purple, but always a pale green, hence the name. The guide Martinez had cut a tree of this variety yielding six or seven cwts. of bark, including *canuto* or bark from the branches; and Gironda had seen a tree in the province of Munecas, in Bolivia, which yielded 10 cwts. of *tabla* or trunk bark alone. The true *Calisaya* of Weddell only yields three or four cwts.

45. I was very anxious to obtain plants of a variety which is said to attain so large a growth, and fortunately met with two, which happened to be growing on the heights of Tambopata.

Cinchona ovata, var. β rufinervis, var. α vulgaris.

46. I was particularly recommended by Dr. Weddell and Mr. Howard to procure some plants of the above species of cinchonæ, which grow at much greater elevations than the calisayas, and I devoted two days to a very laborious search for them, which was rather unsuccessful, though not entirely without result.

47. On the 5th of May I started with this object in view to examine the forest-clad heights of Pacchani, high above the hills over the Yana-mayu, and further to the north. After an ascent of 600 feet, high over the calisaya region, we came to trees of the *Pimentelia gomphosia*, with its bright laurel-like leaves and minute capsules, the *Cinchona pubescens*, and the *Cinchona ovata* (*var. α vulgaris*). The whole day was devoted to a difficult and wearisome search for young plants, but we only found three root shoots, two of the *α vulgaris* and one of the *β rufinervis*.

48. On the 10th of May I passed another day in searching for plants of the *Ovata* species, on some heights called Gloria-pata, immediately above Gironda's clearing. Trees were met with of both varieties, but very few seedlings or root shoots. The *Cinchona ovata*, though at a great elevation, inhabits the very moist parts of the forests, where the trees are covered with dripping moss and hymenophyllums, the latter a sure sign of extreme humidity. They were also in a greater

* Letter to me, September 20th, 1859.

a greater depth of decaying leaves than the calisayas, but little or no apparent soil; and there was much more shade, tree-ferns and palms growing round them. In the zone just below grows the *C. pubescens*, and just above the *C. amygdalifolia* and *Cascarilla bullata*.

49. Altogether 25 plants of the *C. ovata* have been collected, nine of the variety α *Vulgaris*, and 16 of β *Rufinervis*.

Cinchona micrantha (*C. Affinis* of Weddell).

50. This species of cinchona is called by the natives *Motosolo* and *Verde paltaya*. It grows in very low, damp situations, near the banks of streams. I saw one tree, laden with bunches of deliciously sweet small white flowers, actually drooping over the waters of the river Tambopata. Dr. Weddell informs me that the *C. micrantha* sometimes produces a good quality of bark. Letter to me, August 10th, 1859.

51. The *C. micrantha* is found in company with many kinds of palms, tree ferns, bamboos, melastomaceæ, paccays (*Mimosa inga**), *C. pubescens* (*var. Huinapu*), and a *Lasionema*, called by the natives *Carhua-carhua blanca*,† (and apparently different from the *Lasionema cinchonoides* of Weddell,) which is very abundant along the banks of the river Tambopata. Seven good plants of the *C. micrantha* were collected.

General Results.

52. By the 10th of May the collection was sufficiently large to fill the 15 Wardian cases which were provided for its reception at the port of Islay. We had procured 529 cinchona plants, more or less promising, namely :—

Cinchona Calisaya *var.* α *Vera* of Weddell - - -	237
Cinchona Calisaya morada, *C. Boliviana* of Weddell - -	183
Cinchona Calisaya, *var.* β *Josephiana* of Weddell -	75
Cinchona Calisaya verde - - - - - - -	2
Cinchona ovata *var.* α *Vulgaris* of Weddell - - -	9
Cinchona ovata, *var.* β *Rufinervis* of Weddell - - -	16
Cinchona micrantha, *C. affinis* of Weddell - - -	7
	529

53. The plants collected at the Yana-mayu encampment were conveyed in two bundles on the backs of Indians to Lenco-huayccu on the 7th and 8th of May, and again deposited under the shade of trees, with their roots in damp moss, together with the additional plants collected during the days devoted to searches in the forests near Lenco-huayccu.

54. On the 11th of May the collection of plants was prepared for the long journey across the Cordilleras. The plants were placed in rows, with thick layers of damp moss between them, and sewn up in Russia matting, forming four

* Ruiz y Pavon.

† *Carhua-carhua blanca.*—This tree appears to resemble closely the *Lasionema Cinchonoides* of Weddell, who says that its native name is "*Cascarilla Bruta;*" but the guide, Martinez, says that this plant is not the same.

Tree 30 to 40 feet high, growing in moist parts of the valley of Tambopata, near the banks of streams.

Bark lightish brown, marked with white lichens and mosses.

Leaves upwards of eighteen inches long and six to seven broad; dark green above; lighter beneath; veins extending very regularly from the mid-rib, oppositely or alternately pinnated; veins and mid-rib nearly white, especially on the under side; smooth; oblong, acute at both ends; coarse, often bulging between the veins and wrinkled.

Panicles corymbose and multiflower; in threes, and threes again; six to eighteen buds on each branch.

Calyx deep purple and green, leathery; five teeth, very rounded and blunt; limb deciduous; tube connate with the ovary; purplish.

Corolla.—Tube white, tinged with light purple; leathery; five laciniæ, smooth and reflexed.

Stamens five, attached to the middle of the tube of the corolla; exserted; filaments pillose at the base; tinged with purple; anthers a little shorter than filaments, all lying over on the lower side of the flower; bivalve and opening towards the front; light brown colour.

Pistil light green colour; style exserted, but a little shorter than the stamens; stigma bicleft; length of tube of corolla to the end of the anthers, one inch.

four bundles, which measured 2 feet 6 inches by 2 feet. They were marked Nos. 1, 2, 3, and 4—

Nos. 1 and 2 containing *C. Calisaya, vars.* α and β.
No. 3 ,, chiefly *C. calisaya morada.*
No. 4 ,, some *Calisaya morada*, two *C. Calisaya verde, C. ovatas*, and *C. micranthas.*

55. Specimens of rock were collected and marked, in all the localities where cinchona plants were met with. I considered it unimportant to bring away soil, as it appeared to be merely the disintegration of the rock, and the cinchonæ, growing chiefly in moss, seemed to be quite independent of it.

56. All the leaves of the Calisaya trees were more or less eaten by caterpillars, and the roots, especially of the young plants, were frequently attacked by the larva of a beetle, which bored holes through them. When this happened, it was observable that the plant began to throw out roots just above where the larva had deposited itself. I collected three specimens of the caterpillar on the leaves, and one of the animal in the roots, and preserved them in spirits.

The Valley of Tambopata.

57. The whole of the cinchonæ, with the exception of the *Josephiana* variety of calisayas, have been collected in the valley of Tambopata, and I, therefore, endeavoured to collect as much information as possible respecting the soil and climate of that locality.

58. The river Tambopata rises at a place called Saqui, at the foot of the ridge dividing Peru from Bolivia, and, after a course of 20 leagues through a forest-covered ravine, the sides of which rise up abruptly and end in lofty mountain peaks, unites with another river called Pablo-bamba, or San Cristobal, which flows from the other side of the Cordillera of Saqui. The united streams form an important river, which enters the plain country to the eastward, and finally falls into the great river Ynambari or Purus.

59. The sides of the ravine of Tambopata are composed of a rock, which I believe to be a yellow clay slate. When exposed to the weather, it quickly turns to a sticky yellow mud, while below the surface it is very brittle, and easily breaks off in thin layers. Veins of white quartz runs through it, and, as in all the other valleys of Caravaya, gold is found in the bed of the river.

60. The height of the ravine of Tambopata above the level of the sea is between 3,000 and 4,000 feet, and I collected the following information respecting the climate from the natives:—

January.—Incessant rains, with damp close heat both day and night. No sun. Fruits ripen. *C. pubescens* (*var. Huinapu*) in flower.

February.—Weather as in January. Coca harvest. *C. calisaya* in flower.

March.—Less rain, hot close days and nights. Little sun. Bananas ripe. *C. calisaya* and *Pimentelia* in flower.

April.—Less rain, with hot humid nights, and little sun during the day. *C. micrantha* in flower.

May.—A showery month, with little heavy rain. From May 1st to 12th the thermometer ranged from 62 degrees to 71 degrees at 7 A.M., from 69 degrees to 75 degrees at 3 P.M., and from 58 degrees to 68 degrees, the minimum, at night. The trade wind coming up the ravine brought clouds and rain. Month for planting coca and sugar-cane, and what is called the *michca*, or small sowing of maize. Edible roots sown. Coffee harvest begins. *C. micrantha, C. amygdalifolia, C. pubescens, Cascarillas Carua* and *Bullata, Gomphosia*, and *Lasionema* in flower.

June.—Dry and very hot month. Much sun and little rain. A good time for sowing edible roots. A coca harvest early in the month. Oranges and paccays ripen. Cool nights, but a fierce heat during the day.

July.—The driest and hottest month, with cool clear nights. Very few showers. Time for sowing pumpkins, gourds, and water-melons. *C. ovata* flowers.

August.—Generally dry, trees begin to blossom. A month for planting. Bean harvest. *C. Calisaya, Pimentelia*, and *Gomphosia* ripen.

September.

September.—Rains begin. Coca harvest. Time for the blossoming of many trees.

October.—Rains increasing. Paltas ripen. Maize harvest, and time for sowing the *sembra grande* of maize. *C. micrantha*, *C. pubescens*, *C. amygdalifolia*, *Cascarillas Carua* and *bullata*, and *Lasionema* ripen.

November.—Heavy rains. Coca harvest.

December.—Heavy rains. Pumpkins and gourds ripen. *C. ovatas* ripen.

61. Edible roots yield a year after planting, sugar-cane in two years, maize and beans in six months, coca gives three harvests of leaves a year.

62. Almost the whole of the ravine is one huge virgin forest, clothing the sides from the banks of the river to the summits of the mountain peaks. There are a few small clearings in the upper part of the ravine, the produce of which supports the inhabitants, about 20 souls.

Difficulties with the Natives.

63. With regard to the Indians who carried the provisions and plants, they were very suspicious and expected ill-treatment. On two occasions, they had resolved on deserting me and returning to their homes, in which case the failure of the enterprise must have followed. My knowledge of the Quichua language, and of the habits and feelings of the Indians, alone enabled me to manage them, and retain them in my service during a period of perilous and very laborious work.

64. But the principal difficulties arose from the obstacles which the petty local authorities attempted to throw in my way. Señor Gironda, who had been very friendly and had assisted me in various ways, was a justice of the peace, and the only authority in the ravine. On the 11th of May, just after the plants had been sewn up ready for their journey, a letter to Gironda arrived from Don José Bobadilla, the alcalde municipal of the district of Quiaca, saying that he had received positive intelligence that an English stranger had entered the forests to collect cinchona plants, to the serious injury of the people of this country, and ordering Gironda not to permit me to take a single plant, and to send me and the man who had assisted me as prisoners to Quiaca. The rest of the letter, which is in very bad Spanish, relates to other business.* I had reason to believe that a busy, meddling Peruvian, named Don Manuel Martel, had stirred up this opposition, and my opinion was confirmed when I heard that his son was the bearer of the letter. Gironda, though civil and obliging, was very anxious to throw all the plants away, in obedience to his instructions, and I found it necessary to make a rapid retreat, in order to save them.

65. Next day, just before starting, I heard that the ignorant people of Quiaca had been stirred up against me by Martel and Bobadilla, and that they were sending a party down the valley to seize the plants. This news hastened my departure, but I met with other obstacles at Sandia, chiefly caused by the machinations of the same Martel, which gave me considerable trouble. These annoyances obliged me to make a rapid journey, with the plants, direct to Arequipa, without entering any town or village whatever, while the gardener went round by Crucero to get my luggage. This resolution was fortunate, as the gardener found Martel awaiting my arrival at Crucero with the plants, in order to lodge a complaint against their extraction with the Sub-Prefect.

66. Some

* Copy.

"Al Senor Juen de Paz,
"Don Juan de la Cruz Gironda. "6° de Mayo de 1860.

"Teniendo positivas noticias de que sea internado a los puntos de Tambopata un estranjero Ingles, con objeto de estraer plantas de cascarilla, me es de absoluta necesidad pasarle a vm. esta nota para que sin permitir que, en grave perjuicio de los hijos del pais, lo tome ni una planta, por lo que como autoridad debe vm. de aberiguar bien para capturar a el y a la persona quien se propone a facilitarle las dichas plantas, y conducirlo a este; por consiguente comunico a vm. que por su ausencia sean demorado varios decretos superiores de la capital por lo que debe vm. restituirse lo mas pronto posible.

Dios guarde a vm.,
(signed) *José Mariano Bobadilla*,
"Alcalde Municipal del Distrito de Quiaca."

66. Some knowledge and experience of the people with whom I had to deal, and a succession of very fortunate accidents, alone enabled me to overcome these obstacles, which, for some time, threatened the complete failure of the enterprise; and it would certainly be useless to attempt to enter this province for a similar object, at least for some time to come.

Rapid Journey with the Plants from the Forests to the Port of Islay.

67. On the 19th of May, I left the ravine of Tambopata with the plants, and reached Sandia on the 15th. In passing through a forest in the road, one of the mules fell down a precipice for 20 feet, the fall being broken by dense underwood, and more than two hours was occupied in cutting trees and brushwood down to clear a way for him to get out.

68. At Sandia I found great difficulty, and met with much hindrance in procuring the means of proceeding on my journey; but at length I obtained two mules for the plants and an Indian to assist me to load them, and I resolved to make my way direct across the Cordillera, without entering any town or village, to a place called Vilque, where a great fair was going on, and whence I could hire mules to Arequipa. The gardener was sent round by Crucero to pick up my luggage.

69. Since leaving Sandia on April 24th up to May 15th, we had walked over 174 miles, which may not, at first sight, appear very much; but when it is considered that it was chiefly not walking, but scrambling on hands and knees up precipices or through dense forests, and that there was not one day given up to rest, while the supply of food was exceedingly small and precarious, I think it will be considered tolerably good work.

70. On the 17th of May I left Sandia with one Indian and two mules carrying the plants, and halted under a splendid range of frowning black cliffs near the summit of the snowy Caravaya range. On the 18th I reached the summit of the range, and commenced the journey over vast grass-covered plains covered with stiff white frost; after being 11 hours in the saddle, I stopped at an abandoned shepherd's hut built of loose stones. The plants, well covered with the tent and blankets,* were placed by my side during the night, with the thermometer between us, which at 6 a.m. was at 20 degrees, the days and nights bitterly cold, but very fine and generally cloudless. On the 19th I was ten hours in the saddle, and passed the night again in an abandoned hut with the plants beside me, where the minimum of the thermometer was 30 degrees. Two more journeys of similar length, when the minimum during the night of the 21st was 21 degrees, and of the 22d, 16 degrees, brought me to Vilque, where I procured an arriero and mules to convey me to Arequipa. The sufferings during my six days' journey over the lofty plains from Sandia to Vilque were very great; the cold was intense, the work I had with the vicious unmanageable mules was a constant source of anxiety, and I had no food whatever beyond a little parched maize; each day I was upwards of 10 hours in the saddle.

71. Leaving Vilque on the 24th, by forced and rapid marches over an uninhabited and frozen tract of country, exposed to furious gales of intensely cold† wind, I reached the city of Arequipa on the 27th, having travelled over 350 miles of difficult country in 10 days, having to accommodate myself to the pace of a walking Indian and pass much of the time in chasing the vicious mules; I was never less than 10 hours in the saddle.

72. At Arequipa I found the moss which enveloped the plants still damp; but I watered them once or twice during my stay there between the 28th and 30th, during which time the range of the thermometer day and night was between 56 and 60 degrees. On the 31st, I left Arequipa, and crossing the desert, the plants were safely deposited beside the Wardian cases at Islay on June 1st. The gardener arrived at Arequipa on May 29th.

ESTABLISHMENT

* Before leaving Sandia, an extra Russia matting was sewn over each bundle of plants.

† From Vilque to Arequipa the minima of the thermometer were—

On the 23d	26 degrees.	On the 26th	24 degrees.
„ 24th	23 „	„ 27th	36 „
„ 25th	24 „	„ 28th	56, at Arequipa.

Establishment of the Plants in the Wardian Cases.

73. Having written to Mr. Wilthew, Her Majesty's Consul at Islay, immediately on my arrival at Arequipa, he had kindly caused the Wardian cases to be placed in the yard of an English carpenter, and had procured a supply of good soil from the ravine of Mataranes, at the same spot whence I sent a sample for analysis with my letter to Dr. Forbes Watson (No. 2).

74. The plants, which were found on the whole to be in a favourable state, were planted in the cases and well watered during the 2d and 3d of June. The cases being numbered from 1 to 15, a rough account was kept of what plants were deposited in each, some in the flower-pots which had just arrived from England, and those with larger roots loose in the soil.

75. The large-rooted plants without any foliage are in cases, with moss covering the soil, so as to supply them with more moisture. The contents of the Wardian cases are as follows:—

No. 1.	Calisayas (*var.* β *Josephiana*) in pots - - -	50
,, 2.	Calisayas (*var.* α 16 and β 25) - - - -	41
,, 3.	Calisayas (α) - - - - - - - -	34
,, 4.	Calisaya Moradas (*C. Boliviana* of Weddell) - -	38
,, 5.	Calisaya Moradas, in pots - - - - -	42
,, 6.	Calisaya Moradas 14 (*C. micrantha*; 1 large *C. ovatas*)	15
,, 7.	Calisaya Moradas (and the 2 *Verdes*, large, *C. ovatas*)	18
,, 8.	Calisaya Moradas (2 *C. ovatas*, &c., in pots, *C. micranthas* 4) - - - - - - - - -	49
,, 9.	Calisaya (α) in pots - - - - - - -	28
,, 10.	Calisaya Moradas - - - - - - - -	32
,, 11.	Calisayas (α) - - - - - - - -	32
,, 12.	Calisayas (α) and Moradas, unpromising - - -	15
,, 13.	Calisaya Moradas, small and good - - - -	32
,, 14.	Calisayas (α) large - - - - - - -	15
,, 15.	Calisaya Moradas (*C. ovatas*, &c.) - - - -	15
		456
	Plants killed by the cold of the Cordilleras, broken on the journey, or lost - - - - - - - - -	73
		529

76. The flower-pots, most of which were broken on the voyage, are of two sizes, No. 40 and No. 60. The plants will be watered every day and carefully attended to until the day before shipment, when the soil will be battened down and sashes screwed on; in the meanwhile they are kept screwed down, so as to create an artificial atmosphere after being watered, and screened from the heat of the sun at midday. Islay is always exceedingly dry, but June is, on the whole, a favourable cloudy month, thermometer ranging between 64 and 74 degrees.

Seeds.

77. It was my intention to have returned to the forests of Tambopata for seeds of the *C. calisaya* towards the end of July or the beginning of August; but the opposition I afterwards met with convinced me that any attempt to make the collection personally would be worse than useless. Generally speaking, I have no confidence in native agency; nevertheless, under these circumstances, I have thought it my duty to make several arrangements for procuring a supply of calisaya seeds, which, if they fail, will cause no expense, and, if successful, will require an outlay of about 50 *l.* I have good grounds for believing that a supply of several thousand seeds will be forthcoming, but all dealings with natives are uncertain.

Employment of Mr. Pritchett in Huanuco.

78. The Secretary of State having shown his sense of the importance of obtaining as many different species of the cinchona plant as possible, for introduction into India, by authorising me to expend 500 *l.* additional, in procuring plants

plants or seeds from the forests of Huanuco and Huamalies, I have succeeded in procuring the services of a Mr. Pritchett for that purpose. While at Guayaquil, I received a very favourable report of the character and qualifications of that gentleman from Mr. Cope, Her Majesty's Consul General in the Ecuador, and I resolved to employ him, in the event of his coming out to these countries.

79. Mr. Pritchett arrived in Lima on the 10th of April, and was at once supplied with funds to enable him to start for the forests, together with a paper of instructions respecting the species of cinchona plants which are found in Huanuco and Huamalies, with some notes on the mode of collection.

80. During my short stay in Lima, I shall endeavour to have some Wardian cases made for his plants; but I shall, at the same time, instruct him to turn his attention chiefly to the collection of seeds. I trust that, by September, he will have been enabled to collect a good supply of the species found in the Huanuco region, which are so well known to botanists through the work of Ruiz and Pavon, and the accounts given by Poëppig.

Conveyance of the Plants to India.

81. After some consideration, the gardener and I have decided that it will be best to give the plants some time to establish their roots in the flower-pots and cases, previous to their embarkation. I shall, therefore, proceed with them to England by the steamer which passes Islay on the 25th of this month, and expect to arrive at Southampton on the last day in July. The monsoon is not over in the Neilgherry hills, I believe, until the end of September; and it may, therefore, be thought advisable to wait between two mails at Southampton during the warm month of August, but this question will be decided in England.

82. I, of course, propose to accompany my collections to their final home in the Neilgherry hills, as it is very important that I should examine the sites prepared for their reception, or proposed to be used for their future culture, and thus be enabled to supply Dr. Cleghorn and others with all the information I possess. I should also be on the spot when the collections of Mr. Spruce and Mr. Pritchett arrive.

83. John Weir, the gardener, who has accompanied me, has been very efficient in his special duties of packing the plants and establishing them in the Wardian cases, and has displayed much zeal and interest in the enterprise, during the period of his service. I consider him fully entitled to the extra 60 *l.* a year, the receipt of which was to depend on the report I was enabled to make of his conduct.

84. In addition to specimens of rocks and of the animals which feed on the cinchonæ, a collection of dried leaves, capsules, and flowers of the cinchonæ was made; but, owing to the excessive humidity and continual rains, and the impossibility of devoting sufficient time and attention to them, they are in a very damaged state. Specimens of bark, and small branches of cinchonæ and allied species, with their *canuto* bark, were also collected in the forests.

85. Trusting that the numerous deficiencies of this Report will be excused, in consideration of the weak and exhausted state in which I arrived here, and the short time I have had to write it before the arrival of the steamer, while much occupied with other duties connected with the establishment of the plants in the cases,

I have, &c.
(signed) *Clements R. Markham.*

— No. 35. —

From *E. D. Bourdillon*, Esq., to *Clements Markham*, Esq.

Sir, India Office, E. C., 26 April 1860.

I AM directed by the Secretary of State for India in Council, to request that you will despatch to the Governors of Jamaica and Trinidad any small quantity of seeds of the cinchona plant, which may be available for that purpose, without detriment to the supply you may be able to procure for transmission to India, Ceylon, and the Royal Gardens at Kew.

I am, &c.

Clements Markham, Esq., &c. &c. &c. (signed) *E. D. Bourdillon.*

— No. 36. —

From *Herman Merivale*, Esq., to *Clements Markham*, Esq.

[*Note.*—This letter was not received by Mr. Markham until after his return to England.]

Sir, India Office, E. C., 17 May 1860.

YOUR letter, dated 20th March last, detailing your past proceedings, and your future plans in execution of the commission with which you have been entrusted, has been read by the Secretary of State in Council with much interest; and I am directed in reply to state, that in the embarrassing position in which you were placed in consequence of the local information you obtained regarding the position of the *Cinchona Calisaya*, and the obstacles to procuring plants and seeds of that species from Bolivia, Sir Charles Wood is fully satisfied that you exercised a sound judgment as to the course which you decided to follow.

With regard to the mode of transporting your collections to India, Sir Charles Wood has already given you full authority to avail yourself of any opportunity which may be afforded for the transport of the seeds and plants to India, either by sailing or steam ship. He is disposed to agree in the opinion which you have since expressed, that the chances of detention on a sailing vessel, render it inexpedient to select that mode of conveyance. He has, in accordance with your former request, taken the requisite steps for securing the safety of your collections, should you decide on dispatching them *viâ* Panama and Southampton; but he wishes you to understand, that if it should be in your power to charter a steamer direct to India, you are at liberty to make arrangements for that purpose, should you still deem it desirable.

The Secretary of State in Council fully appreciates the difficulties and dangers which you must necessarily encounter in the progress of your arduous mission. He has full confidence in the zeal, energy, and sagacity with which you will meet the obstacles in your way; and he trusts that, notwithstanding opposition, you will return to this country in health and safety, to enjoy the satisfaction of the successful result of your labours.

I am, &c.

Clements R. Markham, Esq. &c. &c. &c. (signed) *Herman Merivale.*

— No. 37. —

EXTRACT from *Clements Markham*, Esq., to the Under Secretary of State for India.

Sir, Steam-ship "Atrato," 28 July 1860.

IN continuation of my letter, dated 9th June 1860, I have the honour to report, for the information of the Secretary of State for India in Council, that I have arrived at Southampton, on board the steam-ship "Atrato," with the Wardian cases, containing my collection of cinchona plants, this day.

2. After the despatch of my letter, dated 9th June, I encountered very considerable difficulty in embarking the plants, owing to the obstacles thrown in my way by the local authorities. Mr. Wilthew, Her Majesty's Consul at Islay, to whom I am much indebted for advice and active assistance, has written a report

 of

of the difficulties I have encountered in the embarkation of the plants, in a despatch to the Foreign Office, by this mail.

3. Before leaving Lima, I despatched two letters to Mr. Pritchett in Huanuco, containing instructions for his guidance, and I have ordered a carpenter at Lima to make six Wardian cases for the reception of his plants.

4. The last tidings I have received from Mr. Spruce are, that he has hired the forests below Huaranda, on the western slope of Chimborazo, where the best red bark is procured, and that he intends to embark his collection on rafts at Ventanas, some way up the river Babahoyo. The forests producing *C. Condaminea* are 15 days' journey from those of Huaranda, and he proposes to send a Dr. Taylor of Riobamba to Loxa, to procure plants and seeds of that species.

5. With reference to Mr. Bourdillon's letter to me, dated 26th April 1860, I have directed Mr. Spruce and Mr. Pritchett to make up two small parcels of cinchona seeds, in case they obtain a sufficient supply, addressed to the Governors of Jamaica and Trinidad, to the care of Her Majesty's Consul at Panama. The gardener, Cross, has passed through Panama, on his way to Guayaquil.

6. The plants are, on the whole, in a good condition, and upwards of 210 are throwing out shoots.

7. I enclose two sketch maps, showing my journey to the cinchona forests of Caravaya, hastily drawn from data, for the construction of maps, consisting of a fixed position at Crucero, and a series of bearings and cross bearings, with a true bearing taken at intervals. These maps should have accompanied my report, dated 9th June 1860.

I have, &c.
(signed) *Clements R. Markham.*

— No. 38. —

From *J. Murray*, Esq., to *T. G. Baring*, Esq., M.P.

Sir, Foreign Office, 20 August 1860.

WITH reference to your letter of the 29th of April 1859, I am directed by Lord John Russell to transmit to you, to be laid before Secretary Sir Charles Wood, a copy of a despatch from Her Majesty's Consul at Islay, reporting the success of Mr. Markham's mission, and his departure for England with specimens of the cinchona plants.

I am, &c.
(signed) *James Murray.*

T. Baring, Esq., &c. &c. &c.
India Office.

Enclosure in No. 38.

From Her Majesty's Consul at Islay, to Lord *John Russell.*

My Lord, Islay, 24 June 1860.

IN reference to a despatch from the Foreign Office, under date of the 30th of April last, I have the honour to inform your Lordship, that I have done all in my power to assist Mr. Markham in the fulfilment of his mission. Mr. Markham leaves this to day, in the steamer, direct for England, *viâ* Panama, taking with him 460 cinchona plants of the calisaya, or best of the species, well secured in Wardian cases, hermetically sealed.

The plants have been allowed to remain here more than a fortnight to repose, and I have had an opportunity of observing during that time how they have thrived, the sprouts, or growth, being very evident in most of them.

The plants were brought down from the interior by Mr. Markham, accompanied by a gardener, wrapped up in matting, in which was a quantity of moss and fern to preserve the dampness; most of them have been planted separately in small flower-pots, the pots embedded in the soil, and battens placed across each row; to prevent their moving, others have been planted in the cases.

Mr. Markham had had many hardships to pass and difficulties to contend with, in procuring the plants. He was for more than ten days in the Montana or forest of Carabaya, which forms the frontier of Peru and Bolivia, accompanied by four Indians, with very little to eat, being obliged to take the the necessaries of life with him, and sleeping under a tent in a very damp atmosphere, and on damp soil.

On his return out of the Montana, an order arrived from one of the petty authorities to seize all the plants, as they were not allowed to be exported. By bribery and persuasion, Mr. Markham

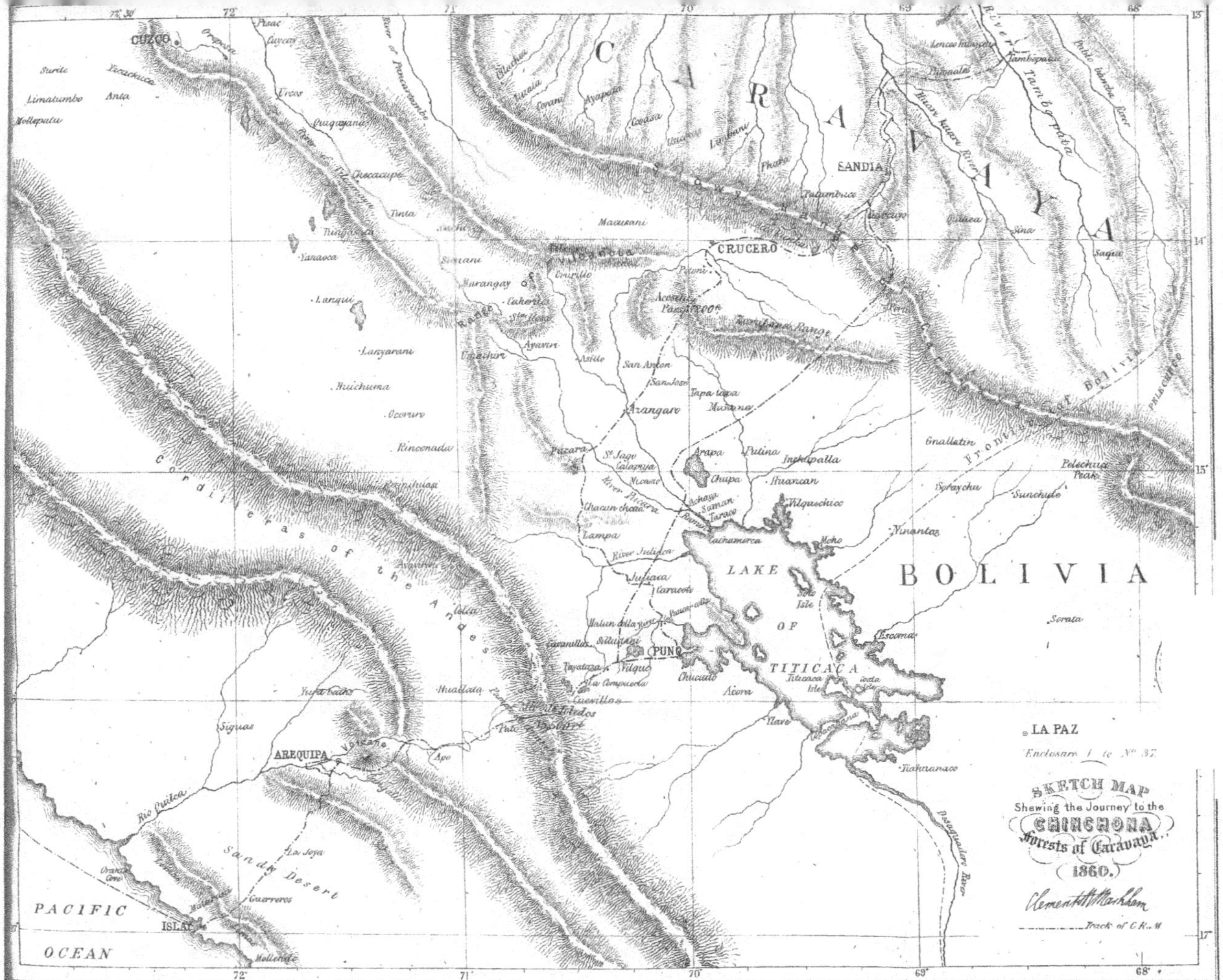

Nº 118 Ordered by The House of Commons to be Printed, 20. March 1863

Henry Hansard, Printer

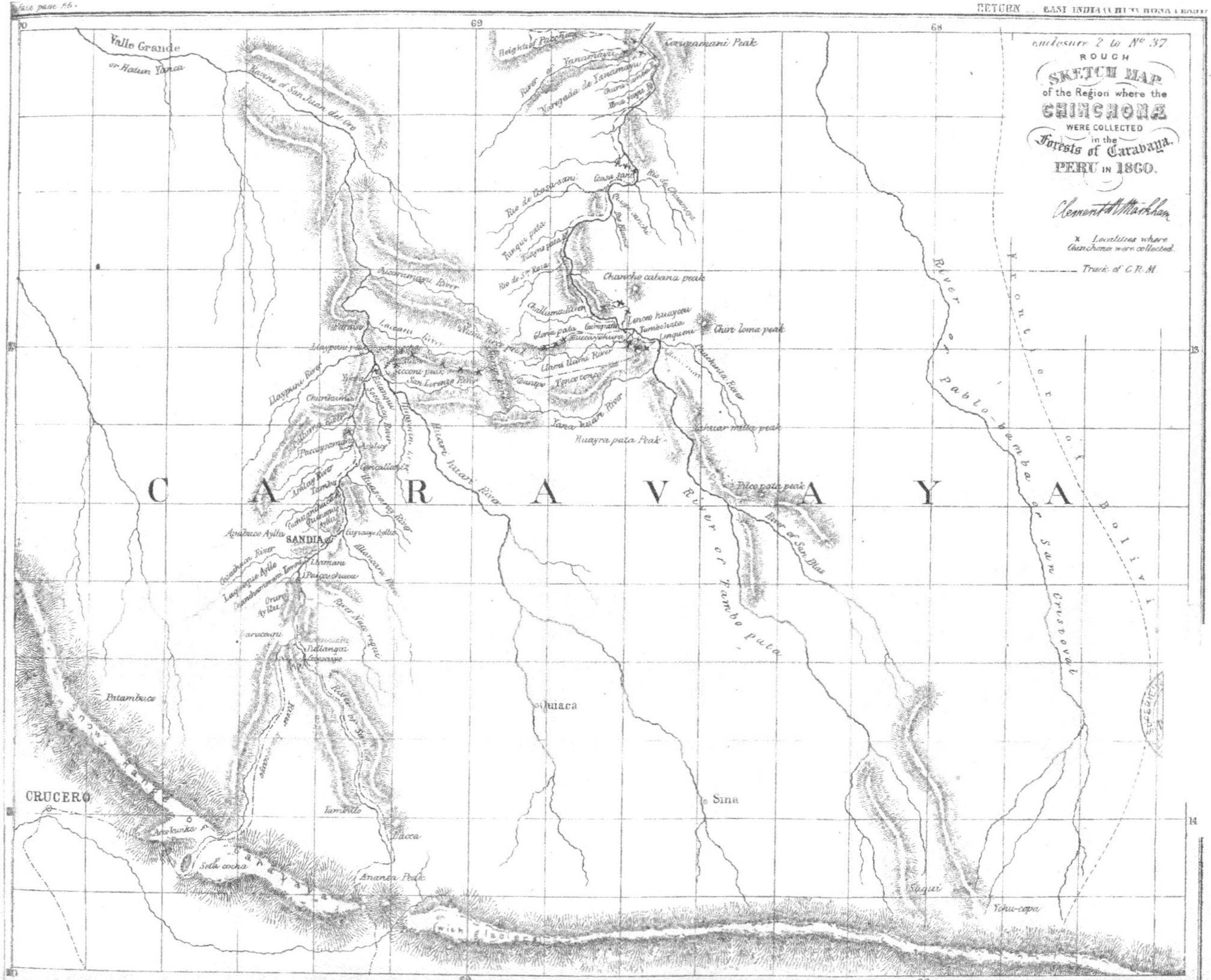
Enclosure 2 to No 37
ROUGH
SKETCH MAP
of the Region where the
CHINCHONÆ
WERE COLLECTED
in the
Forests of Caravaya,
PERU IN 1860.
Clements R. Markham
x Localities where Chinchonæ were collected.
Track of C.R.M.
70
69
68
13
14
C A R A V A Y A
Valle Grande
or Hatun Yunca
Caravamani Peak
Chancho cabana peak
Chiri loma peak
Huayra pata Peak
Pilco pata peak
Yana huari River
River of San Blas
River or Tambo pata
River of Pablo-bamba or San Cristoval
Frontier of Bolivia
Huari huari River
SANDIA
Quiaca
Sina
Patambuco
CRUCERO
Tambillo
Ananea Peak
Saqui
Yanu-capa

Mr. Markham was able to make his escape with them, taking a cross road to avoid molestation, and so arrived safe at Arequipa.

At this port, again, the administrator of the Custom-house objected to the plants being exported, without an express order from the Government and Lima, and Mr. Markham was obliged to proceed to that city to obtain the necessary permission, which, after some scruples on the part of the Minister, he was fortunately able to succeed in doing.

I am not aware that any decree exists prohibiting the exportation of the Cinchona plant, and this molestation on the part of the authorities has proceeded from feelings of jealousy, and from an idea that it is robbing the country of one of its sources of wealth.

Mr. Markham has not been able to take with him any of the seeds, as they are not in a ripe state until the month of August.

I trust that the ultimate object of the Government in sending Mr. Markham on this mission may be obtained.

I have, &c.

The Lord J. Russell. (signed) *C. Wilthew.*

— No. 39. —

From *Herman Merivale*, Esq., to *Clements Markham*, Esq.

Sir, India Office, E.C., 11 August 1860.

I AM directed by the Secretary of State for India in Council to acknowledge the receipt of your letters, dated 9th June and 28th ultimo, the former reporting your proceedings after arrival in Peru, in fulfilment of the Commission with which you were entrusted for obtaining seeds and plants of the Cinchona, and the latter detailing your subsequent proceedings up to your arrival at Southampton on the 28th ultimo, with your collection of plants.

Sir Charles Wood has perused with much interest the detail of your proceedings in Peru, and he directs me to assure you, that he highly appreciates the zeal, energy, and intelligence which have enabled you to form so considerable a collection of plants of the more valuable species of the Cinchonas, as well as to surmount the various difficulties which you had to encounter in the course of your enterprise, whether arising from the natural features of the country to be traversed, the peculiar character of the season, or the jealousy manifested by the population and by the officers of the Government when the object of your expedition became known.

There appears to Sir Charles Wood to be every reason to be satisfied with the measure of success which has attended your arduous enterprise; and your determination to leave the country with the plants, without waiting for the ripening of the seeds of the Cinchonas, is fully justified by the opposition which was subsequently offered to the object of your mission, and which, had your departure been deferred, would probably have led to its entire failure.

Sir Charles Wood is of opinion, that it is highly desirable that you should yourself accompany your collections to India, in order that the experience you have obtained of the situations peculiar to the various species of the Cinchonas may be turned to the greatest possible account, and the Peninsular and Oriental Company have already been requested to reserve accommodation for you on board the steamer leaving Southampton on the 20th instant.

The instructions given to Mr. Pritchett for his guidance in his search for Cinchona plants and seeds in the district of Huanuco have the approval of Sir Charles Wood, and the necessary communication has already been made to Messrs. Gibbs & Co., to make such advances as he may require to the amount which has already been sanctioned.

In conclusion, I have to state that Sir Charles Wood has pleasure in expressing his entire satisfaction with the manner in which you have discharged a duty of great public importance, which you voluntarily assumed when the attempts previously made to meet with a duly qualified person to undertake it had proved fruitless. He has noticed the economy with which your proceedings have been conducted, and he will be prepared, at the close of your labours, to take into favourable consideration your claim to remuneration for the successful performance of an arduous and useful service.

I am, &c.

Clements R. Markham, Esq. (signed) *Herman Merivale.*
&c. &c. &c.

— No. 40. —

From Sir *C. Wood* to the Governor General of India.

My Lord, India Office, London, 17 August 1860.

MR. CLEMENTS MARKHAM, whom I sent on an expedition to the forests of Bolivia in order to procure plants and seeds of the quinine-yielding Cinchona tree, having successfully accomplished his mission, will leave England by the steamer of the 28th instant for Bombay, and thence proceed by sea to Calicut, with the plants in his charge. I transmit herewith, for your information, six copies of Mr. Markham's report of his proceedings while engaged in South America on this undertaking.

2. The Governments of Madras and Bombay have also been advised of Mr. Markham's departure for India by the steamer above mentioned.

I have, &c.
(signed) *C. Wood.*

His Excellency the Right Honourable
The Governor General of India in Council.

— No. 41. —

From *R. Spruce*, Esq., to the Under Secretary of State for India.

Ambato, Republic of Ecuador,
12 March 1860.

Sir,

YOUR letter of November 18, 1859, did not reach me until the end of last month, when we had been for a long time without any correspondence with Guayaquil, on account of the mails being detained by the hostile troops which occupied the road. It was, however, intimated to me some time ago by Mr. Markham that my services had been accepted by the India Government for the object of procuring seeds and plants of the valuable sorts of Cinchona, and I therefore, at the end of last year, laid aside every other occupation to make the necessary preparations for entering on that enterprise. I had besides, during last summer, spent over two months in the forests on the western flank of the Cordillera, at my own expense, and with the sole object of making myself acquainted with the different sorts of Cinchona.

I have now succeeded in hiring all the woods on the western side of Chimborazo (belonging to five different farms) for the purpose of getting out of them seeds and plants of the red bark (*Cascarilla roja*), which is of better quality there than elsewhere, and I hope to enter them in the month of May, when the rains begin to abate.

I am also in treaty with the owners of the woods near Loja which produce the *Cinchona Condaminea,* and hope to obtain license to enter those woods for my purpose. But here a difficulty arises, for, so far as I can make out, the *Cinchona Condaminea* has ripe seeds in the same month as the *Cascarilla roja* (namely, in July), and from Chimborazo to Loja takes 15 days, or if the traveller be overtaken by bad weather, or any of his beasts break down, he may spend 20 days or more on the way. It is therefore clearly impossible that I can be in both places so as to see with my own eyes the seeds of each species taken from the tree, which is the only way to be sure of having the right sort, for the seeds of all Cinchonas are so much alike that they cannot be distinguished without the leaves. To procure the *Cinchona Condaminea,* I should therefore have to send to Loja a competent person in my place, and employ a sufficient staff of labourers to get out the young plants and convey them to the coast; so that although the procuring of seeds and plants of the *Cascarilla roja* (and of some other kinds of less value which grow near it, in a cooler climate) may be accomplished for something less than the 500 *l.* to which my expenses are in the first instance limited, it would considerably exceed that sum to procure the *Cinchona Condaminea* in like manner. As my instructions hardly give me plenary powers on this head, I have written to consult Mr. Cope, and shall be guided by his decision.

I shall

I shall throughout be as economical as possible, and render an exact account of my expenditure. I have horses of my own which I shall make use of as far as I can, and charge only for their keep. It must also be recollected that I am already on the spot, and that no expense is incurred by my coming out or returning.

I shall not fail to make careful observations on the climate and soil of the regions where the different kinds of Cinchona flourish, in accordance with your recommendation.

I remain, &c.
(signed) *Richard Spruce.*

— No. 42. —

From *R. Spruce*, Esq., to *Clements Markham*, Esq.

Dear Sir, Ambato, 14 April 1860.

I wrote a letter to you on the 1st of March, but I learn that it has never reached Guayaquil. I write therefore again, and as the letter goes by the courier of the Corps Diplomatique in Quito, I trust it may safely reach your hands. We have for long had no certain communication with the coast, and I kept three beasts and a man waiting for six weeks to bring up Cross the moment I should hear of his arrival at Guayaquil. The receipt of your letter of January 19th (which reached me three weeks ago) informed me that I must not expect him until May. At the same time I received the box you were so kind as to bring me from England, along with a portion of Mr. Howard's work on Cinchona, but the pamphlet you mention has not come to hand. What was it about? I was in hopes to receive by you Weddell's Monograph, as also the Report of the Dutch Government.

I have hired the forests below Guaranda, on the western slope of Chimborazo, where the best variety of the *Cascarilla roja* is procured. The port where I shall have to embark my collections (on rafts) is Ventanas, a good way up the river Babahoyo.

There is a difficulty about getting the *Cinchona Condaminea*, for the forests of Loja which produce it are 15 days' journey from those of Guaranda, and as both Cinchonas fruit at the same season (July), it is impossible that I can see seeds taken from both with my own eyes, which is the only way to be sure of having the right sort; I propose, therefore, sending Dr. James Taylor (of Riobamba) to Loja, and I have written to ask Mr. Cope if I may venture on this additional expense. Otherwise, I might, next year, gather seeds of it myself and send them to Kew, as I propose making a journey to Loja on my own account.

Your proposal about tying gauze bags round the corymbs of fruit might be good if there were any one "to bell the cat;" but who is to climb within reach of the ends of the brittle ramuli of the *Cascarilla roja?* My plan is, to spread sheets under the tree at the time of cutting or breaking off the branches with seeds.

Mr. Howard is all out about the climate of the *Cascarilla roja*. He has been misled by a worthless book, "Geografia del Ecuador," by one Manuel Villavicencio, which is as full of mistakes as it is of paragraphs.

I will do my best to carry out your instructions respecting the transmission of the Cinchona plants and seeds.

If you find it practicable to dry for me a specimen, with flower and fruit, of every sort of Cinchona you meet with, I shall be exceedingly obliged to you, and I will do the same for you if you desire it.

You must let me know the date of your going to Guayaquil, and I will endeavour to await your arrival there.

Trusting your life and health may be preserved, and that you may have as pleasant a time of it as can be expected in these rough countries,

I remain, &c.
Clements R. Markham, Esq., Lima. (signed) *Richard Spruce.*

— No. 43. —

REPORT on Expedition to procure Seeds and Plants of *Cinchona succirubra*, or Red Bark Tree; with Specimens for the Herbarium at Kew.

From Mr. *Richard Spruce* to the Under Secretary of State for India.

Sir, Guayaquil, 12 October 1860.

THE troubled state of this country, and the interruption of communication between the interior and the coast, have prevented my informing you until now of what I was doing towards carrying out the project of procuring Cinchona plants and seeds. The same causes have interfered seriously with its successful execution; but as I trust that all obstacles have at length been overcome, I shall at present confine myself to a brief account of my operations, reserving for a future occasion a fuller Report, comprising all my observations on the site, meteorology, and accompanying vegetation of the tree producing the *Cascarilla roja*, or red bark.

At the beginning of the present year, I laid aside every other occupation to devote myself to the task assigned me. I had last visited (at my own expense) the Cinchona forests below Alansi, in order to make myself acquainted with the trees producing the barks of commerce; but as I afterwards learnt that the red bark collected about the foot of Chimborazo fetched nearly double the price in the market of that brought from the forests of Alansi and Cuenca, I thought it my duty to endeavour to procure seeds, &c., from trees whose bark was considered the best, although to the eyes of a botanist specimens from all these localities might present no specific difference. The forests of Chimborazo (generally called "of Guaranda," though actually from one to four days' journey from that town) cover an area of perhaps 2,000 square miles. They are rented by two persons, for the purpose of getting out the bark they produce, and I immediately entered into treaty with those persons to allow me to collect as many seeds and young plants as I needed, during the present summer, or dry season. At first, they were unwilling to grant me such permission, at any price; but after a good deal of correspondence, and travelling to and fro, I finally agreed with them that, on payment of 400 dollars, I might take from the forest all I required, provided I did not touch the bark.

It cost me no small amount of inquiry to ascertain what was the best point for a centre of operations, in a range of country so extensive, and accessible with such difficulty; but I finally made out that a place called Limón, where there are a few small cane farms, at the junction of the river Limon with the larger river Chasuán (which is one of those that go to form the river of Guayaquil), was the place where the finest bark had been obtained, and that the settlers, since they found out the value of the bark, had preserved with great care such young trees as were standing on their farms.

I engaged eleven cascarilleros of Guanújo (a village adjacent to Guaranda, where most of the bark collectors reside) to enter the forest with me, as soon as the weather permitted, to search for trees and plants of Cinchona.

I also availed myself of your permission to secure the services of Dr. James Taylor, of Riobamba, for the purpose of procuring seeds and plants of the *Cinchona condaminea* from Loja.

In the spring, I was unfortunately taken seriously ill of a rheumatic and nervous affection, almost amounting to paralysis, which, although it did not incapacitate me from continuing the necessary preparations, rendered it doubtful that I should be able to bear the arduous fatigues of travelling in the forest; I therefore concluded to resign my commission to Dr. Taylor, and send him for the red bark in my room.

The rains did not abate until the end of May, and the 5th of June was fixed on as the day of starting for the forest; for which purpose Dr. Taylor went over to Ambato, where I was residing. Encouraged by his assurance that, if I could only get over to Chimborazo, the climate of the warm forest might probably restore me, and after using for a few days such remedies as he suggested, I started in his company on the 11th of June, my idea being that if I soon get well enough to conduct the enterprise alone, I might then despatch Dr. Taylor to Loja. In the pass of Chimborazo, I was so much exhausted that I had to remain two nights and a day in a hut at a height of nearly 13,000 feet. I rallied, however, and was enabled to reach Guaranda, where I found that my cascarilleros had all been taken

taken as soldiers or militiamen. I remained some days in the vain attempt to procure license for them to proceed to the forest, which was promised me only when the country should be freed of its "tyrants." In their room, I thought myself fortunate in securing four Indians to work under my directions, although they were quite incapable of acting as guides to localities which had remained unsearched in previous years, and to explore which would need excursions into the forest of 10 or 15 days, under the guidance of practised cascarilleros.

At Guaranda, I learnt for the first time (by the passing of diplomatic correspondence for the Honourable C. R. Buckalew, American Minister at Quito) that Mr. Cross, the gardener destined by the India Government to take charge of the Cinchona plants, had arrived at Guayaquil, about the middle of May; and, by the passing of the Spanish Minister through Guaranda for Guayaquil, I was fortunately enabled to write to Mr. Mocatta, Her Britannic Majesty's Consul at Guayaquil, requesting him to forward Mr. Cross to Ventanas, which is the port on the river of Guayaquil where we must embark our collections made at Limon. Such rare opportunities were now my only means of communication with Guayaquil, and I had not another for above three months afterwards.

On the 17th and 18th of June, we descended from Guaranda, by a most precipitous and dangerous track, to Limon,* where we established ourselves in the rancho of one of the settlers. Having reposed a day, Dr. Taylor proceeded to Ventanas—other two days' journey—to await the arrival of Mr. Cross.

After having been a few days at Limon, I so far recovered the use of my limbs as to be able to move about—partly on foot, partly on horseback—and ascertain, by a personal examination, everything which was necessary to be known. I was well satisfied to see, standing about in the cane-fields and near the houses, several fine young trees of the *Cinchona succirubra*, from 30 to 50 feet high, and, as far as I could ascertain, from 13 to 15 years old. Many of them had flowered freely this year, and on several the capsules had attained nearly their full size. They also bore signs of having fruited last year, but no young plants existed beneath them, which was explained by their either standing among cane which had been frequently weeded during the year, or else in open places where cattle had grazed and trodden about. The seedling plants, which I had been assured at Guaranda might be had in any quantity at Limon, proved to be all either shoots from old stools of *Cinchona succirubra*, or young plants and suckers of the worthless *Cinchona magnifolia*, which grows abundantly there, and had fruited during the rainy season, for the capsules were already open and empty on the day of my arrival. Seedlings of *Cinchona succirubra* we could plainly hope to find only in the vicinity of large trees in the virgin forest, and the latter have now become so scarce that, even with the aid of cascarilleros, our finding any such would be uncertain.

When Dr. Taylor had been ten days at Ventanas, a brief note from Mr. Mocatta was left at Guaranda by the Spanish Minister (on his return from Guayaquil to Quito), informing me that Mr. Cross had been taken suddenly ill when about to start for Ventanas. I therefore sent to recall Dr. Taylor, and after his return to Limon our operations were confined to visiting daily the bark trees and watching the progress of the fruit towards maturity, and to studying the accompanying vegetation. Nearly all through the month of July the weather was cool, with a great deal of mist and fog, so that the capsules scarcely increased in size. Many fell off, and some were attacked by a maggot and curled up. On the tree which bore most capsules, the latter began to turn mouldy, the mould being not fungi, but rudimentary lichens—a striking proof of the humidity of the climate. I began to fear we should get no ripe seeds this year, and as the seeds had been especially recommended to me in my instructions from England, it may be imagined how severe was my feeling of disappointment.

About the time of Dr. Taylor's leaving Ventanas, the troops of the Provisional Government of Quito began to march down from the sierra to attack the revolutionary forces, who held Guayaquil and the low country, and, contrary to all expectation, they selected the route by Limon and Ventanas. For six weeks we were kept in continual alarm by the passage of troops, and it required all our vigilance to prevent our horses and other goods being stolen; indeed, one of my horses was carried off, though I afterwards recovered it. It was now too late to think

* Descent from the pass of Chimborazo to Guaranda, in round numbers 6,000 feet (15,000 — 9,000). Ascent from Guaranda to the pass of Llullundóngo 3,000 feet; and descent from Llullundongo to Limon 9,000 feet (12,000 — 3,000).

think of Dr. Taylor's going to Loja. Indeed, if I had had no companion who was independent of the political feuds of the country, I do not see how I could have got on at all; I might literally have perished of hunger. All our provisions had to be procured from Guaranda, and the barley-meal and pease-meal (which are the staple food of the Indians) soon deteriorate in a moist, warm climate; so that we could not get down at a time more than about a month's provisions. My servant, having a little white blood in him, could not stir from the place, or he would have been pressed for a soldier. The Indians could not travel alone, for they might be seized on to carry burdens or conduct laden beasts; so whenever our provisions fell short, Dr. Taylor had to take my horses and an Indian, and go all the long distance to Guaranda to purchase more.

Nearly all this time we were ignorant of Mr. Cross's fate; he might have died, or he might be on his way to join us, we knew not. I selected some fine healthy bark trees which had not flowered this year, and began seriously to think of trying to strike cuttings from them myself; when towards the end of July a vague report reached us that an Englishman, bringing with him a number of boxes, had arrived at Ventanas. On the strength of this, I immediately sent Dr. Taylor thither with horses, and he had the great satisfaction of finding and bringing up Mr. Cross, who reached Limon on the 27th of July. Mr. Cross had had all sorts of obstacles thrown in his way by the forces that held the river, and with the greatest difficulty found men to row his canoes; so that the distance from Guayaquil to Ventanas (which appears so short on the map) had taken him 13 days to travel.

After reposing the following day (Sunday), we had a piece of ground fenced in, and Mr. Cross made a pit and prepared the soil to receive the cuttings, of which he put in above a thousand on the 1st of August and following days. In three weeks some of them had begun to form roots; but in the meantime great difficulty was experienced in securing shade, when rendered necessary by the sudden alternations of fog and bright sunshine. At first, Mr. Cross shaded the cuttings with the fan-like points of the wild cane (*Gynerium saccharoides*) and with plantain leaves, but as these soon shrivelled up, we afterwards made of the fronds of the ivory palm a permanent fall-to roof, which could be elevated and depressed at pleasure. Later on, Mr. Cross put in a great many more cuttings, subjecting them to various modes of treatment (as the whole thing was an experiment), but constant watchfulness was needed to ensure their well-being, for what between caterpillars and burning suns he was sorely tasked to keep them alive.

Towards the end of July the weather took up, and in a few sunny days the capsules made visible advances towards maturity. On the 13th of August, I noticed that the capsules on the finest trees were beginning to burst at the base, and on the following day I had all taken off that seemed ripe, gathering them in this way: an Indian climbed the tree, and breaking the panicles gently off, let them fall on sheets spread on the ground to receive them, so that the few loose seeds shaken out by the fall were not lost. The capsules were afterwards spread out to dry on the same sheets, a process which occupied from two to ten days. The first seeds were taken off at Limon on the 14th, and the last on the 29th of August. Early in September they were all dry.

After bringing up Mr. Cross, Dr. Taylor went to Guaranda to purchase provisions, and on his return I despatched him to San Antonio, Pavon's original locality for the red bark, and two days' journey southward of Limon, where we had learnt that several young trees were still existing, on which flowers had been observed this year.

The climate of San Antonio proved more unhealthy than that of Limon. A hot sun is accompanied by winds out of all proportion cool and strong, so that rheumatic affections and ague prevail. This is, perhaps, the cause also of the backwardness of the seeds at San Antonio, although the bark tree extends lower down towards the Guayaquilian plain than at Limon. Dr. Taylor fell sick almost immediately after reaching San Antonio, had to bleed himself, and finally to go out to Riobamba in quest of remedies. On his return, the capsules were still green, and as he began to fear they would fall off without ripening, he crossed over to Limon to consult with me. The result of our consultation was that he should remain at Limon to assist Mr. Cross, and that I should go to San Antonio, whither I accordingly proceeded on the 12th and 13th of September; having before starting ascertained from Mr. Cross that double the number of plants we should require to fill the cases were already rooted, and only required time to become strong enough to travel.

At

At San Antonio a good many of the capsules had dried up while still unripe, and of those which had ripened some had burst open during the few days that intervened between Dr. Taylor's leaving San Antonio and my arriving there; but happily very few seeds were shed; and in gathering the capsules I profited by my experience at Limon that the seeds rarely fell out for two or three days after the capsules burst, and that the latter closed up again with the dews of night. So by gathering the capsules at day-break not a seed fell out, nor was there any need for the precaution (which, however, I still observed) of extending sheets whereon to receive the capsules as thrown down from the tree. I took off the first seeds at San Antonio on the 14th and the last on the 19th of September.

I had now gathered about 2,500 well-grown capsules, namely, 2,000 from 10 trees at Limon, and 500 from five trees at San Antonio. Good capsules contain 40 seeds each, in some I have counted 42, so that I calculate I have (in round numbers) at least 100,000 well ripened and well dried seeds. Had the month of July been as sunny as it is said usually to be, many more capsules would doubtless have ripened; as it was, only about one flower in ten produced ripe seeds.

Mr. Cross sowed at Limon, on the 16th of August, eight seeds taken at random from those I had gathered there; one of them began to germinate on the fourth day, and at the end of a fortnight four seeds had pushed their radicles. On the 6th of September one had the seed leaves completely developed, and by the 9th of the same month, or 25 days after sowing, the last of the eight seeds pushed its radicle. He also sowed eight seeds gathered by me in 1859, and which had remained nine months in my herbarium; of these, four germinated; I have, therefore, a well-founded hope that good ripe seeds will not speedily lose their vitality, and if daily watched and tended after sowing, will very likely most of them grow.

I had scarcely finished drying my seeds at San Antonio when I received the welcome intelligence that the troops of the Provisional Government had entered Guayaquil, and that, consequently, the communication with the interior was now open; I therefore resolved to proceed to Guayaquil, so as to be able to despatch from thence a portion of my seeds by the first opportunity, and afterwards to await there the arrival of my companions from Limon. My journey from Guayaquil occupied from September 28 to October 6, for I was delayed some days at Bodegas awaiting the arrival of the river steamer.

I now send, by the steamer which leaves Guayaquil for Panamá on the 14th instant, a packet of seeds for Sir W. J. Hooker, at the Royal Botanic Gardens, Kew, and another to the Botanic Gardens in Jamaica. I have not much faith of the trees succeeding at the latter place, on account of the violent winds which I understand occasionally to prevail there, and which would assuredly shatter to pieces the fragile leaves of the *Cinchona succirubra.*

The great bulk of the seeds I propose entrusting to Mr. Cross, and my own opinion is, that it will be best to send them at once to the locality in India destined for rearing the red bark tree. I trust that this locality may be the island of Ceylon, and that if Mr. Cross accompany the seeds and plants thither, he may be allowed to select the site where the experiment is to be tried, and of which I shall have no hopes of success if the soil and climate be not in exact conformity with those of the native forests of the Cinchona.

In conclusion, I feel some satisfaction in stating that, notwithstanding the length of time the task has occupied me, and including the remuneration I have agreed to give Dr. Taylor, the whole expenses have not yet reached 500 *l.*, and I trust that, up to the time when I shall despatch Mr. Cross from Guayaquil, they may very slightly exceed that sum.

I have, &c.
(signed) *Richard Spruce.*

P.S.—I have preserved specimens of every plant I found in good state in the Cinchona forests, and shall have the pleasure of presenting them to the Herbarium of the Royal Gardens at Kew, to illustrate the rich vegetation accompanying the *Cinchona succirubra* at the base of Chimborazo. So soon as I have leisure to put my materials in order, I propose drawing up a fuller report, along with a complete copy of my meteorological register. In the meantime, I have made the following *résumé* of the latter, which may be of use in selecting the locality in India where the experiment is to be tried of rearing the red bark tree.

Résumé of Observations on the Temperature in the Forest of Limon, on the Western Slope of Chimborazo, at about 3,000 feet in altitude.

Temperature of the earth, at a depth of 2 feet, 68½ degrees.

Temperature of the air, from June 19th to June 30th :—

Mean minimum - - - - - - -	61⅓ degrees.
Mean maximum - 74 degrees (temp. at 6½ p.m.,	68¼ degrees.)
Lowest temperature (June 27th) - - -	60¼ ,,
Highest temperature (June 29th) - - -	77 ,,
Mean daily variation - - - - - -	12⅘ ,,
Greatest daily variation (June 27th) - - -	15¾ ,,

For the month of July :—

Mean minimum - - - - - - -	60 ,,
Mean maximum - - - - - - -	72½ ,,
Lowest temperature (July 11th) - - - -	57 ,,
Highest temperature (July 27th) - - -	80½ ,,
Mean daily variation - - - - - -	12½ ,,
Greatest daily variation (July 27th) - - -	21½ ,,

For the month of August :—

Mean minimum - - - - - - -	61⅓ ,,
Mean maximum - - - - - - -	74⅔ ,,
Lowest temperature (Aug. 12th) - - -	59¾ ,,
Highest temperature (Aug. 28th) - - -	80¼ ,,
Mean daily variation - - - - - -	13⅓ ,,
Greatest daily variation (Aug. 28th) - - -	19½ ,,

From Sept. 1st to Sept. 9th :—

Mean minimum - - - - - - -	62¾ ,,
Mean maximum - - - - - - -	72⅛ ,,
Lowest temperature (Sept. 3d) - - - -	61½ ,,
Highest temperature (Sept. 1st and 6th) - -	76½ ,,
Mean daily variation - - - - - -	9¾ ,,
Greatest daily variation (Sept. 4th) - - -	13½ ,,

Temperature of the air at Tabacál, near San Antonio, at an altitude of about 2,600 feet, from Sept. 15th to Sept. 27th :

Mean minimum - - - - - - -	61¾ degrees.
Mean maximum - - - - - - -	72⅔ ,,
Lowest temperature (Sept. 15th) - - -	60¼ ,,
Highest temperature (Sept. 23d) - - -	76½ ,,
Mean daily variation - - - - - -	11 ,,
Greatest daily variation (Sept. 23d) - - -	15½ ,,

The mornings were generally clear and sunny, but mist or fog predominated in the afternoons.

The wind at Limon scarcely ever amounted to a slight breeze. At San Antonio it was rather stronger, but still never of sufficient force to break the brittle leaves of the Cinchona.

The finest trees grow in a stratum of yellow or reddish marl, of immense thickness, and in which few or no stones were intermixed. A specimen of it will be sent in charge of Mr. Cross, along with specimens of the wood, bark, leaves, flowers, aud fruit of the *Cinchona succirubra*.

R. S.

— No. 44. —

Mr. SPRUCE'S REPORT on the Expedition to procure Seeds and Plants of the *Cinchona succirubra*, or Red Bark Tree, to the Under Secretary of State for India, 3d January 1862.

TOWARDS the end of the year 1859, I was entrusted by Her Majesty's Secretary of State for India with a commission to procure seeds and plants of the Red Bark tree, and I proceeded to take the necessary steps for entering on its performance.

Notwithstanding the vast extent of the unreclaimed forests in Ecuador, hardly any part of them is still without an owner, if we except the territory disputed between Peru and Ecuador, on the eastern side of the Cordillera, generally called "Las Montañas del Oriente;" and the forests known to produce the Red Bark are all private property. Some preliminary arrangement was, therefore, indispensable, before I could venture to take away young plants of so rare and precious a tree as the Red Bark. On inquiring about the ownership of the bark woods of Puma-cocha, in the valley of Alausi, which I had visited in 1859, I found they had belonged to a Dr. Bravo (of Cuenca), lately deceased, and that they were now the subject of litigation, so that any treaty made with either of the parties, who claims to inherit them, would most likely be null. I learnt, also, that the red bark,* obtained in that locality, fetched a much lower price at Guayaquil than the bark from the forests about the western foot of Chimborazo (generally called "of Guaranda"), not because the latter was known to contain a greater proportion of alkaloids, which is a test never resorted to here, but because it was of a rather deeper colour, and was brought to market in much thicker slabs. Before detailing the steps I took to obtain leave to collect seeds and plants in the forests of Chimborazo, a brief review of the ascertained distribution of the Red Bark tree along the western slopes of the Quitenian Andes will make what follows more clear.

For a great many years back no red bark has been got out beyond the latitude of 2½° S., or a little to the southward of the river Yaguachi, and its tributary the Chanchán. Possibly, at an earlier period, the tree grew all along the roots of the Andes of Cuenca and Loja, to the limits of the Peruvian desert, in latitude about 5° S., as is indeed intimated by Pavon in his account of this species. To the north, it scarcely passes the parallel of 1° S., where it has been found about the base of the hill of Angamarca, a grassy peak standing north-west from Chimborazo, and considerably to the westward of the main ridge. Within these limits, it occupies a narrow band included between the meridians of 30′ and 40′ west of Quito.† Whether it exists still farther north, about the base of the snowy mountains, Ilinisa and Pichincha, and so on to the river Esmeraldas, is not known, nor does any search appear to have been made for it there. Beyond the limits of Ecuador, on the lower ridges of the Andes of Pasto and Popayan, which run down to the bay of Chocó, we have the conditions of climate and altitude requisite for the growth of *Cinchona succirubra*, but it has not yet been found there. The "Red Bark" of that district is rejected as worthless by the cascorilleros, as I learnt lately from a New-Granadian bark merchant whom I met at Guayaquil; and, on showing my specimens to him, and the figure of *C. magnifolia* in Mr. Howard's work, he immediately recognised it as the "Cascarilla colorada" of the bay of Chocó. Various barks of inferior quality having been called by this latter name, is perhaps the reason why what we call the *true* Red Bark is now known in Ecuador only by the name of "Cascarilla roja,"‡ which is useful as a distinctive appellation, although it does not denote the actual hue of that bark with more accuracy than the older name.

Within the ascertained limits of the true Red Bark it exists (or rather existed up to a recent period) in all the valleys of the Andes which debouch into the Guayaquilian plain. Many years ago it was obtained in large quantities in the valley

* "Red Bark" (with capital initials) indicates the *tree*, and "red bark" the *bark* of the same tree.
† Quito is in 78 degrees 45 seconds, or 5 hours 15 minutes, west of Greenwich.
‡ *Roja* means both *blood-colour* and *fire-colour*.

valley of Alausi, below an Indian hamlet called Linje, on the northern side of the Chanchán (nearly opposite to Puma-cocha, which is on the southern side of the same stream), but it has long been exhausted there.* A race of cascarilleros still survives at Linje, and the adjacent hamlet of Guallanág, who are said to know of a site, which they call Untúm, a long way southward of the river, where there is yet standing a fine "manchon" or clump) of Red Bark; but they refuse to show the track leading thither, probably because no one will pay the price of their secret. Proceeding northward from the valley of Alausi, at the altitude of the Red Bark, we come successively on the valleys of Pallatanga and Chillanes, in neither of which is there a single large Red Bark tree remaining, though some years ago it was abundant. In 1858 I visited Pallatanga, where I could learn of but two young trees still existing. A branch of one of them was brought to me, so much withered as not to be worth preserving, and only sufficient to show that it belonged to some sort of *Cinchona*. In Chillanes, considered at one period the very best locality for this Bark, I am assured that a few slender shoots from old stools are all that remain. Leaving Chillanes and the river Chimbo, whose sources are on the western side of Chimborazo, we come on steep ridges (Cuesta de Angas, Cuesta de San Antonio, &c.), which run down from that mountain.† Towards their base, and in all the intervening valleys, the Red Bark formerly grew in abundance, but at present no large tree of it is known to exist to the southward of the parallel passing through Guaranda. The Bark grounds, which still continue to be worked, are bounded to the south by the ridge which separates the Rio San Antonio from its tributary, the Rio de Tablas, and

* There has lately been published a topographical work on Ecuador ("Geografia de la Republica del Ecuador. Por Manual Villavicencio. New York. 1858,") which, as it is well printed on good paper, and is accompanied by a neatly-engraved map on a large scale, will probably be received in Europe with a degree of credit of which it is utterly unworthy. Besides the errors in description with which it abounds, the dates, distances, heights, and even bearings, can never be depended upon. The author seems to have no clear notion of the difference between north and south, or east and west, as he frequently uses one of those terms by mistake for its opposite. In the map he betrays his utter ignorance of the first principles of geography, by his erroneous numeration of the minutes of latitude and longitude; and the names are often so dislocated that, if he had written them on slips of paper, thrown them into the air, and afterwards stuck them down wherever they alighted on the map, they could hardly have been more out of place. In the whole region of the Red Bark there in not a single town or stream exactly where it ought to be. Linje, for example, is placed on the *south* side of the river Yaguachi, and higher up the stream than the cold village of Sibambe, whereas it is really on the *north* side, far lower down, and near to Guallanág. Even Guaranda, through which the author must have passed scores of times, is placed to the east of the Chimbo, whereas it is actually half a mile to the west of it. Of the course of the Chimbo itself, two accounts, totally at variance with each other, are given in the book, and neither of them agrees with the map. The Rio San Antonio, known by many different local names in its upper part, runs nearly west from the foot of the cuesta all the way down to the river Ventanas, which it enters near Caracol with the name Rio de la Pita. But on the map, the San Antonio and the Pita appear as two distinct rivers, and the former is made to run southward into the river Babahoyo! The work has already been severely criticised, and its more salient errors pointed out, by the Quito press, whose corrections will, however, hardly reach the hands of a single European geographer, and this is why I have thought it necessary to enter here my protest against it, especially as Mr. Howard seems to have been misled by it, in his speculations on the climate of the Red Bark. The only part of it which has really some merit is that which treats of the river Napo, where Villavicencio was stationed as governor for several years. Even the style rises when the author is writing about what he perfectly understands, and whereas the rest of the book is written in very vulgar and often ungrammatical Castilian, when he comes to tell us of the Napo and its inhabitants, his language, if not elegant, is generally clear and forcible.

† It is not well settled to how much of the cordillera the name "Chimborazo," should be limited. When an Indian speaks of "Chimborazo," "Tunguragua," &c., he means merely the snowy summit of those mountains, the adjacent *paramos* having local names, according to the streams which traverse them, or the farms and villages adjacent to them. Proceeding from Chimborazo southward, we have a lofty ridge, not rising in any part of it to the height of perpetual snow, varied here and there by slight depressions, but whose continuity is nowhere broken by any transversal valley. After forming the western boundary of the elevated plain or valley of Tiocajas, it sinks down abruptly from the heights of San Nicolas to the valley of Alausi, at the junction of the Puma-chaca and Chanchán. If the whole of this ridge be considered to belong to Chimborazo, then the forests of Linja are on the western slope of that mountain (as indicated by the person who furnished specimens of the Red Bark to Mr. Howard); but this course would necessitate a similar extension of the limits of Chimborazo on all sides, and we should have to include in it the adjacent mountain, Carguairazo, formerly equally lofty, and separated from it only by a very narrow valley, as also the two "knots" running eastward across the central valley to the foot of the eastern cordillera, the one from Sanancajas, and the other from the northern shoulder of Chimborazo (Paramo de Puenevata), both of which knots include some lofty peaks. I would rather confine the name Chimborazo to the mighty mass which rises abruptly from the plain of Sanancajas on the east, and reposes to the north and south on Puenevata and the Arenal respectively. On the western side, however, I can find no positive break from the summit down to the plain. There is no intervening salient peak, and no ridge whose origin may not be traced to the peak of Chimborazo.

and they form part of five contiguous farms, called respectively El Morado, Matiaví, Sinchig, Talágua, and Salinas, whereof the two former belong to the church of Guaranda, and the three latter (which extend upwards to the *paramos* of Chimborazo, and downwards to the plain of Guayaquil) are the property of General and ex-President Juan José Flores, who, after a banishment of 15 years, has lately returned to take the chief part in the recovery of Guayaquil, from a faction who would have given it up to Peru. Only the high lands of those farms, where there is natural pasturage and ground suitable for the cultivation of potatoes and cereals, have been turned to any account by the proprietors. The middle part is dense, unbroken forest, and in the lower part, which produces the Red Bark, a good many poor people of mixed race from the sierra, and a few liberated slaves from the plain, have formed little cane farms, without asking leave of the owners, or paying any rent. The farms belonging to General Flores have been for some years leased to a Señor Cordovez, who resides at Ambato; and Dr. Francisco Neyra, notary public of Guaranda, rents the farms of the church, but only so far as respects the bark they produce. With these two gentlemen I had, therefore, to treat for permission to take from the bark woods the seeds and plants I wanted. At first they were unwilling to grant me it any price, but, after a good deal of parley, I succeeded in making a treaty with them. whereby, on the payment of 400 dollars, I was allowed to take as many seeds and plants as I liked, so long as I did not touch the bark. They also bound themselves to aid me in procuring the necessary workmen and beasts of burden. Through the intervention of Dr. Neyra, who has throughout done all he could to favour the enterprise, I engaged with his cascarilleros (who all inhabit the village of Guanujo, adjacent to Guaranda), that whilst they were procuring bark for him, they should also seek seeds and plants for me.

From Dr. Neyra I ascertained that a site called Limon would be the most suitable for the centre of my operations. There are many other "Limones" in Ecuador, and there is even another on Chimborazo, by the main road leading to Guayaquil; but the Limon, where I was to establish myself, is at the junction of a stream of that name with the river Chasuán, which runs to the northward of, and nearly parallel to, the river San Antonio, and enters the river Ventanas with the name Siguímbi, at a place called Aguacatál, above the village of Ventanas, while the San Antonio enters the same river much lower down, near the village of Caracol. At Limon existed formerly the finest *manchon* of Red Bark ever seen. It was all cut down many years ago, but I was informed that shoots from the old roots had already grown to be stout little trees, large enough to bear flowers and fruit, and that the squatters (who are many of them cascarilleros of Guanujo), since they got to know the value of the bark, had carefully preserved such trees as were standing in their *chacras* or clearings. Messrs. Cordovez and Neyra have made their depôt for the bark about four leagues lower down the valley, where a stream called Camarón, running down the next transversal valley to the northward, joins the Chasuán.

The intestine war, alluded to in my "Notes" in the "Linnæan Journal" (Vol. iv., p. 176), still continued to rage, and the country was divided into two factions, whereof one held Quito and the whole of the sierra, and the other Guayaquil and the low country. Both maintained as large an army as they could raise in support of their cause, and pressed into their ranks all the suitable men they could lay hold on. Only those of pure Indian extraction were exempt from forced military service; but when the troops were marching about, they continually seized on Indians to carry their baggage and to drive laden beasts. For above a year there had been no mails between Guayaquil and the sierra, and my only means of communication with that port were by the rare passage of some diplomatic agent or courier, or of some foreigner well furnished with passports.

In the last instructions received from England, I was informed by Mr. Clements Markham that Mr. Cross, the gardener chosen to assist me in procuring the bark plants, would come out in December 1859. Before receiving that intimation, I had written to request that he might not come hither before May, for, until the winter rains cease, it is impossible to do anything in the forest, and on the western side of the Quitenian Andes they usually last until the end of May; but it was doubtful if my letter had even reached Guayaquil, so, acting on the supposition that he would come out at the previous date, I had three of my

 horses

horses put up to good feed, and I kept them and a man, for six weeks, in readiness to depart for Bodegas the moment I should hear of Mr. Cross's arrival. At the end of that period a letter, left at Guayaquil by Mr. Markham on his way southward, reached me, from which I learnt that Mr. Cross would not arrive there until May. I had not again a safe opportunity for the coast until early in June, when I wrote to Mr. Mocatta, Her Britannic Majesty's Consul at Guayaquil, requesting him to forward Mr. Cross (in case he had already arrived) up the river to Ventanas, which is the nearest port to the bark woods, on one of the numerous rivers that go to form the Gulf of Guayaquil.

In the account of my visit to Puma-cocha ("Linnæan Journal," l. c.), it will be remarked that I was guided by a person named Bermeo to the locality of the Red Bark tree. When I took leave of him, I informed him that very probably I should return the following year to procure seeds and plants. On the strength of this, towards the end of April, he travelled all the way from Lucmas to Ambato, nearly five days' journey, on foot, to tell me that he had just returned from the woods of Puma-cocha, where he had spent some days, and had found several trees of *Cascarilla roja*, which, though not of large size, were some of them coming into flower. He had besides got a few young plants for me at Lucmas, each in its bamboo pot. I explained to him that, for the present my re-visiting Puma-cocha was out of the question, but that I should be only too glad to have all his plants and seeds, and I fixed the price he was to receive on delivering them in sound condition to the British Consul at Guayaquil. I have only lately learnt that the poor fellow never ventured more from his forest home; indeed, he would hardly have been allowed to reach it again, but for a certificate I gave him, that he was travelling about on my account; and if he had gone to Guayaquil, according to our agreement, and escaped being made a soldier of by the way, he would assuredly not have been allowed to land there, except in uniform.

My preparations for entering the forest being completed, I was awaiting the coming of the dry season, when a severe attack of rheumatism so far disabled me that I determined to delegate my commission to Dr. James Taylor, of Riobamba. Animated, however, by his assurance that in the warm forest I might expect to recover the use of my limbs, I finally resolved to proceed thither in his company. Not to interrupt the rest of my narrative with the continual groanings of an invalid, I may say here, once for all, that the benefit derived from the milder temperature was almost neutralized by the fogs and damp; and, although upheld by a determination to execute to the best of my ability the task I had undertaken, I was but too often in that state of prostration when to lie down quietly and die would have seemed a relief.

We started from Ambato for the forest on the 11th of June. Our road was the same as I had travelled the preceding year, until reaching the *paramo* of Sanancajas, beyond the village of Mocha, where it turns to the right towards the southern shoulder of Chimborazo. In consequence of my having needed two long rests on the way, night came on and found us still on the *paramo*. Thin clouds had enveloped Chimborazo most of the day, but towards evening they gradually cleared away, and after sunset the majestic dome was entirely uncovered, though a slender meniscus of cloud, assuming exactly the form of the cope of the mountain, and still illumined by the rays of the sun (which had set for us) hung for some time like "a glory" over the monarch of the Andes. When this at length melted away, the light reflected from the snow by a clear star-lit sky enabled our beasts to pick their way. It was eight o'clock when we reached the tambo of Chuquipogyo, a solitary house, at between twelve and thirteen thousand feet of altitude. The rude accommodation and the inhospitable climate offered no inducement to a prolonged stay at Chuquipogyo, but, as I was so much exhausted as neither to be able to sleep nor on the following morning to mount my horse, there was no alternative but to remain there all the day and night of the 12th. At seven A.M. of the 13th we resumed our march. The day was fortunately fine, and we had only now and then a few drops of small rain and sleet, instead of the snow-storms with which the traveller has too frequently to contend in the pass of Chimborazo. The vegetation consisted chiefly of hassocks of a *Stipa* and a *Festuca*, so that the general aspect was that of a grey barren waste; but at short intervals we crossed deep gullies whose sides were lined with mosses, and sprinkled with calceolarias, lupines, and other pretty plants. Towards noon we came out on the "Arenál" (the *moraine* of the glacier, near the

the limit of all vegetation.* In a hollow a little below it, was a marsh with a rivulet, one of the sources of the Pastasa, in which I saw, not without surprise, a bed of the large-leaved *Rumex*, which is frequent in similar situations, at from 8,000 to 9,000 feet. The Arenal consists of sand and fine gravel of a pale yellow colour. In one place, the road, for a considerable distance, resembles a broad, smooth gravel-walk in England, so that the only bit of really good road in Ecuador has been made by nature's hand on the crest of the Andes. The vegetation is limited to scattered tufts, or rather hillocks, of a *Valeriana*, a *Viola*, an *Achyrophorus*, a *Werneria*, a *Plantago*, a *Geranium*, a *Draba*, a pretty silky-leaved *Astragalus*, and the elegant *Sida Pichinchesis*, all of which (save the *Astragalus*) have rigid leaves in the characteristic rosettes of super-alpine vegetation, and send enormously thick roots deep down into the loose soil, although even these do not secure them from being frequently torn up by the violent winds and storms that sweep over them. My attention was so much taken up with these interesting plants, and with the immense mass of snow on our right, and in tracing the downward course of ancient lava-streams, which are as visible on Chimborazo as on Cotopaxi and Tunguragua, that I scarcely felt the wind, which swept us along like a gale at sea, and occasionally lifted small fragments of gravel, and hurled them at us. It is scarcely necessary to state that the wind is here always easterly through the day, getting up strong generally about 10 A.M., and rarely continuing to blow with equal force through the night and following morning. Now and then it veers for a moment, and gives the traveller a side blow, which, were he not wary, might unhorse him.

We had left winter behind us on the eastern side of the cordillera, and on our first day's journey, as we looked down the deep valley of the Pastasa, we saw a mantle of dense cloud and rain spread over the forest of Canelos. Even the eastern side of Sanancajas was wet and muddy, but after passing Chuquipogyo the road became nearly dry, and on the western side of the cordillera it was even inconveniently dusty. In the direction of the Pacific not a cloud was visible, though the great distance and the hazy horizon prevented our actually seeing the ocean. So abrupt is the transition from the rainy season, which prevails on the eastern side of the cordillera simultaneously with the dry season on the western.

The Arenal must be near a league across. As we descended from it the whole mountain side became covered with flowers, and nowhere have I seen alpine vegetation in such prime state. *Gentiana Cernua*, with its large pendulous red flowers, formed large patches, and was accompanied by three other species of the same genus, with purple and blue flowers, by *Drabas*, and other alpines. Still descending, the true alpines began to be mixed with half shrubby *Fuchsiæ*, *Calceolariæ*, *Eupatoria*, &c. Even before reaching the zone where these genera grow in the greatest luxuriance, and at less than 2,000 feet below the Arenal, we came on the first tree, a *Polylepis*, forming groves here and there along the declivity. The bark of this tree resembles that of the birch in colour, and in its peeling off in flakes; but if one could suppose an arborescent *Acæna*, it would give a better idea of the pinnate silvery foliage. On the opposite side,—not of Chimborazo, which is bare of trees, but of its sister mountain, Carguairazo,—a *Buddleia* approaches nearest the snow-line. In descending the same side of the cordillera, towards Pallatanga, 10 leagues south of Chimborazo, a *Podocarpus* and a *Berberis* ascend higher than any other tree, while a *Polylepis* (distinct from that of Chimborazo) ceases a thousand feet below them. On Chimborazo, on the contrary, the same *Podocarpus* fails a long way below the first-mentioned *Polylepis*. An accurate discrimination of the species is therefore needed, before we can compare their climatal distribution. I have unfortunately never met any species of *Polylepis* in a good state of flower or fruit.

Still descending, various other trees began to appear, such as *Buddleiæ*, *Myrciæ*, and especially an *Araliacea*, called from its large palmate leaves (which are hoary beneath) "Puma-màqui," or tigers' paw. Here and there the track rounded the heads of *quebradas*, deep and dark, and full of low trees, which were laden with mosses.

At

* I possess a MS. of the late Colonel Hall, containing many valuable hypsometric data,—many of them ascertained in company with Boussingault,—wherein the height of the pass of the Arenal is given at 14,268 feet.

At about half-way down, we came out on a narrow grassy ridge, called the Ensillada (Saddleback), where several long low straw huts had been recently erected, for the accommodation of the soldiery, when marching that way. As we neared the encampment, four raw-looking youths armed with lances rushed out and confronted us, demanding our passports. We had none to show, but our antagonists did not look very formidable, and a shot from one of our revolvers would probably have put them to flight, had I not been furnished with a weapon which I have found far safer and more efficacious in such contingencies, namely, a bottle of strong aguardiente, a taste of which dispelled all opposition to our progress, and also served to induce the guardians of the pass to boil us water for making coffee.

Below the Ensillada we came on steeply-inclined strata of schists, across and down which we went on stumbling for at least a couple of hours; for, as the track runs over their projecting and jagged edges, which no pains have been taken to smooth down, we passed them not without inconvenience and danger. At this stage of our journey we became enveloped in cloud, which filled all the valley of Guaranda, so that we could thenceforth only discern objects near at hand.

We reached Guaranda just after night-fall, having travelled 11 weary leagues from Chuquipogyo. Guaranda is a rather neat little town, with good tiled houses built of adobes, and stands on ground which slopes down to the right bank of the Chimbo, at an elevation of about 9,000 feet. As it is on the main road leading from Guayaquil to the interior, it presents in time of peace a very lively aspect in the dry season, when it is constantly full of travellers and beasts of burden; but when we reached it there were not the least signs of traffic, and only soldiers were to be seen in the streets. The temperature is slightly warmer than that of Quito, and the adjacent hills are grassy, where not under cultivation. From the little I could see of the indigenous vegetation, it appeared interesting. A large *Thalictrum* was abundant, as was also a sarmentose *Labiata*, with spikes of secund scarlet flowers, and a *Tagetes*, called, aptly enough, "Allpa-anis" (earth aniseed), from its scent and its lowly habit.

I was detained several days at Guaranda, partly in purchasing provisions for the forest, including an ox to be taken alive to our rendezvous, and partly in the vain attempt to procure licence for our cascarilleros (who had lately all been enrolled either in the line or the militia) to proceed to the forest; but I had to content myself with the assurance that, until the country was delivered from its present straits, not a single citizen could be spared for any other service. Only one of the cascarilleros, whose rancho we were to occupy, actually accompanied us to Limon, whether with leave or without I never knew, and he was there too much occupied in distilling cane-brandy, and in drinking no small portion of it himself, to be of the slightest use to us in seeking plants and seeds. Through Dr. Neyra's intervention, I secured the services of four Indians of Guanujo, and they proved of the greatest use to us, especially after we began to rear the Bark plants.

As far as Guaranda, two of our boxes had been carried by each beast of burden, but thenceforward, on account of the straitness of the path, they had to be carried singly. On the steep, narrow, and slippery tracks which traverse the western slope of the Quitenian Andes, the beasts of burden are chiefly bulls, called "cabrestillos," whose cloven hoofs enable them to descend with greater security than even mules. Our provisions of potatoes, pease, and barley-meal, &c., had to be carried in sacks so small, that two of them placed on the back of each cabrestillo did not project beyond the animal's sides.

We set forth from Guaranda on the 17th of June, the direction of our route being first northerly, as far as the adjacent village of Guanujo, and then north-west to the pass of Llullundongo, on a ridge of Chimborazo, nearly in front of the Ensillada (from which the deep, wide valley of Guaranda separates it), and at a height of about 12,000 feet. Having surmounted this, we entered on the most precipitous and dangerous descent I have ever passed. The track leads straight down a narrow ridge, varied at wide intervals by level steppes, rarely exceeding a hundred yards across. The soil, from the summit down to the very plain, is a yellowish or reddish loam, wherein the sandy element prevails in some parts, and in others the clayey; and it is of immense thickness, as we could see in the deep gullies worn in the mountain side by the rains, and in the landslips. Angular masses of rock are sparingly imbedded in it, and scattered on the surface, but rounded pebbles are rare.

The

The vegetation in the pass consisted of *Vaccinia* (especially *V. Mortiña* Benth.), *Gaultheriæ*, *Melastomaceæ*, *Compositæ*, &c., disposed in compact shrubberies, with intervening grassy glades. But we had scarcely turned the ridge before the forest became dense and continuous, at first low and bushy, but increasing in height at every step. At about 9,500 feet, we came on the first Cascarilla Serrana, or Hill Bark, and it accompanied us downwards to, perhaps, 8,000 feet. I could distinguish but one species, and the trees were unfortunately in the state most tantalizing to a botanist, the flowers being already fallen, and the capsules too young for examination. It is called indifferently "Cuchicara" and "Pata de Gallinazo," which I believe to be terms merely indicative of the relative facility with which the bark may be stripped off in different individuals, either of the same or of various species.

At three P.M. we reached the Rio de Tablas, a considerable stream of clear water, foaming over large stones; its roar had been audible for the last hour of our steep descent. We crossed it, and on a deserted clearing of some two acres drew up for the night, uniting all our rubber ponchos to make a fall-to roof, to shield us from the night dews. The animals were turned loose to graze on the scanty grass in the clearing, and on the leaves of a *Chusquea* on the edge of the forest.

I have nowhere seen *Melastomaceæ* so abundant as in the forest surrounding our encampment. One species grows to a stout tree 40 feet high, and bears large *pendulous* panicles (a novel feature to me in this order) of blood-red flowers, with large turgid yellow anthers. A lower spreading tree, apparently a *Pleroma*, bore numerous large violet flowers. Other smaller sarmentose species had also large rose or violet flowers. Altogether, I have never seen so gay a forest vegetation, except on the river Uaupés.

We were still in a rather cool region, but the night was dry and the wind very slight, so that we had not to complain of cold. After an early breakfast the next morning, we followed our way, which became still narrower and rougher as we proceeded. We had to climb the high ridge separating the valley of the Rio de Tablas from that of the Chasuán, and then to descend to the latter river, but there were many subsidiary ridges, with intervening hollows, or sometimes nearly level crossings (called "*travesias*"). The track in the precipitous ascents and descents is mostly a gully worn in the soft loamy soil by the transit of men and beasts, to the depth in some places of 10 feet, and so strait, that the traveller, to save his legs from being crushed, must needs throw them on his horse's neck. Here and there, a large stone sticks out, forming a high step, in descending which, there is risk of both horse and rider turning a summerset. In the *travesias*, there is a considerable depth of black tenacious greasy mould, worn by the equable step of beasts of burden into transverse ridges (called "*camellones*," from their resemblance to the humps on a camel's back), with alternating furrows from one to three feet deep. This mould is formed in great part of the decayed leaves of the Suru, a bamboo of the genus *Chusquea*,* which forms almost impenetrable thickets, and whose arched stems and intricate branches, overhanging our way, much impeded our progress. In such places, there was still a good deal of water and mud, for the rainy season was only just over in the forest.

At 6,000 feet, we lost the wax-palm (*Ceroxylon andicola* H. *et* B.), which had accompanied us, though growing very sparsely, from about the upper limit of the Hill Bark. It descends to the same altitude on the eastern side of the cordillera. Lower down, palms began to be tolerably abundant, but of few species. A slender multicaul palm, with the pinnæ so remarkably eroso-truncate as to appear torn; I cannot refer to its genus, for want of flowers or fruit. A *Euterpe*, with

*The *Chusquæ* are bamboos peculiar to the hills, with solid stems, rarely exceeding 30 feet in height, and not preserving an erect position for more than a few feet from the ground; but though I have many times examined them, I could never detect any actual twining in either the stems or the long branches, which merely thread amongst each other and the adjacent trees, so as to form an entangled mass. The *Chusquea*, seen on the way to Limon, rarely descends below 5,500 feet; but what seems the same species, descends in the valley of the Pastasa to 4,500 feet, where it meets the large hollow-stemmed *Guadua*. Another and far slenderer species grows in the valley of Alausi, at about 5,000 feet. In the Andes of Maynas, there is no *Chusquea*, nor (what is more singular) did I see any *Guadua* there. In their stead, an elegant *Merostachys* grows on the hill tops, where the hollow internodes of the sterile stems afford a copious draught of pure water to the thirsty traveller.

with slender solitary stems, forms large beds at from 4,000 to 5,000 feet; and between these limits, we first fell in with the cadi or ivory palm, which extends thence to the plain.

At a very little below 4,000 feet, we came out on the first chacras at Limon, where I almost immediately noted, and with no small satisfaction, a group of three Red Bark trees, each consisting of from two to four stems of 30 feet high, springing from old stools, and bearing a small quantity of fruit. We had still about two miles of gentle descent to the *trapiche* (cane-mill) destined for our habitation, and we reached it early in the afternoon, in the midst of a dense fog.

The *trapiche* stood on a narrow ridge, running eastward and westward, sloping gradually on the northern side to the Chasuán, distant half-a-mile, and very abruptly, or 200 feet perpendicular in about 300 yards, to a tributary rivulet on the southern side. It was merely a long low shed, and a sketch of its internal arrangements may serve for that of all the other trapiches, for which there were about a dozen at Limon. About two-thirds of its length was occupied by the rude machinery and adjuncts of the cane-mill. The remaining third had an upper story with a flooring of bamboo planks, half of it open at the sides, and the other half with a bamboo wall about six feet high, not reaching the roof in any part of it. This was our dormitory, and it was reached by a ladder, merely a tree trunk, with rude notches for steps. On the ground floor was the kitchen, with a wall of rough planks of raft-wood, placed by no means in juxtaposition, but not so wide apart that a dog or a pig could have got through the interstices. The whole fabric was, therefore, abundantly ventilated, and only too frequently filled with fog, as we found to our cost, in coughs and aching limbs, and in mouldy garments, saddles, &c.

Having reposed a day at Limon, Dr. Taylor went on with my horses two days' journey to Ventanas, hoping to find Mr. Cross there, and to bring him up. During his absence, I had to look after killing the ox, and drying the beef, and to repair our dwelling, which was sadly fallen to decay, especially as to the roof. I therefore set the Indians to drag bamboos and palm leaves out of the forest, with which we patched up the hut as well as we could. I visited also all the Bark trees known to exist within a short distance, and was well content to see on many of them a good crop of capsules, which had already nearly reached their full size on the finest trees; on other trees, however, there were only very young capsules, and even a good many flowers, so that I might have obtained at least 30 good flowering specimens; but, wishing to gather as many seeds as possible, I dried only a couple of specimens, which I had afterwards cause to regret, for not one of the late-flowering panicles produced ripe capsules. I learnt from the inhabitants that the trees had been covered with blossom in the latter part of April and beginning of May.

When Dr. Taylor had been 10 days at Ventanas, a brief note from Mr. Mocatta was left at Guaranda by the Spanish minister (on his way from Guayaquil to Quito), informing me that Mr. Cross had been taken suddenly ill, when about to start for Ventanas. I therefore sent to recall Dr. Taylor, and after his return to Limon, our operations were confined to visiting the Bark trees daily, which extended through a zone of about four miles in breadth, and to collecting and studying the accompanying vegetation. As we had a fair share of sun towards the end of June, I was in hopes the fruit would speedily ripen; but nearly all through the month of July, the weather was cool, with a good deal of mist and fog, so that the capsules scarcely increased in size; many fell off, and some were attacked by a maggot and curled up. On the tree which bore most capsules, they began to turn mouldy, the mould being not fungi, but rudimentary lichens, which, whilst it proved that the capsules were still alive and growing, proved also that they were exposed to an atmosphere almost constantly saturated with moisture. I began to fear we should get no ripe seeds, and as the seeds had been especially recommended to me in my instructions from England, it may be imagined how severe was my feeling of disappointment. I had another motive for fearing the same result. The people of Limon had got a notion that I should buy the seeds of them, and one morning, when I made my round among the trees, I found that two of them had been stript of every panicle, undoubtedly by some one who calculated on selling me the seeds. This was very provoking, for the seeds were far from ripe, and all the rest might be destroyed in the same way, so I immediately went round to the inhabitants, and informed them that the seeds would be of no value to me unless I gathered them myself;

myself; and I offered a gratuity to the owners of the chacras where there were trees in fruit, to allow no one to approach the trees except myself and Dr. Taylor. This had the desired effect, and I do not think a single capsule was molested afterwards.

Whilst Dr. Taylor was at Ventanas, the troops of the Provisional Government of Quito began to march down from the sierra, to attack the forces which held the low country, and they selected the route by Limon and Ventanas, along which an army had never been known to pass For six weeks we were kept in continual alarm by the passing of troops, and it needed all our vigilance to prevent our horses and goods being stolen; indeed one of my horses was carried off, though I afterwards recovered it. It was now clear that, unless there had been two of us, both independent of the political feuds of the country, the enterprise must have fallen through. All our provisions had to be procured from Guaranda, and, as they soon deteriorated in a most warm climate, whenever our stock got low, Dr. Taylor had to take my horses and an Indian, and go all the long distance to Guaranda to fetch more. The squatters at Limon, being all highland men, do not take to the food of a warm climate, and they rear no more plantains than suffice to give them an occasional zancocha. About half a day's journey down the valley there were a good many plantains on a deserted farm, and at twice the distance a negro had a fine plantation of them, from which I two or three times got up a mule-load; but the hungry soldiery soon made an end of them, and then even that resource was cut off.

During the long time I had to await the arrival of Mr. Cross, and until the Cinchona seeds ripened, I had ample time for examining the site of the Red Bark tree, and the characteristics of the accompanying vegetation; and I proceed to detail the observations made on those points, up to the period of my departure from the bark forests in September.

The *manchon* of red bark at Limon lies very nearly west from the peak of Chimborazo. The river Chasuán rises on the northern shoulder of that mountain, and runs for a long distance between south and west, till its junction with the Limon (about a mile above our hut), when it turns gradually to the westward, which is thenceforward its general direction until it enters the Rio de Ventanas. At Limon it may be compared to the Wharfe at Bolton Abbey, in size and appearance. The lower part of the Limon has also a westerly direction, from a short distance above its junction with the Chasuán, but in its upper part it runs south-westerly, and its sources seem to be far below the *paramos* of Chimborazo. There are also a vast number of rivulets, tributary to the Chasuán and Limon, and all, as well as the main stream, run with a rapid course, rarely forming cascades of more than a few feet elevation, down deep narrow dales. Even the main valley does not begin to open out until below the region of the Red Bark. The ridge forming the watershed between the Chasuán and the Rio de Tablas subsides very gradually down to the plain, and may be traced nearly to the river Ventanas.

The view from Limon takes in a vast extent of country, both upwards and downwards, and the whole is unbroken forest, save towards the source of the Chasuán, where a lofty ridge rises above the region of arborescent vegetation, and is crowned by a small breadth of grassy *paramo*. Nowhere are there any bare precipices, and a very steep declivity, forming an angle of 60 degrees with the horizon, appearing far away up the Chasuán, is as densely wooded as any other part. The opening at Limon, it will be understood, is purely artificial.

The crystalline waters of the Chasuán and its tributaries, in that part of their course where the Red Bark grows, run over a black or dull blue, shining, and very compact trachyte, which would seem to be the foundation of the Quitenian Andes, for it appears almost everywhere in the lower valleys, on both the eastern and western declivities. In the river Pastasa it occurs at from 3,000 up to 7,000 feet. Generally it is exposed to view only in the bed of the streams, or on their banks, where it often rises into rugged and fantastic cliffs. Over the trachyte at Limon there is to be seen in the bottom of the valleys a fine-grained ferruginous sandstone of a deep brown colour, in thick strata, and usually in large detached masses, lying either horizontally or variously tilted up. I suppose, therefore, that, so far from having been deposited over the trachyte, it is merely the remains of a large bed of rock, which once extended comformably over the whole region, and has been shivered and dislocated by the upheaval of the trachyte itself. It seems the same sort of rock as exists about the base of Tunguragua,

guragua, and forms the lofty cliffs on the southern side of that volcano, where the cataract of Guandisagua comes down at three bounds from the edge of the snow to the warm valley of Capíl, in which grow oranges and the sugar-cane. I have never been able to find any trace of fossils in this rock, and without these my very slight knowledge of geology is insufficient to determine its age; so that when I suppose it to be Silurian, my opinion has no more value than a mere guess. Nowhere in the Quitenian Andes have I seen the stratified rocks, limestones, friable sandstones, and fossiliferous shales, all, I believe, belonging to the lias formation, which constitute the eastern declivity of the Andes of Peru, or at least of the province of Maynas. No bark tree was seen growing on rock of any kind. The soil at Limon is the same deep loamy alluvial deposit, with very few stones intermixed, as we had seen from Llullundongo downwards, nor does a bit of rock crop out in the whole of the descent. The ridges on which the Red Bark grows all deviate little from an easterly and westerly direction. It is far more abundant on their northern than on their southern slope, nor did I see a single tree with flowers or fruit in a southern aspect. The northern and eastern sides of the trees themselves had borne most flowers, and, except on one tree of more open growth than the rest, scarcely a capsule ripened on their southern and western sides. These phenomena are explained by the fact that, in the summer season, the trees receive most sun from the east and north, for the mornings are generally clear and sunny, whilst the afternoons are almost invariably foggy, and the sun's declination is northerly. Another notable circumstance is that the trees standing in open ground, pasture, cane-field, &c., are far healthier and more luxuriant than those growing in the forest, where they are hemmed in and partially shaded by other trees, and that, while many of the former had flowered freely, the latter were, without exception, sterile. This plainly shows that, although the Red Bark may need shade whilst young and tender, it really requires (like most trees) plenty of air, light, and room, wherein to develope its proportions.

From an old man named Toscano, one of the primitive settlers at Limon, I learnt the following particulars. 30 years ago, he and a few others opened the first chacras there. He himself chose a site at more than 4,000 feet elevation, but, finding it rather too cool for his crops, and that the forest was much infested by bears and pumas, which carried off his animals, he afterwards moved about 1,000 feet lower down.* The Red Bark was then very abundant, and on some slopes formed large clumps, with scarcely any intermixture of other trees. The settlers found it made excellent firewood, so they cut it up ruthlessly for that purpose. A good many years ago, it may be 15, it may be more (for the old man's memory is not very perfect for dates), a bark-dealer came to Limon (Toscano believes from Cuenca), who offered the settlers a dollar a piece for every tree they showed him. As the bark was of no value to them, and they still had the wood for firewood, the terms seemed advantageous enough; so the bark-dealer cut down large trees which yielded him 500 lbs. of dried bark each, for the price of a dollar and the expense of getting the bark down to Guayaquil, the whole being only a slight per-centage on the value of the bark to him. In the next and succeeding years other dealers followed the example; every ridge and valley for a great distance around was searched, and the destruction of the bark went on unsparingly. It grew mostly on the farms of General Flores, which were then deserted. Even the cultivated lands in the cool region had run to waste, and the fine corn-mills, for which the General had got machinery from Europe, were in ruins. At length those farms were leased to Señor Cordovez, who had already worked a good deal on bark in New Granada, and the bark-dealers, who had been fattening on other people's property, were excluded. But the mischief was already done, very few large trees were left, and those far apart; nor, since the bark was begun to be worked, can I make out that more than one manchon has been met with at all comparable to that of Limon.

The cascarilleros have found out that the bark is worth money, but neither they nor the greater part of the inhabitants of Ecuador have any correct idea of the use that is made of it in foreign countries; the prevalent opinion being that a permanent coffee or chocolate-coloured dye (still a desideratum in Ecuador) is extracted

* The first chacra reached in descending from Guaranda is still called "Osocahuítú," or the Bears' Den.

extracted from it. I explained to the people of Limon how it yielded the precious quinine, which was of such vast use in medicine; but I afterwards heard them saying one to another, "It is all very fine for him to stuff us with such a tale; of course he won't tell us how the dye is made, or we should use it ourselves for our ponchos and bayetas, and not let foreigners take away so much of it." There is to this day the same repugnance to using the bark as a febrifuge, as Humboldt remarked 60 years ago, and as exists also in New Granada, where cedron and various other substances are preferred to quina. I think I can explain this repugnance. The inhabitants of South America, although few of them have heard of Dr. Cullen, have a theory which refers all diseases to the influence of either heat or cold, and (by what seems to them a simple process of reasoning) their remedies to agents of the opposite complexion; thus, if an ailment have been brought on by "calor," it must be cured by "frescos;" but if by "frio," with "calidos." Confounding cause and effect, they suppose all fever to proceed from "calor." Now, they consider the cascarilla a terribly strong "calido," and justly; so, by their theory (which is the reverse of Hahnemann's), its use could only aggravate the symptoms of fever. A lad employed in the *trapiche*, where we resided, had been to the low country about Ventanas, and on his return was attacked by fever. Decoctions of mallows and barley, and other "frescos," by no means so harmless, were administered, but the patient only got worse. Dr. Taylor indicated the treatment they ought to pursue, and as they would not use bark, I offered to give them quinine; but they had evidently a great horror of it, and had I given it to the lad in the remissions of the fever, they would have mixed nostrums of their own; so that, had the case gone wrong, the blame would have been laid on us. At length, when he was much attenuated, he was taken up to Guanujo, and I never learnt whether he died or recovered, although marsh fevers are generally cured, as if by magic, by simply removing the patient to the cool rarefied atmosphere of the Andes.

Even at Guayaquil, there is such a general disinclination to the use of quinine, that, when the physicians there have occasion to prescribe it, they indicate it by the conventional term "alcaloide véjetal," which all the apothecaries understand to mean "sulphate of quinine," while the patient is kept in happy ignorance that he is taking that deadly substance.

The lowest site of the Red Bark at Limon is at an elevation of 2,450 feet above the sea, where the Chasuán receives the rivulet already mentioned as running below our hut. It is precisely the point where the track from Ventanas leaves the Chasuán (along whose margin it had run thus far, with a gentle ascent from the plain), and begins to ascend the steep cuesta separating the Chasuán from its tributary, the ascent being 350 feet in the first 500 yards; so that where the real ascent of the Andes begins, there also begins the Red Bark. At San Antonio, however, I saw a tree at a height of no more than 2,300 feet; and, if I might believe my informants, trees of immense size have been cut down at points whose height I estimate at barely over 2,000 feet. Following the track leading to Guaranda, the last bark trees growing by the road-side are at a height of 3,680 feet; but leaving the track, and following the hill-side on the left bank of the Limon, there are bark trees scattered about for a distance of a league, and up to a height of near 4,500 feet. On the opposite ridge, or that separating the Limon from the Chasuán, there are also several trees ascending to a still greater elevation, or nearly to 5,000 feet; but I did not take the barometer to these latter, which were all sterile, in consequence of growing in lofty forest.*

From

* In order that my barometrical observations, and the deductions therefrom, may be received with neither more nor less confidence than they merit, I subjoin the following explanations. My barometer (an Aneriod) was sent out to me by the late Admiral Sir Francis Beaufort, and I received it at the Barra de Rio Negro, in the year 1851. At that time, its zero point was considerably higher than it ought to have been, but I did not attempt to rectify it, for I soon found that it was still slowly rising. By observations renewed at various points, and at considerable intervals of time, and especially on my return to the Barra de Rio Negro, after an absence of more than three years, I ascertained pretty accurately the rate of my barometer. In July 1858, I took it to Quito, hoping to compare it there with some mercurial barometer, but I found only two such in the whole city, and both of them out of order. I had, therefore, to content myself with repeated observations at the tablet erected by the French Academicians in the Jesuit's College (now the University), and I have since compared its indications with those registered by Colonel Hall (in the manuscript above alluded to) at various points in the Quitenian Andes. The observations made in the Red Bark forests depend entirely on the mean barometer at Ambato. I hoped to obtain another important element for correcting my instrument on the shores of the Pacific, but when

From the cascarilleros I learnt that although the bark trees growing nearest the plain were generally much larger, yet their bark was by no means so thick in proportion to their diameter as in trees higher up, which I can well believe, for in cutting down trees in the hot plains, I have often been struck with the thinness of the bark compared to that of trees growing in temperate climes. They estimate the circumference of the trees by spanning round them with their fingers, and consequently speak of them as being of so many "cuartas" or spans. (A cuarta is about 8¼ English inches.) The bark is usually not weighed until after being dried; but they have sometimes been curious enough to weigh the fresh bark, and they gave me the following account of the produce of three trees:—

A tree of 5 cuartas (= 3 ft. 5¼ in.) gave 4 quintals of green bark.
A tree of 7½ cuartas (= 5 ft. 2 in.) gave 15 quintals of green bark.
A tree of 14 cuartas (= 9 ft. 7½ in.) gave 9 quintals of green bark.

Seven pounds of green give four pounds of dry bark; but in trees that are not full grown the bark sometimes loses fully half its weight in drying. The tree which yielded 15 quintals of green bark, or 8½ quintals (= 850 lbs.) of dry bark, was the most productive ever cut down. I was shown its site, in the valley of the Limon, at nearly 4,500 feet elevation. A tree almost equal to it was found, in 1859, to north-east of Camaron. The tree, which measured 14 cuartas in circumference, over an English yard in diameter, grew at the lower limit of the Bark region, and the bark was very thin in proportion to the wood. I asked the cascarilleros to point out to me any tree in the forest which seemed to them about the height of these large cinchona trees, and they showed me some of 80 feet, adding that the Red Bark scarcely attained the average height of the virgin forest.

The cascarilleros do not usually go in quest of bark-trees before August, there being generally less fog in that and the following month than at any other period of the year. They go in parties of from four to eight, and each man carries his bag of *mashca* (barley meal), a little toasted maize, salt, lard, onions, and two cakes of *rapadura* (uncrystallised sugar). Those who possess guns take them, as they are necessary for procuring game to eke out their scanty provisions; but the *machéte*, or cutlass, is essential to every one. They descend nearly to the plain, and seek out some ridge which they have never hunted. Two men, called "monteadors," go ahead, opening a narrow track through the brush with their machétes, often a slow and fatiguing process; when they give in, other two take their

when I opened it, on reaching Guayaquil, the pointer had ceased to travel, and, on inspecting the mechanism, I found that the vacuum vase had altogether collapsed, so that my barometer is of no further use to me in the plains.

I calculate the height of Ambato above the level of the sea at 8,567 English feet, by Laplace's formula, from the following elements:—

Lat. 1° 15′ S. Mean bar. 22·218 in. Mean therm. 60 degrees (as it is within a very small fraction).

Mean bar. at surface of Pacific, 30 in., and mean therm. at ditto, 80 degrees (Hall).

I follow Hall in assuming 30 inches for the barometer at the sea level, not taking into account the equatorial depression, generally estimated at one-fifth of an inch. When I came out to the mouth of the Amazon, in 1849, the ship's barometer stood constantly above 30 inches, from about the latitude of Madeira to a long way beyond the tropic, when it gradually sank, and near the equator, where we were becalmed for several days, and afterwards ran for the coast of Brazil as near the actual line as we could, the barometer at noon marked 29·85 in., without any perceptible variation for 13 days together, namely, from June 28th to July 10th. When we ascended the river to Pará, the barometer fell to 29·83 in.

The height above the sea of our hut at Limon I find to be 2,836 feet from these elements:—

Lat. 1½ degree S. Mean bar. 27·1775 in. Mean therm. 67 degrees.

I had not with me in the forest any formula for the calculation of heights, nor unfortunately the correction required for my barometer. I could only be certain that the barometer at Limon indicated a height of less than 3,000 feet, at which figure I roughly assumed it, and as the barometer, on being taken to Tabacal, showed that I had descended some 400 feet, I took the height of Tabacal at 2,600 feet. These heights have proved nearly 200 feet too great, a difference of altitude too small to be accompanied by any appreciable difference of temperature.

I assumed the range of the Red Bark in the valley of Alausi at 3,000—5,000 feet, from Bermeo's rough indications as to how far the tree extended up the Puma-cocha and down the Yaguachi, and it has proved not far from the truth. I gathered an undescribed *Cinchona*, scarcely more than a shrub, at a height of 4,000 feet, on Mount Campana in Maynas. The sub-genus *Cascarilla* (for to me it is no more than a sub-genus, and scarcely even that) has one representative in the Amazonian plain, namely, at the falls of the Rio Negro, and others in the eastern roots of the Andes. The genus *Remijia*, the "Quina-rana," (or bastard Quina) of the Brazilians, rarely ascends out of the plain.

their place. In this way they go up the crest of the ridge until they see no more bamboo in the valleys on each hand, when they know they have passed the limit of the Red Bark, and that it is useless to seek any higher.* If they have been unsuccessful, they betake themselves to a collateral ridge and renew their search. When the day is clear, they can obtain a view over the valleys on both sides, by climbing some high tree; but when it is foggy, they seek only on the ground for the blood-red *Cinchona* leaves, and even these cannot be seen unless close at hand, if the fog be very dense. When their provisions fail they think of returning, and as, by looking out from an elevation and tracing the course of the streams, they can generally tell the direction of Limon, they often arrive there again in a day or two, from points which they had taken 10 or 15 days to reach. If their search has been finally successful, they return almost immediately to the forest, with a larger stock of provisions, and with Indians to assist them, especially in carrying the dry bark to Camaron. The trees being cut down and the roots dug out, the bark is stripped off much in the same way as oak bark in England, but no other tool than the machéte is used. As flat slabs are most appreciated in the market, they rarely make the strips of more than three or four fingers' breadth, for if broader they curl in drying. They have tried to dry broader slabs by fastening the bark to a piece of bamboo, back to back, but as the bark contracts it splits the bamboo. For drying the bark, a stage three feet high is erected, called a "*tendál*," which is precisely the "*muca-en-táua*" used for drying fish on the Amazon. Care must be taken that the flame from the fire beneath the *tendál* does not reach the bark, and if rain be apprehended, the whole has to be roofed over. When the bark is perfectly dry, they have only to convey it to the depôt at Camaron, and receive their 20 dollars per quintal, which is the price usually paid them by Messrs. Cordovez and Neyra; or rather, they have generally received the value in advance, according to the custom of the country, the expenses thus far having been borne by the cascarilleros. From Camaron the bark is conveyed on mules' or Indians' backs to Ventanas, and thence on a raft to Guayaquil, all at the cost of the owners. The entire quantity of the red bark collected in 1859 did not reach 50 quintals, and it was sold for 43 dollars the quintal. In 1860, no red bark at all was got out, so that the trade in it is well nigh extinct.

When the red bark began to be worked at Limon, it was not the custom to strip the bark from the roots; and although a few old stools have since been destroyed for the sake of the bark on their roots, a great number still exist, and have almost without exception grown out again. The shoots grow in a decussate manner, two, four, six, or even eight from the base of the old trunk (of which some six inches has mostly been left), and their vigour and luxuriance is something extraordinary. A few of them have already reached 50 feet in height, and the greater part of them are from 30 to 40 feet. On some stools by the wayside the shoots have been wantonly and repeatedly cut away, and yet others continue to grow out.† Comparing Toscano's account with that of other settlers, it appeared

---

* This bamboo, whose stout hollow stems grow to 80 feet high, abounds in moist flats and hollows in the roots of the Quitenian Andes, on both sides, and I have nowhere seen it at a greater altitude than 5,000 feet, so that it forms an excellent guide to the upper limit of the Red Bark. Wherever it descends to the plain, on either side, it is with dwindled dimensions. On the Rio Negro and the Alto Orinoco it grows nowhere wild, and wherever a grove of it is seen, it uniformly indicates a *Tapéra*, as the sites of ancient *malócas* (villages) are called. Von Martius makes a similar remark respecting the river Japurà, in his interesting "Observatio Geographica," affixed to the "Agrostologia Brasiliensis." "Ipse ego in sylvis ad flumen Japurá ejusmodi densa Bambusearum fruteta triginta et quod excedit pedes alta, conspexi, forsan *Bambusa latifolia*, Kunth, efformata; comitesque Indi, ubi nobis occurrerent, id argumento sibi dicebant esse, olim pagos hic indicos (*Malocas*) fuisse." I have always supposed this bamboo to be the *Bambusa* (*Guadua*) *angustifolia* of Humboldt and Bompland, which those travellers found in the Montana de Quindiu, up to 5,575 English feet; but, as I have never found it in flower, my materials are insufficient to decide the question. All the *Guaduas* seem to have hollow stems, unless a remarkable solid-stemmed bamboo I gathered in flower at the mouth of the Rio Negro (Pl. Exs. 1196), be correctly referred to that genus.

† As the trees grow out again so readily from the crown of the root, I would suggest that, in the event of the attempt to form plantations of the Red Bark in India being successful, when the tress attain a sufficient size to be worth cutting down for the bark, the roots should not be molested, for they extend but a short way from the crown, and really yield a very small quantity of bark, although that is of excellent quality. At Limon, two trees, shoots from old stools, and supposed to be about 15 years old, were marked to be cut down in 1861, when it was calculated they would yield two quintals of bark each.

appeared that not fewer than 13 years, and probably not more than 15 years, must have elapsed since the mass of the Red Bark was cut down at Limon. As the scar of the opposite leaves and stipules forms a complete ring, which is not speedly obliterated, for the rings were distinct even to the very base of some trees, I tried to count the rings, in order to compare their number with the age assigned to the trees; but I found it impracticable whilst the trees were standing, and on two trees we had to cut down, the one for cuttings, the other for its seeds, the rings were unfortunately very indistinct. It was impossible to ascertain how many rings were formed each year, unless I had remained there all the year through. Near the equator, where the amount of light and heat varies so little throughout the year, and plants live under unceasing excitement, the growth of trees goes on almost continuously; not by any means at the same rate in every month, but never suspended entirely, except for a brief period antecedent to the time of flowering. In those plants which are ever flowering, or flower at brief intervals, there can scarcely be any suspension of growth. The ramuli of *Cinchona Succirubra* have from four to six pairs of leaves contemporaneously, but during my stay they were continually lengthening at the point, forming new leaves and throwing off old ones, and I suppose would go on doing so until the month of January at least; nor could I clearly trace any break between the growths of the two preceding years.

In the valleys of the Chasuán and Limon I saw about 200 trees of Red Bark standing. Out of the whole number, only two or three were saplings which had not been disturbed; all the rest grew from old stools, whose circumference averaged from four to five feet. I was unable to find a single young plant under the trees, although many of the latter bore signs of having flowered in previous years. This was explained by the flowering trees growing uniformly in open places, either in cane-fields which had been frequently weeded, or in pastures where cattle had grazed and trodden about. The young plants, which I had been assured I should find abundantly, proved to be either stolons or seedlings (very few of the latter) of the worthless *Cinchona (Cascarilla) Magnifolia*, which grows plentifully at Limon, and must have fruited during the rainy season, as the capsules were all burst open when I arrived there.

Cinchona Succirubra is a very handsome tree, and, in looking out over the forest, I could never see any other tree at all comparable to it for beauty. Across the narrow glen below our hut, and at nearly the same altitude, there was a large old stool, from which sprang several shoots, only one of which rose to a tree, while the rest formed a bush at its base. This tree was 50 feet high, branched from about one-third of its height, and the coma formed a symmetrical though elongated paraboloid. It had never flowered, but was so densely leafy that not a branch could be seen; and the large, broadly oval, deep green and shining leaves, mixed with decaying ones of a blood-red colour, gave the tree a most striking appearance. *C. Magnifolia*, called here "*Cascarillo Macho*" (male bark), grows rapidly to be a large tree. I saw one which must have been over 80 feet high, and I cut down a young tree which measured 60 feet. Saplings of 15 to 20 feet have a very noble appearance, from the large heart-shaped leaves, little short of a yard long; but in full-grown trees, the ramification is so sparse and irregular, and the leaves are so much mutilated by caterpillars, that all beauty is lost. This species sends out stolons from the root, which sometimes form a matted bed, looking like a growth of seedlings. I have not observed the same peculiarity in any other *Cinchona*. The bark of *C. Magnifolia* is of as deep a red as that of *C. Succirubra*, but rather duller, nor do I notice the transverse cracks in the epiderm, that exist in all but very young trees of *C. Succirubra*.

I inquired of the cascarilleros what varieties they distinguished in the Red Bark, and they signalised the following:—

Cascarilla roja de jugo lechoso, with milky juice.
" " *de jugo aguado*, with watery juice.
" " *de hojas crespas*, with wavy leaves.
" " *de hojas llanas*, with plain leaves.
" " *Pata de Gallinazo*, with very adhesive bark.
" " *suelta*, with easily separable bark.

As to the first pair of differences, they appear to depend entirely on the trees being barren or fertile. When the trees are in flower, and especially when the fruit

fruit is ripening, the sap concentrates in the panicles, and only a little watery juice exudes on wounding the trunk. But the cascarilleros did not even know that the trees bore seeds, until my inquiries called their attention to the fact. The seringueros on the Amazon are well aware that, from the time the India-rubber trees begin to flower until the fruit is ripe, they can get little or no milk from them.

At Limon there are trees with plain leaves, and others with leaves in various degrees of crispation, a difference so slight and accidental that it cannot constitute even a variety; nor could I connect it with any variation in soil or exposure.

Trees growing in moist situations are said to have the bark more easily separable than those which grow in dry, stony places, but it also shrinks more in drying. However (and this is the most important point), the cascarilleros have not ascertained that any one of their supposed varieties produces bark superior to the others. Of far greater value is the information derived from Señor Cordovez (who has analysed the red bark collected at various altitudes), that the greater the height at which the tree grows, the larger is the proportion of alkaloids contained in the bark.

Botanically speaking, the Red Bark varies in the breadth of the leaves, and more considerably in the degree of pubescence, although the latter, whether sparse or dense, is always the same short soft down, at once distinguishable from the longer and harsher pubescence of *C. Magnifolia*. Not to burden my report with technical details, I transfer to a supplementary note my description of *Cinchona Succirubra*, drawn up from fresh specimens.

I proceed now to give some account of the other indigenous inhabitants of the Red Bark woods, animal and vegetable.

The *Andine Bear*, chiefly inhabiting the middle wooded region, descends to the lower limit of the Red Bark. On the eastern side of the Andes it rarely goes as low as 3,000 feet.

The *Jaguar* (*Felis onça*) chiefly inhabiting the plain, does not yet seem to have climbed as high as Limon; but at Tarapoto, in the Andes of Maynas, it was abundant up to more than 3,000 feet elevation. The *Puma* or *Leon* (*Felis concolor*) exists not only in the plain, but throughout the wooded slopes of the Andes; it is only too abundant in the roots of the cordillera, and I have seen its footsteps on recent snow at a height of 13,000 feet, on the high mountains to the eastward of Riobamba. "Puma" is the Indian generic name for every sort of tiger, but the Spanish colonists limit it to the red tiger, and call the spotted jaguar "tigre." Bears never troubled our hut, but we had two nocturnal visits from the puma. On one of these occasions the puma seized and was carrying off a little dog, but a very large and fine black dog sprang on the puma, and forced him to let go his hold. By that time the Indians were on foot and running to attack the puma, who only escaped through favour of the darkness. The screams of an animal seized by a tiger are about the most doleful sounds one ever hears in the forest, and after being once heard, their cause can never be mistaken.

The *Wild Pig* (*Poccary*) frequently ascends to Limon, where there are also two orth ree smaller pachyderms.

Two sorts of *Monkeys* are common, one of them almost as noisy as the howling monkey, but of a different genus. I do not know of any monkey which ascends to the temperate region of the Andes.

A pretty red-headed *Parrot*, so small that it might be taken for a parroquet, arrived in immense flocks about the end of July, and took up its summer residence in the Red Bark woods. The same species abounds in the valley of Alausi, where it makes sad havoc of the maize crops, and ascends by day to 8,500 feet, but always descends to Pumacocha to roost. Along with the parrots came *Toucans*, of two species.

Snakes are very frequent, and some of them venomous. Limon seems to be the highest point to which the *Equis* ascends, a large and deadly snake which is a great pest in the plains of Guayaquil; it takes its name from being marked with crosses (like the letter "X") all along the back.

Butterflies I have rarely seen in greater number, and they include at least four species of those large blue butterflies (probably species of *Morpho*) which, on the eastern side, are seldom seen above the hot region. *Cockroaches*, too, ascend higher than I have elsewhere observed. We had four or five species in our hut, none

none of them large, and one very minute species, which often damaged my fresh specimens of plants by mutilating the flowers. It is so abundant at Camaron, 1,000 feet lower down, that it fills the pease and barley meal, and renders them uneatable. *Ants* are far more frequent than in the temperate region, but less so than in the plains. *House flies* are as great a nuisance as at Ambato; and though *fleas* are not quite so numerous as in the cool sandy highlands, there were yet plenty of them (as the Spaniards say), "para el gasto."

Before treating of the indigenous vegetation, some account of the cultivated plants will aid in giving a clear idea of the climate.

The only plant grown to any extent is *Sugar-cane,* and in the Red Bark region only the small white, purple, and black varieties thrive, as they do in sheltered parts of the central valley of the Andes up to 8,200 feet, where they are sometimes exposed to slight frosts. They take two years to ripen. Half a league below Limon, and at a little over 2,000 feet altitude, the *Caña Limeña,* or Lima cane (which I take to be the same as that of Tahiti) begins to flourish, and produces thick stems 15 feet long. It ripens there in 12 months, but in the plain of Guayaquil in eight or nine months, and in the eastern roots of the Andes, as at Tarapoto, it requires no more than six months.

Maize is sparingly grown, and can only be used in a green state, on account of the destructive parrots.

Plantains thrive well, but the climate is still too cool for the large-fruited variety called "Baraganete" at Guayaquil, and "Bellaco," in Maynas. *Bananas,* or *Guineos,* also prosper, as they do even in the temperate region. Other fruits and tubers are grown in such very small quantities as to give the cultivators only an occasional dish. The tuberiferous plants are *Yuca* (*Manihot Aypi*), *Indu* (*Caladii,* sp.), and *Arracacha* or *Zanahoria* (*Arracacha esculenta*).* Two or three sorts of *Frijoles* (*Phaseoli*) are sparingly grown. *Oranges* are well flavoured, but the trees dwindle from becoming overgrown with moss. *Lemons* (from which the site takes its name) have become half wild, and such is also the case with *Citrons. Coffee* thrives admirably, but so little of it is grown, that our stock of the grain was mostly procured either from Guaranda, or from the deserted farm already spoken of. There are some large trees of *Aguacate* (*Persea gratissima*), planted by the first settlers, who would seem to have been fonder of gardens than the existing inhabitants, for on all the deserted sites may be seen remnants of *Coix lachryma, Bryophyllum calycinum,* and occasionally *Datura arborea. Achiote* (*Bixa Orellana*) has been copiously planted, and fruits well; on an old tree by our hut grew no fewer than 10 species of ferns.

Other plants of warm climates, which have been tried, do not flourish. *Cresantia cujete* grows, but never flowers. There is too much fog for rice, and the ears are invariably destroyed by ergot. Scarcely any of the esculent plants of the cool region thrive at Limon; potatoes, for instance, run all to leaf.

As above indicated, Limon was once entirely clad with forest, in which respect it contrasts strongly with the valley of Alausi, where the slopes on both sides are covered with grass, even down to the hot region, and only the lateral valleys and the plateaux are wooded. I cannot doubt that the difference arises from the former being situated in the roots of a snowy mountain, while there is no perpetual snow within a long distance of the latter. I have observed the same difference, referrible to the same cause, along the eastern side of the Andes. After passing the valley of San Antonio, to the southward, there is this intermixture of woods and pajonales all the way to the frontier of Peru. As would naturally

* The tubers of the *Arracacha* are, to my taste, superior to all others except the potato. The flavour is most like that of the parsnip, but far more delicate. The plant, however, does not thrive in either a hot or a cold climate, and the slightest frost kills it. Its range in the Andes is almost limited to the zone between 3,000 and 7,000 feet. The finest *Arracacha* I ever ate grew at 4,000 feet. The length of time the tubers take to ripen (nine or ten months) might seem an insuperable obstacle to the cultivation of the Arracacha in Europe; but I would persevere until I forced it to change its "custom," as the Braziliansbave done with the Manihot, which also ordinarily requires 10 months to ripen; but on the Soliõmes (or Upper Amazon) they have got a precocious variety, called "Mandiocca de tres meses," which, being planted early in the dry season on the rich alluvium left by the retiring waters, ripens its tubers before the site is covered by the next flood.

naturally be expected, the vegetation at Limon is far more luxuriant, and the abundance of ferns, especially in the narrower valleys, is in striking contrast to their scarcity at Puma-cocha. Tree-ferns, of five species, are everywhere scattered in the forest, and add a feature of beauty to the scenery, quite wanting in the valley of Alausi.

I estimate the average height of the virgin forest at Limon at 90 feet; but, as everywhere else in the tropics, there are here and there trees which stand out far above the mass of the forest. The monarch of the forest at Limon is an *Artocarpea*, which, from the leaves and from flowers picked up beneath the trees, I have little hesitation in referring to *Coussapoa*. The following are the dimensions of a tree of this species, which I found prostrate in a recent clearing: length, 120 feet, not including the terminal branches, which had been lopped off, were still 20 inches in circumference, and which would have made it at least 20 feet more. Circumference at 10 feet from the ground, 12 feet 4 inches; from that point narrow buttresses were sent off to the ground on all sides. At 25 feet, the trunk was forked, and the ramification was thenceforth dichotomous, at a narrow angle.

No other tree reaches the dimensions of the *Artocarpea*. A *Lauracea*, called "*Quebra-hacha*" (Break-axe), rises to 110 to 120 feet; its exceedingly hard wood is the usual material for the cylinders of the *trapiches*. My collection contains, unfortunately, very few of the larger trees. On the western slope of the Quitenian Andes there is a great burst of blossom at the commencement of the dry season, that is, towards the end of May, and another of less extent after the rains of the autumnal equinox; so that, as my visit fell between those two epochs, many of the trees were in the same unsatisfactory state as the Hill Bark already mentioned, and others had not yet begun to flower. Besides, I should hardly, under any circumstances, have been at the trouble of cutting down a large tree for the sake of only two or three specimens; and after we began to treat of the Bark plants, the Indians could hardly be spared for any other service.

In proceeding to give a classified list of the plants collected and observed, I shall generally limit myself to indicating their natural order. In order that my attention might not be called away from the main object of the enterprise, I collected very few (often unique) specimens of each plant. Many of them are obviously undescribed, but I have a great repugnance to speaking positively of species, unless I have been able to examine them thoroughly; and even then, for want of herbaria to refer to, I can rarely feel complete confidence in my determinations. I have, therefore, preferred putting the specimens unmutilated into the hands of Sir W. J. Hooker and Mr. Bentham, who may perhaps be induced to name them. The general character of the vegetation may, however, be sketched very intelligibly with very little reference to species.

As I have no work on geographical botany by me, and am quite ignorant of the zones of vegetation into which modern botanists divide the equatorial Andes, I have been accustomed, in estimating the range of plants in altitude, to divide the whole height from the plain to the snow-line into hot, warm, temperate, cool, cold, and frigid regions, nearly in accordance with the common parlance of the inhabitants of the country. To assign precise boundaries to these regions would be as delicate, and indeed impracticable a task, as to say beyond what limits of structure a genus shall not extend, or a species vary. The hot region includes, but is by no means limited to, the plain, for there are very sultry valleys in the roots of the Andes, that of Tarapoto for instance, where, at a height of 1,200 to 1,800 feet, the heat is greater than anywhere on the Amazon. The zone occupied by the Red Bark, decidedly warm through most of its extent, is scarcely more than temperate at its upper limit. For further remarks on the climate, I must refer to the end of this Report. My estimate of the range in altitude of the families, genera, and species, must be considered to relate to only so much of the Andes as is comprised between the equator and the parallel of 7° S. lat. As I have examined some parts of the eastern roots of the cordillera between those limits, I am enabled to institute a comparison between the vegetation existing there, and that of the Red Bark woods on the western side, at corresponding elevations. But I enter into no speculations as to how such plants as *Mimosa asperata* and *Uncaria Guianensis*, which barely ascend to the commencement of the Bark region, to say nothing of of many others, such as *Cratæva tapioides* and *Salia Humboldtiana*, which exist only in the plains on both sides, have ever been able to get over the cold ridge of the Andes, feeling convinced that they have never had to perform so impossible a feat, for plants are assuredly infinitely more ancient than the hills. It would be interesting, however, to ascertain the amount of variation that actually exists between individuals of the same species, growing on the Atlantic and Pacific sides of the Andes.

Sketch of the Vegetation of the Red Bark Forests of Chimborazo (alt. 2,000 to 5,000 feet.)

Gramineæ, 4*.—A good many species of this order were observed, but, as is mostly the case in the dry season, nearly all partially dried up and out of flower; besides that, even in the recesses of the forest, they were sought out and cropped by the starving animals. After the bamboo above spoken of, the arrow-cane (*Gynerium saccharoides*) is the most notable grass, and forms considerable beds, especially near streams. This species is abundant enough on low shores and islands of the Amazon, but it has nowhere spread far from the river-bank, nor (so far as I can ascertain) is it found wild on any of the tributaries of that river, but those which rise in the Andes. On the Rio Negro it is planted, like the bamboo, and a flat of it is highly prized by the possessor. On the Upper Orinoco it does not exist. Even on the Amazon it looks dwindled, and rarely exceeds 18 or 20 feet high; but on reaching the roots of the Andes of Maynas, one begins to see this noble grass in its true proportions. The poles, with which the Cucáma Indians propel their canoes against the rapid current of the Huallaga, are mostly portions of the stems of the arrow-cane. It attains its maximum of development on stony springy declivities, at an elevation of about 1,500 feet above the sea, where a forest of arrow-cane, with its tall slender stems of 30 to 40 feet, each supporting a fan-shaped coma of distichous leaves, and a long-stalked thyrse of rose and silver flowers waving in the wind, is truly a grand sight. The longest stem I ever measured was one I met a man carrying on his shoulder at Tarapoto. From that stem had been cut away the leaves and peduncle, and the base of the stem, which is generally beset by stout-arched exserted roots (serving as buttresses), to a height of one to three feet; yet the residue was 37 feet long, so that the entire length must have been at least 45 feet.

In the western roots of the Andes the arrow-cane is as abundant as in the eastern, but in the red bark woods it no longer grows so tall and robust as it does at half the altitude. In the valley of the Pastasa it struggles up to near 6,000 feet, where its stems are scarcely thicker than the finger. There it meets another *Gynerium* (as I take it to be), called by the Quitenians "*Jucu*," which grows 15 to 20 feet high, and differs from the "*Pintu*" (*G. saccharoides*) in the leaves being distributed throughout the entire length and on all sides of the stem. It grows abundantly by boggy streams, and in morasses on the cold *paramos*, and its stems, called (like those of the *Pintu*) "*caña brava*," enter largely into the fabrication of the poorer class of houses throughout the highlands. I have been unable to find its flowers, nor have I met any one who has seen them.

The other grasses accompanying the red bark comprise several of those rampant forest *Panica* which thread among adjacent branches to a height of 15 feet or more. The long internodes serve as tubes for tobacco pipes and for other similar uses. There are also two broad-leaved "*Gamalotes*" of the same genus. Of grasses frequent in the hot plains, I noted only *Dactyloctenium Ægyptiacum* and *Paspalum conjugatum*.

Cyperaceæ, 1.—This order is scarce, both in individuals and species. The half-dozen species observed belong chiefly to *Scleria* and *Isolepis*.

Araceæ, 4.—As abundant and varied as in the forests of the plains. An arborescent species, called "*Casimin*" by the inhabitants, grows everywhere, even on hills where there is little moisture. The stems reach 10 feet, and are sometimes

* The number affixed to most of the orders indicates how many species of that order I gathered in a perfect state.

sometimes thicker than the thigh, though so soft that a very slight stroke of a cutlass suffices to sever them. The small spathes are fascicled in the axils of the leaves, but of all that I opened the contents were so injured by earwigs and other insects that it was impossible to ascertain the structure of the flowers. A little above, and parallel to the nearly amplexicaul base of each petiole, there is a row of tubercles—undeveloped roots I take them to be, as they quite correspond in position to the aerial roots of the scandent *Araceæ.* Species of *Anthurium* and *Philodendron* are frequent, and their deeply cloven or perforated leaves often assume grotesque forms. One very beautiful climbing *Aroidea*, with shaggy petioles and leaves streaked with deep violet above, purple beneath, I could never find in flower.

Cyclanthaceæ.—Three scandent species of *Carludovica*, all with bifid leaves.

Palmaceæ.—Frequent enough, but of few species. The *cadi*, or ivory palm, is everywhere dispersed, and is precisely the same species as I saw at Puma-cocha. I gathered and analysed the male inflorescence, but the stripping off the fronds for thatch is unfavourable to the development of the fruit, which I never saw in a perfect state. A very prickly *Bactris*, 20 feet high, with five or six stems from a root, grows here and there; and in shady places three or four *Geonomæ* are frequent. The *Euterpe* grows chiefly at the upper limit of the Red Bark. A noble *Attalea* (called "*Cumbi*" and "*Palma real*") extends up the valley of San Antonio to the lower limit of the Bark region. It has a slight beard to the petiole.

Bromeliaceæ.—Many species are perched about on the trees, but none of striking aspect. The presence or absence of this family affords no indication of climate on the equator, for trees of *Buddleia* and *Polylepis*, at the upper limit of arborescent vegetation, are as thickly hung with a *Bromeliacea* as any trees on the Amazon.

Amaryllideæ, 2.—Both herbaceous twiners, the one a *Bomarea*, with pendulous umbels of showy flowers, calyx red, corolla white, with violet spots; an order, so far as my experience goes, entirely absent from equinoctial plains, but tolerably abundant in the temperate and cool regions of the Andes.

Musaceæ.—*Heliconia*, two species.

Zingiberaceæ.—*Cossus*, three species. This is about the highest point at which I have seen any *Cossus* or *Heliconia*, two genera frequent in the plains.

Marantaceæ.—Two or three species of *Maranta* were observed.

Orchidaceæ, 28.—Tolerably abundant, but comprising few handsome species. Most epiphytal orchids love light, and in the dense lofty forest they are rarely seen, and often inaccessible, for they grow on the upper branches of large trees, and descend to the lower branches only on the margin of wide streams, where the whole of one side of the trees is exposed to the light. At Limon, however, in ancient clearings, now become pastures, where a few trees of the primitive forest have been left, and where others have here and there sprung up, despite the treading about of cattle, the branches are laden with orchids and vacciniums; and although none of the former be of remarkable beauty, yet they are in so great variety, and there is such a charm in seeing them on the rugged mossy trees in their native woods, that to me they were always objects of interest. The finest orchid, as to its flowers, is an *Odontoglossum*, with large chocolate-coloured flowers, margined with yellow. I gathered the same species at Puma-cocha, under No. 6,072. As respects foliage, a fairy *Stelis* (*S. calodyction*, Mss.), with roundish pale green leaves, beautifully reticulated with the purple veins, far excels every other plant seen in tha cinchona woods. I found but a single tuft, almost buried in moss on the trunk of a tree. An orchid (genus unknown), with thick coriaceous leaves, curiously spotted with white, a rare feature in epiphytal orchids, was discovered by Mr. Cross. Very remarkable was an *Oncidium*, with numerous peduncles, 10 feet long, twining round one another, and on adjacent plants. Besides the orchids growing on trees, a good many species, allied to *Spiranthes*, grow on the earth and on decayed logs.

The 28 orchids gathered in flower are, perhaps, scarcely a third of the whole number observed. On the slopes of the Andes some orchid or other is in flower

flower all through the year, and almost every species has its distinct epoch for flowering.

In the Andes, epiphytal orchids accompany trees almost to the upper limit of the growth of the latter, and some species are therefore often exposed to positive frost. In 1857 I slept one frosty night on the hill of Guambaló, near Ambato, at a height of about 9,500 feet. In the morning, when the sun came out bright and hot, I saw the maize in the adjacent fields entirely destroyed, the leaves of potatoes and nettles blackened, young shoots of many indigenous plants, even *Vaccinia* and *Gaultheriæ*, bleached and withered; but four epiphytal orchids (one *Stelis*, two *Pleurothallides*, and one *Oncidium*) in full flower, which had been exposed to the influence of the frost, were apparently not the least injured.

Commelynaceæ.—Three species of *Commelyna* seen, chiefly near streams and in cultivated places.

Pontederiaceæ, 1.—A small creeping plant, with white or very pale lilac flowers, probably a *Pontederia*, in springy situations by the Chasuán.

Dioscoreacea.—Only the male plant seen of a *Dioscorea*.

Smilaceæ, 2.—Species of *Smilax*, both with roundish stems and few prickles. One of them, with large cordate leaves, is abundant, but the roots have never been collected in this locality.

Gnetaceæ, 1.— A *Gnetum* (*G. trinerve*, Mss.), apparently parasitic, and remarkable for its three-ribbed leaves. It is the first species of this genus I have seen in the hills, though *Gneta* are common enough in the plains, and especially on the Rio Negro, where the kernel of the fruit is eaten roasted.

Myricaceæ, 1.—A wax-bearing *Myrica*, which descends to 2,000 feet on open beaches of the Rio San Antonio, but was not observed by the Chasuán. The same or a very similar species grows on wide gravelly beaches of the Pastasa. Morona, and other rivers which descend the eastern slope of the Andes; and a good deal of wax is obtained from its fruit, principally by the Jibaro Indians, who sell it to traders from Quito, Ambato, &c., under the name of "Cera de laurél," or laurel wax.

Urticaceæ, 2.—Two or three fruticose *Pileæ* were observed, but the only plant gathered was a tree 25 feet high (growing by the Rio San Antonio), which seems a species of *Sponia*, a genus placed by some authors in *Ulmaceæ*.

Moraceæ.—Here and there grows a parasitical *Ficus*, but the species seemed much fewer than I have observed in other similar localities.

A opeæ.—None gathered, although, as above remarked, the tallest tree of the forest belongs to this order. Two *Cecropiæ* are not unfrequent, and another tree with a tall white trunk and large hoary pedatified leaves, looking quite like a species of the same genus, extends up the slopes of the mountains to 8,000 feet, and has its lower limit above that of the *Cinchona*; but as I have never seen its flowers, and as the *Cecropiæ* are apparently confined to the hot and warm regions, I suppose it may be generically distinct.

Euphorbiaceæ, 3.—The species gathered comprise an *Acalypha*, a *Phyllanthus*, and a small tree of unknown genus. There were besides two *Euphorbiæ* in the cane grounds, and a shrubby *Croton* by the Rio San Antonio.

Callitrichaceæ.—A *Callitriche*, in pools by the Rio San Antonio.

Monimiaceæ.—Three species of *Citrosma* are frequent.

Menispermaceæ.—A woody twiner of this order was noted, probably an *Abuta*, but without flower or fruit.

Cucurbitaceæ, 8.—Plants of this family are abundant, and besides the eight species gathered, some others were seen in a barren state. I gathered two *Anguriæ*, with trifoliolate leaves, and the characteristic scarlet flowers of the genus. One plant, apparently of this order, puzzled me much, for the woody stems, partly twining and partly climbing by means of radicles, and no thicker than packthread, bore a bunch of slender flowers (calyx scarlet, corolla yellow) near the base; but though I pulled down some stems of enormous length, I could

could see no traces of leaves on them. At length, I succeeded in getting down an entire stem, 40 feet long (by no means one of the longest), which had a couple of trifoliolate leaves near the apex. A *Cucurbitacea*, called " *Cidroyota*," which only grows near houses, and has, probably, originally been sown, bears a large pyriform fleshy fruit, corrugated like the rind of a citron (whence the name), which, sliced and cooked along with meat, is very good eating. I dried seeds of it, but they disappeared, having perhaps been carried off by cockroaches.

Begoniaceæ, 4.—Two climbing and two terrestrial species. Of the latter, one is a large coarse plant ten feet high, with leaves resembling those of *Heracleum giganteum*. I have gathered the same or a very similar species on the eastern side of the cordillera. One of the climbing species is very ornamental, from its long pinnate shoots bearing a profusion of roseate flowers and generally purplish leaves. This genus, entirely absent from the Amazonian plain, though it has one representative in that of Guayaquil, abounds on the woody slope of the Andes, especially in the warm and temperate regions.

Papayaceæ.—Two species of *Carica* were seen, both slender simple arbuscules of five to six feet—the one by the Chasuán, the other by the San Antonio. The leaves of the former are boiled and eaten by the inhabitants under the name of " *col del monte*," (wood cabbage). The plants referred to *Carica* require to be carefully re-studied from fresh specimens. The large fleshy, elongate, angular green or yellow fruits of the Papaws and Chamburús look very different from the small, soft, sub-globose scarlet berries of the dwarf *Caricæ*, such as those of the *Cinchona* woods, and other similar ones gathered at Tarapoto, and analysis of both fruits and flowers might reveal more important differences.

Flacourtiaceæ, 1.—A small tree, probably a species of *Bonara*.

Samydeæ.—A *Casearia*, which seems to be *C. Sylvestris*, grows in some abundance, but the fruits were open and empty. This is the highest point at which I have seen a species of *Casearia*, a genus abundant in the plains, especially in woods of secondary growth.

Passifloreæ, 2.—Both species of *Passiflora*—the one a woody twiner (frequently found on the Red Bark tree), with entire leaves, smallish green flowers, and globose berries the size of a cherry; the other a beautiful arbuscule, seen only in the valley of San Antonio, where it grows from the very plain up to 2,600 feet. The slender stems, of from 8 to 14 feet, are usually simple and arched, and the large white flowers grow in small pendulous corymbs from the axils of very large elongate glaucous leaves. It belongs to the sub-genus *Astrophea*, but does not agree with either of the two species (*Passiflora emarginata* and *P. glauca*) found by Humboldt and Bonpland in the Andes.*

Cruciferæ, 2.—Apparently species of *Sisymbrium*, the one growing near streams, the other in open situations; both in very small quantity. This family is entirely absent from the Amazonian plain, nor did I find any *Crucifera* in the lower Andes of Maynas; but in ascending by the Pastasa from Canelos, I came on a *Sisymbrium* at about 3,000 feet, on stones in the mouth of the Topo, by which stream it had probably been brought down from the highlands, where *Cruciferæ* have their normal station, at from 6,000 feet to the snow-line.

Capparidaceæ.—The only species observed was a *Cleome*, a genus which extends from the plain to a great height on the wooded hills.

Sterculiaceæ.—A raft-wood tree; (*Ochromæ*. sp.), is pretty abundant. Another tree of the same order (not seen in flower) appears to be a *Chorisia*.

Büttneriaceæ, 1.—A rampant *Melochia*. *Muntingia Calaburu*, a tree found in the plains on both sides of the cordillera, grows abundantly by the Rio San Antonio, up to 2,500 feet.

Malvaceæ,

* In the " corona" of the flowers, filament and rudimentary anthers are clearly distinguishable in each process, and no doubt can remain that the corona in all *Passifloræ* is really abortive stamens.

Malvaceæ, 2.—Four or five common weeds, whereof *Sida glomerata*, Cav., is the most plentiful, comprise all that was seen of this order.

Tiliaceæ, 1.—A very handsome tree, with a slender straight trunk, reaching 60 feet, very long ramuli, large ligulate serrated distichous leaves, and terminal panicles (sometimes four feet long) of yellow flowers, scented like those of *Tilia Europæa*; it is abundant and ornamental about the middle region of the red bark. Besides this tree, another of the same order (apparently a *Heliocarpus*), growing to about 30 feet, is also frequent, especially in deserted clearings. Except these two species, I saw only a weedy *Triumfetta*, belonging to the same order.

Polygaleæ, 2.—A *Monnina* and *Polygala paniculata*, L. A species of *Monnina* occurs in Maynas, at about the same altitude (a little under 3,000 feet), and this seems the lowest limit of the growth of this genus near the equator. It exists in great abundance at from 6,000 to 10,000 feet, and two or three species ascend nearly 2,000 feet higher. The *Polygala* of the bark woods is the common and almost the only species of the equatorial Andes, on whose western slopes it descends to the plain, and does not seem to ascend higher than 7,000 feet on either side, nor is it common at any elevation. When I recollect the abundance of *Polygala vulgaris* on cold English moors, I am struck with this paucity of *Polygalæ* in the Andes, and still more when I compare it with their abundance and variety on hot savannahs of the Orinoco, and in hollows of granite rocks by the Atabapo.

Sapindaceæ, 1.—A woody climbing *Serjania*, a fine plant, approaching *Paullinia* in character. A *Paullinia* with trigonous stems is frequent, and is the common substitute for rope, where much strength is not required. I saw no flowers of it and only empty capsules. There is also a *Cardiospermum*, which I have seen on both sides of the cordillera up to 7,500 feet, and this is the greatest elevation at which I have noted any *Sapindacea*, an order which abounds in the hot plains.

Malpighiaceæ, 1.—A twiner, with fruit too young to enable me to speak positively of the genus. Plants of this order, which constitute so large a proportion of the vegetation of the plains, diminish rapidly in number and variety as we ascend the hills, and beyond the warm region of the Andes the scandent species entirely disappear; but a *Bunchosia* (probably *B. Armeniaca*)—a tree about the size of our pear-trees—ascends high into the temperate region. On the hills which slope down to the left margin of the Pastasa, this tree grows up to 8,000 feet, and in some places forms large continuous patches, unmixed with any other tree. The edible though rather insipid drupes, as large as a peach, are exposed for sale in large quantities in Ambato and the adjacent towns, under the name of "*ciruelo de fraile*," or friar's plum. They are frequently double, in consequence of only one of the cells of the ovary being sterile, instead of two, as is usually the case, and at Baños a seedless variety is cultivated.

Ternströmiaceæ, 1.—An arbuscule, with opposite leaves and few-flowered peduncles, chiefly from annotinous axils. Two species of the anomalous genus *Saurauja* form trees of about 30 feet, and are conspicuous from their abundance, from their large lanceolate serrated leaves, and axillary panicles of white flowers, resembling those of *Fragaria vesca*. One of the two, with ferrugineo-tomentose leaves, seems quite the same as I have gathered on Tunguragua up to 7,000 feet (Pl. Exs. 5,089). A *Freziera* descends on the banks of the Rio San Antonio to 2,300 feet, and the same species grows on the eastern side of the cordillera, in the valley of the Pastasa, where, however, I have not seen it lower than 4,000 feet.

Clusiaceæ, 3.—One of them, a *Clusia*, abundant and ornamental from its numerous rose-coloured flowers, but the plants nearly all males. A slender half-twining shrub, seen only in fruit, is probably a congener of a doubtful plant with similar habit, gathered at S. Gabriel on the Rio Negro. Two or three other *Clusiæ* were seen, not in flower or fruit.

Marcgraviaceæ, 1.—A *Norantea*, the same as that gathered in the Bark woods of Puma-cocha. *Marcgravia umbellata* is very abundant, and climbs to the tops of the loftiest trees.

Anonaceæ,

Anonaceæ, 2.—The one a *Guatteria*, rather scarce at about 3,000 feet, the greatest elevation at which I have ever observed the genus; the other a small *Anona*, also scarce, it bears an edible fruit, called "*cabeza de negro*," the size of an orange but longer than broad. This order has its chief site in the hot plains.

Ericeæ, Subordo Vacciniace, 6.—Four *Vaccinia*, one *Thibaudia*, and one *Macleania*, all epiphytal shrubs. One of the *Vaccinia*, with fleshy rose or blood-coloured leaves, densely (almost teretely) imbricated on the branches, and with slender red flowers in their axils, looked very pretty on the old trees; but the *Thibaudia* was still more ornamental, from the profusion of its large tubular flowers—calyx and corolla at first yellow, turning red after the bursting of the anthers, and persisting a long time; they unfortunately turn black in drying, so that my specimens give no idea of their beauty. In *Thibaudia* we have a remarkable example of a genus which ascends from the very plain (where, however, it is very scarce) nearly to the extreme limit of lignescent vegetation. *Euericeæ*, on the contrary, according to my observations, do not descend lower than 6,000 feet, on the equator.

Amyrideæ.—Two small trees, of the genus *Icica*, were seen in flower: and some of the tallest trees with pinnate leaves, I have no doubt, from their resinous juice, belong to the same order.

Meliaceæ, 1.—A species of *Trichilia*, called "*Muruvillo*," whose bark is held as a febrifuge, barely enters the bark region at San Antonio, but does not extend up to it at Limon. A tallish tree, with pinnate leaves and very large serrated leaflets, which was putting forth large terminal panicles when I left the woods, probably belongs to this order.

Zygophylleæ, 1.—A fine tree of 40 feet, with large opposite pinnate leaves; it is closely allied to *Guaiacum*, though scarcely referable to that genus.

Podostemaceæ.—The withered remains of at least three species were observed on granite rocks in the River San Antonio, and they are the first of the family I have seen in the Andes, though I have carefully sought for them in streams on both sides of the cordillera.

Oxalidaceæ.—At San Antonio grow two species of *Oxalis*, both of which I have previously gathered, the one on the eastern side of the Andes near Baños, and the other at Pallatanga on the western side.

Caryophyllaceæ.—A solitary species of each of the genera *Stellaria* and *Drymaria* grows very sparingly. In ascending the eastern side of the Andes, I first came on a *Stellaria* at between 2,000 and 3,000 feet. This order, frequent enough in the upper regions of the Andes, seems to exist in the plains at their base, only in the genera *Polycarpæa*, *Drymaria*, and *Mollugo*, all three very scarce on the Atlantic side, but the last-named very abundant on the Pacific side.

Portulaceæ.—A *Portulaca* grows in sandy places inundated by the Rio San Antonio.

Polygoneæ.—A *Triplaris*, apparently identical with that observed at Pumacocha, and possibly distinct from *T. Surinamensis*, extends a little way into the territory of the Red Bark, and in descending from thence becomes more abundant all the way down to the plain, where it is called by the Guayaquilians "*Arbol de frios*," or ague-tree. Its presence, indeed, is a pretty sure indication of a humid site.

Amarantaceæ, 1.—A woody twiner. There are besides two or three weedy plants of this order, probably species of *Telanthera*.

Chenopodeæ.—Two common weeds; one of them being the ubiquitous *Chenopodium ambrosioides*, which grows with almost equal luxuriance in the elevated central valley of the Andes, and in the plains of the Amazon and Guayaquil.

Piperaceæ, 5.—Species of this order are very numerous. I saw perhaps as many as 20, belonging chiefly to the genera *Artanthe* and *Peperomia*. A very fine pepper, resembling *Artanthe eximia*, Miq., but a still handsomer plant, grows

grows towards the lower limit of the bark region. The stem is 20 feet high, slender and perfectly straight, and beset with short, distant, nearly horizontal ramuli, from which hang almost vertically the large, Pothos-like, coriaceous, shining deep blue-green leaves. A multicaul *Artanthe*, 15 to 25 feet high, springs up abundantly in the pastures, where trees of it grow at such regular distances, and are so conspicuous by their yellow-green foliage, that one would suppose them planted. Their ashes afford an excellent lye for soap. On stones by the Rio San Antonio grows a stout *Peperomia*, one to two feet high, subramose, and putting forth axillary fascicles of slender white spadices, which exhale a strong odour of aniseed. When in the midst of a dense patch of it, the scent is almost stifling, though pleasant enough at a short distance. Peppers are equally plentiful in the plains, and throughout the wooded slopes of the Andes.

Lauraceæ, 3.—All small trees, not exceeding 40 feet; but a great many more were observed, including some of the loftiest trees of the forest.

Leguminosæ. Subordo Papilionaceæ, 3.—And several others were observed, but either in poor state or inaccessible. Some of the lofty trees with pinnate foliage, which were not seen in flower or fruit, probably belong to this order. The commonest *Papilionacea* is a *Mucuna*, with herbaceous twining stems, without tendrils, and large yellow flowers. It is the first *Mucuna* I have seen in the hills, but it is equally abundant by the River Guayaquil. Five species of *Erythrina* were seen, two at Limon (one of them being the same as that gathered at Puma-cocha), and the remaining three by the Rio San Antonio. There are also two *Phaseoli*, one *Dioclea*, and another *Phaseolea* with slender spikes of small pale yellow flowers and hard scarlet seeds, of which I have not yet determined the genus. An *Indigofera*, with small pink flowers, w gathered at San Antonio, and the same is frequent in the plain of Guayaquil.

Leguminosæ. Subordo Cæsalpinieæ, 1.—This fine tribe, so abundant in the Amazonian plain, especially on the Rio Negro and Uaupés, where the *Swartziæ*, *Heterostemona*, *Parivoæ*, *&c.*, contest the palm of beauty with the *Vochysiaceæ*, becomes scarce the moment we enter the hills, and is very poorly represented in the Bark woods. My specimens were gathered from the only tree I saw of an obscure-looking *Cassia*. There is, however, one very fine Cæsalpinieous tree, extending up the hills to 4,000 feet, but much more abundant at 2,000 feet. The trunk grows to from 20 to 60 feet, and the branches each bear a coma of very long elegant pinnate pendulous leaves, like those of a *Brownea*. For a long time we could discover no flowers or fruit, but at length Mr. Cross found legumes and abortive flowers, which spring from the naked trunk. The small flowers are crowded on a receptacle comparable to that of a *Parkea*, but are enveloped in orbicular concave bracts, resembling those of a *Cornidia*, gathered on Mount Campana in Maynas. These characters leave me in doubt whether it be really a species of *Brownea*, but, if not, it is undoubtedly closely allied to that genus.

Leguminosæ. Subordo Mimoseæ, 4.—Three *Ingæ* and one *Calliandra*. Other two *Ingæ* were seen without flowers. *Mimosa asperata*, perhaps the commonest of all plants on the muddy shores of the Amazon and the River Guayaquil, struggles up the Rio San Antonio to the lower limit of the growth of the Red Bark, but never seems to flower at that elevation.

Rosaceæ, 1.—A *Rubus*, with numerous small flowers, apparently distinct from *R. Urticæfolius*, poir., which I gathered in Maynas at the same elevation (3,000 feet), and these are the lowest points at which I have observed any *Rosaceæ* near the equator; although plants of this order, especially of the tribe *Sanguisorbæ*, constitute a considerable proportion of the vegetation of the open highlands.

Hydrangeaceæ, 1.—A *Cornidia*. The same, or a very similar species of this truly Andine genus, grows by the Pastasa, on the eastern side of the cordillera, at about 4,000 feet, and other three species were gathered on Mount Campana, in Maynas, at 3,000 feet. I have never seen any *Cornidia* either above or below the warm region.

Cunoniaceæ.—A pinnate-leaved *Weinmannia*, sometimes reaching 80 feet high, is very frequent, and extends down the banks of the Chasuán to perhaps 2,200

2,200 feet. A humbler species descends nearly as low on the Andes of Maynas. On the wooded declivity of the volcano Tunguragua, *Weinmanniæ* constitute a considerable proportion of the vegetation, and extend upwards to at least 11,000 feet.

Lythraceæ.—A *Cuphea*, a small, weak, much-branched under-shrub, with purple flowers, grows gregariously in the pastures, generally accompanied by *Sida glomerata* and a *Stachytarpheta*. By the Rio San Antonio grow other two *Cupheæ*, one of which grows also in the valley of Alausi. This genus, abundant in the plains on both sides of the cordillera, spreads up the hills to 7,000 feet, or through the region of the Red Bark, but scarcely up to that of the Hill Barks. *Adenaria purpurata* grows by the Rio San Antonio up to 2,500 feet, and descends on its banks into the plain, the same as it does by streams on the eastern side of the cordillera.

Onagraceæ, 1.—Three species of *Jussiæa* grow by the Rio San Antonio. In the warm and hot regions this genus takes the place of *Œnothera*, which is frequent in the hills, but rarely descends below 6,000 feet. In other parts of South America, as for instance along the coast of Chili, *Jussiæa* are found inhabiting a cool climate. A single plant of a large-flowered *Fuchsia* was gathered at about 2,700 feet. A similar species occurs very rarely on the eastern side of the cordillera, at a little higher elevation. These are the only instances I know of *Fuchsias* descending so low, their favourite climate being found in the temperate and cool regions of the Andes, say from 6,000 to 11,000 feet.

Melastomaceæ, 9.—The first plant which took my attention at Limon, after the *Cinchona*, was a beautiful epiphytal *Blakea*, growing from 12 to 18 feet high, with large coriaceous leaves and large rose-coloured flowers, from which features, and from its often sitting high up the trees, it has almost the aspect of a *Clusia*. At the base of each flower is a turgid involucre, of four large, orbicular, widely and closely imbricated leaves, within which is secreted a limpid fluid. When the corolla falls away, the involucral leaves close firmly over the calyx, and do not open out, nor does the contained fluid dry up, until the globose roseate berry, the size of a pea, is quite ripe. Another singular character is the syngenesious anthers, with a minute pore at the apex of each cell, through which not a grain of pollen ever escapes, as I satisfied myself by repeated observation; fertilization being effected through the agency of minute beetles, which abound in the flowers, and eat away the inner edge of the anther cells, probably part of the pollen also. This *Blakea* is further worthy of mention for being the plant which the cascarilleros most frequently mistake for the Red Bark; for, though the leaves are somewhat smaller, yet, as they turn red ere they fall off, a dense bushy plant growing near the top of a tree looks at a distance not unlike the crown of the *Cinchona*, while (as observed above), on a view sufficiently near to distinguish the flowers and the texture of the leaves, one would rather compare it to a *Clusia*.

The remaining *Melastomaceæ* offer nothing noticeable, except the scarcity of *Miconia*, the South American genus most abundant in species and individuals, and occurring from the plain to the limits of true forest on the hills. I gathered but one species, which I refer doubtfully to *Miconia*.

Myrtaceæ, 1.—Two or three *Myrciæ*, which are rather scarce. A fine *Eugenia*, called "*Arrayàn*" (but different from the *Arrayàn* of Quito), with very hard, durable wood, and exfoliating bark, grows to a tree of 60 feet or more. Two *Psidia* are frequent; the one (on the beaches by the Rio San Antonio) seems the common *Guayaba* of the temperate region; the other is a timber tree, called "*Guayaba del Monte*," which, although of very slow growth, ultimately reaches the dimensions of the *Arrayàn*, and yields equally valuable timber.

Barringtoniaceæ.—A *Grias*, with the characteristic coma of large elongato-lanceolate leaves, seems to reach its upper limit at about 3,500 feet. It is of rather stunted growth in the Bark region, and does not flower until it gets down into the plain.

Loasaceæ, 1.—A weak branching herb with small white flowers, probably an *Ancyrostemon*. There grows also in the cane-fields a virulently stinging *Loasa*, which

which is too common a weed on the eastern side, at about 5,000 feet. This order, quite absent from the Amazonian plain, accompanies woody vegetation from about 1,200 feet up to 11,000 feet, at the least, and many of the species are climbers.

Umbelliferæ, 4.—Whereof three are *Hydrocotyles*, one of them departing from the habit usual to the South American species, in putting forth erect stems of three to 12 inches from a trailing rhizome. There is also a fourth *Hydrocotyle* (*H. pusilla*, A. Rich.), distinguished by its minute leaves and scarlet fruit, which I gathered at the same elevation on the Andes of Maynas. I have nowhere seen such abundance of *Hydrocotyles* in the forest as at Limon, where they constitute a notable proportion of the ground vegetation. In moist, open situations, on the higher grounds, they are common enough. According to my observations, *Eryngium fœtidum* is the sole representative of the order *Umbelliferæ* in the Amazonian plain, but near Guayaquil there is also a species of *Hydrocotyle*.

Araliaceæ.—Two species of the fine genus *Panax* are not uncommon.

Rubiaceæ, 19.—I think I gathered every plant of this order I saw in tolerable state, but a good many more were observed; on the whole about 30. Of plants peculiar to the warm and temperate valleys of the Andes, never descending to the plain, at least in this latitude, the following may be mentioned:—*Cinchona succirubra* and *Magnifolia*, two *Hameliæ* (one with larger flowers than I have seen in any other species), a *Gonzalea*, and *Rubia Relbun*. Of genera abundant in the plains and rarely climbing the hills are *Randia*, *Uncaria*, *Nonatelia*, *Faramea*, and *Cephaëlis*. *Uncaria Guianensis*, a twiner with formidable aculeiform stipules, has a very remarkable distribution. I have thrice met with it on the Atlantic side of the Andes; viz., first at Pará, near the mouth of the Amazon; secondly, towards the head of the Orinoco; and thirdly, on the hill of Lamas, in the Andes of Maynas. In each of these three localities, so widely separated, it occupies a very limited area. I again met with it about the lower frontier of the bark region, and on the rivers entering the Gulf of Guayaquil it is so abundant as to form a serious obstruction to navigation, especially in the upper part of their course, where the current is rapid, and canoes ascending the stream must necessarily keep close in shore. Of genera peculiar to the highlands, from 6,000 feet upwards, such as *Hedyotis*, not a single representative was seen. Of plants allied to *Cinchona*, the most remarkable is a fine epiphyte, resembling *Buena* and *Hillia* in the large white salver-shaped odoriferous flowers; but the seeds terminate in a long coma, like those of *Echites*, instead of in a short toothed wing, as in those of *Buena*. The habit of *Buena*, indeed, is so much that of an *Apocynea*, that, when I gathered (near Tarapoto) my first species of that genus, I was surprised to observe the large interpetiolary stipules, and the inferior ovary. There is also a handsome tree, growing from 4,000 feet upwards, perhaps allied to *Lüdenbergia*, but with a curious bilamellate crest on the apex of each segment of the corolla. I have previously gathered a congener at Tarapoto, and another on Tunguragua. Two very fine and closely allied species of the tribe *Gardenieæ*, I can refer to no described genus. One of them has leaves of immense size, near a yard long, and they are aggregated at the apex of a usually simple stem, so as to give it the appearance of a palm. The moment I saw it I recollected having observed the same, or a very similar tree, near Santarem, where I could never find flowers, nor did I meet with it elsewhere on the Amazon.

Loranthaceæ, 1.—A *Loranthus*, with numerous small yellow sweet-scented flowers, growing abundantly, especially on *Inga* trees. There are many other species, but no large-flowered ones.

Aristolochiaceæ, 1.—Two *Aristolochiæ* were seen, but in a barren state. A third species, scarcely referrible to *Aristolochia*, was gathered with young flowers. None of the three was seen climbing on the red bark tree.

Lobeliaceæ, 3.—One *Centropogon* and two *Siphocampyli*. One or two other species of the latter genus were seen. The only *Lobeliacea* I have seen in the plain is *Centropogon Surinamensis*, which I gathered at the foot of the granitic mountain of Imei, at the source of the River Pacimoni.

Valerianaceæ,

Valerianaceæ, 1.—A slender twining *Valeriana*. This genus, absent from the plains, begins to be met with in the hills at about 3,000 feet, and extends thence to the very snow-line, going through more phases in external appearance than I know in any other genus.

Compositæ, 3.—So long as I herborised only in the plains, I could never understand how Humboldt had assigned so large a proportion of equinoctial vegetation to *Compositæ*, for, from the mouth of the Amazon to the cataracts of the Orinoco and the foot of the Andes, with the exception of a few scandent *Vernoniæ* and *Mikaniæ*, and of a few herbs on inundated beaches of the rivers, the species of *Compositæ* that exist are weeds common to many parts of tropical America; nor did I meet with more than one arborescent *Composita* (*Vernonia polycephala*, D. C.) in the whole of that immense area. But in ascending the Andes, from 1,200 feet upwards, *Compositæ* increase in number and variety at every step, and include many arborescent species. About midway of the wooded region, and especially in places where the trees form scattered groves rather than continuous woods, *Compositæ* are more abundant than any other family, both as trees and woody twiners, and in the latter form extend nearly to the limit of arborescent vegetation, especially as species of the fine genus *Mutisia*; while on the rigid *paramos* no frutescent plants ascend higher than the *Chuquiraguas* and *Loricarias*; and as alpine herbs, the *Achyrophori*, *Weneriæ*, &c., reach the very snow-line. In the red bark woods *Compositæ* are plentiful, and I should estimate the number of species at near 50. The trees of this order are chiefly *Vernoniæ*, and they abound most in deserted clearings. During my stay a plot was again brought under cultivation which had remained desert for 12 years, during which period it had become so densely and equably clad with a *Vernonia*, whose slender white stems had reached a height of 40 feet, that at a distance it looked like a plantation. Many of the woody twiners are *Compositæ*, chiefly *Senecionidæ*, and as herbaceous or suffruticose twiners there are several *Mikaniæ*. The young shoots of a species of *Mikania* bear very large cordate leaves, usually white over the veins and purple or violet on the whole under surface; but neither it nor the *Aristolochiæ* are known as "*Guaco*" to the inhabitants, who are all natives of the open highlands, and have as yet found names for few plants in the forest. Among shrubby *Compositæ* I noted some *Eupatoria* and two *Baccharides*, but no *Barnadesia*; nor among herbs any *Gnaphalium*, although on the eastern side of the cordillera the two latter genera descend nearly to 3,000 feet. *Tessaria legitima*, D. C., is abundant by the Rio San Antonio. I have come on this tree in the roots of the cordillera on both sides, by all the streams which have open gravelly or sandy beaches laid under water by occasional or periodical floods. Near Tarapoto, and by the Pastasa, in the forest of Canelos, it grows to a straight little tree of 25 feet, and often forms large continuous beds. It ascends nearly to 6,000 feet, and descends into the plain, following the shores of the Amazon, to a little beyond the Brazilian frontier, where it is diminished to a small bush.

When I arrived at Limon, a large proportion of the *Compositæ* were in flower, but there were so many other and more interesting plants in the same state, that when at length I could have turned my attention to the *Compositæ*, their flowers were mostly already shed, for which reason *Compositæ* are very inadequately represented in my collection.

Apocyneæ, 2.—One *Peschiera* and one *Echites*. This order rarely ascends up out of the hot region in the Andes, and in the temperate region I have seen only a single species.

Asclepiadeæ, 4.—All milky twiners. This order, like the preceding, has its principal seat in the hot region, but is by no means confined to it; for two or three slender *Cynoctona* are frequent in the cooler parts of the Andes, trailing over the hedges of cactus and agave.

Solanaceæ, 5.—In this order, also, my collection contains a very small proportion of the species existing in the Red Bark woods. Shrubby *Solana* are almost endless, and two species rise to trees. Two or three species of *Cestrum* also occur as slender trees.

Cordiaceæ, 1.—A *Cordia*, a stout sarmentose species, which threads about among the trees up to a considerable height, though it never actually twines.

 Convolvulaceæ.—

Convolvulaceæ.—This order seems confined to a couple of *Ipomææ*, both occurring very rarely.

Myrsineæ, 2 (or perhaps 3).—The most remarkable of all the plants I gathered is a *Myrsinea*, though, as it grows only at from 5,000 to 7,000 feet, it barely touches the frontier of the Red Bark region. It is an arbuscule of 8 to 10 feet, bearing a coma of large long deep green coriaceous leaves, so that without flower it has quite the aspect of a *Grias*; but above the leaves there is a mass, the size of the human head, of densely packed panicles and minute flowers, all of the same deep red colour. I have not previously seen any *Myrsinea* at all resembling it in habit; but I have examined it sufficiently to state with confidence that it belongs to this order, although probably an undescribed genus.

Labiatæ, 1.—Besides the solitary species gathered, there exist two species of *Hyptis*, one of them apparently *H. Suaveolens;* but this order is always scantily represented in the forest. In cane-fields at San Antonio I saw a *Stachys* with small white flowers.

Verbenaceæ, 2.—One of them a prickly suffruticose *Lantana*, threading among the bushes up to 18 feet in height; the other a woody twiner, with pretty waxy flowers, flesh-coloured externally, but the limb purple within; it is probably a *Citharexylon*, allied to *C. Scandens*, Benth. (gathered on the Uaupés), though the habit is totally different from the arborescent *Citharexyla* which grow in the cooler parts of the Andes. A *Duranta* was noted at San Antonio. A *Stachytarpheta*, which I take to be *S. Jamaicensis*, and is known in Peru and Ecuador as "*Verbena*," seems to follow the steps of man in the cordillera from near the plain up to 10,000 feet. At Limon it exists sparingly as a weed. Another species of the same genus, with very slender spikes and small lilac flowers, abounds in open places.

Gesneraceæ, 17.—The abundance of this family is one of the distinctive features of the Red Bark woods. One group, comprising several species, has a woody rhizome, creeping up the trees, and a few long sarmentose leafy branches. The leaves of each pair are very unequal, and the smaller one sometimes obsolete; the larger one is long, lance-shaped, and, while the rest of the leaf is green, the apex and sometimes part of the margin are stained of a deep red, so as to resemble a lance dipped in blood, whence the native name, "*punta de lanza.*" The axillary flowers are comparatively inconspicuous, and they are partially concealed by large red or blood-stained bracts; they seem to vary considerably in structure in the different species, but I have scarcely examined them, and cannot, therefore, refer these plants with certainty to their proper genus. Another group, whereof two species were seen and gathered, has the long tubular corolla subtended by pinnatipartite sepals, which are so densely beset with stout jointed hairs as to resemble the calyx of a moss-rose, a peculiarity which I do not find noted in any described species of this order. One of the two is a small under-shrub, with the calyx and corolla yellow; the other a slender herbaceous twiner with a scarlet calyx and a dull violet corolla. An *Achimenes*, with pretty scarlet flowers, abounds along the declivities.

Bignoniaceæ, 2.—The one a *Bignonia*, with round stems; the other an *Amphilophium*, with 6-gonous stems; both twiners. Another *Bignonia* was seen, not in flower. I saw no tree of this order, though *Tecomæ* exist both in the plain, and in the cool hill forests. I have never seen any climbing *Bignoniaceæ* at a greater elevation than about 3,500 feet, but they form a large proportion of the scandent vegetation of the hot plains.

Acanthaceæ, 9.—This order is tolerably abundant, and two under-shrubs growing about the lower boundary of the Bark region bear spikes of large handsome scarlet flowers, in appearance like those of a *Justicia*, but different in character. A *Mendozia*, with woody twining stems and umbels of small white verbena-like flowers, grows everywhere.

Scrophulariaceæ, 4.—All humble herbs, two of them species of *Herpestes*, and all rather scarce.

Of

Of *Ferns* and their allies I gathered the following:—

	Species.		Species.
Equisetum - - - - - -	1	Dictyopteris - - - - - -	1
Lycopodium - - - - - -	2	Goniophlebium - - - - - -	2
Selaginella - - - - - -	6	Campyloneuron - - - - - -	5
Polybotrya - - - - - -	1	Niphobolus - - - - - -	1
Rhipidopteris - - - - - -	1	Pleopeltis - - - - - -	3
Elaphoglossum - - - - - -	5	Anapeltis - - - - - -	3
Lomaria - - - - - -	2	Dipteris - - - - - -	1
Blechnum - - - - - -	1	Aspidium - - - - - -	5
Xiphopteris - - - - - -	1	Nephrodium - - - - - -	6
Gymnopteris - - - - - -	1	Lastrœa - - - - - -	11
Tenitis - - - - - -	3	Nephrolepis - - - - - -	3
Adiantum - - - - - -	6	Davallia - - - - - -	2
Hypolepis - - - - - -	1	Cyathea - - - - - -	1
Pteris (including Litobrochia) - -	5	Hemitelia - - - - - -	1
Meniscium - - - - - -	1	Alsophila - - - - - -	4
Asplenium (including Callipteris, Diplazium, and Oxygonium) - -	21	Gleichenia - - - - - -	1
Hemidyctium - - - - - -	1	Trichomanes - - - - - -	4
Didymochlæna - - - - - -	1	Hymenophyllum - - - - - -	5
Polypodium - - - - - -	4	Lygodium - - - - - -	1
Phegopteris - - - - - -	5	Total - - -	131
Goniopteris - - - - - -	2		

From these should be deducted 10 or 12 species gathered beyond the limits of the Red Bark, which will leave (say) 120 species. Within those limits the following ferns were seen, but not gathered, either because they are common throughout tropical America, or from the specimens being imperfect: *Azolla Magellanica*; *Equisetum*, sp.*; *Pteris aquilina*, var. *caudata*; *Gymnogramme calomelanos*, and another species of that genus (Pl. Exs. 4,153), which grows everywhere in the roots of the cordillera on gravelly beaches; *Cyclopeltis semicordata*, a common fern in the hot and warm regions, wherever there are rocks; a loosely pilose *Pteris*, in very ragged condition, gathered previously at Tarapoto (Pl. Exs., 4,667); a *Dicksonia*, of which I saw only young plants and old frondless trunks; several species of *Elaphoglossum*, of which the fertile fronds were shrivelled up, having been in perfection in the wet season, and two or three *Hymenophylla* in the same state; so that if we make allowance for the few species which must have eluded my search, we may safely assume that I left at least 20 ferns ungathered, and the whole number may be taken at 140, that is, of ferns existing in a space not more than four miles long by three-quarters of a mile broad, or of three square miles. Perhaps few parts of the world possess so many species of ferns growing naturally in so small an area.

The five species of tree-ferns gathered in fruit all grow in tolerable abundance, and one of them, an *Alsophila*, with a trunk 40 feet high, large stout pale green fronds, and exactly opposite pinnæ, is perhaps the handsomest tree-fern I ever saw. The *Cyathea* has almost constantly, below its own fronds, a supplementary crown of numerous deep green widely arched sterile fronds of a *Lomaria*, among which spring vertically the slender pectinate fertile fronds; while the trunk is enveloped in a continuous sheath of the soft, pale, but clear green foliage of *Bartramia viridissima*, C. Müll.; the whole forming one of those lovely pictures, which only those who seek out nature in her remotest recesses are privileged to see.

This *Bartramia* was in good fruit, but the greater part of the mosses had fruited during the rainy season, and the number of species was by no means so great as one would have supposed, to see the dense festoons of moss depending from old trees. They are in main part composed of two or three species, which modern botanists would refer to *Trachypus*, of as many *Meteoria*, and of a *Frullania*. *Rhacopilum tomentosum* is frequent, as it is all through the roots of the cordillera, on both sides; and another *Rhacopilum* (*R. polythrincium*, Ms.) grows in some abundance. *Orthotricha*, common enough in the region of the Hill

* Probably a sterile form of *E. Giganteum*. By the Rio de Tablas it grows to 12 or even 15 feet high.

Hill Barks, scarcely descend below 6,000 feet, and at Limon their place is supplied by *Macromitrium* and *Schlotheimia*, both very sparingly represented. *Hookeriæ*, so abundant and ornamental on the eastern slope of the cordillera, in the same latitude and altitude, barely exist at Limon.

Hepaticæ are rather more varied than mosses, and the genus *Plagiochila*, especially, is well represented. Notwithstanding the vast variety of *Plagiochilæ* I have gathered on the Amazon and on the eastern side of the Andes of Peru and Quito, I still found new forms at Limon. The favourite site of this genus is in the warm and temperate region of the Andes. Lower down the number of species diminishes rapidly, and higher up, towards the limit of the forest, the huge masses of robust *Sendtneræ*, *Lepidoziæ*, and in some places of *Frullaniæ*, leave little room for the delicate *Plagiochilæ*. *Lejeuniæ*, on the contrary, are hot country plants.

Of Lichens, the foliaceous species are remarkably scarce. Epiphyllous lichens, whose abundance and variety is so notable a feature of the vegetation of the Amazon, seem to attain their upper limit in the Red Bark woods. The trunks of the trees are generally too well covered with mosses to leave much room for the development of crustaceous lichens. Still a good many species exist, chiefly *Graphideæ*, and I did not notice any lichen on the Red Bark which does not grow indifferently on other sorts of trees. They present no peculiarity indicative of a tropical country, if I except the occasional occurrence of a red-fruited *Ustalia*, a genus prominent for its abundance and beauty among the epiphlæous lichens of the Amazonian plain. There is sometimes an approach to that whitening of the trees which was one of the first things that took my attention on the Amazon, where one sees trunks so completely and uniformly invested by the shining white crust of lichens (mostly *Graphideæ*) that at a little distance it might be mistaken for the epiderm.

Reserving the important subject of climate to be last discussed, I resume my narrative of operations.

In the month of July, two young men at Limon, who were owing money to Dr. Neyra, determined to go in search of Bark trees, and I offered to pay them liberally if they should find any seeds or seedling plants for me. They returned from the forest after an absence of seven days, having seen neither Bark trees nor seedlings, and the weather, they said, was too foggy and wet to renew the search with any chance of success. Nevertheless, we planned an expedition in quest of plants, which Dr. Taylor was to conduct, accompanied by two Indians to carry provisions, and a man of Limon to act as guide. But when everything was in readiness for their starting, a report reached us that an Englishman, bringing with him a number of boxes, had arrived at Ventanas. On the strength of this I immediately sent Dr. Taylor thither with horses, and he had the great satisfaction of finding the Englishman to be Mr. Cross. Ventanas, however, was so full of soldiery, and was so likely to be soon the theatre of a conflict (for the opposing army lay encamped only a few leagues lower down the river), that Dr. Taylor very wisely had the materials for the Wardian cases removed about three hours' journey up the river, to a farm called Aguacatál, where they were not likely to be molested.

Mr. Cross had had all sorts of obstacles thrown in his way by the forces that held the river, and with the greatest difficulty had found men to row his canoes, so that the distance from Guayaquil to Ventanas (which appears so short on the map) had taken him 13 days to travel. He finally reached Limon on the 27th of July, looking pale and thin from his recent illness, and from the sleepless nights passed on the river, but anxious to set to work immediately. We had no young plants for him, nor any expectation of obtaining them, but I was satisfied that cuttings would succeed, although it would necessarily be a tedious process to root them well. The owner of the *chacra* of Oso-cabuitu showed me some sprigs, cut from an old stool of red bark, which he had stuck into the ground by a watercourse four months previously, and they had all rooted well. Mr. Cross also agreed with me that the success of the process was certain, and that the question was merely one of time, which only experience could solve. After reposing the following day (Sunday), we had a piece of ground fenced in, and Mr. Cross made a pit, and prepared the soil to receive the cuttings, of which he put in above a thousand on the 1st of August and following days. He afterwards

wards put in a great many more, subjecting them to various modes of treatment; and he went round to all the old stools, and put in as many layers from them as possible; but only those who have attempted to do anything in the forest, possessing scarcely any of the necessary appliances, and obliged to supply them as far as possible from the forest itself, can have any idea of the difficulties to be surmounted. Glass was the only thing for which we could find no substitute, and to get up to Limon the glasses of the Wardian cases was not to be thought of, over roads so strait and rough, where even the surest footed beast goes on continually stumbling. So we made our frames of palm-fronds, our buckets of bamboos, and invented similar contrivances for other needful articles. The closed communication with Guayaquil was felt to be a sore obstacle, as we might have sent thither for canvass and other things required for the plants, and also for a little wine and porter for the invalids.

The mornings were always cool and sometimes dull, but at seven o'clock or so, the sun would often come out blazing hot. In the afternoons, when the fog seemed to have set in for the day, it would sometimes clear away for a brief space, and admit the scorching rays of the sun. On these occasions, and on the days of sustained heat, the only means of keeping the plants from withering was to give them abundance of water; and then there was the risk, on the other hand, of their damping off. Water was supplied to the *trapiche*, for the service of the still and for culinary purposes, by a small *acéquia* (canal) carried along the hill side from the head of a rivulet about a mile off. We had by this means generally sufficient water for our plantation, but as the *acéquia* was ill-made and protected by no fence, the cattle, roaming about, generally trod and dammed it up at least once every day, when the Indians had to seek out and repair the damaged spots. But when the supply of water failed just at the moment of one of those outbursts of sun, there was no alternative but for all hands to run with buckets down to the deep glen, where there was a considerable stream, although the steep ascent from it was very toilsome. In a few weeks the cuttings began to root, and then they were attacked by caterpillars, which also had to be combated. In short, it is impossible to detail here all the obstacles encountered, and which only Mr. Cross's unremitting watchfulness enabled him to surmount. As his labours have been crowned by success, he may perhaps give a separate account of them, which will necessarily be fuller and more accurate than any I could furnish.

The passage of troops still went on for some days after Mr. Cross's arrival at Limon. A good deal of rain had fallen in the upper woody region, and the roads were horrible. The poor beasts of burden, ill-treated and with their heavy loads ill-adjusted, had their backs worn into sores, and many of them sunk under their burdens. Wherever a beast gave in, there it was turned adrift. In the warm forest, maggots soon filled their sores and ate into their very entrails; so, after wandering about for a time, most pitiable objects, they at length nearly all died. Between Guaranda and Ventanas not fewer than 300 dead horses and mules strewed the track and the adjacent forest, and above 20 carcasses were laid within nose-shot of our hut. I set the Indians to roll them into ditches and hollows, and cover them with branches and earth, but the horrid smell turned their stomachs, and they never half performed the task. During the day, whilst we were going about, we did not feel so much inconvenience, but, when the night breeze filled our hut with the vile odour, we found it impossible to sleep. Now, I smoked awhile, and then I lay down, covering my face with a handkerchief wetted with camphorated spirit, but all in vain. When I considered the fate of those poor animals, and still more that of their unfortunate owners, from whom they had been taken by force, and who, in losing perhaps their only mule, had no means left of conveying to market the produce of their industry, and thereby supporting their families, it will not be wondered at that I cursed in my heart all revolutions. Grave, indeed, must be the motive of complaint, which a people can have against its rulers, to justify it in taking up arms to obtain redress.*

Towards

* I may here relate an incident bearing on the same subject. Whilst Dr. Taylor was bringing up Mr. Cross from Ventanas, a body of some 800 men, whose commander I had known at Ambato, arrived from Guaranda. As usual, they bivouacked at Limon, and when I turned out on the following morning, I saw my four Indians prisoners in the hands of the soldiery, and one of them, with his hands tied behind him and a rope round his body, about to be dragged off towards Ventanas.

Towards the end of July the weather took up, and in a few sunny days the fruit of the bark trees made visible advances towards maturity. On the 13th of August I noticed that the finest capsules were beginning to burst at the base, and on the following day I had all taken off that seemed ripe, gathering them in this way,—an Indian climbed the tree, and breaking the panicles gently off, let them fall on sheets spread on the ground to receive them, so that the few loose seeds shaken out by the fall were not lost.* The capsules were afterwards spread out to dry on the same sheets, and the drying occupied from two to ten days. The first seeds were gathered at Limon on the 14th, and the last on the 29th of August. Early in September they were all dry.

Mr. Cross sowed, on the 16th of August, eight of the seeds I had gathered; one of them began to germinate on the fourth day, and at the end of a fortnight four seeds had pushed their radicles. On the 6th of September one had the seed leaves completely developed, and by the 9th of the same month, or on the 25th day after sowing, the last of the eight seeds pushed its radicle. One of the seedlings was afterwards lost by an accident, but the remaining seven formed healthy little plants, and, when embarked at Guayaquil, along with the rooted cuttings and layers, bid as fair as any of the latter to reach India alive. He had previously sown, at Guayaquil, eight *Cinchona* seeds gathered by me in 1859, and which had remained nine months in my herbarium; even of these, four germinated, and the remaining four might possibly have grown also, had they not been carried off by mice. It is, therefore, clearly proved that well ripened and properly dried seeds do not lose their vitality for a much longer period than their excessive delicacy would lead one to suspect.

Before gathering the seeds at Limon, I had cast about to see if there were any seeds to be had elsewhere. From Camaron I learnt that the few shoots from old stools that existed in the valleys to the east and north-east of that site were all far too young to bear fruit; but I ascertained that fruit had been observed in the valley of San Antonio, on a few young trees that still existed there. After bringing up Mr. Cross, Dr. Taylor went to Guaranda to purchase provisions, and on his return I despatched him to Tabacál, a cane-farm belonging to Dr. Neyra, about a league below San Antonio. Tabacál proved still more unhealthy than Limon, and Dr. Taylor had scarcely arrived there when he was taken ill, had to bleed himself, and finally to go to Riobamba in quest of remedies.† On his return the capsules were still green, and, as there was reason to fear they might fall off without ripening, he went over to Limon to consult with me. The result of our consultation was that he should remain at Limon to assist Mr. Cross, and that I should go to Tabacál, whither I accordingly proceeded on the 12th and 13th of September. The distance is really very short, perhaps not more than 12 or 15 miles in a direct line; but there is no road thither unless by way of Guaranda, which would take four days. I followed the route already taken

---

Ventanas. Among the beasts of burden which accompanied the troops, this poor fellow had recognised his own mule,—his *only* mule,—as dear to *him* as Sancho's ass was to Sancho, and, with the aid of his companions, had contrived to abstract it during the night, and hide it away in the forest. In the morning the mule was missed, and my Indians were immediately denounced as the delinquents, for they had been seen handling the mule the previous evening. I confess my indignation was at that moment at the boiling point, and I wished for a hundred "Rifle Volunteers," to put the whole disorderly rabble to rout. However, I had given up half my dormitory to the colonel, and had treated him with as much hospitality as lay in my power, so that I had some right to expect he would not deny any request of mine; and, accordingly, after a short parley with him, he ordered the Indians to be released. Thus I kept my Indians, and the Indian kept his mule, which was all we wanted.

* This process was not unattended with risk to the Indian, on account of the brittleness of the branches of the Bark tree. One small tree had had so much bark stripped off near the root that it was much decayed at that part, and began to crack when the Indian attempted to climb it; so, with the consent of the owner, I had it cut down to obtain the few good capsules it bore. It was one of four shoots from a large old stool, the other three shoots having been previously cut down. Its entire length was 33 feet, and to first branch 18 feet; circumference near base, 12 inches; bark cracked longitudinally, scarcely transversely; rings too obscure to be counted.

† About the end of August, whilst Dr. Taylor was at Tabacál, seven cascarilleros, who had obtained leave of temporary absence from military service, came to Limon, and started for the hills, between the valley of Chasuán and that of Tablas. They were absent 14 days, during which time they found but three Bark trees, the largest of which they calculated might yield three quintals of dry bark; they did not see seeds on any of them, nor had they fallen in with any young plants. They ought to have gone again to get the bark, but what with the war which still continued to rage, and the rainy weather which set in at the end of September, the trees were left to stand until another year.

taken by Dr. Taylor, namely, along the path to Guaranda as far as the crest of the first ridge, and thence down to some cane-farms on the Rio de Tablas, considerably lower than the place where we had bivouacked in the month of June. Thus far there was some sort of track, but from Tablas to Tabacál, across the high ridge separating the two valleys, there had been none until Dr. Taylor opened one with the aid of an Indian. So far as I could judge from the vegetation, Tablas is about 5,000 feet high. *Cinchona magnifolia* grows abundantly, and extends some way further up the valley; and at half a league further down, I saw two trees of *C. Succirubra*, but both unfertile.

The farm of Tabacál is at a height of 2,403 feet above the sea. The valley of San Antonio opens out there into a broad basin (evidently once a lake), but again contracts about a mile lower down, between cliffs of the same trachyte and ferruginous sandstone as exist at Limon. At the upper end of the basin, a mile and a half from the farm-house, the road from Guayaquil to Guaranda leaves the bank of the river and ascends the steep *cuesta* of San Antonio, whose foot is about 2,500 feet above the sea, coinciding remarkably with the height of the foot of the *cuesta* of Limon. The river is from five to ten yards wide, and about three feet deep, but three or four feet deeper in the rainy season, when the broad beaches, strewed with blocks and rounded fragments of granite, are inundated. Along the beaches extend straggling thickets of a *Myrica*, a *Psidium*, *Muntingia Calaburu*, *Tessaria legitima*, and several other trees and shrubs indicated in the foregoing enumeration. In little pools float a *Callitriche*, an *Azolla*, and a *Riccia*. On stones in the stream itself the scorched remains of *Podostemeæ* were abundant.

The Red Bark tree grows here and there in the valley, beyond the beaches, and up the cuesta to above the church of San Antonio.* The ground is everywhere stony, and both the site and climate are evidently less favourable than at Limon, for the Bark trees are more stunted and the fruits much more backward. There is a penetrating coolness in the wind at Tabacál and San Antonio, which the indications of the thermometer do not explain, though its effects are sensible enough, not only on man, but on other animals and on plants. Agues and slow-continued fevers prevail throughout the year, but especially in the rainy season. There are scarcely any cockroaches or house-flies at Tabacál, nor did I see or hear in the adjacent woods any monkeys, parrots, or toucans. A good many of the capsules of the Red Bark had dried up while still unripe, and of those which had ripened some had burst open during the few days that intervened between Dr. Taylor's leaving Tabacál and my arriving there; but happily very few seeds were shed, and in gathering the capsules I profited by my experience at Limon, that the seeds rarely fell out for two or three days after the capsules burst, and that the latter closed up again with the dews of night.† So by gathering the capsules at daybreak not a seed fell out, nor was there any need for the precaution (which, however, I still observed) of extending sheets whereon to receive the capsules when thrown down from the trees. I took off the first capsules at San Antonio on the 14th, and the last on the 19th of September.

I had now gathered about 2,500 well-grown capsules (without enumerating many smaller ones), namely, 2,000 from ten trees at Limon, and 500 from five trees at San Antonio. Good capsules contain 40 seeds each; in some I have counted 42; so that I calculated I had (in round numbers) at least 100,000 well-ripened and well-dried seeds. Some small turgid (almost globose) capsules contained only from two to four seeds, as large and ripe as any in the largest capsules, while other capsules of the ordinary length, but slender, proved to contain only abortive seeds, and were accordingly rejected in the drying. Had the month of July been as sunny as it is said usually to be, many more capsules would doubtless have ripened; as it was, only about one flower in ten produced ripe seeds.

I had scarcely finished drying my seeds at Tabacál, when I received the welcome intelligence that the army of General Flores had obtained possession of Guayaquil,

* Of the once large village of San Antonio nothing now remains but the church, and the few existing inhabitants of the parish are scattered about in farms.

† The placentas generally fall out along with the seeds, but they are rarely ejected by the bursting of the capsule. The old empty capsules continue to hang on, sometimes, until the trees blossom again.

Guayaquil, and that the communication between the coast and the interior was re-opened. I therefore resolved to proceed to Guayaquil, and despatch from thence a portion of my seeds by the first opportunity.

I started from Tabacál on 28th September. The road thence to Guayaquil follows the right bank of the river, as far as to where the latter is confined to a deep chasm (to avoid which some rough ground has to be climbed), and then crosses to the left bank. The descent is really very gradual, but seems more steep than it really is, because the river tosses and foams among the huge stones which impede its course. As we descended, it was interesting to mark the gradual transition to the vegetatiou of the hot region. Leguminous trees, so scarce in the hills, began to be frequent. A bombaceous tree (*Chorisiæ*, sp.) here and there adorned the forest with its numerous purple flowers. *Cinchona magnifolia* was budding for flower; it accompanied me to within 1,000 feet of the plain. Enormous figs, with a long cone of exserted roots, straddled over the decayed remains, or often only over the site of the tree which had served to support them in their infancy, and which they had strangled to death after establishing for themselves a separate existence.

At about 1,500 feet elevation, I met a *Myristica*, which by the leaves I could not distinguish from that form of *M. sebifera*, which has been called *M. Mœsa* by Pöeppig, and which grows about Tarapoto, at the same altitude. A little lower down I saw the first *Neea*, and near it a *Vismia*, not one of those weedy species diffused throughout tropical America, but a handsome tree, resembling *V. uvulifera* (from the *Casiquiarc*). These three genera seem rarely to ascend above the hot region.

Five leagues below Tabacál the road again passes by a broad pebbly ford, to the right bank at Pozuelos, where we drew up for the night, thoroughly wetted by a soaking shower, which had accompanied us for the last hour and a half. Pozuelos is a miserable little bamboo village, but notable for its extensive orangeries, which produce the finest fruit in Ecuador. Here the valley opens out wide, and by an almost imperceptible descent mingles gradually with the plain. The river becomes muddy, still, and tolerably deep, much like the Wharfe at Tadcaster. The vegetation is now unmistakeably tropical, and there is as noble forest around Pozuelos as I have anywhere seen. Palms are far less varied than on the Amazon, but the *Attalea* above-mentioned grows immensely tall and stout. An *Astrocaryum*, whose clustered trunks are perfect *chevaux-de-frise*, from the long flat prickles with which they are beset, is very frequent. *Mimosœ* are abundant, and so are papilionaceous twiners, among which I noted an *Ecastaphyllum*. The beautiful arborescent *Passiflora* (*Astrophea*) grows far larger than at San Antonio, and I could not help now and then stopping my horse under its stems, which here and there bent gracefully over our path, to admire the large pendulous glaucous leaves and the clusters of white flowers; but I sought in vain for ripe berries. In marshy places there are beds of rank ferns (*Lastrœœ* and *Diplazia*), and in pools an *Eichhornia* and a *Pontederia*. The common weeds of hot countries begin to appear, such as *Asclepias curassavica* and *Tiaridium Indicum*, the latter of which I had not seen since leaving the Amazon.

A few leagues below Pozuelos the forest gets gradually lower, until at length we emerge on broad savannahs covered with *gamalote*, in which there are only scattered trees or distant groves of *Cratœva tapioides* and a *Cochlospermum*, and along the streams dense entangled thickets. Multitudes of fine sleek horses roam over the savannahs, but the few cows that are to be seen are very lean, the foliage of the *gamalote* being too harsh for them, although not for the horses.

Bodegas, which we reached towards night of the 29th, is a small town at the confluence of the river of Bodegas (or Babahoyo) with that of Ventanas (or Caracol), their united waters constituting what most foreigners consider the river of Guayaquil, though the natives call it merely the Rio Grande, and limit the name " Ria * de Guayaquil " to the estuary, from the mouth of the river Daule (just above the city) down to the ocean. In the rainy season, the site of Bodegas is a large lake, and only the upper storeys of the houses are inhabitable, the lower storeys being deep under water. The communication with Guayaquil (distant 45 miles)

* " Ria " corresponds to " flumen," as " rio" to " fluvium."

45 miles) is maintained by means of a small steamer, but it had been hired by the Government for the conveyance of troops, and its movements were very uncertain. I was detained until October 6th, awaiting its arrival at Bodegas, and about midnight of the same day I reached Guayaquil.

I found Guayaquil in some confusion, and crowded with people; besides the number of troops that still occupied it, there was so great an influx of visitors from the interior and from foreign ports, on account of the renewal of the commerce, which had been long suspended, that I with great difficulty found a lodging. I then immediately set to work to pack up my seeds, and to draw up a brief report, to accompany parcels of them which I had been instructed to forward to the Royal Gardens at Kew, and to Jamaica. These I despatched by the steamer for Panamá on the 14th of the same month.

Before I left Tabacál a note from Mr. Cross, brought by one of the Indians, informed me that all was going on well, but he could still give no definite opinion as to how long the plants would take to become strong enough to travel. I therefore waited as patiently as I could for further news from him, which was rather difficult to obtain, as there were no means of communicating with Limon, except by way of Guaranda. I was so cramped for room that I could not open out and arrange the dried plants I had brought with me; and as this was almost the only occupation in which I could have employed myself, I soon grew heartily sick of Guayaquil, although the place is lively enough, not only from a good deal of traffic concentrated in a small space, but from almost daily fires (to which the frail materials of which the houses are constructed render it constantly liable), from frequent earthquakes, and from occasional revolutions. On one day, the 12th of October, we had four earthquake shocks, and along the coast, as at Manta, seven shocks were felt the same day. A violent shock at 2 p.m., of October 26th, shook a good deal of plaster from the walls. It is, however, wonderful to see how far these wooden houses will bend over and rise up again. At length, in November, I heard from my companions in the forest, that by the end of the month they calculated the plants would be sufficiently rooted to travel. I therefore resolved to proceed to Aguacatal, so as to have the Wardian cases put together, and a raft constructed there in readiness to receive the plants.

On November 24th I proceeded to Bodegas. There was then no obstacle to the navigation of the river, but as almost everybody was going to a feast in a neighbouring village, I had much difficulty the following day in procuring a canoe and a couple of men to take me up to Aguacatal, where I arrived at 3 p.m. of the 27th.

For two nights previous to my leaving Guayaquil slight showers had fallen, but in the forests, in the roots of the Cordillera, a good deal of rain had already fallen, and the rivers were rising. The flow of the tide extended to only half a league above Bodegas, though in the height of summer it reaches halfway to Ventanas, or nearly to the point where the mud on the beaches begins to be mixed with small pebbles. Between Ventanas and Aguatacal there are two short rapids over gravel, and ascending still higher the stones become gradually larger and more numerous, though the river is still of considerable volume, and sufficiently open to admit of being navigated by large rafts. From about five leagues below Ventanas upwards, there is no more savannah, and there are fine cacao plantations along the riverside, but by no means continuously. Aguacatal consists chiefly of one large farm-house, and of several smaller ones scattered along the bank, so that there is quite a little colony, and, singularly enough, nearly all the inhabitants are descendants of two Chinese, brought hither from Manilla in the time of the Spaniards. Their industry is almost limited to the cultivation of cacao, and of a small proportion of coffee, but their thriftier habits enable them to live much more comfortably than the lazy descendants of liberated Africans, who constitute the majority of the squatters in the plain. The materials for the cases had been deposited at the farm-house, where I accordingly took up my residence, and from whose owner, Don Matias de la Cruz (son of one of the afore-mentioned Chinese), I received great kindness and assistance. At Ventanas I found a negro carpenter to aid me in putting the cases together, but he was used to only rough work, and to nails of the largest calibre, so that if I had not put in most of the nails with my own hands, the cases would have been split in pieces. This taskoccupied me two days, and I then cast about for a raft. Hands were scarce, and I found that to cut down the needful balsa trees

and

and bamboos, and drag them to the beach, would be a work of some time and expense; so, by Don Matias's advice, I bought of an old negro, who lived a long way higher up the river, a raft he had just completed, with the intention of selling or hiring it to some one who had cacao to take to Guayaquil. The usual price was 100 dollars (which included the pay and keep of the raftsmen on the voyage), but on my representation that my cargo would be less trouble to him than cacao, he agreed to let me have the raft for 90 dollars.

Rafts for conveying cacao to Guayaquil are denominated according to the number of *cargas* (or loads) they are made to carry. A *carga* of cacao is 90 lbs. weight at the farm, but on reaching Guayaquil the Church puts in its decimating hand, and reduces the *carga* to 81 lbs. Hence a *Balsa de cien cargas* is one made to carry 9,000 lbs. of cacao, and similarly of a balsa of 200 or 400 *cargas*, which last is the largest size that can navigate the river Ventanas. The raft I purchased was of 250 *cargas*, and it proved of exactly the dimensions we needed for accommodating the plant-cases, and giving us space for cooking and sleeping. It was composed of 12 trunks of raft-wood, 63 to 66 feet long, and about a foot in diameter, ranged longitudinally, so as to occupy a width of 15 feet, and kept in their places by five shorter pieces tied transversely and widely apart, extending nearly to the root end of the trunks, but leaving a considerable space free towards their point, for the convenience of working the raft. The five cross pieces were covered with bamboo planking, so as to form a floor 36 feet long by 10½ feet broad, which was fenced round with rails to a height of three feet, and the whole roofed over and thatched with leaves of *Maranta Vijao*. For carrying cacao, the fence has to be lined with bamboo boards, so as to form, with the flooring, a sort of large bin. The rope used in binding together the constituent parts of the raft was the twining stem of a *Bignonia*, nearly terete, but marked by four raised lines, overlying four deep grooves in the substance of the stem, and alternating with four shallower grooves. When the stem is twisted to enable it to be tied, it splits lengthwise along those grooves into eight strips, which, however, still pull together, and offer very great resistance to transverse fracture.*

The cases were all in readiness, and the raft brought down the river and moored in front of the farm-house, but Mr. Cross did not arrive with the plants until the 13th of December. Some difficulty had been experienced in procuring the requisite number of beasts of burden, and the making of cylindrical baskets to contain the plants had proved a tedious task; besides that, the tying up each plant in wet moss, and the packing them in the baskets, were delicate operations, which Mr. Cross could trust to no hands but his own. There had been not a few falls on the way, and some of the baskets had got partially crushed by the wilfulness of the bulls in running through the bush; but the greater part of the plants turned out wonderfully fresh. We had the cases taken down to the raft, and Don Matias lent us a couple of men to carry thither the earth, sand, and dead leaves necessary for making the soil to put in the cases. Mr. Cross put as many plants into the cases as he could possibly find room for, and only rejected a few that were so much injured by their journey from Limon that they were not likely to survive the voyage to India, the whole number put in being 637. As we might expect some rough treatment on the descent to Guayaquil, we did not venture to put on the glasses, but in their stead stretched moistened strips of calico over the cases, which seemed to answer admirably. As Mr. Cross wished the plants to be firmly established in their new residence before moving them from Aguacatal, I determined to delay our departure until the latest possible moment;

---

* I have long known that the strongest of all *lianas* are *Bignonias*, and I have many times trusted my life and goods to their strength. In the "*malos pasos*" of the Huallaga, canoes are dragged up the most dangerous places by means of from one to four stems of *Bignonia*, according to the size of the canoe and the weight of its cargo. I have never known the *lianas* to break, and as I have sat in my canoe, anxiously watching its slow upward progress, my only care was that the *lianas* were securely fastened to the prow, or lest the sudden bursting of a whirlpool beneath the canoe should tear them from the hands of the Indians, as they with difficulty held their way along the rocky shore.

In the Guayaquil district, as on the Amazon, the aërial roots of various *Aroideæ* and *Carludovicæ* are the common substitutes for string, but *Bignonia* stems are always preferred, wherever strength is essential. Of all the Aroideous roots, the strongest seem to be those of the curious genus *Heteropsis* (*Timbotitica* of the Amazon, *Támshi* of Maynas). At Limon and San Antonio, as already mentioned, the trigonous stems of a *Paullinia* supply the place of string.

moment; that is to say, so as to reach Guayaquil and fasten up the cases before the arrival of the steamer of the 28th.

During my stay at Aguacatal, I made a small collection of plants, and copious notes on the character of the vegetation; but although a comparison of the latter made at the mouth of the Chasuán, and perhaps not 150 feet above the sea-level, with those made higher up the same stream, in the region of the Red Bark, could not fail to be interesting, I omit them here, in order not to swell out further this report, already of an inordinate length. Two facts only I will mention—1st, on the broad stony beach at Aguacatal, *Salix Humboldtiana*, *Adenaria purpurata*, and *Tessaria legitima* grew together in such abundance that I could almost fancy myself still on the Amazon, about the mouth of the Huallaga, where those three plants grew together in precisely the same way; 2nd, in the woods behind Aguacatal I saw a few young trees of the *Jéve*, or india-rubber tree, which formerly abounded throughout the upper part of the Guayaquilian plain, but has now become very scarce from the barbarous custom of cutting down the trees to obtain the milk, instead of tapping them, as in Brazil. From the accounts previously given to me of this tree, I was prepared to find it something very different from the *Siphoniæ* of the Amazon, and a sight of it showed at once that it was an *Artocarpea*. It is said to grow to an immense tree, but the largest specimen I saw did not exceed 60 feet, and it had on it female flowers and fruit. In habit and in the structure of the involucres, it reminds me most of *Naucleopsis*. From *Brosimum* it is distinct enough by the multiflorous receptacles, but it should be compared to Aublet's *Perebea*.* The milk is nauseous, not sweet-tasted as in *Siphonia*, and it contains only 30 per cent. of pure caoutchouc. Whether from some peculiarity in the chemical constitution of the milk, or whether the same thing would take place with the *Siphoniæ*, I know not, but it is a singular fact, that if taken up the Andes immediately after being collected it does not coagulate there. Señor Cordovez, who has an india-rubber manufactory at Ambato, keeps the milk of the *Jéve* in hide vats in an open corridor, where it retains its fluidity for two months at the least.

After my arrival at Aguacatal the weather was occasionally showery, but the rains were evidently heavier towards the source of the river, which would suddenly rise several feet, and then rapidly lower again; so that we had to watch our raft night and day, lest on the one hand it should be carried away by the floods or the onslaughts of driftwood, or on the other hand should be left high and dry by the sudden receding of the waters. At 11 P.M. of December 22d, heavy rain came on at Aguacatal, and did not cease until 9 A.M. of the following day, when the river had risen much, and continued rising through the day; the next night still heavier rain fell, clearing off at about 8 A.M. of the 24th, which was the day fixed for starting on our voyage. Our raftsmen were three in number, as far as to Bodegas, but thence to Guayaquil, where the river is wider, and is therefore not subject to sudden rises and falls, we needed only two. As soon as the rain ceased, we got the glasses of the cases put on board, and when our raftsmen had taken their last "trago" with their friends, and said their last "Adios," (always a lengthy process) we left Aguacatal; Don Matias, at parting, foretelling us a speedy but perilous voyage.

The oars used in navigating these rafts are merely bamboos, about 20 feet long,

* Desirous of leaving the analysis of the flowers and fruits to better hands, I have not yet examined them; but I add here my notes made from the living plant, which, along with my specimens, may enable the genus and species to be correctly determined:—

Arbor 60—100 pedalis, *ramis* primariis secundariisque subconfertis, angulum acutum adscendentibus, pinnatim ramulosis. *Cortex* caudicis subsulcata, ramulorum cicatricibus stipularum oblique annulata. *Ramulorum* apice crescentium pars novella distiche foliosa pilis breviusculis ferrugineis pilosa. *Succus* turbide lactens copiosus sapore amaro-acrido.

Folia cujusque ramuli sub 10, petiolo brevi $\frac{1}{2}$—$\frac{3}{4}$ unciali piloso, media $11\frac{1}{2} \times 5\frac{3}{4}$ unc. (inferiora sensim minora) elongato-oblonga acute apiculata basi profunde cordata, denticulata, dentibus singulis fasciculum pilorum gerentibus, subcoriacea, supra sparse strigillosa læte viridia, subtus pallidiora ad venas elevato-reticulatas ferrugineo-pilosa; *venæ* primariæ sub 20-jugæ angulo 80° e costa egredientes, sensim sursum curvatæ, prope marginem subito arcuato-anostomosantes; venæ intermediæ sub-quaternæ mox cum venis secundariis crebriusculis obliquis anostomosantes.

Stipulæ $2\frac{3}{4} \times 1\frac{1}{2}$ unc. amplexanti-convolutivæ tenues pallidæ pilosæ deciduissimæ, venis 20 longitudinalibus a basi ad apicem usque percursæ.

Receptacula ad axillas foliorum annotinorum (sæpius jam decisorum) sessilia, solitaria, ad *Anonarum* fructûs instar squamosa, diametro semunciali, fructu aucta.

Fructus baccati in massam fere hemisphæricam concreti, aurantiaci miniative, insipidi.

long, half their thickness being cut away for about a yard at the outer end, so as to form a sort of scoop. Two oars were fixed in the prow, and a third oar in the stern, the latter being worked by the old black who had sold me the raft. The river had risen almost to its winter level, and we swept along rapidly. At 2 P.M. we were already eight leagues away from Aguacatal, near a site called Cataráma, below which the river is narrowed in some places to 30 yards, and the navigable channel is further straitened by the trees (chiefly species of *Inga*), which hang far over the water. Add to this that the river ran like a sluice, and that the turns were frequent and abrupt, and it will be seen how difficult it was to maintain our clumsy craft always in the mid-stream. Although the men tugged hard at their oars, they could not save us from being frequently brushed by the trees; and at length, at a sharp turn, the raft went dead on, and through a mass of branches and twiners that hung over to the middle of the river. The effect was tremendous; the heavy cases were hoisted up and dashed against each other; the roof of our cabin smashed in; and the old pilot was for some moments so completely involved in the branches and the wreck of the roof, that I expected nothing but that he had been carried away. He held on, however, and at last emerged, panting and perspiring, but with no further injury than a smart flogging from the twigs, which, indeed, none of us entirely escaped. There have been instances on this river of a man being hooked up bodily by the formidable *Uncaria Guianensis*, and suspended in mid-air, whilst the raft passed from under him.

Our deck now presented a lamentable sight, but we had little time for ascertaining the amount of damage, as at every turn a similar peril awaited us. We, in fact, twice again ran into the bush, not quite so violently as before, but each time adding to the damage already sustained. We had calculated on reaching Caracol that day, and might still have done so before nightfall, but that there were some bad turns ahead, which, as the men were already much fatigued, we could not expect to pass without very great risk; so at 4½ P.M. we brought to, with some difficulty, at a place where the bank was free from trees, and made fast for the night. We then set to work to clear away the wreck of sticks and leaves which strewed the raft, and to repair the roof, which was completed by moonlight. The cases had received only a few slight cracks, and had none of them turned over, but the leaves of the precious plants were sorely maltreated. The night was fortunately dry, but we slept little, for if the river had gone down much in the night there was great danger of part of the bank falling in and swamping the raft, and at every bit of loose earth that fell, I turned out to see if any more considerable fall was to be apprehended. The river, however, remained stationary, and early in the morning we resumed our voyage, Mr. Cross lending the aid of his strong arms to the stern oar. As far as Caracol the river continued narrow and winding, and at various points we barely cleared the bushes, but nothing more serious happened to us than the loss of a few loose cloths, which were hooked up by a pendulous mass of the *Uncaria*. From Caracol downwards the river grew wider, and the banks were less overhung with wood, so that we went on with more security. We passed Bodegas a little after noon, and continued on down the river of Guayaquil. Soon after nightfall we had got as far as to where the influence of the tide was still felt, and as it was ebbing, we profited by it to hold on our way until two o'clock of the following morning, when the flood tide obliged us to lay by. Thenceforward we got on slowly, on account of having to wait between tides; but we reached Guayaquil at noon, on the 27th, without any further accident, and I immediately went on shore and sought out a carpenter, to assist Mr. Cross in nailing laths over the soil and in fixing on the sashes. By 5 P.M. of the 28th everything was completed. The plants, thanks to Mr. Cross's tender care of them, bore scarcely any traces of the rough treatment they had undergone in their descent from Limon, and in their late voyage from Aguacatal, and the only thing against them was that they were growing too rapidly, owing to the increased temperature to which they had lately been subjected. We had the cases put on board a launch and conveyed alongside the mole, to be in readiness for embarking on the steamer which was expected that night.

The steamer we were awaiting usually entered Guayaquil, on her way from Panamá southward, at 6 to 8 P.M. of the 28th of each month, and, after taking on board the mails, &c., sailed again before daybreak. At Payta she left that part of her cargo destined for Panamá, to be picked up by a steamer from Lima,

which

which passed Payta on the 1st of the month, *en route* for Panamá, but did not touch at Guayaquil. However, the Panamá steamer did not come in until the night of the 31st, all too late to catch the Lima steamer at Payta, having been detained at Panamá (as we afterwards learnt) four days, awaiting the overdue Atlantic mails. On the 30th a large goods steamer came in, which goes to and fro between Lima and Guayaquil. She was not to sail again until the 2d of January, and the plants, if sent by her, would have to remain at Payta until the 13th or 14th, when another steamer should pass from Lima to Panamá; but, as there was no alternative, we had them put on board her, and commodiously arranged on the poop-deck. I then took leave of Mr. Cross and the plants, satisfied that so long as they were under his care, they were likely to go on prosperously, and having done all I could on my part to conduct the enterprise to a successful issue. During its performance, all engaged in it had run frequent risk of life and limb; but a far greater source of anxiety to me were the *contretemps* (a few only of which have been indicated in the preceding pages) that every now and then threatened to bring our work to nought. It is difficult for those who live in a country of peace and plenty, but above all of good roads, to appreciate the obstacles that beset all undertakings in countries where none of those blessings exist. Most fervently do I desire that the experiment of forming plantations of cinchonas in the East Indian possessions of the British Crown may be successful. I have seen enough of collecting the products of the forest to convince me, that *whatever vegetable substance is needful to man, he must ultimately cultivate the plant producing it.* Whilst the demand for such precious substances as Peruvian bark, sarsaparilla, caoutchouc, &c. must necessarily go on increasing, the supply yielded by the forest will decrease, and ultimately fail. My operations in the Red Bark woods have only partially opened the eyes of the Ecuatoreans to this fact, but have in a high degree excited their jealousy, at the prospect of another nation participating in the possession of a treasure which they have not known how to preserve from deterioration and proximate destruction, but which, with a little foresight, might have been rendered an endless source of wealth to their country. The proof of this jealousy may be seen in the following extracts from a decree promulgated by the Convention of Ecuador, under date 1st May 1861:—

"The National Convention of Ecuador considering,—

"1. That only three American nations possess in their forests the precious quina tree:

"2. That this territorial wealth, having been at the mercy of all kinds of speculations, has fallen into disrepute, and that those who work on it are laying waste the quina-bearing forests, both those belonging to the nation and those which are private property, without any profit either to the latter or to the public treasury,—

"Decrees:

"Art. 1. The Executive shall ordain the necessary regulations to compel those who cut down quina trees to plant, around each tree cut down, six plants or shoots of the same sort.

"Art. 2. It shall also forbid every person, whether native or foreigner, to make collections of plants, cuttings, or seeds of quina trees, and shall take the necessary precautions to prevent those articles from passing the ports and frontiers of the republic; and on those who break this decree shall impose the penalties of confiscation of the said articles, and of a fine of 100 dollars for every plant or cutting, and for every drachm of seed found in their possession."

These are the most important provisions of the decree. Another article proposes inviting the other *two* quina-producing nations, Bolivia and New Granada (forgetting or not knowing that quina exists also in Peru), to unite with them in the prohibition; and other articles forbid the exportation of the bark itself, from which quinine is to be extracted on the spot. The whole decree is framed on the dog-in-the-manger principle, and it is needless to point out its errors in fact, and its retrograde tendency. There is no harm in sticking six branches into the ground, beneath each tree cut down, and leaving them to Providence; but it is a great mistake to suppose that so rude an expedient will suffice to maintain the bark tree, even at its present reduced rate of production, much less to restore the forests to their pristine state, or to make them what they might be.

METEOROLOGICAL REGISTER * kept at *Limon*, on the River Chasuán, on the Western Slope of *Chimborazo*, in Lat. 1° 30′ S., Long. 79° 20′ W., and at a Height of 2,836 Feet above the Sea.

—	Barometer.		Thermometer.			WIND AND WEATHER.
	Maximum.	Minimum.	Min.	Max.	6½ p.m.	
1860:						
18 June	–	–	–	–	–	Cool easterly wind 2—6 a.m.; then clear hot sun, with very slight westerly wind until noon; afterwards calm, with dense fog till night.
19 ”	27·150	–	–	–	–	⊙ Cool strongish easterly wind 2—6 a.m.; rest of day calm. Day clear and hot till noon; foggy in afternoon, with gentle rain 3—5 p.m.; afterwards clear.
20 ”	–	27·040	–	73	–	Cool wind 1—6 a.m. Day sunny and nearly calm. Sky almost cloudless till near noon; then about half obscured.
21 ”	–	–	–	–	–	Windy before daylight. Day moderately sunny, with no fog.
22 ”	27·140	27·055	–	–	–	Night and morning calm. Day sunny, occasionally overcast, with gentle cool wind till 4 p.m.; then calm and drizzling till 5½ p.m. Slight shower, 7 p.m.
23 ”	27·115	–	61½	75	69½	Cold strong wind 1—6 a.m. Day clear, hot, and windy till 1 p.m.; then foggy and calm till 2 p.m.; afterwards sunny, with gentle westerly wind.
24 ”	27·125	–	62	68	–	Cold strong wind 0—6 a.m. Sunny till noon; then foggy till night, with drizzle from 3 to 4 p.m.
25 ”	27·105	27·075	61½	75	–	Cold wind 0—6 a.m. Sunny till noon; afterwards foggy.
26 ”	27·150	27·095	61½	75½	67	Cold wind 4—6 a.m. Day sunny, with mist on hills to eastward in afternoon, but clear in valley of Limon.
27 ”	–	–	60½	76	–	Windy 6—7 a.m., and occasionally through day, which was clear and hot till nightfall.
28 ”	27·150	–	–	76	–	Cool easterly wind 5—7 a.m. Day clear and hot, with gentle westerly wind.
29 ”	27·150	–	–	77	–	Cool easterly wind 5—7 a.m. Day clear and very hot till after 2 p.m., when fog began to come on, and towards evening passed to drizzling rain.
30 ”	27·150	–	61	70	–	Cool easterly wind 5—6½ a.m. Sky clear in morning, becoming obscured towards noon. Afternoon foggy, calm, and in evening drizzling.
1 July	27·215	27·135	61	68	–	Dull and nearly calm till noon. Fog and rain 0—8 p.m. An earthquake at 9 a.m., coming apparently from northward, with a rumbling noise; then gentle undulations, lasting near a minute, and ending with a smart shock.
2 ”	–	–	62	70	–	● Nearly calm; sunny till near noon, then mostly overcast, but no fog.
3 ”	–	27·155	61	76	–	Cool easterly wind 6—7 a.m., then gradually gentler, and at 9 a.m. veering to westerly. Clear and sunny till 1½ p.m., afterwards foggy.
4 ”	–	27·125	58¾	75	–	Clear morning, with easterly wind 6—7 a.m. Day sunny till 11 a.m., then obscured at intervals until 1 p.m.; afterwards foggy and drizzling.
5 ”	–	27·120	61	70	–	Wind easterly 6½—7 a.m.; through rest of day variable. Mostly dull; foggy from 10 a.m. (partially clearing away at 2 – 3 p.m.) throughout.
6 ”	–	27·110	62	71	–	Cool westerly (to north-westerly) wind almost throughout. Sunny till near noon, then foggy till 3 p.m.; sunny again till 4 p.m. (when greatest temperature was attained); then foggy till night.

* In offering a copy of my Meteorological Register, I have to apologise for its deficiency of information on several important points. The instruments which it was proposed to send out to me never came, and the only instruments I possessed were the Aneroid barometer above spoken of, and a thermometer, whose scale ascended only to 112°, nor was it possible to procure any others in the Andes. I felt much the want of a hygrometer, and of an additional thermometer for observing the temperature in the sun of the air and earth, and also the temperature of the streams. Mr. Cross had bought at Guayaquil a small thermometer, which served us for ascertaining the temperature of the earth, at a depth of two feet, for several days; but as he afterwards required it for regulating the temperature of his pit, these observations were discontinued. In the equatorial Andes, from 8,000 feet and upwards, a thermometer buried in the shade at the depth of a foot gives remarkably equable indications throughout the year; but such is by no means the case in equatorial plains. I supposed that by doubling the depth required at 8,000 feet, I should obtain equable results at 3,000 feet; but experiment has proved that I ought to have gone deeper; for the thermometer, buried at a depth of two feet for 12 days, varied to the extent of one degree and a half during that period.

During my travels in South America, I have been accustomed to note the diurnal maximum and minimum of the barometer, which near the equator is rendered easy by their recurrence at nearly the same hour each day. As I have never had any one to assist me in my observations, I have rarely been able to register the nocturnal maxima and minima, but the few I have noted go to show that the diurnal maximum exceeds the nocturnal by the same quantity that the nocturnal minimum exceeds the diurnal; so that the mean of all the four terms does not sensibly differ from that of either of the pairs.

After my departure from Limon, Mr. Cross continued to register the temperature and the state of the weather; but I had not time to extract more than the chief results of his observations, which I shall give consecutively with those of my own.

Meteorological Register kept at *Limon*, on the River Chasuán, &c.—*continued.*

—	Barometer.		Thermometer.			WIND AND WEATHER.
	Maximum.	Minimum.	Min.	Max.	6½ p.m.	
1860;						
7 July	27·200	–	62½	75	–	Gentle wind 6½—7 a.m.; afterwards nearly calm. Slight fog till 7 a.m., then sunny till 11 a.m., when a slight shower, followed by a brief clear interval; afterwards foggy and showery till night.
8 ,,	27·150	27·125	60	74	–	Gentle cool wind in morning. Sunny till noon; foggy and showery in afternoon.
9 ,,	–	27·165	60	71	–	Cool wind throughout. Sunny till 11 a.m., then foggy; after 2 p.m. again nearly clear.
10 ,,	27·210	27·135	60	70	–	Cool variable wind 7 a.m. throughout. Mostly overclouded; flying mists on slopes, but no fog till 6 p.m.
11 ,,	27·215	27·175	57	06½	–	Very cold day, though calm; sunny till 9 a.m., then overcast and misty.
12 ,,	27·195	27·125	59	71¼	–	Very gentle cool southerly (to westerly) wind throughout. Sky often overcast, but no fog to-day.
13 ,,	27·175	27·095	61	70	–	Very slight variable wind. Sunny in early morning, then mostly overcast, and in afternoon foggy.
14 ,,	27·185	27·115	59	74½	–	Cold blasts of wind occasionally from midnight to sunrise; afterwards nearly calm. Sunny till 10 a.m., then overcast till 1 p.m., and again sunny till evening.
15 ,,	27·210	27·145	60	75	..	Calm day. Dull and cool in morning, then sunny till noon; misty 0—3 p.m., then again sunny; windy 9—12 p.m.
16 ,,	27·200	27·145	59	72	–	Cold gusty wind 0—7 a.m. Sunny till 11 a.m.; afterwards misty, and towards evening foggy.
17 ,,	27·195	27·145	58	74½	–	Gusts of wind 0—6 a.m. Fine and mostly clear day, though sun occasionally obscured between 1 and 3 p.m. Misty after sunset.
18 ,,	27·175	27·110	58	75	–	☉ Morning very cold and windy. Day sunny, with flying mists about noon. Foggy after sunset.
19 ,,	27·175	27·115	59	71½	–	Wind slight. Dull and cold till 7 a.m., then sunny until noon. Afternoon misty, and towards evening foggy.
20 ,,	27·175	–	58	73	–	Calm; moderately sunny till near noon, then misty, and towards evening foggy and drizzling. Several explosions from the volcano Sangay heard this day, and at 7½ p.m. a very long one ended with a perceptible trembling of the earth.
21 ,,	27·175	–	59	73½	–	Gentle easterly wind in morning; sunny till 3 p.m.; then foggy till 5, when fog cleared away.
22 ,,	27·175	27·125	59	69	–	Gentle westerly wind throughout. Fair, but mostly dull, with flying mists occasionally in afternoon.
23 ,,	27·205	–	60	73½	–	Gentle westerly wind 9 a.m.—3 p.m. Sky mostly obscured by thin cloud, through which sun rarely shone; dropping at 1 p.m.
24 ,,	27·225	27·155	59	72	–	Cool westerly wind 9 a.m.—1 p.m. Sunny till 1 p.m., then overcast; after 5 p.m. foggy and showery.
25 ,,	27·205	27·135	62	75½	–	Calm; sunny till 2 p.m., then misty, and towards evening foggy and showery (smart rain on hills above Limon).
26 ,,	27·235	–	–	68	–	Calm and cool; foggy (with brief clear intervals) and showery throughout.
27 ,,	27·185	27·125	59	80½	–	Gentle westerly wind. Clear hot day.
28 ,,	27·185	–	62	75¼	–	Nearly calm; sunny till 3 p.m.; then dull, with flying mists, and in evening foggy.
29 ,,	27·235	27·150	64	70½	–	Very slight wind. Foggy throughout, except a brief interval between 11 and 12 a.m.
30 ,,	27·250	–	61	69½	–	Calm; sunny till 8 a.m., then gradually obscured; afternoon misty, and at 4 dropping (thunder to westward).
31 ,,	27·195	27·125	62	76	66½	Gentle wind and clear sky till noon; then foggy and calm till night.
1 August	27·175	–	–	72	–	● Calm, mostly dull, and in afternoon foggy.
2 ,,	27·175	27·090	–	70¼	–	Misty in morning; foggy in afternoon (heavy rain on the hills these two days).
3 ,,	27·155	27·095	–	71	–	Sky mostly overcast, but foggy only after 4½ p.m.
4 ,,	27·135	27·060	60	74½	–	Gentle cool north-westerly wind until 2 p.m.; then calm, sunny, with light cloud, till 2 p.m.; then overcast, and after 3 foggy.
5 ,,	27·150	27·080	60	72	–	Gentle cool westerly wind throughout. Sky mostly overcast, with light cloud; foggy 3—5 p.m.; then partially clearing away.
6 ,,	27·175	–	62	74	–	Calm in morning; cool (westerly, veering to southerly) wind in afternoon. Moderately sunny till 1 p.m.; then foggy, and towards evening drizzling.

Meteorological Register kept at *Limon*, on the River Chasuán, &c.—*continued.*

—	Barometer.		Thermometer.			Temp. of Earth at 2 feet.	WIND AND WEATHER.
	Maximum.	Minimum.	Min.	Max.	6½ p.m.		
1860:							
7 August	27·175	–	62	78	–	68	Cool easterly (to south-easterly) wind at daybreak, and again from 6½ to 10 p. m.; remainder of day nearly calm. Fine sunny day, with gentle rain 4—5 p. m.
8 „ -	27·240	27·175	62	78	–	68	Nearly calm; sunny till 2 p. m., then dull, and in evening rather misty.
9 „ -	27·225	27.175	61	74	–	69	Cool westerly wind from daybreak to sunset, getting up again near midnight. Clear and sunny till noon, then overcast; foggy after 2 p. m., with a shower at 4.
10 „ -	27·225	27·135	60	79¼	–	69	Cool strong easterly wind 0—7 a. m.; gentle westerly through rest of day. Clear and very hot till 2 p. m., then misty till evening.
11 „ -	27·220	27·155	61	76	–	69½	Cool strong easterly wind 4—6½ a.m., then nearly calm, but again windy from 8 p.m. through night. Sunny and clear till 1 p.m., then misty till night.
12 „ -	27·225	27·170	59¾	77¼	–	68	Cool easterly wind 0—7 a.m. Clear and hot till 2½ p.m., then misty, and from 4—4½ drizzling fog, afterwards partially clear.
13 „ -	27·225	27·150	61	72½	–	68½	Cool easterly wind 5—7 a.m. Warm but cloudy, and after 4 p.m. foggy. (Thunder on hills to eastward in afternoon, as also yesterday).
14 „ -	27·250	27·175	64	73	–	68½	Calm day; dull and warm in morning; from 6½—8 a.m. foggy, then clear till near noon; afterwards overcast, and from 2 p.m. foggy and showery, with brief sunny intervals.
15 „ -	27·255	27·185	63	70	–	68¼	Mostly overcast; foggy 7—8 a.m., and again after 2 p.m., with showers 3—4½ p.m.
16 „ -	27·260	27·185	61	71	–	69	⊙ Calm through day; cool southerly wind 7 p.m. nearly through night. Fog 6½—8 a.m., then clearing away (but sky overclouded) till 2 p.m., after which misty and occasionally dropping.
17 „ -	27·235	–	61¼	79	6	68⅓	Southerly wind, in gusts, 0—2 a.m.; south-westerly 8 a.m.—4 p.m. Clear and hot till 2½ p.m., then gradually overcast, but not misty.
18 „ -	27·205	27·175	61	75½	–	68½	Calm at daybreak, but cold westerly wind 6½—12 a.m. Sunny and hot, after 2 p.m. overcast; a shower at 4 p.m., then misty till night.
19 „ -	27·225	27·145	60½	72½	–	–	Cool strongish westerly wind 7 a.m.—2 p.m. Fine day, but with a good deal of light cloud; misty at 3 p.m., soon clearing away.
20 „ -	27·265	27·20	60½	67¼	–	–	Wind slight, cool, south-westerly, varying to north-westerly towards evening. Dull day, with flying mists throughout.
21 „ -	27·225	27·175	61½	70½	–	–	Cool northerly wind 7 a.m.—12 p.m. Sunny till 8 a.m., then overcast; showers at 1 and at 3 p.m.; after 5 p.m. foggy.
22 „ -	27·215	27·160	62	77¼	–	–	Cool wind, mostly westerly, but varying to northward and southward till 4 p.m.; again windy after 8 p.m. Clear and sunny till 4 p.m., then showery, and misty till night.
23 „ -	27·225	27·175	63	78½	–	–	Gentle cool westerly wind, and bright sun till 4 p.m., afterwards foggy.
24 „ -	27·245	27·180	62½	76½	–	–	Westerly wind till 6 p.m. Foggy in morning; bright sun 8—11 a.m., then foggy till 1 p.m.; sunny 1—2½ p.m., then mist and showers till night.
25 „ -	27·225	27·175	60½	78½	–	–	Strong wind 4 a.m.—4 p.m.; easterly till 8 a.m., then westerly (varying to southerly). Fine sunny day, with mist only 5—6 p.m.
26 „ -	27·265	27·205	61½	79¼	–	–	Strong south-westerly wind 8 a.m.—4 p.m. Clear and sunny till 4 p.m., then partially overcast.
27 „ -	–	–	60¾	77	–	–	Puffs of south-westerly wind before daybreak (and again after sunset); cool easterly wind and clear sky 5—8 a.m., then cloudy and sultry till 6 p.m., afterwards foggy.
28 „ -	27·245	27·200	60¾	80¼	–	–	Cool gusty wind before daybreak; day nearly calm; very sultry; overclouded after 3 p.m.; flying mists in evening.
29 „ -	27·275	27·205	61	71½	–	–	Calm and dull, with rain, 4—4½ p.m., but from 5 to 6 p.m. clear sky and bright sun.

Meteorological Register kept at *Limon*, on the River Chasuán, &c.—*continued.*

—	Barometer.		Thermometer.			WIND AND WEATHER.
	Maximum.	Minimum.	Min.	Max.	6½ p.m.	
1860:						
30 August	27·285	27·200	61	70	–	Calm till 3 p.m., then westerly wind till 6 p.m. Fog from before daybreak to 7½ a.m., then mostly dull (with drops of rain at noon) till 3 p.m., afterwards sunny.
31 „ -	27·275	27·185	63	77	–	● Cool northerly wind 4—6 a.m., calm till afternoon, then westerly till 4 p.m., and at 4½ p.m. southerly. Overcast till noon, then sunny till 3 p.m. Smart rain 4½—6 p.m.
1 Sept. -	27·280	27·180	–	76½	–	Cool easterly wind 4—6½ a.m., afterwards nearly calm; gentle north-westerly wind 3—4 p. m., then again calm.
2 „ -	27·275	27·220	63¾	69	–	Cool westerly wind; puffs of southerly wind after nightfall. Foggy throughout, with occasional drizzle.
3 „ -	27·275	27·225	61½	70	–	Calm; showery before daybreak; sunny till 11 a.m., then dull, with flying mists and showers till evening.
4 „ -	–	27·175	63	76½	–	Cool southerly wind 3—6 a.m., then westerlytill 3 p.m. Clear till 3 p.m., then slightly misty.
5 „ -	27·250	27·175	61¾	72½	–	Wind cool easterly 5½—6½ a.m., then gentle westerly. Sunny till 11 a.m., then overcast; after 4 p.m. foggy; showers from 7 p.m. through night.
6 „ -	27·250	27·200	63¾	76½	–	Calm; showery before daybreak, and misty till 7 a.m., then sunny, with light clouds, throughout.
7 „ -	27·275	27·195	64	69	–	Easterly (to north-easterly) wind 6—7 a.m., then mostly calm. Rain before daylight; misty after 7 a.m., and in afternoon occasionally foggy.
8 „ -	27·275	27·185	62¾	73	–	Slight wind before daybreak, afterwards calm. Flying mists till 10 a.m., then clear, but cloudy.
9 „ -	27·225	27·140	62	70	–	Nearly calm throughout. Overcast, save a sunny interval between 10 and 11 a.m. (Fog on hills above Limon, down to 5,000 feet. Rain to eastward in evening).
10 „ -	–	–	–	–	–	Gentle westerly wind. Rain 0—2 a.m.; day warm, but mostly overcast; foggy after 2 p.m. (Thunder showers to eastward 0—3 p.m.)
11 „ -	–	–	–	–	–	Nearly calm; clear till 10 a.m., then misty till night.
						Journey from Limon to Tablas.
12 „ -	–	–	–	–	–	Clear hot day, with strong westerly wind in afternoon.
						Tablas to Tabacál (San Antonio).
13 „ -	–	–	–	–	–	Moderate westerly wind. Clear till 9 a.m., then overcast, and afternoon misty.
14 „ -	–	27·375	–	–	–	Strong westerly wind 8 a.m.—3 p.m., then calm. Sunny until wind fell, then misty.
15 „ -	27·445	27·395	60½	73	–	⊙ Weather almost exactly as yesterday.
16 „ -	27·635	27·535	61	75¾	–	Wind cool, easterly 6—7 a.m; strong westerly 8 a.m.—3½ p.m., then calm. Sunny till 3½ p.m., then misty on hills.
17 „	27·615	27·560	63	72	–	Strong wind till 3 p.m., easterly in early morning, then westerly. Sunny till 3 p.m., then obscured (mist on hills down to 500 feet above Tabacál).
18 „ -	–	27·590	63	71½	–	Strong wind 6 a.m.—4 p.m., easterly till 7½ a.m., afterwards westerly. Sunny till 4 p.m., then overcast. Misty on hills in afternoon.
19 „ -	–	–	59½	–	–	Calm in morning; strong westerly wind 8 a.m.—3½ p.m., then calm. Sunny until wind fell.
20 „ -	27·680	27·615	60½	73	–	Calm in morning; strong westerly wind 8 a.m.—2 p.m. Moderately sunny till 2 p.m., afterwards dull, with mist on hills above Tabacál.
21 „ -	27·675	27·600	61	70	–	Cool westerly wind 8 a.m.—6 p.m., and again 7—9 p.m. Mostly overcast, after 2 p.m. misty (as on hills through day).
22 „ -	27·680	27·600	61	70½	–	Strong cool westerly wind 7 a.m.—4 p.m. Clear till 10 a.m., then overcast, and in afternoon misty on hills to within 500 feet of Tabacál.
23 „ -	27·700	27·605	61	76½	–	Strong westerly wind 7 a.m.—4 p.m., then gentler, and dying away about 8. Clear hot day, with flying mists only on hills.
24 „ -	–	27·575	61¾	71	–	Strong cool wind, easterly 5½—7 a.m., then westerly till 4 p.m. Moderately warm, but with much mist on hills.
25 „	27·630	27·560	64	72	–	Strong westerly wind 7 a.m.—3 p.m. Moderately warm, but mist descending low on hills, and after 3½ p.m. filling valley itself.

Meteorological Register kept at *Limon*, on the River Chasuán, &c.—*continued.*

—	Barometer.		Thermometer.			WIND AND WEATHER.
	Maximum.	Minimum.	Min.	Max.	$6\frac{1}{2}$ p.m.	
1860:						
26 Sept. -	27·680	27·610	63	76	–	Wind easterly in morning; strong cool westerly wind 7 a.m.—4 p.m., then nearly calm. Very hot till 4 p.m, then overcast, and on slopes misty.
27 „ -	–	–	63	72	–	Mostly calm, cloudy, and after 3 p.m. foggy and drizzling.
						Tabacál to Pozuelos.
28 „ -	–	–	–	–	–	Westerly wind till 2 p.m., then calm. Sunny in morning, at noon overcast; rain from 2—3 p.m.
						Pozuelos to Bodegas.
29 „ -	–	–	–	–	–	Nearly calm till noon, then smart westerly breeze.
30 „ -	–	–	–	79	–	Calm till noon, then very gentle westerly wind. Overcast, and in evening hazy.

I subjoin a few deductions from the foregoing Register, and such additional observations as seem necessary to afford a clear notion of the climate of the Red Bark woods:—

1. *Barometer*, as observed at Limon, from June 19th to September 9th, 1861:—

	Inches.
Mean maximum - - - - - - - - -	27·207
Mean minimum - - - - - - - -	27·148
Mean of maxima and minima - - - - - - -	27·1775
Mean daily range - - - - - - - - -	·059
Entire range for the above period (viz., between 27·055 inches on June 22d, and 27·285 inches on August 30th)	·230
Greatest variation in one day (on September 1st) - -	·100
Least (on July 8th) - - - - - - - -	·025

The observations made at Tabacál (San Antonio) from September 14th to September 27th, give the following results:—

	Inches.
Mean maximum - - - - - - - - -	27·634
Mean minimum - - - - - - - - -	27·550
Mean maxima and minima - - - - - - -	27·592

The mean daily variation of the barometer in the Amazon valley, at Barra do Rio Negro (a nearly central point), is ·111 inch, as deduced from observations made in 1851, and again in 1855, at both of which periods precisely the same result was obtained.

It is well known that at great elevations above the earth's surface the atmospheric tides become less sensible, and that as we ascend still higher they at length become imperceptible; but in ascending from the plain to the summits of the Andes, the range of the barometer at various points differs widely, not only on account of difference of altitude, but in a much greater degree from difference of soil, climate, and exposure. In the hot and comparatively dry valley of Tarapoto (alt. 1,500 feet), where the climate is a perpetual summer, the prevailing sunny weather being varied by only an occasional thunderstorm, the mean diurnal range of the barometer is near two-tenths of an inch; but I have not yet collated the whole of my observations so as to be able to state it precisely. In the equally dry plains of Ambato (alt. 8,500—9,000 feet), where reigns an almost invariable spring, and where the small quantity of rain that falls during the year descends usually in gentle showers, the mean range of the barometer is exactly one-tenth of an inch, or nearly twice as great as in the foggy Bark woods at one-third of the altitude.

2. *Thermometer*,

2. *Thermometer*, at Limon, from June 19th to December 8th,—*

Mean minimum - - - - - - - - - -	61½°
Mean maximum - - - - - - - - - -	72⅕°
Mean of minima and maxima - - - - - - -	66¾°
Mean temperature at 6½ P.M. - - - - - - -	67¾°
,, ,, of warmest month (August) - - -	68°
,, ,, of earth, at a depth of 2 feet - - -	68½°
Highest temperature observed (July 27th) - - - -	80½°
Lowest (July 11th) - - - - - - - -	57°
Entire range - - - - - - - - - -	23½°
Mean daily variation - - - - - - - -	10½°
Greatest (July 27th) - - - - - - - -	21½°
Least (October 31st) - - - - - - - -	3°

It will be remarked that the gradual increase in the mean temperature of the air was very nearly contemporaneous with the augmented elasticity. The warmest weather was undoubtedly between July 27th and September 26th. On clear days the maximum temperature was attained at from 2½ to 3 P.M.; but as it usually came on misty at noon, or even earlier, there was from that moment rarely any increase of heat, but, on the contrary, very often a sudden decrease. On July 15th the thermometer fell from 75° at noon to 65° at 3 P.M., a fall of 10° in three hours, which, on the equator, is sufficient to cause a sensation of great cold.

According to my own experience, on passing the equator to southward, the lowest temperature throughout the year is in the month of July, about 20 days after the summer solstice. At Limon the minimum temperature was on July 11th. At Tarapoto (lat. 6½° S.) it fell on the 9th of July in two consecutive years (1855 and 1856). In July 1857 I was at Baños (lat. 1° 35′ S.); but I had no instrument wherewith to ascertain the temperature (which I felt to be intensely cold), having had to abandon all my goods in the forest, on my recent disastrous journey from Canelos. At Daule, near Guayaquil, the minimum temperature (63¾°) occurred on the 7th of July of the present year (1861).†

By collating the thermometrical observations in each month, we obtain the following results:—

Month.	Mean Minimum Temperature.	Mean Maximum Temperature.	Mean of Maxima and Minima.	Lowest Temperature.	Highest Temperature.	Mean Variation in 24 Hours.	Greatest Variation in 24 Hours.	Least Variation in 24 Hours.	Mean Temperature at 6 p.m.	Total Range during Month.
	°	°	°	°	°	°	°	°	°	°
June - -	61⅓	74	67½	60¼ (27th)	77 (29th)	12⅔	15¾ (27th)	6 (24th)	68¼	16¾
July - -	60	72½	66¼	57 (11th)	80½ (27th)	12½	21½ (27th)	6½ (29th)	-	23½
August - -	61⅓	74⅗	68	59¾ (12th)	80¼ (28th)	13⅓	19½ (28th)	6¾ (20th)	-	20⅓
September -	62⅓	72½	67½	60 (16th)	80 (19th)	10¼	20 (19th)	5 (30th)	68½	20
October - -	62	70	66	60 (21st)	74 (24th)	8	13 (24th)	3 (31st)	67⅗	14
November -	62½	71	66½	58 (29th)	75 (30th)	8⅓	16 (29th)	5 (14th)	67⅙	17
December -	62	71½	66¾	- -	- -	9½	- -	- -	67¾	-

3. *Winds*.—In mountainous countries it is difficult to ascertain the exact direction of the wind, except on the peaks and on the crests of the main ridges. In a deep narrow valley, the wind generally blows either up or down it, whatever be its direction on the adjacent summits. A similar effect takes place on narrow rivers, bordered by lofty forest; thus, on the Casiquiari, and on the upper part of the Rio Negro and of the Orinoco, the wind usually blows either up or down

* Deduced from my own observations up to 11th September, and from Mr. Cross's after that period. The temperature at half an hour after sunset, which various circumstances usually prevented me from noting, was, after my departure, constantly registered by Mr. Cross.

† In the Amazonian plain I have never seen the thermometer below 70°.

down the stream. I have, therefore, not attempted to indicate the exact direction of the wind at Limon, nor any but its more marked variations. In general at daybreak (5 A.M.) an easterly wind was blowing, which had sprung up either at midnight or in the early morning hours—rarely at three or four hours after sunset of the previous evening,—and it seldom lasted for more than an hour after sunrise. Then there was a lull for an hour or two, until the day wind got up, rarely blowing for half an hour together in any fixed direction throughout the month of June; but on the 3d of July it began to blow with some steadiness from the westward, although it did not get fixed in that quarter until July 22d, after which date the wind was westerly, as a rule, from 9 A.M. (or earlier) until the afternoon fog came on. Sometimes the westerly day wind was preceded by a calm instead of the usual easterly morning wind. Northerly and southerly winds were generally gusty and of brief duration. The direction of the wind at Limon is, doubtless, influenced by the proximity on the one hand of the snowy ridge of the Andes, and on the other hand of the hot savannahs and sandy deserts of the Guayaquilian plain, bordering on the ocean. A tract of country of considerable breadth, lying along the coast of Ecuador, from Puná to near Cape San Francisco, differs little in soil and climate from the sandy deserts on the coast of Peru, and is rarely visited by more than two or three days of gentle rain throughout the year. Every day, as this sandy plain becomes heated by the solar rays, or very often not until it reaches its maximum heat, there is a rush of cold air from the ocean; but as the prevailing wind along the Pacific coast is southerly, the westerly current that would otherwise be generated is modified into a south-westerly one. In the rainy season this phenomenon is confined to the neighbourhood of the coast, for the savannahs of the Guayaquilian plain are mostly inundated; but in the dry season, when the same savannahs become dry or even dusty flats, westerly (to south-westerly) winds prevail in the after-part of the day, over the whole plain, and far up the valleys that debouch into the plain from the cordillera, especially those which are of considerable width, and whose slopes are in great part covered with grass, which becomes brown and parched in the dry season. At Guayaquil, the phases presented by the wind on a summer's day are generally the following:—At daybreak there is a cool easterly (to north-easterly) breeze. After sunrise there is a brief lull, and then a gentle variable wind springsup, its direction being modified by two nearly equal and contrary forces, the influx of cold air from the Andes, and an opposing current from the ocean. At 3 p.m. the south-west wind begins to prevail, and comes on at first in gusts, then in a sustained current of considerable intensity. At sunset it softens for a while to a gentle breeze, but about 7 p.m. it comes on again with greater violence than before, and rarely abates before 3 a.m. of the following day. This may be taken as the type throughout the whole plain, although apt to be much modified by peculiarities of local configuration, such as savannah, or forest, or the proximity of one of those wooded ridges which intersect the plain transversely to the normal direction of the wind.

I regret that, for want of an instrument to measure the intensity of the wind in the bark woods, I can give no precise information on that head. Compared with the violent winds in the central valley of the Andes, or even with those of Guayaquil, the wind at Limon never exceeded a gentle breeze. In the valley of San Antonio it was a little stronger, and still more so in the valley of Alausi; but in the latter locality its full force was displayed only above the red bark region. A question which has much excited my attention is, up to what elevation does the westerly wind prevail on the Pacific side of the Andes? I have felt it up to 10,000 feet; and yet whenever I have passed the crest of either branch of the Andes, I have found an easterly wind blowing there. I think I have collected evidence to show that on the equator the easterly wind, due to the earth's rotation, prevails at all hours in the upper regions of the atmosphere; the principal fact which points to such a conclusion being, that when the volcano Sangay is more active than ordinary, there are showers of volcanic dust or fine ashes, throughout the Guayaquilian plain, and even far out to sea. There was a fall of volcanic dust from Sangay, at Guayaquil, in the month of June of the present year, beginning on the night of the 23d, and continuing, with brief intermissions, through the five following days. But on the 18th of July as much dust fell as on all the days together of the previous fall. The shower came on at 9 a.m., when a gentle south-westerly wind was blowing. A little later the wind veered to eastward, and blew strongly, when the dust began

began to fall thicker, appearing in the air like drizzling rain. The whole sky was obscured by a lurid purple haze, and objects at a little distance seemed enveloped in fog. In the space of two hours I collected about an ounce of dust on a cardboard measuring 2¼ square feet. A little before sunset the sky became clear, and no more dust was seen to fall; but I am informed by a gentleman of Guayaquil, that all through the year, when the weather is perfectly calm, a sheet of paper spread on the ground collects a sensible quantity of volcanic dust, recognisable by its slightly saline and sometimes sulphureous taste.*

4. *Humidity.*—On the western side of the Quitenian Andes, south of the equator, the summer or dry season is considered to commence on the 1st of June, and to end on the 31st of December, the remaining five months constituting the winter or wet season. As we advance to the northward of the equator those seasons become reversed, so that the rainy season at Panamá, for instance, coincides nearly with the dry season at Guayaquil, and the steamers which run between Guayaquil and Panamá encounter winter at one extremity of each trip, all through the year. On the eastern side of the cordillera, from the equator southwards, the wet season is certain to last from March until November, and even the remaining months are in some years so rainy that there is no really dry weather throughout the year. The climate of the central valley is modified by this opposition of seasons to east and west of it, as also by the nature of the soil, and the greater or less proximity of snowy peaks; so that, in proceeding along it, we find a different climate (as relates to the phases of humidity and dryness) at every few leagues. We have now, however, to sketch only the general character and the more marked phases of the dry season in the Red Bark woods of Chimborazo.

The days on which there was neither mist, fog, nor rain at Limon, between the 18th of June and the 8th of December, were only the following:—†

June 20, 21, 26, 27, 28.
July 2, 10, 12, 14, 27.
August 17, 26, 31.
September 1, 12, 14, 17, 19, 20, 21, 23, 24, 25.
October 14, 15, 23, 24.
November 29, 30.
December 1, 2.

Although there were but three days in August in which there was no visible moisture in the lower atmosphere, yet the days were generally clear and sunny until a later hour, and there was more sustained heat than in the previous months. The formation of cloud in the Bark woods on those days when the upper

* Sangay is perhaps the most active volcano on the face of our globe. Since the day when it was first seen by the Spaniards (now more than 300 years ago), it has been in continual eruption, whereas most other volcanoes have had their periods of repose; but as it stands in the midst of uninhabited forest (for the village of Macas is at least two days' journey away), its eruptions rarely cause any damage to the dwellings of men. Its position is in the eastern cordillera, in latitude about 2° S., longitude 78° 33′ W. It is crowned by a great breadth of perpetual snow, or rather of alternating layers of snow and ashes, and even, it has been asserted, of modern trachyte. In the adjacent parts of the central valley of the Andes, as, for instance, at Riobamba, its explosions are rarely and indistinctly audible; but as we descend the forest-clad slope of the western cordillera, and especially when we reach the plain, they are clearly heard. At Bodegas, although distant 80 geographical miles in a direct line, the reports are so loud and distinct that they often cause people to start who have been accustomed to hear them every day of their lives. The sound is more like the roar of cannon than that of thunder, though easily distinguishable from both after a little experience. The explosions are ordinarily from one to two hours apart, rarely at intervals of only a quarter of an hour, though I have a few times heard two explosions within five minutes. At Guayaquil they are distinctly heard, although above 100 miles away; and I am assured that the sound not unfrequently reaches the very coast, at a distance of 2½ degrees of longitude from the volcano.

† It will be noted that I have used the term "mist," when, although the air was filled with visible vapour, the evaporation was still so great that there was no sensible deposition of dew; but when the vapour was denser, and moistened objects in contact with it, I have called it "fog." There was, of course, no precise limit between those two phases; and as mist passed into fog it was curious to stand in the forest, and remark how some trees were already dripping whilst others remained dry. Generally, condensation takes place earliest on smooth shining leaves, and latest on hirsute or tomentose leaves; but considerations of this nature will by no means explain all the variations observed; and there can be little doubt that every plant has its peculiar temperature, necessary to be taken into account in studying the phenomena of its existence.

upper atmosphere was tolerably clear, was usually on this wise. Five leagues below Limon, and on the farther side of the valley of Camaron, a long wooded hill, rising to about 6,000 feet, shuts up the view to the westward, down the valley of the Chasuán. As the sun declined from the meridian, mist began to form on the eastern declivity of this hill, and went on increasing in volume until its projecting margins were caught by the westerly wind, and carried up the valley. At the same time a similar process was going on about and above Limon, on all those slopes which the sun's rays no longer reached, or on which they fell very obliquely. As the day wore on, the mist continued to increase and to descend lower and lower, until it sometimes reached Limon at the same moment as the mist from below. But whether the valley were filled entirely with mist blown up from the hill of Camaron, or in part from the lowering of the stratum of visible vapour to the altitude of Limon, that event was always the signal for the dropping of the westerly wind, the refrigeration of the atmosphere stopping the draught up the valley; but when during the night the general easterly wind resumed its suspended sway, it gradually swept away the mist, so that there was usually none at sunrise. The afternoon mist generally enveloped our hut, and extended some distance lower down the valley. At Tabacál, on the contrary, it often hung a few hundred feet above the farm. By observations at these two points, I deduce that the average height of the base of the evening cloud on the flanks of this part of the Andes is about 2,500 feet.

When I ascended the Quitenian Andes from the eastern side, and reached the central valley, whose medium height is about 9,000 feet, I saw, not without surprise, the clouds hung as high overhead as they had been in the Amazonian plain which I had lately left. In the Andes there are two distinct and often simultaneous formations of cloud, in consequence of there being two sets of condensing surfaces, the snowy summits and the wooded slopes. The space between the snow and the forest forms a zone whose perpendicular breadth varies from 3,000 to 8,000 feet, its lower limit being often far below the absolute upper limit of forest, in consequence of the nature of the soil forbidding any continuous growth of trees. Nearly the whole of the central valley is comprised in this zone, and the loose volcanic sand which prevails in many parts of it (as at Ambato and Riobamba) gets heated by the sun to a greater degree than even the white beaches of the Amazon and Tapajoz; so that there is rarely any formation of mist, and between sunrise and sunset the snow-clouds nearly always float at a vast height above the valley; while, on looking down from it to the eastward, we may see the forest clouds spread out below our feet.

During the time I remained in the Bark woods, say from about the summer solstice to a little after the autumnal equinox,* there was no heavy or long-continued rain; but on the hills, at a few thousand feet above us, heavy rains, mostly accompanied by thunder, were frequent. From July 24th to August 2d it rained heavily there every day.† There is a rainy zone on the flanks of the cordillera, where as a rule rain may be expected every day in the year; but I can do little more here than merely indicate the fact of its existence. Its limits vary with local configuration, and with the proximity of a snowy mountain, or the contrary; but to determine them on any parallel would require a long series of observations. On the western declivity of Chimborazo this rainy zone would seem to extend from 5,000 to 9,000 feet altitude, and the maximum of humidity is, perhaps, about midway of it, or at about 7,000 feet. Throughout the wooded slopes of the Andes, fogs or gentle showers may occur at any altitude, in the midst of the finest weather; and even in the plain, when (in proceeding from the coast) we reach the point where forest begins to prevail over savannah, there are occasional slight showers in the dry season, although fog is very rare until reaching about 500 feet elevation. At Guayaquil itself, during the same period, two or even three months may pass without a drop of rain falling. In this respect the climate of Guayaquil contrasts notably with that of Pará, where, throughout the dry season, a thunder shower at 2 p.m. is expected every day.

In the western cordillera, and in the plains at its base, south of the equator, the continuity of the dry season is broken by a rainy fit commencing a few days after

* It will be understood that I speak of those epochs as they occur in the north temperate zone.

† At Guaranda, situated in a wide grassy valley to the eastward of these rainy woods, and at only a short distance from them, not a drop of rain fell during that period.

after the autumnal equinox, and called by the inhabitants "*el Cordonazo de San Francisco* (St. Francis's Girdle).* I have happened to be travelling in the western cordillera at that epoch in three consecutive years, viz., 1858, 1859, and 1860. In the year 1858, the weather began to be broken on the 22d of September, but the heaviest rains (accompanied by violent thunder) were from 28th September to 1st October—precisely the four days which I spent in passing from Riobamba to Pallatanga. In 1859, the rains came on on 28th September, when I was on my way from Guataxi (in the valley of Alausi) to Riobamba, and continued till 8th October. They were heavy in the forests and on the *paramos* (where the snow lay down to 12,000 feet), but in the central valley there were only gentle showers. In 1860, at the same epoch, I descended from San Antonio to Guayaquil, and the rains began the day I started (28th September). At Bodegas the sky was overclouded and the weather showery from 30th September to 5th October. At Guayaquil the *cordonazo* was represented by heavy rain on the 3d and 4th of October.

At Limon it came on to rain heavily on the 26th of September, nor did the weather ever fairly take up again after that period, as may be seen by the following *résumé* of the observations made by Mr. Cross, from the 12th of September to the 8th of December:—

Weather mostly fair, though misty or foggy in the afternoon, till past the equinox. On the 26th the rains came on, and from that date until the 13th October the mornings were cloudy, sometimes foggy, and the afternoons rainy (rarely merely foggy), the rains being heavy, and sometimes lasting all through the night.

The 14th and 15th of October were fine days, clear of fog, but from thence to the end of the month and until the 28th of November, though the mornings were usually clear and sunny, the sky became overclouded before noon, and in the afternoons there was either rain or dense fog.

The 29th and 30th of November, and the 1st and 2d of December were clear, hot days; 3d and 4th of December were tolerably fine days, though misty towards evening; on the 5th there was fog and rain in the afternoon, and on the 6th, 7th and 8th the day was foggy throughout.

I have thus sketched, as intelligibly as my materials will allow, the summer or dry season in the Red Bark woods of Chimborazo for the year 1860, and the question naturally arises, "If such were the dry season, what must the wet season be?" The answer, as I received it from the settlers at Limon, is that, whereas in the summer the early part of the day is often sunny, in the winter it is usually foggy, and that the fogs of the afternoon and night in summer are represented by heavy rains in winter. They added that, after a night of unusually heavy rain, the following day was sometimes sunny until noon. When I reached Limon, I saw evidence in the quantity of partially dried-up mud, and in the deep *camellones*, that the winter rains must have been severe. Still Limon is decidedly drier than the forest of Canelos, at the same altitude and on the same parallel, on the eastern side of the Andes, which is surely the point of maximum humidity on the face of this globe, and where the very trees seem to serve no other purpose than to hang ferns and mosses on.

The type of the rainy season at Guayaquil seems to be as follows:—In the month of November slight showers begin to fall occasionally, but it is not until about 10 days after the solstice that heavier rains come on, and winter is considered to have fairly commenced. As the ground becomes moistened, the sea breezes abate, and there is more sustained heat, though the maximum temperature each day is, perhaps, scarcely equal to that of the finest summer months. Still, all through January and well into February the quantity of rain that falls is not great; the showers are heavy, but of brief duration, and two or three fair days together occasionally intervene. March is the rainiest month in the year, and April is often very little drier. In May the rains begin to abate, and towards the

* St. Francis's day is the 4th of October. Throughout South America, the periodical alternations of dry and rainy weather are laid to the account of those saints whose "days" coincide nearly with the epochs of change. But if the weather be rainy when it ought to be fair, or if the rains of winter be heavier than ordinary, the blame is invariably laid on the moon. One would think that, *en revanche*, any occurrence of fair weather, when rainy weather had been expected, would be placed to the credit of the same planet, but such is not the case.

the end of the month there is rarely more than an occasional slight shower, so that after the 1st of June there is usually unbroken dry weather.

The last rainy season has, however, shown marked deviations from the above type. The rainiest part of the season occurred at its customary epoch, namely, from 26th February to 30th March, and the most terrific thunderstorm of the whole winter was on the night of 22d March. But the last day of March was clear and hot, without a drop of rain, and all through April there was fine sunny weather, with very rarely a gentle shower, so that summer seemed to be setting in two months before its time, and the farmers began to fear a season of excessive drought. However, at eight p.m. of the 30th of April, heavy rain came on, and did not abate until sunrise the following day. Thenceforth, nearly throughout the month of May, the weather was wet, though the rains were less violent than in March, and rarely accompanied by thunder. On the 27th of May the weather again took up, that day and the next being quite fair, although up to 28th June there was frequently drizzling rain; so that, by the prolongation of the wet season beyond its usual period, the equilibrium was restored, and on the whole an average amount of rain was considered to have fallen.

NOTE on CINCHONA SUCCIRUBRA, Pavon, and some allied Species.

Chinchona succirubra, Pavon :—

Hab.—In sylvis primævis cordilleræ occidentalis Andium Quitensium, præcipue ad radices montis nivosi *Chimborazo*, alt. 2,000—5,000 ped. Angl. (610—1520 metr.) supra mare.

Descr.—*Arbor* pulcherrima, 50—80 pedalis; caudice recto circumferentiâ 4-usque ad 10-pedali; comâ symmetricâ elongatâ, ramis infimis longioribus deinde superioribus sensim decrescentibus paraboloideâ, vel ramis infimis iis proxime sequentibus sub-brevioribus ovoideâ.

Cortex, caudicis ubi lichenibus non obvelatus est fuscobadius, haud profunde longitudinaliter rimosus, demum etiam rimulis transveralibus fissus; ramulorum annotinorum rufescens, novellorum e viridi cinerascens secus apicem rubescens.

Succus ecoloratus, cortice autem inciso, in lucem aeremque susceptus exinde sæpius albescit, postea sensim rubescit.

Rami decussati, angulo 50°—80° adscendentes, teretes, e foliorum stipularumque cicatrisibus annulati; novelli tamen tetragoni foliosi fragiles succosi, pube brevi deciduâ densiuscule vestiti.

Folia opposita decussata, cujusque ramuli 4—6 paribus contemporalibus, cujusque paris inter se subæqualia raro valde inæqualia, sæpe perfecte ovalia, secus paniculas ovato-ovalia, raro rotundato-ovalia, basi in petiolum sensim abrupteve attenuata, apice abrupte acuta vel levissime acuminata rarius rotundata, nitida subcoriacea (fragilissima tamen) læte viridia ad luteum potius quam ad cœruleum vergentia, ætate tota sanguinea, suprà sparse decidue puberula et inter venas plus minus bullato-elevata, subtus pubescentia, raro in utraque facie glabrata; venis 11—12 cujusque lateris, angulo 56°—59° cum costâ tereti (siccando complanatâ) efformantibus, subtus prominulis, â costâ ultrà medium rectis dein sensim incurvantibus et prope marginem anastomosantibus; petiolo tereti, e folii laminâ decurrente suprà lineis duabus parum elevatis percurso, tomentello. Folia ramulorum tenuiorum nonnunquam ovali-vel etiam obovato-lanceolata.

Stipulæ interpetiolares deciduæ erecto-patulæ ligulato-oblongæ obtusæ ad costam carinatæ, basi subventricoæ superne explanatæ, reticulato-venosæ, sub-puberulæ, juniores pallide virides, adultiores basi roseæ vel etiam totæ sanguineæ.

Pedunculi ex axillis foliorum superiorum minorum lanceolatorum (etiam ad bracteas lineari-lanceolatas subulatasve redactorum) orti, subinde paniculam elongatam pedalem vel etiam sesquipedalem efformantes, tomentosi, bis terve decussatim pinnati dein trichotomi; divisionibus basi bracteatis sæpe indistincte

oppositis

oppositis v. plane alternis. *Pedicelli* calycesque basi bracteolis minutis rigidis sanguineis ovato-lanceolatis basi utrinque unidentatis suffulti.

Calyx parvus dense appresso-puberulus; *tubus* subturbinato-hemisphæricus; *limbus* cupulatus fere ad medium usque in lobos 5 lato-triangulares carinatos, apicibus sinubusque acutis, fissus, pubescens raro subglabratus, persistens.

Corolla calycem fere 5-ies excedens, extus dense puberula, ante anthesin clavata postea hypocratcrimorpha; *tubus* elongato-truncato-obconicus, intus glaber; *limbus* e lobis 5 patulis valvatis elongato-ovato-lanceolatis, margine apiceque villis densis albis (siccande flavidis) barbatis.

Stamina, corollæ tubum paululum superantia; *filamenta* glabra compressa à basi fere ad medium usque cum corollâ concreta; *antheræ* elongatæ lineares.

Stylus teres; *stigma* subemersum e lobis duobus ovato-lanceolatis crassis faciebus unisulcis erecto-patulis constans.

Capsula stricta curvulave tenui-ovoideo-fusiformis à basi dehiscens, valvulis dorso costis 5 parum elevatis percursis.

Semina anguste subovali-lanceolata sæpius asymmetrica, alâ margine lacero-fimbriatâ ciliatâ, basi angustata et ibidem integra bilobave.

The above description was drawn up from fresh specimens, and I have omitted only a few microscopic details which are common to the genus and the tribe.

The normal form of the leaf is undoubtedly oval, tapering decidedly at the base, less (or not at all) at the apex. In the vast majority of plants, the form of the leaf is modified in proximity to the inflorescence, and where the leaves pass insensibly into floral bracts, the modification is often considerable; so that (in collecting plants) where no leaves of the normal form existed on a flowering ramulus, or so nearly adjacent to it that they might be comprised in the specimen without making the latter of inordinate size, I have, whenever practicable, dried leaves of a sterile branch separately; and, indeed, that ought perhaps always to be done, for the presence or absence of stipules, and their exact form when present, can often be ascertained only by inspecting the growing apex of a barren branch. But, as Klotsch has described the leaves of this *Cinchona* as "ovato-ovalia," I took some trouble to ascertain if this were really the prevailing form, and I measured, on leaves taken from several trees, the distance of their conjugate axis (or line of greatest breadth) from the base and apex. This line was, in nearly all cases, farther from the base than from the apex, so that had not the attenuation of the base always exceeded that of the apex, the leaves ought to have been obovate. With my pencil I completed the oval, so as to cut off the tapering base and apex, and on measurement I generally found it an almost exact ellipse. I add the dimensions of a few of the leaves I measured, including both normal and extreme forms; where it is to be observed that, in the first factor, the first member represents the distance of the widest part of the leaf from the base, and the second from the apex, so that the sum of the two members gives the entire length of the blade of the leaf. The dimensions are in English inches and decimal parts.

Leaves taken from terminal ramuli of a luxuriant tree of 30 feet, from which I gathered some good seeds:—

No. 1, (4·8+4·65) × 6·7 inches.
No. 2, (5·1+4) 6·5 inches.

Leaf of a shoot 8 feet high, from an old stool:—

No. 3, (4·3+3·6) × 5·15 inches.

Leaf of a very vigorous branched shoot, 12 feet high:—

No. 4, (5·7+6·5) × 9·85 inches.

Fallen leaf from a tree of 25 feet:—

No. 5, (4·7+5·3) × 7·65 inches.

Leaf of a slender shoot from near the base of a large tree:—

No. 6, (2·3+1·7) × 2·4 inches.

Abstraction being made of the tapering bases and apices, the form of the leaves Nos. 1 and 3 is exactly oval, of No. 2 obovato-oval, of No. 5 ovato-oval, of No. 4 rotundato-ovate, and of No. 6 obovato-lanceolate. The petiole in all these leaves, except the last, was from 2 to 2·2 inches long; and the accompanying stipules measured 1·5 × ·55 inches. From four to six pairs of leaves, and three or four pairs of stipules, usually coexist on each ramulus.

As to the texture of the leaves, were they not so fragile, they are in nearly all cases thick enough to be called coriaceous. Fallen leaves are softer and tougher, and on picking up a blood-red leaf I have been struck by its similarity in look and feel to a piece of morocco leather. It is singular that even in dried specimens the leaves do not break so readily as when fresh. It is rarely possible to predicate accurately the texture of leaves from dried specimens. Fleshy leaves of *Peperomiæ*, *Begoniæ*, various *Gesneraceæ*, &c., become quite membranaceous, or even transparent, by drying. Coriaceous leaves, of a naturally dry constitution, such as of laurels, change very little in drying; but young juicy leaves of any plant are apt to dry very thin.

The degree of pubescence varies considerably; but never are the leaves entirely naked, and rarely are they so pubescent beneath as to be called tomentellous. The nature of the pubescence is pretty constant to one type—short, soft, and never appressed hairs.

The panicles, usually not more than nine inches long, sometimes reach 12 or even 18 inches. The type of the inflorescence seems to be, as in most *Cinchoneæ*, the triflorous cymule, a terminal sessile flower and two lateral ones on short stalks; but as one of the latter is often obsolete (its place, however, being indicated by the presence of three bracteoles, one pedicellar and two calycine), and as there is sometimes an extensive dislocation of the normally opposite ramification of the peduncles, the ultimate disposition of the flowers occasionally puts on the appearance of a contracted raceme.

The length of the calyx is ·15 inch, of the corolla ·7 inch (tube ·5, limb ·2), and of the capsule 1—1·4 inch.

Cinchona Magnifolia, growing along with *C. Succirubra*, is easily distinguished from it by the form and the immense size of the adult leaves, and by the dull red-brown colour of the aged ones. The largest leaf measured was 26½ × 22 inches, and the thick fleshy petiole seven inches more. The leaves are nearly always more rotund than those of *C. Succirubra*, *cordate at the base*, the apex cuspidato-acuminate; yet leaves adjacent to the panicles taper at the base as in the leaves of *C. Succirubra*, and those of young plants and suckers are ovali, or obovato-lanceolate, and attenuated at the base and apex. The veins make a very wide angle with the costa, towards the cordate base depressed below the horizontal line, and therefore greater than 90°, and they begin to curve gently upwards from their very insertion. The pubescence is longer and harsher than in *C. Succirubra*. The capsules, compared with those of other *Cinchonæ*, are as enormous as the leaves. I gathered one that was eight inches long, and the seeds are proportionally elongate.

I proceed now to state the result of a comparison of the specimens of *Cinchonæ*, collected in 1859 in the valley of Alausi, with those of *C. Succirubra* from Chimborazo. The *Cascarilla roja* seen at Puma-cocha in that valley was merely a slender drawn out shoot, and the dried specimens from it are extremely membranaceous. The following is my note on the leaves: *Folia*, elongato-ovalia v. obovato-lanceolata basi longe-attenuata, pilis paucis adspersa, recentia crassiuscula succosa siccando membranacea. I have seen quite similar leaves on drawn-out shoots at Limon; and from the milky juice of the Puma-cocha plant, I have no doubt it is the same species; but no one could safely assert this from the dried specimens alone, without having seen the living plants.

The specimens gathered in the same valley under the name of *Cascarilla cuchicara* consist of two forms, the one with nearly glabrous, the other with densely pubescent leaves. The latter alone possesses flowers and good fruit, and, until I saw how *C. Succirubra* varied in respect of pubescence, I inclined to consider it distinct from the former. It was gathered in the forest of Yalancay, below the heights of San Nicolas, on the northern side of the river Chanchan, and under

under rather adverse circumstances, for I came on the tree at nightfall, and when I had still some distance of very broken ground to travel to reach my resting-place. Whilst one of my men climbed the tree, and hastily broke off a few branches, the other cut off pieces of bark from its trunk, which were those sent to Kew under the name "*Cuchicara.*" In the dusk I could not distinguish what we had got, but on opening my vasculum the following morning, I found some good capsules, a few fragmentary flowery panicles, and besides the rather imperfect leaves attached to the latter, only young leaves at the apex of two sterile ramuli. From those materials the following brief description has been drawn up, chiefly with reference to the differences from *C. Succirubra*.

Ramuli petiolique cinereo-tomentosi. *Folia* (juniora) 4·6×2·8 unc. *oblonga utrinque acuta* vix attenuata, secus paniculas late ovata, supra nitida et præter ad costæ dimidium inferiorem glabrata, subtus cinereo-tomentella; *venis primariis* 9—10-*jugis angulo* 41°—42° *adscendentibus* fere ad ¾ usque suæ longitudinis rectisde in incurvis et secus marginem anastomosantibus. *Paniculæ subcorymbosæ Calyx* eo *C. Succirubra duplo major*; tubus turgidior; limbus sanguineus glabratus rugulosus, lobis subacuminatis, *sinubus excavatis*. *Corollæ* saturate lateritiæ tubus paullo crassior *stamina sat longe superans*; limbi lobis subbrevioribus apice margineque supra medium parce barbatis. *Capsula* uncialis oblonga ovoideo-fusiformis eâ *C. Succirubræ crassior*. *Semina latiora robustiora,* subovalia parum lacera a basi ad medium usque ciliata.

The other *Cuchicara* was obtained at Llalla, on the southern side of the Chanchan, about the wooded roots of the *paramo* of Azuay. It was out of flower, and the capsules had nearly all shed their seeds; but after a long search I found a few capsules which had still some seeds left. They were mostly much abbreviated—nearly globose—but on the same panicle were two longer capsules of quite the same form as those from Yalancay. The following are my notes on this *Cinchona*.

Ramuli, petioli foliaque nitida, præter *fasciculos pilorum ad venarum* (raro etiam ad venularum), *axillas* glabrata. *Folia* 7·5×4·5 unc. *oblonga* v. subovalia brevissime acuminata, basi sensim sub attenuatâ; *venis primariis* 10-*jugis angulo* 42°—43 *adscendentibus*. *Stipulæ* iis *C. Succirubræ* subconformes.

It will be remarked that in both these forms the leaves have the same general outline, the margins nearly parallel towards the middle (therefore rather oblong than oval), proportion of length to breadth as five to three, and that the veins are inserted at the same angle. But I find no fascicles of hairs in the axils of the veins in the pubescent, as there are in those of the smooth variety, and this is really the only difference of importance. They can hardly be varieties of *C. Ovata*, for in Fitch's beautiful figure of that species the leaves, even of a barren shoot, are represented somewhat ovate, by no means oblong, and the angle of the veins is greater than 50°. Were I to be guided by the description in De Candolle's *Prodromus*, I should consider the *Cuchicara* only a variety (and a very slight one) of *C. Condaminea*, H. B. K.

The specimens gathered at Llalla under the name "Pata de Gallinazo," are liable to the same animadversion as those of the "*Roja*" from Puma-cocha; for they were taken from a young plant eight feet high, growing in deep shade, to which circumstance may safely be attributed the want of redness on the veins, noted in my "Visit to the *Cinchona* Forests." I have now sedulously compared the specimens with those of the *cuchicara*, and can find no tangible difference. The leaves have the same general outline, the venation, and the tuft of hairs in the vein axils. They are more decidedly acuminate, and very acute; but the same peculiarity is to be seen in the leaves of young plants of *C. C. succirubra* and *magnifolia*.

I have, &c.
(signed) *Richard Spruce.*

Chonana, near Guayaquil,
22 September 1861.

Note respecting the Map.

The accompanying Map is intended to illustrate both the present Report on the expedition to procure seeds and plants of *C. Succirubra* by Mr. Spruce, and his former visit to another part of the "red bark" region in 1859, an account of which was printed in the Journal of the Proceedings of the Linnean Society.

This region, comprising the forests on the western slopes of Chimborazo and Asuay, and the courses of the rivers which fall into the Bay of Guayaquil, has never been correctly laid down in any map. Many of the rivers mentioned by Mr. Spruce are not to be found in the best atlas, and the courses of many of those which are marked are quite incorrect. Very few of the names of places, too, in Mr. Spruce's Report are to be found in any existing map, and those which are marked are frequently in wrong positions. All the positions depend on that of Guayaquil, while scarcely a single authority agrees as to the longitude of that town.

	°	′	″	
Villavicencio gives the longitude of Guayaquil in	80	9	51	W.
Inman - - - - - - - - -	79	56	0	W.
Raper - - - - - - - - -	79	52	7	W.
Admiralty chart - - - - - - -	79	51	0	W.
Arrowsmith and others - - - - -	79	50	0	W.
Keith Johnston - - - - - - -	79	43	0	W.
English Cyclopædia of Geography - - -	79	23	0	W.

By far the fullest map of this region is that which was published by Villavicencio, in 1858, to accompany his work on the geography of Ecuador; and I have, therefore, been obliged to take Villavicencio's map as a guide for the courses of the larger rivers, and the positions of the principal places, for want of a better.

But Mr. Spruce, in a note at page 66, states that Villavicencio is not to be depended upon, and mentions several errors in his map. In the accompanying map I have corrected these errors, in accordance with Mr. Spruce's statement, and I have marked the places and courses of rivers which are mentioned in Mr. Spruce's Report, but which are not to be found in any map, as nearly as possible according to his descriptions. Of course, with data so insufficient accuracy is not attainable, but at the same time the present map is fuller and more accurate than any that has before appeared, comprising the "Red Bark" region of Ecuador, and all the places and rivers mentioned in Mr. Spruce's Reports will be found in the positions assigned to them by him, or as nearly so as was possible, while retaining Villavicencio's positions for Guayaquil and the other chief towns. Both the longitudes of Villavicencio, and those of the Admiralty Chart, are indicated on the map.

Lucmas and Limon, though they are merely small farms, are marked in capitals, because the former was Mr. Spruce's head quarters during his visit to the Cinchona forests in 1859, and the latter during his operations in 1860.

(signed) *Clements R. Markham.*

India Office,
3 January 1862.

Map to illustrate Mr. SPRUCE'S REPORTS on the "RED BARK" REGION OF ECUADOR.

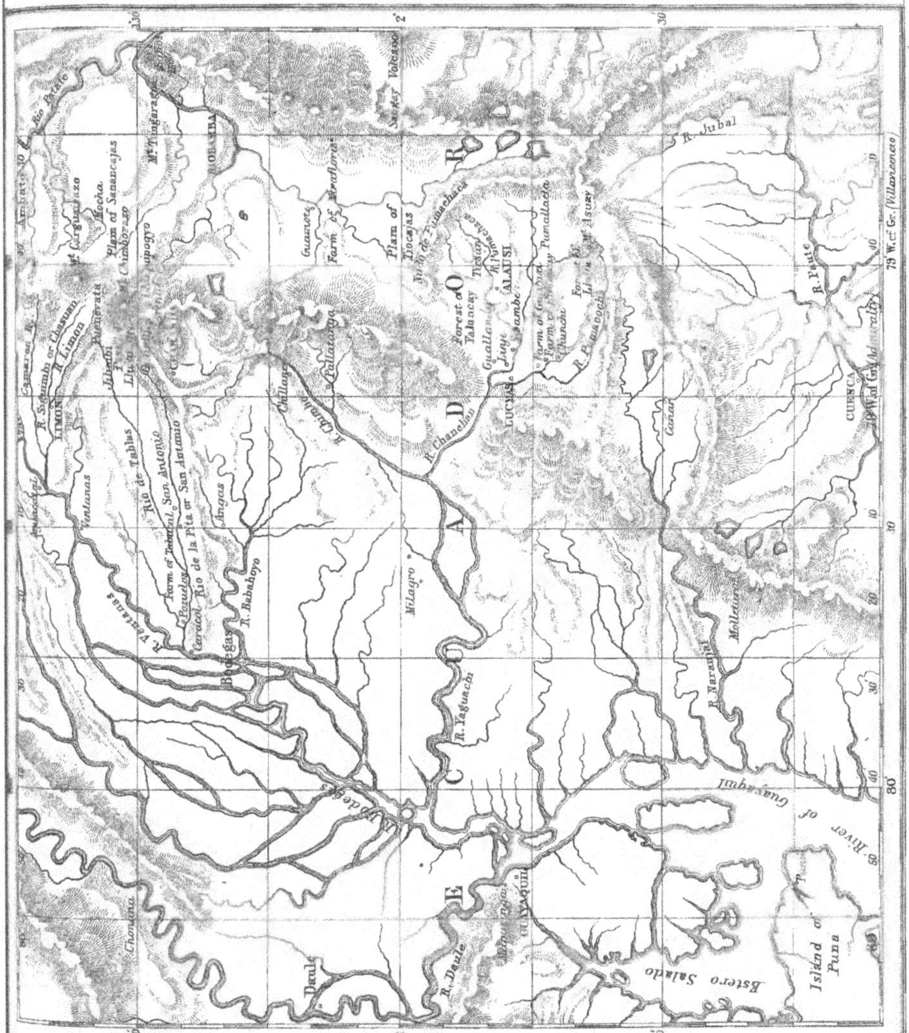

— No. 45. —

COPIES of CORRESPONDENCE relating to the Employment of Mr. *Pritchett.*

MEMORANDUM.

ON 19th December 1859, Mr. Pritchett addressed the Under Secretary of State for India, stating that he had been in communication with Mr. Markham, and that he had offered to procure cinchona plants from the Peruvian province of Huanuco. He was informed, in reply, that Mr. Markham had authority to pay 500*l.* to any one whom he might think proper to employ in the Huanuco forests.

In a letter dated 16th December, in reply to one from Mr. Pritchett, Mr. Markham had stated that he would employ him if he came out to Peru at his own expense, before Mr. Markham left for the interior.

Mr. Pritchett did not arrive while Mr. Markham was in Lima, but, when Mr. Markham started for the interior, he left Mrs. Markham in full possession of his views and intentions, in case Mr. Pritchett should arrive during his absence.

— No. 46. —

Mr. *Pritchett* to Mr. *Markham.*

My dear Sir, Lima, 10 April 1860.

I ARRIVED here yesterday from Southampton. Having applied to Messrs. Gibbs & Co. for your instructions, I was extremely sorry to find that the answer received was that none had been left by you, and that they recommended me to communicate with you by letter.

Knowing how precarious is the chance of any letter now finding you, and even should I receive your answer to this within two months of the present time, how large a part of the season will have gone away, I earnestly beg of you to answer this as early as possible, sending me instructions, and authorising Messrs. Gibbs to advance me enough to pay the expense of mule hire in the interior.

I have, &c.
(signed) *G. J. Pritchett.*

— No. 47. —

Mrs. *Markham* to Mr. *Pritchett.*

Arequipa, April 1860.

MRS. MARKHAM is sorry to inform Mr. Pritchett that Mr. Markham has already left this for the interior, therefore the best thing for Mr. Pritchett to do will be to proceed immediately to the forests of Huanuco, and if possible to bring down plants and seeds to unite with Mr. Markham's collection.

Mrs. Markham is not aware whether Mr. Pritchett has already received any instructions, and, therefore, it may be best to repeat what Mr. Markham wishes Mr. Pritchett to do, which is to collect young plants, and if possible seeds, of the three following species of cinchonæ, namely, *C. nitida, C. micrantha,* and *C. glandulifera.*

C. nitida may be distinguished by its bark being of a clear grey colour, from the silvery lichens which almost entirely cover it. The parts not covered by lichens are of a chesnut colour. Its leaves are lanceolate-obovate, capsule narrow, twice as long as broad, corolla roseate, and very fragrant. It is known in commerce as "grey bark," and also as "*Quina Cana Legitima,*" and is especially found at Panatahuas, Casapi, Cuchero, and near Huanuco.

C. micrantha may be known by the white colour of its bark, and greater roughness of surface; when cracked it is more fibrous, and of a light cinnamon brown

brown colour. The leaves are broadly ovate, rather downy underneath at the base of the veins. Panicle very large, brachiate, many flowered. Corolla white, and densely silky. Capsule three times as long as broad. Contrary to the usual habit of cinchonæ, this species is met with in the bottoms of valleys, and on the banks of rivers. It is known as "*Cascarilla de Chicoplaya, de flor frequeña*," and is distinguished from other species round Huanuco by the pleasing white colour of its flowers. "*Pata de Gallinazo*" is the bark of the younger and upper branches of this species, so called from the black scrawly lichen (graphis) which grows on the exterior. It is found in the cool and shady tracts of Chicoplaza, Mownon, and Cuchero, growing in low damp situations.

C. glandulifera.—This is the most valuable species of the three. Its bark is known by its dark colour, only here and there varied by small greyish green spots, and the inside should be the colour of a ripe orange, shading into fiery brown. Leaves ovate, lanceolate, on the upper side smooth and shining, on the under side hairy. Corolla pale rose colour, velvety on the tube, and woolly inside the limb. Capsule three times as long as broad. Known in commerce as "*Cascarilla Negrilla.*" It is found in Panatahuas, Chicoplaza, Mownon, and Cuchero, but is rare, only being met with on the higher mountain ridges. It flowers in February and March. Mr. Howard has also mentioned to Mr. Markham that a valuable species known as "*Cascarilla de Hoja de Oliva*" is found on the Cuesta del Carpis and near San Rafael, and that the *C. Uritusinga* of Loxa has been found in Chicoplaza.

Arrangements will be made with Messrs. Gibbs for advancing the necessary money (500 dollars) to Mr. Pritchett, who had better leave directions for having his letters forwarded, in case Mr. Markham should have any further instructions for him. If Mr. Pritchett leaves Lima as soon as possible he will be at Huanuco in the beginning of June, and may have the plants down to the coast in time to meet Mr. Markham.

— No. 48. —

Mr. *Pritchett* to Mr. *Markham.*

My dear Sir, Lima, 17 May 1860

I BEG to acknowledge receipt of 500 dollars received from Mrs. Markham by last steamer, also a letter containing instructions, in accordance with which I shall leave to-morrow morning for Huanuco, and hope to be successful in bringing down seeds of the different cinchonas mentioned. I shall leave my address with Messrs. Gibbs.

I have, &c.
(signed) *G. J. Pritchett.*

— No. 49. —

Mr. *Markham* to Mr. *Pritchett.*

Sir, Lima, 15 June 1860.

I ARRIVED at the port of Islay on the 1st instant with my collection of Cinchona plants, and shall convey them to India by the steamer which leaves Islay on June 24th. On reaching Arequipa I received your letters, dated from Lima on April 10th and May 7th, and a copy of Mrs. Markham's instructions to you.

I conclude that you are now about to enter the Cinchona forests of Huanuco or Huamalies, and that you will be fully engaged in the work of collecting before you can receive this letter, in which I propose to transmit my final instructions before leaving the coast. You will see that I have succeeded in completing my collection of plants much earlier than I had expected.

Mrs. Markham has already supplied you with information respecting the three species of Cinchona to which you should turn your attention; and you will observe that the principal localities to be examined are in the vicinity of Huanuco; or else, like Chicoplaya, in the ravine of the river Monzon, in Huamalies, which I think ought also to be explored.

The

The plants should, if possible, be young seedlings; but you will very likely find great numbers of root shoots, springing from trunks of trees which have been cut down, with good roots of their own. These also should be collected, and, if too tall, cut down to a length of about 18 inches, and relieved of leaves and top hamper.

For transport across the cordillera, the plants should be packed in layers of damp moss, and sewn up in packages of warm matting, or banana leaves.

Your attention should be particularly directed to the collection of seeds. You should ascertain the time they are ripe, and take them just before the capsule opens, and the seeds are scattered. This operation will require considerable care. Mr. Spruce proposes to spread sheets under the trees at the time of cutting or breaking off the branches bearing capsules. When collected, the seeds should be dried, carefully kept dry, and occasionally aired. On arriving at Lima, they should be delivered to Mr. Petrie at Callao, the agent of the Pacific Steam Navigation Company, with a request that he will forward them to England.

As soon as the plants arrive in Lima, you will establish them in Wardian cases, which I have ordered to be made here for that purpose, and forward them to Southampton; but I will write to you more fully on this subject in a few days.

Much must, of course, be left to your own discretion in this important enterprise, and the information you obtain on the spot will be a much better guide to you than any instructions that I can transmit with regard to the localities to be examined; but I would particularly recommend the forests along the course of the Mownon, and those near Chinchao, and the Cuesta del Carpis.

You should take notes of the soil, climate, and position in which the Cinchonæ grow, and forward a report of your proceedings to the India Office immediately on your arrival at Lima. Dried specimens of leaves, flowers, and capsules should also be procured, if possible, and transmitted. Wishing you health, and success in this undertaking,

I have, &c.
(signed) *Clements R. Markham.*

— No. 50. —

Mr. *Markham* to Mr. *Pritchett*.

Sir, Lima, 29 June 1860.

You will receive this note at the same time with another dated the 15th instant. With regard to your collection of plants and seeds of the Cinchonæ, I have ordered cases to be made here for the reception of the plants on their arrival, by a carpenter named Lewis, whose workshop you can find out from the clergyman here, the Rev. J. Henry. You can establish the plants in the carpenter's yard, and have them removed to Callao on the day the steamer sails, and you will find no difficulty in procuring fresh soil. There will be six cases.

The cases should be filled with soil to a depth of eight or nine inches, and the plants should be planted in rows from the back to the front of the case. This should be done as soon as possible, as every day that they are out of the soil lessens the chance of their growing. The distance from plant to plant must be regulated by their size, but in the case of their having much foliage, it is better that they should be rather wide apart, as the crowding of the leaves is always injurious, often inducing mildew and mould. After being planted, the plants should be well watered; and if the cases are not to be immediately moved, they should be sprinkled from time to time as they get dry.

On the surface of the soil, between each row of plants, a flat piece of wood should be placed, three or four inches wide, extending from the back to the front of the case, held firmly down by two other pieces extending the whole length of the case—the one being nailed to its back and the other to its front. The one along the back should be put in before the plants. The under edge of this batten ought to be just far enough above the surface of the soil to allow the ends of the cross battens to be inserted under it. By this means the soil and plants are kept from being disturbed in the operation of moving the cases.

When the cases are to be finally closed, the soil should be in a medium state, as regards moisture, and all the dead foliage should be removed. They should be made as air-tight as possible by means of putty and paint.

 The

The seeds should be made up in paper parcels, about half an ounce in each, which should all be put in a canvas bag, and kept hanging during the voyage in some airy part of the ship, such as the captain's cabin. The paper should be of an absorbent nature, so as to dry up any moisture coming from the seeds, such as common brown paper.

In addition to the main packet of seeds, you are to make up two smaller ones, to the address of the Governors of Jamaica and Trinidad, to the care of Her Majesty's Consul at Panama, and the large packet is to be sent to the address of the Under Secretary of State for India.

You should make arrangements with Mr. Petrie at Callao about the shipment of the Wardian cases in the first steamer for Panama, on the upper deck, and you will pay Lewis, the carpenter, for them; but I will request that the sum may be repaid to you, and not included in the 500*l.*, so you should send in an account of it.

Wishing you every success,

I have, &c., in great haste,
(signed) *Clements R. Markham.*

Note.—In the event of Mr. Pritchett meeting with any opposition from the local authorities in embarking his plants, I have supplied Mr. Jerningham, Her Majesty's Consul-General at Lima, with a copy of the letter from the Minister of Finance to the Superintendent of the Custom-house at Islay, ordering him to allow my plants to be embarked, which will be an unanswerable argument.

Clements R. Markham.

— No. 51. —

From *G. J. Pritchett*, Esq., to *Clements R. Markham*, Esq., India Office, London.

Sir, Lima, 13 September 1860.

On the 16th ultimo, the day on which I arrived in Huánuco from the bark districts of Cocheros, Casapi, Pampayaco, and others, where I had been engaged the previous two months in examining the most favourable spots for carrying out my object of obtaining seeds and plants, I had the pleasure of receiving your two favours of 15th and 29th June, from Lima, containing for my guidance some further particulars, in addition to those already received, of the distinguishing characteristics of the different species of barks to be observed, and also instructions as to the packing and delivery of the seeds and plants.

Although the arrival of these letters to my hands has been so tardy, I may, nevertheless, venture to hope that no prejudice has been thereby caused to the execution of my mission, as every particular, with the exception of only one unavoidable item, has been complied with. The collection, for instance, of seeds, to which you desire that special attention should be paid, in preference to that of young plants, I had already determined on before leaving London, where I learnt from Mr. Veitch, that he thought success more likely to be achieved through the ripe and carefully gathered seeds than by means of the plants. If it had been otherwise, and the plants had been considered more desirable than the seeds, it would have proved very costly for me, as the carriage from the bark woods to the coast ranges from 25 dollars to 30 dollars per cargo of 12 arobas.

I was therefore the more glad to find that the instructions received by me in Huánuco, on my return from the Montaña, had been already and fortunately anticipated, as I have obtained a good quantity of ripe seed, well dried, and most carefully packed, and which will be delivered in perfect order, according to your letter. I could greatly have increased the quantity, had I not been obliged to return to Lima by the end of August. I have also been very much hindered from getting seed earlier, by the season having been unusually wet and unfavourable for its ripening, so that it was only within the last fortnight of my being in the forest that the greater part of the seed was gathered, it only then having become sufficiently ripe for the purpose.

Should it be necessary, it would not be difficult to make arrangements for an annual supply from the Huánuco district of considerable quantities, both of seeds and plants.

My

My departure from Huánuco for Lima was on the 21st ultimo, and I am sorry to say that my arrival at the latter place was not in sufficient time to embark the plants in the steamer of the 29th. My first care on arrival there was to get the plants established in the Wardian cases, which was done in the course of a few days, as soon as the carpenter had finished his work, and admitted of so doing. The expenses and cost of the Wardian cases, including shipping, railway, &c., are 186 dollars.

By the present steamer, the following are shipped to the care of C. T. Bidwell, esq., Panama; viz.—

Six Wardian cases, plants, containing 10 in each, addressed to the Under Secretary of State for India.

One bale, containing one packet, addressed, Under Secretary of State for India, containing 24 doz. ½ oz. papers, *C. micrantha* seed, var. *Provinciana.*

18 doz. ½ oz. papers, *C. nitida* seed.

8 doz. ½ oz. papers, *C. micrantha*, var. *Pata di Gallinazo.*

One packet, addressed, H. E. the Governor of Jamaica, containing,—

6 doz. ½ oz. papers, *C. micrantha* seed, var. *Provinciana.*

4 doz. ½ oz. papers, *C. nitida.*

One packet, addressed, H. E. the Governor of Trinidad, containing,—

4 doz. ½ oz. papers, *C. micrantha*, var. *Provinciana.*

4 doz. ½ oz. papers, *C. nitida.*

all of which I trust will arrive in perfectly good order at their respective destinations.

I shall embark in the present steamer, and hope to have the pleasure of seeing you about the middle of next month. My address will be as before, the Fishery, Boxmoor, Herts.

I am, &c.
(signed) *G. J. Pritchett.*

—No. 52.—

LETTER from *G. J. Pritchett*, Esq., to the Under Secretary of State for India.

Sir, Boxmoor, Herts, 9 July 1861.

THE particulars of the circumstances causing the delay of my report on the bark districts of Huanuco, which I visited last year for the purpose of collecting certain species of the plants and seeds of *Cinchona* peculiar to it, are already before you.

I have now the honour to submit, for your information, the following details:—

Having obtained letters of introduction in Lima, and made what preparations were needful in that city, in the way of waterproof tent for the forest, as well as warm clothing for passing the cordillera of the Andes, I took my departure from that city on the 18th May, leaving there a letter to be forwarded to Mr. Markham, intimating my having done so.

The city of Huanuco was reached on the 28th, a distance of eighty leagues. It is situated on the eastern slope of the Andes.

This being the last point for procuring mules, as well as preparing provisions, it was necessary to remain here some days to carry out these objects. In the meanwhile, I was engaged in procuring as much local information as possible, in connexion with my object.

A very short time proved how interested the community of Huanuco are in the products of the neighbouring forests. I was welcomed by the governor of the place, and everything that would in any way contribute to success was placed at my disposal. Through the kindness of several of the residents, I was enabled to obtain the services of a Bolivian, who had in former years been engaged in getting out bark, to a considerable extent, and was well acquainted with the several most interesting spots in the forest for that purpose.

The time of my arrival in Huanuco was unusually favourable for gaining information on every point that might be necessary, and ready and eager replies were given to my inquiries, in consequence of the expectations of the inhabitants being at the highest respecting the future prosperity of their city, on account of a grand a grand road, which was already commenced, for connecting the province of Huanuco with the river Ucayali (about fifty leagues to the east), the largest and most important of the southern tributaries of the Amazon.

Arriving at this time, with introductions from members of the Government in Lima, and not having anything to do with the usual objects that take people to Huanuco, it was impossible that the popular mind could allow me to pass unnoticed. To me, therefore, was assigned the post of emissary from the Government for ascertaining the most suitable point on the Ucayali which should be made the terminus of the road, with the view of connexion with the Amazon by large steamers on the former river.

Provisions of dried meat, biscuit, lard, rice, tea and coffee, sugar, spirits, tin teapot and mug (the spirits being the most important of all in the damp forest) being ready, I left the city of Huanuco for the forest on the 9th June, having been delayed there twelve days by these indispensable preliminaries.

The route to the bark district (I should say to the centre of the district, as it extends from north to south over a distance of at least from forty to forty-five leagues) lies to the eastward, the first part of the road, for about five leagues, being down the valley of Huanuco, and more or less along the river's bank. Sugar-cane estates occupy the land on either side, whose products supply the mineral district of the Cerro de Pasco with large quantities of the aguardiente, the rum of the country, and is a source of extensive support and profit to the inhabitants. The whole of the cultivation is by irrigating canals from the river, a system most thoroughly understood by all the Indian population of South America.

Leaving the valley of Huanuco, the road strikes off to the left, in a northerly direction, gradually ascending from the river, in the direction of the highest part of the chain of mountains, at the top of which is Carpis, and at a distance of about two leagues is the village of Acomayo. This is the halting-place generally adopted by travellers leaving Huanuco, on account of eggs and alfalfa being both obtainable here, and the necessity for giving a good rest to the mules before attempting the pass of the mountain. It was my fate to both ascend and descend this mountain on foot, on account of the unusually unfavourable state of the road at the time of my entering the forest.

The great mountain range of Carpis may be considered the outpost of this part of the forest. On one side, from its towering elevation, you look over the boundless sea of forest vegetation to the eastward; on the other, in the direction of the cordillera and Huanuco, the prospect consists of every form of bare rock and arid mountain, except in those few instances where the bed of a valley is visible, and the green patches of irrigation can be distinguished.

On the forest side, the vapour and cloud which rise are continually bathing the woods, which seem at this spot to be the perpetual focus for the converging clouds. They are carried over the tops of the range towards the more heated plains of Acomayo, and bear with them in that direction, for a short distance, their beneficial and nutritive influence, though it does not extend above a league or a league and a half.

The atmospheric changes which rapidly take place at this point are very great, every vicissitude of temperature being experienced here within a few hours—at one time, a raging tempest of rain and wind; at another, the calm, tranquil, leaden atmosphere of chilling cloud and fog. I presume the almost fathomless depths of the water-worn abysses of the forest, the great proximity of their sides to each other, at the same time that they are under the influence of a tropical sun, will account for these phenomena.

Carpis contains many specimens of trees of the *Cinchona* species; among them the *C. purpurea* immediately arrests attention, on account of the distinctive character of its foliage; it is very abundant here, as well as in other parts of the forest which I visited. I presume it made more impression on me here, as I saw it for the first time.

C. nitida is common on the north-east side, and at the upper part of the mountain.

C. obovata, the source of the olive-leafed, but known there as the *lucumo*-leafed species, is met with in small quantities, but with characteristics so decided that I could have no doubt of its being the species so called. It required several days' examination before it could be discovered, and I had almost despaired of finding it, when the last day brought success.

C. micrantha,

C. micrantha, var. Provinciana and *var. Pata de Gallinazo*, are both inhabitants of the lower levels of the mountain. Other species were met with, which may be valuable; but as my object was confined to those above named, and my time was exceedingly limited, it was urgent for me to make the most of the short remaining season, and dedicate the whole of my energies to carrying it out in the most effective manner possible.

I lost the opportunity of seeing an important distinctive character of the *Cinchonas* by arriving on the ground too late to see the trees in flower, so I was obliged to be guided by other peculiarities, in which I trust I have been successful.

The nature of the ground, the dense and lavish character of the vegetation, which is exuberant beyond expression, have hitherto effectually kept this region in a perfect state of seclusion and almost entirely unknown, except to the few natives who, in naked loneliness, have been urged by hunger to thread their way through the brakes and sloughs of its rank wastes, when escaping from the thrall of some oppressive estate owner, or pursuing the chase of some wild animal for food to support the exertion necessary for threading the difficult mazes of the entangled woods.

Chinchao is the first village met with in descending the valley of the river of Casapi, of which Carpis is the head. It gives its name to a cinchona district in the neighbourhood, on both sides of the valley, from which specimens of cinchona have been brought, and sometimes also applies to the chain of lofty hills or mountains on the left bank, which connects the crest of Carpis with the important bark mountain of Cayumba, within a league or so of the river Huallaga, to which the river of Huanuco is tributary.

On this chain of hills the same species of cinchona are met with: in the upper parts, the *nitida* and *obovata*, and in the lower, the *purpurea* and *micrantha*.

Chinchao is the only village of this valley, consisting of about 20 huts and a church.

The coca hacienda of Casapi was reached on the 13th June, having passed, on the way down the valley, the different coffee and coca haciendas for the cultivation of those products.

Casapi.—This hacienda is an extensively cleared portion of the forest for the cultivation of the coca shrub, whose leaves are greatly appreciated among the labourers of the country as a stimulant of a peculiarly supporting character—many nights and days of laborious watching and exertion being undergone by the assistance of its strange properties.

To the miner it is considered indispensable, and the important mineral district of Pasco, which contains many thousand inhabitants, would be a desert were it not for the strange energy imparted to the miner by the use of the leaf of this invaluable shrub.

It is masticated, with the addition of a small quantity of caustic lime, which is carefully introduced to the chewed mass at the end of a small stick. "Hualqui" is the name of the hide bag containing the coca leaves, and "poto" that of the small *maté* containing the lime.

Casapi is situated at the lower or eastern end of the valley, where it joins the main valley of the River Huallaga. This was the first scene of continuous exploration. It was here that I was joined by my guide, who did not join me for 10 days after my arrival.

In the meantime, I proceeded to make use of all the means at my disposal, by availing myself of the people of the hacienda to show me the tracks and intricacies of the neighbouring woods, all which was most kindly permitted by the owner of the establishment, who is the son of the gentleman who entertained Dr. Pœpig when he visited these parts. With this assistance, I was enabled to examine the whole of these woods before the arrival of Juan, my guide. The result of the exploration proved how active had been the operations of the collectors in the time of former bark speculations; for, with but rare exceptions, every tree had been felled, and nothing was left to subsequent collectors but to wait till the younger plants should come to their full maturity.

It was evident that this was not the spot for my purpose.

Casapillo is situated on the high land which is formed by the junction, at an acute angle, of the Casapi valley with that of the Huallaga. Its height above the woods of Casapi is between 400 and 500 feet.

 The

The only species found here was the *C. nitida*, whose only habitat is airy situations; but, as in the case of Casapi, it had been visited by the collectors, and every cinchona tree had been felled; the spot was soon abandoned for search in others of better promise.

The extent of this wood, which is on a high spur of land which comes from the range of hills in the direction of Pillao, is several square leagues.

Cocheros.—The mountain called San Cristoval de Cocheros is situated at about three leagues from Casapi, close to the Huallaga. The owner of these haciendas told me that it had never been visited by collectors, and that I could prosecute my search in its woods as much as I pleased. It rises, an isolated mountain, from the low land at the conflux of the two rivers, to a height of about 1,200 feet above them. This point is about the centre of the bark district of Huanuco.

It has on the north, or lower down the Huallaga, within a 15-league radius, the following bark-producing stations: Chicoplaya, San Antonio, Tingomaria, Huachipa, Cayumba, Patayrondas, besides others on the Monzon River. On the south, in the direction of Panao, Pampayaco, Lanzabamba, Jaupe, Mallgo, Iguacará, and Pillao.

On the arrival of Juan (my bark guide), I immediately set to work to determine the capacity of our new scene of labour for producing cinchona seed, and daily were the trips made into its woods for that purpose. But it was soon clear that, however much was met with, and seemed merely to require a few days to ripen, nothing could be done for the present, as the capsules were only recently formed.

During this pause, which was unavoidable, it seemed desirable to have other woods, known to contain the *nitida* and *micrantha* species, examined at the same time, to ascertain the state of the seed there, which, if more forward, could have been harvested before the Cocheros seed was ready. None, however, was found to possess the advantages of this spot for my purposes. I therefore determined to make the entire collection of seeds and plants from this point, and commenced at once to fix on the trees in the most forward state, so as to watch the gradual maturing of the seeds, both of the *nitida* and *micrantha*. It seemed as if a few days would be sufficient for the purpose, yet several weeks elapsed before the first lot of seed was gathered.

The Governor of Tingomaria sent me several specimens of bark from his neighbourhood, and offered me access to the woods of his district; but the swollen state of the river, which had for a long time prevented any communication from below, and having the species I required so near at hand, made me thank him for his kindness without availing myself of it.

He sent several specimens, which proved to be of the *micrantha* and other species found in Cocheros.

From the reports brought me by people engaged by me in the search for the *nitidas* and *micranthas* as well as the *C. obovata* in the mountains of Pillao, I have no doubt that this district to the south of Cocheros, with the intermediate points enumerated above, would yield a prodigious quantity of these barks, should the time ever arrive of its attaining a commercial value.

Huachipa was reported to me, by an old Spaniard, and formerly a collector, as containing the *C. obovata*. We searched there for it, however, without success.

The first examination of Cocheros gave very little promise of good. I commenced at the east corner of the mountain, on the lower side next the river, and gradually rose along the south-east face, in a zigzag direction, till the summit was reached. Here an abundance of *C. nitida* trees was met with, having a fair quantity of seed, though in the early part of the ascent I was greatly disappointed at meeting with only few, but very fine, specimens of the *nitida* and *micrantha* species. I was somewhat reconciled, however, with the reflection that it was probable the sunny side of the mountain would prove more favourable to the cinchonas, more particularly those requiring warmth and moisture, and I looked forward to the morrow to try the correctness of the surmise. Early next day, our course (the starting point being the same as yesterday) was directed due north, parallel with the line of the river; and having ascended sufficiently high to be well in with the *micranthas*, which already showed greater development than on the south-east side, we continued in a horizontal direction along this face of the mountain, meeting with a most satisfactory show of the *var. Provinciana*. We marked

marked the trees as we entered, by way of precaution, so as to arrive at the same spot on a subsequent visit, which had to be repeated a great many times before felling the trees for gathering the seed.

The *var. Pata de Gallinazo* is scarce on this mountain, as well as on every other we visited, compared with the *var. Provinciana.* They both grow to very large size, and the foliage is somewhat similar, but they are easily distinguished by the bark.

Some of this species I found to be as large as 30 inches diameter, and a noble and elegant appearance many of them have among their brethren of the forest, rising in some instances as high as 70 feet.

Our day's work confirmed me in the determination to take this point as a fair specimen of the district. The supply of trees and seeds being so ample, and the field of exploration being so comparatively near to the coca hacienda before named, made this spot suitable also for the drying process, so very needful for the delivery of the seed in good condition on the coast.

Being entirely satisfied as to the existence of the seeds at this point, I now only felt great anxiety about the weather. Although it was then about the middle of the dry season, heavy soaking rains were still falling from day to day, and the seed seemed to make no progress whatever towards maturity.

Towards the latter part of July the weather broke up, and the sun began to make impression on the solid banks of clouds that filled the valleys. Though clouds were the prevalent visitants during this so-called dry season, there were occasions, during some portions of the day, when the sun unveiled, and even penetrated to the very underwood of the forest.

But even to the last day of my remaining here, when we had nearly a fortnight's fine weather, with only an occasional shower, the tracks were still deep with mud, and only in the exposed situations could the mud be found less than ankle-deep. This fortnight of fine weather was the harvest that was necessary to be fully improved.

The rapid ripening of the seed kept as many hands as I could procure from the hacienda occupied in felling the trees, and stripping them of their seed. After various trials, I found that the felling of the tree was the best way of proceeding under my present circumstances. My time was very short, and the quantity of seed suddenly ripened so plentiful, that to attain my object of getting a good supply of it I could afford to be extravagant; and although much more seed was lost than what was gathered, still my limited time compelled me to adopt this plan.

During the fortnight we were engaged in this work, seven large trees were felled daily, and denuded of their capsules. At this same time the drying process had to be attended to in the hacienda, and every advantage to be taken of the sunshine, while the seeds were carefully protected from the breeze, which, with our utmost care, did not fail to deprive us of some of them. Our spoil having been so hardly earned, ensured this part of our operations being carried out with a jealous care, and the loss in this respect was reduced to a minimum.

By the 13th August, when it was necessary for me to leave, in order to arrive in Lima by the end of the month, the seeds were all carefully put up in outside wrappings of tar-cloth, and every precaution taken to protect them from external influence. The small plants had been brought in and packed in bundles, between layers of the cryptogamous parasites of the coca shrub, overlaid with coverings of palm-branches bound tightly together, and then enveloped in several thicknesses of the woollen fabric of the country, called "xerga."

If it had not been for the great expense of carriage to the coast, I should have brought more plants, as it would have been equally easy for me to have despatched from this district 100 cargas or loads of cinchona plants as the half load to which I was compelled to limit myself, and which I felt exceedingly unwilling to conform to.

During the journey down, I had the plants soaked morning and evening, except those few days on which we were passing the cold region of the Cordillera.

They were in perfect health when put into the Wardian cases in Lima, as also when they arrived at Southampton; I having, during the passage home, made it my business to attend to them, so as to preserve the temperature at as equable a state as possible.

With regard to the geology of the district in and around Cocheros, Casapi, Carpis, the Tingo, &c., the rocks are of the primary formation, and, in many localities,

localities, highly disintegrated, large masses of hornblende, felspar, and micaceous minerals existing in great quantity.

The warmth of the climate (I allude to where the sun's rays are not intercepted by foliage), together with the almost constant moisture of the atmosphere (for it should be borne in mind that my visit was during the dry season), are no doubt highly conducive to disintegration, and hence the great fertility of the soil, derived, after the lapse of many centuries, from this particular class of rock.

Among all the distinct mineral species which abound on the surface of the earth, none are so rich in potash as felspar. This substance is very generally distributed in every direction, derived doubtless from the plutonic rocks by gradual disintegration. All the cinchona tribe are said to require a large quantity of potash for their full development, and hence the reason of their attaining such large proportions in this province.

The felspar which I brought to England, and which I have had examined by an eminent chemist, is pronounced by him to be, in conjunction with other mineral bodies, that best suited to form a rich and prolific soil, when heat and moisture have broken up its particles, rendering it thereby fit for assimilation by the plant.

There is also another mineral which is very abundant, viz. steatite, a silicate of magnesia and alumina. It derives its name from the soft and almost greasy texture it presents, resembling the solid portions of tallow or fat stearic acid. In the republics of South America the natives call it "jabocillo," or soapstone, for a similar reason. The vast quantities which abound in the Huanuco districts generally render them very interesting, both to the geologist and the mineralogist.

I cannot say, however, that I think the geology of the district, or, rather, the geological formation of the rocks (the primary source of the soils on which the cinchona plants grow), to be the sole cause of their flourishing here better than in other parts of the world, as in many other portions of South America, particularly in Chili, Bolivia, and Columbia, I have noticed the same description of minerals with comparatively little alteration. The whole chain of the Andes, from Cape Horn to the Isthmus of Darien, consists essentially of a species of granitic rock, termed "Andesite," differing somewhat from granite (properly so called) and from syenite, which was formerly supposed to constitute the great mass of that chain.

The region about Coquimbo, in Chili, is thickly strewn with disintegrated felspar. Mica, hornblende, and steatite also abound; but the climate of these countries, especially near the coast, precludes the possibility of the growth of the cinchona, it being very dry, with cold south-easterly winds. Nearer to Cape Horn, indeed, much rain falls, but that frigid latitude is also adverse to the growth of a plant so essentially tropical. Hence a climate is also necessary as well as a soil, even though the cinchona may find in the latter, to a certain extent, a fitting and congenial pabulum.

The climate of these districts is essentially moist and warm. The difference in degree, however, between that of the lower parts of the mountains, the habitat of the *micranthas*, and the higher, where the *nitidas* are chiefly found, is very striking, and too much stress can scarcely be laid on this characteristic. I was prevented making observations with my thermometer, as it was disabled on its way down the valley of Casapi. The difference I speak of, therefore, is that of the sensible heat. That I am not mistaken is proved by the perceptible change so remarkable in the character of the vegetation. For instance, within a vertical distance of 200 to 250 feet, it is scarcely possible for it to pass unnoticed. Another important condition, which favours the greater development of the vegetation of the lower levels, is the greater depth and infinitely richer quality of the soil. This is the natural result of the heavy rains, which carry with them the most rich and soluble parts of the upper grounds, and deposit them on the lower, accumulating there its stores of incalculable vegetable wealth.

It merely remains to me to express my wish that the results of my collection of seeds and plants in India, will confirm my present impression, that the service which I had the honour of being entrusted with was not inefficiently carried out.

I have, &c.

(signed) *G. J. Pritchett.*

— No. 53. —

From Sir *C. Wood*, Bart., Secretary of State for India, to His Excellency the Honourable the Governor in Council, Fort St. George; dated London, 17 August 1860.

Para. 1. I HAVE to inform you that Mr. Clements Markham, who was sent to South America last December, to procure a supply of the quinine-yielding cinchona plants, for introduction into India, has arrived in England, with a supply of both varieties of the *C. Calisaya*, and also a few plants of the *C. ovata* and *C. micrantha*.

2. Of these plants 216 are already throwing out shoots, and 53 more still retain life; being 60 per cent. of the number originally planted in the Wardian cases in the Peruvian port of Islay.

3. Mr. Markham will sail for Calicut, by way of Bombay, on the 27th inst., and it is important that the necessary preparations for the conveyance of the plants from the port of Calicut to the sites prepared for their reception in the Neilgherry Hills should be completed before his arrival.

4. The report forwarded by last mail, six additional copies of which are now transmitted, will have placed Dr. Cleghorn and Mr. McIvor in possession of all the details connected with Mr. Markham's expedition, and will have led them to anticipate his arrival by preparing the necessary sites for the cultivation of the plants.

5. Collections of cinchona plants and seeds of other valuable species from the north of Peru, and from Ecuador, will probably arrive in India towards the end of the present year.

6. I have to request that you will advance to Mr. Markham, during his stay on duty in your Presidency, such sums from time to time as you may be satisfied he requires for his own personal expenses, and for the efficient performance of the duty entrusted to his charge.

— No. 54. —

From *H. Cleghorn*, Esq., M. D., Conservator of Forests, to *J. D. Bourdillon*, Esq., Secretary to Government, Revenue Department, Fort St. George, dated 20 September 1860.

I BEG to enclose for the consideration of Government the accompanying letter of Mr. W. G. McIvor, Superintendent Ootacamund Garden, with an estimate of money required for preparing a site for the cinchona plants, expected almost immediately. The following suggestions upon Mr. McIvor's proposal occur to me:—

1. The 50 acres alluded to which lie convenient for superintendence should be reserved specially for the purpose.

2. Ten acres of forest might be prepared immediately, in anticipation of Mr. Markham's arrival. The cart track should also be made. Mr. McIvor has Mr. Markham's pamphlet and report, and knows what amount of shade should be left.

3. The timber felled should be lotted and sold by Mr. McIvor; the proceeds will be available for the preparation of the ten acres. In adddition to this, I would suggest a grant of 2,000 rupees, to be accounted for as expended.

4. The simultaneous cultivation of peppermint, &c., is a good suggestion; but until Mr. Markham's arrival, I should not propose more than the preparation of ten acres. So far as I know, Mr. Markham has from 600 to 700 plants, all of course of small size; allowing for losses in transit, and the proportion to be sent to Mr. Thwaites, in Ceylon, this area will suffice; moreover, Mr. Markham may

consider other sites preferable, or may advise the trial of experiments in several localities for different species.

5. I have not heard of Mr. Markham's having reached England, but his arrival in India should be telegraphed at once to Mr. McIvor, from Calicut or Madras, according to circumstances.

— No. 55. —

From Mr. *W. G. McIvor*, Superintendent Government Gardens, to Dr. *Cleghorn*, Conservator of Forests; dated Ootacamund, 12 September 1860.

WITH reference to the order of Government, under date the 18th ultimo, No. 1220, I have the honour to enclose an estimate of the money required for the preparation of the cinchona site indicated in paragraph 9 of your letter dated the 31st July 1860, No. 83, and beg to solicit the favour of your making application to Government for the sanction of the amount required.

2. In the estimate I have included the cost of a bandy road from the cantonment of Ootacamund to the cinchona plantation, as this will enable us to cart manure at a small cost.

3. As the cinchona trees will be planted wide, and as several years will elapse before they cover the ground, I would suggest that peppermint be planted over the whole extent of the land, and the essence prepared for the medical department; this to be sold at what is considered its fair value. I make this proposition in order to economise the expense of this experimental planting, as I anticipate that the returns from the peppermint will in a great measure meet the expenses of keeping up the plantation.

4. In an experiment of this kind, where it is important to show that it can be profitably conducted, every exertion should be made in order to increase the returns from the undertaking; as a great drawback to the extension of the cultivation of the cinchona will be the length of time the plant requires to come to maturity.

5. I have just learned that Mr. Markham arrived in Southampton on the 28th of July, with a large supply of cinchona plants in good condition, and that they were to be dispatched to India by the first steamer in August; it is, therefore, probable that they may have already reached Madras; and as no preparation has been made for their reception, I will proceed at once with the work, in anticipation of the sanction of Government, and trust you will approve of this course, as I am most anxious for the success of the undertaking and the preservation of the plants, which would be endangered to a certain extent were they to arrive when entirely unprepared for their reception.

— No. 56. —

ORDER by the Madras Government, 28 September 1860.

1. COPY of the Despatch above recorded will be communicated to the Acting Conservator of Forests, the Collector of Malabar, and the Superintendent of the Government Gardens, Ootacamund.

2. Mr. McIvor will proceed at once to Calicut, there to await Mr. Markham's arrival. The Collector will afford all needful aid for facilitating the transit of the cases to their destination, and will also furnish Mr. Markham, on his arrival, with such funds as he may require to meet his personal expenses.

3. Copies of Mr. Markham's report to the Secretary of State will be forwarded to the Acting Conservator of Forests, Mr. McIvor, the Superintendent of the Láll Bágh at Bangalore, and Mr. Holl (overseer) at Coonoor.

4. In

4. In his letter, dated 20th inst., the Conservator of Forests submits a letter from Mr. McIvor, detailing the steps which he proposes to take in pursuance of the Order of Government, dated 18th ultimo. The Government approve Dr. Cleghorn's recommendations; the 50 acres selected will, accordingly, be marked out and reserved specially for the cinchona plant. The other arrangements are as follows: 10 acres of the above to be immediately cleared and prepared, the cart track to be made, the felled timber to be sold, and the proceeds to go towards the expenses. A grant is also sanctioned of 2,000 rupees, to be accounted for when expended.

5. Pending the arrival of Mr. Markham, Mr. McIvor will confine the cultivation of peppermint to the 10 acres which are to be first cleared. The Government will be prepared to extend this permission, should Mr. Markham see fit to recommend it.

To the Collector of Tinnevelly.
,, Resident of Travancore.
,, Collector of Sea Customs, Madras.
,, Commissary General.
,, Acting Conservator of Forests, with printed copy of Mr. Markham's report.
,, Collector of Malabar.
,, Superintendent Government Gardens, Ootacamund, with printed copy of Mr. Markham's report.

To Mr. New, Superintendent, Láll Bágh, Bangalore, with printed copy of Mr. Markham's report.
To Mr. Brown, Horticultural Gardens, Madras.
To Mr. E. Holl, Overseer, Coonoor, with printed copy of Mr. Markham's report.
To the Accountant General.

— No. 57. —

From Mr. *Clements R. Markham*, to the Secretary to Government, Madras; dated Ootacamund, 22 October 1860.

I HAVE the honour to report, for the information of the Governor of Madras in Council, that I arrived at this place, with the cinchona plants which I had collected in the forests of South America, on the 12th instant.

2. I enclose a copy of my report* to the Under Secretary of State for India, in which will be found a detailed account of the present state of the plants, and my opinion respecting the site selected by Mr. McIvor for their cultivation.

*Mr. Markham to the Under Secretary of State for India, 20 October 1860.

3. With the sanction of the Secretary of State for India, I have employed agents in other parts of South America, distant from the region whence I have already procured a collection of plants of the *Cinchonæ Calisaya* and *ovata*, to collect plants and seeds of other valuable species. I expect that these additional cases of plants (15 or 20 in number) will arrive at Bombay towards the end of the year, whence a portion will be sent to Ceylon, and the remainder to Calicut, for transmission to the Neilgherries.

4. Pending the arrival of these additional plants, I propose, with the sanction of the Madras Government, and in pursuance of instructions which I have received from the India Office, to visit several of the mountainous regions of this Presidency, with the view of ascertaining whether any or all of them are suitable for the cultivation of the cinchona plant.

— No. 58. —

From Mr. *C. Markham* to the Under Secretary of State for India; dated Ootacamund, 20 October 1860.

I have the honour to report, for the information of the Secretary of State for India in Council, that I arrived in these hills, with the cases containing cinchona plants, on the 12th instant.

2. Before leaving Bombay, I did not send any of the cases to Ceylon, because, after the treatment they had already received, I was unwilling to trust them on board the Peninsular and Oriental Company's steamers, without some one specially in charge of them; but I have arranged that seven of the cases out of Mr. Spruce's collection shall go to Ceylon, and exchanges can afterwards be made between the plantations in Ceylon and the Neilgherries.

3. On the 3d instant, I sailed from Bombay in Her Majesty's steamer "Pleiad," I. N., which had been placed at my disposal, by order of Sir George Clerk, for this service. The cases were landed at Calicut on the 7th, and sent up the river Beypoor on the same evening, in canoes. Much difficulty was experienced by the coolies in conveying such heavy loads up the Sispara Ghaut; but every facility was supplied by Mr. Grant, the Collector of Malabar; and Mr. MacGregor, one of the assistant collectors, rendered most efficient assistance, by superintending the conveyance of the cases to the summit of the ghaut, where they were taken charge of by Mr. McIvor, the superintendent of the Government gardens at Ootacamund. The cases arrived in the Government gardens, without any accident, on the 12th instant, and the plants were immediately examined by Mr. McIvor.

4. The plants had suffered very much from the delay of six days at Bombay, and during the voyage to Calicut many of them began to droop; but notwithstanding all they had gone through, a number were still throwing out green fresh-looking shoots when the cases were opened at Ootacamund. The roots, however, were found, on examination, to be all more or less attacked by decay, and it was at once apparent that the chief reliance must be on the cuttings which could be obtained from the shoots thrown out by the plants during the voyage. Mr. McIvor obtained 207 cuttings, more or less promising; and he also potted the plants, after carefully removing the decayed wood, in the hope that some might form new roots, and that others might continue to throw out shoots, whence additional cuttings might be obtained: 125 of these original plants were potted.

5. It is now more than a week since the collection arrived at Ootacamund, and already upwards of 50 of the cuttings have begun to grow; and 10 of the original plants have begun to sprout, whence more cuttings will be obtained. Thus the successful introduction of the *Cinchonæ Calisaya* and *ovata* into India is certain; and there is every reason to hope that, with the aid of Waltonian cases, which are now being constructed, I shall see as many cinchona plants before leaving India as I originally collected in the forests of Caravaya.

6. This success, as regards all that has led to it since the arrival of the plants in India, is entirely due to the skill and intelligence of Mr. McIvor, and to his great experience in the propagation of plants.

7. I have examined the site selected by Mr. McIvor for the first cinchona plantation, and consider it exceedingly well adapted for the purpose. The site is a sholah or wooded ravine, at the back of the range of hills which rises behind the Government gardens, and which entirely protects it from the west winds; whilst another high ridge completely screens it from the east. It is 7,450 feet above the level of the sea, and, from its sheltered position, is warmer by several degrees than Ootacamund. Like the thickets where the *Cinchonæ* grow on the pajonales of Caravaya, in Peru, it is surrounded by steep grassy slopes, with a vegetation analogous to that of the Caravayan pajonales. Thus the tree rhododendron takes the place of the purple melastoma, a large white lily that of the liliaceous sayri-sayri; while the gaultheria, lycopodia, and gallia appear to be almost identical in the two regions. The vegetation of the interior of the ravine also resemble that of the pajonales of Sandia to some extent. It contains osbeckias,

osbeckias, holly, cinnamon, michelias, vaccinium, sapota, &c., with an undergrowth of lobelia, acanthus, and ferns, and nine species of cinchonaceous shrubs. The temperature appears to be almost identical with that of the pajonales above the valley of Sandia, in Peru, and the spot receives a moderate supply of rain and mist during both monsoons. It is true that this wooded ravine is more elevated, by nearly 1,500 feet, than any point in Caravaya where I found the cinchona growing; but Ootacamund is more than two degrees nearer the equator, and the temperature of the two places appears to be nearly the same. It is no small advantage, too, that the ravine is so near the Government gardens, and that the cinchona plantation will thus have the benefit of Mr. McIvor's constant supervision.

8. These are my reasons for believing that the site already chosen will be suitable for the cultivation of *Cinchonæ.* The Madras Government has sanctioned a grant of 2,000 rupees for clearing the portion of the ravine intended for cultivation, and for making a cart track to Ootacamund; and Mr. McIvor has made an excellent suggestion (to plant the spaces between the Cinchona trees with peppermint; the essence to be prepared and sold, so as to meet the expenses of keeping up the plantation, in the interval that must elapse before the Cinchona trees can become profitable), which has also been sanctioned.

9. While believing that the site already selected will be found well adapted for the cultivation of the *Cinchonæ Condaminea, ovata,* and also of the *Calisaya,* especially in its shrubby form; I yet consider it very important that another experiment should be tried at a lower elevation, more particularly if, as I fully expect, the *Cinchonæ micrantha* should be amongst the species which are expected to arrive from South America. I intend to go with Mr. McIvor to select a site for this purpose, somewhere in the direction of the Wynaad hills, as soon as the weather becomes finer.

10. When the cinchona becomes a cultivated plant, there is every reason to believe that, like coffee, and I believe cinnamon, it will be found most profitable to grow it in its shrubby form; that more bark will be obtained from the shrubs than from trees, occupying the same space of ground; and that the shrubs, from being grown at a greater elevation, will yield a larger percentage of alkaloids. There will, at the same time, be a stronger inducement to undertake the cultivation as a shrub, because the plantations will be necessarily in much healthier situations. The natives of this country, as well as those of Bombay, are fully alive to the value of quinine; and it is probable that they, as well as European settlers, will hereafter be willing, and even anxious, to cultivate the plants which yield it.

11. With reference to a paragraph in Mr. Merivale's letter to me, dated the 11th of August 1860, I propose, "in order that the experience I have obtained of the situations peculiar to the various species of the cinchonas may be turned to the greatest possible account," to visit the Pulney hills, in Madura, those on the borders of Tinnevelly and Travancore, those of Wynaad and Coorg, and those of Mahableshwur, in Bombay, with the view of ascertaining whether any or all of these are suitable for the cultivation of the cinchona plant. I trust and believe that my observations will prove useful hereafter; though at present, on account of the absence of settlers, and from other causes, there may be little prospect of Cinchona plantations being soon established in some of the above-named regions.

— No. 59. —

From *C. R. Markham,* Esq., to *J. D. Sim,* Esq., Acting Secretary to Government, Revenue Department, Fort St. George; dated Ootacamund, 30 December 1860.

Sir,

1. With reference to an article in the "Madras Daily Times," mentioned in an order received by Mr. McIvor to report upon the state of the cinchona plants, I consider it right to address the following remarks to you, for the information of the Governor in Council. I am told that the article in question, which has attracted

attracted the notice of the Government, is intended to convey the idea that the service upon which I am employed will end in failure; and I address the following remarks to you, in order to give the Government the assurance that, humanly speaking, it is scarcely possible that such can be the result of the experiment the conduct of which has been entrusted to me.

2. When I was appointed to perform this service, I took measures to procure plants and seeds of the four most valuable kinds of cinchona bark known in commerce—namely, the *Calisaya* or yellow bark, the grey and crown barks, and the red bark.

3. The trees yielding these barks grow in regions separated by many hundreds of miles from each other. I undertook to procure the *Calisaya* species myself, and entrusted the collection of the other species to agents thoroughly qualified for the work.

4. The Government is aware, from my report, dated June 1860, that, after much difficulty, I succeeded in embarking upwards of 400 *Calisaya* plants in good condition, at the Peruvian port of Islay, a considerably larger number than was collected by M. Hasskarl for the Dutch Government. Unfortunately, no steamer was provided in the Pacific to convey the collection by a direct route to India; and it became necessary to take it by the circuitous route of the West Indies and the overland journey to Calicut. The extreme heat of the Red Sea must have done the plants much injury; as at the time they were in England, they were seen by Mr. Veitch, and by the foreman at Kew Gardens, who considered them to be in excellent condition. In my report, dated 20th October 1860, I stated that, on the arrival of the plants at Ootacamund, the roots were all decayed, but that Mr. M'Ivor had obtained 207 green cuttings, and 125 wood cuttings, from which all decayed parts which were visible had previously been carefully removed. I added, that 50 of the green cuttings had already begun to show signs of growth, as well as 10 of the wood cuttings.

5. I regret to say that the strong hopes which we then entertained have been disappointed. The green cuttings subsequently went off, as well as many of the wood cuttings; and Mr. McIvor considers that they must have been all more or less tainted by decay. A few of the wood cuttings are still alive and green, and some of them may eventually grow, though I scarcely think it probable.

6. But my object in writing this letter is to give the Government the assurance that the success of this very difficult and important experiment does not depend on the plants which have already arrived, and that disappointment, in one or more instances, is a very different thing from the entire failure of the attempt to introduce these inestimable plants into India.

Calisaya species.

7. With regard to the *Calisaya* species, in the event of our losing all the plants now at Ootacamund, such a calamity will by no means involve failure. I left 17 young *Calisaya* plants at Kew Gardens, and Sir William Hooker has succeeded in procuring four or five *Calisaya* plants raised from seeds formerly transmitted by Dr. Weddell, from which he has struck cuttings; so that next year a second supply of cinchona plants of the *Calisaya* species will be forwarded to India. I have also taken measures to procure a supply of *Calisaya* seeds from Peru; and if my agent should fail me, I am acquainted with others, residing on the spot, whose services I shall be able to obtain, to collect and transmit seeds next season. Thus, it will be seen that the successful introduction of the *Calisaya* species is not dependent on the plants which have already arrived; and the same remark is equally applicable to the species yielding grey and red bark.

Species yielding grey bark.

8. I employed an agent to procure seeds and plants yielding the grey or crown bark of commerce, who has succeeded in performing that service, and his collection has already arrived at Bombay. The grey barks sell at a high price, and are much used in the form of decoctions and infusions. Of the plants yielding this bark, 56 arrived at Southampton last October, eight of which were dead, and were left at Kew Gardens, and the remainder, "being good strong plants, and apparently well rooted,"* were forwarded to India. These plants arrived at Bombay on the 15th of December, having been delayed very much, from some cause as yet unaccounted for. I am sorry to have to report that, on their

* Report of a gardener sent from Kew, to examine these plants at Southampton.

their arrival, all except six were found to be quite dead, and that those which retain life are reported to be in a precarious state. But as with the *Calisaya* species, so with those yielding the grey or crown bark, one disappointment is very far from involving the failure of the experiment.

9. A box of seeds of the grey bark species is now on its way from Bombay, and I have no doubt that Mr. McIvor will be successful in rearing them. A portion of these seeds will be transmitted to the Government Gardens in Ceylon. Seeds have also been sent to the islands of Jamaica and Trinidad, where they will be raised in the hill districts; and from thence, if the seeds now on their way to Ootacamund should fail (which there is no reason to expect), young plants will hereafter be forwarded to India. Cuttings also may possibly be struck from the two plants left at Kew.

10. The species yielding the red bark of commerce, which is only second in value to *calisaya*, and which, according to the latest market prices in London, is now more esteemed than any other species, will also be introduced into this Presidency. I engaged the services of an agent to collect plants and seeds (of the *Cinchona Condaminea* and of the species yielding red bark), who is well known as a botanist, and is eminently qualified, in all respects, for the undertaking. No tidings have yet arrived of the approach of his collection; but 15 cases of plants and a supply of seeds may now be expected in India by every mail. Portions of the seeds of these species, also, will be left at Jamaica, Trinidad, and Kew Gardens, so as to insure the experiment from possible failure. **Species yielding red bark.**

11. It will be seen, by the above remarks, that one or two disappointments were from the first anticipated, but that so many precautions have been taken to prevent the entire failure of this most important experiment, as to render it, so far as human means can avail, almost impossible. The successful propagation of the cinchona, from any plants or seeds which arrive in a healthy condition at Ootacamund, is ensured by the skill and experience of Mr. McIvor.

12. I remain at Ootacamund until the arrival of the cinchona seeds, now on their way from Bombay. I shall then return to Bombay, by way of Coorg and Wainád, previous to my departure for England; and from Bombay I shall have the honour of transmitting to you, for the information of the Governor in Council, a copy of the final report which it will be my duty to address to the Under Secretary of State for India, after having examined the hill districts of the Neilgherries, Pulneys, Wainád, Coorg, and Mahableshwur.

— No. 60. —

From Dr. *Macpherson*, Inspector General of Hospitals, to the Secretary to the Principal Inspector General, Medical Department.

Sir, Madras, 19 December 1860.

1. In my letter No. 42, dated Singapore, 1st September last, I reported to the Principal Inspector General that an unforeseen detention in the Straits Settlements determined me to proceed to Java, with the double object of procuring a passage to Labuan, and personally to examine into the mode of culture and propagation of the cinchona tree, which I understood had been successfully introduced into that island from South America.

2. On the 20th October following, I reported that I had failed to get a passage to Labuan, but that I had free access to the Government cinchona plantations and nurseries, and that it was my intention to embody the knowledge I had acquired regarding the culture and propagation of this valuable tree, in a translation from the Dutch of a pamphlet entitled, "Kina Kultur in the Island of Java," presented to me by the authors, Drs. Junghuhn and DeVrij, two gentlemen in the service of the local government, in special charge of the plantations.

3. I am now engaged in drawing up a report in reply to the queries of the Royal Commission on the sanitary state of the Indian Army. On the completion of this work, it will be my duty to inspect the military establishments in the province of Pegu. But before proceeding thither, although I have not yet

received the treatise referred to above, I will without further delay convey to the Principal Inspector General, for the information of Government, the result of my observation and inquiries, as these may be of some service in advancing the active endeavours now being made to naturalize on our mountain ranges probably the most important genus in the whole Botanical Materia Medica.

4. The medico-botanical history of cinchona, introduced into Europe in 1640, is still imperfectly understood, and all relating to it continues a subject of intricate and important inquiry. Of the 26 species admitted, 12 furnish a part of the barks of commerce. They are all either tall shrubs, or lofty evergreen trees, adorned with beautiful shining leaves, two inches long by two broad, rising from 30 to 40 feet in height; the older and thicker stems have now become scarce; those now found seldom exceed six inches in diameter; but when protected by dense forest, they rapidly run up to 40 or 60 feet in height.

5. The tree is supposed to be indigenous in a meridianal distance through Columbia, Peru, and Bolivia, extending from the 11th degree north to the 20th degree south of the line, growing on rich surface-mould, covering a substratum of mica slate and gneiss, at an altitude of from 4,000 to 8,000 feet above the sea, where the temperature is equable, and varies between 59 and 66 degrees of Fahrenheit.

6. The cascarilleros or peelers usually destroy the tree by stripping off its bark as it stands; whereas were they to cut it close to the ground, young shoots would spring up, which would in their turn become fit for peeling in from six to twenty years. This reckless destruction, coupled with the enormous demand for quinine in Europe, has occasioned so great a scarcity, that the authorities in Upper Peru contemplate placing an interdict on the exportation of bark for a series of years. It is asserted that 800 to 900 trees are cut down in order to furnish 11,000 pounds of bark, and that 25 to 50 ounces, or 1½ to 3 per cent., are the two extremes of quinine from 100 pounds. The sum expended by the Indian Government in the purchase of this valuable medicine is stated to exceed five lacs of rupees annually. Madras consumes, on an average, 2,090 lbs. of bark and 451 of quinine. Great Britain imports annually about 400,000 lbs. of bark, and retains towards 120,000 lbs. for home consumption.

7. In the year 1852 M. Hasskarl was commissioned to proceed to Bolivia by the Dutch Government to procure specimens of the cinchona tree. He was unable to penetrate into the forests, but both plants and seeds were conveyed to him by the cascarilleros or bark collectors. The only knowledge, therefore, which this gentleman acquired regarding the growth of the plant, &c., was from these individuals. He arrived in Java in December 1854 with 21 boxes, containing the five species of the tree noted in the margin, and also a supply of seed belonging to each species.

Cinchona Calisaya.
" Lacumaefolia.
" Lanceolata.
" Succirubra.
" Lancifolia.

8. He selected for his plantation the slope of the Geday mountain, about 100 miles from Batavia, varying in elevation from 3,500 to 4,500 feet above the sea, which he effectually cleared of forest: only one seed out of 1,000 germinated, and most of the young trees on being planted out speedily died, and of all the trees imported only two survived. Ignorant of the habitudes of the plant, three mistakes were committed:

(1.) The elevation was insufficient.

(2.) The ground should not have been cleared, for the fungi generated by the decaying roots of the forest trees proved pestilential to the growth of the cinchona tree, as is shown in the specimen of the root herewith sent of one that struggled on for six years.

(3.) The superficial vegetable mould being too light, the tender roots were unable to penetrate the volcanic turf beneath, so spread out horizontally, which checked their growth. This, however, turned out a most fortunate mistake, for the trees, although stunted in growth, and made to resemble the artificially formed dwarf forest trees found in Chinese gardens, being thus forced into early maturity, flowered and seeded freely.

9. The Government of Netherlands India felt that hitherto they were experimenting in the dark. To guard, therefore, as much as possible against further failure, they nominated on liberal salaries Dr. Junghuhn, a gentleman of

of distinguished scientific attainments, and an eminent naturalist, as sole custodian over the Cinchona plantations, and associated with him, Dr. De Vrij, an accomplished professor in chemical and agricultural science in the University of Leyden, to analyse every plant that died, with reference to the quantity of the valuable alkaloids contained in each, the soil producing them, &c., so as to trace all that was hurtful to their growth, and to arrive at some sound conclusion respecting the proper elevations for their propagation.

10. Complete success may now be said to have rewarded the labors of these gentlemen; many of the old plants were carefully removed to new localities more inland, numerous cuttings were secured from others, and much care was devoted to the germination of the seedlings from the seed referred to in paragraph 3. In the margin is given the number of healthy young trees planted in six different forests: there are besides well-stocked nurseries, and a good supply of seed in hand.

Cinchona Calisaya	15,819
" Lucumæfolia	9,20,068
" Lanceolata	45
" Succirubra	35
" Lancifolia	14
Total -	9,35,981

11. For the nurseries, a sheltered part of the forest is selected and cleared sufficiently for the erection of ranges of narrow ridge roofed nurseries, open on both sides. Here beds are formed, and scaffolding for pots or cut bamboos for the seed raised fully 18 inches from the ground. The mould is a rich coffee coloured or black, freed from all decaying or dead roots, leaves, &c., and without manure or other artificial substance. The seed which does not exceed a carroway seed in size, is placed on the surface of the mould, watered twice daily from the squeeze of a sponge, and not exposed to the sun until it has germinated, when the sun is admitted from 6 to 8 a.m. If too much water be given, cryptogams destroy the seed, and the plant is so tender that a slight touch will destroy it as it sprouts. Under favourable circumstances the seed germinates in five to six weeks. But they should never be thrown away, until by the aid of a glass the seed is found to have decayed, for they have been known to germinate after a year's exposure on the soil.

12. Less water is now required for the young plant, which should remain in pots from six to 12 months, according to their vigour or otherwise. They should never be planted out until they have attained a length of at least six inches, and look strong and healthy. Cuttings are treated in the same way. But they are more difficult to deal with than seeds, and never make such good trees. The tree thrives best in the densest forest, and the southern decline of hills is that most suitable for its growth. The best forests are those which have the largest trees, and especially where the *Quercus Fungiformus* is found, a tree of the beech species, having powerful buttresses, and attaining great height.

13. Nurseries succeed best at, or under 4,000 feet. The Cinchona Calisaya grows only between 5,000 and 5,800 feet. The other species will flourish at a greater elevation. Those planted under 5,000 feet yield little quinine, but the best elevations have yet to be ascertained. The tree is at first very slow in growth, but when it has taken root and gains strength, it springs up rapidly. Holes three feet every way should be dug, and the mould freed from stones and foreign substances, replaced and raised like an inverted saucer, so as to let the water run freely off from around the stem of the plant. The holes should be in concentric circles through the forest, *i.e.*, from a given line, circles are formed, and sufficient only of the forest is cleared in order to be able to replace the plants if necessary, remove the weeds, &c. Each tree is distant 15 to 20 feet, according as the ground is available; at first they were protected by a bamboo fence; but now the Cinchona plantations, having extended over so many hundred acres, simple bows are placed around and tied at the top to protect the plant from injury from wild animals, &c. An insect, a kind of *darmestes*, about the size of the head of a pin, sometimes works into the medulla, where it deposits its egg and kills the young plant.

14. Chemical researches have shown a considerably larger amount of quinine in the plants grown in the Island of Java than in any yet imported from South America. As shown in paragraph 6, three per cent. appears the largest average in the latter, whereas five per cent. was discovered in the former, the alkaloid being present in the leaves and roots as well as in the bark of the stem, which is an encouraging assurance of success. Overseers, usually steady old soldiers, are placed in charge of the plantations; the 1st class receive 125 rupees, the 2d

 100 rupees,

100 rupees, and the 3d 75 rupees per month. From 200,000 to 300,000 plants are the fixed number in each plantation.

15. My hurried departure from Singapore did not enable me to procure the necessary letters of introduction to officials in Java, a point of etiquette absolutely necessary when information is sought, nor did my short stay in the island give me sufficient time to make the full observations I desired. I did my best to procure correct information, but I may be in error in some of the particulars above recorded. Had I gone there commissioned by Government, with proper documents, I might have secured from the authorities both seeds and young plants for experiment on our mountain ranges, which would be much more likely to succeed than any direct importations from South America.

16. I am confirmed in this latter assurance, by the receipt this day, of a communication from the British consul in Batavia, through whose influence, when there, I endeavoured to procure a supply, of which the following is an extract:—

"Although you did not take the right way to procure quinine plants, you had hardly left the island when all began to regret their apparent churlishness. If you get the Governor of Madras to address the Governor General of Netherlands India personally, requesting a supply for an experiment on your mountains, and offering in return any of the products of India that he may desire, the supply will be granted."

17. Having been over the chief mountain ranges within the Presidency of Madras, I was to some extent in a position to contrast their physical aspect with the features of the elevated forest lands which have proved successful for the growth of the Cinchona tree in Java. The climate and soil too on our hills, I conceive to be equal for this purpose to anything observed in that island. I believe also I am correct in stating that the *Cinchona excelsior* is indigenous in some of our forests, circumstances which may be considered to augur favourably for the success of the earnest endeavours now in progress to naturalize the tree in India.

18. I am impressed with the conviction that the same success which has rewarded the unremitting exertions of the Dutch in Java ought also to attend similar efforts on the part of our Government. I trust I may be excused for suggesting that immediate advantage be taken of the liberal offer conveyed to me through the British representative in Batavia. It has been through the exertions of his Excellency, first as Minister for the Colonies at the Hague, and second as Governor General of Netherlands India, that the experiment which forms the subject of this letter, was entered on and brought to a successful issue, and I have no reason to doubt the sincerity expressed in a desire to reciprocate the respective advantages possessed by the two countries.

19. The 77th and following paragraphs of Mr. Markham's letter to the Under Secretary of State for India, dated Peru, 9th June 1860, refers to expected supplies of seed and plants from South America. His Excellency the Governor will observe from this report that no ordinary amount of care is necessary, in all stages of its growth, to habituate the plant within our tropics, and he will doubtless direct such measures to be carried out, prior to their arrival, as to the selection of site, preparation of mould, formation of nurseries, &c., &c., as will aid in the success of the experiment.

— No. 61. —

LETTER from *C. R. Markham*, Esq., to the Under Secretary of State for India.

Sir, Bombay, 26 February 1861.

IN this letter I propose to submit, for the information of the Secretary of State for India in Council, a report of the present prospects of the experiment now in process for the introduction of Cinchona plants into India; of my proceedings during my stay in India; and of the conclusions I have been led to form, respecting the measures which it will be advisable to adopt in order to ensure the success of of this important attempt. It is my intention to return to England by the steamer which leaves Bombay on 12th March.

2. It is with deep regret that, in the first place, I have to report that the sanguine hopes of the final recovery of the collection of plants which arrived in the Neilgherry Hills last October, prematurely expressed in my letter dated 20th October 1860 (No. 7), have been disappointed. I will recapitulate the prospects, as they now appear, of successfully introducing the various species of Cinchonæ into India; and, though as regards the plants and some of the seeds which have already arrived they are sufficiently unpromising, it will be seen that there is no reason to apprehend the eventual failure of the experiment.

3. The species which it is intended to introduce into India are,—I. the *Cinchona Calisaya*; II. those yielding grey bark; III. those yielding red bark and the *C. Condaminea*; and IV. those which yield the barks imported from New Granada. I will notice these in their order.

4. I. The *C. Calisaya.*—In my Letter, dated 20th October 1860 (No. 7), I reported that, out of the collection of plants which I conveyed to the Neilgherry Hills, Mr. M'Ivor had obtained 207 green cuttings, and 125 wood cuttings, from which all visible appearances of decay were first carefully removed. I added that, during the first week, upwards of 50 of the green cuttings, and 10 of the wood cuttings were showing signs of growth, and that success was certain. My conclusion, partly dictated by the intense anxiety I felt on the subject, was premature. On the four days following the despatch of my letter, there was incessant rain accompanied by heavy mist; the atmosphere of the gardens resembled that of the interior of a Wardian case, and the green cuttings all began to droop and look sickly. Every endeavour was made to save them, two Waltonian cases were constructed, in order to subject some of them to a bottom heat of 75 degrees, and force them to take root; but warmth, though it tends to draw out the roots of cuttings, also increases the rapid spread of decay if any exists, and this experiment was, therefore, only tried on a portion of the cuttings. In spite of all our efforts, the green cuttings went off one after the other, the last one lingering until late in November. The wood cuttings continued to look promising for a considerable time longer; but decay made its appearance in them also, a fatal taint seemed to pervade them all, and, when I finally left the Neilgherry Hills, on the 10th of January 1861, only eight retained life, of which one, *C. Calisaya*, had a green healthy looking bud, and was very promising. It was healing over the portion of the bark which had been cut, a thing which none of the others had ever attempted to do. In a letter, dated 10th February, Mr. M'Ivor tells me that these surviving cuttings remain nearly in the same state, but that a little decay is making its appearance here and there in some of them; so that I am unable to entertain hopes of the ultimate recovery of more than one.

5. On my arrival at Alexandria, 175 of the plants were covered with leaves and green sprouts, and were looking fresh and healthy; so that the mischief must have been caused by the intense heat of the Red Sea, and of Bombay during the six days that I was delayed there. It is much to be regretted that a steamer was not furnished, to convey the collection direct from the west coast of South America to India. I feel certain that, in that case, a great number of plants would have been saved; though it is right to add that, out of the 400 Cinchona plants procured by M. Hasskarl for the Netherlands Government, which had the advantage of being conveyed by the direct route to Java, only *two* have survived.

6. The loss of the Cinchona plants, which I had collected with so much labour and difficulty in the Peruvian forests, is most disastrous, but not I trust irreparable. Before leaving England, I sent 17 small Calisaya seedlings to Kew, respecting which Sir William Hooker says, in a letter, dated 8th January 1861, that two continued to show signs of *real* life, though he did not expect to keep them through the winter. In a letter, dated 18th August 1860, he informed me that he had obtained five plants of *C. Calisaya*, which had been in gardens in England for some years, from which he was striking cuttings. There is reason to hope, therefore, that a case of *C. Calisaya* plants may be sent to India, at the same time with the seedlings raised at Kew from the seeds of the grey and red barks. I also think that I shall be able to procure a supply of seeds of the *C. Calisaya* from South America,

America, by means of the 50*l.* which has already been sanctioned for that purpose; and there is a prospect of the Netherlands Government in Java being induced to exchange some of their plants of *C. Calisaya* for those of species which we possess and they do not, a subject on which I shall submit some further observations presently.

7. II. *The Cinchonæ yielding Grey Bark.*—The collection of plants and seeds of Cinchonæ yielding grey bark made by Mr. Pritchett in the forests of Huanuco arrived in England in October; and a gardener from Kew reported that "46 were good strong plants, apparently well rooted." * Two of the plants and a portion of the seeds were left at Kew Gardens; the remaining plants and seeds being despatched to India on the 10th of November. They arrived at Bombay on the 13th of December, when Dr. Birdwood, who was directed to examine them by Sir George Clerk, found the seams of some of the cases gaping, the soil utterly parched and dried up, "just like powder in a druggist's shop," and the plants in a hopeless condition. All, except six,† were quite dead, several being mere cuttings without the sign of a root, and one a small branch torn roughly from a tree, and stuck in the soil of the case. The six survivors had the pith discoloured and the bark soft, and Dr. Birdwood reports that the dead plants in the cases appeared to have lost all life for at least three or four weeks.

8. At the same time, a packet of seeds of the *Cinchonæ nitida, micrantha,* and of the variety of *micrantha* known to the bark collectors as "*Pata de Gallinazo,*" arrived at Bombay, but did not reach Ootacamund until the 13th of January, when they had lost their vitality, and Mr. M'Ivor entertains no hope that any will come up. He has sent a portion of these seeds to Ceylon.

9. Nevertheless, there is every prospect that the grey bark species will eventually be introduced into India; as the seeds left at Kew are coming up in great quantities, and the seedlings will probably be ready for transmission to India in the course of next autumn.

10. III. *The Cinchona yielding Red Bark and C. Condaminea.*—I have received copies of Mr. Spruce's Report, and have felt much pleasure at the great ability, perseverance, and zeal, with which he has conducted the service entrusted to him. I have also heard from Sir W. Hooker, in a letter, dated 8th January 1861, that the supply of seeds sent to Kew by Mr. Spruce are doing well, many having already germinated, and that three tin cases of seeds, since transmitted by Mr. Spruce, reached England early in January, and will be forwarded, some to India and some to Ceylon, without delay. These seeds have arrived at Bombay in good condition, and have been despatched by post, to Ootacamund. I trust that Mr. Spruce will not forward the cases of plants until the severity of the winter in England is passed.

11. Mr. Spruce reports that he was unable, during the season of 1860, to take any steps for the collection of seeds and plants of the *C. Condaminea*; but the Secretary of State in Council will probably authorise him to do so, during that of 1861.

12. IV. *Cinchonæ which yield the Barks imported from New Granada.*—It will, perhaps, be remembered that, respecting the region of New Granada, one of the four from which I considered it advisable that the different species of Cinchonæ should be procured, a letter was addressed to the Colonial Office, but that no steps were taken by that department to procure the species of New Granada. I now find that that eminent botanist, Dr. Karsten, presented some seeds of the *Cinchona Condaminea* (*var. δ lancifolia*), one of the New Granada species, to the Dutch Government, and that there are now 14 healthy young trees of that species in Java, some of which might be exchanged for a few plants of species which we possess, and which the Dutch have not. I now propose to submit a few remarks on the letter of Dr. Macpherson, Inspector-general of Madras Hospitals, to the Secretary to the Principal Medical Inspector General, dated 19th December 1860 (No. 50), reporting his visit to the Cinchona plantations of Java; ‡ especially with respect to procuring this New Granada species, and, perhaps, some plants of the *C. Calisaya*, by a system of exchange.

13. Dr.

* Report dated 20th October. † Since dead.

‡ Proceedings of Madras Government, 11th January 1861, Nos. 166 and 167.

13. Dr. Macpherson supplies a few particulars respecting the cultivation of Cinchonæ in Java, in addition to those already given from Dr. Junghun's Report, translated in my pamphlet ("Notes on the Culture of Cinchonas"); but Mr. M'Ivor assures me that the system of culture adopted by the Dutch is most erroneous (as described to him by Dr. Macpherson), and as the sites selected by them in Java were not chosen by any one who had visited the Cinchona forests of South America, little dependence can be placed on their suitability, while the Java experiment is as yet too recent to admit their superior knowledge on the ground of experience. Dr. Macpherson, however, quotes a letter from the British Consul at Batavia to himself, stating "that if the Governor of Madras addresses the Governor General of Netherlands India, personally, requesting a supply (of Cinchona plants) for an experiment in India, and offering in return any of the products of India that he may desire, the supply will be granted."* How far this liberality, on the part of the Dutch authorities, can be advantageously accepted by the Madras Government, is worthy of consideration. There can be no doubt that the Dutch have the *C. Calisaya* (15,819 trees) raised, partly from the two surviving plants brought by M. Hasskarl, and partly from seeds sent to Paris several years ago by Dr. Weddell; but I have reason to doubt whether they have any plants of the *C. succirubra*, the red bark species. Dr. Macpherson names that species among those in Java, and gives the number of trees at 35, but it is not mentioned in Dr. Junghuhn's report. Mr. Spruce is probably in a position to bear out my opinion that the Dutch are mistaken in supposing that they possess that species. We, however, now have a large supply of the seeds in India; and, as it is of equal value with the *C. Calisaya*,† the Dutch authorities, when they ascertain that they have not got it, will, probably be quite ready to exchange plants of *C. Calisaya* for those of so valuable a species. It will, of course, be unnecessary to make any application, unless our own endeavours to introduce the *C. Calisaya* end in failure.

14. The Dutch also have 14 trees of a New Granada species, the *C. lancifolia*, and they would probably be quite ready to exchange some of these plants for those of equal value which we possess in Mr. Pritchett's collection, namely, the *C. nitida* and *C. micrantha*.

15. The other species given in Dr. Macpherson's list are quite worthless. The *C. lucumæfolia* (920,068 plants) originally called *C. ovata* by M. Hasskarl, is of very doubtful character; and the *C. lanceolata* (45 plants) is probably not a Cinchona at all, the name not appearing in Dr. Weddell's list, nor in those of any of the established modern authorities.

16. If any proposal for exchanges should eventually be made, it will be very important that a person well acquainted with the appearance of the different species should be sent to receive the plants in Java, so as to prevent mistakes. This might be done by one of the gardeners who have been in South America, who will accompany the plants which will hereafter be sent from Kew to India, and whose services will be required at the Cinchona plantation in the Neilgherries.

17. I now proceed to submit the observations I have made, and the conclusions I have formed as to the suitability of the various hill districts in the Madras and Bombay Presidencies for Cinchona cultivation. Those districts are the Neilgherry Hills, Wynaad, Coorg, the Pulney Hills, the Anamallays, and Shervaroys, the hills near Courtallum in Tinnevelly, and the Mahabaleshwur Hills in Bombay. I have examined all except the Anamallays, Shervaroys, and Courtallum, it being impracticable to form any Cinchona plantation in the Anamallays, for many years to come, as there are no European residents, and the Shervaroys and Courtallum not possessing sufficient elevation, and being ineligible from other causes.

18. *The Neilgherries and Wynaad.*—In my letter dated October 20th, 1860, (No. 7), I described the site already selected by Mr. M'Ivor, near the Government gardens at Ootacamund, and stated my reasons for believing that it will prove

* Para. 16.

† Market prices in London in 1860.—*C. Calisaya* bark, 2*s.* 8*d.* to 3*s.* per lb. Red bark, 3*s.* 6*d.* to 7*s.* per lb.

prove suitable for the cultivation of those species of Cinchonæ which flourish at the highest altitudes, namely, the *C. nitida*, *C. Condaminea*, and a variety of the *C. Calisaya*.

19. Early in November, I went, with Mr. M'Ivor, in the direction of Wynaad, to select another site for a Cinchona plantation, at a somewhat lower elevation, and where the available land would be more extensive than in the ravine already chosen near the gardens. The conditions most favourable for the production of quinine in the bark of Cinchona plants are those of continuous vegetation, with a mean temperature of from 60 to 70 degrees of Fahr., varying according to the species, an almost constant supply of moisture, and an elevation of from 5,000 to 8,000 feet. In every part of the western ghauts the vegetation is subjected, during at least three months in the year, to an amount of dryness which is never known in the forests in South America; but I have seen no locality in India which more nearly meets the requirements of a Cinchona plantation than that which we selected on this occasion. It is, or was, within the Wynaad district, and the land belongs to the Nair Rajah of Nellamboor, in Malabar, who will be quite willing to let it to the Government; but it is in fact a portion of the northern slope of the Neilgherry Hills. The site is close to the travellers' bungalow at Neddiwuttum, near the crest of the ghaut on the road leading from Ootacamund to Manantoddy. The forest covers a declivitous slope, at an elevation of about 5,000 feet, and extends to the verge of the steep descent into the table land of Wynaad. There is a good supply of water in the forest, and the soil is rich, its base being a mixture of syenite and laterite, curiously combined in strata. In this forest, amongst other plants, I found the *Hymenodictyon excelsum* (called by Roxburgh *Cinchona excelsa*, but excluded from the list of Cinchonæ by Weddell), an *andromeda*, wild yam, cinnamon, pepper, coffee, wild ginger, an *osbeckia* with purple flowers, and numerous ferns and orchids. Moss, in great quantities was hanging from the branches and trunks of the trees, a sure sign of great moisture. This jungle is within the narrow limits of the region which receives the monsoons. Though protected, to some extent from the south-west, it receives a full share of the monsoon during the summer, and is also refreshed by the north-east monsoon, coming across Mysore, from October to December. During the remaining months it is not without mists and heavy dews in the nights, until the south-west monsoon again commences in May. Eventually, the plantation might be extended for a considerable distance to the east and south, at the same elevation, to the falls of the Moyaar, a tributary of the Cauvery, and even further still, in the direction of Kalhutty. The travellers' bungalow, which is never used, would be available as a residence for the gardener in charge of the plantation.

20. The road which passes by Neddiwuttum, leads to the coffee estates in Wynaad, of which there are now upwards of 40 belonging to European settlers; thus the planters will often pass the Cinchona plantation, and, when its success is secured, it is to be hoped that some of them will undertake the cultivation in the forest lands immediately above the line of their own coffee estates. Unfortunately, the coffee plantations in the Neilgherries are all on the southern side, near Coonoor and Kotagherry, which is too dry for the Cinchonæ, being outside the region of the south-west monsoon. The *C. succirubra*, yielding red bark, the *C. Calisaya*, and *C. micrantha* may all be cultivated in the forest which has been selected at Neddiwuttum.

21. *Coorg.*—Next to the sites selected in the Neilgherries, the mountainous district of Coorg appears better adapted for the growth of the Cinchona plant than any other part of the western ghauts. Tadiandamol, the highest peak of Coorg, is 5,780 feet, and its capital Mercara 4,500 feet above the sea. During January, February, and March scarcely any rain falls, but the valleys are seldom without moisture, and during my visit in January, heavy dews were frequent in the morning and evening, and at sunrise there were always long streaks of low-lying clouds resting on the sides of the ravines. At this season the belts of jungle, both on the Mysore and Malabar sides of Coorg, are scorched up with excessive dryness (a condition never known in the South American forests with which I am acquainted), but this was not so much the case in the loftier parts of the Coorg districts. In April and May there are frequent showers, from June to August the rain comes down in torrents, in September and October there are showers,

showers, in November Coorg receives rain from the north-east monsoon in small quantities, and December is foggy. The fall of rain on the western side of Coorg, the only part suitable for Cinchonæ, averages 150 inches. The mean of the thermometer at Mercara in 1836, during the hottest month, was 78 degrees, and during the coldest 63 degrees, the average temperature being about 65 degrees.

22. I examined the country in the neighbourhood of Mercara, and found a locality to which I had been directed by Dr. Macpherson, which is well suited for a Cinchona plantation. It is four miles from Mercara, by the side of the road to Mangalore. Its elevation must be a li tle over 4,000 feet, and the forest, about a mile long, extends in breadth from the road, down the steep sides of a ravine, to the valley at the bottom, which is bare of trees. It contains many tall trees, though not growing close, and the underwood is very dense, consisting of five kinds of ferns, a solanum, a lobelia, &c. There were also *cinnamon*, *hymenodictyons*, *tree ferns*, and *melastomaceæ*, and the general character of the flora appeared suitable for the growth of Cinchonæ. In this, the driest season, I found two small streams trickling through the underwood. Further down the Mangalore ghaut there are several flourishing coffee plantations, and when a Government Cinchona nursery is successfully established in their neighbourhood, the planters may also undertake the cultivation. There are probably many other sites equally suitable for the growth of Cinchonæ in Coorg, but none so conveniently situated as regards Mercara. Labour, as is also the case in the Neilgherries, is chiefly procured from Mysore, the coolies coming up after their own work is done.

23. *Pulney Hills.*—In the Madura district, the Pulney or Varragherry Hills, like the Neilgherries further north, branch out in an easterly direction, from the main line of the western ghauts. United to a portion of the Animallay range at their western end, they stretch out into the Madura plains for a distance of 50 miles, and average a breadth of 15 to 20. They are divided into two parts, a lower series of hill and dale to the eastward, averaging a height of 4,000 feet, where there is a great deal of forest, some cultivation, and several villages inhabited by people of the Velleler caste; and a loftier region to the westward, averaging 6,000 feet, with mountain peaks, the highest of which, Permanellie, attains an elevation of 7,500 feet. The formation consists of gneiss, traversed by veins of felspar, and the soil in the eastern part is a light reddish loam, yielding crops of garlick, mustard, two kinds of millet, besides groves of plantains, and lately the villagers have formed several small coffee gardens. In the western and loftier part, the soil is very poor, being a heavy black peat, several feet thick, with a yellow stiff clay as a subsoil. The rains on the Neilgherry Hills have the effect of mixing the decaying grass with the decomposed rock, and a rich soil is thus formed; but on the Pulneys this does not appear to be the case; the one becoming a black peat, the other a stiff clayey subsoil. These remarks apply to the interior valleys, but on the outer slopes, looking over the plains of Madura, there is a good soil in places, and magnificent forests at the foot of a perpendicular wall of gneiss, which forms the southern ridge of the Pulneys. There are also fine forests in the sheltered ravines, in which I observed trees of the following genera: *michelia, myrsine, rhodomyrtas, symplocos, bignonia, crotalaria, passiflora, osbeckia, jasminum, millingtonia, cinnamomum, dodonæa, monocera, sahota,* besides a variety of cinchonaceous shrubs, such as *hymenodictyon, hedyotis, lasianthus,* and *canthium.* Tree ferns abound near streams, and, like the Neilgherries, the grassy plains are dotted with tree *rhododendrons, gaultherias, lobelias, hypericums,* and ferns. I was told that, during the season of the south-west monsoon, the Pulneys only receive passing showers, and in corroboration of this, I missed the *Berberis Mahonia,* a plant which, on the Neilgherries, is never found beyond the range of the south-west monsoon. The Pulneys, however, receive the full benefit of the monsoon from the north-east.

24. There are several damp, well-wooded ravines near the settlement of Kodakarnal, where the species of Cinchonæ, which prefer great altitudes, might be established. When these plants are thoroughly rooted in the Neilgherries, a few might advantageously be sent to the Pulney Hills, under the care of the gardener employed by the collector of Madura, Mr. M'Ivor having previously selected a suitable site. As the villagers have lately introduced the coffee plant, it

it is not improbable that they might also be induced to undertake the cultivation of the plant yielding quinine, of the value of which they are well acquainted.

25. *The Anamallay Hills* probably possess several localities suitable for Chichona plantations, but being very feverish, and no European being yet established on them, it will probably be many years before they could be made available.

26. *The Shervaroy Hills*, in the Salam district, only attain a height of 3,000 feet, and, being quite out of range of the south-west monsoon, they are both too low and too dry for the growth of the Cinchona plant.

27. *The Hills near Courtallum*, in Tinnevelly, enjoy the full benefit of both monsoons, but the highest waterfall at Courtallum is only 2,000 feet above the sea. Localities, however, may hereafter be found between Tinnevelly and Travancore, with an elevation of 3,000 to 4,000 feet, where the *C. micrantha* and even the *C. succirubra* might thrive.

28. *The Mahabaleshwur Hills.*—The only part of the western ghauts, within the Bombay Presidency, which attains an elevation sufficient for the growth of Cinchonæ, are the Mahabaleshwur Hills, the highest part of which is 4,700 feet above the sea, in latitude 18 degrees north. These hills are composed almost entirely of laterite, overlying the basalt of the Deccan, and the soil is exceedingly poor and shallow. The mean temperature of the hottest month is 73 degrees, of the coldest 62 degrees, the average for the year 65½ degrees; but the climate, in every other respect, is most unfavourable. From October to the end of April scarcely a drop of rain falls, and everything is dried up, the Mahabaleshwur Hills receiving no portion whatever of the north-east monsoon, too wide an extent of land intervening between them and the Bay of Bengal. In May there are showers, and from June to September there is an unceasing deluge of rain, the fall being estimated at from 250 to 300 inches. The most essential requirement for the growth of Cinchonæ is a continuous supply of moisture; and in a climate where, for upwards of six months in the year, they would be exposed to excessive dryness, they certainly would not live. In addition to these climatic obstacles, there is a great want of forest trees in the jungles, which would supply a sufficient amount of shade, the vegetation of the scanty thickets consisting chiefly of such shrubs and small trees as *memecylons, jasmines, indigoferas, crotolarias, eugenias,* with an undergrowth of *solanums, gentians, ferns,* and *curcumas.* I visited both Coorg and Mahabaleshwur in the driest and most unfavourable time of the year, but the advantage, both as regards vegetation and moisture, were incomparably in favour of Coorg; indeed, I should say that there was no part of the western ghauts, of similar elevation, so entirely unsuited for the growth of Cinchonæ as the Mahabaleshwur Hills.

29. Ten miles to the eastward of the station at Mahabaleshwur, and immediately overlooking the valley of the Krishna, there is a place called Paunchganny. It is under 4,000 feet above the sea, entirely exposed to the cold east winds during the dry months, the surrounding hills are destitute of jungle affording suitable shade, and altogether it is the last place where Cinchona plants would be likely to thrive. I regret this, because at Paunchgunny there is a small experimental farm beloning to a retired apothecary of Sir J. Jeejeebhoy's hospital; application has been made for some plants, and no doubt all possible care and attention would have been bestowed upon them.

30. *Khasia Hills, Penang, Tenasserim.*—The Cinchona plant, in its native forests, is entirely confined to the tropics, and it seems likely that the greater variation of temperature in the extra-tropical regions would render any part of the Himalaya range unsuitable for its culture. Nevertheless, under cultivation, it may be found possible to extend the area of the Cinchona region, and the Khasia Hills, in the Bengal Presidency, where the necessary elevations can be obtained, may hereafter supply another site for a plantation, though, in the first instance, it would be imprudent to attempt the experiment in any other region than that which most nearly resembles the Cinchona forests of South America. In the Island of Penang, and in the Tenasserim Province, the necessary climate and elevation may also be found.

31. *Ceylon.*—On the whole, it will probably be found that the hill country of Neurellia, in Ceylon, which possesses the necessary elevation, and is within the region

region of both monsoons, will be found as good a locality as any which I have described in the peninsula of India; and I am glad to hear, from Mr. Thwaites, that many of the coffee planters are extremely desirous of trying the cultivation of cinchonas on their estates. Mr. Thwaites has received some seeds of *C. micrantha* from Kew, which have not germinated, and there is little hope that those sent him by Mr. M'Ivor will be more successful. A good supply of Mr. Spruce's seeds will, however, have reached Ceylon by this time.

32. In conclusion, I have to submit some observations respecting the measures it will be advisable to adopt in conducting the future operations connected with this most important experiment, the success of which will establish as a native of India the plant yielding the most valuable drug—as regards tropical countries—that is known in medicine, the supply of which now costs the Government upwards of 50,000 *l.* a year.

33. I would recommend that the experiment should in the first place, and until the propagation of plants by cuttings has rendered success certain, be confined to the two sites already selected, near the gardens at Ootacamund, and at Neddiwuttum, and that its management should be entrusted to Mr. M'Ivor, whose zeal, intelligence, and experience as a practical gardener, and knowledge on this special subject, probably exceed those of any other person to be found in India.

34. There is every reason to hope that, before the close of the year, Mr. M'Ivor will have, in the greenhouse at Ootacamund, a goodly supply of healthy young plants of the species of *C. Calisaya*, *C. succirubra*, *C. micanthra*, *C. Condaminea*, and *C. nitida*, raised from plants and seedlings sent from Kew, and from Mr. Spruce's seeds; and it should be remembered that, as regards the *C. Calisaya* especially, if only one or two good healthy plants could once be established at Ootacamund, it would be easy to propagate them, in two or three years, to almost any extent. The Madras Government has already made the necessary grant for expenses connected with clearing and planting the site near the gardens, and a similar grant will be necessary for the plantation at Neddiwuttum. As soon as the plants are sufficiently strong for planting out, it will be requisite that Mr. M'Ivor should be assisted by a European gardener, to be resident at Neddiwuttum; and he is now anxious that Weir, the gardener who went with me to South America, should be employed on that duty.

35. When I left Bombay in October, Weir was accidentally left behind; and as, on my arrival at Ootacamund, Mr. M'Ivor said that his services would not be required, I telegraphed to Bombay to have him dismissed and sent back to England. Unfortunately, he had already been despatched to Calicut in a native boat,* and having been three weeks at sea, eventually reached Ootacamund.† Regretting exceedingly the additional expense which this mistake has caused, I sent him back to Bombay, and he sailed for England on the 12th of January. Mr. M'Ivor, having fully instructed Weir in the best method of packing plants for long voyages, having demonstrated to him the errors usually committed by the nurserymen in England, and considering him a steady and honest man, who would be very useful to him when the plantations are fairly begun, is now very anxious that he should be sent out in charge of the cases which will, hereafter, be transmitted from Kew, and that he should be appointed as his assistant in the cinchona plantations. When the operations are extended, it will be of great importance to secure the services of Cross, the other gardener who has been in South America, to take charge of the plantation in Coorg, under Mr. M'Ivor's superintendence.

36. As soon as the plantations in the Neilgherries are thoroughly established, I would recommend that a third plantation should be formed in the forest already described in Coorg, on the Mangalore road, and in the vicinity of the coffee estates, and also that some plants should be established on the Pulney Hills, in charge of an intelligent native—Mr. M'Ivor having previously selected a site and given the necessary instructions. M. Levinge, the Collector of Madura, has expressed

* Letters to the Under Secretary of State for India from Bombay Government, General Department, Nos. 21 and 25 of 1860.

† Letter from Mr. Markham to Secretary to Government, Bombay, October 15th, 1860.

expressed his willingness to do all he can to ensure the success of the experiment. He tells me that, to the westward of Kodakarnal, he can find forests nearly resembling those of Neddiwuttum, and which receive the south-west monsoon; and thus, under his auspices, the experiment in the Pulneys would have every prospect of success. The staff eventually required for the conduct of the cinchona experiment would thus consist of—Mr. M'Ivor, to superintend the whole, especially the plantation near the gardens; two European gardeners, one at Neddiwuttum, and the other at Coorg; a native with some education on the Pulneys, and the necessary number of native overseers and labourers.

37. The large forest trees would, at first, be left standing in the plantations, to protect the plants from the sun, the gales of wind, and heavy rains; and further reflection has confirmed me in the opinion that it will be most advantageous to cultivate cinchonas as shrubs, in the same way as coffee and cinnamon, and not to allow them to run up as trees, for reasons which I have already stated in my letter, dated 20th October 1860 (No. 7). Mr. Howard, the quinine manufacturer, informs me that, though the large bark from trees is preferred, and yields rather the most quinine, the bark from small branches also commands a good price. Shrubs would, undoubtedly, suffer little from the bark being removed from their smaller branches, while large trees would never recover from the loss of the bark from their trunks; indeed, such a system would resemble that which has proved so destructive to the cinchona trees in South America. To cut the trees down, and trust to root-shoots springing up from the stumps, though not equally objectionable, would require a lapse of many years between the felling of one tree and the maturity of its offspring, and would, I think, be a most erroneous system to adopt.

38. As cinnamon is the only other plant which is cultivated for its bark, I have procured a few particulars respecting its culture in Ceylon from Mr. Thwaites. In the cinnamon gardens the young shoots are peeled twice during the year, at a particular period of growth, when the bark comes off readily. This particular time is known at once by the peelers, from the appearance of the young shoots, and the process of peeling is then a very expeditious one, with practised hands. Young plants are raised from seeds in nurseries, and planted three feet apart, when they are a foot or 18 inches long. They will commonly bear peeling in three or four years after being transplanted, if in a favourable locality, and properly attended to. The roots are earthed up frequently, to keep the soil loose and free from weeds.

39. From the Government cinchona grounds it may be expected that a considerable quantity of quinine-yielding bark will eventually be collected; and though the process of extracting quinine may be too difficult, and require too much skill, as well as expensive materials difficult of transit, to give any prospect of its being carried on *in situ*, there can be no reason why a manufactory should not be established in the Presidency town, so as to avoid the costly necessity of sending the bark to England. I have had conversations with many coffee planters on the subject, and I think it likely that, as soon as they know that the Government experiment has been successful, they will be willing to undertake the cultivation of cinchona plants on their own account; and for this reason it is an advantage that the Government cinchona nurseries should be in the vicinity of the coffee estates. Should this be the case, the cinchona would soon be as important an addition to the products of the hills, in a commercial point of view, as coffee has already become.

40. The impression that the natives can with difficulty be induced to undertake the cultivation of any new plant is certainly erroneous as regards Southern India. In Wynaad upwards of 2,000 acres is taken up for coffee cultivation by natives; in Coorg, where coffee was only introduced about six years ago, I scarcely saw a single hut to which a small coffee garden was not attached; and the villagers in the Pulney Hills have also commenced its cultivation. Maize is grown to some extent in Mysore, and the extent to which the cassava (*Jatropha manihot*), only lately introduced, is now cultivated in Travancore is quite remarkable. There is every reason to suppose that the natives will be equally ready to cultivate a plant yielding quinine, the value of which is so well known to them.

41. The seeds of the *chirimoya*, generally considered the most delicious fruit in the world, of the *aji* or Peruvian capsicum, and of the *Schinies molle*, which I brought

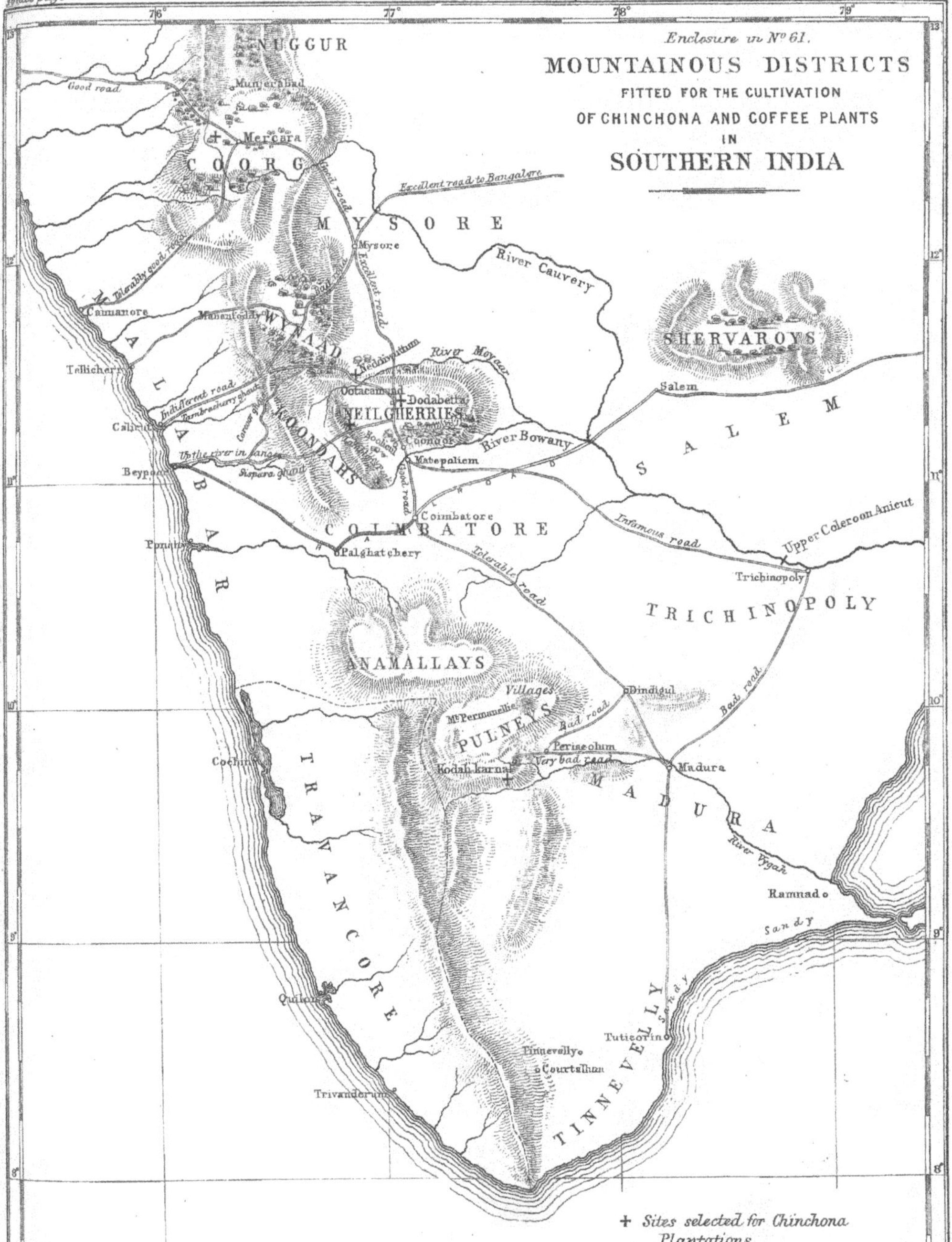
Enclosure in No 61.
MOUNTAINOUS DISTRICTS
FITTED FOR THE CULTIVATION
OF CHINCHONA AND COFFEE PLANTS
IN
SOUTHERN INDIA
NUGGUR
Good road
Mercara
COORG
Excellent road to Bangalore
MYSORE
Mysore
Excellent road
River Cauvery
SHERVAROYS
Cannanore
WYNAAD
Tellicherry
Ootacamund
Dodabetta
NEILGHERRIES
Indifferent road
Calicut
KOONDAHS
River Bowany
Coonoor
Salem
SALEM
Beypoor
Coimbatore
COIMBATORE
Palghatchery
Infamous road
Upper Coleroon Anicut
Trichinopoly
Tolerable road
TRICHINOPOLY
ANAMALLAYS
Villages
Dindigul
Bad road
PULNEYS
Bad road
Very bad road
Cochin
Madura
MADURA
TRAVANCORE
River Vygah
Ramnad
Sandy
Quilon
Tuticorin
Tinnevelly
Courtallum
Trivanderum
TINNEVELLY
MALABAR
76°
77°
78°
79°
8°
9°
10°
11°
12°
13°
+ Sites selected for Chinchona Plantations.
Coffee Plantations.
Signed,
Clements R Markham

brought from Peru, are coming up well at Ootacamund. The *chirimoya* will probably succeed well at Bangalore, the *aji* in all the warm parts of India.

I have supplied Mr. M'Ivor with Dr. Weddell's "Quinologie," and with memoranda on the species of cinchonæ yielding red, grey, and crown barks, collected from the works of Humboldt, Ruiz and Pavon, Caldas, Poeppig, and others. It is important that he should also have Mr. Howard's work, now in process of publication by Lovell Reeve, of Henrietta-street, Covent Garden ("Nueva Quinologia de Pavon").

Copies of this report will be transmitted to the Governments of Bombay and Madras.

I have, &c.
(signed) *Clements R. Markham,*

— No. 62. —

From *D. Macpherson*, Esq., M.D., Inspector General of Hospitals, on special duty at Ootacamund, to *J. D. Bourdillon*, Esq., Secretary to Government, Revenue Department, Fort Saint George; dated Ootacamund, 5 February 1861.

Sir,

1. HAVING, pursuant to my instructions, dated 11th January 1861, No. 85, visited the Neilgherry Hills to inspect and report on the sites selected for an experimental nursery and plantation for cinchona plants and seeds expected from South America, I now proceed to state how far they resemble those which have proved successful in Java, and to make some general observations on the subject.

2. When *en route* to the hills, I had the pleasure of an interview with Mr. Markham, and received from him information regarding the habitat of the plant in its native country, which, with my inquiries in Java fresh in my mind, I have found useful in arriving at the results I am now about to record.

3. Three sites have been selected on the Neilgherry Hills for the quinquina (I use this term as, from its analogy to the active principle of the cinchona plant, it is that adopted in Java and by many of the best writers) plantations. I minutely explored these in company with Mr. M'Ivor, the superintendent of the Horticultural Gardens. The first is a scantily-wooded *sholá* embracing the sides of a ravine, having an eastern aspect, ascending from the Horticultural Gardens, and stated to embrace an area of 50 acres. The lowest part of this, the "Dodabet site," on which it is proposed to cultivate the plant, is 7,830, and the highest 7,950, feet above the sea; to this locality a road about six feet in width, and in length about one mile, has been partially constructed, and the underwood in the *sholá* is now being cleared. The chief attractions in this position are the numerous varieties of the cinchona family found there, and because of the altitude; for the best-informed writers allow "that the bark containing the largest amount of the alkaloid is obtained from trees growing at the greatest elevation, and that the stunted shrubby varieties of the plant, the cinchona *Calisaya Josephiana* for instance, which is found at an elevation of 9,500 feet, are particularly good when their growth is owing to the altitude of their position." But the same authorities inform us "that the best trees inhabit dense woods and aspire to rise above the tops of the highest trees;" and Mr. Spruce, engaged in collecting plants, &c., in South America, states, "that the finest trees grow in a stratum of yellow or reddish marl of immense thickness, and in which few or no stones were intermixed." Now, the site under review, although it possesses elevation, is wanting in luxuriance of vegetation; the forest trees are too cramped and scanty to give sufficient shade, the soil is generally a superficial superstratum of black vegetable mould on disintegrated granite, or on masses of trap protruding on the surface, and it is deficient in moisture. It bears no resemblance to those sites on which the plant flourishes in Java; and until we are in possession of plants of the *Calisaya Josephiana*, no further expense should, I think, be incurred on this spot.

4. As regards the important matter of the best elevation for the propagation and cultivation of the plant, I may here state that Humboldt and others give it a range in its native country of from 5,000 to 10,000 feet. Mr. Markham, at paragraph 19 of his Report to the Under Secretary of State, dated 9th June 1860, states, "I had but slight opportunities of observing the temperatures of the pajonal region about 5,000 feet above the sea, where the *Cinchona Josephiana* is found;" and in paragraphs 57 and 60, "the whole of the cinchonæ, with the exception of the *Josephiana* variety, have been collected in the valley of Tambopata, the height above the level of the sea being between 3,000 and 4,000 feet." Mr. Spruce, in the Appendix to his Report, speaks of "the Forest of Limon, on the western slope of Chimborazo, at about 3,000 feet in altitude, and that of Tabacál, near San Antonio, at an altitude of 2,600 feet," these being the two positions wherein he made the collection shortly expected here; and finally, in Java, the recognised elevations which a succession of experiments, conducted with much care for a period of seven years, have established, are, for the nurseries, between 3,000 and 4,000 feet only, while the plantations range from 3,000 to 6,000 feet. Now, with these facts before us, it must, I think, be admitted that we are risking our seeds and plants by attempting to propagate them in the Government Gardens at Ootacamund, the elevation of the lower greenhouse where they are placed being 7,478, and that of the upper 7,596 feet above the level of the sea.

5. To conduct the experiment with any prospect of success, I would urge the Government without loss of time to adopt the system now working so successfully in Java, and direct the preparation of nurseries under efficient superintendence on the sites selected for the plantations, and at the more moderate elevations than the Government Gardens afford.

6. In the selection of the sites, consideration was very properly bestowed on those adjoining the trunk-roads leading to the Neilgherry plateau. The second of these is the "Avalanche site," on the highway from Calicut, and 15 miles from Ootacamund: it commences north-east from the Travellers' Bungalow, distant about a mile, and covers an area of some 1,000 acres, nearly the whole of which might be made available for the varieties of the plant which inhabit the more elevated ranges in the Andes. The black superstratum of soil is rich and deep, generally free from stones; it is well watered, the vegetation is rich and luxuriant; the forest trees are of great size, abounding in rhododendrons one of which, at an elevation of 7,075 feet, in good health, I found to measure at two feet from the ground, 12 feet 9 inches in circumference, and more than 3½ feet in diameter; and the following varieties of plants common to the cinchona regions, and found also in the forests selected for the growth of the plant in Java: coffee, holly, ivy, cinnamon, tree-ferns, palms, peppers, bloberries, leseanthus, melestomaceæ (*Osbeckia*), magnolia, spoceneæ, and an undergrowth of ground orchides, ferns, acanthus, aroidæ, myrtaceæ, and small bamboos, with numberless gigantic climbers. The large trees are covered with moss and orchides, indications of humidity, and there are open well-sheltered glades, similar to the pajonal region where the *C. Josephiana* is found. The steep declivities which the plant prefers, sufficiently overshadowed by trees, are numerous, and the ravines indicate a subsoil of decaying schist much discoloured with red oxide.

7. The Avalanche Bungalow faces to the north, and the aspect of the forest is north-east and south-east; the former is unquestionably the best exposure in these latitudes. Because of the passage of the sun to the south during the dry and cloudless season, the rays fall direct on a north-east aspect; the very opposite state of matters have induced the Dutch in Java to select a southern exposure for their quinquina plantations. The parched appearance of the southerly and western aspects at this, the period of drought on the hills, the contracted circumference of the sholás, and the cramped vegetation on these, compared to that seen on the other surfaces, is of itself a sufficient indication that a northern and eastern exposure is that which holds out the best chances of success in the undertaking the Government are now entering on. The elevation of the Avalanche Bungalow above sea is 6,725 feet; the thermometer in the sun at 9 a.m. stood at 53 degrees; this may be said to be the lowest margin of the forest. The centre elevation is 6,740 feet, and the thermometer at 11 a.m. indicated

dicated in the forest shade 65 degrees. On a grass ridge mid-summit, passing over to a scrubby sholá having a south-western aspect, the elevation was found to be 7,180 feet, and the thermometer in the sun 70 degrees at noon. The forest continues luxuriant to an elevation of 7,800 feet above the sea, when it ceases, the grass hill ascending about 40 feet higher; here the thermometer at 1 p.m., in the sun, indicated 74 degrees of Fahrenheit.

8. There is but one objection to this site, viewing it on the Java standard, viz., the want of a low elevation for nurseries; but otherwise there are so many well-protected favourable spots on the site for this purpose, especially with the aid of a glass-house, and the position appears to be so well adapted for the more valuable species of the plant, *i. e.*, the *Calisaya* and *ovata*, the Travellers' Bungalow in its proximity, in which the overseer in charge could reside, and the fact that a large burgher population, available as labourers, inhabit the vicinity, are circumstances which will weigh favourably with Government in according their sanction to establishing the "Avalanche site" as one of the proposed plantations. In elevation it is nearly equal to the "Dodabett site," far surpassing it in other respects, and there is another nearly equally extensive and in every respect favourable forest, descending to a lower elevation, about six miles from the bungalow.

9. I shall denominate the third situation selected for a quinquina plantation the "Neddivattam site," it being contiguous to the Travellers' Bungalow of the same name, 17 miles from Ootacamund, at the summit of the pass leading from that place to the western coast. This forest has also a north-east and a north-west aspect, and it covers an area of about 400 acres, in an undulating descent on the flank of the mountain, to the plateau land of Wainád. It shares in both monsoons, receiving a medium fall from each, a very desirable circumstance. In luxuriance of forest it is fully equal to that described under the "Avalanche site," and the flora springing up on every side promises equally well for the future success of the cinchona plant. Unfortunately, about one-half of this forest only is available; this half is strikingly illustrated by Mr. Spruce's words: "The finest trees grow in a stratum of yellow and reddish marl, of immense thickness, and in which few or no stones are intermixed." The main portion of the space is occupied by an avalanche, in which the whole of the surface soil from the highlands has been swept down and deposited a depth of from 50 to 80 feet. But nowhere in the better part of this space is the superficial rich, black, or coffee-coloured mould under 4 to 6 feet; the substratum appears to be granite and trap, in process of disintegration. A large stream passes down the centre of the space, entering from the summit, which can be conveyed in any direction for irrigation purposes. The prevailing undergrowth is that seen in the Andes, viz., the *Acanthus*, the *Melestomaceæ*, &c., and the exact same small fern which covered the plants imported by Mr. Markham. The *Hymenophyllum* grows on many of the forest trees. Elevated green hills protect the spot from the force of the south-west monsoon, and the trees increase in magnitude, and are overhung with rich drooping folds of moss in the more protected positions—indications of the humid character of the climate, and its germinating properties for nurseries. There is a very convenient elevated spur for overseers and storehouse about the centre, upwards of an acre in extent, having a full command of water.

10. The following give the barometrical and thermometrical indications on the 22d January 1861:—

Highest Locality.

Greatest elevation on the forest skirt	- - - -	6,150 feet.
At 9 A.M. thermometer on surface	- - - -	67 degrees.
" " 18 inches beneath surface	- -	66 "

Spur for the House, &c.

Elevation	- - - - - - - - - -	5,550 feet.
Thermometer in stream adjoining, 10 A.M.	- - -	54 degrees.

Centre Locality.

Elevation	- - - - - - - - - -	5,220 feet.
Thermometer 18 inches beneath surface at noon	- -	65 degrees.
" on surface "	- -	68 "
" 4 feet above surface "	- -	73 "

Lowest

Lowest North-east Aspect.

Elevation	- - - - - - - - - -	4,530 feet.
Thermometer 18 inches beneath surface at 2 P.M.	- -	73 degrees.
,, on surface	,, - -	71 ,,
,, 4 feet above surface	,, - -	74½ ,,

Lowest North Aspect.

Elevation	- - - - - - - - - -	5,430 feet.
Thermometer 18 inches beneath surface at 3 P.M.	- -	73 degrees.
,, on surface	,, - -	71 ,,
,, 4 feet above surface	,, - -	76 ,,

On the Andes in April and May, the mean of the observations given by Mr. Markham is 68 degrees, and from July to September that by Mr. Spruce is 66 degrees—the temperature of the earth 2 feet beneath the surface being 68½ degrees. The character of the soil generally on the surface is a rich black vegetable mould 18 inches in depth, beneath which is a fine, red, coffee-coloured, friable, porous marl; and thus the slope descends to the Wainád plain, where the elevation varies from 3,800 feet upwards.

11. The chief objection to this position is its limited extent; for a large portion of it, as already stated, is too stony for planting. But contiguous to, or rather adjoining on, it westward, with a similar aspect, is another forest equal in extent, and possessing the same character of flora and soil. This land is Mr. Ouchterlony's property; the possession of it would very much add to the value of the proposed plantation. On my intimating this to Mr. Ouchterlony, he generously offered to hand it over to Government, stating: "I regard the experiment to introduce the cultivation of cinchona into the country of so much vital importance, that I should be happy to assist it in any way in my power; and as you seemed to think the forest adverted to a desirable locality for it, I shall be willing to transfer my title and interest in the forest for the object of the cinchona plantation, should the Government desire to possess it." Mr. Ouchterlony's original note is enclosed.

12. Although the two sites just described have a striking resemblance to those which have proved successful under the Dutch Government in Java, they are wanting in the "trees, with buttressed roots of stupendous size," referred to in the 26th paragraph of Mr. Markham's report above quoted, and found throughout the Java forest plantations. Trees of this sort are common, however, on the Western Gháts; in the Annamully, and in the Coorg forests, which I have visited, where are found also "the wild plantain, gigantic climbers, and tree-ferns," found in the cinchona forests of South America and in Java. In a letter from Mr. Markham, just received from Mercara, he calls my attention to such a site "four miles down the Mangalore Ghát, where I came to the conclusion that it would be an excellent site for nurseries, better than any forest tract I have as yet examined to the south-east and south." When *en route* to the low country, I propose to visit this place; it will only take me a few miles out of my direct road to Madras, and I will then be able to speak of it from personal examination.

13. I take the liberty to submit, that the period has arrived for Government to determine on the extent to which this great experiment is to be conducted. As stated in my former report, the early endeavours of the Dutch in Java ended in failure, and so it continued until science and chemical research were called in to aid. With the exception of three cuttings made from the plants introduced by Mr. Markham, viz. :—

1. Cinchona Calisaya.
1. ,, ,, Josephiana.
1. ,, ovata.

—which, under the skilful management of Mr. M'Ivor, superintendent of the Government Gardens here, may yet become robust plants—and the few left at the Royal Botanical Gardens, Kew, that gentleman's importation of 456 plants are dead. The collection of plants transmitted by Mr. Pritchett from Lima were dead on arrival at Bombay, and the valuable assortment of seeds forwarded by the same

same gentleman, comprising the varieties denominated the red, crown, and grey barks of commerce, or the—

Cinchona micrantha.
,, provinciana.
,, nitida.

are stated to have suffered a delay in their transmission to this place of six weeks at Lima, and 27 days at Bombay—a circumstance which, of necessity, must injure their vital property. Mr. Spruce, in his letter dated 12th October 1860, to the Under Secretary of State, at page 4 intimates the despatch, "by the steamer which leaves Guayaquil for Panama on the 14th October, a packet of seeds," collected by himself, with much care; and four months have now nearly elapsed, without any intimation of its being received. I venture to suggest, that the Government address the Home and Bombay authorities on the necessity of expediting the despatch of plants and seeds in each case under the care of a competent gardener, whose services may be made available, if necessary, on the several sites selected for their propagation.

14. Mr. Spruce, botanist, now at Ecuador, writes to Mr. Markham on 5th July 1859: "The testimony of all the bark collectors goes to prove that the bark trees are rapidly verging to extinction. I am credibly informed that in some of the cinchona forests in Ecuador there does not remain a single tree large enough to produce seeds." If, therefore, it be established that "the plant containing the most valuable medical substance the earth produces" will flourish on mountain ranges, at elevations from 2,600 feet upwards, according to Mr. Spruce's statement, private enterprise will doubtless soon find it their interest to extend its cultivation, even although the prospect of remunerative return may embrace a term of seven years. But to establish this fact, Government must, I submit, as has been done in Java, be prepared to enter on the experiment with vigour, and simultaneously, in order to secure a better chance of success, to open nurseries and plantations in different localities. The scale I suggest for our immediate wants (and not a day should be lost in preparing nurseries— the most important, and, at the same time, the most difficult part of the undertaking), are the two plantations indicated on the Neilgherries, the one in Coorg, and hereafter another on the less accessible Annamullies, with efficient gardeners resident at each place, and overseers under them, together with an educated and intelligent botanist, possessing a knowledge of analytical chemistry, to conduct the whole. The services of John Weir, who accompanied Mr. Markham, ought, I think, to be secured. He has returned to England. He might come out in charge of some of the plants left at Kew Gardens. The services of Mr. Cross, the gardener who accompanied Mr. Spruce, will also be valuable in conducting the experiment. Apart from the interest which their researches may have created in them, numerous particulars regarding the growth of the plant in its natural state can be applied by them in its cultivation in this country.

15. I submit that in the new and difficult field of inquiry Government are now entering on, and the imperfect knowledge we possess of the chemical history of the quinquina barks, the employment of a superintendent possessing a special knowledge of the subject is of much importance. As a guarantee against mistakes, he ought to be provided with the means, by continuing analytical inquiry, to enable him to ascertain at what period the alkaloids develope themselves, and the constituents which add to or detract from this development. In connexion with this part of the subject, I take the liberty to introduce the name of Dr. Croneman, a young Dutch gentleman in private practice at Bandong in Java, in the neighbourhood of the quinquina plantations. This gentleman accompanied me over the plantations, and I was much pleased with his intelligence and general knowledge of all relating to the growth and propagation of the plant, and its chemical analysis. It was evident to me that he took a warm interest in the subject from a love of natural science alone; for I knew he held no appointment under Government, nor yet could he anticipate advancement through me. Subsequent inquiry through Dr. DeViy, Dr. Junghuhn's coadjutor in charge of the quinquina plantations, satisfied me that this young man was much devoted to science, had a good knowledge of botany and geology, was a very fair draftsman, and, through Dr. DeViy, had acquired some knowledge in analytical chemistry. He possesses an imperfect knowledge of the English language so far as writing it, but can read and speak it with some freedom.

Without holding out any prospect of procuring employment for him under the British Government, before leaving Bandong I ascertained from Dr. Croneman that an engagement of the sort, which would advance his interests, would be agreeable to him. He promised to continue to devote himself specially to the subject on my informing him that, if an opportunity occurred, I would bring his name and qualifications to the notice of the Government of Madras. I hope I may be pardoned for now doing so, and also for the length of this communication.

Mr. Markham having applied to me for a copy of my former report, and also of any I may send in to Government from this place, may I beg you will obtain sanction to forward these to him to Bombay? I also solicit that a copy of this report may be sent to the head of my department, as I am unable to obtain a copyist here to prepare it. A small supply of seeds having been distributed by Mr. M'Ivor to parties at Bangalore, the Wainad, &c., I would suggest that my report on the cultivation of the cinchona plant in Java be placed on the editors' table for their information.

— No. 63. —

FROM *D. Macpherson*, Esq., M.D., Inspector General of Hospitals, to *J. D. Bourdillon*, Esq., Secretary to Government, Revenue Department, Fort Saint George; dated Mercara, 20 February 1861.

Sir,

1. ADVERTING to my letter to you, No. 7, dated 5th February, from Ootacamund, I have now to bring to your notice, for the information of Government, that having fully examined the site selected by Mr. Markham in this locality, I am enabled to report that it bears even a closer resemblance to the quinquina plantations in Java than the two sites which I approved of on the Neilgherry Hills.

2. The forest referred to occupies a position to the left, between the third and fifth milestones down the Mangalore Ghat from this place. The trees are of great magnitude, chiefly the open and continuous buttressed species, clustered with orchideous plants and rich drooping moss. Tree-ferns, small bamboos, cardamoms, and underwood, similar to that described in my former letter, give cover to a rich, deep, brown mould, free from stones. The forest trees are somewhat distant one from the other, and the foliage above is very lofty, so that, when the entire underwood is removed, there will be a free circulation, with abundance of light and shade. The ground undulates from ridges down into ravines, with running streams. These ridges average in elevation from 3,400 feet above the sea, the ravines gradually descending 100 to 150 feet. The temperature of the atmosphere at 8 A.M. in the sun indicated 85 degrees of Fahrenheit, in the shade four feet above the surface 69 degrees, in the surface $67\frac{1}{2}$ degrees, and 18 inches beneath $61\frac{1}{2}$ degrees—its aspect being N.E. and N.W.

3. Unfortunately, the extent of this forest is circumscribed, barely, I should say, 100 acres. But from its open character, it will receive a larger number of trees than a similar space on the localities examined on the Neilgherries; and its elevation, equable temperature, and genial climate make it a valuable locality for a nursery, and one of the earliest experimental plantations. Distant about three miles from this site, on the same side of the ghat, immediately above a coffee clearing by Mr. Bain, is a forest ascending up to 4,000 feet, and well adapted for a quinquina plantation, into which, as the space in that first referred to became occupied, trees could be introduced, with the same good prospect of success.

4. I beg to suggest that application be made to the Commissioner of Mysore, to reserve the above two sites for Government purposes, as otherwise they may pass into the hands of coffee planters, who, by felling the forest, would render it useless for the introduction of the cinchona tree.

— No. 64. —

FROM Captain *H. R. Morgan*, Officiating Conservator of Forests, to *J. D. Bourdillon*, Esq., Secretary to Government, Revenue Department, Fort St. George; dated Ootacamund, 1 April 1861.

Sir,

1. IN forwarding a letter * and tabulated statement from Mr. McIvor, Superintendent Government Gardens at Ootacamund, I have the honour to request you will submit it to Government for their decision.

* Dated 30th March 1861, No. 37.

2. As Dr. Macpherson has requested in his letter No. 7, dated 5th February 1861, paragraph 15, that his report may be laid on the editors' table, for the information of those who have obtained a supply of seeds, perhaps Government would have no objection to lay my report, No. 418, dated 28th March 1861, and the accompanying report of Mr. M'Ivor's, also on the editors' table, for the information likewise of those who have obtained seeds.

— No. 65. —

FROM Captain *H. R. Morgan*, Officiating Conservator of Forests, to *J. D. Bourdillon*, Esq., Secretary to Government, Revenue Department, Fort Saint George, dated Ootacamund, 28 March 1861.

Sir,

1. WITH reference to G. O. No. 552, of 9th March 1861, ordering all further propagation of seed to be put a stop to in the glass-house at Ootacamund, &c., I have the honour to request you will bring to the notice of Government the following discrepancies which exist in Dr. Macpherson's first and second reports on the cinchona plants, and which, I would respectfully point out, invalidate the whole of his remarks, and render his information of no value.

2. In letter No. 1, Dr. Macpherson ascribes the failure and death of the plants to a "want of elevation," only 3 to 4,000 feet, and in letter No. 8, Dr. Macpherson recommends a site in Coorg as admirable, though the elevation is only from 3 to 4,000 feet. Again, in paragraph 13 of No. 1 letter, Dr. Macpherson admits that "those planted under 5,000 feet yield but little quinine," and in the face of this admission recommends Coorg and condemns the Dodabetta site.

3. In paragraph 12 of letter No. 1, Dr. Macpherson says, "the southern decline of hills is that most suitable for its growth," and in letter No. 2, paragraph 7, contradicts himself and says, "the northern is the best."

4. In paragraph 9, letter No. 1, it is stated that "five per cent. was obtained" (this was under peculiar circumstances) from stunted plants which had died through being planted on a substratum of volcanic tuff (lava) on an exposed situation. There is no evidence to show that the general yield of the Java cinchona is five per cent. of quinine.

5. In "Notes on the Culture of Cinchona," page 13, Dr. Junghuhn "considers that the elevation for the culture of the cinchona is to be found at 5 or 6,000 feet above the sea." At page 15, Howard, the greatest authority, says: "The higher and colder the place of growth was, the more value was attached to the bark." Again, page 15: "Those cinchonas which are rich in alkaloids, inhabit the peculiar cloudy region of the Andes, in which, during the rainy season, which continues for nine months in the year, a steady rain is only interrupted during the day by short gleams of sunshine, interchanging with clouds and mist; whilst in that part of the year which answers to our winter, cold nights, in which the temperature of the air descends to freezing-point, are followed by days in which the rays of the sun, piercing here and there through the thick clouds, raise the temperature to 77° Fahr., whilst the leaves are kept almost constantly bedewed by the continual mists. The mean temperature of this region is about 55° Fahr." Dodabetta itself is 52° Fahr.; the mean temperature of the Dodabetta site is about 55° Fahr.; that of Coorg may be reckoned about 75° Fahr. Again, page 17: "The bark of those trees which grew in this ravine, far above the

the normal limits of the forest-growing cinchona, gave 3½ per cent. of sulphate of quinine, whilst the bark obtained from the cinchona of the lower-lying forest scarcely afforded one per cent."

6. From the above, it is clear that Dodabetta is the best site, and Coorg the worst, for producing quinine. The lowest height in Java (see page 6 "Cinchona cultivation") for plantations is 4,700 feet, not 3,000, as stated by Dr. Macpherson in paragraph 4, letter No. 2; the highest about 7,500, just the height of the Dodabetta site; mean temperature 57°. In paragraph 7 of Mr. Markham's letter to Government of 22d October 1860, he approves of the Dodabetta site. *C. nitida*, plants of which are now growing in the glass-house of the gardens, "grow on high mountains in cold situations" (*vide* page 21). It is true that *C. succirubra* is said to grow at an elevation of only 3,000 feet (Mr. Spruce's report); but this elevation is not to be relied upon, as neither aneroid nor mountain barometer was in the possession of Mr. Spruce, and the probability is (supposing it to be a good quinine-yielding plant) that the elevation was not under 6,000 feet, as the locality ranges over 12,000 feet of elevation.

7. Dr. Macpherson states that the Dodabetta site consists of granite and trap-rock. I can see none. The rock is gneiss, the substratrum is decomposed felspar and hornblend—the former yielding 11 per cent. of potash, a most valuable ingredient for forming alkali; the latter supplies 13 per cent. of lime. Had we only trap and granite, the situation would be very indifferent. The surface mould is in many places two feet deep. The trees, in a clump which I measured, consisting of seven, averaged two feet in diameter and three feet from the ground, quite large enough for our purpose. Again, the Neddiwuttum site is spoken of in paragraph 9, letter No. 2, as "a stratum of yellow or reddish marl." Now marl is a compound of clay and lime, of which we have none on these hills. Mr. Spruce is probably mistaken also about marl, what is more probable, is a compound of mica and felspar, the greasy feeling being due to the mica: nothing could be better than this for a substratum, as mica gives for the formation of alkali 9 to 14 per cent. of potash, and felspar 13 per cent. There can be found a hundred suitable sites on these hills, with a substratum of the above.

8. In paragraph 11, letter No. 1, Dr. Macpherson speaks of raising seed under "narrow ridge roofed nurseries" (thatched?) "open on both sides." The only seed I know of that is grown in this manner is mushroom-spawn. I am confident that if this plan is to be carried out, not a seed will germinate at Neddiwuttum. In my former letter, No. 343, dated 28th January 1861, I recommended that the seed should be made over to Mr. McIvor, to be raised under glass, and I now again would most respectfully urge upon Government the absolute necessity of raising the seed under glass at present. A small quantity of seed has been distributed to different parties, in various situations, for trial, and if they are successful, more can be sent.

9. With glass we can command any temperature between 60° and 90°, quite sufficient for raising seed. If the seeds expected by Mr. Cross are now planted in the nurseries at Neddiwattum, recommended by Dr. Macpherson, the monsoon will commence before they can germinate (those in the glass-house at Ootacamund having taken more than 60 days), and they must mildew and rot. The same will happen to the plants if planted out before they have made strong roots.

10. In paragraph 13, letter No. 2, Dr. Macpherson speaks of "chemical research" as having achieved success for the Dutch. I would remark that a good practical gardener would have done more for them, and further that, as far as quinine-yielding plants go, they have yet to attain success.

11. In paragraph 14, letter No. 2, an intelligent botanist possessing a knowledge of "analytical chemistry" is recommended. Mr. Howard, the great manufacturer, will soon settle the value of the bark; a better chemist we could not have.

12. In conclusion, I would observe that the Dutch have by no means accomplished success: they have grown some 90,000 plants (in the large glass house at Ootacamund we can store away 80,000 plants until fit for planting out), but they have yet to prove that those contain quinine. Had Dr. Macpherson given the market quotation of the bark, or an analysis by an English chemist, instead

instead of the results of a partial experiment of an enthusiastic Dutchman, we might have had some proofs of success. It is notorious that neither the Java tea or coffee is considered good, whereas our Kangra tea surpasses the Chinese, and our Neilgherry coffee equals Mocha. With the exception of the expedient for raising seed, which every practical man versed in arboriculture must condemn, Dr. Macpherson has told us nothing but what we knew before, (*vide* "Notes on the Culture of the Cinchona," *passim*, by Mr. Markham, 1859); and the result of Dr. Macpherson's visit to Java has been, to recommend here what he condemned in Java, and paralyse our efforts by introducing an impracticable plan for raising plants from seed. Fresh seeds, according to Mr. Spruce, take from 4 to 25 days to germinate; old seeds, according to Mr. McIvor, from 60 to 90 days under glass. What time they will take in Dr. Macpherson's nurseries, supposing they ever germinate, it is impossible to say. The sandal-wood tree, if grown in a moist and shady situation, does not yield the same scent as that grown on partially exposed situations. Tea, if grown in a low latitude and elevation, commands no price in the market, and the like reasoning holds good with the cinchona; the higher the situation, the greater the production of alkaloid.

— No. 66. —

FROM Mr. *W. G. McIvor*, Superintendent Government Gardens, Ootacamund, to *J. D. Bourdillon*, Esq., Secretary to Government, Madras; dated Ootacamund, 30 March 1861.

Sir,

1. I HAVE the honour to solicit the favour of your having the goodness to submit, for the consideration of the Right Honourable the Governor in Council, the following remarks on the subject of Dr. Macpherson's report, dated the 5th February 1861 :—

2. I am induced to bring the circumstances under which this report was written to the notice of Government, being convinced, by practical experience and personal knowledge, that the order of Government under date 9th March 1861, if carried out, will render almost certain the entire failure of the important experiment now in progress for the introduction of the quinine-yielding cinchonas into India.

3. In my first interview with Dr. Macpherson, and while about to enter into botanical and horticultural subjects, he informed me that he was "entirely ignorant of botany and gardening;" that he had been selected by Government to inspect and report on the sites, simply because he had seen the cinchona plantations in Java, and the practice of the Dutch in "successful operation." He informed me that, as he had been sent here, he wished to give a good report to Government on the "whole subject," requesting my assistance with information. This I most readily gave, placing in his hands notes of all that has been published in English on the subject; also the valuable work of Dr. Weddell in French, together with the manuscript notes of Mr. Markham, at the same time pointing out and explaining the parts bearing on the subject in connexion with my experience of this climate.

4. Dr. Macpherson, in his report, lays much of this information before Government as the result of his own investigation and personal knowledge; and I would have been glad to have passed over in silence Dr. Macpherson's adoption of this rather unusual course, had it produced no bad results. But when his report has produced an order endangering the experiment, I feel myself called upon, by duty to your Honourable Government, to myself, and to the country, to detail with plainness and candour the facts which have led Government to place (as I will presently show) unmerited confidence in the opinions of Dr. Macpherson.

5. In paragraph 3 of his report, Dr. Macpherson gives altogether an incorrect description of the "Dodabetta site." Firstly, it is not "a scantily wooded shola," but on the contrary is composed of trees of the ordinary size and height prevailing

vailing in the best forest or "sholas" on these hills, as the Conservator of Forests can testify, having at my request taken the measure of a clump of trees near the centre of the site. Secondly, it has not an "eastern aspect," but nearly a contrary one, the aspect being north-west. Thirdly, the soil is not "generally a superficial superstratum," as proved by specimens* from 1 to 10, taken from various parts of the forest. Fourthly, the soil does not rest on disintegrated granite —*vide* specimens from 11 to 15, both included. Fifthly, no "masses of trap" are found in any part of the site. Sixthly, it is not deficient in moisture, as can be proved by the register of the last 20 years kept in the Government Observatory at Dodabetta, and established by the specimens of the branches and bark, Nos. 16 to 18. Dr. Macpherson has omitted to give in his report the observations he made with the thermometer on this site, which I supply.†

6. In paragraph 4 of the report under review, Dr. Macpherson states: "Now, with these facts before us, it must, I think, be admitted that we are risking our seeds and plants by attempting to propagate them in the Government Gardens at Ootacamund, the elevations being 7,478 and 7,596 feet above the level of the sea." Such assertions as the above are very objectionable, because they convey the impression that Dr. Macpherson had given facts to prove that plants could not be propagated, or seeds raised, at such elevations; whereas Dr. Macpherson did not quote (nor can he quote) a single fact to prove his position, but simply his own opinion, founded as it is on a total want of knowledge of the subject. But I, on the contrary, have much pleasure in being able to state, for the information of Government, the very gratifying fact that many fine seedlings of three varieties of the cinchona are now growing, and have been reared, in the very places Dr. Macpherson condemns; and I state, without fear of contradiction, that no such favourable place can be found in India for rearing the cinchonas as the gardens under my charge.

7. In paragraph 5 of Dr. Macpherson's report, he urges your Government "without loss of time to adopt the system now so successfully working in Java." In paragraph 8 of his report of the 19th December 1860, we are informed of the extent of this success in Java, and that with the Dutch, "only one seed out of one thousand germinated." We have already raised over 3 per cent. of our imported seeds, and more are daily coming up, so that at the lowest estimate I have in this respect obtained 30 times the results of the Dutch; and I trust this important fact will induce the Government to reconsider paragraph 5 of their order of the 9th instant, No. 552, and more especially as the operation of this part of the order deprives the experiment of the advantage of the efficient appliances possessed by the garden for rearing seeds and propagating plants, and thus places Mr. Markham in a wrong position, with reference to his unwearied exertions for its success. On this part of the subject I would most respectfully remark that Dr. Macpherson, apparently alarmed

---

* Specimens of Soils from Dodabetta Site.

No. 1,	from first ridge,	six inches below the surface.	
„ 2,	from second ridge,	do.	do.
„ 3,	from first valley,	do.	do.
„ 4,	from third ridge,	do.	do.
„ 5,	from second valley,	do.	do.

Specimens of Rocks.

No. 11, from first ridge.
„ 12, from second do.
„ 13, from first valley.
„ 14, from third ridge.
„ 15, from second valley.

Specimens of Subsoil.

No. 6,	from first ridge,	six feet below the surface.	
„ 7,	from second ridge,	do.	do.
„ 8,	from first valley,	do.	do.
„ 9,	from third ridge,	nine feet below	do.
„ 10,	from second valley,	do.	do.

Forwarded by Banghy.

Specimens of Branches and Bark.

No. 16, from centre of site.
„ 17, upper limit.
„ 18, lower limit.

† Temperature of air from 12th December to 11th January, the coldest season in the year—

Mean	59½ degrees.
Lowest	54 „
Highest	67 „

Temperature of earth 63 degrees, at 18 inches below the surface.

Temperature of water in the stream under dense shade at 6 a.m., 52½ degrees; at 6 p.m., 54 degrees; in the water there was no variation throughout the month.

alarmed at the effects likely to be produced on the experiment, so far counter-orders this order of Government, that in paragraph 6 of the notes drawn up for my guidance, he directs that I will use my discretion in retaining a portion of the seeds and plants at the garden. The Conservator of Forests, in his letter No. 409 of the 21st, directs that I will put a "stop to any further attempt to propagate seeds or rear plants in the garden;" the order of Government being plain to this effect, I am at a loss how to proceed.

8. In paragraph 8 of Dr. Macpherson's report, he approves of the northern exposure of the sites I have selected; but he does not explain to Government the fact, that on his first inspection he entirely condemned the sites because of this exposure, distinctly informing me that "nothing but a southern exposure would suit the cinchonas, and this they had proved by long experience in Java:" all my arguments were used in vain to persuade Dr. Macpherson of the altered conditions of the climate which required altered circumstances. I named coffee estates which had failed and been parched up on south exposures, mentioned the greater capability of the coffee plant to endure drought and extremes of climates; and as it had failed, how could we expect to be successful with the cinchonas? Although these questions were unanswerable, they would have proved quite unavailing had it not been for the fortunate circumstance that while inspecting the Avalanche site we came on a narrow ridge, where I was enabled to show Dr. Macpherson at a glance the wonderful difference in the vegetation, caused by exposure only, between the two forests which lay at our feet (one facing the north, and the other the south): this accident brought conviction to his mind, otherwise Dr. Macpherson would have recommended your Government to have changed every site to the south, and thus brought the most certain destruction on the undertaking.

9. I pass over paragraphs 7, 8, and 9, not because they are free from error of description, but because they do not contain anything seriously calculated to mislead the Government.

10. While describing the soil of Neddiwuttum site in paragraph 10, Dr. Macpherson states that "the character of the soil generally on the surface is a rich black vegetable mould, 18 inches in depth, beneath which is a fine, red, coffee-coloured, friable, porous marl." Marl, in any shape whatever, has not been found on the Neilgherries, and certainly none on the Neddiwuttum site.

11. In Dr. Macpherson's letter to Government, dated Mercara, 20th February 1861, No. 8, a site on the Mangalore Ghàt is strongly recommended for a cinchona plantation, the average of the "ridges" being given as "3,400 feet above the level of the sea." Prior to leaving the Neilgherries, Dr. Macpherson asked for and received my opinion on this site; he mentioned that he had seen Mr. Markham at Mysore, and recommended that gentleman to visit it. I pointed out to Dr. Macpherson that it is given as a rule, by every authority on the subject, that cinchona trees growing below 5,000 feet are deficient in quinine, although it is true that the largest cinchona trees are found at much lower elevations, even down to 1,000 feet, but, in the words of Dr. Lindley, many of these species "yield as little quinine as a willow." The object of this experiment is to produce quinine, and I submit the Government should call for further information before expending a large sum of money on the plantations on the Mangalore Ghàt. Without any disrespect to Dr. Macpherson, I will quote him self as an authority against the measure he now recommends Government to adopt. In his letter to Government, dated Madras, 19th December 1860,* No. 50,

---

* Dr. Macpherson to Government, Madras, 19th December 1860, No. 50.

Paragraph 8.—Nurseries succeed best at, or under, 4,000 feet, the *Cinchona calisaya* grows only between 5,000 and 5,800 feet, the other species will flourish at a greater elevation. Those planted under 5,000 feet yield little quinine.

Dr. Junghuhn in his report, dated 1st July 1858, gives the elevation of the lowest plantation in Java at 4,704 English feet, the highest at 7,875 feet, and the plantation on the Gedog-Badah, as from 6,852 to 7,000 English feet above the level of the sea.

Humboldt gives the elevation—

For Quilled bark at - - - - - - - -	9,000 feet.
" Grey bark at - - - - - - - - -	6,500 "
" Yellow or Calisaya bark at - - - - - -	6,200 "
" Red bark - - - - - - - - -	4,500 "

No. 50, and at paragraph 8, Dr. Macpherson states that he (Hasskarl) "selected for his plantation the slope of the Geday mountain, about 100 miles from Batavia, varying in elevation from 3,500 to 4,500 feet above the level of the sea," remarking that, "ignorant of the habitudes of the plant, three mistakes were committed:" first, the elevation was insufficient—namely, the elevation of 3,500 and 4,500 feet he states to be insufficient, although 100 and 1,600 feet higher than the highest ridges of the site recommended in Coorg. When on the subject of elevation I give at the foot the opinions of the best authorities, by which it will be seen that we have much to learn on this point; and the safest way to attain this knowledge is by careful though inexpensive experiments, which the Neilgherries offer greater facilities for conducting than any other part of India. In conducting these experiments, it should always be borne in mind that the highest point at which the plant will flourish, and the greatest exposure it will bear without injury, is the most favourable for the production of quinine, because vegetable alkaloids (such as quinine) are not drawn from the earth, but are formed by the action of the leaves when exposed to light and air, and the power of this action is increased by elevation and a rarefied atmosphere.

12. I shall now proceed to notice the practice of the Dutch in Java, not from a wish to criticise their mode of operations, but because I am directed "carefully to carry out their practice." Long experience, in many instances dearly bought, has taught me the difficulty of carrying out a practice, however perfect and successful in other localities or countries, because of the great difficulty of faithfully applying the details of the practice to the varied local circumstances. But when a practice opposed to every principle of horticulture and vegetable physiology is attempted to be carried out, certain failure must of necessity follow.

13. The description given by Dr. Macpherson of what he saw in Java must convey to the mind of every man acquainted with horticulture a painful picture of the want of knowledge of the Dutch in these matters. But in justice to the gentleman in charge of the plantations in Java, I mention that many important discrepancies occur between their published accounts and that given by Dr. Macpherson, the instance given in the foot* being selected, as Dr. Macpherson grounds on it the whole change of the culture in Java; but as my object is simply to deal with this matter in so far as the accounts have misled Government, I shall only notice the operation as described by Dr. Macpherson.

14. In paragraph 14 of Dr. Macpherson's letter of the 19th December 1860, No. 50, it is stated, "chemical researches have shown a considerably larger amount of quinine in the plants grown in the Island of Java than in any yet imported

---

Howard, Karsten, and Poeppig give nearly the same elevation for all the varieties of bark except the red bark.

Markham gives the best elevation for grey and crown barks at from 6,300 to 7,000 feet.

For Calisaya bark	- - - - - - - -	5,000 feet.
Spruce for red bark	- - - - - - - -	3,000 „

Weddell for the *C. ovata* (which Howard says is the red bark) gives an elevation of 5,900 to 7,500 feet.

NOTE.—The probable cause of these discrepancies may be found in the fact, that in the neighbourhood of high mountains, the temperature of the valleys are much reduced at night, because the cold air generated on the mountain tops, being of greater specific gravity, descends rapidly, displacing the warm air of the valleys. Consequently, the region of the different species of cinchona will be lowest where the mountains are high, and their tops covered with snow, and highest where the mountains are comparatively low. *W. G. McIvor.*

* Dr. Macpherson, to Government, Madras, 19th December 1860, No. 50, paragraph 8 * * * "2d. The ground should not have been cleared, for the fungi generated by the decaying roots of the forest trees proved pestilential to the growth of the cinchona tree, as is shown in the specimen of the root herewith sent of one that struggled on for six years."

In Mr. Clements Markham's translation of Dr. Junghuhn's report, at paragraphs 3 and 4, a very different account of the cause of fungi is given: "The attacks of the Rhizanthes, which are also met with at Tjiniruan; but the plants here have been rendered more liable to them, by the great wooden stakes that Hasskarl had driven in, to protect the young plants from the stormy winds, so close as to injure their roots; and as the ends of the stakes decayed in the earth, they were attacked by fungi. . . . .

The strong south-west winds, which prevail during the rainy season, they blow with such force, that several cinchona trees have been half cut through by the strong cords by which Hasskarl, without the production of soft moss, had caused them to be tied to the stakes.

imported from South America," * * * "three per cent. appears the largest average in the latter, whereas five per cent. was discovered in the former." That this result is most encouraging is a fact beyond all dispute; it is probable also, because in cultivation plants can be placed in more favourable conditions for the production of certain secretions than usually happens in nature. Dr. Macpherson does not state it, but it is certain that this gratifying result must have been obtained from the plants exposed to light and air, *i. e.* grown on the site effectually cleared of forest, as it is as impossible for a cinchona plant to produce quinine when grown in dense shade, as for an animal to be fed without food. Dr. Macpherson details the system now followed in Java—namely, that of planting the trees under dense shade without even clearing away the underwood—as a complete success: experience will prove the reverse, and will one day establish the fact that, having gone from one extreme to the other, the Dutch are retrograding instead of progressing in the culture of the cinchona for the production of quinine, and that they are now, figuratively and literally, working in the dark. I append the opinion of Dr. Lindley* on this subject, and this can be supported by hundreds of authorities, and the fact of everyday experience with all plants, as no plant can thoroughly elaborate its juices or perfect its secretions in dense shade.

15. I would further remark that our experiment, so far as it has gone, will bear favourable comparison with that of the Dutch. Dr. Hasskarl's expedition to South America cost the Government, I am informed, 10,000 *l.*, and occupied upwards of two years, and was productive of less results than the expedition of Mr. Markham has already been, if nothing more comes from it than the plants now growing in the gardens. On this subject I would remark, that I learn from Mr. Anderson that he brought plants of the *Cinchona Calisaya* to Ceylon; I also received from that gentleman seeds of the species noted at the foot.† More of these and other species may shortly be expected from Kew, and more are daily coming up here, so that at the lowest estimate I may safely say, that one-tenth of the results to be fairly expected from Mr. Markham's expedition have not yet developed themselves. The two cuttings (one of *Cinchona Calisaya* and one of *C. ovata*), are still alive, but show no signs of growth.

16. Appended is a detailed report of the seeds reared here, the time they have taken to germinate, and the various modes of treatment adopted.

17. With reference to planting seeds on the plan adopted in Java, namely, that of sowing them in beds, "one seed in a pot or bamboo" under thatched sheds, and watering them "twice daily from the squeeze of a sponge," is so absurd that I am confident, on reconsideration, your Honourable Government will not require such a mode to be put into practice: few persons have any idea of the care and attention required to rear these small and delicate seeds, especially after a long journey and exposure to many vicissitudes of climate.

18. With reference to selecting the "Dodabetta site," now condemned by Dr. Macpherson, and the work stopped for the present by Government, I have the

* Lindley's Theory and Practice of Horticulture, page 70.—"It is to the action of leaves; to the decomposition of their carbonic acid, and of their water; to the separation of the aqueous particles of the sap from the solid parts that were dissolved in it; to the deposition thus effected of various earthy and other substances, either introduced into plants, as Silex and metallic salts, or formed there, as the vegetable alkaloids; to the extrication of nitrogen and, probably, to other causes as yet unknown—that the formation of the peculiar secretions of plants, of whatever kind, is owing; and this is brought about principally, if not exclusively, by the agency of light. Their green colour becomes intense, in proportion to their exposure to light within certain limits, and feeble in proportion to their removal from it, till, in total and continued darkness, they are entirely destitute of green secretion and become blanched or etiolated. The same result attends all their other secretions: timber, gum, sugar, acids, starch, oil, raisins, odours, flavours, and all the numberless narcotic, acrid, aromatic, pungent, astringent, and other principles derived from the vegetable kingdom, are equally influenced, as to quantity and quality, by the amount of light to which the plants producing them have been exposed."

† Mr. Anderson to Mr. McIvor, Calcutta, 8th March 1861.—"I also brought out three plants of the *Cinchona Calisaya*, which I sent up to Peradenia in charge of Mr. Thwaites, head-gardener; one was a large plant three feet high. It arrived in excellent order."

Cinchona micrantha provinciana.
C. micrantha Pata de Gallinazo.
C. succirubra.
C. nitida.
C. Without name.

* Dated India Office, London, 9th June 1859, No. 21; also dated India Office, London, 17th August 1860, No. 42.

the honour to state that, in the first instance, the Secretary of State for India* requested information from Dr. Cleghorn and myself on the subject of the sites best suited for the cultivation of the cinchonas. Ill-health prevented Dr. Cleghorn from visiting the localities and selecting the sites. Prior to that gentleman leaving for home, he left this duty entirely to myself, stating, "it could not be left in better hands." At the time I felt myself insufficiently informed to accept so great a responsibility, and although I named the sites which appears suited, I recommended that they should not be finally adopted until we had the benefit of Mr. Markham's personal knowledge of the natural localities of the plants. That gentleman on his arrival here inspected this site, and on a careful comparison of what he observed on the Andes highly approved of it. Mr. Markham, being here for a short time only, had not an opportunity of observing the moisture of the climate. The observations made by Mr. Markham were forwarded to Mr. Howard, the best judge in Europe of such matters, and that gentleman's opinion is given in the foot-note.† Subsequent observations and inquiries confirm in my mind that this site is eminently suited for the experiment, and it is most unfortunate that the work should have been stopped at the very time the plants requiring a high elevation are growing in the gardens.

19. I most respectfully beg to solicit that your Honourable Government may be pleased to place this experiment on the Neilgherries entirely under my management, or release me from any connexion with it.

20. I make this request having been taught, in the early stages of the garden,‡ the utter impossibility of conducting operations, either to the satisfaction of Government or myself, when constantly interfered with by parties possessing no practical knowledge of the matters in which they would direct. I therefore trust that the success I have attained in these gardens may be taken into consideration, and that Government may repose the same confidence in me they have hitherto done. My long experience (13 years) on these hills, and consequently my possession of local knowledge in horticultural matters, which must prove of great advantage in conducting this experiment, is a subject worthy of the consideration of Government. I possess testimony to my attainments in botany, vegetable physiology, and horticulture from the most eminent men in Britain§; and not only do I possess this knowledge, but that I am qualified to apply it with judgment

---

† From Mr. Markham, 10th February 1861.—"I have heard from Mr. Howard, who thinks the site for a cinchona plantation in the shola behind the gardens well chosen if it be not too dry, that is, if it is moistened with sufficient showers."

"The conditions favourable for the production of quinine are evidently those of a continuous vegetation with a mean temperature of from 60° to 70°, varying a little according to the species."

(No. 126.) Public Department.

‡ "Extract from the Minutes of Consultation, dated 9th February 1853," paragraph 8.—"In originally appointing a Committee (Extract Minutes of Consultation, 20th June 1848), the Government distinctly declared that interference with the gardener in professional matters should be avoided. It was difficult to state how far the control of the Committee should extend, but it was intended that it should be of a general character; that, in fact, they should merely see that the superintendent was carrying out the objects for which the garden was established, and not that he should be placed entirely under their orders and deprived of all power of acting without their instructions."

Paragraph 9.—"The progress which the gardens have since made renders it desirable that this control should be still more relaxed, and the Government think the most expedient plan now is to place the gardens and their establishment entirely under the management of Mr. McIvor, who has shown himself equal to the task, and who will have an additional stimulus to exertion by being made wholly responsible for its success or failure."

§ Sir W. J. Hooker, in "London Journal of Botany," June 1847.—"A separate work was still much needed upon the Hepaticæ, and we have now the pleasure to announce an excellent little volume on these, the labour of Mr. W. Graham McIvor, at this time attached to the Royal Gardens, Kew. While resident in Scotland, and since his sojourn in England, this botanist has been indefatigable in his researches after these beautiful plants, and has consequently been eminently successful, and no less so in the accurate determination of the species."

Professor Lindley bears similar testimony to my botanical attainments.—"Gardeners' Chronicle and Agricultural Gazette" for 1848, page 20.

From Mr. Westwood, Botanic Gardens, Dollar, 1st November 1845.—"I may with confidence recommend him to your notice, as one who is likely to employ the energies of an active mind to advantage in any department of his profession."

From

ment and develope it with success, is established by numerous minutes by the Government of Madras; also the Secretary of State for India, and the late Court of Directors have honoured me with frequent and creditable mention of my "zeal, skill, and activity;"* from the Secretary to the Government of Madras, dated 12th January 1859, No. 3; from the Honourable Court of Directors to Madras Government, dated 5th August, 1857, No. 51, and others.

21. Should your Honourable Government think fit to place the cinchona plantations on the Neilgherries entirely in my hands, I will accept the responsibility of their success or failure. I do not promise to conduct the experiment throughout without mistakes, but I fear not to guarantee to Government greater results, and at far less cost, than they will obtain in Coorg or elsewhere.

From Mr. J. McNab, Royal Botanic Gardens, Edinburgh, 8th December 1847.—"I would consider you eminently qualified for any situation, either horticultural, botanical, or combined, that may occur at home or abroad."

From Mr. Cuthbertson, Yorkshire, 8th December 1847.—"He has a thorough knowledge of gardening in all its branches; in short, he is a most enterprising young man, and it is very rare to find a young man to equal him."

From Mr. J. Smith, Curator, Royal Botanic Gardens, Kew, 11th December 1847.—"Therefore, viewing his general good conduct, his practical knowledge of gardening, and his botanical knowledge, I have no hesitation in considering him a most efficient person to fill the gardener's situation now vacant in India."

"Minute by the Honourable the President.

* "I have visited the garden, and entirely agree with Dr. Cleghorn that Mr. McIvor deserves great credit for the manner in which he has laid it out. The garden is both a beautiful pleasure-ground and a valuable public institution for the improvement of indigenous and the naturalization of foreign plants; and it has been formed from the commencement by Mr. McIvor, with great industry and artistic skill, out of a rude ravine.

"The advantage of Mr. McIvor's science and experience will be in a great degree lost, if means are not taken to train up under him persons who can profit by his teaching, and if he is not relieved from mere clerical work.

"Ootacamund, 24th February 1861. (signed) "*C. E. Trevelyan.*"

"Extract from the Minutes of Consultation, under date the 15th March 1859 (No. 328).

"The Governor in Council has much pleasure in giving effect to this order of the Home authorities, being of opinion that Mr. McIvor has fully earned this augmentation of salary by his zealous and intelligent discharge of his duties; and he desires to express his sense of the great improvement which Mr. McIvor's care, and skill, and judgment have effected in the garden."

Revenue Department.

Proceedings of Madras Government, 15th May 1860 (No. 781).

Paragraph 5.—"They concur with Dr. Cleghorn that the Superintendent deserves great credit for his imporant application of moss, whereby, at once, young plants intended for transplanting are better prepared than formerly for removal, and can be transported at less than one-tenth of the usual cost, while the garden space is also economized.

(signed) "*J. D. Bourdillon,*
"Secretary to Government."

REPORT showing the NUMBER of CINCHONA SEEDS reared at the Government Gardens, Ootacamund, with a detailed Account of the various Modes of Treatment.

Names of Species.	Nature of the Soil in which sown.	Amount of Shade.	Amount of Water.	Preparation of Seeds before Sowing.	Number of Days before Germination took place.	Number which Germinated strongly.	Number which Germinated weakly.	Total Number of Seedlings.	REMARKS.
No. 1. Cinchona micrantha, variation Provinciana.	A mixture of three equal parts—one of burned earth, one of sand, and one of very old cow-dung.	Shaded in bright sunshine only.	Watered sparingly at first, and only when the soil was dry on the surface.	Steeped for four hours in oxalic acid.	62	61	16	77	All the seeds were sown in flower-pots well drained, and the soil boiled, in order to destroy the grubs and larva of insects, which would otherwise devour the seeds or young plants as they began to grow. After the soil is boiled, it is allowed to dry, then mixed in a dry state, and put into the pots. It is important it should be mixed dry, otherwise it hardens.
No. 2. Ditto - - ditto -	Ditto - - ditto - - -	Ditto - - ditto -	Watered morning and evening.	12 hours in lime -	–	None	None	None	
No. 3. Ditto - - ditto -	In brown loam selected by Dr. Macpherson.	Shaded throughout, except in the mornings and evenings.	Ditto - - ditto -	Steeped four hours in oxalic acid.	64	None	1	1	
No. 4. Ditto - - ditto -	In black loam selected by Dr. Macpherson.	Ditto - - ditto -	Ditto - - ditto -	None - - -	–	None	None	–	
No. 5. Ditto - - ditto -	A mixture of equal parts of loam, burned earth, and leaf-mould.	Shaded in bright sunshine only.	Watered as No. 1 -	None - - -	65	None	8	8	
Cinchona micrantha, var. Pata de Gallinazo.	Soil prepared as at No. 1 - -	Ditto - - ditto -	Ditto - - ditto -	Steeped as No. 1 -	63	18	6	24	
Ditto - - ditto -	Soil as No. 1 - - - -	Ditto - - ditto -	Ditto - - ditto -	None - - -	–	None	None	–	
Cinchona nitida -	Soil prepared as at No. 1 - -	Ditto - - ditto -	Ditto - - ditto -	Steeped four hours in oxalic acid.	66	46	14	60	
Ditto - - ditto -	Prepared as at No. 4 - - -	Ditto - - ditto -	Ditto - - ditto -	None - - -	68	None	2	2	
						125	47		
				TOTAL Number of Seedlings - - -				172	

In the treatment of these seeds, they appeared to be impatient of too much shade and moisture, soon becoming mouldy and rotting off. The seeds were sown on the surface, and covered with a thin coating of finely cut moss. The black and brown loams, as used in Java, seemed to retain too much water, and are certainly unsuited for rearing old seeds. Fresh-gathered seeds, possessing great vital power, may grow in loam, but not so freely as they would in soil prepared as at No. 1. The seeds are easily distinguished when they begin to germinate, as they strike their radicles into the ground with great force, considering the small size of the seed; the radicle being established in the ground, the plumule is raised up with the seed on the top of it, where it remains three or four days; then it falls off, and the seed-lobes (*Cotyledons*) expand. I give this description of the process of germination, as I find it is not described in any of the works I possess.

(signed) *W. G. McIvor,*
Superintendent, Government Gardens.

Ootacamund, 30 March 1861.

Enclosure 1, in No. 66.

From *D. Macpherson*, Esq., M.D., Inspector General of Hospitals, to *J. D. Sim*, Esq., Secretary to Government, Revenue Department, Fort Saint George; dated (on the tour of inspection) Rangoon, 24 July 1861.

Sir,

1. Consequent on the nature of my duties within these provinces during the past four months, copies of Captain Morgan's and Mr. McIvor's letters, and the Government order thereon, bearing on my report to you, dated 5th February, No. 7, only reached me a few days since.

2. With regard to his (Captain Morgan's) remarks and criticisms on my public reports to Government in matters relating to the introduction of cinchona into India, I feel it incumbent on me to reply as follows:—

3. In the first paragraph of his letter, dated 28th of March last, No. 418, Captain Morgan asserts "that the existence of certain discrepancies between my first and second reports invalidates the whole of my remarks, and render my information of no value." On this he proceeds to show—

The first "discrepancy," which relates to the subject of "elevation" for the growth of cinchona trees, asserting that in my letter No. 1, I condemn what I recommend in letter No. 8. Had Captain Morgan quoted correctly, he should have said that in the former I stated nothing from my own knowledge. I merely reported the result of experiments made in Java, specially observing, in the same paragraph from which he quotes, "but the best elevations have yet to be ascertained." In the latter I gave my opinion, as directed, on what appeared to me to be the best plan to pursue in our experiments; an opinion, as far as relates to the Dodabett and Coorg sites, I still maintain to be correct.

The second instance of "discrepancy" relates to the "southern decline" of the hill being recommended in my Java report, whereas in my Neilgherry letter I state "that the northern is the best." Captain Morgan is correct; and I am indebted to Mr. McIvor's superior knowledge in horticulture, as graphically described in paragraph 8 of his letter, for "bringing conviction to my mind by his unanswerable arguments."

4. Paragraphs 4, 5, and 6 of Captain Morgan's letter call for no observations.

5. Captain Morgan states, in paragraph 7 of his letter, that I incorrectly describe the Dodabett site, as consisting of "disintegrated granite, or masses of trap protruding on the surface." The "rock," he says, "is gneiss, the superstratum is decomposed felspar and hornblende, the former yielding 11 per cent. of potash, a most valuable ingredient for forming alkali" (what is potash but an alkali?) "and the latter supplies 13 per cent. of lime." Now, as gneiss "is a slaty or secondary granite, as when granite passes by several perceptible gradations into gneiss" (*vide* Humble's Dictionary of Geology), and as "trappean rocks are composed of two minerals, felspar and hornblende" (*vide* Lyall's Geology, page 463), Captain Morgan's assertion is only opposed to mine in terms dissimilar, but of corresponding signification. Such being the case, in Captain Morgan's own words, the Dodabett site "is a very indifferent situation."

6. Captain Morgan, in observing on the word "marl," used by me in my Neilgherry letter, says, "Now marl is a compound of clay and lime, of which we have none on these hills." He forgets that in four lines above this remark he alludes to the presence of 13 per cent. of lime in the composition of the substratum on the Dodabett site. Lyell, at page 13, states that the "word marl is used ambiguously, and is applied to substances in which there is no lime, as to the red loam, usually called red marl in certain parts of England. Agriculturists are in the habit of calling any soil marl which falls to pieces readily on exposure to the air." It was in its agricultural signification that I applied the term, the construction alone which a practical gardener like Mr. Weir or Mr. Spruce employed it.

7. Captain Morgan discovers other "discrepancies" in my statements, which are as easily demolished as the above have been. But I have more important duty on hand than to waste time in confuting assertions by one who criticises my official acts in the style which pervades his letter; nor indeed would I have taken the trouble to do what I have done, had it not been for the endorsement on the Government order of the 16th April 1861, No. 855, which induces me to solicit that the same publicity which was given to the documents under reply may also be accorded to this.

Enclosure 2, in No. 66.

Order of the Madras Government, 16 April 1861.

1. The papers above recorded relate to the prosecution of the attempts to introduce the cinchona tree into South India. It is unnecessary to review them at length; and the Government will merely notice those points on which orders are required.

2. It was directed in the order of the 9th March, No. 552, that the site at the back of the Government Garden at Ootacamund should be abandoned, and also that a stop should be

be put to attempts to raise cinchona plants and seeds at the garden. In deference to the opinion expressed by Mr. Markham, as well as by Mr. McIvor, the Government now modify that order, and give permission to continue the operations at the garden ravine site, as well as to retain at the garden for the present the plants brought by Mr. Cross, and sow the seeds, as the Neddiwattum site is not ready, and does not contain the necessary appliances.

3. The Governor in Council, however, desires that this last-mentioned site, which Mr. Markham considers (paragraph 19) to be eminently well suited to the purpose, shall be prepared as soon as possible, and a portion of the plants transferred to it. The Government had hoped to engage the services of Mr. Cross to have immediate charge of this plantation; but from Captain Morgan's letter of the 9th April, they learn that he is unwilling to remain in India. The Government have applied to the Secretary of State to send out Mr. Weir, and they will repeat the request, now it is found that Mr. Cross does not desire to remain.

4. For the present the Government plantations will be confined to these two sites; but seeds should be distributed to those coffee planters in Wainâd and Coorg who may wish to try and rear them. After the result of the experiment on the Neilgherries shall be known, the Government will be prepared to commence operations at the site selected in Coorg, which Mr. Markham (paragraph 21) agrees with Dr. Macpherson in regarding as well suited to a cinchona plantation.

5. In accordance with Mr. Markham's recommendation (paragraph 33), the operations at both the sites now fixed on, viz. the garden ravine and Neddiwuttum, will be entrusted to Mr. McIvor. Captain Morgan will report, after consulting with him, as to the arrangements to be made for the immediate superintendence of the operations at Neddiwattum, until the arrival of Mr. Weir or some other qualified gardener from England.

(True extract)

(signed) *J. D. Bourdillon*,
Secretary to Government.

To the Conservator of Forests.
,, Board of Revenue.
,, Inspector General of Hospitals.
,, Superintendent Government Gardens, Ootacamund.

— No. 67. —

From the Government of Madras to Sir *Charles Wood*, dated Madras, 24 April 1861.

Proceedings of Government, 16th April 161, Nos. 265 to 271.

We have the honour to forward for your information the papers specified in the margin, relating to the introduction of the cinchona tree into South India.

2. Mr. Cross arrived at Ootacamund on the 9th April, with 463 plants of the *C. succirubra* and six *Calisaya* plants, all in good order. As many as 172 plants had also been raised from seed in the Ootacamund Gardens up to the 30th March.

3. You will observe that Mr. McIvor, of the Ootacamund Government Garden, a man of much intelligence and skill in his calling, disputes the justice of Dr. Macpherson's views as to the proper management of the seeds and plants, and that he is partly supported by Mr. Markham, in a despatch* written from Bombay to the Under Secretary of State for India, of which a copy was sent to us. In deference to the opinions thus expressed, we have modified our order of the 8th March, No. 552, and permitted Mr. McIvor to continue the operations at the garden ravine site, and also to have a nursery fur cinchonas in the garden.

* Dated February 26th 1861, No. 8.

4. We were desirous to engage Mr. Cross, recently arrived in charge of plants, to have charge of the Neddiwattum plantation; but he is unwilling to remain in India. We beg, therefore, to repeat the request contained in paragraph 4 of our former Despatch, that Mr. Weir may be engaged and sent out, with as little delay as possible, to have charge of that plantation. Mr. Weir appears to be peculiarly well fitted for the charge; but if he should not be willing to come, then we beg that some other competent gardener may be sent out.

5. We

5. We have resolved that, for the present, the Government plantations shall be confined to these two sites; but we have directed that seeds shall be distributed to those coffee planters in Wainád and Coorg who may wish to try and rear them. After the results of the experiments on the Neilgherries shall be known, we shall be prepared to commence operations at the site selected in Coorg, which Mr. Markham (paragraph 21) agrees with Dr. Macpherson in regarding as well suited to a cinchona plantation.

6. In accordance with Mr. Markham's recommendation (paragraph 33), we have entrusted the operations at both the sites now fixed on, viz., the garden and ravine at Neddiwuttum, to Mr. McIvor. Captain Morgan, our Acting Conservator of Forests, has been directed to report, after consulting with him, as to the arrangements to be made for the immediate superintendence of the operations at Neddivattam, until the arrival of a qualified gardener from England.

7. It is desirable that a second gardener should be sent out from England, to have charge either of the Coorg plantation or of that at the Avalanche site on the Neilgherries, whichever may be formed first. We would request you to send out such a person without delay; because, until such new plantation shall be undertaken, he may be very usefully employed, under Mr. McIvor's instructions, in acquainting himself with the habits of the cinchona plant and its mode of treatment.

— No. 68. —

From *Clements Markham*, Esq., to the Under Secretary of State for India in Council.

Sir, Valetta, 8 April 1861.

I HAVE great pleasure in reporting, that I met the gardener, Cross, at Aden, on board the Peninsular and Oriental steamer "Orissa," on the 19th of March, with 15 cases of cinchona plants, in excellent condition, consisting of about 600 *C. succirubra*, and six *C. Calisaya*, from Kew—the latter not being in so hopeful a condition, but still alive. The Red Sea was very cool, the thermometer being at times as low as 65 degrees, so that the plants have not been exposed to any great heat, and their stems, leaves, branches, and roots were in the most perfect state possible

2. Before I left Bombay, arrangements had been made for transmitting the plants to Calicut, in Her Majesty's steamer "Pleiad," without a day's delay, so that long ere this they ought to have arrived at Ootacamund and Ceylon.

3. Though, in the course of this experiment, more than one disappointment has been encountered, yet the present prospects of final success are encouraging, and a large measure has already been achieved. The species yielding red bark, the most valuable next to the *Calisaya*, has by this time been safely introduced, in large quantities, into India and Ceylon. Six plants of *C. Calisaya* have now reached Ootacamund, in addition to those of my collection, which still survive, and Sir William Hooker has been very successful in striking cuttings from ae, *C. Calisaya* at Kew; so that I trust another case may be transmitted to India, in the next cold season, of that inestimable species. The plants of the collection brought by Mr. Pritchett, which have already been transmitted to India, have failed; but his seeds have germinated freely at Ootacamund, as well as at Kew and in Jamaica, and young plants of these species may also be sent to India in the next cold season.

4. Thus, although, as was to be expected, several failures and disappointments have taken place in the course of an experiment of such great difficulty, and requiring, to ensure success, such a combination of favourable circumstances, as well as of various kinds of knowledge, energy, and forethought—yet, in consequence of the numerous precautions which have been taken, both by orga-

 nizing

nizing three distinct expeditions and by establishing depôts to fall back upon both at Kew and in the West Indies, there is now a good prospect of establishing in the hills of Southern India, and in Ceylon, all the species of cinchona plants which yield alkaloids of medicinal value.

5. The knowledge acquired, by personal observation, of the native forests of the *C. Calisaya* by myself, and of those of the *C. succirubra* by the gardener Cross, will have been of great advantage in comparing them with analogous sites in the Indian hills, and in imparting such knowledge to Mr. McIvor; so that he will enter upon the superintendence of the cinchona plantations in India with a tolerably full acquaintance with the requirements of the plants, as regards climate, soil, and elevation.

6. I regret to say, that Cross declines to remain in India, and desires to return to England as soon as possible; so that it will be necessary to secure the services of some other gardener, to assist Mr. McIvor in the superintendence of the cinchona plantations. Such help, even if the experiment is to be conducted on the very smallest scale, is absolutely essential. The Dutch Government in Java, who are determined to spare no expense in ensuring the introduction of this invaluable plant, have organized a much larger staff, consisting of a superintendent, with a salary of 1,200*l.* a year, with no other duty, an agricultural chemist, and a numerous staff of gardeners and labourers.

7. I shall defer any further observations and suggestions respecting the service on which I have been employed, until my arrival in England; and trusting that the Secretary of State in Council will, on the whole, be satisfied with the way in which I have performed the duty the conduct of which has been entrusted to me,

I have, &c.
(signed) *Clements R. Markham.*

— No. 69. —

From *Clements Markham*, Esq., to the Under Secretary of State for India.

Sir, Torquay, 30 May 1861.

I HAVE great pleasure in reporting, for the information of the Secretary of State for India in Council, that I have received a very favourable account of the state of the cinchona plants in the Neilgherry Hills, from Mr. McIvor, down to the 23d ultimo.

2. Of the six plants of *C. Calisaya*, he is certain of saving four, and perhaps five.

9. Of the seeds of *C. succirubra*, upwards of 100 have already come up, and Mr. McIvor makes certain of 70 to 80 per cent. of the remainder.

4. He already has a fine stock of strong young seedling plants of *C. nitida* and *C. micrantha*.

5. Of the plants of *C. succirubra*, 463 in number, which arrived at Ootacamund early in April, Mr. McIvor reports that he will save the whole.

7. With reference to my memorandum, dated 17th May 1861, I now find that, in consequence of the receipt of a copy of my report, dated Bombay, February 26th 1861, and of a letter from Mr. McIvor, the Madras Government have modified their order of 9th March 1861, No. 552, with regard to their concurrence in the recommendations of Dr. Macpherson; and in their order of 16th April 1861, No. 855, they direct that the operations at the Dodabetta site may be resumed, and that the propagation of seeds and raising of plants in the Government Gardens may be continued. Most fortunately, Mr. McIvor, feeling that the removal of the tender cinchona plants would ensure their destruction, had ventured to delay his obedience to the previous order of the Madras Government,

Government, and thus the only mischief which has been caused by Dr. Macpherson's interference, has been a delay of more than a month in the preparation of the important Dodabetta site.

7. The directions contained in the Despatch, which has lately been approved, have thus been anticipated by the Madras Government, who, in their order of 16th April, have entirely cancelled their previous order of 9th March; but these contradictory orders point out the great importance of placing the cinchona experiment in charge of one competent and responsible person, who would not be exposed to constant interference from officers who are entirely ignorant of the subject on which they offer opinions to the Government.

8. The proceedings of Dr. Macpherson are an example of the mischief which such interference may cause. In consequence of having visited the cinchona plantations in Java, and written a short account of what he saw, the Madras Government ordered him to proceed to the Neilgherry Hills, and report upon the sites selected by me for cinchona cultivation. Those sites were selected, and the other arrangements connected with the experiment were made, by me in communication with Mr. McIvor, after a careful and unremitted study of the subject for nearly two years, after a minute examination of the cinchona forests of South America, and after having made myself thoroughly acquainted with the proceedings of the Dutch in Java, through the published accounts of Dr. Junghühn, the superintendent. Yet the recommendations of Dr. Macpherson, which, if carried into effect, would have ensured the destruction of the plants and involved the abandonment of one of the sites, were at once adopted by the Madras Government, without any reference either to myself, although specially sent to India by the Secretary of State to select these sites, or even to Mr. McIvor.

9. It is true that, more than a month afterwards, the Madras Government cancelled the order in which they had adopted the recommendations of Dr. Macpherson, but in the meanwhile the mischief might have been done; and hereafter the recommendations of any other officer equally ignorant of the subject might with equal reason be adopted, and retard the success, or even cause the entire failure, of this important experiment.

10. For these reasons I would venture to urge most strongly, that the whole charge of the experiment should be placed in the hands of Mr. McIvor, who is willing to undertake the responsibility. In his letter to the Madras Government, dated 30th March 1861, he requested that the matter might be placed entirely in his hands, or that he might be released from any connexion with it. This appears perfectly reasonable, for Mr. McIvor cannot be expected to undertake any responsibility, if he is to be exposed to constant interference from Dr. Macpherson. The whole management of the experiment, both as regards the measures to be adopted for clearing the sites and cultivating the plants, and as regards the engagement of labourers, should, I submit, be placed entirely under Mr. McIvor's management, and he should be responsible to, and in direct communication with, the Government.

11. The Madras Government has now ordered both the sites on the Neilgherry Hills to be prepared as soon as possible, and all the operations to be entrusted to Mr. McIvor; but his proceedings are to be reported through Captain Morgan, the Acting Conservator of Forests, instead of his being placed in direct communication with the Government. The plants, when planted out, will run many risks from elks and pigs, at first; and Mr. McIvor proposes to retain all the original plants in the Government Gardens, where no accident can befall them, and to propagate from them, planting out only those which have been propagated. The original stock would always be retained for the purpose of propagation, and by these means there would be many thousands of plants ready to plant out by next spring.

13. The superintendence of this important and very difficult experiment will entail much toil and expense, as well as anxiety; and the Secretary of State in Council will probably consider that Mr. McIvor should be allowed 300 rupees per month. The Dutch superintendent, I understand, is in the receipt of 1,200 *l.* a year, with the rank of a resident (equivalent to our collectors), or

nearly four times the sum; although we have achieved twenty times the success of the Dutch, in half the time, and at half the cost. While the Dutch only have one valuable species, we have procured the best species of cinchonæ, yielding red, grey, and yellow barks; while they only saved one plant, which was conveyed direct from South America, we have secured several hundreds; while only one in a thousand of their seeds came up, from 70 to 80 per cent. of ours are germinating; and while their single expedition to South America cost them 10,000 *l.*, and lasted two years, our three expeditions will have cost under 5,000 *l.*, and will have taken only one year. With far greater economy, we have attained a considerably larger measure of success; the attempt is of greater importance to our vast Indian Empire than to the small island of Java; and therefore, while the Dutch superintendent of cinchona plantations, for that duty alone, receives a salary of 1,200 *l.* a year, it does not appear that 360 *l.* will be too much for the gardener who undertakes the superintendence in the Neilgherry Hills. Special qualifications, not easily met with, are required for the post; the duties will entail much toil, expense, and anxiety, and the responsibility will be great. A smaller allowance would, I think, be insufficient, and Mr. McIvor is ready to undertake the duties for 300 rupees per month.

14. It is gratifying to find that the gardener, Cross, who has personal knowledge of the forests where the *C. succirubra* grow, is of opinion that the site selected by me at Neddiwattum is peculiarly well adapted for the cultivation of that valuable species, and, indeed, that the plants will grow better there than in their native forests, the soil being superior.

15. Cross has refused to remain in India, and the Madras Government have requested that Weir, the man who accompanied me to South America, may be sent out to work under Mr. McIvor at the Neddiwuttum site. Unfortunately, Weir has, I believe, already sailed for Brazil in the employment of the Horticultural Society, and it will therefore be necessary to engage the services of some other man. I have now to request that I may be authorized to search out and engage a gardener for this service, with a salary of 150 *l.* a year to begin with, increasing at the rate of 10 *l.* a year, but with the understanding that he shall not forsake the service of Government during a specified term of years. Unless some such understanding is come to, and a yearly increase of salary is allowed, it seems hopeless to suppose that a gardener of any attainments will remain in Government employ in India, when he is almost certain to be tempted by far more advantageous offers from private persons.

16. In a former letter, I suggested that I should be authorized to arrange with Mr. Spruce to procure a supply of seeds of the *C. Condaminea* for the sum of 100 *l.* In Mr. Spruce's letter, dated Guayaquil, 12th October 1860, he reports the obstacles which prevented him from procuring a supply during last season, but he has since offered to perform this service for the above sum. *C. Condaminea* (the tree growing in the Loxa forests, and yielding the crown bark of commerce) is the only very valuable species which is not yet introduced into India. It is the earliest known species, the *Cinchona officinalis* of Linnæus, the plant specially described by La Condamine, Humboldt, and Pavon, and is still of great commercial value. The sum required by Mr. Spruce for procuring seeds of this species is exceedingly small in comparison with the importance of the object to be gained; and I, therefore, venture again to request that I may be authorized to make arrangements with Mr. Spruce for procuring a good supply of *C. Condaminea* seeds for the sum of 100 *l.*

I have, &c.
(signed) *Clements R. Markham.*

— No. 70. —

From *E. Hammond*, Esq. to *Herman Merivale*, Esq., C. B., India Office.

Sir, Foreign Office, 2 October 1861.

In compliance with the request conveyed in your letter of the 15th of June last, Earl Russell instructed Her Majesty's Acting Consul-General at Guayaquil to pay to Mr. Richard Spruce the sum of 100 *l.*, for the the purpose of procuring a supply of seeds of the *Condaminea* species of quinine-yielding cinchona trees from the forests of Loxa; and I am directed by his Lordship to transmit to you, for the information of Secretary Sir Charles Wood, a copy of a Despatch from Mr. Mocatta, stating that Mr. Spruce declines the offer made to him on account of ill-health. Consular, No. 30. 28 August 1860.

I am, &c.
(signed) *E. Hammond.*

Enclosure in No. 70.

From Her Majesty's Vice-Consul at *Guayaquil* to Lord *John Russell.*

My Lord, Guayaquil, 28 August 1861.

In conformity with your Lordship's Instructions, contained in Mr. Murray's Consular Despatch, No. 5, of the 28th June last, I acquainted Mr. Richard Spruce with the wishes of Her Majesty's Secretary of State for India, and I have now to inform your Lordship that Mr. Spruce declines the offer made him, on account of the infirm state of his health.

I have, &c.
(signed) *Francis Mocatta.*

— No. 71. —

From Her Majesty's Vice-Consul at *Guay aquil* to the Secretary of State for India.

Sir, Guayaquil, 13 September 1861.

I have received instructions from the Foreign Office to pay to Mr. Richard Spruce the sum of 100 *l.* for the purpose of procuring a supply of seeds of the *Condaminea* species of quinine-yielding cinchona trees, and to draw upon you a bill for 100 *l.* at seven days after sight.

Mr. Spruce having declined the offer on account of ill-health, I have engaged the services of Mr. Robert Cross, the gardener recently employed in assisting Mr. Spruce.

As from the proceeds of my bills on the India Office,—		£.	*s.*	*d.*
In 30 March 1860 - - - - -	for	200	–	–
In 28 May 1860 - - - - -	„	500	–	–
In 7 November 1860 - - - -	„	250	–	–
In 14 January 1861 - - - -	„	50	–	–
say - - -	£.	1,000	–	–
Mr. Spruce drew only for - -		926	8	3
leaving a balance in my hands of - - - -	£.	73	11	9
in favour of the India Office, I have to advise you that I have this day drawn upon you, at seven days' sight, merely for the sum of - - - - - - - - - -		26	8	3
to complete the sum of - - - - - -	£.	100	–	–

which I am instructed to pay for the aforesaid purpose.

I have, &c.
(signed) *Francis Mocatta,*
Her Britannic Majesty's Acting Consul General.

— No. 72. —

From Her Majesty's Vice-Consul at *Guayaquil* to the Secretary of State for India.

Sir, Guayaquil, 14 December 1861.

Referring to my letter of the 13th of September last, I have the honour to inform you that Mr. Robert Cross has returned successful from the forests of Loxa, bringing with him, after undergoing many hardships and overcoming the greatest difficulties, about 100,000 seeds of the *Condaminea* species of quinine-yielding trees, which I forward by this day's mail.

Of the 100 *l.* which I was authorized to place at his disposal, he has disbursed for the expenses of his mission the sum of 41 *l.* 16 *s.*, and I would suggest that I may be authorized to draw upon you, at seven days after sight, for that amount, in order that Mr. Cross may receive the clear sum of 100 *l.* as remuneration for services of so important a character.

Enclosed I have the honour to hand you his report,

And to be, &c.
(signed) *Francis Mocatta*,
Her Britannic Majesty's Vice-Consul.

—No. 73.—

From *R. Cross*, Esq., to the Under Secretary of State for India.

Sierra de Cajanuma, near Loxa,
Sir, 9 November 1861.

On my arrival at Guayaquil, I learned from Mr. Mocatta, Her Britannic Majesty's Vice-Consul there, that Mr. Spruce had declined going for the seeds of *C. Condaminea* to Loxa. It was further stated to me that the Government of Ecuador had passed an edict prohibiting the exportation of either seeds or plants of the quina tree, under a penalty of 100 dollars for every plant, and for every drachm of seed.* However, after consulting with Mr. Mocatta, I undertook to go to Loxa and make a collection of seeds of the *C. Condaminea*.

I left Guayaquil on the 17th of September, and proceeded in an open rowing-boat to Santa Rosa, a small town near the Gulf of Guayaquil, which I reached on the 20th. I had some difficulty in procuring mules at this place, as they are sometimes lost in crossing the first ridge of the cordillera. However, on the morning of the 21st, I succeeded in engaging the services of a peon and mules, and left Santa Rosa,† following the track which leads to Zaruma.‡ The road, or rather pathway, leads through a dense forest, which was exceedingly damp and swampy; and we encamped for the night at the base of a lofty mountain ridge, amidst incessant rain and thick dark fogs. On the 22nd, we ascended the first ridge of the cordillera, the rain still continuing, and stayed all night at an Indian hut on the mountain summit. This day, in crossing a lofty precipitous ridge, one of our mules slipped into a deep ravine, and was dashed to pieces. During our ascent, I saw many young trees of the "Red Bark," growing at an elevation of 8,000 or 9,000 feet. On the 23d we reached Zaruma, a small town situated at the base of the eastern slope of the first ridge of the cordillera. At Zaruma I found an English surgeon, suffering from paralysis, who had resided for several years in Loxa. In course of conversation with this person, I made inquiries concerning the locality of the cinchonas, but could not glean any information on that

---

* *See* Mr. Spruce's Report, p. 103.—*C. R. M.*

† Santa Rosa is the port for the province of Loxa, near the shores of the Gulf of Guayaquil, and almost due south from that town. Santa Rosa is about 80 miles from Guayaquil, by sea.

‡ Zaruma is in latitude 3° 36′ south, and about 5,000 feet above the level of the sea. A good deal of sugar is sent to Guayaquil from the surrounding district. The distance from Santa Rosa to Zaruma, on Villavicencio's map, as the crow flies, is 15 miles, and from Zaruma to Loxa 38 miles.—*C. R. M.*

that point. I did not, however, make known the special object of my journey, as I had previously learned elsewhere that the doctor was in the service of the Republican Government.

On the 24th, having procured a peon and fresh mules, I left Zaruma, and began to ascend the second ridge of the cordillera. The central ridge, unlike the one I had just crossed, is barren and dry, and is in many places strewn with large masses of vitrified rocks, which are frequently mottled with the pseudo-bulbs of several species of *Orchideæ* and stunted *Cacti* and *Agave*. The mountains over which we passed were furrowed by ravines of immense depth, in which there was not a single drop of water to be found, and the aspect of the whole was of the most barren character imaginable. Our course continued over a series of ridges until dusk, when we halted for a few hours, so as to have moonlight to pursue our journey. At about 1 A.M. on the 25th, we resumed our way over extensive paramos, covered by a very coarse species of *gramineæ*, and stunted shrubby *mimosæ*. Some of the mountain ridges over which we this day passed, were narrowed to a breadth of not more than four feet, and presented on each side almost perpendicular precipices, from 3,000 to 4,000 feet in depth.

On the 27th we reached Loxa, which is situated at the base of the eastern slope of the second ridge of the cordillera.*

On the 28th I hired a peon and mules, and proceeded eastward, to reach the mountains of Zamora, a tract of country traversed by wild Indians. After a fruitless search of three days, I returned to Loxa. I did, indeed, find a species of cinchona, the bark of which is sometimes mixed with that of the *condaminea*, but it is of little value.

On the 1st of October I left Loxa, and went about eight miles to the southward, to a low long ridge of hills, called the Sierra de Cajanuma, where I had heard the *C. Condaminea* was to be found growing. As I travelled along the pathway which traverses this mountain slope, I found several young trees of the *C. Condaminea*, growing in steep, precipitous places, but no seeds were to be seen. However, I directed my course to an Indian hut, which was situated on a little rounded eminence near the summit of the mountain, intending to remain there for the night.

I found the possessor of the hut to be an experienced bark collector; and so, although it afforded but little shelter from the cold winds which sweep over the stony paramos, yet I could see at once that situated as it was, far from public roads or other dwellings, it was well suited for the accomplishment of the work. I, accordingly, located myself in a little shed at the end of the hut, wherein was a quantity of cinchona bark, and which, although favourable for the drying of seeds, was so cold that I have sometimes been compelled, during windy nights, to seek shelter in the bottom of a neighbouring ravine. I afterwards searched the lower slopes of this mountain for seeds, but although I found a considerable number of young trees, I could only gather half-a-dozen capsules. October being the month in which the seeds of *C. Condaminea* ripen, I was afraid I should not be able to secure (owing to the great scarcity of seed-bearing trees) a sufficient quantity before the season had passed away. One day, however, on passing along the bank of a steep ravine, I happened to look over a projecting rock, and saw growing on the steep slope beneath a number of fine young trees of the *C. Condaminea*, some of which bore a few panicles of seed, which, on examination, I found to be perfectly ripe. After this discovery, I continued to search all the ravines on the sierra, on which I am at present located, from sunrise to sunset, some of which I had to descend by means of the trailing stems of a species of *passiflora*, and in this way almost all the seeds sent were collected.

On the accessible slopes of the sierra, there are in general but few cinchona trees to be seen, owing, in part, to the annual burning of the slopes, and, in part, to the continual cropping of the young shoots by cattle.

The Sierra de Cajanuma, which forms part of the central ridge of the cordillera, is about eight miles to the south of Loxa. This and the adjoining mountains are mostly composed of primitive rocks,† which have, like those of the Neilgherries

* Loxa is about 6,800 feet above the level of the sea.—*C. R. M.*

† Caldas and Humboldt say that these rocks are micaceous schists and gneiss. *Semanario*, p. 281.—*C. R. M.*

Neilgherries in India, been tilted up and heaped together by volcanic action. The rock is, in many places, in a state of decomposition, and large portions are frequently tumbling down from the more elevated summits. The alluvial deposit in the ravines where the *C. Condaminea* is found growing is shallow, in many places not more than six inches in depth; and I have often gathered seeds from trees which were growing in clefts of rock where there was not a single ounce of soil to be found.

The *C. Condaminea* is a slender-growing tree, from 20 to 30 feet in height, and from 8 to 10 inches in diameter at the base. But few trees are to be seen of these dimensions. The plants from which the bark of commerce is now taken are, in general, not more than 8 to 10 feet in height. When the plants are cut down, three or four young shoots or suckers in general spring up; but this does not always happen, as some of the more industrious cascarilleros frequently pull up the roots, and bark them also. The bark is taken from the smallest twigs; thus the annual growths are sometimes taken, especially if they are strong. The plants are sometimes found growing in little clumps, and sometimes solitary, but always in dry situations. The temperature of the cinchona region ranges from 34 to 70 degress Fahrenheit; it seldom, however, falls below 40 degrees, and rarely rises above 65 degrees. The general range of the temperature is from 45 to 60 degrees Fahrenheit.

The vegetation on the Sierra de Cajanuma is, in general, of a semi-arborescent character, but some of the higher summits, being entirely destitute of soil, are barren. The vegetation on this and the surrounding mountains is altogether remarkable, combining, in the deeper ravines, species in general prevalent in tropical and cold-temperate climates. In the bottoms of the ravines grow a species of alnus, probably *A. glutinosa, Pteris aquilinæ, Melastomæ, Peperomias*, palms, and two species of tree-ferns, growing from 30 to 35 feet in height. On the slopes, and throughout the low-lying country in the immediate neighbourhood of Loxa, barley, maize, peas, and potatoes are cultivated. The climate is certainly very similar to that of the Neilgherries, but the alluvial deposit is shallower, and is, in consequence, less favourable for the cultivation of maize, &c.

Three distinct species of cinchona are collected in the mountains of Loxa—the *C. Condaminea*,* *C. crespilla* (?) and *C. ochiluma* (?)† The latter species is not of much value. The *C. crespilla*,‡ however, is a good bark, not much inferior to the *C. Condaminea;* and I have succeeded in collecting, after several long journeys up the Sierra Grande, a few seeds of this species also. The *C. crespilla* grows at high elevations, in a deposit of peat, and where the temperature sometimes falls to 27° Fahrenheit.

I am of opinion, that the *C. Condaminea* will succeed well on the Neilgherries. There are several ravines immediately above the bungalow on the Neddiwattum site, which will, I believe, be found suitable for the cultivation of this species. If the temperature does not fall below freezing-point on the Dodabetta site, it may be planted there also, and in similar situations, at about the same elevation, throughout the Neilgherries. In making plantations of cinchonas, extensive ravines ought to be selected, and the shrubs cut down and burnt. A fence should then be made along the summits of the banks, to prevent the burghers and todahs from feeding their cattle among the cinchona trees. The trees ought to be planted about seven or eight feet apart, for, after the first cutting, three or four growths of suckers will in general spring from each root; so that, in planting, this ought to be kept in view. It will not be necessary to make great roads for the conveyance of manure; indeed, such would be superfluous, as the soil on any part of the Neilgherries is quite rich enough to grow successional cuttings of the *C. Condaminea* for centuries.

The

* The *C. Condaminea*, the seeds of which have been collected by Mr. Cross, appears to be the *C. Chahuarguera* of Pavon, some account of which will be found at the end of this report, taken from Mr Howard's work.—*C. R. M.*

† Probably intended for *Hoja de lucma.—C.R.M.*

‡ The *C. crespilla* is probably a variety of *C. Chahuarguera*, growing at a greater elevation. Mr. Howard says that the *C. crespilla* bears the same relation to the normal and large-grown *C. Chahuarguera*, as the *C. Josephiana* of Weddell does to the normal *C. Calisaya*. It will be very important to ascertain how far circumstances may have influenced the change.—*C. R. M.*

The principal aim should be to get the species multiplied as rapidly as possible, and form extensive plantations; for I am persuaded that the *C. Condaminea* will succeed on the Neilgherries.

I have, &c.
(signed) *Robert Cross.*

P. S.—Since writing the foregoing, I have returned to Guayaquil, with nearly 100,000 seeds of *C. Condaminea.* I trust, on arrival in England, they may be sent immediately to the Neilgherries. The seeds, together with this report, I deliver into the hands of Mr. Mocatta, Her Britannic Majesty's Consul at Guayaquil.

Guayaquil, 12 December 1861.

— No. 74. —

From *E. D. Bourdillon*, Esq., Secretary in the Public Department, to *T. Pycroft*, Esq., Chief Secretary to Government, Fort St. George.

Dear Sir, India Office, 17 January 1862.

1. HEREWITH is transmitted a parcel of seeds of the *Cinchona Condaminea*, which arrived from South America by the last mail. It is addressed to Mr. W. G. McIvor, and it is very important that it should be transmitted to its destination at Ootacamund with all possible dispatch.

2. Fifty copies of Mr. Cross's report, together with some notes on the *C. Condaminea*, compiled by Mr. Markham, will be forwarded by the next mail; and 40 copies of Mr. Spruce's report on his expedition to procure seeds and plants of the "Red Bark" are now transmitted, for the information of Mr. McIvor and others, who are entrusted with or interested in the cultivation of the cinchona plants in India.

3. Ten additional copies of Mr. Spruce's report will be forwarded, with Mr. Cross's reports, by next mail.

— No. 75. —

ORDER thereon, 17 February 1862.

1. ORDERED, that the sealed packet containing the receipt for a box of seeds sent through the Peninsular and Oriental Company by the Southampton mail steamer of the 20th January 1862, received from the Secretary of State, be forwarded to the Collector of Sea Customs; and that he be requested, with reference to para. 1 of the Despatch above recorded, to take steps without delay for clearing the box above referred to, and dispatch it to Mr. McIvor, the superintendent of Government Gardens at Ootacamund, by the nearest route with all practicable expedition.

2. The 50 copies of Mr. Cross' report and 40 of that of Mr. Spruce, alluded to in para. 2 of the said Despatch, will be duly distributed on their arrival.

(signed) *C. G. Master,*
Deputy Secretary to Government.

— No. 76. —

From *W. G. McIvor*, Esq., Superintendent Government Cinchona Plantations, to *J. D. Sim*, Esq., Secretary to Government, Madras.

Sir, Ootacamund, 12 March 1862.

1. WITH reference to the Order of Government, dated 17th ultimo, I have the honour to inform you that I received from the Collector of Sea Customs on the 4th instant, in good condition, the packet containing the seeds of *Cinchona Condaminea* and *C. crespilla*.

2. It affords me much pleasure to be able to acquaint you, for the information of Government, that a few of the same batch of seeds, which I received in a letter from Mr. Markham on the 16th ultimo, are germinating freely. On the 16th day after sowing, I found that twelve seeds had germinated, and to-day, being the 23d day, upwards of 200 seedlings have germinated, or over 50 per cent. of the total number of perfect seeds received. Judging from this result, I have little doubt that we will be able to rear nearly the whole of the seeds received on the 4th instant.

3. The Government will observe, that in this sowing of seeds, the time in which the first seeds germinated has been reduced from 62 to 16 days, and that within the 23d day a larger proportion of the seeds have vegetated than was previously effected in three months. I mention this fact, as perhaps no stronger one could be given, to show the daily improvement we are making in attaining a more perfect knowledge of the nature and treatment of these plants.

— No. 77. —

From *W. G. McIvor*, Esq., Superintendent Government Gardens, Ootacamund, to *J. W. Breeks*, Esq., Private Secretary to His Excellency the Governor.

Sir, Ootacamund, 4 June 1861.

1. IN reply to your letter of the 30th ultimo, I have the honour to furnish, in a brief form, for the information of his Excellency the Governor, the following remarks on the subject of your inquiries :—

What has been done in rearing the cinchona plants on the Hills.

2. The first sowing of cinchona seeds was made here in January last. In sowing these, I was influenced by the descriptions given of their treatment in Java, and the excessive amount of shade, moisture, and retentive soil there believed to be necessary for the germination of the seeds. I soon discovered that the seeds began to mould and damp off, and almost despaired of succeeding in rearing any; however, of this batch, from 3 to 4 per cent. germinated. The next sowing was made in the early part of March, and the soil used was of a much freer nature, one-half being composed of burned earth; of this sowing, from 15 to 25 per cent. germinated. Encouraged by this result, the third and last sowing, which was made in the beginning of April, the soil used was composed nearly entirely of burned earth; and of this sowing, about 60 per cent. germinated—of one of the varieties (*provinciana*) about 90 per cent. These results convince me that the great difficulties said to attend the rearing of the seeds, and the cultivation of the plants, do not so much lie in the nature of the seeds themselves, or of the plant, as in our ignorance of the proper treatment to be adopted.

At present I have in the gardens upwards of 2,000 plants in very promising condition. Some of the 463 imported plants are at the present moment in the most luxuriant state of health, and the remainder are now rapidly recovering from the disease and damage contracted in the Wardian cases, with a vigour which I have only seen equalled in one or two instances in the numerous species of plants I have introduced into these gardens.

3. I possess

Cultivation of the cinchonas on the Neilgherries.

3. I possess but little information on this subject, as the cultivation of the plants has hitherto not been attempted, except in Java, and this is so recent that valuable data cannot be gathered from what has been done there; their results, moreover, have as yet been unsatisfactory. It appears to me that much erroneous matter has been published with reference to the cultivation of these plants, and that we have everything to learn. For example, it is an established opinion, by parties entitled to consideration, that the plants should be grown under the partial shade of forest trees. In April last I planted three plants of the red bark, two under shade, and one in an open spot surrounded by brushwood or undergrowth. All these plants are growing luxuriantly; but since the setting-in of the monsoon, which happened on the 29th ultimo, the plants under the shade have been injured by their leaves being cut to pieces by the constant drip from the forest trees, while the plant shaded by the brushwood continues in the most luxuriant state of health, with its leaves uninjured. This experiment would indicate brushwood to be the proper shade for the plants; but from its limited nature, I do not feel myself justified in coming to this conclusion until I have made further experiments in the track thus indicated. As I have already remarked, the opinions of the authors who advocate partial shade are worthy of consideration, they having seen the plants in the various aspects of their natural forests; and in such localities they must of necessity, in the struggle for life which prevails throughout nature, grow in the shade of other plants; but these authors inform us that the cinchonas strive to overtop the forest trees to obtain light and air. On this subject I am much perplexed, but am daily gaining knowledge; so that, before any extensive planting is undertaken, I shall have satisfied myself, by actual experiment, which method will be most advantageous. The drip from large forest trees proves injurious to all plants grown under them; and I am of opinion, that while we select all that is advantageous in the natural localities of the cinchonas, we should reject all that we find detrimental. For example, Mr. Bruce informs us that he found wheat growing wild in Upper Egygt, struggling for existence among rushes and other weeds; but no one would adopt this principle in its cultivation: in like manner, too much shade may prove injurious to the cinchonas.

4. In the forests on the Andes the cinchona trees are cut down and stripped of their bark, and it is a generally preconceived opinion that this plan should be adopted in cultivation; but although this may be necessary, and even advisable, in the wild state, it appears a most ruinous system to put into operation in cultivation: not only is it unsuitable to the man of limited means, who requires a quick and uniform return on his capital, but it also necessitates the destruction of the plantation to produce a return at all, and this after waiting 10 or 12 years. To obviate these inconveniences, it occurred to me that the plants in cultivation should be induced to branch as near the ground as possible, and on the third year, say, the two branches at A A are cut off from their bark, they would immediately throw out fresh shoots below the line at A A. From these shoots one or two should be selected to take the place of branches removed. In the fourth year the branches at B B would be cut off in like manner, and so on until the sixth year, when the new brances formed at A A could again be removed, and so on for any number of years.

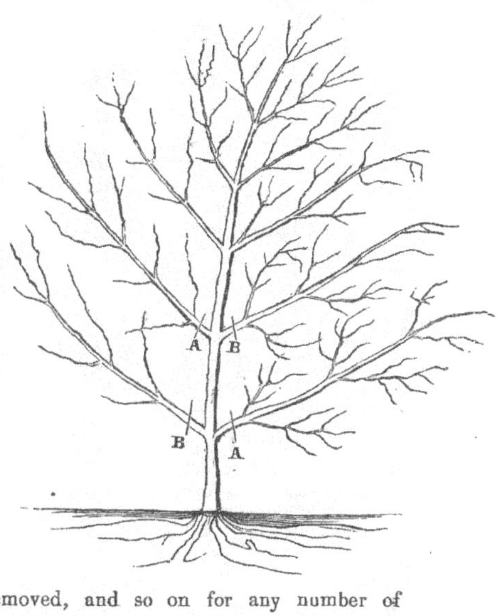

5. This treatment would ensure a quick, uniform, and constant supply of bark;

and if the pruning (as I may term it) be judiciously carried out, the trees would be benefited rather than injured by the removal annually of a few of their branches.

6. Mr. Markham, to whom I have spoken on this subject, considers it the best plan that can be adopted in the cultivation of the plants. There is, however, one objection to it:—it is, that the price of quill-bark (bark from branches) is of a little less value than the bark from the trunks. In the London market the trifling difference of 1*d.* to 2*d.* per pound is quoted. Howard, the great quinine manufacturer, in reply to the queries of Mr. Markham on this subject, states:—

"As to the plancha (trunk) bark and canuto bark (the bark of smaller branches), the former is preferred, and yields rather the most quinine; but the quill canuto also commands a good price."

Suitable sites.

7. The sites selected near the gardens and at Neddiwattum are, I consider, well suited, and perhaps better than any other sites which could be found on the Neilgherries, from their being so conveniently accessible; but doubtless, hundreds of other sites as well suited in soil and climate could be selected. The Dodabetta, or site near the garden, has been selected entirely for an experimental plantation—*i. e.*, a plantation in which to test what amount of exposure or shade, and description of shade, of soils and subsoils, are best suited to the growth of cinchonas, and the development of their alkaloids. This site contains a great variety of exposures, and also a great variety of soils; and thus offers, for this special purpose, advantages which it would be difficult to meet elsewhere. The Neddiwattum site is a large forest of perhaps 400 acres of as fine land as is to be had on the Neilgherries, well sheltered, and in every respect, so far as I am aware, well suited to the growth of all the varieties of the cinchona, and here will be the principal Government plantation; but it is most important that we should have a higher site for experiments, in order to prove whether the cinchonas will or will not grow over the whole extent of the plateau of the Neilgherries, and this could not be established by any amount of success which we might obtain at Neddiwattum. If it proves that the cinchonas can be cultivated over the whole plateau of the Neilgherries, it will establish a fact the importance of which cannot at present be estimated, because it will open an immense field for European enterprise and energy, and, in combination with this profitable employment of capital, it will place Europeans in a healthy and invigorating climate.

Eventual disposal of plants now propagating.

8. I would propose to retain all the plants here (with the exception of a few, which will be required for experiments) till June or July next year, which is the best planting season of the year. By that time, if sufficient means are placed at my disposal, I trust to have from 50,000 to 80,000 plants ready to put out into the Neddiwattum site. My object in detaining the plants here are two: the first is to facilitate the propagation, and the second is—while we are thus accomplishing an important object in increasing our plants, we are (during the same time, which will extend over a year), by planting a few plants out under various circumstances and in different positions, ascertaining by actual experiment which is the safest method to be adopted in making our extensive plantations.

Prospect of success.

9. As I have already remarked, the plants have taken to the climate in a manner which has only been equalled by one or two of the numerous species of plants I have successfully introduced; and I am convinced that, if our operations are conducted with skill, we may obtain a success altogether unprecedented.

What I consider necessary to ensure success.

10. To ensure success, it appears to me indispensable that the officer in charge of the experiment should be left to the free exercise of his own judgment, and not required to follow any prescribed method of cultivation, which cannot lead to other than bad results. I am convinced of this, because I have gained more correct information from my short observation of the plants under cultivation, than from all that has been written and said upon the subject. If sufficient caution is exercised in conducting this experiment, and the officer in charge possesses ability to trace the effects produced on the plants under cultivation to their true causes, there exists little danger of any serious error being committed. The Government will be expected to afford efficient means, and to allow an establishment sufficient to carry out the operations to the greatest extent practicable

practicable; and it would be detrimental for the Government in future to issue orders stopping operations without reference to the executive officer, or the benefit of his opinion on the subjects the Government may be recommended to adopt. I express myself more freely in this private communication on the subject, than I did in my official correspondence, as great injury has been done to the experiment by the Order of Government of 9th March 1861, No. 552. His Excellency being anxious to obtain correct information will, I trust, excuse me for bringing this to his notice. Although what has been done here has been attempted to be deprecated to Government, I am aware, from the care and skill which I have devoted to the rearing of these seeds and plants, that when reports from other quarters of their results are received and compared, that it will be established that our success is quite unequalled. From the commencement of the cultivation of these plants (and this is the most critical period), I have had to do everything with my own hands, as I have not a man in my establishment who possesses sufficient knowledge of the nature of the plants to be entrusted even to water them. One over-watering might cause the death of the whole of the seedlings, by causing them to damp off; it is therefore of the utmost importance that a well-educated European gardener be sent out from England as soon as possible, and as the experiment progresses, two more well-educated gardeners will be required.

11. This is merely a brief outline, more founded upon supposition than any fact which I have had to guide me with reference to their cultivation; and it may prove that some alterations in these plans may have to be adopted during the progress of these experiments.

P.S.—A few leaves, showing the injurious effects of the drip, are forwarded for the information of his Excellency. The drip passes through the newly-developed leaves like a shot, and shatters and breaks the older ones.

— No. 78. —

From the Right Honourable Sir *C. Wood*, Bart., Secretary of State for India (Public), to His Excellency the Honourable the Governor in Council, Fort St. George.

Sir, India Office, 2 July 1861.

1. I HAVE considered in Council your letter in the Revenue Department, dated 24th April, No. 63 of 1861, reporting that, "in deference to the opinions" of Mr. Markham and Mr. McIvor, you have modified your order of 9th March, No. 552, respecting the abandonment of the site for cinchonæ cultivation at the back of the Government Gardens at Ootacamund, and the relinquishment of further attempts to raise plants from seeds or cuttings in the Government Gardens. In this determination you have anticipated the directions contained in my Despatch, dated 7th June (No. 25) 1861.

2. It is, in my opinion, very desirable that the management of the cinchona experiment should be placed in the hands of Mr. McIvor, at least for the present, free from the control of other officers, and that he should, as regards this duty, be placed in direct communication with your Government.

3. The important operation of introducing the cinchonæ into India has now been successfully effected, and it is my opinion that the measures for the cultivation of these valuable plants should be framed, as far as possible in accordance with the habits of the growth of the cinchonæ in their native forests in South America, and not with reference to the mode of culture pursued by the Dutch in Java. It will, nevertheless, be well that Mr. McIvor should be kept informed respecting the proceedings of the Dutch; and as the reports of the superintendent are published in Germany, Mr. McIvor can be supplied with accurate and reliable information from time to time respecting the progress of the cinchona experiment in Java.

4. The superintendence of the cinchona plantations in the Neilgherry Hills will involve great responsibility, as well as considerable toil and anxiety; and qualifications not easily found are required for the post. I shall, therefore, be willing to sanction any reasonable allowance which you may deem it right to propose for Mr. McIvor, for the performance of this important duty.

5. With reference to paragraph 3 of your Order of the 16th April, I have to inform you that the gardener Weir has accepted other employment, but that a gardener with the requisite acquirements will be engaged and sent out to Ootacamund with as little delay as possible.

— No. 79. —

MINUTE by Sir *William Denison.*

1. I FORWARD herewith a letter addressed to my private secretary by Mr. McIvor, enclosing an estimate of the cost of the buildings to be erected, that of clearing the land, &c., for next year's plantation of the cinchona plants, and also of the permanent establishment which will be required to keep the plantations in order.

2. To this must be added :—

(1). The cost of the propagating-house, which is in progress, and will soon be completed, for which a sum of about 1,500 rupees was granted, but which will, according to Mr. McIvor, be finished for about 2,000 rupees; probably, it would be as well to insert 2,500 rupees as the cost of this, including contingencies.

(2.) Mr. McIvor's salary as superintendent.

3. These additions will raise the estimate for capital expended upon the preparation of a plantation of 160 acres to 31,076 rupees, and the annual outlay to, say, 13,200 rupees, or 1,100 rupees per month.

4. I think, however, that this will be money well laid out. The number of trees which an acre will carry is about 700, say 650; and as it is estimated that each tree will produce (after, say, 10 years' growth) 5 lbs. weight of bark annually, the yield per acre will be 3,250 lbs. (say 3,000 lbs.), and for 160 acres 480,000 lbs., or upwards of 200 tons. At 6 *d.* per pound, which I believe to be a low price, this will give 12,000 *l.* per annum as the return upon the 160 acres—the annual expense of management, &c., being 1,320 *l.*

5. It will be seen that in the estimate a sum is taken for trenching the ground for the plants. Mr. McIvor, in his wish to keep down the estimate of first cost, proposed to put the plants in pits; I, however, suggested the propriety of trenching a portion of the ground at all events, in order to ascertain whether this would not secure a better growth than the system which he was about to adopt: this, if found to be necessary generally, will add to the first cost of the plantation, but it will be well repaid by the improved growth of the trees.

6. It appears to me that Mr. McIvor might be empowered to conduct the whole of the work, including the erection of the buildings, subject to the condition that the work, when completed, should be examined and approved by the District Engineer. It is absolutely necessary that the work should be pushed on vigorously, in order that the land should be fenced in, trenched, and prepared for planting by the end of May 1862; and the house for the overseer and men must be ready by the same time. If the responsibility of the whole is thrown upon Mr. McIvor, the Government will know to whom any blame of neglect will attach; but if the Department of Public Works is placed in charge of the erection of the buildings and wall, &c., there will be of course, in case of failure, mutual accusations between the department and Mr. McIvor, and the Government will not have it in its power to decide which was in fault. I forward herewith a return of the number of plants at present in the garden. I saw two or three

three yesterday, which had been planted out in the garden, and these appeared healthy; those in the propagating-house were in the best possible condition. Mr. McIvor was busily engaged in increasing the number by laying and making cuttings; he expects also to receive a large fresh supply of seed in October, and by the end of May 1862 to have plants enough to fill the land which he will have ready; while in the course of 1862, and the first half of 1863, he will have plants sufficient to fill 200 or 300 additional acres. The sum mentioned in the estimate will be required at once, and must be inserted in the supplementary estimate, leave being given to Mr. McIvor to proceed at once with the preparation of the land, the construction of buildings, and the wall, the object of which is to keep pigs, &c., out of the plantations; he must also be directed to send in an estimate for the Budget of 1862-63, including in that the cost of the additional clearing at Neddivattum, and the establishment for this, and for the year's plantations also. These latter will not of course be required in full strength till the middle of 1862, as the estimate for first cost provides for trenching the ground and planting out the young plants.

7. I think it would be advisable that, as proposed by Mr. McIvor, the gardener who is expected to arrive should be placed in the position of deputy—that is, should be empowered to act in all cases for Mr. McIvor both in the Botanic Garden itself, and in charge of the cinchona plants—and, as before stated, that the whole establishment should be withdrawn from the control of the Conservator of Forests.

(signed) *W. T. Denison.*

— No. 80. —

From Mr. *W. G. McIvor*, Superintendent Botanical Gardens, to *J. W. Breeks*, Esq., Private Secretary to His Excellency the Governor of Madras.

My dear Sir, Ootacamund, 16 August 1861.

1. I HAVE the honour to enclose the estimate for the formation of the cinchona plantations on the Neilgherries, amended as suggested by his Excellency the Governor.

2. I would most respectfully propose that the European gardener engaged by the Secretary of State be placed in charge of the propagating department, and, in addition to this duty, he be required to act as my deputy in the garden during my occasional absence at Neddivattum.

3. The propagating-house sanctioned by order of Government, No. 1,328, dated 3d July 1861, being urgently required for our rapidly increasing number of plants, the work was immediately begun by me, and will shortly be completed, according to a plan and specification furnished by the engineer. This officer has also furnished an estimate, amounting to 3,680 rupees. I however believe that I will be able to finish the work, according to plan and specification, for 2,000 rupees. I would recommend that this work, when finished, be examined and reported on by the engineer, and I would wish this done with all the buildings I may erect, as a course likely to prove satisfactory to the Government and myself.

4. I enclose, for the information of his Excellency the Governor, a report of he number and condition of our cinchona plants.

ESTIMATE of Cost of Cinchona Plantations on the Neilgherries.

PARTICULARS.	Cost of forming the Plantation with Buildings, Roads, &c.			Cost of Fixed Establishment.		
	Rs.	*a.*	*p.*	*Rs.*	*a.*	*p.*
NURSERY AT OOTACAMUND.						
Building and other Contingent Charges.						
To house for the European gardener, to consist of two main rooms 12 feet × 12 feet, and 4 verandah rooms, 6 feet × 12 feet. Walls to be built of burnt brick in clay. Fireplaces, chimneys, and corner of brick in chunam, and plastered with chunam throughout. Roof to be constructed of teak-wood, and covered with tiles. Doors and windows and flooring of two main rooms of teak-wood. Verandah rooms to be floored with flat tiles - - - - - - - - -	1,200	–	–	—		
To building a wall 756 yards in length, to enclose nursery ground, 5 feet high and 14 inches thick, of burnt brick laid in clay, at 1 rupee per yard - - - - - - -	756	–	–	—		
Contingent charges, at 10 per cent. - - - - - -	195	9	7	—		
Fixed Establishment.						
European gardener, probable, 150 *l.* per annum - - - -	-	-	-	125	–	–
Head propagator - - - - - - - - - - -	-	-	-	35	–	–
Two first assistants, at 10 rupees each - - - - - -	-	-	-	20	–	–
Three second ditto at 7 ,, ,, - - - - - -	-	-	-	21	–	–
Six gardeners - at 6 ,, ,, - - - - - -	-	-	-	36	–	–
Six ditto - - at 5½ ,, ,, - - - - - -	-	-	-	33	–	–
One peon - - at 7 ,, ,, - - - - - -	-	-	-	7	–	–
TOTAL - - - *Rs.*	2,151	9	7	277	–	–

To forming a Plantation of 50 Acres of Cinchona Trees on the Dodabetta Site.

PARTICULARS.	Cost of forming the Plantation with Buildings, Roads, &c.			Cost of Fixed Establishment.		
	Rs.	*a.*	*p.*	*Rs.*	*a.*	*p.*
Building and other Contingent Charges.						
To house for overseer, to consist of two main rooms, 12 feet × 12 feet each, and two verandah rooms, 6 feet × 12 feet, to be constructed with burnt brick laid in clay, and bamboo roof covered with tiles. Teak-wood doors and windows - -	560	–	–	—		
To houses for 20 coolies, to be constructed with brick built in clay; bamboo roof, covered with tiles. Teak-wood doors and windows - - - - - - - - - - -	200	–	–	—		
To felling 40 acres, at 10 rupees per acre. Sopping and clearing 40 acres, at 7 rupees per acre. Pitting 40 acres, at 10 rupees per acre. Trenching 10 acres, at 180 rupees per acre. Carriage of plants for 50 acres, at 2 rupees per acre. Filling in holes, planting, and shading, at 5 rupees - - - -	3,230	–	–	—		
The proceeds from the sale of firewood may be estimated to cover the cost of enclosing and finishing the construction of roads.						
Contingent charges, at 10 per cent. - - - - - -	399	–	–	—		
Fixed Establishment.						
One overseer - - - - - - - - - - - -	-	-	-	40	–	–
One maistry - - - - - - - - - - - -	-	-	-	10	–	–
Five gardeners, at 6 rupees each - - - - - - -	-	-	-	30	–	–
Twenty coolies, at 5½ ,, ,, - - - - - - -	-	-	-	110	–	–
TOTAL - - - *Rs.*	4,389	–	–	190	–	–

ESTIMATE Cost of forming a Plantation of 100 Acres of Cinchona Trees on the Neddivattum Site.

PARTICULARS.	Cost of forming the Plantation with Buildings, Roads, &c.			Cost of Fixed Establishment.		
	Rs.	*a.*	*p.*	*Rs.*	*a.*	*p.*
Building and other Contingent Charges.						
To house for overseer, with quarters for superintendent, to contain four main rooms 12 feet × 14 feet each, and six verandah rooms, 12 feet × 7 feet each. Walls to be constructed of burnt brick laid in clay. Chimney and corners of brick in chunam, and plastered with chunam throughout. Roof to be constructed with teak-wood king-beams; rafters of jungle-wood, with bamboo reapers, and covered with tiles - -	1,750	–	–	—		
To out-houses, one kitchen 10 feet × 12 feet, and two out-houses, 10 feet × 15 feet each, constructed as above - -	330	–	–	—		
To tool-rooms and storerooms, each 10 × 15 feet, constructed as above - - - - - - - - - - - -	250	–	–	—		
To houses for 100 coolies, to consist of 30 rooms, 7 × 10 feet each, constructed as above - - - - - - -	1,000	–	–	—		
To enclosing 100 acres with a wall 5 feet high and 14 inches thick with burnt brick laid in clay, and trench outside 4 feet wide, 2½ feet deep, at 1 rupee per running yard of 3,900 yards - - - - - - - - - - - - -	3,900	–	–	—		
To felling 100 acres, at 15 rupees per acre. Sopping and clearing, at 15 rupees per acre. Pitting 80 acres, at 20 rupees per acre. Trenching 20 acres, at 200 rupees per acre. Carriage of plants, at 6 rupees per acre. Filling holes, planting, and shading, at 8 rupees per acre - - - - - - -	10,000	–	–	—		
To forming cart-roads 12 feet wide, over 100 acres of land, including from public road to plantation, or about 4½ miles, at 300 rupees per mile - - - - - - - - -	1,350	–	–	—		
To two teak-wood bridges over streams, 10 feet span each, and 8 feet wide, with stone abutments, at 85 rupees each - -	170	–	–	—		
To tools: 200 pickaxes, at 2 rupees each; 200 felling-axes, at 2 rupees each; 100 bill-hooks, at *Rs.* 1-8 each; 200 momaties, at 1 rupee each; 12 steel digging forks, at 4 rupees each; 24 steel spades, at 2 rupees each; 12 crowbars, at 3 rupees each - - - - - - - - - - - -	1,282	–	–	—		
Contingent charges, at 10 per cent. - - - - - -	2,003	3	2	—		
Fixed Establishment.						
One overseer - - - - - - - - - - - -	-	-	-	70	–	–
One head maistry - - - - - - - - - - -	-	-	-	15	–	–
Two peons, at 7 rupees each - - - - - - -	-	-	-	14	–	–
Fifty coolies, at 6 rupees each - - - - - - -	-	-	-	300	–	–
Office Establishment.						
One writer, at 20 rupees; books, stationery, ink, quills, &c., 3 rupees - - - - - - - - - - - -	-	-	-	23	–	–
TOTAL - - - *Rs.*	22,035	3	2	422	–	–

(signed) *W. G. McIvor,*
Superintendent Botanical Gardens.

Government Gardens, Ootacamund,
16 August 1861.

ABSTRACT of Estimate of Cinchona Plantations on the Neilgherries.

PARTICULARS.	Cost of forming the Plantations with Buildings, Roads, Tools, &c.	Cost of Fixed Establishment.
	Rs. a. p.	*Rs. a. p.*
NURSERY AT OOTACAMUND.		
Buildings and other contingent charges	2,151 9 7	—
Fixed establishment	- - -	277 - -
DODABETTA PLANTATION.		
Building and other contingent charges	4,389 - -	—
Fixed establishment	- - -	190 - -
NEDDIWUTTUM PLANTATION.		
Building and other contingent charges	22,035 3 2	—
Fixed establishment	- - -	399 - -
Office establishment	- - -	23 - -
TOTAL - - - *Rs.*	28,575 12 9	889 - -

Government Gardens, Ootacamund,
16 August 1861.

(signed) *W. G. McIvor,*
Superintendent Botanical Gardens.

REPORT on the Number and Condition of the Cinchona Plants in the Government Gardens at Ootacamund, on the 9th August 1861.

NAMES.	NUMBER.	REMARKS.
Cinchona succirubra, or red bark	1,517	The imported plants are all in very promising condition, many of them being in the most luxuriant state of health. The largest of the plants measure 2 feet 6 inches to 2 feet 10 inches high, and some of their leaves measure 7½ inches by 11⅛ inches. The average growth of the month being 1¾ inches. The maximum growth made by the most luxuriant shoots being 7 inches. The first of our seedlings are from 6 to 7 inches high, and from 6 to 8½ inches in diameter across the leaves;—the average growth of the month being about 1½ inches, while the maximum monthly growth made by the most vigorous plants is 2½ inches.
Cinchona calisaya, calisaya bark	6	
Cinchona nitida, genuine grey bark	804	
Cinchona micrantha, var. Provinciana	896	
Cinchona micrantha, var. Pata de-Gallinazo	42	
Species without name	271	
TOTAL - - -	3,536	

Government Gardens, Ootacamund,
9 August 1861.

(signed) *W. G. McIvor,*
Superintendent Botanical Gardens.

— No 81. —

ORDER of the Madras Government, 7 September 1861.

1. IN their Order of the 16th April last, the Government directed that the cinchona experiment should for the present be restricted to the garden ravine and Neddivattum sites, the Horticultural Gardens being also made available as a nursery and propagating place, and in any other way that might be found advisable. Under

Under these orders, therefore, operations on any other site will not be undertaken without the express permission of Government.

Superintendence of operations.

2. In the same order, the operations at the selected sites were entrusted to Mr. McIvor; but doubts having arisen as to the exact degree of authority which it was intended to vest in him, the Government, in their order of the 3d July last, gave him full and entire control over the operations, holding him answerable for his conduct of them, and restricted the intervention of the Conservator of Forests to periodical inspections and reports, without, however, the power of interference except by order of Government.

Mr. McIvor's remuneration.

3. In the order of the 3d July, the Government also resolved to apply to the Secretary of State for permission to raise Mr. McIvor's salary from 200 rupees to 300 rupees per mensem, in consideration of the additional responsibility and labour which this important experiment will entail on him. The Secretary of State has expressed his willingness to sanction any reasonable remuneration which this Government may propose. The Government are now in a better position to judge of the probable labour, &c. which will devolve on Mr. McIvor, and resolve to recommend that Mr. McIvor's salary be raised from 200 rupees to 350 rupees during the first year, and to 400 in the second. This remuneration is for his services as superintendent of the gardens as well as of the cinchona operations. The grant will take effect from the commencement of the current official year, and provision for it will be made in the supplemental budget.

Assistant gardeners.

4. The Government, in April last, applied to the Secretary of State to send out Mr. Weir, as an assistant to Mr. McIvor. Mr. Weir, however, has accepted other employment; but another skilled gardener, G. Batcock, has been engaged*. He will be placed, on arrival, under Mr. McIvor's orders, and will act as his deputy both in the horticultural garden and the cinchona plantations. His salary is to be 150 *l.* per annum, commencing from the 20th August 1861, and increasing at the rate of 10 *l.* yearly. His engagement is for five years, and he is to have a suitable residence, or an allowance for house-rent.

* Despatch, 16th July 1861, No. 35. C. O. 4th instant, No. 1760.

Estimates of expenditure.

5. In paragraph 5 of the order of the 3d July 1861, Government sanctioned the immediate construction of a propagating-house, at a cost of about 1,500 rupees; and in paragragh 6, Mr. McIvor was called upon for a statement of the probable monthly expenses of the experiment. Mr. McIvor has now submitted estimates to the following amount:—

	Capital.	Current Monthly Expenditure.
	Rs.	*Rs.*
Propagating-house in the gardens, estimated by the District Engineer at 3,680 rupees, but which Mr. McIvor hopes to complete for	2,000	—
House for European gardener	1,200	—
Wall round nursery	756	—
Contingencies	196	—
European gardener, at 150 *l.*	- -	125
Eighteen under-gardeners	- -	145
One peon	- -	7
Nursery at Ootacamund	4,152	277
For a plantation of 50 acres on the Dodabetta or garden ravine site:—		
Overseer's house	560	—
Coolies' quarters	200	—
Clearing, pitting, trenching, and planting (fencing and roads being covered by sale of timber)	3,230	—
Contingencies	399	—
Overseer	- -	40
Under-gardeners	- -	150
Dodabetta site	4,389	190

	Capital.	Current Monthly Expenditure.
	Rs.	*Rs.*
Plantation of 100 acres at Neddiwuttum :—		
Overseer's house	1,750	—
Out-houses	330	—
Tool and store rooms	250	—
Coolies' quarters	1,000	—
Enclosing site with wall	3,900	—
Clearing and planting	10,000	—
Cart-roads	1,350	—
Two bridges	170	—
Tools	1,282	—
Contingencies	2,003	—
Overseer	- -	70
Fifty-one under-gardeners	- -	315
Two peons	- -	14
Neddiwuttum site	22,035	399
Writer and stationery	- -	23
Mr. McIvor's allowance - - - *Rs.*	- -	150

6. The aggregate estimate thus amounts to an outlay of capital of 30,576 rupees, or (say) 31,000 rupees, and a monthly charge of 1,039 rupees, or 12,468 rupees per annum. To the latter charge an addition of 150 rupees will have to be made in the second year, on account of the increase then proposed for Mr. McIvor, and that due under his agreement to George Batcock, who in each successive year will also draw 10 *l.*, or 100 rupees extra.

7. Thus, for an outlay of 3,100 *l.* and an annual charge of about 1,300 *l.*, the Government will have a nursery and two plantations of 160 acres of cinchonas. Each acre will contain about 700 trees, and each tree is estimated, after (say) 10 years' growth, to produce 5 lbs. weight of bark annually, for which 6 *d.* per pound is a low price. Taking, however, 650 trees to the acre, and 3,000 lbs. weight only of bark, the annual produce would be 480,000 lbs., worth 12,000 *l.* per annum, as the return on a capital of 3,100 *l.*, and an annual outlay of 1,300 *l.* The experiment, however, cannot be regarded as a mere money speculation; if successful, its results will be of incalculable benefit to the public.

8. The estimate includes a provision for trenching a part of the land. Mr. McIvor, in his anxiety to keep down the first cost, proposed to put the plants in pits. The trenching of a portion of the land was suggested by the President, and if found successful will be extended; and the improved growth of the plants will compensate for the additional expense of this mode of preparing the ground.

9. The Government resolve to authorize Mr. McIvor to conduct the whole of the operations, including the erection of the buildings, subject to the condition that the work, when completed, shall be examined and approved by the District Engineer.

10. The work will be pushed on vigorously, in order that the land may be fenced, trenched, and prepared for planting by the end of May 1862. The houses for the overseers and labourers must also be ready by that time.

11. The Accountant-General will accordingly provide, in the supplemental budget, for an outlay of 31,000 rupees on buildings, &c., and of 7,000 rupees for establishments, or 38,000 rupees in all. Pending the sanction of the Supreme Government to the budget, the Collector of Coimbatore will be authorized to make such advances as may be necessary from time to time on Mr. McIvor's receipts, to be subsequently adjusted. The Accountant General will furnish the Collector with the necessary instructions.

12. The Accountant General will also instruct Mr. McIvor to prepare his budget estimate for the year 1862-63, in due form and time.

13. Under

13. Under the orders already noticed, Mr. McIvor has been placed in an independent position as regards the cinchona experiment, and the Governor in Council resolves to place the botanical gardens similarly under his entire control. The preliminary operations of the cinchona experiments are conducted in the Botanical Gardens, where the propagating house now sanctioned will be constructed, and it will be embarrassing if Mr. McIvor has not full power over the gardens as well as the cinchona plantations. Mr. McIvor will, therefore, be under the direct orders of Government in both these departments, as laid down in General Order, 3d July last.

14. These proceedings will be commuicated to the Secretary of State and the Goverment of India.

(signed) *J. D. Sim*,
Secretary to Government.

—No. 82.—

From the Government of Madras to Sir *Charles Wood.*

Madras, 6 July 1861.

1. We have the honour to forward, in continuation of our Despatch of the 24th April last, further papers relative to the experiment, which is now being tried on the Neilgherries, of introducing the cinchona tree into Southern India.

2. Mr. McIvor has complained of certain remarks made by Dr. Macpherson, as disparaging his mode of treating the cinchona seeds, and requested an inquiry; but we informed him that compliance with his request was uinecessary, as the fact of our having entrusted him with the charge of the cinchona operations on the Neilgherries, was itself a proof that he had not lost our confidence. Captain Morgan, on his part, offered to draw up a paper of information as to proper sites, treatment of seeds, potting plants, erecting glass-houses, &c.; but although we appreciated his offer, we considered the preparation of such a paper to be unnecessary at present.

3. We desire to draw your particular attention to the very interesting reports of Mr. McIvor, which will be found recorded in our Proceedings of the 3rd July; and we feel confident that you will be gratified to receive such promising accounts of the experiment so far as it has progressed. "At present," Mr. McIvor writes, "I have in the gardens upwards of 2,000 plants in very promising condition. Some of the 463 imported plants are at the present moment in the most luxuriant state of health, and the remainder are now rapidly recovering from the disease and damage contracted in the Wardian cases, with a vigour which I have only seen equalled in one or two instances in the numerous species of plants I have introduced into these gardens." There has been some misapprehension as to the degree of power which we intended to vest in the superintendent of the Horticultural Gardens at Ootacamund in respect to this experiment; we have, therefore, placed this matter beyond doubt, by giving Mr. McIvor full and entire control over the operations, holding him answerable for his conduct of them. The Conservator of Forests will, however, periodically inspect and report on his operations, but he is not to interfere with them, except by our express orders. We believe this to be the most judicious course, because very little is yet known of the culture, &c. of the plant, and the experiment is manifestly one which needs professional knowledge and experience, and constant care; and in Mr. McIvor's zeal and ability we have great confidence.

4. Our great object at present is to propagate a large number of plants, leaving the establishment of plantations in different localities to follow hereafter, when a sufficiency of plants has been raised to place the experiment beyond risk of failure; and with this view, we have prohibited the gratuitous issue or sale of seeds and plants until the experiment is safe, and have granted 1,500 rupees for the construction of a propagating-house: when the introduction of the plant is beyond doubt, we shall afford every facility to persons desirous of cultivating it.

5. In consideration of the much additional trouble and responsibility entailed on Mr. McIvor, we beg permission to raise his allowances from 200 rupees to 300 rupees at once, as we do not think it fair that his remuneration should be deferred until the work is accomplished. We consider him justly entitled to the additional salary we have proposed, and considering the importance of the experiment entrusted to him, we hope you will accede to our recommendation. We address you on this subject, instead of the Government of India, because this experiment has been carried on under your direct instructions.

— No. 83. —

From Sir *C. Wood* to the Governor of Madras.

Sir, India Office, London, 9 August 1861.

1. WITH reference to para. 3 of my Despatch, dated 2d July (No. 27) 1861, I now transmit 50 copies of the translated report of the Dutch superintendents of cinchona plantations in India. In the same packet 50 copies are transmitted of a pamphlet, compiled by Mr. Markham, containing botanical descriptions (together with notes and observations) of all the species of cinchonæ now growing in India; and 50 copies of Mr. Pritchett's report on the cinchona region of Huanuco, in Northern Peru.

2. You will also supply one or more copies of these pamphlets to the different agricultural and horticultural societies in India, in order that the useful information they contain may be as widely circulated as possible.

I have, &c.
(signed) *C. Wood.*

His Excellency the Honourable
the Governor in Council, Fort St. George.

—No. 84.—

From the Right Honourable Sir C. *Wood*, Bart., Secretary of State for India, to His Excellency the Honourable the Governor in Council, Fort St. George.

Sir, India Office, 14 September 1861.

1. I HAVE considered in Council your letter in the Revenue Department, dated 6th July (No. 89) 1861, transmitting further correspondence respecting cinchona cultivation; and I learn with great satisfaction, from the interesting reports of Mr. W. G. McIvor, the increasing numbers and highly flourishing state of the cinchona plants under his charge.

2. Your resolution to entrust Mr. McIvor with "full and entire control over the operations," is in accordance with the opinion expressed in my Despatch of the 2nd July last; and in conformity with the intention which I then stated, I authorise, in compliance with your present recommendation, the increase of Mr. McIvor's salary from 200 rupees to 300 rupees per mensem.

— No. 85. —

From Sir *C. Wood* to the Governor General.

My Lord, India Office, London, 2 July 1861.

I HAVE considered in Council your letter dated the 26th of April, No. 25 of 1861, forwarding a communication to the Governor General of the Netherlands India, on the subject of measures to be adopted relative to the introduction of the cinchona plant into India.

2. You

2. You will have perceived from my Despatches, dated 7th June (No. 25) and 2d July (No. 27) 1861, to the Madras Government, that the conclusions to which they were led by Dr. Macpherson's representations, were erroneous. That Government has since seen occasion to modify the view then adopted. From more recent intelligence, it appears that the plants in some instances, and the seeds generally, in the Government gardens at Ootacamund, are progressing very favourably. You will also perceive from the above-mentioned Despatches, that I have directed the Madras Government to leave the management of the undertaking in that Presidency under the immediate control of Mr. McIvor, the superintendent of the Government gardens at Ootacamund, who, from his experience in gardening, and from the advantages he has derived from personal intercourse with Mr. Markham and the gardeners under him, who have studied the nature of the trees in their native forests, appears in every way suited to the post. It will, therefore, be unnecessary to enter into any engagement for the services of Dr. Croneman, or any other gentleman connected with the Dutch Government, with reference to the cultivation of this plant in the Madras Presidency. With regard to the cultivation of the cinchona, which you may think it expedient to adopt in other parts of India, it will probably be better to depend mainly upon the plants and seeds obtained under the present expedition, than to trust to the exchanges which may be made with the Dutch Government, whose largest collection, there is ground to believe, consists of a species of the plant of a very inferior description.

I have, &c.
(signed) *C. Wood.*

— No. 86. —

From the Government of India to Sir *Charles Wood*, Secretary of State for India.

Sir, Fort William, 25 July 1861.

In continuation of our letter, No. 25, dated the 26th April, we have the honour to transmit, for your information, the accompanying copy of a communication, dated the 13th ultimo, from the Governor General of the Netherlands India, regarding a supply of cinchona plants and seeds. We also forward copy of the reply made to his Excellency, and of a letter addressed to the Government of Fort St. George.

2. We purpose, either next month or in September, to send Dr. Anderson, the officiating Superintendent of the Calcutta Botanical Gardens, to Java, to receive charge of the plants and seeds which are promised by the Netherlands Government.

We have, &c.,
(signed) *Canning,*
H. Rose,
H. B. E. Frere,
R. Napier.

Enclosure 1, in No. 86.

From the Governor General of Netherlands India to His Excellency the Viceroy and Governor General of British India.

Buitenzorg, 13 June 1861.

In reply to your Excellency's letter of the 23rd April 1861, No. 816, I have the honour to inform you that the successful issue of the cultivation of the Peruvian bark in the Island of Java enables me to place at the disposal of the British Government 500,000 seeds, about 100 or 200 seedlings of the *Cinchona lucumæfolia,* and from 50 to 100 plants of the *Cinchona Calisaya.* These seeds will be forwarded as soon as possible.

As to the young plants, it is the opinion of Dr. Junghuhn, principal inspector of the said cultivation, that they should be carefully packed in boxes, according to the method prescribed by Ward, and entrusted (during the transit) to the charge of an intelligent person, well instructed beforehand in the mode of treating them.

 To

To ensure as much as possible the safety of this consignment, Dr. Junghuhn has suggested the appointment of Mr. Markham to this mission, an arrangement which will have the advantage of bringing these two gentlemen together, and affording Dr. Junghuhn the opportunity of imparting to Mr. Markham whatever information his personal experience has enabled him to collect.

This proposal seems to me the more deserving of your Excellency's attention as, in the opinion of Dr. Junghuhn, Dr. Groneman of Bandong, who accompanied Mr. Macpherson over a part of the plantations, and who is alluded to by your Excellency towards the end of your letter, is not equal to the important task which your Excellency would seem inclined to entrust him with.

To promote the undertaking in question, I have deemed it advisable to subjoin here some general rules to be observed in regard to the cultivation of the cinchonas:—

1. The seeds should be set for the purposes of germination in borders, situated from 4,500 to 5,000 feet above the level of the sea, and well sheltered.

2. The *Cinchona Calisaya* succeeds best in Java at an elevation of from 5,000 to 5,700 feet, whilst the *Cinchona lucumæfolia* can be planted even 1,300 feet higher.

3. To prevent the shoots from degenerating and not attaining their full perfection, the plantation of the bark should always be under the shelter of forests.

Dr. Junghuhn is of opinion that it is of the highest importance to select the ground in accordance with these data.

Enclosure 2, in No. 86.

From his Excellency the Earl *Canning*, Viceroy and Governor General of India, to his Excellency the Governor General of the Netherlands India (No. 1391).

19 July 1861.

I have had the pleasure of receiving your letter, dated the 13th June, on the subject of a supply of cinchona plants and seeds, and I beg to tender to your Excellency my warm acknowledgments for the liberal spirit in which my request in this matter has been responded to.

2. I propose that some competent person should proceed to Batavia by the mail steamer of next month, in order to receive charge of the plants and seeds which your Excellency is kind enough to promise. Mr. Markham, whose name has been suggested to your Excellency by Dr. Junghuhn as a proper agent for the purpose, is at present in England, and his services cannot, therefore, be made available; but care will be taken to select an intelligent person well fitted for the important duty, and with the advice and assistance of Dr. Junghuhn, I shall feel little doubt of the attainment of a successful result.

3. Again offering to your Excellency my cordial thanks for your courteous and friendly communication, I remain, &c.

Enclosure 3, in No. 86.

From *W. Grey*, Esq., Secretary to the Government of India, to *T. Pycroft*, Esq., Chief Secretary to the Government of Fort St. George.

19 July 1861.

In continuation of my letter, No. 844, dated the 23d April, I am directed to forward, for the information of his Excellency the Governor of Madras in Council, the accompanying copy of the communication received from the Governor General of Netherlands India, regarding a supply of cinchona plants and seeds, and to state that the Governor General in Council proposes, either next month or in September, to send Dr. Anderson, the officiating superintendent of the Calcutta Botanical Gardens, to Java, to receive charge of the plants and seeds which are promised in this communication.

2. Dr. Anderson will be instructed to convey the plants to Madras, using his discretion, however, as to leaving any of them in Ceylon, which it may appear to him hazardous to carry on. Due notice will be given hereafter of the period at which Dr. Anderson may be expected to arrive at Madras, in order that arrangements may be made by the Madras Government for the prompt removal of the plants to the localities selected for them.

— No. 87. —

From Sir *Charles Wood* to Lord *Canning*.

My Lord, India Office, London, 24 October 1861.

I HAVE considered in Council your letter, dated 23d July (No. 51) 1861, informing me of the measures you have taken, with regard to the offer of the Governor General of Netherlands India to place a number of plants and seeds of two species of *Cinchonæ* at your disposal. I observe that the Dutch Government offers 50 to 100 plants of *C. Calisaya,* and this addition to the small stock of that valuable species in the Neilgherry Hills will be very acceptable; but, at the same time, I have to inform you, that it has been decided by the first botanists in this country, that the species, called by the Dutch, *C. lucumæfolia,* of which they offer 500,000 seeds and 50 to 100 seedlings, is quite worthless. I, therefore, desire that no expense whatever be incurred in connexion with this species; and that, if not too late, the liberal offer of the Dutch Governor be accepted, only so far as the plants of *C. Calisaya* are concerned.

2. A copy of this Despatch will be transmitted to the Madras Government.

I have, &c.
(signed) *C. Wood.*

—No. 88.—

Extract from *W. Grey,* Esq., Secretary to the Government of India, Home Department, to *T. Pycroft,* Esq., Chief Secretary to the Government of Fort St. George.

Sir, Fort William, 9 December 1861.

1. I AM directed to forward to you a copy of a report submitted to the Government of India by Dr. Anderson on his return from Java, together with a copy of the reply made to him.

2. Dr. Anderson will leave for Madras to-morrow morning, and will arrive, therefore, simultaneously with this letter. His first care will be to superintend the removal of the plants which he has in charge to the Neilgherry Hills, for which it is hoped that all necessary preparations will have been made under the orders of His Excellency the Governor in Council.

Enclosure in No. 88.

From *Thomas Anderson,* M.D., Officiating Superintendent of the Botanic Gardens, Calcutta, to *W. Grey,* Esq., Secretary to the Government of India.

4 December 1861.

1. I have the honour to report my return to Calcutta on the 28th November from Singapore, with seven Wardian cases containing 412 young and very healthy plants, and 400,000 seeds of species of cinchona, obtained from the cinchona plantations in the Island of Java. I have secured a passage to Madras by the mail steamer of the 10th; the plants ought, therefore, to reach their destination at Ootacamund about the middle of this month. In a demi-official letter from Java, dated 26th October, I briefly reported my progress up to that date. The plants I have now brought were made over on the 7th November at the nursery of Tijaneroian on the Malabar Mountains, 180 miles from Batavia.

2. Dr. Junghuhn most liberally placed at my disposal, 100 plants of *Cinchona Calisaya,* about 300 of *C. Pahudiana,* and six of *C. lancifolia.* Of the first of these species I considered only 56 plants strong enough to undergo the risks of the long voyage to Madras, and accordingly I had the number of *C. Pahudiana* increased to 350. A larger number of *C. lancifolia* was also offered to me, but only six seemed at all likely to survive the journey. Of those six one has died, the only casualty among the 412 plants. *C. lancifolia* is in the young state a succulent rank plant, forming little or no wood, and accordingly exceedingly liable to damp off when transported to a warm climate. From Tijaneroian the Wardian cases were brought by coolies to Batavia, under the charge of the principal native gardener of the Calcutta Botanic Gardens. He rode alongside of them all the way, travelling only by

by night, and resting with the plants by day, under the dense shade of a fig-tree (*Ficus nitida*) found in all Javanese villages. I went in advance with Dr. DeVrij to examine the original cinchona plantations of the Dutch, where all the original plants from South America are, and where also all the accidents and failures occurred which at first threatened the entire extinction of the experiment. At Buitenzorg, I halted for the arrival of the cinchona plants; and after having seen them again, I proceeded to Batavia, to make arrangements for their voyage to Singapore. My great aim was to detain the plants as short a time as possible in the hot climate of Batavia. The cases reached Batavia late on the night of the 13th November, and were shipped on board the Batavian and Singapore steamer on the evening of the 14th. I sailed from Batavia on the morning of the 15th. After a pleasant passage of three days through a perfectly smooth sea, we arrived at Singapore on the evening of the 18th. My intention was to have remained at Singapore until the arrival of the Peninsular and Oriental Company's steamer from Hong-Kong, and to have proceeded by it to Galle, there to land the cases and wait the arrival of the mail steamer from Suez, and by it take a passage to Madras. However, on my arrival at Singapore I found the Calcutta and Hong-Kong steamer "Lightning" about to sail for Calcutta, and I at once saw the advantage of proceeding by that route in preference to going by Galle. By going to Calcutta the plants would have 10 or 12 days in a cool climate, almost identical, in temperature at least, with that of the cinchona plantations of Java; they would have every convenience for resting in shade, and abundance of careful attendance, and would also escape the risks which would be incurred by landing and re-shipping heavy cases in the harbour of Galle in the hurry of coaling and landing cargo. Lastly, no time would be lost, as by this route I shall reach Madras quite as soon as if I had gone by Ceylon. After leaving Penang, a fungus appeared on nearly all the plants, and this rendered necessary the unpacking and re-packing of all the plants in the cases, a work which has occupied the head European gardener and several natives for three days. All traces of the fungus have been most carefully removed, and the moss with which the pots were packed has been dried. Advantage was also taken of this shifting of the plants to dispense with two unwieldy Wardian cases lent to me in Java. The plants contained in these were placed in three light cases of the pattern used in this garden. I stated in my demi-official letter that the information freely imparted to me by the scientific gentlemen in charge of the cinchona cultivation was one of the most important parts of my mission. Much of this information referred to questions of proper elevation above the sea, mean temperatures of atmosphere and soil, exposure to sunlight, clearing of the forests, nature of the soil, and position of the plantations on the mountains, as well as to points of purely chemical interest. There can be no doubt that, on the whole, there will be greater difficulties to contend with in introducing cinchona into India than have been experienced by the Dutch in Java. Dense forests possessing a moist climate, do not occur extensively in Southern India at elevations from 3,000 to 6,500 feet high, which may be taken roughly as the two extremes at which the cultivation of species of cinchona will be most successful. The site selected at Ootacamund is, as Mr. Markham allows, at least 1,500 feet above the highest elevation at which *C. Calisaya* is found in Bolivia, and 2,000 feet higher than the upper limit at which, after numerous experiments, it has been found possible to grow that species in Java, four degrees nearer the Equator than Ootacamund. Mr. Markham seems to forget that the lines of mean temperature are, even near the Equator, not parallel with degrees of latitude, and how much more do they vary when the points compared are mountain chains whose every phase of climate is influenced by local causes? If the *Cinchona Calisaya* is planted in a scantily wooded "Shola" whose elevation is 7,830, and the highest 7,950 feet above the sea, the young plants will most certainly be lost. Besides elevation and meteorological considerations, it is also necessary, in selecting a site for a cinchona nursery, to take into account the proximity and extent of forest that will be available for the permanent site of the trees. It will cause a large increase of expense at the first planting, and great additional labour in attending to the trees afterwards, if the product of a nursery must be distributed over circumscribed patches of forest far removed from each other. A small ravine containing a forest about a mile broad, and whose upper limit is only 4,000 feet above the sea, will accommodate a very small number of trees requiring dense shade, and whose height when full grown will probably exceed 80 feet. Such a patch of forest at Mercara is described by Mr. Markham as well suited for a cinchona plantation. Judging from the papers published by the Madras Government, the same remark applies to all the sites chosen in Southern India. Forests of the limit of 1,000 acres, and the Neddiwuttum site of 400 acres would be stocked by the hundredth part of a year's produce of a Java cinchona nursery. In Java, where the Dutch have entered on the cultivation on a most extended scale, the nurseries, which are only nine in number, are in the centre of vast forests where many square miles of forest are available for receiving the young trees from each nursery. In many places on the volcanic range of the Malabar in Java, I have ridden for three or four hours through a plantation of cinchona extending for 4 or 500 yards on each side of the path. Such liberal views of what is necessary for the success of so important an undertaking as the naturalization of the quinine-yielding cinchonas contrast strongly with the imperfectly formed plan on which this cultivation has been commenced in India.

3. In reading the official papers published by the Madras Government, I have also noticed that no provision seems to be made for selecting different sites for the various and numerous species already introduced into the nursery at Ootacamund. It may be generally said, that each species of cinchona requires a peculiar treatment for it to attain its highest development

development, and this is shown by each species of cinchona being found in South America within limits suitable to itself alone. This fact has been fully admitted by the Dutch, and they have attempted to imitate in the nurseries and plantations the natural conditions in which each species is found. This difference among the species has also attracted the notice of Mr. Thwaites, the director of the Royal Botanic Gardens of Ceylon, and who is charged with the superintendence of the introduction of cinchona into that island. He tells me, that that valuable species, *C. succirubra*, is quite a tropical plant, and succeeds well at Peradenia, the tropical botanic garden of Ceylon. Of course such a species cannot be expected to flourish in sites ranging from 7,000 to 7,800 feet in elevation. I have many other facts to record and many more remarks to make, suggested by what I have observed in Java; but it is quite impossible for me to allude to them now, with all the pressing duties of my office, which must be attended to before I leave for Madras. I shall, however, have the honour to submit this report in an extended form, embracing the whole subject of the introduction of cinchona, soon after my return from Madras.

4. In conclusion, I consider it my duty to recommend that a definite plan should be drawn up, in the most liberal spirit, having for its aim the means of procuring the largest possible amount of quinine in the shortest possible time. Its details ought to include provision for the immediate establishment of nurseries on all the mountain ranges suitable for the cultivation of any of the species, and where large tracts of forest are available, such as the Khasia Hills, the Eastern Himalayas, the mountains extending from Chittagong down to the Malayan Peninsula. On all of these ranges at least *C. succirubra* will thrive, and it is one of the richest in quinine of all the species of cinchona. A nursery and plantation might at once be organised at the northern slopes of the Khasia, where the rainfall is only 150 to 200 inches in the year, and where forests are tolerably abundant. Should this be sanctioned, I would propose to leave in the Botanic Garden of Calcutta a sufficient number of the plants I brought from Java to commence a plantation, and seeds to form a nursery. I would suggest that not more than 10 plants of *C. Calisaya* and about 60 of *C. Pahudiana* be left here; to these I can add 32 seedlings of various species which were raised here in April, and which in two months will be strong enough to stand the journey to the Khasia Hills. With a little care these plants I propose to leave here can be kept in perfect health until the middle of March.

— No. 89. —

From *W. G. McIvor*, Esq., Superintendent Government Gardens, Ootacamund, to *J. D. Sim*, Esq., Secretary to Government, Revenue Department.

Sir, Ootacamund, 2 August 1861.

1. WITH reference to the order of Government on the introduction of the cinchona plants from Java, I have the honour to solicit the favour of your being good enough to bring to the notice of Government, that the value of the species and the correctness of the names given to some of these plants in Java is at present involved in much doubt and uncertainty.

2. In a letter which I had the honour to address, on the 18th ultimo, to the private secretary to his Excellency the Governor, I mentioned, "that the bark (and specimens of the leaves and flowers) of the cinchona, called by the Dutch *lucumæfolia*, have recently been forwarded from Java to Mr. Howard for analysis. The bark has proved to be worthless, and the species to be one of no value, and is now named *Cinchona Pahudiana*."

3. Although these remarks are forwarded on private information, it is of such a nature as will not admit of doubt as to their correctness. Moreover, I see that the information which I received has since been confirmed by the public notice of the plant by J. E. Howard, Esq., in the proceedings of the Linnæan Society of the 2d May 1861, and also in the "Gardener's Chronicle and Agricultural Gazette" of 25th May, as a new species, but one of little value, except as a botanical specimen, the flowers being very ornamental.

4. This species was first called "ovata" by Hasskarl, and since "lucumæfolia" by Dr. Junghuhn, and now named "Pahudiana" by Howard, in honour of the Governor General of Java. It is very probable that Dr. Junghuhn was not aware of the result of Howard's analysis and investigation at the date of the correspondence recorded in the Proceedings of Government. I observe that a large number of this species has been very liberally offered by the Governor General of Java, and I consider it my duty to give this brief but plain statement of the facts connected with this plant, so far as I have been able to ascertain them, in

in order to enable your honourable Government to decide as to whether it is advisable or otherwise to incur the cost of introducing and cultivating this species.

5. The *Cinchona Calisaya*, of which from 50 to 100 plants are also liberally offered, is a species of undoubted value, and its introduction may be worthy of consideration. However, we already possess six plants of this species, in very fine health, and 50 or 60 more are expected from Kew in October; we have also every reason to expect a large supply of seeds from Peru, but we cannot possess too many plants of this valuable species. Seeds of this species from Java would be very desirable, as their transit would cost little.

6. The third species they have in Java, named *lancifolia*, is also very valuable, but none of this is offered, and it is questionable if they could be spared, as 14 is given as the total number of plants in Java. This (the *lancifolia*) is only a variety of the *Condaminea*, which grows on high and exposed situations. I learn from Mr. Markham that he has made arrangements with Mr. Spruce for the extensive introduction of seeds of the *Condaminea*, and I am informed that I may expect the seeds to reach me in November.

7. The other species in Java, *Cinchona lanceolata*, is very doubtful, but no analysis has been made of it, as they have, as I believe, only a few (45) plants.

8. I enclose, for the information of Government, a report on the number and condition of our cinchona plants, taken on the 9th July; since that time about 400 more seedlings have come up.

9. I also beg to enclose copy of hints for the treatment of plants in Wardian cases, which may prove useful to the gentleman entrusted with the importation of the plants from Java; the treatment there described has been practised here for many years with the best results.

— No. 90. —

REPORT on the Number and Condition of the Cinchona Plants in the Government Gardens at Ootacamund, on the 9th July 1861.

NAMES.	NUMBER.	REMARKS.
Cinchona succirubra, or Red Bark -	1,204	The imported plants are in a very healthy and flourishing condition, the leaves on some of the red bark plants measuring 11 × 7 inches. Average growth of the month, 1½ inches; height of largest plants, from 2 feet 4 inches to two feet 7 inches. The first of the seedlings are 4¼ inches high, and furnished with from two to three pairs of branches; some of the leaves measure 2½ × 1¼ inches. Average growth of the month, 1¼ inches. More seedlings are coming up daily.
Cinchona calisaya, Calisaya Bark -	6	
Cinchona nitida, genuine Grey Bark - - - - - -	714	
Cinchona micrantha, var. Provinciana - - - - - -	802	
Cinchona micrantha, var. Pata de Gallinazo - - - - - -	36	
Species without name - - -	211	
TOTAL - - -	2,973	

Government Gardens, Ootacamund,
9th July 1861.

(signed) *W. G. McIvor*,
Superintendent Botanical Gardens.

Hints on packing and conveying Plants in Wardian Cases.

THE cases to be furnished with a false bottom, raised about two or three inches above the true bottom by bars of wood of the thickness required, being nailed on the underside; through this false bottom holes are bored at regular distances; over these holes let a few broken pieces of pot be placed, and over this a layer of of moss—the case being filled with soil to within two or three inches of the level of the glass, and the plants carefully planted pretty close together, so as to allow of a case containing 35 or 50 plants according to their size.

The best sort of soil I believe to be formed of equal parts of leaf-mould, turfy loam, and sand; these should be mixed in a dry state, and if possible spread out and exposed to the action of the sun for a few days prior to being put into the cases.

During the voyage the plants should have plenty of light and air, in fine weather one side of the case being left open for two or three hours morning and evening; the soil being every three or four days turned up on the surface to the depth of about half an inch, with a small pointed stick, and always kept rough (never smooth) on the surface.

The object of this is to allow the air to circulate among the soil, and this circulation of air is also facilitated by the false bottom. This is, perhaps, one of the most important things to be attended to in transporting plants in Wardian cases, as the action of air on the soil keeps the roots in fine condition, and entirely prevents the formation of mildew and damp, which so frequently prove fatal to the roots of plants in Wardian cases. The plants should have water when the surface becomes decidedly dry, but they should not be soaked with water: the proper amount of moisture to preserve roots in a healthy state, is only what the soil can retain in its cavities by the force of attraction. The principal object of the false bottom is to allow any excess of water to drain off into a place where it cannot sour the soil, and yet not to be lost, for as the soil becomes dry above the water, it will be attracted to it. The true bottom of the cases should be watertight, and in stormy and bad weather, the cases should be shut up tight, to prevent the possibility of salt water getting to the plants; but should this happen, which it ought not to do, the only means of preserving the plants is immediately to wash them with fresh water.

Ootacamund, 22 July 1861.

(signed) *W. G. McIvor*, Superintendent Botanical Gardens.

— No. 91. —

From *W. G. McIvor*, Esq., Superintendent Government Gardens, Ootacamund, to *J. D. Sim*, Esq. Secretary to Government, Revenue Department.

Sir, Ootacamund, 6 August 1861.

1. On re-perusing the correspondence recorded in the order of Government, dated 29th July 1861, and with reference to my letter of the 2d instant, I fear I have not entered so fully on the subject of the importation of cinchona plants from Java as its importance requires. I would, therefore, most respectfully explain that from the 500,000 seeds of the *Cinchona lucumæfolia* liberally offered by the Governor General of the Netherlands India, we may expect to rear upwards of 400,000 plants, as this is a species most luxuriant in its growth, producing seeds of greater vital powers than the ordinary species of cinchona.

2. To afford suitable accommodation for this number of plants will cost about 10,000 rupees, and to attend to them will require one man to every 2,000 plants, or an establishment of 200 men for the first year; at the end of the first year, the land necessary to plant this number of plants may be estimated at 1,200 acres; at 50 rupees per acre, for preparing, pitting, and planting, will cost 60,000 rupees. The establishment necessary to keep up this extent of land, at two men to the acre, gives 2,400 men, at six rupees each, or a monthly expenditure of about 14,000 rupees, not including overseers, tools, &c. I believe this will prove an unprofitable expenditure of public money, and one which will only lead to ultimate loss and disappointment; and, under these circumstances, I respectfully beg to explain that I cannot be responsible for the results in the cultivation of this species.

3. The course I purpose to pursue in this important undertaking, is only to cultivate species of known and established value; all that are the least doubtful, should only be grown to a limited extent, and after they have fairly and unmistakeably

mistakeably developed their qualities, their cultivation can be extended, or otherwise.

4. This line of procedure appears to me indispensable, to avoid disappointment, as not only many, but the majority of the species of cinchona, are worthless for the production of quinine.

P.S.—Since writing the above, I observe that Professor Lindley, in a review of Howard's work, states: "We have omitted to mention the appearance of the seventh part of Mr. Howard's superb work on Cinchonas, or Illustrations of the Neuva Quinologia of Pavon. It contains figures of *Cinchona Uritusinga, nitida,* and *Pahudiana,* a new species now cultivated in Java by the Dutch, but of inferior quality; it seems, however, to grow freely, and would be a good hothouse shrub, bearing panicles of pale vermilion flowers as large as lilacs."

— No. 92. —

From the Chief Secretary to the Government of Madras to *W. G. McIvor,* Esq., Superintendent of Government Gardens, Ootacamund.

Sir, Fort St. George, Madras, 14 December 1861.

I AM directed by his Excellency the Governor in Council to inform you that Dr. Anderson, of the Bengal Medical Service, has been deputed by the Government of India to visit the Neilgherries, for the purpose of inspecting the nurseries of the cinchona plants there, and of satisfying himself as to the prospect which they give of ultimate success.

2. Dr. Anderson will leave Madras to-morrow morning, and may be expected at Ootacamund on the 17th instant. I am to direct that you will place yourself in communication with him, and will afford him all possible information and assistance in furtherance of the duty with which he has been charged.

(signed) *T. Pycroft,* Chief Secretary.

— No. 93. —

From Mr. *W. G. McIvor,* Superintendent Government Cinchona Plantations, to *T. Pycroft,* Esq., Chief Secretary to Government, Madras.

Sir, Ootacamund, 20 January 1862.

WITH reference to your communication of the 14th ultimo, No. 1649, I have the honour to acquaint you, for the information of Government, that during Dr. Anderson's stay on these hills, I furnished that gentleman with every information regarding our operations; and at his request he was carefully instructed in our process of propagation and cultivation of the cinchonas, which the filling of our new propagating-house afforded him the means of observing in all its details. Dr. Anderson expressed himself highly gratified by our system of propagation from layers, being a method not usually adopted, and one which greatly facilitates our means of increasing these valuable plants. Dr. Anderson has also been furnished with the plans of our propagating-house, in order that he may erect two similar buildings on the Himalayas, so as to enable him perfectly to follow the method of propagation practised here.

2. So far as our operations have yet extended, our success is indisputable and quite unequalled, but a difference of opinion exists between Dr. Anderson and myself as regards one of the next steps I am about to take, namely, that of planting out 75 acres of cinchona plants without the shade of forest trees; this Dr. Anderson thinks, will prove disastrous, although there can be no objection to this opinion being placed on record; in order, however, that the Government may be satisfied that I have not come to any hasty conclusion as to the various modes of culture it is desirable to pursue in our experiments, I beg to be permitted to detail the facts which have influenced me in forming an opinion.

3. As

3. As already brought to the notice of Government, we propose planting during this year in all 150 acres. Of this 75 acres will be planted under various degrees of shade of forest trees, and 75 acres planted without any shade of forest trees.

4. With reference to the first method, the advantages which it offers are these:—the cultivation can be conducted with little skill, as under dense shade all will be left to nature, and in reality no cultivation required; the plants would also look well to the casual observer, although drawn and watery. Its disadvantages are these:—the period when we can expect quinine, or bark, will not arrive until our cinchona plants overtop the forest trees and expand their heads in the open sunshine, and this will take from 40 to 60 years; and it is doubtful if some of the most valuable species of cinchona would ever overtop the forest, but die out, as described at para. 11; the plantations would also have to be felled to obtain the produce.

5. It will be observed, that under this system of cultivation, and with the necessity of destroying the plantations to get the produce, the growth of Peruvian bark would never become an article of private enterprise; and it is doubtful if Government plantations would ever be found on a scale sufficiently large to affect the value of quinine in the market.

6. With reference to the second system, its advantages are:—if successful, it will furnish bark in eight years from the date of planting, and in 12 years the bark will become an article of commerce. The plantations will not have to be cut down or destroyed in order to obtain the produce, but uniform and constant yearly supplies of bark will be procured without any damage whatever to the trees. Thus the production of Peruvian bark will be placed within the reach of the ordinary speculator, and even within the reach of the man of limited means; and as it would be profitable, it will no doubt soon become an extensive article of produce. Its disadvantages are these:—to get the trees over the first year or two of their growth will require a great amount of skill and attention. The ground, being cleared of the forest, will be exposed to the full effects of evaporation and radiation, and this in a limited degree, although beneficial in promoting the fertility of the soil, in excess no doubt will be injurious, but this injurious action can be more simply and efficiently combated by other means than the shade of living trees.

7. The arguments against this method advanced by Drs. Macpherson and Anderson, who visited the cultivation in Java, have received my full and serious consideration, and from all I can gather the whole seems to have originated in a misconception of facts. It is believed by Dr. Junghuhn, the principal director of cinchona cultivation in Java, that the cinchona trees in their natural localities on the Andes "grow in damp forests overshadowed by trees." But the greatest authority* contradicts this conclusion and their practice, and states that the only species they have cultivated to any extent, viz., the *C. lucumæfolia*, or, as it is now called, *pahudiana*, "grows in a very sandy micaceous soil, on dry sunny hills without much shelter from the sun." But were it so that the cinchona trees grew in damp forests overshadowed by trees, still it would be difficult to come to a conclusion more erroneous than that in cultivation such was desirable or necessary; because, in the localities where plants are indigenous, there is always one or more conditions the most favourable to the perfect development of the plant, but there are also other conditions which are injurious, and one of these is invariable overshadowing and overcrowding.

8. Our minds not being fixed as to the best culture to be applied to a newly introduced plant, the absurdity of the above conclusion does not appear in such full relief as if the same principles and facts were advanced to guide us in the treatment of plants long in cultivation. Suppose any one were to dictate to the agricultural world that they must grow their tea, coffee, cotton, wheat, barley, &c. &c. &c., among thorns, briars, and weeds, because they must of necessity grow

* Howard's 7th No. of Nueva Quinologia de Pavon.

grow under such circumstances in a state of nature, it would be received as the production of a wandering mind, although the facts would be correct, and only the conclusion erroneous. All terrestrial plants which have been brought into economic cultivation from the beginning of the world up to the present time have been found to be benefited by full exposure to the light of heaven; and no facts have yet been advanced to show that the cinchonas are likely to form an exception to this general rule.

9. In coming to a conclusion as to the course desirable to be followed in our experimental cultivation, I have been much guided by the opinions of Mr. Markham. This gentleman, commissioned by the Secretary of State for India, visited South America in 1860, penetrated into the cinchona region, and, being an excellent observer, noted with great minuteness the various influences as affecting the growth of these valuable plants. Mr. Markham visited India at the end of the same year, and, by numerous notes and a long personal intercourse, conveyed to me every particular of his observations, and this intercourse afforded us the great advantage of being able fairly to discuss the best means of applying a system of culture suited to meet the different conditions of our climate.

10. The correctness of Mr. Markham's observations has stood the test of practical experience, without failing as yet in one instance; and it would be unreasonable to conclude they will fail when applied to the future stages of our operations, especially as his means of observation have been of the most perfect nature. I do not for a moment doubt the high scientific attainments of Dr. Anderson; but this gentleman has only seen in Java the plants in a very doubtful state of cultivation, and therefore is more liable to form an erroneous opinion. Moreover, the Java system of rearing seeds had at the instance of Dr. Macpherson a fair trial here, and when compared with the results we otherwise obtained it proved a failure.

11. The opinions of Mr. Markham are also borne out by every authority who possessed the same advantages as himself, namely, that of studying the habits of the cinchonas in their natural localities. Mr. Howard believes that the cinchonas "delight" in exposure to "free air, cold, water, and sunshine." Poeppig states, that with the bark collectors "all stems were rejected, even when they stood in very promising groups (*Manchas*), if the soil was damp and the valleys warm and without a current of air." Dr. Karsten states, "For the bark of the cinchona growing in the ravine described, high above the actual limits of the forest, gave three-and-a-half per cent. sulphate of quinine, whilst that from the lower-lying forest scarcely yielded one per cent." Weddell suggests, that in cultivation the cinchonas be planted in cleared ground along with faster-growing plants; and this would no doubt be a good system, were it not that the faster-growing plants would take up a great proportion of the nourishment from the soil, which would be more profitably stored up in the cinchonas. Mr. Cross, a very intelligent young gardener, engaged by Mr. Markham to assist him in his mission, states in the notes he furnished to me: "I observed that many of the red bark trees, when growing under dense shade, lost a portion of their branches, and sometimes all of them, during the wet season; or, if not, they assumed a weak climber-like habit, which, if exposed suddenly at any time to influences of a damp or dry nature, would be likely to cut them off altogether."

12. Much has already been, and no doubt will be, demonstrated in actual cultivation, to show various modifications in applying the principles above given, with the greatest advantage to the conditions of our climate and soil; but, until this experience is had, it appears safest for us to endeavour to administer to the plants in the highest degree, those conditions which have been ascertained to be most favourable to their perfect development on the Andes, and to remove or mitigate such as are injurious.

13. Our present success is only comparatively satisfactory, and this we can only expect to be the case in our future operations; as had I possessed at the beginning the same experience I have even now, nearly double the results would have been obtained; also with reference to our system of cultivation and propagation,

gation, although comparatively perfect, yet no doubt it will ultimately give way to one very much superior, when we become better acquainted with the nature of the plants; but these improvements will be effected only by a modified application of the same principles, as we cannot expect to violate with impunity any of the laws which govern vegetable life.

14. I shall now briefly notice the present condition of our experiment, as the coldest and the greatest part of our dry season has now passed away, and it gives me much pleasure to be able to state that all our cinchona plants in the open air have borne this unusually severe winter without injury. In September last I planted at Neddiwattum six plants of different species in a cleared spot on the highest and most exposed point of the site, and all of these have not only borne the cold and drought without injury, but it has never checked their growth, and at present the plants are in the finest possible state of health, their leaves of the deepest green, some of which measure 9 by 12 inches.

15. At Ootacamund I planted 15 plants between May and August, and 12 of these were of the red bark; being the most tender species, I wished to test the amount of cold and exposure it would bear. Here the cold of December checked the growth of these plants, but has not in the least injured them; the leaves still keep their deep-green colour, and measure from 7 to 9 inches. This plant is evidently more hardy than we at first supposed, as a plant of *Fuchsia serratifolia* (growing within two feet of the red bark) had the points of its tender shoots killed by frosts, while even the young leaves of the red bark were not touched.

16. The plants in our propagating-houses continue to grow with their usual vigour. The largest of those growing as specimens measure 4 feet in height, and the circumference of the stem above the ground measures 3¼ inches, at 18 inches above the ground 2½, and at 3 feet 2¼ inches. The strongest growing plant that we have, is one that has been layered and consequently short, but the circumference of the stem at the ground measures over 4 inches. The total number of our plants at present is about 9,000, of eight different species. Of these upwards of 3,000 have attained a size fit for propagation; the others are necessarily small, but making satisfactory progress. Dr. Anderson was furnished with 204 plants of our most valuable species for introduction in Bengal, and 16 have been forwarded to Mr. Maltby for the Rajah of Travancore. On taking the plants out of the Wardian cases which Dr. Anderson brought from Java, they were all more or less affected by rot and fungi at the roots. Three of the *Calisayas* have died since being transplanted, two more are doubtful, but the others seem to be recovering.

(No. 284).

ORDER thereon, 22 October 1862, No. 2263.

1. THE Government consider this report very satisfactory.

2. Mr. McIvor will forward brief monthly reports of the progress of his various operations, noting especially the condition of the plants at Neddiwuttum.

(signed) *T. Pycroft*, Chief Secretary.

Enclosure in No. 93.

REPORT on the Number and Condition of the Cinchona Plants in the Government Gardens at Ootacamund and Neddiwuttam on the 31st January 1862.

NAMES.	Number of Plants.	Value per lb. of Dry Bark in the London Market.
		s. d. s. d.
1. Cinchona succirubra, or Red Bark	6,580	2 6 to 8 9
2. Cinchona Calisaya—Calisaya, or Yellow Bark	67	2 10 „ 5 –
3. Cinchona lancifolia, Brown Bark	4	1 8 „ 2 10
4. Cinchona nitida, or Genuine Grey Bark	1,000	1 8 „ 2 9
5. Cinchona species without name	308	1 8 „ 2 10
6. Cinchona micrantha, var. Provenciana	1,713	1 8 „ 2 9
7. Cinchona Peruviana, or Grey Bark	60	1 8 „ 2 10
8. Cinchona Lucumafolia of the Dutch, or Pahudiana of Howard	425	No value.
Total Number of Plants	10,157	

REMARKS.—The whole of the plants are in very fine condition, many of them being in the most luxuriant state of health. The largest of the plants are from 3½ to 4½ feet in height, and some of their leaves measure over 12 by 18 inches. The circumference of the stem of the largest plant measures 3½ inches at the ground, at 18 inches above the ground the same stem measures 2¼ inches, and at 3 feet above the ground 2¼ inches.

The thickness of the bark in these plants is very remarkable, being in some instances a quarter of an inch, and on the smaller stems the average thickness considerably exceeds that of the wood. About 3,000 plants have been placed in the nurseries in the open air; these are making very satisfactory progress. For experiment, six plants of different species were planted out in September last, in a cleared spot, on the highest and most exposed part of the Neddivattam site. All of these plants have borne the cold and drought without injury, their growth not having been in the least checked. At Ootacamund the growth of the red bark plants was checked by the cold and drought of December and January; but the weather now being more mild, they have again begun to grow. Of the cuttings put into the new propagating house in the beginning of January, about one-half of them were found on the 28th to be rooted, the roots varying from a quarter to one and a half inch in length; all species seem to root alike freely on a bottom heat. The number of cuttings lost from damp and accidents has averaged from 6 to 10 per cent. With the *Calisayas*, which takes long to root without bottom heat, we obtained the following results:—of 24 cuttings put in on the 1st of January, at the end of the month two had died, 11 were rooted, and the remaining cuttings had quite heeled over and begun to emit roots, which will be perfectly developed in from 8 to 12 days. On removing the plants brought by Dr. Anderson out of the Wardian cases, they were all found to be more or less affected with rot and fungi at their roots; since being transplanted, three plants of the *Calisaya* have died, two are doubtful, as also one of the plants of *C. lancifolia*; the others are now recovering, and seem to have fairly taken to the soil.

(signed) *W. G. M'Ivor*,
Superintendent Government Cinchona Plantations.

— No. 94.—

From *Thomas Anderson*, Esq., M.D., Officiating Superintendent Royal Botanic Gardens, to *W. Grey*, Esq., Secretary to the Government of India.

11 February 1862.

I HAVE the honour to report my return from the Neilgherries on the 13th January, after having made over to Mr. McIvor at Ootacamund 50 plants of *Cinchona Calisaya*, Wedd. in excellent condition, with the exception of one sickly and one almost dead, 284 plants of *C. Pahudiana*, Howard in perfect health, also four plants of *C. lancifolia*, Mut. in excellent order. These four are the only plants of *C. lancifolia* that have ever been introduced into India. I have thus completed the special duty with which I was entrusted, and nothing now remains for me but to lay before His Excellency the Governor General in Council the results of my investigations in Java and in the Neilgherries, as well as of my study since 1854 of the subject of the introduction of the species of cinchona into India.

2. In

2. In my demi-official letters addressed to you, and in my public letter No. 326, dated 4th December 1861, I have remarked on the very liberal manner in which the plants and seeds of cinchona were given to me by the Dutch authorities; but as none of these communications were adapted for publication, I shall here briefly detail my proceedings in Java, as well as the manner in which I was received there.

3. I reached Batavia on the 5th October, and on reporting my arrival to Alexander Loudon, Esquire, the General Secretary, I was invited to proceed at once to Buitenzorg, in order that I might have an interview with the Honourable M. Prins, Acting Governor General, and to present my letters from the Government of India. After an audience with His Excellency, orders were passed, allowing me the free use of the Government post-horses during my travels, and a passport to visit all parts of Java was also presented to me. Orders were also issued to Dr. De Vrij, the gentleman charged with the chemical investigation of the bark of the cinchona, directing him to meet me at Bandong, a large town in the centre of the western portion of the island, and in the vicinity of the cinchona plantations. I had apartments given to me in the palace of Buitenzorg, until the carrying out of these arrangements would permit my departure for Bandong. At Bandong I met Dr. De Vrij on the 14th October, and the next morning we started in company for Loro Kedeol, a temporary wooden dwelling erected for Dr. Junghuhn at 6,500 feet in the vicinity of the cinchona plantations on the Kendeng Mountains, distant about 50 miles from Bandong. There we awaited the arrival of Dr. Junghuhn, who joined us on the following day accompanied by Baron Von Richthofen of the Prussian embassy to Japan. We resided for some days at Loro Kedeol, making daily excursions to the cinchona plantations, and also visiting two active volcanoes. I made very extensive collections of plants illustrative of the flora of this mountain chain, having engaged for this purpose about 20 coolies, who worked under the guidance of my two trained plant collectors. I took advantage of Baron Von Richthofen's being of our party, to have the observations confirmed which I made on the geology of the mountains selected for the cultivation of cinchona. That gentleman is travelling as geologist to the Prussian embassy, and is also known by a large work on the Geology of the Tyrol. On all occasions I was accompanied by Dr. Junghuhn, who carefully pointed out to me the experiments he had made in the various cinchona nurseries, explaining fully all the details, and satisfying my curiosity on every point. During our rides through the primeval forests, sites suitable for cinchona plantations were always noted, and the reasons for selecting them freely discussed.

Dr. Junghuhn, from his extensive knowledge of the natural history of Java, was able to give me information of the most valuable kind concerning the distribution of the trees and plants occurring in the cinchona plantations. In his great work on Java, and in his "Plantæ Junghuhinanæ," to which most of the first botanists of Europe have contributed monographs, these facts of botanical geography are all recorded, but they acquired additional interest and value when communicated by Dr. Junghuhn on the scene of his labours and with special reference to the cinchona cultivation. After visiting six nurseries and the adjoining plantations, and examining the cinchona plants that were to be made over to me, we returned to Bandong, which I made my head quarters, and where my botanical collections were accumulated. After a few days at Bandong spent in arranging and examining my collections, Dr. De Vrij and I started for Limbang, the residence of Dr. Junghuhn, at the foot of the great active volcano Tankuban Prahu. Here we found Dr. Junghuhn suffering from a severe attack of dysentery, caused by exposure while travelling during the past six weeks; when I left Java, three weeks later, he was still seriously ill. Dr. De Vrij and I ascended to the summit of the volcano, and we also visited the recently formed cinchona nursery on this mountain, and the young plantation in the forest. I found it was impossible for me to reach Batavia, as I had hoped, in time for the first steamer in November. I was therefore able to devote some days to visit the district of Garood, an extensive plateau, about 2,000 feet above the sea, called, on account of its wonderful beauty and fertility, the Garden of Java. It is surrounded by lofty volcanic mountains, and to their slopes also Dr. Junghuhn has proposed to his Government to extend the cultivation of cinchona. We spent four days here, ascending three active volcanoes, one of which had recently

recently erupted, exploring the forests on their sides, and visiting also one of chose depressions in the mountain side where the skeletons of animals suffocated by noxious gases are constantly to be found. We saw in it the recent skeletons of a wild hog and of *Felis minima.* On my return to Bandong, I despatched the native gardener, whom I had brought from Calcutta, to the nursery of Tjaneroen, in order to accompany and take charge of the Wardian cases containing the cinchona plants, on their journey to Batavia. After again visiting Limbang to take leave of Dr. Junghuhn, I proceeded on my way to Batavia accompanied by Dr. De Vrij. We diverged, when about halfway to Batavia, in order to visit Tjibodas, the only cinchona plantation I had not seen, except one in the eastern part of the island. The plantation of Tjibodas is the one in which occurred all the accidents and failures that attended the introduction of the plant into Java. We spent four days here, passing one night on the summit of the Pangerango, the loftiest mountain in the west of Java, 10,000 feet high. Dr. De Vrij then returned to Bandong, and I pursued my journey towards Batavia. At Buitenzorg I had the honour of an interview with his Excellency Baron Von Sloet, the Governor General of the Netherlands India, who had arrived from Holland during my absence in the interior. When thanking his Excellency for the facilities that had been given me for seeing all that had been done for rendering the experiment successful in Java, I took the opportunity of mentioning that several very valuable species of cinchona had been received in British India, besides *C. Calisaya;* and that I was authorised to state that, if desired, plants of these would be placed at the disposal of the Dutch Government. I reached Batavia on the 11th November, and sailed on the 15th for Singapore. There I found the China steamer about to sail for Calcutta, so I at once took a passage by it, arriving in Calcutta on the 28th November.

4. At the Botanic Gardens here the plants were carefully cleaned and re-packed by Mr. Scott, the head gardener, a portion of them being retained to form the nucleus of a nursery in the Khasia Hills.

5. On the 10th December I sailed for Madras with the greater portion of the cinchona plants, and an experienced native gardener to take charge of them. All the necessary arrangements had been made at Madras for my proceeding to the Neilgherries, so that there was no delay or detention, and I arrived at Ootacamund on the 17th December.

As I mentioned in the commencement of this report, only two plants had suffered from the journey. Mr. McIvor was directed by his Excellency Sir William Denison to put himself in communication with me, and to afford me all possible information and assistance in furtherance of the duty with which I had been charged. The short period that my duties in Calcutta allowed of my spending in the Neilgherries, was entirely devoted to the study of the cultivation of cinchona in these mountains. All the sites that Mr. McIvor had selected were carefully visited, their geology, meteorology, and botany examined, and their characteristics noted; while the hitherto very successful cultivation and propagation of *Cinchona succirubra*, and other valuable species, in the conservatories and recently erected propagating-house in the Government gardens at Ootacamund, were fully explained to me in all their details.

6. I took advantage of my possessing eight empty Wardian cases, in which I had brought the cinchona plants from Java, to bring to Calcutta a large quantity of all the available species of cinchona at Ootacamund, to add to the stock reserved for the experiment in this Presidency. These arrived in tolerable order, considering the loose manner in which Mr. McIvor, from want of time, was obliged to pack them. About 13 plants out of 204, the entire number received, have been seriously damaged; the remainder, in the present genial climate of Calcutta, have quite recovered, and are as healthy as they were at Ootacamund.

7. I cannot conclude this portion of my report without referring to the great interest taken in my expedition by the officials of the Government of Netherlands India. I was received with marked courtesy by the Honourable M. Prins, President of Council, then Acting Governor General. From this gentleman, and from Alexander Loudon, Esq., General Secretary to Government, I received most valuable assistance and direction. To the Resident of the Preanger Regencies I am indebted for the promptness with which the ample relays of coolies were provided for the carriage of the Wardian cases, as well as the horses for my own use,

use, during the long journey from the cinchona plantations to Batavia. To Mr. Yellinghaus, Assistant Resident at Bandong, my thanks are due for constant services rendered during my prolonged stay in his district; and to the Native Prince, the Regent of Bandong, whose guest I was for several days at his resting-houses in the more inaccessible districts, where he sent furniture and servants for my use. Above all, I desire to bring to the notice of his Excellency the Governor General in Council, the unremitting kindness and attention of Dr. Junghuhn and Dr. DeVrij, and the unreserved manner in which all information that I could desire on our daily journeys was imparted to me. Messrs. Jardine, Skinner & Company, and Messrs. Apcar & Company, liberally allowed me to take the Wardian cases containing the cinchona plants, to and from Singapore, free of charge in their steamers. The same privilege was granted by the Peninsular and Oriental Company on my return from Madras with the cinchona plants.

8. The season is now too far advanced for the despatch of plants to Java; and the plants at the Neilgherries are not at all adapted for transmission to a distance, as plants artificially propagated, as they have been, cannot bear the risks of a long journey without a few months' preparation. Of those I brought the short journey from the Neilgherries to this, I lost nearly 10 per cent., while the plants from Java, which were seedlings, can hardly be said to have suffered at all. I shall reserve a set of plants from the first cuttings made from the plants from Madras, at present in the Botanic Gardens here, and by a preparatory process they will be rendered hardy enough for despatch to Java about the middle of November. I shall communicate with Dr. Junghuhn concerning the necessary arrangements for the transport of the plants from Singapore, where I shall send them in charge of one of the native gardeners who accompanied me to Java. The species of which I shall be able to send plants to Java are *Cinchona succirubra* of Pavon (not the plant known under that name in Java, which I consider a variety of *C. ovata*), *C. nitida*, *C. micrantha*—all valuable quinine-yielding species.

General Account of the Introduction of Cinchonas into Java and India.

1. The importance of such a subject as the introduction of cinchona into India, and the ignorance among gardeners of the proper methods of treatment of the various species, from the fact that no species of the genus has ever been cultivated except in Java, have given rise to a series of pamphlets and letters containing a great deal of irrelevant matter. I have before me six pamphlets, containing 286 pages of printed matter, besides 142 pages of printed correspondence, on this subject, which, with the exception of one or two short letters, have all been published during the last nine months. Of these, four pamphlets are translations, by Mr. Markham, of Latin botanical descriptions of species of cinchona, from the works of the well-known authors, Weddell and Howard, and notes extracted from the publications of the German botanists and travellers Karsten and Poeppig. The remaining two pamphlets are inaccurate translations of Dr. Junghuhn's second report on the cinchona in Java, one by Mr. Markham, the other by Mr. Fraser, under the auspices of Dr. Macpherson.

2. In this report Dr. Junghuhn gives an interesting account of the first introduction of the plant into Java. It is, therefore, unnecessary for me to enter into any details now, beyond stating that the first plants were introduced in the end of 1854. Mr. Hasskarl, the horticulturist who brought the plants from South America, and Mr. Teysmann the gardener (*hortulanus*), in charge of the Botanic Gardens Buitenzorg, were entrusted with the cultivation of the plant. Their efforts were followed with so little success, that in 1856 the direction of the cultivation was made over to Dr. Junghuhn. Dr. DeVrij, Professor of Chemistry at Rotterdam, was afterwards appointed to assist Dr. Junghuhn in the chemical researches into the quality of the cinchona bark produced in Java. The result of their exertions is that from 43 plants of *C. Calisaya* Wedd., 30 of *C. lancifolia* Mut., two of a variety of *C. ovata* (called *C. succirubra* by Dr. Junghuhn, but not that species), and 64 of *C. Pahudiana* Howd., have been produced about 8,000 plants of *C. Calisaya*, and more than half a million of *C. Pahudiana*, and a corresponding increase in the number of the other species.

3. In Java, the principal plantations are situated on the Kendeng and Malabar range of mountains, in the southern portion of the island, in south latitude

 7 deg.

7 deg. 20 to 25 min., and east longitude 107 deg. 20 to 35 min. These mountains, rising from the plateau of Bandong, 2,000 feet above the sea, to 6,000 or 7,000 feet, are covered to their summits with a dense forest of gigantic trees. The forest is continuous, except where broken by the sight of a solfatara or the crater of an active or extinct volcano. On leaving the rice cultivation of the plateau, and commencing the ascent of the mountain, to reach, for example, such a plantation as that of Kawa Tjividei, we pass first the beautiful and extensive coffee plantations; the coffee plants (untopped) are 20 or 30 feet high, their stems covered with mosses or with such orchids as *Vanda tricolor*, and *Cœlogyne speciosa* or *Javanica*. Trees of *Erythrina Indica* have been planted among the rows of coffee trees, to give the shade which they require Occasionally, especially as we approach the upper border of the plantations and the ascent becomes steep, specimens of that giant of the forests of the Malayan Archipelago *Liquidamber altingiana* are noticed raising their bare smooth stems, without a branch or an epiphyte, to the height of 150 or 180 feet, where they terminate in a leafy head. On leaving the coffee gardens, we enter a dense forest, where on every hand we see the tree-ferns *Alsophila contaminans*, several species of *Cyathea*, the wild plantain, many broad-leaved *Zingiberaceæ* such as *Amomum*, *Hedychium*, *Elletaria*, *Pininga*. The forests are choked with an undergrowth of these plants and with *Araliaceæ*, such as *Sciadophyllum*, *Panax*, and other scandent shrubs, with *Urticeæ* and numerous *Rubiaceæ* such as *Morinda*, *Canthium*, *Vangueria*, *Paederia fœtida* and *tomentosa*, *Pavettæ* of several species, and *Chasalia*. The numerous branches of these bushy shrubs become entwined with prickly-leaved scandent palms, principally *Plectocomia* and *Calamus*, and a sub-scandent bamboo, which I referred to the beautiful species *Bambusa elegantissima*, Hassk. Gigantic figs occur in this region, and, with their enormous aërial roots and high well-branched stems, form the most striking objects in the vegetable kingdom. With the exception of the Rasamala (*Liguidamber Altingiana*), the stems of the trees are covered by a dense mass of epiphytic orchids, ferns, *Lycopodia*, and mosses; they hang from the branches in long festoons, and quite conceal the bark on all parts of the tree. Conspicuous among these epiphytes is the *Asplenium Nidus-avis*, whose mass of plantain-like light-green leaves, closely appressed to the trunk, may be observed on almost every tree. On the forked branches of some of the older trees, at this elevation (5,000 feet), the *Rhododendron Javaniacum*, an epiphyte with deep orange-coloured flowers forming a large head, attracts attention even from a distance. As we ascend through the dripping forest, the vegetation changes with the altitude, and at 6,500 feet types of a temperate flora are more abundant, though mingled with tropical forms able to resist the somewhat lower temperature. The larger forest trees are *Podocarpus cupressina*, *P. Junghuhniana*, *P. Nereifolia*, *Memecylon costatum*, *Astronia macrophylla*, and *M. laurifolia*, *Gordonia Wallichii* with several Laurineæ, especially *Tetranthera* and *Cyclodaphne*. The abundance of oaks is also a peculiar feature in these forests; such species as *Quercus spicata*, *Pseudomolucca Sundaica nitida* and *Junghuhn*, with the nearly allied genera of *Lithocarpus* and *Castanea*, are common. Shrubby *Melastomaceæ*, indicative of the dampest climates, grow epiphytically on the stems of the trees, having their roots buried in the thick covering of mosses, hymenophylla, and other ferns. One of the most beautiful genera of this order is *Medinilla*, of which 16 species are found in these forests. Two species of *Polyosma* represent the gooseberries and currants of the northern forests of Europe and America, and the temperate genus *Rubus* abounds in species. Epiphytic *Solanaceæ* and *Cyrtandreæ* also occur constantly in the moistest spots, proving the perpetual humidity of these forests.

4. The dense foliage and the mass of spongy matter in the shape of mosses, entwined roots of epiphytal orchids, and ferns suspended overhead on the branches, intercepts a great deal of the heavy rain, and forms an effectual shelter for the traveller, who has, however, a more serious inconvenience to fear than rain from the falling of dead branches, broken off under the weight of moisture in their mossy coating. The upper zone of these mountain regions, from 7,500 to 10,000 feet, possesses a vegetation of even a more temperate character, such as one or two species of *Clematis*, *Thalictrum*, *Ranunculus*, *Violaceæ* and *Berberideæ*, *Saxifragræ* represented by the Himalayan genus *Astilbe*, the temperate *Rhododendrons*, *retusum* and *albiflorum* with *Gaultheriæ*, and several species of *Vaccinium*, and one species of the eminently American genus *Gaylussacia*.

lussacia. As we approach the craters of the active volcanoes, the luxuriant forest becomes stunted and scorched, even blackened, by the action of noxious gases, and is at length succeeded by a peculiar volcanic flora, consisting of a few gregarious plants, which are able to resist the irritating fumes of the sulphuretted hydrogen and other gases given off from the crater. Among these plants are *Leucopogon Javanicus*, *Gaultheria punctata* and *leucocarpa*, *Thibaudia vulgaris*, *Syzygium rostratum*, with *Pteris incisa* and *Selliguea*.

5. The climate of these forests is one of almost equal temperature with abundant moisture. There is no markedly dry season, as in Southern India and the Western Himalayas; but the rainy period, commencing in the end of September, lasts until the end of June, but occasionally rain falls throughout the entire year, as happened in 1861. The annual rainfall varies from 180 to 250 inches, according to the exposure, but the moisture in the atmosphere is much greater than any amount of rainfall would indicate. On all the mountains of Western Java, the dew-point, during nine months of the year, is at saturation.

6. All the cinchona forests are at those elevations where the afternoons are misty and rainy. Such a record as the following may be taken as a general account of the meteorological conditions of nearly every day for nine months, and sometimes for the entire year, at the height of 6,500 feet:—At sunrise (the thermometer being about 48 or 50 degrees) the sky is unclouded, and the sun shines brightly and warmly until 10 o'clock; while the valleys and plains below are hidden in a dense covering of clouds, out of which the higher ranges of mountains stand like islands in a sea. As the air becomes warmer and the sun's heat increases, these clouds rise up from the plain and begin to ascend the mountains, or, more properly, the moisture in the ascending warm currents becomes condensed on coming in contact with a colder upper stratum of air on the mountains, and about 11 o'clock the sun is hidden at all elevations above 4,500 feet, while it shines brightly in the plains. On the summit of the Panerango, 10,000 feet high, I observed my thermometers, which at 6 P.M. stood at 47 degrees Fahrenheit, rise at 9 P.M. to 49 degrees under the influence of a heavy fall of warm rain, brought up by a moist wind from below. This rise to 49 degrees was equal to four degrees above the proper temperature, which at 9 P.M. ought to have been 45 degrees. About an hour after noon, rain commences, and increases in quantity until near sundown, ceasing gradually about midnight, the clouds sinking down into the valleys. After midnight, the temperature is lowered by radiation under the almost cloudless sky. The range of the temperature is, however, small, both for the daily variation and the annual range. The difference between the maximum and minimum is from 10 to 12, while, from the proximity to the equator, the annual variation at Bandong is only about 2½ degrees.

7. Observations on the temperature of the air and the rainfall have been instituted at all the cinchona plantations of Java, except the small one in the eastern part of the island. The mean annual temperature of the cinchona nurseries varies from 62 to 66 degrees, and it is at these temperatures that the plants thrive best, when placed in the forest.

8. *Geological structure.*—The mountains on which the cultivation has been commenced are all volcanic in their structure, the rocks being principally trachyte and its varieties. In the neighbourhood of the more active volcanoes, such as Mount Gedeh, where the cinchona garden of Tjiboddas is placed, a deep layer of volcanic dust covers the soil. The steep slopes of the precipitous porphyritic mountains of the extreme west of the island have been avoided.

9. *On the Dutch method of cultivating Cinchonas.*—The nurseries for the propagation of the cinchonas are always at the lowest point of the site selected for the plantation, in order that the delicate process of germination may be carried on in the warmest spot. A tolerably flat place is chosen for the overseer's house and the nurseries, and it is usually cleared from all trees and brushwood. The nurseries are long and narrow raised beds of earth, arranged in terraces on the gentle slope, and protected from the sun and rain by low sheds, lightly thatched. Under these sheds, the young cinchona plants are raised from seed in bamboo pots, placed on the beds of earth. At the nursery of Tjineroen there are one or two propagating pits (slightly sunken glazed houses) for the artificial propagation of such species as do not bear

bear seed. In these houses the valuable species *C. lancifolia* has been largely increased by cuttings. In the open nurseries, where the seedlings are raised, the following plan is pursued:—The bamboo pots, made by cutting a thick bamboo transversely below each joint, are placed closely together on the earthen bed after having been filled with finely-sifted rich soil. The seeds to be sown in them are soaked over night in water, and in the morning each seed is taken up and placed, by means of a pair of fine wooden forceps, on the surface of the earth, a few grains of fine sand or earth being sprinkled over it to prevent the seed being blown away; water is very sparingly given until the seed germinates. In about 60 days the seed germinates, and the young plant is left undisturbed until it is large enough to be planted out in the forest. Handling the young plant causes it to droop and decay, and I have frequently seen the young plants die after only touching the leaves on one occasion. Many of the seedlings perish in the earlier stages, often from unaccountable causes, and frequently from "damping off," a term used by gardeners for decay caused by too much moisture and deficiency of light and air. Dr. Junghuhn recommends the removal of the lower pair of leaves from the plants when they are about six or nine months old, but I fear that doing so only tends to draw up and weaken the plants. When the seedlings are about a year or 18 months old, and have acquired a height of 12 inches, they are planted out in the forest in the sites which it is intended they shall permanently occupy. The planting is commenced at first in the immediate vicinity of the nursery, in cleared, well-dug circles about six feet in diameter. From the neighbourhood of these circles, brushwood and the over-hanging trees are cleared away, so as to admit the light perpendicularly, while the side-lights are somewhat excluded. The plants are thus removed from any drip from the trees, while they have the full advantage of rain and a considerable amount of sunlight. The plants in the forest accordingly look healthier and hardier than do the seedlings grown under the dense shade of the thatched sheds. To protect the young plants from being broken by the falling limbs of trees, three strong posts are placed over them, being tied at the top over the plant so as to form a cone. Considerable damage was received at first from the partiality of *Cervus munjak*, a species of barking deer, for the tender shoots of the cinchona; but this danger is now avoided by a strong palisade of bamboo being placed round each circle until the tree has grown beyond the reach of this animal. After the ground near the nursery has been filled with plants, the circles are made along the footpath in the forest leading to the cinchona plantation and from it. Again, roads at right angles are cut through the forest, and these in their turn are planted. Thus, through time, the forest becomes intersected by footpaths cutting it almost into square patches filled with cinchona trees. After the trees are planted out, the only care they require is to be kept free from weeds and brushwood, to keep the paths clear, and to remove dead and over-hanging branches from over the young trees. These operations, from the sowing to the planting out, and the tending of the trees afterwards, are all carried on in each plantation by the establishment attached to it. Thus, each nursery and its plantation are under the charge of a European gardener, who resides at the nursery, where also the little settlement for the native labourers is placed. Each nursery has been chosen with a view to there being several thousands of acres of forest available for the reception of the young plants, a method by which all expenses are diminished, while the important duties of supervision are efficiently discharged by the European overseer. In the forest the trees grow rapidly, the internodes of the stem elongate, and the leaves become much developed in size. The shutting out of the side-lights and nearly all the rays of the sun, except those from directly overhead, causes the plants to become drawn up and to grow rapidly in height: I do not consider this an unhealthy condition, as it is the state of the tree in its native forests as well as of all the trees of a tropical forest grown under the circumstances I have detailed. At the plantation at Tjiboddas, I observed plants of *Cinchona pahudiana* that had been only five or six years in the forest, and their height was about 25 or 30 feet, with a well-developed stem devoid of branches in its lower part, and with the leafy head (*coma* of botanical descriptions) stated to be characteristic of the cinchonas in their native localities. When the tree has acquired its full height, probably 60 or 70 feet, the trunk will become proportionally thick; for when it has reached its full stature, the crown of leaves, important organs of nutrition in all plants, will continue to perform their functions under the addi-

-tional

tional stimulus they will receive from the strong light to which they will become exposed on attaining the average height of the other forest trees. Such also is the opinion of the Dutch gentleman in charge of the cultivation, with the important addition that they do not expect to obtain quinine in its full proportion until the trees have acquired their full development in thickness as well as stature. That will not be attained under 40 or 50 years in the case of *Cinchona Calisaya* and *C. Pahudiana*, and, probably, of *C. micrantha*, *C. nitida*, and *C. lancifolia*. *Cinchona Pahudiana* is the only species in Java that continues to bear seed, *C. Calisaya* having ceased to do so after the first occasion; some important observations have been made in regard to this process. Until very lately, the only plants that yielded seed were those in the fully-cleared ground of the Governor General's strawberry garden at Tjiboddas, on the slopes of the active volcano, Gedeh. These plants, from exposure to the sun and air, are mere leafy bushes, 10 or 15 feet in height, with a stem dividing at one or two feet from the ground into numerous branches, more in the manner of standard apple-trees than of the healthy young plants of the same species in the adjoining plantation in the forest, with their well-formed stems and definite head of leaves (*coma* of Weddell and other botanists). The first seed yielded by these plants was of excellent quality, affording a percentage of 60 or 70 seedlings. After the first year, the seeds began to degenerate, and out of a recent sowing of 20,000 seeds, only about 200 germinated. The plants are evidently all dying from the unnatural position in which they are placed. The good seed that is now obtained in Java is all the produce of a healthier plant of *Cinchona Pahudiana*, planted partially in full sunshine at the nursery of Tjineroen. It has begun to yield seed much too soon, for it has not yet acquired the half of its full height. The untoward effects of unnatural conditions in the seed has had greater influence on the more delicate species: *C. Calisaya*, a plant of it even more stunted and leafy than *C. Pahudiana*, has borne seed only once, though it continues to produce flowers abundantly. Both it and several plants of *C. Pahudiana* were covered with flowers, and the last also with seed, during my visit to Tjiboddas and Tjineroen; and I was allowed to take specimens from both species for the Royal Herbarium of Kew, as well as that of the Calcutta Botanic Gardens.

10. Observations made on many thousand plants of *Cinchona Pahudiana* and of *C. Calisaya*, show that the latter species requires a lower elevation, and therefore a higher temperature, for its successful cultivation than the former. At the plantation of Kawa Tjividii, 6,230 English feet above the sea, *C. Calisaya* grows much slower than it does at the plantation Reon Gœnong, 1,030 feet lower: these trees, of the same age as those at that plantation, are also much more vigorous, under the increase of nearly four degrees on the mean annual temperature of the upper plantation. Dr. Junghuhn finds that 5,300 feet ought to be the upper limit for *C. Calisaya*.

11. On my arrival in Java, Dr. DeVrij was engaged on some valuable researches on the alkaloids in the various parts of a plant of *C. Pahudiana*: these were discontinued, of course, while he was travelling with me, but they had advanced far enough for me to learn the general results. He had confirmed DeLondre's discovery, made about 20 years ago, that the roots of cinchonas contained a larger proportion of alkaloids than the bark. In the roots of a tree of *C. Pahudiana* only two years old, there was no wood with bark formed, but the herbaceous stem yielded nine-hundredths of a grain of quinine. These important discoveries induced Dr. DeVrij to propose to his Government that, instead of waiting until the trees are fully developed before attempting to procure quinine, an experiment should be made for the purpose of testing his discovery on a large scale. The result that Dr. DeVrij expects is, that quinine in considerabe quantity would be obtained from the roots of trees about three or four years old: such a process would necessitate the destruction of the plants for the sake of their roots; the success would depend, besides, on there being several trees which bore seed abundantly, in order to keep up the supply.

12. In concluding this general account of what I observed in Java, I may state that I was greatly impressed with the advantage, in every way, of having so important an experiment directly under scientific superintendence. I particularly noticed that where the meteorology and botany with the general geology of the mountains were known, there was little difficulty in selecting the proper elevations for the various species of cinchona, and that, from a

knowledge of the habitats of the cinchona, there was no attempt made to grow them in such unnatural places for a shade-loving tree as cleared gardens, and at elevations either above or below their proper limits. If the experiment had all along been under scientific management, all the early errors which nearly threatened the extinction of the cinchonas in Java would have been avoided.

General Report on the Cultivation of the Species of Cinchona in the Neilgherries.

It is now more than 20 years since Dr. Royle recommended the introduction of the cinchona into India, and in 1852 he endeavoured to carry out his own suggestion by sending out to Calcutta seeds of *Cinchona Calisaya* procured for him by M. Weddell, who travelled in the cinchona forests of Bolivia from 1845 to 1847; these seeds were sown in the Botanic Gardens of Calcutta, but none of them germinated. In February 1853, Mr. Fortune, when on his way to China, brought six plants of *Cinchona Calisaya* from England by the overland route; these plants were sent to the Botanic Gardens of Calcutta, where one died soon after its arrival: the others were kept in the Botanic Gardens here for more than a year after their arrival, and were ultimately sent to Darjeeling, where they were planted in the open air, at a site considerably above what will prove to be the upper limit of this species in Sikkim. The introduction of the Peruvian-bark trees into India was also strongly recommended by Dr. Falconer, while he was superintendent of the Botanic Gardens here, in a paper published by the Agricultural and Horticultural Society. In 1855, I forwarded a communication on the same subject to the Medical Board. The assurance contained in these reports, that the cinchonas would succeed in India, induced the Government to recommend their introduction: the Court of Directors gave a favourable answer to the recommendation, but no steps were taken to carry out the experiment until after the mutiny.

2. In 1859 Mr. Markham, a clerk in the India Office, was appointed by Lord Stanley to proceed to South America, to procure plants and seeds of the best species of cinchona for transmission to India. As Mr. Markham's only qualification for this duty appeared to be a knowledge of the country where some of the cinchonas are found, acquired during travels in South America, his appointment was regarded with great surprise by scientific men; and Dr. Lindley, in the "Gardeners' Chronicle," predicted the entire failure which ultimately attended Mr. Markham's efforts, founding his opinion on Mr. Markham's ignorance of botany and science generally. A practical gardener accompanied Mr. Markham to South America. After an absence of nearly nine months, Mr. Markham arrived at Ootacamund with the remainder of 400 plants of *Cinchona Calisaya* originally shipped at the South American port. These plants were in Wardian cases, and had been brought from South America by one of the West Indian line of mail steamers to Southampton, where the cases were transhipped to the Peninsular and Oriental steamer for transport to Bombay. From Bombay Mr. Markham conveyed them by a special steamer to Calicut. On the 24th December 1860, all Mr. Markham's plants at Ootacamund were reported as dead. Simultaneously with Mr. Markham's expedition, arrangements were made to obtain seeds and plants of the valuable species *C. succirubra* through Mr. Spruce, the well-known botanist, who has now spent 12 years in South America as a botanical traveller and collector. Mr. Cross, a practical gardener, was sent out from England to assist Mr. Spruce, as well as to accompany the plants collected by them to their destination in India. The first result of their efforts was the dispatch to England and the West Indian Islands of a quantity of good seed of *C. succirubra*. Seeds of *Cinchona micrantha*, *C. nitida*, and *C. Peruviana*, sent from Huanaco by Mr. Pritchett, an agent engaged by Mr. Markham, arrived at the Royal Gardens at Kew about the same time as those sent by Mr. Spruce. Sir W. Hooker entrusted packets of all these species to my care, for sowing in the Botanic Gardens, Calcutta, and for distribution to the Botanic Garden at Ceylon, and to the gardens at Ootacamund. The seeds sown at these places germinated well. A large quantity of the seeds of the four species of cinchona were also sown at Kew, in the propagating-house built expressly for them by the orders of the Secretary of State for India. In January 1861, I brought out with me from England two plants of *Cinchona Calisaya*, for the cinchona nursery at Ceylon. These arrived in perfect health, and have been extensively propagated. The gardener Cross arrived at Ootacamund on the 9th April 1861, with 463 plants of

Cinchona

Cinchona succirubra procured by Mr. Spruce and himself. These plants were brought by the same route as Mr. Markham adopted, viz., mail steamer from Chagres to Southampton, and the Peninsular and Oriental Company's steamer *viâ* Southampton to Bombay, and then steamer to Calicut. Mr. Cross had with him six plants of *Cinchona Calisaya*, propagated in England from old plants which had existed for several years in England as curiosities, and which had been added to his stock at Southampton. All his plants, although they had been six months in Wardian cases, were in such excellent health that Mr. McIvor was soon able to propagate them artificially to such a degree, that from 507 plants of *C. succirubra*, the stock on the 9th May 1861 (463 of which were brought by Mr. Cross), there were on the 1st January 1862, 5,200 plants. From my own experience of the difficulties attending the transporting of so delicate plants by long sea-voyages, and especially of the trying journey in the Red Sea, I am certain that Mr. Cross deserves a large share of credit for the great success that has so far attended our efforts to introduce the cinchonas.

The plants of *C. Calisaya*, *C. lancifolia*, and *C. Pahudiana*, brought by me from Java, are the last addition to the number of species and plants of cinchona in India.

3. *General Condition of the Experiment in the Neilgherries.*—The introduction of the cinchonas into India is still in the first stage. With the exception of a few plants recently placed in the open-air nurseries at Neddiwattum, all the cinchona plants in the Neilgherries are growing in the conservatories in the Government Gardens at Ootacamund, where, protected from the vicissitudes of the weather, and in a recently erected house, even under the influence of artificial heat, they are growing luxuriantly. Under such favourable circumstances, the plants receive at once every condition necessary to their perfect health that an almost hourly observation of their wants indicates. They have been placed under these circumstances for two reasons:—In the first instance, from there being no one in the Neilgherries who could point out the sites on those mountains best adapted for receiving the plants; and thus they were considered to be safer under the protection of a glass-house, and now they are retained there in order to be artificially propagated to the greatest possible extent. The great success that has followed, and the result, compared with the early efforts of the Dutch, show that this is the wisest plan that could have been adopted. The 463 plants of *Cinchona succirubra* brought by Mr. Cross in April 1861, with the plants of this species raised from seed, had been multiplied on the 31st December to 5,200, and his six *C. calisayas* to 11, not one of Mr. Markham's having survived. It is hardly necessary to extend this report by referring to the minutiæ of Mr. McIvor's method of propagating the plants, beyond stating generally that each plant, as soon as it has attained a sufficient size, is artificially propagated by being "layered." In the recently erected propagating-house, where artificial heat can be applied to the soil by flues passing under the beds of earth, this process of layering will be carried on at double the rate, as the layers can then be removed from the stock plant as soon as the smallest roots appear; and on being placed in the heated soil these roots grow rapidly, and the newly-formed plant is in its turn ready to be increased from every internode. In this branch of the cultivation, Mr. McIvor has brought all the varied resources of highly advanced English gardening to promote the object he has in view—the obtaining the largest number of plants in the shortest possible time.

4. *Of the Sites for the Cinchona Plantations in the Neilgherries.*—As regards experiments or observations on the suitable localities of the Neilgherries for the cultivation of cinchona, we are as far from possessing them now as before the introduction of cinchona at all. I maintain that the successful rearing of the cinchonas in the greenhouses at Ootacamund is no more a proof that the climate of the Neilgherries is adapted for their cultivation, than the fact that many thousands of seedlings, as well as cuttings, are now existing in perfect health in the cinchona nursery at Kew, would lead us to expect that the plants will grow in the open air in England. The great difference that exists between the climates of the South American cinchona forests and the Neilgherries ought to have received greater attention than it has; and in the selecting of sites, convenience of access from Ootacamund should have been made subservient to the greater consideration of climate. A few sites have been chosen on the Neilgherries for the permanent plantations of the cinchonas, but none of them answer to the accounts given

given of the cinchona forests of South America, nor to those in which the cinchonas succeed in Java. A few remarks on the physical aspect, climate, and botany of the Neilgherries will allow of a comparison being made with the account I have already given of Java, and also with the brief notice I shall add of the physical features of the forests of the Andes.

5. *Of the physical Aspect of the Neilgherries.*—The elevated plateau of the Neilgherries has its central point in about north latitude 11 deg. 30 min.; its greatest breadth is nearly 50 miles from the north-east to south-west, while in another direction the breadth diminishes to 20 miles. The lowest point of the plateau, where its steep escarpment running down to the plains commences, is about 6,000 feet. Its surface is diversified by rounded grassy hills and flat-bottomed valleys, the result of denudation by marine action. The loftiest of these hills is Dodabetta, about 8,700 feet above the level of the sea, and situated close to the station of Ootacamund. The bare unwooded hills and valleys, with trees only in the ravines and very sheltered spots, give a bleak and uninviting aspect to the upper region of these hills. The sides of the hills running up to the crest of the plateau are more or less wooded throughout, but the botanical character of the forests and the size of the trees vary much on the different aspects of the escarpment, the contrast being greatest between the northern and southern slopes.

6. *Geological Structure of the Neilgherries.*—(See Memoirs of the Geological Survey of India, vol. i. part 2.)

The rocks of the Neilgherries consist of the varieties of gneissose rocks, composed principally of quartz, hornblende, felspar, and garnet. A few dykes of trap occur in some parts. A good fertile but rather shallow soil, in many parts very stony, is formed by the disintegration of these rocks. The best soil is formed in the deeper ravines that have been long covered by trees, and where the decayed vegetable matter forms a stratum of some depth; I frequently noticed good soil of great depth on the less abrupt slopes on the north-western and western sides of the plateau.

7. *Meteorology of the Neilgherries.*—I have been able to find no very trustworthy observations on the temperature of any of the stations on the Neilgherries, and none of the hygrometric state of the atmosphere. Mr. McIvor spoke to me of the density of the atmosphere, but I fear that he must have misapplied the term, as barometric records, the index of the density of the air, are not of the slightest value with reference to vegetation, except when they are made for the purpose of determining the altitudes of mountains. The climate of the Neilgherries partakes of the nature of that of the plains by which it is surrounded. Of these, the Carnatic on the east receives the shortest and irregular north-east monsoon in November and December, the Neilgherries receiving a few passing showers in some parts, the north-eastern slopes receiving more than those further removed, while in some portions rain scarcely falls at all during this monsoon. The greater portion of December and the whole of the months of January, February, March, and April are very dry. In May, only a few showers occur, and now and then there is a day of heavy rain. The rainfall at Ootacamund from the 1st November to the end of May, from the average of seven years' observation, amounts to only 14 inches. Small as this amount is, in order to prevent errors, it is necessary to state that during seven years, only one inch of rain fell in December, while not a drop was recorded for the three following months. During this period irrigation is absolutely necessary in the coffee plantations, especially on the eastern aspect of the hills, and even in the Wynaad on the moist side. The south-west monsoon, commencing in June, blows with great violence along the western coast of India, and extends to the western slopes of the Neilgherries and to the Koondahs. Its greatest force is spent on the western crest of the plateau and the hills rising from it, so that comparatively little rain occurs towards the centre of the table-land, though the atmosphere is very moist. Hardly any rain passes over the Neilgherries to the Carnatic. During the remaining five months of the year, about 22 inches of rain fall, making up almost 48 inches on an average of seven years' observation at Ootacamund. We have thus the climate of the Neilgherries, as regards rainfall and moisture in the atmosphere, divided into two periods; a long one of comparative drought with 13 inches of rain occurring in its two last months, with one inch distributed over the other four; second, a period shorter than the previous one, during

during which rain falls with comparative regularity and abundance during five months, to the amount of 22 inches at Ootacamund. The temperature of the Neilgherries, like that of all hilly countries, varies from mere local causes. In a low marshy valley on a clear night in December or January, when radiation is excessive, I have seen the thermometer sink even to 24 Fahr., while a self-registering minimum thermometer which I had placed on the Dodabett Hill, nearly 1,000 feet higher, and partly shaded by trees, recorded only 31 degrees. These cold nights are followed by days of comparatively great heat, the thermometer rising to 60 and 61 degrees, giving a range of 37 degrees for the lower localities, and almost 28 degrees for the higher and drier ones. Through the clear atmosphere which exists at this dry season, the sun shines with great power; so great, that on one occasion my black bulb thermometer, placed in the full sunshine, at 11 a.m., rose to 177 degrees. The dryness of the air during these seven months is also very great, my hygrometers (dry and wet bulb thermometers) indicated 11 deg. 9 min. as the dew point. Records of the temperature and rain-fall at Ootacamund observed during a series of years are published in Mr. Smoult's edition of Dr. Baikie's Memoir on the Neilgherries. These tables give a maximum temperature of 76 degrees, a minimum of 31 degrees, and a mean annual temperature of 56 deg. 5 min. The conclusion from these data is that Ootacamund possesses a very equable climate. The locality where these observations were made must have been one of the most favourable in Ootacamund, as I recorded much lower temperatures than any observed either by Dr. Baikie or Mr. Ross, and that too without my having chosen the coldest spot in Ootacamund. During the short time I remained in Ootacamund, I was able to make a very few observations on the temperature and humidity of the air, and those I succeeded in obtaining were most carefully made with good instruments. The instruments I had with me were two good self-registering minimum thermometers, an excellent thermometer by Greiner of Berlin, and a very delicate one by Newman, and a second less delicate one by the same well-known maker. I also used a mountain thermometer by Newman, graduated to fifths of a degree. This I used as a black bulb thermometer. My hygrometer was constructed from a thermometer by Greiner, and another by Newman.

METEOROLOGICAL OBSERVATIONS AT OOTACAMUND.

Minimum Temperature on Grass at Ootacamund.		Of the Air at 7 A.M.	Of the Air at 10 A.M.	Of the Air at 2 P.M.	Of the Air at 6 P.M.	Of the Air at 10 P.M.	Humidity of the Air from Three Observations.
22 December 1861	16° Fahr. - - -	34°	53°·5	60°·3	47°	33°·5	0°·668
23 December „	Minimum 3 feet above the ground, 24° Fahr. -	- -	- -	59	- -	28	—
24 December „	Minimum 3 feet above the ground, 14° Fahr.	26	—	—	—	—	—

On the night of the 24th December:—*Eucalypti*, a few acacias from Australia, roses, geraniums, fuchsias, and many other soft-wooded garden plants, were destroyed; besides several indigenous shrubs, such as *Berberis Nepalensis* and *Aristata* and *Lobelia excelsa*, were blackened by the frost. At an elevation 600 feet higher than the compound, where the above observations were made, the air felt drier and warmer, and this was confirmed by the thermometer, which at noon stood at 60 deg., while the humidity of the atmosphere was only 0·417, or nearly absolutely dry.

8. This short sketch of the climate of the Neilgherries is applicable to all the central portions of these hills. The slopes present considerable differences, according to their exposure; but their climates vary only in the quantity of rain that falls during the monsoon. Thus while Ootacamund receives only 48 inches of rain (or 63 inches according to some) in the year, and the average rain-fall over the Neilgherries is about 90 inches, the Koondahs, which receive the full force of the south-west monsoon, are stated to have a rain-fall of 250 inches. All, however, possess the marked dry season of the year. This dryness of the air

air and soil would not exist if the Neilgherries were more elevated. Mountains covered with perpetual snow have constant sources of moisture from the amount of evaporation given off by the snow as well as from the perennial streams that have their origin in the melting snow.

9. *Botany of the Neilgherries.*—The vegetation of the Neilgherries wants greatly the luxuriant character of the temperate forests of the Himalaya. The trees above the crest of the plateau accordingly partake more of the character of brushwood than forest. The trees existing in the "sholas" and filling up the ravines are rather scattered; they are generally slow-growing species, and apparently of great age. Their trunks are short, much branched and gnarled; most of them are evergreens, with hard leathery smooth shining leaves, adapted for withstanding a dry cold climate, where extremes of heat and cold are found. With them, and forming the undergrowth, there occur annuals springing up at the commencement of the rains, flowering soon, and fruiting before the dry weather commences. With these annuals, plants with perennial roots and rapid growing succulent stems are mingled. In the warmer forests, such as those below the western and north-western crests of the plateau, the forest after November is almost impenetrable, from the intricate way in which those dried-up stems of these plants are entwined. This state of rest indicates an absence of that important character of the South American cinchona forests mentioned by most travellers, and also by Mr. Markham—continuous vegetation. The period of rest which occurs in the vegetation of the Neilgherries is entirely owing to the long continued drought. It does not occur in South America nor in Java, because these countries possess a perpetually humid climate, and it exists only slightly in the moist sub-tropical forests of Sikkim. The common trees of the Neilgherries sholas are *Michelia Nilagirica, Myristica Malabarica* (in forests up to 5,500 feet), *Cleyera, Gymnanthera* and *Gordonia obtusa, Stemonurus fœtidus;* one or two species of *Microtropis, Photinia Notoniana;* two species of *Eugenia* and *Cinnamomum.* The brushwood consists of a few *Aralias, Turpinia Nepalensis, Berberis Nepalensis,* and *B. aristata Celastrineæ* and *Rhamnaceæ, Pittosporum tetraspermum, Leguminoseæ;* one or two *Melastomacæ, Rubiaceæ,* belonging to the genera *Wendlandia, Canthium, Lasianthus, Coffea, Grumelia, Psychotria.* A few large *Vernoniæ* are also frequent; *Acanthaceæ* have gregarious species, such as *Phelobhyllum, Stenosiphonium Russellianum;* several species of *Strobilanthus,* principally of the old section, *Endopogon; Barleria,* and several species of *Thunbergia,* all climbers. The large *Lobelia excelsa* is very abundant everywhere. Two species of *Vaccinia* and one of *Gaultheria* are rather common shrubs. The gnarled trunks of *Rhododendron arboreum* distinguish it as one of the slowest growing of the Neilgherry trees. In warmer woods, a species of *Calamus* is common, and with it tree ferns of no great size occur, but only in the moistest hollows. A few epiphytic orchids are common on the branches of trees in the less elevated forests below the crest of the range. Among the species I observed at Neddiwattum were *Pholidota bimricata,* a little *Bolbophyllum,* a species of *Trias, Eria Dalzellii, Dendrobium Microchilon,* with *Eria Mysorensis* in the lower parts. A strange pellate-bulbed *Dendrobium, D. Microbullon* was rather common, closely adpressed to the bark of the trees. The large luxuriant sections of *Dendrobium, Cymbidium* and *Vandas,* as well as the large perennial terrestrial orchids of the moist Java forests, are entirely absent. Hygroscopic ferns, Lycopodia and mosses, indicatives of the dry and wet seasons of these mountains, covered the branches of the trees. At the season I was there they were dried and shrivelled up in all the forests I visited, except where they were moistened by the spray of small cascades. *Tremantodon Schmidii cuneifolius, Dicranum albescens* and *densum; Tortula Orthodonta, Fumaria connivens;* one or two species of *Philonotis, Neckera flabellata, Æqualifolia Arcuans,* and *parvula;* also a moss, detected by Mr. M'Ivor, *Stereodon Ivoreanus,* are those occurring among a host of other species.

10. Any sites for the permanent cinchona plantations in such a country want, therefore, that important condition of a perpetually moist climate all the year round. With the exception of one, the sites that have been chosen are certainly the most favourable localities that could be found in the Neilgherries. The Dodabetta site seems to me to be very unsuitable, and this opinion, based first on the printed reports of Mr. Markham, Dr. M'Pherson, and Mr. M'Ivor, was quite confirmed when I visited it. Its elevation is too great for any species but

C. lancifolia

C. lancifolia and *C. micrantha*, and for them I consider it too dry. It is situated behind and joins on to the Government gardens, and extends from 7,830 feet to 7,950 feet above the sea; it is of small extent, containing only about 50 acres, and some acres must be deducted from this in computing the available ground on account of the rock cropping out through the soil as well as the steep declivities of some parts. Mr. M'Ivor, who seems to have chosen this locality, and who has recommended Government to spend a considerable sum of money in cutting down the bushes and making footpaths through the wood, has evidently formed a very erroneous idea of its climate. Thus Mr. M'Ivor informed me that the rain-fall was 80 inches, which must be an error, as not half a mile off 48 inches are given by Dr. Baikie and Mr. Ross as the rain-fall, while 63 inches is the maximum I can find for Ootacamund, and that probably refers to the summit of Dodabetta, where the observatory was placed. Mr. M'Ivor showed me a spot in this ravine where he told me that I would find the climate "perfectly moist," and that it was the dampest part of the shola, and so it also seemed to me to be, but my hygrometer indicated 15 degrees between the wet and dry bulbs, or a humidity of only 0·417, saturation being indicated by 1·000. During nearly every day in December and January the thermometer must fall to nearly the freezing point, for at the place indicated by Mr. M'Ivor as the warmest and moistest in the site, my minimum fell on the night of the 23d December to 31 degrees, and there were many colder nights than this even during my short stay in the Neilgherries. I found nearly all the residents of Ootacamund judging of frost merely by the presence of hoar frost. The existence of hoar frost of course is ample proof that the thermometer has at least reached the freezing point, but as hoar frost is merely frozen dew depending on the presence of moisture in the air, its absence does not show that a low degree of cold has not occurred. Accordingly, where my thermometer indicated 31 degrees there was no hoar frost, although the thermometer was one degree below the point at which hoar frost is formed. The humidity of the air at 7 a.m. on the 23d in this shola was only 0·747. It is much to be regretted that no observations of any value were made in this ravine before choosing it as a site for cultivating cinchonas; it seems to have been chosen during the rainy season when the climate all over the hills is moist. I visited the Neddiwattum site a few days after my arrival at Ootacamund, and I spent three days at the Neddiwattum bungalow, for the purpose of examining the site more leisurely. I made a series of observations on the temperature and humidity of the air which show only such differences between those made at Ootacamund as are the result of the lower elevation. This forest is of considerable extent, stretching from the crest of the plateau at 5,800 feet to much below the open cinchona nursery in the centre of the forest, about 4,500 feet elevation. Some of the trees are of considerable size, though the majority are small both in height and thickness of stem, and I saw almost none above 70 feet in height. *Sterculia guttata*, *Michelia Nilagirica* and *Myristica Malabarica* were among the loftiest I observed. The vegetation generally presented very markedly the usual characteristics of a region where the year is divided into a wet and a dry season. The forest was choked up by dried remains of the vigorous vegetation of the past rainy season, consisting principally of *Strobilanthes viscosus*, *lupulinus*, *Heyneanus* and allied species of *Acanthaceæ*. The mosses and most of the ferns were dried up, and in a state of rest. The days were clear with bright powerful sunshine, and the atmosphere very dry; the nights were cloudless, and from the great radiation, the cold towards morning was always very intense; the thermometer, above 6,000 feet, falling generally to the freezing part in open spots. The thick banks of mist which collected every night over the Wynaad coffee plantations never ascended above 2,500 feet, and in the morning they were dissipated by the powerful rays of the sun.

11. Of the climate at the other periods of the year I could only judge by the reports from the residents in the hills. All agreed in one statement, that the climate becomes excessively dry in February, March, and April, and that comparatively no rain falls for five or six months, while during the four months from the beginning of June until the end of September, the moisture is abundant. At this site above 50 acres of forest have been cleared from trees, and it is further intended to trench this extent of land with the view of preparing it for a plantation of cinchona without shade. Such a procedure is quite opposed to

to all we know of the habits of the genus, as well as the opinion of so great an authority as Weddell, as well as the experience of the Dutch in Java. Until we know that the cinchonas will succeed in the Neilgherries under conditions as similar as possible to those in which they are found in South America, such a proposed mode of cultivation as I have alluded to above, seems to me to be very premature. Neither will there be any medium between perfect success and complete failure, and all the probabilities point to the latter result as the most probable.

12. The following few, but very carefully made meteorological observations, were noted during my visit to the Neddiwattum site:—

25th December.—Temperature of air at the Neddiwattum Cinchona Nursery at 1.30 p.m., 60 deg. 5 min.; at 6 p.m. 53. of soil in shade, and three inches below surface, 55; humidity of the air at 1.30 p.m. 0·632. At Neddiwattum Bungalow, at 5,800 feet elevation, the temperature of air at 8 p.m., 53 deg.

26th December.—At the Bungalow at 6 a.m., 34 deg. 5 min. In sheltered spot under trees at 7 a.m., 40 deg.; at the open Nursery a minimum thermometer exposed all night, 39 deg.; at 7.30 a.m. in open air, 41 deg.; under trees, 50 deg.; temperature of air at Bungalow at 11 a.m., 61 deg.; humidity of the air at Bungalow at 11 a.m., 0·596; humidity of air close to a stream in the forest adjoining the Bungalow, noon, 0·708; temperature of air at Bungalow at 10.30 p.m., 47 deg. 5 min.

27th December.—Temperature of air at Bungalow at 6 a.m., 35 deg.; at the cinchona nursery by minimum, 42 deg. Greatest daily variation observed at the nursery, 21 deg. 5 min.

13. Arguing from these observations, the open cinchona nurseries at nearly 5,000 feet are too high for *Cinchona succirubra*, but as regards temperature they are very suitable for *Cinchona Calisaya*, *C. nitida*, and perhaps *C. Peruviana*, and probably one or two degrees too warm for *C. micrantha* and *C. lancifolia*. The other site was at the Avalanche Bungalow, but as no planting will be commenced there for some years, it is quite unnecessary to enter into details concerning it. The result of my personal observation, as well as of my inquiries, satisfied me that there is an abundance of localities of the above character obtainable in the Neilgherries for the cultivation of the less temperate species of cinchona, such as *C. succirubra*, *C. Calisaya* and probably *C. nitida* and *Peruviana*, as well as *C. Pahudiana*. For the temperate species, of which we now possess *C. micrantha* and *C. lancifolia*, and among which *C. Peruviana* may require to be classed, the higher portions of the Neilgherries, though cold enough, are too deficient in moisture and continuous forest to allow of their being successfully cultivated. For such temperate species, that will almost withstand a slight fall of snow, we must look for a proper home in the moist region of Darjeeling, and the damp deep inner valleys of eastern Kumaon. Fortunately, the largest number of plants in the Neilgherries belong to that very valuable species, *C. succirubra*, and it is that species which I am certain that from necessity, as well as choice, Mr. M'Ivor will be obliged to cultivate most extensively. The following short extracts, taken from well-known writers on the subject of cinchona, and from the reports of Messrs. Markham, Spruce, and Pritchett, will show the climatological requirements of each species:—

14. *Cinchona succirubra*, a native of the equatorial portions of the Andes, near Mount Chimborazo, from the line to two degrees south latitude. Mr. Spruce, who visited the forests on more than one occasion, says that the tree is found at the base of the mountain, and that some of the lands formerly occupied by this species are now cleared for the cultivation of sugar-cane. His observations show it to be the most tropical of all the species of quiniferous cinchonas. The climate, as described by Mr. Spruce, is exceedingly moist; even in July, one of the dry months, there was "a great deal of mist and fog;" rudimentary lichens formed on the seed capsules of *C. succirubra*, a striking proof of the humidity of the weather. The elevation of the forest is 3,000 feet above the sea, and the mean temperature from the 19th June until the 27th September, is a small decimal less than 68 deg. The minimum temperature observed was 59 deg. 32 min., and the maximum 80 deg. 5 min. The temperature of the earth at two feet under the ground, 68 deg. 5 min. During the period of these observations the

sun

sun is north of the line, so that probably the summer is two degrees warmer, which would raise the mean annual temperature to nearly 70 degrees. In a letter to Sir W. Hooker, dated the 20th October 1859, Mr. Spruce has entered fully into the botany of the forests of the western slopes of the Quitenian Andes, where *C. succirubra* is found, so that I am enabled to form an opinion of the character of the flora existing along with *C. succirubra*. He says, "The Cascarilla roja (the Spanish name of *C. succirubra*) seems to grow best on stony declivities, where there is, however, a good depth of humus, and at an altitude of from 3,000 to 5,000 feet above the sea. The temperature is very much that of a summer day in London,* though towards evening each day cold mists blow down the valley from Azuay, and for five months in the year, from January to May, there is almost unceasing rain. To prove further the tropical character of *C. succirubra*, several species of palm are found along with it. These are, two species of *Phytelephus*, or irony palm, a species of *Carludovica*, a species common on the Amazon; *Triplaris Surinamensis* was also very abundant. "In general, the arborescent vegetation seemed scanty in species and uninteresting. There were also a few figs, and on the steep declivities there were patches of low forest, consisting chiefly of *Clusiæ*, *Thibawdiæ*, and *Melastomaceæ*. Two small *Trichomanes* crept along the branches of shrubs, but terrestrial ferns were all but absent."

From what I have observed of this species both in the Royal Gardens at Kew, where the seeds germinate in the propagating house with a temperature of 78 deg. for the day, and 10 or 12 degrees colder by night, from the fact that none of the seedlings of this species raised in Calcutta last March, have suffered in the least degree, and from the temperature of the glass houses at Ootacamund, in which the species succeeds admirably, ranging from 55 deg. at night to 78 and 80 deg. for the maxima, I am convinced that *C. succirubra* is a very tropical species. The nurseries at the Neddiwattum site are therefore too high, as they are situated at what will prove to be the upper limit of the successful cultivation of this plant, and the patches of forests cleared for the young plants are still 500 feet higher. Mr. M'Ivor has placed out in the Government garden at Ootacamund some plants of this species; when I saw them they were sickly, from being at least 2,500 feet above their highest limit.

15. *C. Calisaya* is a lofty tree of considerable thickness of stem common in the forests of Bolivia and Caravaya. Weddell says it grows in the hottest forests of Caravaya and Bolivia at an elevation of 5,000 to 6,000 feet above the sea. His account of its habit shows that it is a shade-loving tree, and he believes that the shrubby variety *C. Calisaya var. Josephiana*, is merely the result of the exposure of some plants to the influence of bright sun-light. His remarks on this subject are worth translating, especially as Mr. Markham in his extracts from Weddell's book has omitted them. He says—"I have for long thought that this variety might constitute a distinct species, but a more attentive and complete study in its native place has convinced me that it is nothing but a peculiar form of the type *C. Calisaya*, to which I have referred it. I have at the same time little doubt but that the districts which it now occupies were formerly covered with forest, and which having been destroyed, doubtless by conflagration, this plant has assumed a shrubby form, resembling in this many other plants of Brazil, which may be observed having a different proportion, according as they exist in the plains or the forest. Accordingly, it is probable that the cultivation of quinine trees will not succeed unless we apply to them the conditions necessary for the plants to raise themselves. It will be necessary always for this reason that they should have the society of other trees growing a little more rapidly than themselves, in order to afford a salutary shade during the first years of their existence." See Weddell's Histoire Naturelle des Quinquinas, p. 32.

Mr. Markham, in his report, is not very explicit in his remarks about the climate of the *Cinchona Calisaya* districts. A spot where this species grew abundantly was 5,422 feet above the sea, and at a nearly similar height the lowest temperature observed was 53 degrees and the highest 67 degrees. This was in May, corresponding in season to our month of November, and at five degrees

* Mean temperature of a day in July in London is about 68 or 70 degrees.

degrees further from the equator than Ootacamund. Even Neddiwattum, only 5,000 feet, is far too cold even for this species, and probably much too dry, according to the data of the climate of the Caravayan forests furnished by Mr. Markham, who states that the rains last for nine months.

16. I have a number of statements concerning the cinchona forests of South America, all of which describe the abundant moisture the trees delight in. It would extend this report too much to classify them under the various species we have under cultivation. To cite two of them, Weddell says of *C. micrantha*—" It grows in the shady moist woods of the mountain;" and again, " of all the cinchonas which I have studied in the living state, *C. micrantha* is the one which delights most in humid places. In the provinces of Carabaya I have met with it close to torrents. Under these circumstances, the leaves acquire a larger development there than they do in drier places."

17. Of *Cinchona lancifolia*, the same author says—" According to Humboldt, *C. lancifolia* extends high up the mountains; the upper limit of its zone is below 9,500 feet. The individuals which grow at this elevation are exposed during the cold nights to a temperature near 32° Fahrenheit." Karsten, writing generally of the best species of cinchona, says — " The scrobiculate-leaved cinchona, rich in alkaloids, inhabits the misty region of the Andes, where, in the nine months' rainy season, the constant rain is only interrupted in the day by interchanging sun rays and fog clouds; whilst in the season corresponding with winter, cold nights, in which the temperature sinks, and the dark azure sky is lighted by the glittering brilliancy of innumerable stars, follow days in which the rays of the sun, warming the atmosphere to 76 degrees, now and then penetrate the thick fog which lies almost constantly on the damp foliage of the forest. The average temperature of this region is from 53 degrees to 55 degrees Fahrenheit."

" The less healing, generally large-leaved, unscrobiculate cinchona, occupying a more extensive district, and living in some measure in common with the Ladenbergia genus, is more rarely refreshed by falling showers and rising fogs in the dry season, when it has to bear a temperature rising to 96 degrees, whilst in winter it falls to 40 degrees of heat in the morning, and rain generally follows the sunny morning hours, from midday to midnight only."

The cinchona,* with the small fruit, scrobiculate leaves, and rich in alkaloids, is confined to 11 degrees north and south of the centre point of the district of Loxa. It descends only to a height of 6,500 feet above the sea, from the cold summits of the mostly snow-capped mountains, where it sometimes reaches the upper limits of the growth of trees, *i.e.* 11,500 English feet.

18. Mr. Pritchett, referring to the forests of Huanaco, where *Cinchona nitida*, *C. micrantha*, and *C. Peruviana* are found, says—" On the forest side the vapour and cloud are continually bathing the woods, which seem at this spot to be the perpetual focus for the converging clouds. At one time, a raging tempest of rain and wind; at another, the calm, tranquil, leaden atmosphere of chilling cloud and fog."

" Although it was then about the middle of the dry season, heavy soaking rains were still falling from day to day. Towards the latter part of July the weather broke up, and the sun began to make impression on the solid banks of clouds that filled the valleys. Though clouds were the prevalent visitants during this so-called dry season, there were occasions during some portions of the day when the sun unveiled, and even penetrated to the very underwood of the forest. But even to the last day of my remaining here, when we had nearly a fortnight's fine weather, with only an occasional shower, the tracks were still deep with mud, and only in the exposed situations could the mud be found less than ankle-deep." " The climate of these districts is essentially moist and warm."

19. I am indebted to Mr. M'Ivor for the following tabular statement of the number of species and plants of cinchona in the Neilgherries on the 31st December 1861 :—

REPORT

* *C. micrantha*, Ring et Paron.

REPORT on the Number and Condition of the Cinchona Plants in the Government Gardens at Ootacamund and Neddiwuttum on the 31st December 1861.

NAMES.	Number of Plants.	Value per lb. of dry bark in the London market.
		s. d. s. d.
1. Cinchona succirubra	5,200	2 6 to 8 9
2. Cinchona Calisaya	59	2 10 to 5 0
3. Cinchona lancifolia	4	1 8 to 2 10
4. Cinchona nitida	1,050	1 8 to 2 9
5. Cinchona sp. without name	314	1 8 to 2 10
6. Cinchona micrantha	1,497	1 8 to 2 9
7. Cinchona Peruviana	64	1 8 to 2 10
8. Cinchona Pahudiana of Howard	425	No value.
TOTAL Number of Plants	8,618	

(signed) *W. M'Ivor.*

The plants brought by me from Ootacamund require to be deducted from this statement to give the actual number of plants that were in the Neilgherries when I left on 4th January.

20. The following statement gives the number of cinchona plants in the Botanic Gardens, Calcutta, on the 1st February, arranged according to the species and under sources whence I obtained them. The plants are in very good health, and *Cinchona succirubra, C. Calisaya* and *C. Pahudiana* are growing most vigourously, and seeds *C. Pahudiana* are coming up daily :—

TABLE showing the Number of each Species of Cinchona in the Botanic Gardens, Calcutta, on the 19th January 1862.

Name of Species.	From Ootacamund.	Raised in Botanic Gardens, Calcutta.	From Java.	Total.
C. succirubra, Pav.	87	4	- - -	91
C. Calisaya, Wedd.	- - -	- - -	6	6
C. nitida, R. et P.	56	11	- - -	67
C. micrantha, R. et P.	43	13	- - -	56
C. Peruviana, Howd.	4	1	- - -	5
C. Pahudiana, Howd.	- - -	- - -	59	59
C. sp. Ignot	3	2	- - -	5
	193	31	65	
GRAND TOTAL of Plants of Cinchona in the Botanic Gardens, Calcutta				289

21. I would recommend the following plan as the best that could be pursued with the view of introducing the cinchona into the mountain ranges of the Bengal Presidency.

By my possessing plants of all the species of cinchona that have as yet been introduced into India and Java, the experiment is in reality a year in advance of the time when I obtained permission to commence the cultivation in the Khasia hills. I then intended to commence operations with only *Cinchona Calisaya, C. succirubra* and *C. Pahudiana,* of all of which I had specimens, and I had then no hope of obtaining the large supply of the other three species which I have since then received. If I should have obtained these additional species next year, I would then have recommended the extension of the cultivation to the Darjeeling ranges. This I consider must be done this year, in preference to commencing in the Khasia hills, where sites for the temperate species cannot be found. I would therefore request permission, under the orders of the Government of India, to proceed with all the cinchona plants to Darjeeling, immediately after the expiration of my duties as professor of botany and examiner in medicine in the middle of March. It will be necessary to secure the services of a European gardener or overseer,

overseer, to remain in charge of the cinchona nursery at Darjeeling, and to act under my orders. I would instruct such a person in all the details of propagating, as practised so successfully by Mr. M'Ivor, and also in such parts of the Dutch system as seem to me worthy of imitation. I should further commence at once to prepare to test the value of Dr. DeVrij's suggestion, by allowing a sufficient number of seedlings of *C. Pahudiana* to grow rapidly in a warm site, with the intention of destroying them after three years for the sake of their roots. This I shall be able to do as I possess about 400,000 seeds of *C. Pahudiana*. One of my first steps at Darjeeling would be to obtain at least 1,000 acres of suitable land on the lower and outer ranges of Darjeeling. After selecting such a spot, a house would require to be built for the accommodation of the European gardener, also a propagating house after the model of the last one built at Ootacamund, expressly for the propagation of cinchona, a plan of which I possess, also a hut for two or three native gardeners from the Botanic Gardens, Calcutta. If such a plan should be sanctioned, I can safely promise that after 12 months there will be cinchona plants enough in Darjeeling to commence a nursery for the more tropical species in the Khasia hills, besides supplying the Dutch next November with the plants promised to them. With the assistance of a propagating house, *Cinchona succirubra* will be increased in 10 months by 500 per cent., while without such aid, perhaps an increase of only 20 per cent. will be the result. The larger the scale on which this cultivation is commenced, the greater will be the return, and the sooner the yield of quinine. The aim ought to be to throw the greatest quantity of quinine into use in the shortest space of time possible. This can only be effected by taking full advantage of the high state of perfection to which English gardeners have carried artificial propagation until we possess seed-bearing trees, and by the scientific superintendence of the whole experiment, and most especially of the selection of sites for each species. If this plan is sanctioned, I would solicit that the following estimate of the probable expenditure for the next year be favourably considered, and further that I may be allowed to engage the services of a European gardener without delay. For such a person a salary of 150 rupees a month, and a dwelling house (or an equivalent until a house could be built,) would be sufficient for the first year, but to secure a good and trustworthy man, it will be necessary to promise an increase to 200 rupees a month after the first year:—

Approximate Estimate for the Expenditure of the proposed Cinchona Plantation in the Bengal Presidency for the Year commencing 1st April 1862.

	Rs.	*a.*	*p.*
Salary of one European gardener at 150 rupees per mensem -	1,800	–	–
Two native gardeners at 14 and 12 rupees each per mensem -	312	–	–
15 coolies at 5 rupees each per mensem - - - - -	900	–	–
My travelling expenses to and from Darjeeling - - -	500	–	–
Travelling expenses of the gardener to Darjeeling - - -	200	–	–
Transport to Darjeeling from Calcutta 14 Wardian cases containing cinchona plants - - - - - - - - -	300	–	
Travelling expenses of two native gardeners from Calcutta to Darjeeling - - - - - - - - - - - -	50	–	
Building a propagating house, with apparatus for heating the house, as per detailed estimate and plan - - - - -	2,500	–	–
Total - - *Rs.*	6,562	–	–
10 per cent. on the total amount to allow for contingencies -	656	4	–
Grand Total - - - *Rs.*	7,218	4	–

(signed) *Thomas Anderson.*

— No. 95. —

From *W. G. McIvor*, Esq., Superintendent Government Chinchona Plantations, Neilgherries, to *J. D. Sim*, Esq., Secretary to Government, Revenue Department, Fort St. George, Ootacamund, 9 May 1862.

Sir,

I HAVE the honour to acknowledge the receipt of the Order of Government of the 30th April 1862, No. 931, directing me to submit any observation I may wish to offer on Dr. Anderson's report to the Supreme Government, dated the 11th February 1862.

2. The successful cultivations of chinchona in India is a subject of such vast importance, that the Government will, I trust, excuse the candour and detail with which I proceed to discuss the merits of the report, as it is most important that all facts connected with this experiment be fairly and plainly represented, so that they may be understood, and duly appreciated by Government.

3. From a careful perusal of the report, the unfair manner in which the condition and prospects of our experiment is depreciated, combined with the disparagement of the great success and exertions of Mr. Markham, and the various discrepancies which the evasion of these facts necessitate, renders the object and meaning of the report difficult to be understood. Although the time which has elapsed since the report was written is comparatively short, nevertheless it has been sufficient to place Dr. Anderson in the position of offering arguments and opinions against developed facts, as our plants in the open air have now passed through the whole of this unusually dry and cold season, not only without injury, but they have, during the whole time, preserved the finest possible state of health, many hundreds of them having made shoots in this so-called fatal season of from 9 to 12 inches.

4. It is endeavoured to be shown, at page 4, paragraph 8, of the report under review, that our plants on the Neilgherries, from being artificially propagated, cannot bear the risks of a long journey; or, in other words, that they are more delicate than the Java seedlings, which Dr. Anderson had frequently seen "die after only touching the leaves on one occasion." Our young plants are subjected to as much handling as ordinary forest trees in an English nursery, and that they are better suited to bear a journey, is established by the results described by Dr. Anderson, who, in the first instance, states that "of those I brought the short journey from the Neilgherries to this, I lost nearly 10 per cent., while the plants from Java, which were seedlings, can hardly be said to have suffered at all." But this is an exaggeration of the losses with our plants, as at paragraph 4, Dr. Anderson informs us that "about 13 plants, out of 204, the entire number received, have been seriously damaged; the remainder, in the present genial climate of Calcutta, have quite recovered, and are as healthy as they were at Ootacamund." And again, at page 25, paragraph 20, Dr. Anderson states that 193 of the plants from Ootacamund were "growing most vigorously" on the 11th February, 1862; it thus appears that the loss of the plants from Ootacamund was less than 5½ per cent. The number of plants which Dr. Anderson delivered at Ootacamund, compared with those which he retained in the Calcutta Botanical Garden, and the number he originally received from Java, shows that the loss in transit of the Java plants was fully three times as much as the loss sustained on the plants he took from Ootacamund.

5. Another instance of extraordinary disparagement occurs at page 14, paragraph 4. where Dr. Anderson states, "I maintain that the successful rearing of the cinchonas in the greenhouses at Ootacamund is no more a proof that the climate of the Neilgherries is adapted for their cultivation than the fact that many thousands of seedlings, as well as cuttings, are now existing in perfect health in the chinchona nursery at Kew, would lead us to expect that the plants will grow in the open air in England." This sentence conveys, as Dr. Anderson must be well aware, the most erroneous impression that can possibly be conceived, because in England the difference between summer and winter precludes the possibility of chinchonas ever being grown there; but how different is this climate, our extreme variation between summer and winter, taken from the observation of T. G. Taylor, Esq., made at Dodabetta, for 10 years, shows the extreme variation of temperature here

here to be 25·25 degrees; the variation in England in usual seasons is 43·7 degrees, and in severe winters frequently 80 degrees. Dr. Anderson was here in the depth of the most severe winter we have had for 25 years, and the greatest cold that has ever been registered on the Neilgherries occurred at that time; yet, notwithstanding, Dr. Anderson saw hundreds of plants turned out daily into the nurseries in the open air at Neddivattum, without sustaining the slightest damage. Moreover, Dr. Anderson also saw six plants of different species, which had been placed out in September last in a cleared spot in the highest and coldest part of the Neddivattum site, which, at the time he saw them (December), all the species were in the finest possible state of health, although they had then passed through the coldest part of the season.

6. Dr. Anderson, in page 13, paragraph 3, shows that he was quite conversant with the object of our plants being placed in the glass-houses,* and states this to be "the wisest plan that could have been adopted," and it is unaccountable why this advantageous system of cultivation should have been in the very next paragraph converted into the means to impress upon the Government the very erroneous idea that the climate of the Neilgherries is as unsuited to the cultivation of cinchonas as the climate of England. I cannot pass over without remarking the rather confusing discrepancies in the report with reference to the sites. At page 3, paragraph 5, Dr. Anderson states, that "all the sites that Mr. M'Ivor had selected were carefully visited; their geology, meteorology, and botany, examined, and their characteristics noted." And again, at page 14, paragraph 3, while speaking of our plants, Dr. Anderson states, "they have been placed under these circumstances for two reasons—in the first instance, from there being no one in the Neilgherries who could point out the sites on those mountains best adapted for receiving the plants, and thus they were considered to be safer under the protection of a glass-house." And again, at page 14, paragraph 4, "the great difference that exists between the climates of the South American chinchona forests and the Neilgherries ought to have received greater attention than it has, and in the selecting of sites convenience of access from Ootacamund should have been made subservient to the greater consideration of climate." Also in page 19, paragraph 10, "with the exception of one, the sites that have been chosen are certainly the most favourable localities that could be found in the Neilgherries." I submit that the information which Dr. Anderson possessed did not justify the remarks above quoted, as Dr. Anderson was aware that all the sites were either selected or approved by gentlemen who had visited the chinchona forest of South America, and made a careful comparison of our climate with that of the chinchona regions of the Andes. And on reflection Dr. Anderson must admit that this gave their opinions infinitely greater weight than his own, which was necessarily formed on descriptions he had read of the climate of the Andes, as Dr. Anderson never visited the chinchona regions; and he cannot hold that reading a description of a subject can convey a more correct conviction than personal observations and experience. We all know how liable we are to misconceive and misapply a fact we have read or heard described, and that Dr. Anderson is not beyond the liability of falling into this error is illustrated at page 22, paragraph 14, of his report, where he quotes what Mr. Spence describes as the seriously damaging effect of wet weather on the plants to be a condition highly favourable and necessary for their development. It is plain to the most ordinary reader that Mr. Spence, from page 2 to 4 of his report of the 12th October 1860, speaks of the unusually damp season on the Andes as being likely to frustrate his undertakings, which, in his own words, was only rendered successful when, "towards the end of July, the weather took up, and in a few sunny days the capsules made visible advances towards maturity." Any one reading the severe losses of 1860, owing

* Mr. McIvor to Secretary to Government, 9th May 1861, No. 59, paragraph 11:—"The plants brought out by Mr. Cross have been transplanted in our glass-houses, and are now favourably progressing in the process technically termed 'hardening off.' By this process they will in a few weeks be able to bear exposure without injury, and although they could then be transplanted in the Neddivattum site without the loss of a single plant, I would consider it very unadvisable to put them there, because a few plants put out into an immense forest swarming with wild animals would be liable to be entirely destroyed in one night, however well they may be fenced. Moreover, it is of the utmost importance that all the original plants be retained here, as this would greatly facilitate their propagation, and give us a stock of plants in 14 or 15 months, which otherwise could not be had for many years."

owing to the wet harvest, would not have fallan into a more serious error had he conceived that a wet harvest was highly beneficial, by causing the crops of grain to grow and rot in the ear.

7. Dr. Anderson endeavours to depreciate Mr. Markham's success and exertions to an extent which the facts of the case do not justify; with reference to the charge set forth of this gentleman's "ignorance of botany and science generally," the result of Mr. Markham's expedition entirely rejects. The cinchona seeds which Dr. Anderson himself brought to India were the produce of Mr. Markham's expedition, many hundreds of plants in Ceylon and Jamaica are the produce of the same; and we now on the Neilgherries possess upwards of 30,000 plants of nine of the most valuable species of chinchona,* all the result of Mr. Markham's exertions. In short, the success has been such as never before to be equalled by any endeavour on record to import plants; and, are we to believe this success to be the result of chance, directed by ignorance? Dr. Anderson might have been consistent, and instead of taking all the credit of conveying the plants from Java, to himself, he should have conferred it on the native gardener who accompanied him. Not only was Mr. Markham qualified to carry the importation of the plants with which he was entrusted to its present successful issue, but that gentlemen gave much further proof of his ability by affording such information and observations as has secured the successful management of the plants after their introduction. The correctness of this is now well established, for those who have attended to Mr. Markham's observations on the management of the plants have met with great success: while those who have either neglected or despised his theory, have met with comparative failure; and this indeed is the case with Dr. Anderson, who raised from Mr. Markham's seeds in the early part of last year, "about 80 seedlings," and the table given at paragraph 20 of his report, shows that these had decreased on the 11th February last to 31.

8. At page 11, paragraph 12, Dr. Anderson observes that "in concluding this general account of what I observed in Java, I may state that I was greatly impressed with the advantage in every way of having so important an experiment directly under scientific superintendence." It is difficult to trace the facts which made this impression on Dr. Anderson's mind; none capable of doing so are described in his report, nor are they to be found in the results of the Java experiment; but the contrary, for we find that the scientific gentlemen in charge of the operations in Java (perhaps through ignorance, or perhaps because the plant was hardy and grew rapidly) cultivated to a large extent, and at great cost an entirely worthless species of chinchona, to which they had erroneously attached the name of a valuable sort; these gentlemen were unable to discover their error, and unwilling to admit it when first pointed out; but now the fact has been indisputably established by the examination and analysis of Mr. Howard, both of specimens and bark from the Java plant, and also of the same species from its natural locality on the Andes. Again referring to paragraph 2 of Dr. Anderson's report, it appears Dr. Junghuhn has, in another instance, erroneously attached the name of *C. succirubra* to another worthless sort. Even in India we have examples of folly of this sort, which exceeds that of Java. An eminent

* LIST of the Number and Species of Chinchona Plants in Cultivation on the Neilgherries, on the 30th April 1862.

Botanical Names.	Commercial Names.	Number of Plants.	Value in the London Market, per lb. of dry Bark.	REMARKS.
			s. d. s. d.	
1. Chinchona succirubra - -	Red bark - - -	14,450	2 6 to 8 9	All in fine health.
2. Ditto - Calisaya - -	Yellow bark - -	237	2 10 to 7 –	Do. do.
3. C. Condaminea Var, Uritusinga	Original loxa bark -	1	2 10 to 7 –	Unhealthy.
4. C. Condaminea Var, Chahaurguera	Rusty crown bark - -	8,000	2 10 to 7 –	All in fine health.
5. C. Condaminea Var, Crespilla -	Fine crown bark - -	105	2 10 to 6 –	Do. do.
6. C. lancifolia from Java - -	Crown bark - - -	1	1 8 to 2 10	Unhealthy, affected by fungi.
7. C. nitida - - - -	Genuine grey bark -	2,922	1 8 to 2 9	All in fine health.
8. C. Species without name - -	Fine grey bark - -	1,211	1 8 to 2 10	Do. do.
9. C. micrantha - - -	Grey bark - - -	3,786	1 8 to 2 9	Do. do.
10. C. Peruviana - - -	Finest grey bark - -	357	1 8 to 2 10	Do. do.
11. Pahudiana from Java - -	Unknown - - -	425	Worthless.	—
	TOTAL No. of Plants - - -	31,495		

eminent medical gentleman of the Bombay service attached the name of *C. succirubra* to the wild Brinjal or *Solanum giganteum*, and so successfully, that the Governor of that province was induced to visit, and to express himself highly gratified by the appearance of the young Brinjal plantation which the medical gentleman in charge had honoured by the designation of *C. succirubra*. But it cannot be facts of this natnre in which the advantage of scientific superintendence was made plain to Dr. Anderson. It is true that at page 11, paragraph 11, an "important" discovery of Dr. De Vrij is detailed, namely, that "in the roots of a tree of *C. Pahudiana*, only two years old, there was no wood with bark formed, but the herbaceous stem yielded nine hundredths of a grain of quinine," or a quantity so infinitely small that it cannot be comprehended: 480 grains make one ounce, this gives 5,330 trees to produce an ounce of quinine; at 25 feet apart, the distance the plants are placed in Java, this number will cover upwards of 60 acres. Dr. Junghuhn estimates the cost of "labour alone," for transplanting each plant from the seed bed to the forest, at one florin; this makes the cost of the quinine 5,330 florins per ounce, or 533 *l.*; and this does not include grubbing up the roots, tending the plants for two years, &c., which would increase the cost to at least double, or 1,000*l.* per ounce, and "these important discoveries" Dr. Anderson proposes to "commence at once to prepare to test." Surely, to the mind of every man the value of this discovery is plain, except indeed it be not so to the scientific man, who views his subjects from a lofty eminence, and disdains to think for a moment of its practical value.

9. In operations of this sort a correct knowledge of the science of horticulture is very necessary, and when combined with the knowledge of the practice also, together with the powers of correct reasoning, its advantages are enormous. It enables us to receive all theories with doubt when opposed to the laws which govern vegetable life. It points out to us our own shortcomings, and suggests the means of improvement. When matters go wrong it enables us to trace the true cause and apply proper remedy. But we have no record of the success of science, combined with practical ignorance, in this form, alas! science has ruined hundreds of men possessed of great energy and talent.

10. It was to be expected that the chinchonas on their introduction to India would have to struggle against the wildest theories, in the most conflicting opinions, with reference to their cultivations; as in all ages newly imported plants of great value have suffered more or less from this cause, and from the beginning I have been anxious to mitigate this to such a degree as not seriously to retard our progress, notwithstanding we have suffered to some extent, and may still suffer. I would therefore most respectfully submit for the consideration of Government the desirableness of giving us time to develope our results prior to gentlemen being deputed to report on the position of our experiment. For unless the gentlemen so commissioned have themselves gained greater results in the cultivation of the plants than we have, together with long experience of our climate, their reports can only confuse and embarrass the Government; while they are discouraging to those intrusted with the responsible and arduous duty of bringing the experiment to a successful issue. I may mention that had a commission been deputed to visit and report on the prospects of the chinchona experiment in Java, so recently after their commencement, as Dr. Anderson was deputed to the Neilgheries after the beginning of our operations, only two sickly plants would have been found in that island. That the reports are perplexing to the Government has been well established by the matter laid before them by Dr. Macpherson, who persuaded Government that chinchona plants could not be grown, or seeds raised in our glass-houses at Ootacamund. It has long ago been admitted by all parties, that we have grown our cinchonas in the glass-houses with unequalled success; and in a few months I hesitate not to state that all parties will be compelled to admit that our cultivation in the open air is equally successful.

11. In experiments of this sort the preliminary operations are the most difficult to accomplish, because every day adds to our experience and knowledge of the nature of the plants. Our success in the preliminary operations is indisputable, and it is mere trifling to argue that we will fail in the future stages; for if we were successful when we possessed only a slight knowledge of the nature of the plants, it is only reasonable to expect that we will be more successful when our knowledge becomes perfected by long observation and practical experience.

12. The remarks on the climatological characters of the sites on the Neilgherries,

gherries, described from paragraphs 10 to 14 of Dr. Anderson's Report, are calculated to give a very erroneous impression of the climate. The only perfect meteorological table for a whole year in my possession is that recorded at the Government Observatory, Dodabetta (the highest point on the Neilgherries), and published in the report of T. G. Taylor, Esq., H. C. Astronomer, dated Madras Observatory, 15th February 1848. The extracts at foot* are taken from this record, and entirely contradict the impression conveyed by Dr. Anderson. The variation of our climate is, as it indeed must be from our position near the equator, very little, the lowest temperature registered during the year being 40 degrees, while the highest was 67 degrees. I may observe that the mean temperature of the Dodabetta site is about 2½ degrees warmer than the summit of Dodabetta, and the Neddivattam plantation at its upper limits is about five degrees warmer, while its lower limits is about 15 degrees warmer. Dr. Anderson selected for his observations a land-locked hollow, or the coldest part that could have been found in Ootacamund, and this is evident from his own report, as we are told in paragraph 7, that "on the night of the 24th December, eencalypti, a few accacias from Australia, roses, geranium, fuchsias, and many other soft-wooded garden plants, were destroyed; besides several indigenous shrubs, such as berberies, nepalensis and aristata and lobelia, excelsa, were blackened by frost." The plants which Dr. Anderson states to have been killed formed the principal growth all over the Neilgherries; so it must have been in some peculiar locality where Dr. Anderson observed the facts he describes. Dr. Anderson has been very unhappy in the selection of the facts he uses to impress us with an idea of the aridity of this climate. Referring to the dry season, he states that "during this period irrigation is absolutely necessary in the coffee plantations, especially on the eastern aspect of the hills, and even in the Wainád on the moist side." There is not a coffee plantation either on the Neilgherries or in the Wainád irrigated. His description of the botany also conveys an erroneous impression, as we have no plants in these forests with perennial roots and rapidly growing succulent stems "springing up at the commencement of the rains," fruiting and dying before the dry weather. The dried-up stems to which Dr. Anderson alludes being the stems of endopogon, barberia, and strobilanthus; these are plants which grow from five to seven years before flowering, and immediately they have flower and produce seed they die away; and this happened to be the case with many of the species last year, their dead stems filling the jungles at the time of Dr. Anderson's visit. With this tribe of plants Dr. Anderson is well acquainted botanically, but he would seem not to have studied their habits of growth.

13. With reference to our proposed plan of cultivating the chinchonas in the open ground without the shade of living trees, is a plan not opposed to the opinions of the great authorities on chinchona cultivation; nor is it, as Dr. Anderson states, opposed to the opinion of Dr. Weddell.† But it is certainly opposed

* Months.	Fall of Rain.	Lowest Temperature Registered.	Highest Temperature Registered.
	Inches.	*Min.*	*Max.*
January	1·2	40·0	62·8
February	7·43	41·2	61·0
March	3·61	43·5	67·0
April	19·80	40·0	66·0
May	4·86	46·3	65·8
June	4·55	44·0	60·0
July	7·41	44·3	59·0
August	9·32	44·5	59·1
September	7·52	41·8	59·0
October	12·49	42·8	58·8
November	11·85	42·9	58·8
December	12·28	41·0	60·4
Total - - - *Inches*	102·14	42·47	61·35

† "I have no doubt that the Indian plantations will amply compensate the trouble and expense of maintaining them. With respect to conducting them we have as yet little or no experience. The only reason I can adduce for planting the young chinchona trees under the protection of a

opposed to the practice of the Dutch in Java; and I have explained in detail the reasons and necessity for this mode of cultivation in my letter to Government of the 20th January last. That the Dutch in Java have grown a worthless species under dense shade is no argument why we should cultivate the valuable species under similar conditions; but the contrary, as they have failed in the cultivation of the only valuable species they possess, namely, *C. Calisaya.* It is proverbial "that ill weeds grow apace," under the most adverse circumstances they can be placed in; and so exists the *C. Pahudiana* in Java under its adverse conditions. My own experience in the cultivation of chinchonas has been short, still it is sufficient to enable me to state that we will meet with great success in open cultivation. The observations and facts on which this opinion is formed will be detailed at length in my annual report, which I trust shortly to forward to Government.

— No. 96. —

MINUTE by Sir *William Denison.*

1. It appears to me that Dr. Anderson has mistaken the conditions of the experiment now making upon the Neilgherries as to the cultivation of the different species of chinchona. The object has been to ascertain whether, in a climate differing in many respects from that in which the chinchona is found, it may not be possible, by care and attention, to acclimatize the plant so as to perpetuate and cheapen the supply of a medicine, the importance of which in a country like India it is impossible to over estimate.

2. The Government and its agents are perfectly cognizant of the difference between the climate of the Neilgherries and that of the slopes of the Himalayas; they did not depend upon the brief experience of Dr. Anderson, who in a residence of about a week on the Hills in the depth of winter, could hardly be supposed to have acquired sufficient knowledge of the plan to have been able to lay down dogmatically either the laws which regulate the weather, or the action of this upon plants raised from seeds or cuttings in the locality itself, but they feel that there are quite sufficient grounds both in the statement of Mr. Markham who selected the site, and in those of others who have visited the experimental plantations in Java, to justify a belief that the chinchona in some of its most valuable species may be profitably cultivated on the Neilgherries, and they see nothing in the present paper of Dr. Anderson which would induce them to stop the

---

slight shade afforded by other trees is that these plants, in their native country, have appeared to me never to grow beyond the state of shrubs when under other conditions; it may thence be inferred that the safest way of proceeding would be to plant the cinchonas at convenient distances in a quincunx alternately with some more fast growing trees, which may be cut away when no longer required. It is evident that the advantage to be reaped from this disposition must mainly depend upon the proper choice of these intervening strangers, it being kept in mind that they are placed there to protect and not to choke.

"Perhaps an equally good result might be obtained by planting the chinchonas without any intermixture, but very close together, so as to make them run up, and then thinning them out as might be required. At all events, it seems to be an essential point that, for a certain period, the soil and trunks of the young trees should be protected from the direct influence of the scorching sun, as plants so exposed have generally appeared to me to have a stunted growth.

"My reason for recommending the young plants to be placed in the open field, jointly with young trees of some other order and rather more fast growing than them, originated from the fact of my having always seen the Calisaya tree dwarf and stunted when growing in exposed or entirely open situations; whether the same thing takes place with other species seems doubtful, as Mr. Spruce says that the red bark tree thrives in open ground.

"At all events, I should never recommend planting any of these trees in the dense shade of the forest; in such a situation the greater part of them would evidently soon be smothered.

"If I have said that shade appeared indispensable to the trees at an early age, I never meant that they should have too much of it. I think that the trees in India ought to be planted in open ground, and close enough (if unmingled with other trees) to oblige each other to run up, sufficient space and air being gradually provided by judicious pruning and thinning out. A most important condition of success may be found in the choice of the proper time for planting out, the best being probably the beginning of the rainy season."—9 March 1862.

the experiment which has been commenced in such a satisfactory manner by Mr. McIvor.

3. This report should be sent to Mr. McIvor with a request that he would examine and give an opinion upon the various statements made.

(signed) *W. T. Denison.*

Enclosure in No. 96.

REPORT on the Number and Condition of the Chinchona Plants in cultivation on the Neilgherries, on the 30th April 1862.

Botanical Names.	Commercial Names.	Number of Plants.	Value in the London Market per lb. of dry Bark.	REMARKS.
			s. d. s. d.	
1. Chinchona succirubra - - -	Red Bark - - -	14,450	2 6 to 8 9	The whole of the plants are in the finest possible state of health, with the exception of *C. lancifolia* and *C. Chahuarguera.* Our plants in the open air within the last two months in rapidity of growth, general health, and luxuriance, having much exceeded those in our glass houses. The *C. lancifolia*, lately imported from Java, being affected by fungi at the roots, it is doubtful if we will be able to save it. As several cuttings of this sort although successfully rooted, the fungi, which apparently spreads along the pith, has attacked these rooted cuttings and killed them. The *C. Chahuarguera* only lately imported, and has suffered much during the voyage, the whole of the leaves and part of the young shoots having been dried up; still as it seems not to have contracted any disease, I hope it will recover. In the portion of our nurseries under the protection of the shade of living trees layers made in this position on the 3d January were found not to have rooted on the 27th April, while layers made at the same time in the open sunshine were found rooted by the end of the same month or in 28 days. The growth under the shade has also been unsatisfactory, not having in in any case exceeded four inches in the last two months, while in the same period many hundreds of the plants in the open ground have grown from 12 to 16 inches. Nothing can exceed the luxuriance and bright healthy look of the leaves in the open sunshine, while the leaves on the plants under the shade are pale, and covered with small hairs.
2. ,, Calisaya - - - -	Yellow Bark - -	237	2 10 to 7 –	
3. ,, Condaminea Var. Uritusinga	Original Loxa Bark -	1	2 10 to 7 –	
4. ,, Condaminea Var. Chahuarguera.	Rusty Crown Bark -	8,000	2 10 to 7 –	
5. ,, Condaminea Var. Crespilla -	Fine Crown Bark -	105	2 10 to 6 –	
6. ,, lancifolia from Java - -	Crown Bark - -	1	1 8 to 2 10	
7. ,, nitida - - - - -	Genuine Grey Bark -	2,922	1 8 to 2 9	
8. ,, species without name -	Fine Grey Bark - -	1,211	1 8 to 2 10	
9. ,, micrantha - -	Grey Bark - - -	3,786	1 8 to 2 9	
10. ,, Peruviana - - - - -	Finest Grey Bark -	357	1 8 to 2 10	
11 ,, Pahudiana from Java - -	Unknown - - -	425	Worthless.	
	TOTAL Number of Plants - -	31,495		

Government Gardens,
Ootacamund, 12 May 1862.

(signed) *W. G. McIvor,*
Superintendent Government Cinchona Plantations.

OPINIONS on the proposed method of cultivating Chinchona on the Neilgherries.

Mr. Howard's opinion.—"I have read and carefully considered the proposed plan of cultivation in India; and have no hesitation in saying, I think Mr. McIvor is right in his views as to the best mode of planting out the chinchona; always supposing sufficient care is used to protect them for a year or two. With reference to the yield of quinine and bark which may be obtained by lopping and pruning the branches, I will let you have a specimen of *C. Calisaya*, which must have been grown as a shrub, and contains 4 per cent. of quinine, so that a large produce may be realized in this way."

Dr. Weddel's opinion.—"I have no doubt that the Indian plantations will amply compensate the trouble and expense of maintaining them. With respect to conducting them we have as yet little or no experience. The only reason I can adduce for planting the young Chinchona trees under the protection of a slight shade afforded by other trees, is that these plants, in their native country, have appeared to me never to grow beyond the state of shrubs when under other conditions. It may thence be inferred that the safest way of proceeding would be to plant the Chinchonas at convenient distances in a quincunx alternately

nately with some more fast growing trees, which may be cut away when no longer required. It is evident that the advantage to be reaped from this disposition must mainly depend upon the proper choice of these intervening strangers, it being kept in mind that they are placed there to protect and not to choke.

"Perhaps an equally good result might be obtained by planting the chinchonas without any intermixture, but very close together, so as to make them run up, and then thinning them out as might be required. At all events it seems to be an essential point that, for a certain period, the soil and trunks of the young trees should be protected from the direct influence of the scorching sun, as plants so exposed have generally appeared to me to have a stunted growth.

"My reason for recommending the young plants to be placed in the open field, jointly with young trees of some other order, and rather more fast-growing than them, originated from the fact of my having always seen the Calisaya tree dwarf and stunted when growing in exposed or entirely open situations, whether the same thing takes place with other species seems doubtful, as Mr. Spruce says that the Red Bark tree thrives in open ground.

"At all events I should never recommend planting any of these trees in the dense shade of the forest. In such a situation the greater part of them would evidently soon be smothered.

"If I have said that shade appeared indispensable to the trees at an early age, I never meant that they should have too much of it. I think that the trees in India ought to be planted in open ground, and close enough (if unmingled with other trees) to oblige each other to run up, sufficient space and air being gradually provided by judicious pruning and thinning out. A most important condition of success may be found in the choice of the proper time for planting out; the best being probably the beginning of the rainy season. —9 March 1862."

Mr. Markham's opinion.—"There can be no doubt that the correct method of cultivating the chinchonas is planting them out in the open, with plenty of light and air, they may require slight shade from the direct rays of the sun at first. The only really fine, well grown plant of *C. Calisaya* that I saw in Caravaya was one that had been planted in the middle of a clearing, entirely exposed; those in the forest were poor struggling things in comparison."

Mr. Spruce's opinion.—"The ridges on which the Red Bark grows all deviate a little from an easterly and westerly direction. It is far more abundant on their northern than on their southern slope, nor did I see a single tree with flowers or fruit in a southern aspect. The northern and eastern sides of the trees themselves had borne most flowers, and except on one tree of more open growth than the rest, scarcely a capsule ripened on their southern or western sides. These phenomena are explained by the facts that, in the summer season the trees receive most sun from the east and north, for the mornings are generally clear and sunny, whilst the afternoons are almost invariably foggy, and the sun's declination is northerly. Another notable circumstance is that the trees standing in open ground, pasture, cane-field, &c., are far healthier and more luxuriant than those growing in the forest, where they are hemmed in and partially shaded by other trees, and that while many of the former had flowered freely, the latter were without exception sterile. This plainly shows that, although the Red Bark may need shade whilst young and tender, it really requires (like most trees) plenty of air, light and room, wherein to develope its proportions."

Mr. Cross' opinion.—"In forming plantations of the Red Bark, I would cut down wholesale the entire forest, and allow it to deaden and dry, and then set it on fire. This should be done immediately before the rainy season, the plants should then be planted about 2½ or 3 yards distant. By the time that the rains are over, the plants will be large enough to shade each other's roots, it is the roots that require shading (not the tops) to prevent the too rapid evaporation of moisture from the ground during the sunshine. If done in this way, the Red Bark plants would soon grow up into a magnificient evergreen forest. Only that portion of the forest required for planting should be cut down and burned. By burning, the land is cleared of all noxious insects and will be in a fine healthy state for receiving the plants: and by the time that insects begin to accumulate again, the plants will be established and fully developed; and so will be beyond the attack of insects."

(True Extracts.)

(signed) *W. G. McIvor,*
Superintendent Government Chinchona Plantations.

— No. 97 .—

ORDER of the Madras Government, 22 October 1862.

1. THE foregoing papers have reference to the experiments now being made upon the Neilgherries in the cultivation of the different species of chinchona. The Government resolve to bring them to the notice of the Secretary of State.

2. The following table shows the number of plants of each kind on the 31st August 1862:—

	Botanical Names.	Commercial Names.	Number of original Plants and Date of Receipt.	Number of Plants on the 30 April 1862.	Number of Plants on the 31 August 1862.	Value per lb. of Dry Bark in the London Market.
						s. d. s. d.
1.	C. succirubra - -	Red Bark - - -	457, April 1861	14,450	30,150	2 6 to 8 9
2.	C. Calisaya - -	Yellow Bark - -	6, April " - ; 48, Dec. " -	237	1,050	2 10 to 7 0
3.	C. Condaminea, var. Uritusinga - -	Original Loxa Bark -	1, April 1862 -	1	41	2 10 to 7 0
4.	C. Condaminea, var. Chaharguera -	Rusty Crown Bark -	Seeds, Feb. "	8,000	20,030	2 10 to 7 0
5.	C. Condaminea, var. Crespilla - -	Fine Crown Bark -	" Feb. "	185	236	2 10 to 6 0
6.	C. lancifolia - -	Pitayo Bark - -	4, Dec. 1861 -	1	1	1 8 to 2 10
7.	C. nitida - - -	Genuine Grey Bark -	Seeds, Feb. "	2,922	8,500	1 8 to 2 9
8.	C. species without name - - -	Fine Grey Bark - -	" Feb. "	1,211	2,440	1 8 to 2 10
9.	C. micrantha - -	Grey Bark - - -	" Feb. "	3,786	7,400	1 8 to 2 9
10.	C. Peruviana - -	Finest Grey Bark -	" Feb. "	357	2,295	1 8 to 2 10
11.	C. Pahudiana - -	Unknown - - -	250, Dec. "	425	425	Worthless.
		Total number of Plants -	766	31,495	72,568	

[*Note.*—Average present propagation about 10,000 per mensem.]

3. The Dodabetta plantation extends at present over 60 acres, of which 15 have been already occupied, while the remaining 45 are in various stages of preparation, and will be planted before the end of the current year.

4. The Neddivattum site comprises 150 acres, of which 21 have been planted, and the remainder more or less prepared. The actual plantation will be extended from 21 to 100 acres in the course of the present calendar year.

5. The Government are much gratified at the decided success attained in the propagation of the plant. Mr. McIvor's mode of culture, from the outset, is explained in full detail in the fifth of the papers recorded above (paragraphs 22 to 40), and nothing can be more satisfactory or promising than its results.

6. In the early part of last season, the experiment of planting out was first tried, and has been attended so far with marked success. Six plants were placed out in a cleared spot on the highest part of the Neddiwuttum site, about 6,200 feet above the level of the sea. These plants, including the most delicate variety (*C. succirubra*), have stood the cold of the winter, the drought of the spring, and the rain of the monsoon, and are now in the most vigorous and healthy condition, ranging in height from 36 to 42 inches, although only 15 months old. In fact, there seems little reason to doubt, that by proper care and attention, the plant may be cultivated in the open air on the Neilgherries with success.

7. The Government will not enter upon any lengthened discussion of the different views entertained by Dr. Anderson and Mr. McIvor as to the culture of the plant. The system adopted by Mr. McIvor has the support of Messrs. Markham, Cross, and Spruce, who alone have seen the plant growing in its natural habitation. It is consistent with the recognised principles of horticulture and, above all, has proved eminently successful in practice. The cultivation of the chinchona is still an experiment; but so far as present experience extends, the plan of open

planting has been most successful, and the Government will not abandon a system which has in every respect been attended with such satisfactory results. At the same time, the experiments under shade will not be discontinued, 55 acres on the Dodabetta site, and 15 at Neddivattum, having been reserved for that purpose.

— No. 98. —

EXTRACT from Sir *C. Wood* to Lord *Canning*.

My Lord, India Office, London, 8 February 1862.

I HAVE considered in Council your letter dated 21st December (No. 97) 1861, forwarding correspondence relating to Dr. Anderson's recent deputation to Java; and I approve the acknowledgments made under your orders to the Governor-General of Netherlands India, for the courteous treatment accorded to Dr. Anderson, and for the collection of Chinchona plants and seeds placed at the disposal of that gentlemen.

2. With reference to the communication addressed by you to the Madras Government on the 9th of December 1861, that Government will no doubt be glad to receive any information which Dr. Anderson may be able to afford as to the cultivation of the Chinchona in Java; but I am of opinion that, in the conduct of the important experiment which is now proceeding in so highly satisfactory a manner, Mr. McIvor should be left to carry out his plans without interference on the part of other officers, and the Madras Government will therefore continue to be guided by the instructions on this point communicated to them in my Despatch of the 2d July (No. 27) 1861. It is, however, by no means my wish to limit the experimental cultivation of the Chinchona to those localities which have been already decided on, and I entirely approve your intention to send some of the plants obtained from Java to a site on the Khassia hills.

His Excellency the Right Honourable
The Governor General of India in Council.

— No. 99. —

From the Secretary of State for India, to His Excellency the Right Honourable the Governor General of India in Council.

My Lord, India Office, London, 31 May 1862.

Para. 1. I HAVE considered in Council your Despatch of 28th February last, forwarding a copy of a further report by Dr. Andersou on the results of his recent deputation to Java, and containing his views as to the cultivation of the Chinchona plant in India.

2. I am fully aware of Dr. Anderson's ability, and this report contains evidence of the zealous interest with which he has studied the question. But I must, nevertheless, disapprove of the terms in which he has thought proper to express himself regarding Mr. Markham and his labours.

3. It is to him that India is primarily indebted for the acquisition of the Chinchona. He has studied the plant attentively in its native country, and I believe that many of his conclusions, derived from observation there, have been corroborated by science at home. But the transplantation is as yet an experiment only: there is much to be learnt which practice only can teach. And it is surely better for scientific men to recognise this fact, and not to allow such difference of opinion as they may feel respecting a project as yet uncertain to interfere with courteous communication of sentiments, or with co-operation as far as possible.

4. I have, therefore, only to repeat the expression of my desire, that no interference should take place, on the part of Dr. Anderson or anyone else, with the prosecution

prosecution of the experiments now proceeding in the Madras Presidency under the charge of Mr. McIvor.

5. But I have also to repeat the approval, conveyed in my Despatch of the 8th February last, of the intention of your Government to take measures for the cultivation of the Chinchona at Darjeeling, or elsewhere in that region, if a suitable spot can be obtained, with the aid of the abundant supply of plants which can, apparently, be derived from Ootacamund. Dr. Anderson will, I presume, be charged with the conduct of these operations, and will have an opportunity of testing the success, in India, of that mode of cultivation of which he has been led to approve.

6. Such further investigation as I have been able to make, has rather tended to confirm the opinion, though opposite to that apparently entertained in Java, that the *C. Pahudiana* is one of the less valuable kinds of Chinchona. I should think it unwise to be at any great expense in propagating it; but I do not wish that Dr. Anderson should be prohibited from making the experiment regarding the whole subject, as one on which the amplest information is desirable, and can only be obtained by degrees.

I have, &c.
(signed) *C. Wood.*

— No. 100. —

NOTE on the Cultivation of Chinchonæ, by Mr. *Spruce.*

Chanduy, near Guayaquil, June 1862.

MR. MARKHAM'S notions on the cultivation of *Chinchonæ* entirely coincide with my own. If some empiric, who has never seen the *Chinchonæ* in their native country, has sufficient influence to induce the Indian Government to attempt to cultivate Chinchona plants according to some method distinct from the one proposed by those who have had that advantage, by all means let him be made responsible for the result.

The plan pursued by the Dutch, of growing the Chinchonas in the shade of dense forests, has always seemed to me most erroneous, and the person who devised it has read the lesson afforded by a study of the conditions of their existence on their native soil quite differently from what I have done. One of the first things that struck me in the great Amazonian forest was, the struggle for existence maintained among the individual plants which compose it. Not only (as among animals) are the more robust species and individuals continually harassing and displacing the weaker ones, but a parent tree (so far from cherishing) actually smothers thousands of its offspring beneath its own shade. Every place seems occupied, and of the seedlings which spring up under the large trees, not one in 10,000 can be expected to arrive at maturity, or to lift its head beyond the gloom, except an outlet be made for it by the decay and fall of its parent, or of some neighbouring giants of the forest. But let the same seedlings be planted in recently cleared ground, and nearly every one will prosper. I have seen the experiment tried, and the only indispensable precaution is, that it be done in the rainy season, when neither natural nor artificial shade is needed, but would, on the contrary, be positively prejudicial.

There are tribes of plants, always of humble growth and usually of obscure appearance, which naturally seek the shade. The sub-order *Coffeaceæ* (of the great order *Rubiaceæ*) has many examples of this propensity, and the coffee-tree itself is one of the most notable. In South American forests, the numerous species of *Psychotria* and other genera allied to *Coffea*, are nearly all shade-loving plants; but even these, granted their normal conditions of temperature and humidity, grow perfectly well in the full glare of sunshine; and I suspect they seek the shade because they find there a sufficient and unvarying humidity, rather than to avoid the light. The sub-order *Chinchoneæ*, and especially the species of *Chinchona* itself, mostly seek to rise into the full influence of the light before they display their gaily-coloured flowers, whose development is essential to the permanence of the species. The officinal *Chinchonæ* are nearly all forest trees,

trees, and those which are not have for companions bushes as humble as themselves.

My opinion is that, if the same climate can be found in India as the red bark tree possesses in its native country, no shade at all will be required after the plants are once well rooted. The fogs which prevail in the woods of Chimborazo are an all-sufficient shade, and it is only during four months in the year (June, July, August, and September) that the trees are exposed to (I would rather say enjoy) about six hours' sun per day. I believe if you consult Mr. Cross, you will find his opinion coincide with mine as to the expediency of allowing to the Chinchona plants the full influence of the light and air, provided that the necessary misty atmosphere and the freedom from violent winds can be secured.

As Mr. Howard has found slender quill-bark of *C. succirubra* so productive in alkaloids, Mr. McIvor's plan of growing the *Chinchonæ* as bushes or low trees, and of reaping an annual crop of bark from their lopped branches (similarly to what is practised with the Cinnamon), is well worth trial. Chinchona trees are only sparsely branched, but they are very patient of mutilation, and speedily put forth pairs of branchlets for every branch that has been lopped, if only one or two leaf-nodes have been left on. So much pruning might, perhaps, cause the trees to flower and fruit more than is desirable, but that can only be determined by experiment. Even if the trees were cut down, once for all, when arrived at maturity, I cannot but think that their cultivation (on an extensive scale) would be eventually remunerative. The man who plants a wood of oaks or elms cannot hope to live to cut down the trees for timber, but every year his plantation increases in value, and is so much capital at accumulative interest; and the same would be the case with a plantation of Chinchonas. In whatever way the question of pecuniary profit or loss may be decided, it is clear that, if we will have quinine, we must plant Chinchonas. In the forests where, a few years ago, Mr. Karsten speculated that the Chinchona trees would never be exhausted, I am informed that, at this moment, people are digging up old roots, the scanty supply of bark thus obtained being all that is now to be had there.

— No. 101. —

From *W. G. McIvor*, Esq., Superintendent Government Chinchona Plantation, Ootacamund, to *J. D. Sim*, Esq., Secretary to Government, Revenue Department, Fort St. George.

Sir, Ootacamund, 31 May 1862.

1. I HAVE the honour to forward herewith the report on the Government cinchona experiment on the Neilgherries, for the official year ending the 30th ultimo. The accounts, which form an appendix to this report, require further examination, and will be forwarded hereafter.

2. I trust the Government will not consider that I have strayed from the legitimate subject of this report, by entering into a minute detail of our system of cultivation, my object being to endeavour to place in the hands of our assistants such information as may prove useful to them in the management of the plants. Should the Government approve of this, and be pleased to sanction the report being printed in a convenient pocket form, I respectfully beg to solicit the favour of being supplied with 50 or 100 copies for the use of the establishment, and for distribution to those anxious to try chinchona cultivation in this country.

REPORT on the Government Chinchona Experiment on the Neilgherries, for 1861–62.

1. It is now little more than a year since we fairly began the cultivation of the quinine-yielding chinchonas on the Neilgherries; and although our operations are necessarily in the first stages, the information which has been obtained with reference to the nature and requirements of the plants, their propagation and cultivation,

cultivation, and the general success which has attended our efforts, will, I trust, render this report not uninteresting. With the view of rendering the various subjects treated more easily referred to, I have arranged them under the following heads:—

Introduction of plants; reasons for attempting to introduce and cultivate in India.

2. The supply of Peruvian bark has for many years been inadequate to the demand—hence the steady and yearly increase in the price of this valuable medicine; and without any apparent hope of this state of the market giving way to a better, as the chinchona forests of South America are rapidly disappearing before the axe of the *cascarilleros*, it is evident that the produce of the Andes cannot long continue to meet the demands of European markets. In 1859, the Secretary of State resolved to attempt the introduction and cultivation of the various species of quinine-yielding chinchonas into India; and an expedition was organised in the early part of 1860, under the direction of Clements R. Markham, Esq., with a view to accomplishing this undertaking. Mr. Markham was assisted by Messrs. Spruce and Pritchett, as also by two practical gardeners, one of whom Mr. Cross, a very intelligent and enterprising young man, has aided much by his perseverance and judgment in bringing the introduction of the Peruvian bark to its present satisfactory issue; and it reflects much credit upon the Secretary of State, the judgment displayed in the selection of the agents employed to carry out this very hazardous and difficult part of the undertaking.

3. At the commencement of this expedition, Mr. Markham resolved not to cease in his exertions until all the various species and varieties of commercial value were successfully imported to India; and this, indeed, has been nearly accomplished, as we now possess nine of the most valuable species known in commerce. Three species or varieties in addition are known to produce rather inferior descriptions of bark, and these, although of less value than the species we possess, will, we trust, be introduced also, as their qualities may fairly be expected to improve under cultivation in this country, as indeed has been the case with most plants when imported and cultivated in other countries. For instance, we find that sugarcane, a native of this country, was exported to the West Indies in 1506; and although a few shoots only were successfully transplanted in their new abode, so well did they thrive, and so rapidly was the cultivation extended, that by the beginning of the 18th century, no less than 800 ships were employed in conveying this one product from the West Indies to different parts of the world. Rice also, a native of this country, was accidentally imported into America, where its cultivation extended with such surprising rapidity, and the quality of its produce so much exceeded that of India, as to be worth double the price in the market. Cotton, also a native of this country, was introduced into Egypt with equal results; so much indeed did it improve in quality, that even up to the present day, ordinary Egyptian cotton commands a price fully a half higher than the finest grown in India.

4. The present condition of our chinchona experiment holds out great promise, that its importation into India will be attended with results equal to those I have described as being effected by the introduction of sugarcane into the West Indies, rice to America, and cotton to Egypt.

Species and varieties introduced, their nature and value.

5. In dealing with this subject, I have considered it desirable not to encumber this report by botanical descriptions, and shall therefore proceed briefly to notice the species introduced, their commercial value, localities, and habits of growth.

Chinchonas yielding Quinine.

6. "*Cinchona succirubra*" the "*Cascarilla Colorada*" or "Genuine Red Bark" of commerce.—This species grows to a lofty tree, and is the most valuable known, being the richest in alkaloids, which generally amount to as much as 3 to 4 per cent., and thus "fair average samples are valued in the market at more than twice the price of calisaya bark." The present price of red bark varies from 2*s.* 6*d.* to 8*s.* 9*d.* per lb. of dry bark. This sort is also hardy, its range of growth extending from 3,000 to 8,000 feet; the plant, according to Mr. Spruce, prefers open ground, with "plenty of air, light, and room wherein to develop its proportions;" "the bark is thin in proportion to the diameter of the trees when growing at low elevations, and thick in proportion when growing at high elevations." The amount of alkaloids are also much affected by elevation. Mr. Spruce informs us that "Senor Cordovez (who has analysed the red bark collected at various altitudes) found that the greater the height at which the trees grow, the larger is the proportion of alkaloids contained in the bark." Of this species we now possess upwards of 14,000 plants, all in very fine health.

7. "*Chinchona Calisaya*" or "Yellow Bark of Bolivia."—This species grows to the height of a large forest tree, and was long considered the most valuable of all the medicinal barks; and certainly it was so, until the discovery of the red bark. The present price of calisaya or yellow bark varies from 2*s.* 10*d.* to 7*s.* per lb. Of this species we have evidently two varieties, very distinctly marked even when growing under the same conditions. According to Mr. Markham and Dr. Weddell, "the tree Calisaya grows on declivities and steep rugged places of the mountains 5,000 to 6,000 feet above the sea, in the hottest forests of Caravaya and Bolivia." Subsequently, Mr. Markham in writing of this species states, "There can be no doubt that the correct method of cultivating the cinchonas is planting them out in the open, with plenty of light and air; they may require shade from the direct rays of the sun at first. The only really fine well-grown plant of *Chinchona Calisaya* that I saw in Caravaya was one that had been planted in a small clearing entirely exposed; those in the forest were poor straggling things in comparison." Of this species we possess 237 plants in fine health; it is equally as hardy as the red bark, and as easily propagated.

8. "*Chinchona Condaminea,*" var. *Uritusinga*; the "*Cascarilla fina,*" or "Original Loxa Bark."—This species, which, in the days of La Condamine, was a noble and lofty forest tree, is now almost extinct, the trees of a large size having entirely disappeared from the Andes; it is rich in alkaloids, good specimens giving a total of 3·8 per cent., and in this respect it equals the Calisaya bark of Bolivia. It was common on the mountains of Uritusinga, and grows at elevations from 6,000 to 8,000 feet; a general opinion prevails among the cascarilleros that the bark of this species "differ in quality according as it is exposed to the morning or evening sun." Of this sort we possess only one plant, liberally presented to the Indian Government by J. E. Howard, Esq.,; it arrived here on the 18th April 1862, and although much damaged by the journey is now in very promising condition.

9. "*Chinchona Condaminea,*" var. *Chahuarguera;* the "*Cascarilla Colorado del Rey,*" or "*Cascarilla Amarilla,*" or the "Rusty Crown Bark" of English commerce, and of equal value to the preceding. This is nearly allied to the Uritusinga, inhabiting the same localities, but perhaps growing at greater elevations. In the days of Pavon this was a slender tree of little more than 24 feet in height, and is considered to be the species that produced the bark which cured the Countess of Chinchon. At the present time, Mr. Cross informs us, "but few trees are to be seen of these dimensions. The plants from which the bark of commerce is now taken are, in general, not more than 8 to 10 feet in height. When the plants are cut down, three or four young shoots, or suckers, in general spring up; but this does not always happen, as some of the more industrious cascarilleros frequently pull up the roots, and bark them also. The bark is taken from the smallest twigs; thus the annual growths are sometimes taken, especially if they are strong." Mr. Cross also observes, that "the alluvial deposit in the ravines

ravines where this species is found growing is shallow, and in many places not more than six inches in depth." Of this sort we now possess upwards of 8,000 seedlings, and more are daily coming up. This sort is very hardy, and promises to be one of easy cultivation, and well suited to the highest ranges of these hills, especially the Dodabetta site.

10. "*Chinchona Condaminea*," var. *Crespilla* (*C. Crispa Tafalla*) or "fine Crown Bark."—This species is a small shrub, and contains a smaller quantity of alkaloids than the preceding; still it brings a high price in the market, being a "very fragrant and pretty-looking bark." It grows at great elevations, from 7,000 to 10,000 feet, in a deposit of peat, and where the temperature sometimes falls to 27° Fahr." We possess 105 seedlings of this species, which will no doubt prove well suited to the highest part of the Dodabetta site.

11. "*Chinchona lancifolia*" from Java, or "Crown Bark."—This is a species of third value; it is also hardy and easily cultivated, inhabiting the high and cold regions of the Andes; when growing in exposed situations, it produces a good bark. I regret, however, to state that this species cannot be considered as successfully introduced. Four plants of this sort were imported by Dr. Anderson from Java in December 1861; at the time they arrived the plants appeared in good health, but on removing them from the Wardian cases they were found to be affected by rot and fungi at the roots. They made some progress after being transplanted, and two of their tops were layered and successfully rooted. In January one of the plants died, and towards the middle of March the others were evidently affected by fungi and becoming sickly; as soon as the decay was observed to be making progress, the rooted tops were removed and placed in fresh earth, and promised to do well. By the end of March, the three original plants had died, and by the 15th April one of the rooted tops began to show symptoms of decay, and speedily died away. On examination it was found that the fungi had extended along the pith. We still possess one rooted layer, but it is doubtful if it will survive, as I fear it is also tainted with disease, and may any day die off.

Chinchonas yielding Chinchonine.

12. "*Chinchona nitida*," "*Quina cana legitima*," or "Genuine Grey Bark."—This is a lofty tree, abounding in the higher regions of Huanuco; its predominant alkaloid is cinchonine, and is consequently of less value than the preceding species, which belong to the class yielding quinine; the analysis of the bark from which our seeds were gathered gave 2·22 per cent. of alkaloids, consisting chiefly of cinchonine: Mr. Howard has, however, found quinine in samples of the fine grey barks of commerce. This species grows in exposed places, at elevations from 6,000 to 8,000 feet, and is said to delight in "free air, cold, water, and sunshine." Of this sort we possess about 3,000 plants, all in very fine health.

13. Chinchona species without name. Allied to the above, and raised from seeds gathered by Mr. Pritchett, near Huanuco. Mr. Howard is of opinion that this species may prove to be identical with *Chinchona obovata* of Pavon. It is said to be a "good bark," and extensively imported with the grey bark of commerce. We now possess upwards of 1,000 plants of this species, and we considered it desirable to stop the extension of the propagation of this plant, until we receive more correct information of its identity and value.

14. "*Chinchona micrantha*," the "*Cascarilla Provinciana*," or Grey Bark.—This is a lofty tree, inhabiting warm and damp forests, where it attains a great circumference—one tree frequently yielding from 200 to 250 lbs. of dry bark. The bark is generally rich in alkaloids, yielding as much as 2·70 per cent., principally consisting of cinchonine. Of this species we possess upwards of 3,700 plants.

15. "*Chinchona Peruviana*," the "*Cascarilla Pata de Gallinazo*," or "finest Grey Bark."—This species attains the height of an ordinary-sized tree in the Forest of Cocheros, where it is still abundant, growing at a lower elevation than *Chinchona nitida*, and yields a bark of considerable value; the bark of the trees our seeds were collected from, when analysed by Mr. Howard, yielded three per cent. of alkaloids, "comprising chiefly chinchodine and chinchonine." It thus ranks among the most valuable of the grey barks. Of this species we possess 357 plants, all in good health.

16. "*Chinchona Pahudiana*," the "*Cascarilla Crespilla Chica*" from Java.—This species was met by Dr. Hasskarl in the neighbourhood of Uchubamba, on the eastern side of the second Cordillera, "at an elevation of 5,500 to 6,000 feet above the level of the sea, in a very sandy micaceous soil, on dry sunny hills, without much shelter from the sun." A large number of this species were imported from Java by Dr. Anderson, and a few also were raised here from seeds obtained from the same source. We possess 425 plants of this sort, and as it is of no commercial value, the number will not be further increased.

17. The Dutch in Java, having fallen into the very serious error of erroneously attaching the name of a well-known and valuable species to this worthless plant, had proceeded in its cultivation "to a much greater extent than its properties at all warrant." This discovery indicated the necessity of caution on our part with reference to the value of our plants, and the correctness of the names attached to them; and an investigation of this subject, also made under the direction of Mr. Markham, together with the valuable assistance of Mr. Howard, has led to the most satisfactory results; and I believe that a doubt cannot be entertained as to the correctness of the names attached to our species, as in many instances the bark of the trees from which the seeds were gathered, and the layers procured, was subjected to analysis, in order to prevent the possibility of mistake.

Selection of sites for cultivation.

18. As early as June 1859, the Right Honouarble the Secretary of State for India called for information on the subject of the best localities in this Presidency for the cultivation of chinchona; and the Right Honourable Sir C. Wood, in a Despatch, dated 17th August 1860, directed that sites might be selected and "prepared for the cultivation of the plants." At that time we felt our informaton inadequate to enable us to perform this very important task with that degree of certainty required; although the sites likely to prove suitable were named, it was suggested that, prior to their final adoption, they should be examined and approved by Mr. Markham. It will be observed from what has already been said, that the various species of cinchona require different elevation and exposure, and only by a person thoroughly conversant with the subject could so very important a task as the selection of sites be expected to be successfully accomplished. Mr. Markham visited India towards the end of 1860, and feeling a difficulty in forming a correct opinion, owing to his inexperience of this climate, requested my aid in this matter. While on the Andes, Mr. Markham noted with great minuteness the various influences affecting the growth of the chinchonas: these observations were placed in my hands, which, combined with a long personal intercourse, enabled us fairly and impartially to discuss the altered conditions of our climate, and the consequent modifications required to be possessed by the sites we selected, in order to ensure success. It was felt at the time that much would have to be developed by practical experience; and so far as our operations have progressed, the correctness of the opinions originally formed by Mr. Markham have been faithfully developed.

19. It was proposed to confine our operations in the first instance to two sites—namely, one suited for the experimental cultivation of the higher-growing species, while the other was selected for such species as require a warmer temperature. With this view, the site near Neddiwuttum was fixed upon for our first operations, possessing as it does several advantages with reference to exposure, and varying in elevation from 4,500 to 6,300 feet above the level of the sea. The species to be cultivated here at the lowest elevations is the red bark of Ecuador, and the yellow or Calisaya bark of Bolivia, and on the higher elevations the crown barks of Loxa and the grey barks of Huanuco. The site at Dodabetta is of limited extent, being originally but a little above 60 acres; however, since the receipt of the *Chinchona crespilla*, we have included in this site about 25 acres more, as being likely to suit the habits of this species; and I trust that this arrangement will meet with the approval of Government. This site possesses a great variety of exposure, and a great variety of soil also, and thus offers great advantages for an experimental plantation. The species intended to be cultivated here are the *Chinchona nitida*, or genuine grey bark, and varieties of *Chinchona Condaminea*, namely, the original Loxa bark, the rusty crown bark, and fine crown barks of commerce. Northern exposures have been selected for all the sites; this has been considered desirable, as the sun's declination is southerly during our dry and

and cloudless season; consequently, the northern slopes of the hills are much more moist during this season than the southern slopes, which receive the rays of the sun at nearly a right angle; consequently, they become parched and dried up; and this we considered would be injurious to the cinchonas, and consequently avoided selecting southern exposures for our plantations.

20. The great losses which have generally been sustained by placing newly imported plants at once out in the open air, suggested to us the desirableness of placing our plants in the first instance under the protection of glass. This gave us the power of rapidly increasing the plants, while it offered the great advantage of enabling us to note with much accuracy the various conditions affecting their health and growth; and this was rendered of more importance, as the information we originally possessed with reference to the cultivation of these plants was so vague and ambiguous, and in many cases indeed so conflicting, contradictory, and absurd, that it rendered the attainment of early practical knowledge of great value; while we based our theory of cultivation upon the observations of Mr. Markham and the other agents employed in introducing the plants to India. Our first care was to ascertain the conditions on the Andes most favourable to the perfect development of the plants; it was also necessary to ascertain and fairly understand such conditions as were unfavourable. **Cultivation; outline of system pursued.**

21. In the system of cultivation pursued here, we have simply endeavoured to administer to the greatest extent possible those favourable conditions, and to mitigate or remove the adverse ones. Although this system has been met by great opposition by gentlemen in this country, it is nevertheless one which has secured to us the great success we have obtained in so short a period; because the true principles of cultivation clearly point out, that while we follow nature in all that is beneficial, we should assuredly reject all that is injurious. Under this impression, we have latterly followed the system of open cultivation in every respect; we rear our seeds, strike our cuttings, and place out our plants in the nurseries, using as little shade as possible, and our results have incontestably established its great advantages.

22. The first sowings of our imported seeds took place in February 1861, and no certain data being given, our first operations were necessarily experimental, and consequently a number of the seeds were lost by being sown in too retentive a soil, and supplied with what (to chinchona seeds) proved to be an excess of moisture. The greatest success obtained in our first attempts was by the use of a soil composed almost entirely of burned earth, on which nearly 60 per cent. of the seeds germinated, the temperature of the earth being kept above 70 degrees Fahrenheit. The period required before germination took place varied from 62 to 68 days. **Cultivation; propagation by seeds.**

23. A supply of seeds recently received of the valuable varieties of *Chinchona Condaminea* have made more satisfactory progress; these were sown on the 11th February 1862, on a very light open soil, composed of a beautiful open felspathic sand, with a small admixture of leaf-mould. Our experience with the first seeds plainly indicating that the chinchonas are very impatient of an excess of moisture, great care was taken in the preparation of the soil used in this sowing. The leaf-mould was, in the first instance, exposed to the sun for two or three days and thoroughly dried; it was then heated to about 212 degrees Fahrenheit, in order to destroy all grubs or larvæ of insects; after being allowed to cool, it was brought into the potting-shed, and watered sufficiently to make it moist, but only to that degree of moisture that the particles of soil would not adhere together when pressed firmly with the hand—that is, the earth, on being laid down, was sufficiently dry to break and fall into its usual form. The leaf-mould and sand in this state of moisture were mixed together and the pots filled, the surface lightly pressed down, and the seeds sown thereon being lightly covered with a sprinkling of sand. The pots were then plunged into beds of moist sand, on a bottom heat of about 75 degrees Fahrenheit; these were never watered in the strict sense of the word; when the surface became dry they were merely sprinkled with a fine syringe, just sufficient water being given to damp the surface, but never to penetrate or consolidate the soil. Under this treatment the seeds began to germinate very strongly on the 16th day after sowing, and still continuing to germinate, the principal art appears to be to keep the soil in a uniform state of moisture, but never wet. The least excess of moisture causes the seeds to

mould and damp off in thousands, while, as a matter of course, if kept too dry, they become parched up. As soon as the seeds have germinated, they are carefully pricked out into fresh earth (prepared as above described). This operation is a very delicate one;—the radicle being carefully raised out of the original seed-pot is removed to the new pot, being carefully covered with soil, while the seed lobes are kept well above the surface; in this way from 25 to 50 seedlings are transplanted into a five-inch pot, and then treated in every respect the same as the seeds, that is, they are never watered, the surface being merely sprinkled and the pots plunged in beds of damp sand, as before stated, to keep the soil in that medium state of moisture in which it was when first placed in the pots. The necessity for this care is to prevent the seedlings from damping off, to which they are very liable when treated otherwise; it also greatly facilitates their growth and the formation of roots, the earth in which they are placed being so perfectly open that it is readily affected by the action of the atmosphere, and thus kept in the most favourable condition for promoting vegetation. When treated in this way, our seedlings have made an average growth in one year of over 30 inches, while many of our seedlings which were raised and grown on a retentive soil have not attained the height of three inches in the same period.

Cultivation; propagation by layers.

24. As soon as our imported plants and seedlings had attained sufficient size, they were propagated by being layered, as illustrated in the margin; in this way, they were found to root readily in about six weeks or two months at the latest, and the plants being bent down, it caused them to break, or throw out shoots from every bud along the whole length of the stem, and not only this, but many latent buds were developed, and a fine growth of young wood produced for succeeding layers and cuttings. In this way, each plant was treated as it gained sufficient size, namely, from eight to ten inches in height, until we had procured about 3,000 layered plants. Beyond this, we have not extended our stock of plants for propagation, as we calculate that 3,000 plants will always yield us as many layers and cuttings as we can possibly require. The principle of layering we have adopted is somewhat different from that usually practised, as we found the juice of the chinchonas, when cut, flowed so freely from the wound, that if merely placed into the soil, it was apt to cause mildew and rot. To remedy this, a piece of perfectly dry brick is placed into the cut as soon as it is made; this absorbs the juice, and effectually prevents the ill effects it produced.

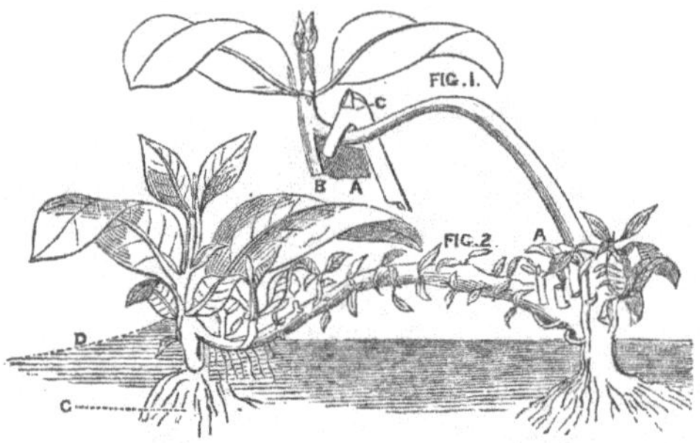

Fig. 1.—Layer as prepared for laying down. A, the piece of Brick; B, the tongue; C, the peg.
Fig. 2.—Represents the same plant, six weeks after being laid. C, the rootlets; D, the surface of the soil.

25. The layers, when well rooted, are removed from the parent plant, potted off, and kept in a close atmosphere for a few days, until they become established. In removing the layers, great care must be taken; for if they are cut off before the shoots shown in Figure 2, at A and B, have attained a good size, and fairly developed their leaves, the stock or parent plant is almost certain to die off. The reason of this is, the sap flows into the plant with equal vigour, but cannot be elaborated because of the removal of the leaves attached to the layer, and consequently it ferments and causes rot in the parent plant. So marked and undoubted is this fact, that if our trees are at any time cut down for their bark, not one in ten will survive; hence appears the necessity of the mode of cultivation detailed from paragraphs 38 to 40.

Cultivation; propagation by cuttings.

26. Our object being to produce the largest number of plants in the shortest possible space of time, our attention was early turned to growing the chinchonas by cuttings; and in this respect also, our first operations were not attended with the success desired. We soon discovered that cuttings from old wood, or rather from

from wood of three or four months' growth, was difficult to root, requiring from two to three months, and that it frequently damped off. It soon became plain, that the youngest wood that could be procured was the best adapted for making cuttings, as young tender shoots, a fortnight or three weeks old, formed roots in a very short space of time, the majority of these cuttings being invariably rooted within a month; it is, however, difficult to deal with this description of wood, and to secure success requires a great amount of care. The earth in which these cuttings are placed, is prepared as before described for the seeds; it is, however, kept a little drier. The cuttings, on being made, are placed around the sides of the pots, the cut end of each being pressed firmly on a piece of dry brick, as shown in the illustration in the margin. Each pot contains from 20 to 25 cuttings, and as they are filled, they are immediately removed to the propagation frames, and plunged into beds of damp sand on a bottom of about 80 degrees Fahrenheit.

FIG. 3.

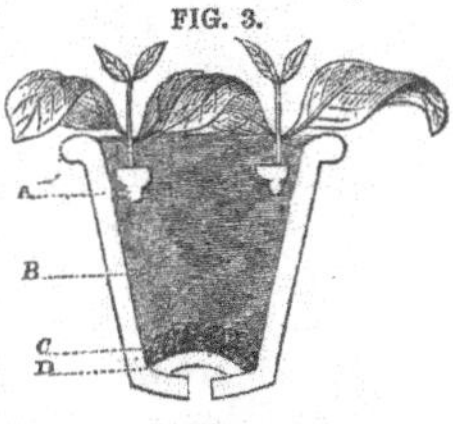

Fig 3.—Showing cuttings as placed in the pot, with the ends on a piece of dry brick. A, the brick; B, the soil; C, moss; D, potsherds.

27. The cuttings are now carefully watched, and their leaves moistened by a fine syringe when the atmosphere in the cases appears dry; they are, however, never watered, it being very necessary to ensure success to avoid this, as we have invariably found, that when the earth is once watered, it causes the cuttings to damp off, and seriously retards their rooting. The cause of this appears to be, that the cuttings not only suffer from excess of damp; but the soil when watered in the usual way, after the cuttings are placed in the pots, by its expansion and adhesion from the action of the water, the particles of soil are forced far too close together to be beneficial for the development of roots. With young wood, our losses with cuttings has recently not averaged 3 per cent. In removing the cuttings from the stock plants, one or two pairs of leaves and buds should, if possible, be left between the plant and the part cut; this is done in order not to decrease the succeeding supplies of young wood, which would be the case if the cut was made close to the parent stem. Another circumstance very necessary to be attended to in order to ensure success, is to be careful to place each cutting as it is made into the pot, with the cut end on a piece of dry brick; this must be attended to, because where the cut is made, the juice begins to flow, and this juice, if not immediately absorbed by the dry brick, causes mildew and rot. When the cuttings are placed in the cases, they are exposed to as much light as they can bear without flagging.

28. In December last, it occurred to me, that the plants could be successfully propagated by leaves with the bud attached; and as this method offered very considerable advantages in producing a large number of plants from a limited supply of wood, we resolved to attempt the experiment, which has been carried out most satisfactorily. The figure in the margin illustrates the method by which this is accomplished; the whole secret of success depends entirely on the amount of moisture given; if this is supplied in excess, they rot immediately, even in a day; but if sufficient care is exercised, the losses will not exceed 3 or 4 per cent., and this percentage has not been exceeded by many thousands we have propagated in this way: by this method, fine plants are obtained in every respect resembling strong, healthy seedlings. The period required to form roots is nearly the same in all the species, varying from three to

Cultivation; propagation by buds.

FIG. 4.

Fig. 4.—1. Represents the bud A, prepared for placing in the pot, showing the cut part B, upon the brick C.
2. A pot of buds of *Chinchona Calisaya* 41 days after planting.
3. A bud of *Chinchona succirubra* also 41 days after planting.

to six weeks. In the figure above given, the pot on the left represents six *Chinchona Calisaya* buds put in on the 30th January last, which were all rooted in 41 days after, being the date on which the drawing was made by Mr. Batcock. This drawing on the right, represents a rooted bud of the Red Bark put in at the same time. It may be observed, that it is not indispensable that a leaf be attached to the bud; this is no doubt a great advantage, although we have struck many buds without any leaf attached.

29. The usual way in which we prepare the buds is to remove the point of the shoots for a cutting; the stem is then divided near the middle of each internode, split down the centre, and immediately placed upon the brick in the pot, the bud itself being covered with about a quarter of an inch of soil, while the leaf, of course, projects above the surface; the pots are then plunged in damp sand, and treated in every respect the same as the cuttings.

Cultivation under the shade of living trees.

30. The entire adoption of this system has been endeavoured to be forced upon Government by the scientific gentlemen who have visited and who conduct the Java plantations. It is, however, a system of very questionable utility, as it has been in operation in Java for many years without producing the desired results; it moreover seems to have been adopted from a want of confidence in discriminating between the conditions which are beneficial, and those which are injurious in a state of nature, hence a slavish imitation of what has been described as the natural conditions under which the plants grow in their indigenous localities on the Andes. In cultivation, this implicit imitation of all the natural conditions under which plants must of necessity grow in a wild state, has invariably led to bad results; as indeed it must of necessity do, because the whole art of culture is vested in the very simple art of administering to the plants such conditions only as are conducive to their perfect development, and of removing or mitigating to the greatest extent possible such conditions as are injurious. To give a near example:—When coffee cultivation was attempted in Ceylon and in the Wainád, numerous intelligent and enterprising gentlemen imitated nature in this respect, and planted their coffee under shade; after eight or ten years, it was discovered that no return whatever could be obtained under such circumstances; and after this amount of time lost, money expended, and hopes disappointed, they had to begin and fell the whole of the shade, to the almost utter destruction of the plantations: and although we have been subjected to the criticisms of "obstinacy" and "stubbornness" in recommending a different course, I feel that it must be admitted that had we accepted arguments or opinions against facts daily developed before our eyes, together with the practical experience of generations, we would have given cause for much more serious strictures.

31. With the concurrence of Government, we have arranged to plant this season 75 acres of chinchona plants under various degrees of shade of forest trees; but only a few acres of this will be under dense shade, as our present experience has taught us that under such conditions cinchona plants cannot flourish. The main cause of this is that the roots of the forest trees immediately fill up the holes into which the chinchona plants are placed, thus depriving them of nourishment at the roots, while they are choked above for want of light and air. The production of alkaloids also cannot take place until the cinchona plants have overtopped the forest trees and expanded their heads in the open sunshine to enable them perfectly to elaborate their juices, and as this will require a period of 40 or 60 years, and the necessity for the destruction of the plantation to obtain the produce even after this lapse of time, this system, I fear, cannot be considered as one at all desirable to be followed.

32. The further suggestion, which has recently been recommended by Dr. Anderson to the Government of India, to grow *Chinchona Pahudiana,* because "nine-hundreth of a grain of quinine" had been found in the roots of one of these plants by Dr. De Vrij, seems insufficient to justify an expenditure of money in order to test the value of this discovery, as at this rate, to produce an ounce of quinine will require 5,330 trees. It is, however, added, that this had confirmed De Londre's discovery, made about 20 years ago, "that the roots of cinchonas contained a larger proportion of alkaloids than the bark." Unfortunately, De Londre himself gives an account directly the reverse of that above quoted as the results of his discovery, namely, that he obtained a much smaller proportion of quinine in

in the roots than in the bark, and that this small quantity was impure, incrystallizable, and consequently of no value. In order that the Government may not be misled, I may mention that De Londre's discovery refers to the roots of chinchonas producing bark rich in alkaloids, hence so far from going to prove the correctness of the discovery of Dr. De Vrij, its tendency is to prove the reverse; for if the roots of cinchonas producing bark rich in alkaloids only yielded a very small quantity of impure quinine, the conclusion is plain that a species such as the *Chinchona Pahudiana* which contains little or no alkaloids in its bark, must have still less in its roots.

33. In the early part of last season, several plants of different species of chinchona were planted out under different conditions, in order to test experimentally which would be the safest system of cultivation to pursue. These plants have been carefully watched and treated in every respect alike, and the result has been that the plants placed without the protection of any living shade has made the most satisfactory progress, and borne the dry and cold weather without the least injury. The plants placed under living shade were found to be damaged in some degree during the rains by the incessant drip; however, on the weather clearing up, they threw out fresh leaves and quickly recovered, but towards the end of the dry season these plants were found to be suffering considerably from the drought; on taking a few of them up, it was found that the holes in which they were placed had become filled by the fibres of the roots of the forest trees in the neighbourhood, which had drawn up the whole of the moisture and nourishment from the soil in which they were planted. The average growth of the plants under shade from the end of September 1861 to the 14th May 1862, has been about three inches. Cultivation in the open ground.

34. In putting out the plants which were placed in the open without any living shade whatever, we saw from the first that we had to combat with the young plants the bad effects of excessive evaporation, during our dry season, under a bright and scorching sun; we also saw the injury likely to be done to the plants by excessive radiation during bright and cloudless nights. To obviate these disadvantages, the plants were sheltered on the approach of the dry weather by a rough enclosure of bamboo branches with the leaves adhering to them, so as to give the plants sufficient shelter both from the effects of evaporation and radiation. The manner in which this is accomplished is illustrated in the margin. In addition to this shade of the branches of bamboos, the soil around the roots of the young chinchona plants was covered with one or two inches in thickness with half-decayed leaves, and the plants thus treated have a very great luxuriance which has not been exceeded by any of the plants in our propagating-houses. To ascertain the cause of this luxuriance, a few plants were examined at the end of the dry season, when the soil about the roots was found perfectly moist, and thousands of young roots of great strength had penetrated the covering of decayed leaves. The following table illustrates the growth of six plants placed out in a cleared spot on the highest and coldest part of the Neddivattum plantation:—

FIG. 5.

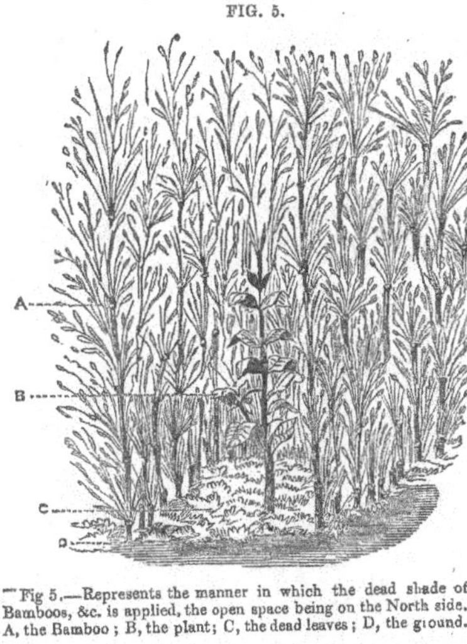

Fig 5.—Represents the manner in which the dead shade of Bamboos, &c. is applied, the open space being on the North side. A, the Bamboo; B, the plant; C, the dead leaves; D, the ground.

	Height of Plants when planted on the 29th September 1861.		Height on the 14th May 1862.	
		Inches.	*Feet.*	*Inches.*
No. 1.	Chinchona succirubra	9	2	5
– 2.	Ditto - ditto	4	2	3
– 3.	Ditto micrantha	$3\frac{1}{4}$	1	4
– 4.	Ditto - ditto	3	1	4
– 5.	Ditto nitida	$3\frac{1}{2}$	1	7
– 6.	Ditto - ditto	3	1	6

35. This result cannot but be viewed as most satisfactory; it establishes beyond a doubt that our chinchona plants will grow well under open cultivation, and thus the experiment will no doubt secure to us all the advantages we can desire. It is not only upon these six plants that this opinion is founded, but also on observations made upon many hundreds of plants placed out in our nurseries in December last; a portion of our nurseries were left partially shaded by living trees, while other portions were entirely open; at the end of March the plants shaded by living trees had scarcely made any progress, while those in the open portion of the nursery had grown upwards of a foot; we therefore cut down the whole of the trees which shaded the nursery with the exception of one, which could not be felled without damage to the young plants.

Cultivation; outline of proposed system.

36. From the observations made under the preceding head, I would respectfully recommend to the Government that in our operations of next season, the principle of open cultivation alone be pursued. This system is not, in fact, so great an outrage "on the habits of the genus" or on the opinions of authorities on chinchona cultivation as recently represented by Dr. Anderson. The description already given of the plants abundantly proves this fact. And with reference to the opinions of authorities, with the exception of the gentlemen in Java, they are unanimous in pronouncing this open system of cultivation to be right; even Dr. Weddell,* who has been frequently quoted as entertaining a different view of the matter, distinctly approves of this system of culture.

37. The advantages of open cultivation are such as cannot fail to carry conviction to the mind of every man who will give the subject a moment's serious consideration, as it enables us at once to place our plants out under the most favourable conditions to promote their growth. The soil is not impoverished by the roots of neighbouring trees, the plants cannot suffer from drip, nor from the effects of evaporation or radiation, as the dead shade affords them, in this respect, a far more efficient and certain protection than could possibly be given by any living shade, while instead of impoverishing it enriches the ground; it also possesses the incomparable advantage of being entirely under our own control, it can

* "My reason for recommending the young plants to be placed in the open field, jointly with young trees of some other order, and rather more fast-growing than these, originated from the fact of my having always seen the calisaya tree dwarfed and stunted when growing in exposed or entirely open situations; whether the same thing takes place with other species seems doubtful, as Mr. Spruce says that the red bark tree thrives in open ground.

"At all events I should never recommend planting any of these trees in the dense shade of the forest. In such a situation the greater part of them would evidently soon be smothered.

"If I have said that shade appeared indispensable to the trees at an early age, I never meant that they should have too much of it. I think that the trees in India ought to be planted in open ground, and close enough (if unmingled with other trees) to oblige each other to run up, sufficient space and air being gradually provided by judicious pruning and thinning out. A most important condition of success may be found in the choice of the proper time for planting out, the best being probably the beginning of the rainy season."

(signed) *H. A. Weddell.*

(True Extract)

(signed) *W. G. McIvor,*
Superintendent Government Chinchona Plantations.

can thus be adjusted exactly to suit the seasons. In the wet weather, when shade would be decidedly injurious by promoting the growth of fungi and causing rot, it can be removed; while, in the dry season, it can be increased to any extent necessary. It also enables us at once to place the plants under the most favourable conditions for the development of the alkaloids, and under this system of cultivation I have no doubt that many of the species will give a supply of bark, in from six to seven years after planting, and that in eight to ten years they will give a large yearly supply. This artificial shading will of course be required until the plants attain sufficient size to cover the ground, which will probably be in two years or less.

38. In a state of nature all products are reaped in the most improvident and reckless manner possible; but the moment the plants are brought into cultivation this must cease, and the harvesting of the produce of the present year must be effected in such a manner as not to injure that of succeeding years. Although in the forests of the Andes the trees are cut down and stripped of their bark, such a system can never be profitably put into operation in cultivation, and another more suited must therefore be devised. I would suggest that our trees be planted in such a manner as to secure the constant and uniform yearly supply of bark by simply lopping and pruning the trees; if this operation is conducted with skill, the plants will be benefited rather than injured by the yearly removal, before the middle of the dry season, of a certain portion of their branches. This will not retard the growth of the plants, nor indeed can any damage arise from an attempt to carry out this system, which has been brought to the notice of Mr. Howard, and that great chemical authority considers "that a large produce may be realized in this way." Proposed treatment for the yearly production of constant and uniform supplies of bark.

39. In the first years, probably from the sixth to the eighth after planting, the produce will be comparatively small, and be entirely of the description known in the market as quill bark, but after the 12th year of the growth of the plants a large proportion of the loppings and prunings will produce what is known in the market as flat or trunk bark. As an argument against this system, it has been advanced that chinchona plants do not throw out any branches, but this is a mistake, as we have some plants, although a little more than 15 months old, with 11 to 13 branches, and some of these branches themselves measure 3½ feet in length, and the secondary branches one foot four inches. There is certainly nothing in the habits of all the species of this plant but what promises to be admirably suited to this method of cultivation; and from our own observations I feel convinced that much, if not the whole, success of the cultivation depends upon our results in this part of the operation. For if, as stated by the Dutch in Java, the plants will not attain sufficient size to produce bark under 40 or 50 years, then chinchona cultivation can never become of commercial importance, but this is not at all likely to be the case; for if our plants continue to attain the same rate of growth as they have done, we have every promise of a small supply of bark even before the lapse of the period mentioned above, and we can reasonably expect that our plants, when once well established, will attain greater luxuriance than they have hitherto done.

40. In order to obtain the greatest produce from our plantations at an early date, it appears to be desirable to place our plants rather close together, and with this object in view in our operations of this season we have prepared to place the shrubby varieties at a distance of from seven to eight feet apart, which will give about 889 and 680 plants respectively to the acre; the layer-grown species at nine and ten feet apart, which will give about 537 and 435 plants to the acre. This of course would be much too close to remain to attain their full size, but when they begin to crowd and impede the growth of each other they can be thinned out; and this operation will no doubt furnish a large supply of bark, as they will probably not require to be thinned out before the 12th year of their growth, as when they first begin to crowd sufficient light and air will be afforded by lopping and pruning a portion of the branches.

41. The propagating-house sanctioned by Government in July last was finished by the end of December, and has been found most complete and efficient in its working details; some delay was caused in the progress of this work owing to the heavy rains in October and November, as also by the inexperience of the workmen in erecting a building, it was found difficult to get the furnaces Progress of operations.

furnaces and flues built in such a manner as to give a steady and efficient heat to the soil in the propagating frames. This, however, was successfully accomplished, and the house in full working order and filled with plants by the 1st of January. The house contains fifteen propagating frames, and each of these holds about 1,200 cuttings, or in all sufficient space for about 18,000 cuttings; the house also contains as much space as that occupied by the propagating frames for the growth and propagation of plants by layers and for hardening off such plants as are rooted. The cost of this building amounts to about 2,100 rupees.

42. *House for European Gardener.*—This building was completed by the latter end of January, at a cost of about 1,350 rupees; at the suggestion of His Excellency the Governor, who visited the work at the time the foundations were being laid, the rooms were enlarged, and the house now contains two main rooms 12×14, three verandah rooms, one being 7×14, the other two 6×14, with open verandah 7½×14, together with kitchen, store-rooms, and pantry.

Overseer's house, Dodabetta Plantation.—This building is not yet quite finished, but is in a very forward state. In estimating for this building it was proposed to be done temporarily, namely, with bamboo roof; but, as our operations progressed, I considered it desirable to construct this as also a house for the Head Propagator in a permanent and durable manner, and consequently the buildings have been substantially erected with burnt bricks, the corners, jams, and chimneys being laid in chunam, and the whole of the timber and roofs of teakwood. I hope to be able to finish these buildings in this substantial manner for only a trifle more than the estimates for the temporary buildings, and I trust the Government will approve of the alteration.

Propagator's house.—This has been erected close to the propagating-house, as it was found indispensable that the Propagator should be on the spot in order to give the plants and cuttings that amount of attention which is necessary to ensure success. This buiiding will be completed in a few days.

Coolies' quarters.—These have been built with burned bricks, teak rafters, and bamboo reepers.

43. The difficulty experienced in getting artizans to proceed to Neddiwnttum, has rendered it now impossible to get the permanent building there completed before the setting in of the rains; therefore small but comfortable temporary buildings, with teakwood doors and windows, have been erected for the assistant superintendent in charge of the plantation, as also for the overseers, with store and tool houses, and accommodation for about 200 workmen. The permanent buildings will be proceeded with immediately the rains are over; all the materials, including doors, windows, &c., being finished there will then be no delay.

44. *Felling.*—On the Neddiwnttum plantation about 85 acres have been felled, cleared, and prepared for planting this season; and as our work was much delayed last season by the forest not being felled in time, I considered it desirable to fell about 50 acres for next year's planting, so that our work may not be delayed at the commencement of next season. On this plantation about 15 acres have been cleared for planting under the shade of living trees, and on the Dodabetta site about 55 acres have been prepared for placing out the plants under various degrees of living shade; in only a small portion has the underwood been cleared away, and here the chinchona plants will be placed out under dense shade; but the greatest portion of the land is almost entirely cleared, only sufficient living trees being left to give efficient shelter and slight shade. Here also five acres are entirely cleared of forest; consequently the results on this plantation will enable us to form a correct opinion of all the advantages and disadvantages likely to accrue from the two systems of cultivation, and all the intermediate stages between them.

Trenching and pitting.—After the roads being either formed or marked out, our trenching and pitting operations were begun; at Neddiwnttum ten acres of trenching have been completed, and on the Dodabetta site about 21 acres of land has been trenched, and 25 acres pitted. The whole of this site will be prepared by the end of May, when with the approval of Government we will proceed to pit and trench the 25 additional acres on this site intended for the cultivation of *Chinchona crespilla.*

45. *Enclosures.*

45. *Enclosures.*—As above mentioned, the difficulty of getting artizans to proceed to Neddinuttum, the walls to enclose this plantation have not been begun, although many of the bricks have been made; it has therefore been found necessary to enclose this site with a strong temporary fence. The Dodabetta site is nearly enclosed by a turf wall and ditch on three sides, and on the fourth by a wooden fence; the brick wall around the nurseries is now in progress.

46. *Increase of Plants.*—Next in importance to that of introducing a valuable plant is its increase and multiplication, and with this object in view great attention has been given to this part of our operations, which has been much facilitated by the efficient working of the new propagating-house. The following table gives the number of plants on the 30th April, or at the end of the official year:—

Botanical Names.	Commercial Names.	No. of Plants.	Value in the London Market per lb. of Dry Bark.	Remarks.
			s. d. s. d.	
1. Chinchona succirubra -	Red Bark - -	14,450	2 6 to 8 0	In fine health.
2. Do. Calisaya - -	Yellow Bark -	237	2 10 to 7 –	Do. do.
3. Do. Condaminea, var. Uritusinga -	Original Loxa Bark	1	2 10 to 7 –	Promising.
4. Do. Condaminea, var. Chahuarguera -	Rusty Crown Bark	8,000	2 10 to 7 –	In good health.
5. Do. Condaminea, var. Crespilla - -	Fine Crown Bark	105	2 10 to 6 –	Do. do.
6. Do. lancifolia from Java - - -	Crown Bark- -	1	1 8 to 2 10	Unhealthy.
7. Do. nitida -	Genuine Grey Bark	2,922	1 8 to 2 9	In fine health.
8. Do. species without name - -	Fine Grey Bark -	1,211	1 8 to 2 10	Do. do.
9. Do. micrantha - -	Grey Bark - -	3,786	1 8 to 2 9	Do. do.
10. Do. Peruviana - -	Finest Grey Bark	357	1 8 to 2 10	Do. do.
11. Do. Pahudiana from Java - - -	Unknown - -	425	Worthless -	Do. do.
	Total number of Plants -	31,495		

Although this increase is highly satisfactory, we have been materially retarded in this respect by supplying, at the end of December last, to Dr. Anderson, for cultivation in Bengal, 204 well-established plants of different species of chinchonas, the greater portion of these being of the most valuable species we possess; these by this time would have produced many thousands. Still, the distribution of these plants will be more beneficial to Government than if they had been retained here; should the localities selected for their cultivation prove suitable, the plants will no doubt be increased with the same rapidity as has been attained here. With our red bark plants the increase of the year is upwards of 2,000 per cent., and equal results have been attained with all the species in proportion to their value:—that is, species of less value have not been propagated to such an extent.

47. General difficulty was experienced, especially in the first stages of our operations, in getting together a tolerably efficient establishment; and although this condition of affairs has lately considerably improved, still we are far from possessing an establishment with the general requirements necessary for conducting operations of this description. This, indeed, was to be expected, as the cultivation of the plants is new; and even in organizing an establishment for any undertaking, it requires time to bring it to an efficient state of working. In the propagating department, the effects of carelessness and ignorance in the management of the plants were productive of the most serious losses. I have been much assisted since the arrival of Mr. Batcock in October last; and I have every reason to be highly satisfied with the intelligence, ability, and zeal with which he has performed the duties entrusted to him. Mr. Patmore, the head overseer on the Establishments.

 Neddiwuttum

Neddiwuttum plantation, has also taken a great interest in his work, exhibiting an unusual amount of skill in the management of the plants, and is in every respect well qualified for promotion. Mr. Lyall, the European gardener recently engaged by the Secretary of State, arrived here on the 18th ultimo, and has been placed in charge of this plantation. The other overseers, although willing and anxious to give satisfaction, have exhibited a want of knowledge in the management of the plants and the direction of labour, which I have found great difficulty in improving. Every endeavour, however, is being made to obtain men possessing the various qualifications required.

48. *Office.*—I have seriously felt the want of a good accountant and office manager, the salary (40 rupees) at present allowed being insufficient to secure the services of a man possessed of the abilities required. Mr. Hollis, recommended by the Forest Department, conducted the office duties until the end of October last, when, being offered a higher salary by the coffee planters, he left this employ without due notice, or delivering over the records and account of his office, which put me to much inconvenience.

Concluding remarks.

49. So far as our operations have progressed, this experiment has been eminently successful, both as regards the number, genuineness, and value of the species introduced, their increase and cultivation. The very important fact has also been established, that the climate of the Neilgherries is suitable for the growth of all the most valuable species of chinchona, and that the plants possess as great power of withstanding extremes of wet and drought as is generally the case with evergreens. It has also been ascertained that the chinchonas, like nearly every other plant, has a distinct period of growth, which extends over about nine months of the year, the remaining three months being one of comparative rest. This has especially been clearly demonstrated by our seedlings in the glass-houses, for although the temperature and moisture was kept nearly uniform through the year, yet towards the season of rest the growth of the plants became less rapid, the upper leaves assuming a leathery texture, while the lower leaves became red and fell off, thus exhibiting the usual signs of a definite season of rest: this was the case with all the species, but not so marked in the *Chinchona nitida*, although this species also exhibited unmistakeable signs of a season of comparative rest, while immediately on the return of spring the whole of the species began to grow with renewed vigour. I record these observations, as it is generally believed that the conditions most favourable for the growth of these plants "are those of continuous vegetation;" and although this is literally correct, because vegetation never fairly ceases, yet it conveys somewhat an erroneous impression; for it is evident from the indications the plants themselves have given of their nature, that to urge them to an equal continuous growth would do serious damage, by preventing the perfect elaboration of the juices of the plants, a condition to which they are undoubtedly subjected in their natural localities on the Andes, and this condition is, no doubt, essential to their well-being.

50. Our plants have, in the most satisfactory manner possible, passed through all that we had to fear from the effects of this climate,—namely, the dry season, and hailstorms, to which we are liable in the spring of the year. Our dry weather certainly presents no insurmountable difficulty to the successful cultivation of the chinchonas, and it is likely to prove highly beneficial in promoting the production of alkaloids: the only difficulty our dry season presents is that it renders the operations with the young plants more difficult for a year or two, but when once the plants are fairly established, it cannot be productive of any inconvenience whatever. It is indeed very questionable if our dry season, especially on the western side of the Neilgherries, is so severe or of so long continuance as that of the cinchona region on the Andes, as we frequently read of the jungles there being periodically set on fire, while here the drought has seldom been experienced sufficiently severe to render this possible. The hailstorms, as they happen before the young leaves of spring are expanded, do comparatively little damage to the plants. From the effects of hail our chinchonas have not suffered more than any other introduced plants which luxuriate all over these hills.

51. Although the increase in the number of the plants of last season has been very satisfactory, still we may expect far greater results this year, as we now possess a more perfect knowledge of the system of propagation, and more efficient appliances,

appliances, so that during this year we may calculate on producing at least 150,000 plants. I would therefore respectfully suggest, that the plants be offered for sale to the public in January next, at the following rates,—namely, 500 rupees per 1,000; 300 rupees for 500; 200 rupees for 150; 100 rupees for 50, or 4 rupees per plant for any number under 50. We have now numerous applications for plants, both from planters in this Presidency and from Bombay; and as the number required is generally large, I thought it desirable to fix a low price upon the plants when a thousand or upwards are taken by one purchaser: and I think it is more desirable that our plants be sold to private individuals than gratuitously distributed, which is apt to lead to the loss of the plants, because persons do not generally value that which they receive for nothing, whereas those who purchase plants at a fair price establish by this act that they value and consequently will take care of them; moreover, it will induce purchasers to propagate and increase the plants themselves, and thus greatly facilitate the extension of their cultivation.

52. In concluding this report, I beg to tender my grateful acknowledgments to his Excellency Sir William Denison and the Government of Madras, for the confidence they have reposed in me while conducting the operations of this important experiment through its most critical stages, and at a time when the correctness of our own views had not been practically developed, and many conflicting theories pressed upon Government. My best acknowledgments are also due to Clements R. Markham, Esq., for much valuable assistance and information, which has greatly contributed to the successful development of this undertaking; also to J. E. Howard, Esq., for his contribution of the valuable species of *Chinchona Uritusinga*, and for much important scientific information.

(signed) *W. G. McIvor*,
Superintendent Government Cinchona Plantations.

Government Gardens, Ootacamund,
31 May 1862.

— No. 102. —

From *W. G. McIvor*, Esq., Superintendent Government Chinchona Plantations, to *J. D. Sim*, Esq., Secretary to Government, Revenue Department.

Sir, Ootacamund, 27 June 1862.

WITH reference to the order of Government, under date the 23d June 1862, I have the honour to inform you, with reference to the application of Mr. Lascelles for chinchona plants, that by the planting season next year, we will have available for distribution, probably, between 20,000 and 30,000 plants. In conversation, this gentleman mentioned 10,000 as the probable number of plants he intended to purchase: this quantity will, no doubt, be available for Mr. Lascelles, and will leave sufficient plants for the supply of other applicants.

— No. 103. —

Memorandum from *W. G. McIvor*, Esq., Superintendent Government Chinchona Plantations, Ootacamund, dated 6 September 1862.

1. I WOULD respectfully submit that the progress of the chinchona experimental cultivation, and the present very promising condition of the plants, are such as to justify more extended operations than those already proposed. I would therefore recommend that, in addition to the land (150 acres) proposed to be opened at Neddiwuttum during the present official year, a new plantation, of at least 100 acres, be opened to the east of the Pycara Waterfalls, as this is a site which will no doubt prove well suited for the cultivation of all the species

of cinchonas, and especially for the most valuable sorts, such as *C. succirubra*, *C. Calisaya*, and *C. Condaminea*. In opening this plantation, I would recommend that the land be cleared of forest and trenched—that is, in the first instance, lines of trenches to be made three feet wide and two feet deep, and ten feet apart, for the *C. succirubra* and *C. Calisaya*, and eight feet for *C. Condaminea*: this will leave an intervening space of five and seven feet in each row of untrenched land, which can be turned over after the planting is finished; or, perhaps, portions of it may be trenched over with the greatest advantage, immediately before the roots of the plants reach the untrenched land.

2. I would also submit, for the consideration of Government, that the pay of the office manager be increased from 40 to 50 rupees per mensem, and that the salary of the second writer be increased from 25 to 40 rupees, and that he be required to furnish security to the extent of 2,000 rupees, and to perform the duties of pay-clerk or shroff.

3. Subjoined is an estimate of the cost of this new work.

ESTIMATE COST of forming a Plantation (of 100 acres) of Chinchona Trees on the East of the Pycara Waterfalls.

PARTICULARS.	Cost of forming the Plantation with Buildings, Roads, Tools, &c.			Cost of Fixed Establishment.		
	Rs.	*a.*	*p.*	*Rs.*	*a.*	*p.*
Building and other Contingent Charges:						
To house for the assistant superintendent, to consist of two main rooms, 12 × 12, and four verandah rooms, 6 × 12. Walls to be built of burnt brick in clay. Fireplaces, chimneys, and corners of brick in chunam, and plastered with chunam; roof to be constructed of teakwood, king-beams, rafters of jungle-wood, and covered with thatch; doors and windows of teakwood - -	1,200	–	–	—		
To out-houses, one kitchen, 10 × 12, and two out-houses, 10 × 15, constructed as above - - - - - - - - - -	330	–	–	—		
To tool-rooms and store-rooms, each 10 × 15, constructed as above	250	–	–	—		
To houses for 100 coolies, to consist of 30 rooms, 7 × 10 each constructed as above - - - - - - - - - -	1,000	–	–	—		
To enclosing 100 acres with strong wooden fence, five feet high -	750	–	–	—		
To felling 100 acres, at 15 rupees per acre; lopping and clearing, at 15 rupees per acre; trenching 100 acres in lines, 3 feet wide, 2 feet deep, at 80 rupees per acre; shading plants, at 7 rupees per acre; carriage of plants and planting, at 6 rupees per acre -	12,300	–	–	—		
To forming cart-roads, 12 feet wide, over 100 acres of land, at 300 rupees per mile - - - - - - - - - - -	1,350	–	–	—		
To tools.—200 pickaxes, at 2 rupees each; 200 felling-axes, at 2 rupees each; 100 billhooks, at 1½ rupees each; 200 mamooties, at 1 rupee each; 12 steel digging-forks, at 4 rupees each: 24 steel spades, at 2 rupees each; 12 crowbars, at 3 rupees each -	1,282	–	–	—		
A propagating-house - - - - - - - - - - -	2,000	–	–	—		
Contingent charges, at 10 per cent. - - - - - - - -	2,046	–	–	—		
Fixed Establishment:						
1 Assistant superintendent - - - - - - - - -	-	-	-	125	–	–
2 Peons, at 7 rupees each per mensem - - - - - - -	-	-	-	14	–	–
TOTAL - - -	22,508	–	–	139	–	–

(signed) *W. G. McIvor*,
Superintendent Government Chinchona Plantations.

Government Gardens, Ootacamund,
6 September 1862.

MINUTE by Sir *William Denison.*

I VISITED Neddiwuttum a few days ago, and found the state of the plantation to be as follows:—

1. At the top of the hill, a height of about 6,000 feet above the sea, a number of plants had been in the ground for upwards of a year; they had been exposed to the cold of the winter, the drought of the spring, the wet of the monsoon, yet nothing could look more healthy and flourishing than the whole of these. The tenderest species, *C. succirubra*, seemed to flourish best, for a plant not more than 15 months old was three feet six inches high. Farther down the hill a piece of ground, about 68 acres in extent, has been cleared and prepared for plants; this site occupied two sides of a valley, and was sheltered by belts of trees on the ridges, separating it from the adjacent valleys. About 18 acres of this were planted, and the plants looked healthy and flourishing. The planting had been delayed by the wet weather, but Mr. McIvor expected to plant at the rate of about 10 acres per week. In an adjacent valley, at a lower level, about 180 acres had been felled and partially burned, and below this again, was the propagating-house and the nursery for young plants. The permanent buildings for the coolies and superintendent had yet to be erected, and the fence round the plantation to be completed. Great credit, however, is due to Mr. McIvor, for the energy which he has shown in pushing on the experiment, and for the amount of work which he has got through; nothing can look better than the plants, and everything seems to me to testify to the success of the experiment. I should therefore be disposed to recommend that this should be pushed on steadily and regularly, and that 150 acres should be added annually to the plantations, for a period of nine or ten years at least, at the expiration of which period, we shall be able to ascertain whether Mr. McIvor's views as to the possibility of getting a return from the loppings and prunings of the trees, are correct. Should they be so, the size of the annual plantation may be diminished.

2. I have proposed to plant 150 acres annually, because I am of opinion that the Government will have to depend very much on its own exertions to provide chinchona bark to an extent at all commensurate with its consumption. It is perfectly true that many persons have asked for plants, and professed their intention of making plantations; but looking to the fact that they must, under any circumstances, remain without any interest upon their outlay for nine or ten years, and that this outlay will amount, with interest, to about 100 *l.* per acre, I do not think that any great extent of land will be planted. Should the lopping and pruning produce the quantity of bark anticipated by Mr. McIvor, the return will be sufficient to repay the capital expended in about 10 years, inclusive of interest; but the supply will not be large enough to produce any great effect on the market-price of quinine, which will go on increasing until the trees now planted arrive at their full growth, say 40 years, when the return might amount to 40,000 lbs. of bark per acre, or for 180 acres six millions of pounds. The cost to the Government would be at the utmost, supposing there to be no return in the interval, about 1,000 *l.* per acre, and the return, even at present prices, would be at least 16,000 *l.* per acre.

3. With reference to the accompanying proposal from Mr. McIvor, that he should be allowed to make a new plantation at Pycara, at a cost of 22,508 rupees, I should recommend that it be acceded to, to this extent—that he should be allowed to clear away the timber from 100 acres during the dry season, when alone it can be done with advantage, and that for this purpose he should be allowed to expend 3,000 rupees, while he should also be allowed to build a propagating-house and houses for the superintendent and the coolies, at a cost not exceeding 4,000 rupees; the remainder of the work to be included in the estimate for 1863-64, which must also include the completion of the plantations to the extent of 300 acres, and the clearance of the ground (150 acres) for the plantation of 1864-65. The other propositions of Mr. McIvor seem reasonable.

September 1862. *W. T. Denison.*

ORDER of the Madras Government, 2 October 1862.

1. ON a consideration of the President's minute above recorded, in which his Excellency has detailed the success of the cinchona plantation at Neddiwattum, and has strongly recommended the gradual extension of these plantations, the Government resolve to sanction the proposal made by Mr. McIvor to form a new plantation at Pycara, at a total cost of 22,508 rupees; limiting, however, his operations during the current year to clearing away the timber from 100 acres during the dry season, when alone it can be done with advantage. To carry into effect this commencement of the new plantation, 3,000 rupees will be allotted to Mr. McIvor.

2. A further sum of 4,000 rupees will be allowed for building a propagating-house, and houses for the superintendent and coolies.

3. Mr. McIvor will make provision for the remainder of the work in framing the budget estimate for 1863-64, in which should also be included the completion of the plantation to the extent of 300 acres, and the clearing of 150 acres for the plantation of 1864-65.

4. The Government approve also of the proposal made by Mr. McIvor to increase the salaries of the office manager and of the second writer from 40 to to 50 rupees, the second writer being required to furnish security to the extent of 2,000 rupees, and performing the duties of shroff. Application will, accordingly, be made to the Government of India for sanction to this increase of salaries.

5. Mr. McIvor will be called upon to report whether the additional expenditure sanctioned in this order can be met from the sums entered in the budget for 1862-63 for the cultivation of cinchona.

(signed) *T. Pycroft*,
Chief Secretary.

— No. 104. —

From the Government of Madras to Sir *Charles Wood*.

Madras, 23 October 1862.

1. WE have the honour to forward, for your information, papers regarding the cultivation of the chinchona on the Neilgherry Hills.

2. We beg to draw your attention especially to the Minute recorded by our President, after a personal inspection of the plantation at Neddivattum.

3. The following table shows the number of plants of each species on the 31st August last:—

Botanical Names.	Commercial Names.	Number of Original Plants and Date of Receipt.	Number of Plants on the 30th April 1862.	Number of Plants on the 31st August 1862.	Value per Pound of Dry Bark in the London Market.
					s. d. s. d.
1. C. succirubra - - -	Red Bark - -	457, April 1861	14,450	30,150	2 6 to 8 9
2. C. Calisaya - - -	Yellow Bark -	{ 6, April ,, 48, Dec. ,, }	237	1,050	2 10 to 7 –
3. C. Condaminea, var. Uritusinga.	Original Loxa Bark	1, April 1862	1	41	2 10 to 7 –
4. C. Condaminea, var. Chahar-guera.	Rusty Crown Bark	Seeds, Feb. ,,	8,000	20,030	2 10 to 7 –
5. C. Condaminea, var. Crespilla	Fine Crown Bark -	,, Feb. ,,	105	236	2 10 to 6 –
6. C. lancifolia - - -	Pitayo Bark - -	4, Dec. 1861	1	1	1 8 to 2 10
7. C. nitida - - - -	Genuine Grey Bark	Seeds, Feb. ,,	2,922	8,500	1 8 to 2 9
8. C. (species without name) -	Fine Grey Bark -	,, Feb. ,,	1,211	2,440	1 8 to 2 10
9. C. micrantha - - -	Grey Bark - -	,, Feb. ,,	3,786	7,400	1 8 to 2 9
10. C. Peruviana - - -	Finest Grey Bark -	,, Feb. ,,	357	2,295	1 8 to 2 10
11. C. Pahudiana - - -	Unknown - -	250, Dec. ,,	425	425	Worthless.
TOTAL Number of Plants - - -		766	31,495	72,568	

Note.—Average present propagation, about 10,000 per mensem.

4. We

4. We need not comment on this table, which is enough in itself to show the great success attained in the propagation of the plant.

5. The Dodabetta plantation extends over 60 acres, of which 15 have been planted out, and 45 have been cleared and prepared in different stages. A further extent of 45 acres will be planted in the course of the current year. Of the entire area only five acres will be entirely cleared for the reception of plants, while 55 acres will retain various degrees of shade as an experimental measure.

6. The Neddiwuttum site comprises 150 acres, of which 21 have been planted, and 129 acres, more or less, prepared. A further extent of 79 acres will be planted in the course of the current calendar year. It is to this latter plantation that our President specially refers in his Minute, to which we have above called your attention; and we doubt not that you will be gratified to learn the flourishing condition of the plants generally, and in particular of six plants which were planted out experimentally on 29th September 1861, on the highest part of the site, about 6,200 feet above the sea. These plants (including the most delicate variety, *C. succirubra*) have stood the cold of the winter, the drought of the spring, and the wet of the monsoon without any artificial protection, and were in the most vigorous and healthy condition, ranging in height from 36 to 42 inches, although only 15 months old.

7. We do not deem it necessary to trouble you with any lengthened remarks on the difference of opinion between Dr. Anderson and Mr. McIvor as to the culture of the chinchona plant. The system adopted by Mr. McIvor is supported by Messrs. Markham, Cross, and Spruce, who alone have seen the plant growing in its natural habitat, is consistent with the recognised principles of horticulture, and, above all, has proved eminently successful in practice. Granting that the cultivation of the chinchona is still an experiment, it seems to us that we should be guilty of great want of judgment if we abandoned a system which has in every respect been attended with such satisfactory results. As already remarked, 55 acres of land are being tried with varying degrees of shade, in order that every mode of culture may be practically tested; but we are bound to say that, so far as our present experience extends, the plan of open planting has been most successful, the trees in open ground being far healthier and more vigorous than those under the shade of living trees, and this in proportion to their exposure to the influence of the atmosphere.

8. Mr. McIvor's mode of culture from the outset is explained in full detail in his report of the 31st May 1862, and we need only add that nothing can be more satisfactory or promising than its results.

9. The rapid propagation of plants has enabled us to offer a considerable number for sale early next year, at the moderate price of 4 annas (or 6*d*.) each. In fixing this rate, we have been influenced by a desire to encourage the cultivation of the plant by private individuals, owing to the expenses of cultivation, and the long period which must elapse before returns can be expected. We are not sanguine of the investment of private capital in this speculation, and therefore, while extending every legitimate encouragement to private enterprise, we purpose yearly to add to the Government plantations. We have directed Mr. McIvor to clear 100 acres, at a site differing in aspect from that at Neddivattum, during the ensuing dry season (when alone this operation can be advantageously performed), and to build a propagating-house and quarters for the superintendent and coolies, at an aggregate cost of 7,000 rupees. The planting out of this new site will not be undertaken until 1863-64.

10. We consider that Mr. McIvor is entitled to very great credit for the able and energetic manner in which he has conducted the important experiment entrusted to him, and that he has well merited the increased salary allowed to him in modification of that proposed in our Order of 3d July 1861.

From

— No. 105. —

From *W. G. McIvor*, Esq., Superintendent Government Chinchona Plantations, Ootacamund, to *J. D. Sim*, Esq., Secretary to Government, Revenue Department, Fort St. George.

Sir, Ootacamund, 13 November 1862.

WITH reference to the Order of Government of the 22d ultimo, No. 2263, I have the honour to enclose the report for last month of our progress in the cinchona operations, and would add that we have begun the permanent buildings both at Neddiwuttum and at Pycara, that upwards of 200 acres of forest have already been cleared for the next season's planting, which makes the total extent of our plantations, more or less prepared, 410 acres.

REPORT on the Number, Distribution, and Condition of the Chinchona Plants on the Neilgherries, on 31 October 1862.

No. of Species.	Botanical Names.	Commercial Names.	Number of Plants.	Value per Pound of Dry Bark in the London Market.
				s. d. s. d.
1	C. succirubra - -	Red Bark - -	39,268	2 6 to 8 9
2	C. Calisaya - -	Yellow Bark - -	1,346	2 10 to 7 –
3	C. Condaminea, var. Uritusinga.	Original Loxa Bark -	820	2 10 to 7 –
4	C. Condaminea, var. Chaharguera.	Rusty Crown Bark -	27,957	2 10 to 7 –
5	C. Condaminea, var. Crespilla.	Fine Crown Bark -	287	2 10 to 6 –
6	C. lancifolia - -	Pitayo Bark - -	1	1 8 to 2 10
7	C. nitidia - -	Genuine Grey Bark -	8,542	1 8 to 2 9
8	C. (species without name.)	Fine Grey Bark -	2,514	1 8 to 2 10
9	C. micrantha - -	Grey Bark - -	8,110	1 8 to 2 9
10	C. Peruviana - -	Finest Grey Bark -	2,477	1 8 to 2 10
11	C. Pahudiana - -	Unknown - -	425	Worthless.
		TOTAL Number of Plants	91,747	

TABLE II.

MEMORANDUM of the Growth of the 11 Plants planted on the Second Denison Plantation at Neddiwuttum, on 30 August 1862.

Number of Plants.	Height in Inches when Planted 30 August 1862.	Height in Inches on 31 October 1862.	Growth in Inches during Two Months.	By whom Planted.
1	23	31	8	His Excellency Sir W. Denison.
2	16½	28	11½	
3	19	25	6	
4	15	23	8	
5	27	36	9	
6	20	28	8	
7	21	30	9	J. W. Breeks, Esq. - -
8	18	28	10	Dr. Sanderson - -
9	20	26	6	J. D. Sim, Esq. - -
10	20	32	12	Lieutenant McLeod - -
11	18	30	12	P. Grant, Esq. - -

REMARKS.

1. The total number of plants placed out permanently in the plantations is 35,000; and although many of these were only recently transplanted, all are making satisfactory progress.
2. The increase by propagation during last month was 11,291, being considerably above the average of the last two months.
3. The *Chinchona lancifolia* continues to make satisfactory progress, and I believe it may be safely stated that the introduction of this valuable species is now secured.
4. TABLE II. exhibits the growth of 11 plants, planted out by his Excellency the Governor and other gentlemen, on the 30th August 1862; these plants have been selected as their heights were noted at the time of being transplanted; and as they are all of the most valuable species, namely, *C. succirubra*, a correct record of their rate of growth in this climate will no doubt prove interesting. All the other species continue in the finest possible state of health, and are making equal progress to the Red Bark.

Government Gardens, Ootacamund,
6 November 1862.

(signed) *W. G. McIvor*,
Superintendent, Government Chinchona Plantations.

— No. 106. —

REPORT on the Number, Distribution, and Condition of the Chinchona Plants on the Neilgherries, on the 30th November 1862.

No. of Species.	Botanical Names.	Commercial Names.	Number of Plants.	Value per Pound of Dry Bark in the London Market.	REMARKS.
				s. d. s. d.	
1	C. succirubra - -	Red Bark - -	42,184	2 6 to 8 9	During last month, no plants having been placed out in the plantations, therefore the number of plants permanently planted out is the same as in October, namely, 35,000, all of which are making very satisfactory progress. The average growth of last month, as will be observed by Table II., is 6½ inches, which exceeds the average growth of September and October by two inches.
2	C. Calisaya - -	Yellow Bark - -	1,372	2 10 to 7 –	
3	C. Condaminea, var. Uritusinga.	Original Loxa Bark -	850	2 10 to 7 –	
4	C. Condaminea, var. Chahuarguera.	Rusty Crown Bark -	37,781	2 10 to 7 –	
5	C. Condaminea, var. Crespilla.	Fine Crown Bark -	464	2 10 to 6 –	
6	C. lancifolia - -	Pitayo Bark - -	1	1 8 to 2 10	
7	C. nitida - -	Genuine Grey Bark -	8,565	1 8 to 2 9	
8	C. species without name.	Fine Grey Bark -	2,542	1 8 to 2 10	
9	C. micrantha - -	Grey Bark - -	8,148	1 8 to 2 9	
10	C. Peruviana - -	Finest Grey Bark -	2,594	1 8 to 2 10	
11	C. Pahudiana - -	Unknown - -	425	Worthless.	
	TOTAL Number of Plants - - -		104,926		

TABLE II.

MEMORANDUM of the Growth of the Eleven Plants, planted on the Second Denison Plantation, at Neddiwuttum, on the 30th August 1862.

Number of Plants.	Height in Inches when Planted, 30th August 1862.	Height in Inches on the 31st October 1862.	Height in Inches on the 30th November 1862.	Growth in Inches during November 1862.	By whom Planted.
1	23	31	38	7	His Excellency Sir W. Denison.
2	16½	28	33	5	
3	19	25	31	6	
4	15	23	32	9	
5	27	36	43	7	
6	20	28	34	6	
7	21	30	35	5	J. W. Breeks, Esq.
8	18	28	35	7	Dr. Sanderson.
9	20	26	32	6	J. D. Sim, Esq.
10	20	32	39	7	Lieutenant McLeod.
11	18	30	37	7	P. Grant, Esq.

The increase by propagation during the month is 13,179, which considerably exceeds the results obtained in any previous months. The largest plant we possess is now 6 ft. 9 in. high, with branches from three to five feet in length; the stem, measured at half a foot above the ground, is 5¾ inches.

(signed) *W. G. McIvor,*
Superintendent Government Chinchona Plantation.

Government Gardens, Ootacamund,
December 1862.

— No. 107. —

REPORT on the Number, Distribution, and Condition of Chinchona Plants on the Neilgherries, on 31 December 1862.

No. of Species.	Botanical Names.	Commercial Names.	Number of Plants.	Value per Pound of Dry Bark in the London Market.
				s. d. s. d.
1	C. succirubra - -	Red Bark - -	45,352	2 6 to 8 9
2	C. Calisaya - -	Yellow Bark - -	1,448	2 10 to 7 –
3	C. Condaminea, var. Uritusinga.	Original Loxa Bark -	872	2 10 to 7 –
4	C. Condaminea, var. Chahuarguera.	Rusty Crown Bark -	46,751	2 10 to 7 –
5	C. Condaminea, var. Crespilla.	Fine Crown Bark -	664	2 10 to 6 –
6	C. lancifolia - -	Pitayo Bark - -	1	1 8 to 2 10
7	C. nitida - -	Genuine Grey Bark -	8,591	1 8 to 2 9
8	C. species without name.	Fine Grey Bark -	2,569	1 8 to 2 10
9	C. micrantha - -	Grey Bark - -	8,304	1 8 to 2 9
10	C. Peruviana - -	Finest Grey Bark -	2,729	1 8 to 2 10
11	C. Pahudiana - -	Unknown - -	425	Worthless.
	TOTAL Number of Plants - - -		117,706	

REMARKS.

The planting season having passed, the number of plants placed out in the plantations remain as in October, namely 35,000; these are now well established, and are making satisfactory progress.

The increase by propagation during last month is 12,780, being a little above the average results obtained during the last six months.

TABLE II.

MEMORANDUM of the Growth of Eleven Plants of *C. succirubra*, planted on the Second Denison Plantation at Neddiwuttum, on 30 August 1862.

Number of Plants.	Height in Inches when Planted, 30 August 1862.	Height in Inches on 30 November 1862.	Height in Inches on 31 December 1862.	Growth in Inches during December 1862.	By whom Planted.
1	23	38	41	3	His Excellency Sir W. Denison.
2	16½	33	37	4	His Excellency Sir W. Denison.
3	19	31	34	3	His Excellency Sir W. Denison.
4	15	32	36	4	His Excellency Sir W. Denison.
5	27	43	48	5	His Excellency Sir W. Denison.
6	20	34	40	6	His Excellency Sir W. Denison.
7	21	35	38	3	J. W. Breeks, Esq.
8	18	35	37	2	Dr. Sanderson.
9	20	32	38	6	J. D. Sim, Esq.
10	20	39	42	3	Lieutenant McLeod.
11	18	37	42	5	P. Grant, Esq.

Table II. exhibits the growth of 11 plants, planted out by his Excellency the Governor and other gentlemen on the 30th August 1862; the average growth of these plants for last month being only four inches, or two-and-a-half inches less than in November. This growth is, however, considerable, as December is one of the coldest months in the year, and the season at which most plants begin to winter. The whole of the plants in the nurseries and propagating houses continue in fine health.

Government Gardens, Ootacamund,
7 January 1863.

(signed) *W. G. McIvor,*
Superintendent Government Chinchona Plantations.

— No. 108 *A.* —

REPORT on the Number, Distribution, and Condition of Chinchona Plants on the Neilgherries, on 31 January 1863.

No. of Species.	Botanical Names.	Commercial Names.	No. of Plants.	Value per Pound of Dry Bark in the London Market.	REMARKS.
				s. d. s. d.	
1	C. succirubra - -	Red Bark - -	47,507	2 6 to 8 9	The total number of plants planted out permanently in the plantations remain as formerly, namely 35,000. These continue to make very satisfactory progress, having now passed through the month of January, the driest and coldest in the year, not only without injury, but their growth has scarcely been retarded by the cold and drought. It may therefore be concluded that our dry and cold season on the Neilgherries will not form any impediment to the successful cultivation of cinchonas.
2	C. Calisaya - -	Yellow Bark - -	1,424	2 10 to 7 –	
3	C. Condaminea, var. Uritusinga.	Original Loxa Bark -	891	2 10 to 7 –	
4	C. Condaminea, var. Chahuarguera.	Rusty Crown Bark -	54,790	2 10 to 7 –	
5	C. Condaminea, var. Crespilla.	Fine Crown Bark -	739	2 10 to 6 –	
6	C. lancifolia - -	Pitayo Bark - -	1	1 8 to 2 10	
7	C. nitida - - -	Genuine Grey Bark -	8,296	1 8 to 2 9	
8	C. species without name.	Fine Grey Bark -	2,579	1 8 to 2 10	The increase by propagation during last month is 11,689, being rather under the average results of the last six months. Deducting the plants sent to Bengal and elsewhere, together with the number lost in transplanting, gives the total number of plants at present 127,671.
9	C. micrantha - -	Grey Bark - -	8,247	1 8 to 2 9	
10	C. Peruviana - -	Finest Grey Bark -	2,772	1 8 to 2 10	
11	C. Pahudiana - -	Unknown - -	425	Worthless.	
	TOTAL Number of Plants - - -		127,671		

TABLE II.

MEMORANDUM of the Growth of Eleven Plants of *C. Succirubra*, planted on the Second Denison Plantation at Neddiwuttum, on 30 August 1862.

Number of Plants.	Height in Inches when Planted, 30 August 1862.	Height in Inches on 31 December 1862.	Height in Inches on 31 January 1863.	Growth in Inches during January 1863.	By whom Planted.
1	23	41	45	4	His Excellency Sir W. Denison.
2	$16\frac{1}{2}$	37	40	3	
3	19	34	38	4	
4	15	36	40	4	
5	27	48	52	4	
6	20	40	41	1	
7	21	38	41	3	J. W. Breeks, Esq.
8	18	37	40	3	Dr. Sanderssn.
9	20	38	40	2	J. D. Sim, Esq.
10	20	42	48	6	Lieutenant McLeod.
11	18	42	46	4	P. Grant, Esq.

Table II. exhibits the growth of 11 plants, planted out by his Excellency the Governor and other gentlemen on the 30th August 1862, the average growth of these plants for last month being about $3\frac{1}{2}$ inches, or half an inch less than in December; but when it is considered that a maximum growth of six inches was obtained in this month, it will be observed how little effect our dry and cold season has on the plants.

(signed) *W. G. McIvor,*
Superintendent Government Chinchona Plantations.

— No. 108 B.—

REPORT on the Number, Distribution, and Condition of Chinchona Plants on the Neilgherries, on 28 February 1863.

No. of Species.	Botanical Names.	Commercial Names.	No. of Plants.	Value per Pound of Dry Bark in the London Market.	REMARKS.
				s. d. s. d.	
1	C. succirubra - -	Red Bark - -	48,989	2 6 to 8 9	The total number of plants planted out permanently in the plantations remain as formerly, namely, 35,000. These plants have now passed through the dry and cold season in the most satisfactory manner; the weather now becoming mild, with appearance of rain, indicating the close of the winter season. The increase by propagation during last month is 8,068, being about 3,500 plants under the average results of the last six months, this reduction being caused by the want of space to harden off the plants.
2	C. Calisaya - -	Yellow Bark - -	1,480	2 10 to 7 –	
3	C. Uritusinga - -	Original Loxa Bark -	927	2 10 to 7 –	
4	C. Condaminea -	Select Crown Bark -	51,012	2 10 to 7 –	
5	C. Crespilla - -	Fine Crown Bark -	825	2 10 to 6 –	
6	C. lancifolia - -	Pitayo Bark - -	1	1 8 to 2 10	
7	C. nitida - - -	Genuine Grey Bark -	8,312	1 8 to 2 9	
8	C. species without name.	Fine Grey Bark -	2,595	1 8 to 2 10	
9	C. micrantha - -	Grey Bark - -	8,326	1 8 to 2 9	
10	C. Peruviana - -	Finest Grey Bark -	2,847	1 8 to 2 10	
11	C. Pahudiana - -	Unknown - -	425	Worthless.	
	TOTAL Number of Plants - - -		135,739		

TABLE II.

MEMORANDUM of the Growth of Eleven Plants of *C. succirubra*, planted on the Second Denison Plantation at Neddiwuttum, on 30 August 1862.

Number of Plants.	Height in Inches when Planted, 30 August 1862.	Height in Inches on 31 January 1863	Height in Inches on 8 February 1863.	Growth in Inches during February 1863.	By whom Planted.
1	23	45	48	3	His Excellency Sir W. Denison.
2	16½	40	44	4	
3	19	38	41	3	
4	15	40	43	3	
5	27	52	54	2	
6	20	41	43½	2½	
7	21	41	44½	3½	J. W. Breeks, Esq.
8	18	40	44	4	Dr. Sanderson.
9	20	40	42	2	J. D. Sim, Esq.
10	20	48	51	3	Lieutenant McLeod.
11	18	46	52	6	P. Grant, Esq.

Table II. exhibits the growth of 11 plants planted out by his Excellency the Governor and other gentlemen on the 30th August 1862, the average growth of these plants during last month being 3¼ inches, or a quarter of an inch less than in January, which, allowing for the shortness of the month of February, gives merely the same results. The height of the largest plant we possess is now 7 feet 2 inches, with branches from 3 to 5¼ feet in length. The stem, measured half a foot from the ground, is 5¼ of an inch in circumference.

(signed) *W. G. McIvor.*
Superintendent Government Chinchona Plantations.

APPLICATIONS for CHINCHONA PLANTS.

		No.
G. Dawson, Esq.	Ootacamund	1,000
J. Chesson, Esq.	Mahableshwar	500
W. Chambers, Esq.	Ootacamund	1,000
A. R. Lascelles, Esq.	Ootacamund	10,000
T. De Facien, Esq.	Kattarey	5,000
C. Vincent, Esq.	Kattarey	5,000
J. Pierie, Esq.	Calicut	2,000
W. Stainbank, Esq.	Hullikul	1,000
J. H. Schnarrie, Esq.	Ootacamund	5,000
W. Southey, Esq.	Wallaghaut	1,700
E. T. FitzGerald, Esq.	Calcutta	800
Major Morgan	Ootacamund	1,000
	TOTAL	34,000

MEMORANDUM of CHINCHONA PLANTS DISTRIBUTED.

F. N. Maltby, Esq.	Travancore	16
Dr. Junghuhn	Java	56
A. R. Lascelles, Esq.	Ootacamund	12
M. Anderson, Esq.	Jamaica	2
Dr. Wiehe	Bombay	10
Dr. T. Anderson	Calcutta	554
Dr. Jamieson	Saharunpore	107
Professor Lees	Calcutta	61
Rajah of Travancore	-	521
	TOTAL	1,339

— No. 109. —

MEMORANDUM by Mr. *Markham.*

(Sent to Mr. McIvor, *viâ* Southampton, 19 February 1863.)

THERE has been much confusion in the nomenclature of the species of chinchona from the forests of Loxa, three varieties of which are now growing on the Neilgherry Hills. They are all classed by Dr. Weddell under the head of *C. Condaminea*, and hitherto the varieties have been called, in Mr. M'Ivor's Reports—1. Uritusinga. 2. Chahuarguera. 3. Crispa.

Dr. Hooker, in a recent number of the "Botanical Magazine," has named the species *C. officinalis*, reverting to the original name given by Linnæus. Dr. Hooker says: "When once the law of priority is departed from without perfectly "good cause, the door is opened to endless future change, and consequent con- "fusion. The genus was founded upon the one plant called 'quinquina,' by La "Condamine, to which Linnæus gave the specific name of *C. officinalis*. This "name, which appears to us in every way unobjectionable, and which was adopted "by Vahl and Lambert, Willdenow, Lamarck and Rœmer, and Schultes, was "changed by Humboldt and Bonpland to *C. Condaminea*, on grounds which we "consider insufficient."

It is, therefore, proposed that the name of *C. officinalis* should be adopted for this species now thriving in India, out of deference to the opinion of so high an authority on systematic botany as Dr. Hooker.

With regard to the three varieties of this species now growing on the Neilgherry Hills, it is proposed to adopt the following names, with the concurrence of Sir William and Dr. Hooker:—

1. That now called *Uritusinga* was the original variety discovered by La Condamine, and it should therefore bear his name, var. *Condaminea*.

2. That now called *Chahuarguera* is the identical plant figured in Plate X. of the great work of Humboldt and Bonpland (the unshaded branch with capsules). It ought, therefore, to bear the name of one or other of those eminent naturalists. A species of chinchona has already been called after Humboldt, and it is, therefore, proposed to call this variety *Bonplandiana*.

3. The variety *crispa* of Tafalla requires no alteration.

We have, therefore—

C. officinalis 1. Var. *Condaminea*.
2. Var. *Bonplandiana*.
3. Var. *crispa*.

Clements R. Markham.

18 February 1863.

— No. 110. —

From the Secretary of State for India to His Excellency the Honourable the Governor in Council, Fort St. George.

Sir, India Office, London, 2 January 1863.

Para. 1. I HAVE considered in Council your letters, in the Revenue Department, dated October 10th (No. 73), October 23d (No. 75), and November 18th (No. 82) 1862, transmitting the proceedings of your Government connected with the cultivation of chinchona plants on the Neilgherry Hills.

2. The complete success which has hitherto attended this important experiment is very satisfactory, and I am of opinion that it has now reached a stage at which it has become necessary to take effective steps both to ensure the steady annual increase of the area of the Government plantations in the Neilgherries, and the introduction of the chinchona into other hill districts.

3. I, therefore, approve of your resolution to plant 150 acres annually, for at least 10 years, so that, at the end of that period, there may be a prospect of obtaining a very large harvest of quinine-yielding bark. No return can be expected

expected before that time, so far as bark is concerned; but I take this opportunity of calling your attention to the supplement to the "Calcutta Gazette" of October 15th (No. 54) 1862, in which it is stated that an infusion of the leaves of *C. succirubra*, which had spontaneously fallen from plants in the Darjeeling nursery in June and July, had been administered to patients suffering from intermittent fever, who were cured without any other medicine whatever. If the cinchona leaves can thus be turned to account, a return on the outlay may be obtained almost immediately, while great additional benefit will be derived from the cultivation of the plants. The medicinal properties of the leaves can be tested on a very much larger scale in your Presidency than at Darjeeling, and I desire that measures may be taken for obtaining an analysis of the leaves, and that a supply may be sent to some one of the Government hospitals for trial.

4. Chinchona cultivation should be introduced into the other hill districts of your Presidency, as well as into Coorg. The two great objects of the experiment are—the provision of an abundant and certain supply of bark for the use of hospitals and troops, and the spread of the cultivation throughout the hill districts, in order to bring the remedy within the reach of frequenters of jungles, and of the native population generally. Your Government has very justly observed that "the experiment cannot be regarded as a mere money speculation," nor are the commercial advantages that may be derived from it to be considered as other than a secondary consideration; though of course a return for the outlay, and the spread of chinchona cultivation by private enterprise, are very desirable in themselves.

5. The Collectors of Coimbatore and Madura, in concert with Mr. McIvor, should be directed to take the earliest opportunities that offer, of introducing chinchona cultivation into the hill districts of their collectorates; and a request to the same effect should be sent to the Commissioner of Mysore, with respect to Coorg, where there are many coffee planters who would doubtless be willing to undertake this cultivation.

6. Your resolution to offer a certain number of plants for sale every year, at a moderate price, will have the important effect of extending the cultivation over a wider area. Two companies have already been formed in London, for the object of cultivating chinchona, in combination with coffee and tea, in the Western Neilgherries and Wynaad; and I observe that Mr. Lascelles, the agent of one of these companies, has already bespoken 10,000 out of the 20,000 plants which are to be sold this year. Chinchona, when grown together with coffee, is likely to be a profitable investment, especially if the leaves can be turned to account, notwithstanding the greater length of time that must elapse before any profit can be expected from the former. I am, therefore, inclined to take a more hopeful view of the prospect of capital being invested in this speculation than your Government has been able to do; and I desire that every legitimate encouragement may be extended to individuals or companies who may undertake chinchona cultivation.

7. I cordially approve of the increase of salary which you have allowed to Mr. McIvor, to whose great skill as a propagator, and zeal and intelligence in superintending the experiment, the success which has now been attained is mainly due.

8. The monthly reports from the superintendent of chinchona plantations should be transmitted to me as soon after receipt as possible, and, in addition to the number and condition of the plants and the area under cultivation, they should also contain information respecting the number of plants sold or otherwise disposed of, the localities to which they are sent, and the prospects of cinchona cultivation by private enterprise.

9. In your letter, dated October 10th (No. 73) 1862, you report the dismissal of the gardener Lyall. In the accompanying papers there is sufficient evidence of negligence and insubordination on his part to justify his dismissal, and I must, therefore, express theopinion that the lenity with which he has been treated was wholly undeserved.

— No. 111. —

From *Herman Merivale*, Esq., C.B., to *J. E. Howard*, Esq.

Sir, India Office, 16 June 1862.

I AM desired by the Secretary of State for India in Council to convey to you his best thanks for your valuable present of a fine plant of *Chinchona Uritusinga*, which will be a very important addition to the number of quinine-yielding species of chinchona plants already acclimatized in the Neilgherry Hills.

Sir Charles Wood has much pleasure in being able to inform you, although, through the carelessness of the railway authorities at Avenashy, the plant suffered very severely in its transit across the hot plains, that it has recovered from the damage it then received since its arrival in the Neilgherry Hills, and that it is now considered to be safe.

I have, &c.
(signed) *Herman Merivale.*

J. E. Howard, Esq.,
2, Lordship-lane, Tottenham, N.

— No. 112. —

MEMORANDUM by Mr. *Markham*.

India Office, 17 June 1862.

I HAVE on several occasions explained the reasons which make it important to introduce the *C. lancifolia* of New Granada into India, the only valuable species of chinchona which has not been established there. I would now propose that I should be authorised to employ the gardener Cross, who is now in South America, to procure a supply of seeds of this species. I have great confidence that he will do his work thoroughly and expeditiously, as well as economically. Last autumn he overcame great difficulties in procuring seeds of *C. Condaminea* near Loxa, and got a large supply of the best varieties, which were in excellent order on arriving in India, and came up by thousands. *C. lancifolia* and other valuable kinds in New Granada are important; they thrive at very great altitudes, and yield the alkaloid called chinchonidine as well as quinine.

Clements R. Markham.

Note.—Mr. Markham's proposal was approved by the Secretary of State in Council on 20th June 1862.

— No. 113. —

From Sir *C. Wood* to Lord *Elgin*.

My Lord, India Office, London, 24 January 1863.

Para. 1. WITH reference to my Despatch, dated 31st May 1862 (No. 48), I now transmit a translated extract from a number of the "Flora," a German botanical periodical (together with the original), containing letters from M. Hasskarl, the gentleman formerly in charge of the chinchona culture in Java, by which it appears that, owing to the unfavourable reports of scientific men in Holland, the Government of Netherlands India have determined to put an entire stop to the further cultivation of *Chinchona pahudiana* plants in Java.

2. M. Hasskarl was the introducer of this species from South America.

3. Under these circumstances, it does not appear to me advisable that any further expense should be incurred in the cultivation of this species in Darjeeling.

4. I have

4. I have perused with interest Dr. Anderson's letter, in the supplement to the "Calcutta Gazette" of 15th October 1862 (No. 54), in which he reports that four cases of intermittent fever have actually been cured by the use of an infusion of chinchona leaves without any other medicine whatever. I desire that any reports from Dr. Anderson on the progress of the experimental cultivation of chinchona plants may be transmitted to me without delay, as well as any accounts of the chemical analysis of chinchona leaves, or bark, which you may receive from the Chemical Examiner to your Government.

I have, &c.
(signed) *C. Wood.*

His Excellency
The Right Hon. the Governor General
of India in Council.

Enclosure in No. 113.

EXTRACT from No. 21 of the "Flora" of 1862, a German Periodical published at Ratisbon, on the Cultivation of Chinchona in Java.

WITH reference to what was said last year in this Paper (pp. 224 and 608, &c.), I should not withhold from your readers the decision of the Minister of the Colonies, in the Second Chamber of the Dutch States General, in reference to this culture. A doubt had been expressed whether, in the great spread of chinchona cultivation, a wrong method might not have been adopted; and the Minister replied:—

"The belief that the culture of the least valuable species of cinchona would be useful and profitable, is the reason that so many trees have been grown in Java, of the kind first known as *C. ovata*, then as *C. lucumæfolia*, and now as *C. Pahudiana*. A tree of this species has been chemically analyzed by Professors G. F. Mülder, and F A. W. Miquel; and in consequence of the joint report of these gentlemen, the Indian Government have determined to put an entire stop to the further cultivation of *C. Pahudiana*. At the same time, the Governor General has considered whether it will be advisable for the Government to continue the chinchona cultivation, or whether the time has come for handing it over to private enterprise."

(signed) Dr. *J. K. Hasskarl.*

Königswinter, 23 May 1862.

THE following is from the "Niewen Amsterdamsch Handelsen Effectenblad," No. 151, 2 June 1862:—

IN the sitting of the Second Chamber, the question was brought forward, whether it would be advisable to leave the culture of the chinchona to private enterprise; and I may be permitted, with modesty, to give my opinion on this subject.

It would appear to me, that the culture must be undertaken by Government, to whom it is not essential that the return should be rapid. It appears that the chemical researches of Messrs. Mülder and Miquel do not support those of Dr. De Vrij (given in the "Batavischen Handelsblattes" of 14th September 1861, p. 607, &c.), and in this case the hope of chinchona cultivation being undertaken by private enterprise disappears.

(signed) *J. K. Hasskarl.*

— No. 114. —

REPORT on the Botanical Gardens, Calcutta, from April 1861, to April 1862, by *T. Anderson*, Esq., M.D.

(EXTRACT).

THE most important event in the history of the Botanic Gardens for the past year, is the share the gardens have had in the introduction of the quinine-yielding *Chinchonæ* into India. I was directed last September to proceed to Java, *viâ* Singapore, to procure plants and seed of the species of cinchona cultivated by the Dutch; also to examine the method of cultivation adopted in that island, and afterwards to proceed to Madras to report on the prospects of the success of the experiment of cultivating the chinchonæ in the Neilgherries. The results of this mission are fully detailed in my report to the Government of India. I derived

derived great assistance from the varied resources of the Botanic Gardens, in carrying out my operations connected with this important subject. The native gardeners that accompanied me were lent from the Botanic Gardens, as also were the Wardian cases for the transport of the plants.

The chinchona plants were brought to Calcutta from Java, before they were taken to Madras. During the 14 days they remained in Calcutta, they were so carefully tended by Mr. Scott that, when they reached their destination at Ootacamund, only a mortality of one per cent. had occurred during the entire period spent on the journey from Java to the Neilgherries. While I was in Calcutta, before proceeding to Madras, I received the sanction of Lord Canning to a proposal to commence the cultivation of chinchona in the mountains of the Bengal Presidency; and, as a nucleus of this cultivation, I was authorised to leave a few plants of *Chinchona Calisaya* and *C. Pahudiana* in the Botanic Gardens, pending arrangements for their final destination. This occurred in the beginning of December. While I was at Ootacamund, I procured 204 plants belonging to four other species of chinchona besides those I obtained in Java. Several of these plants were destroyed between the foot of the Neilgherries and the railway station, by the upsetting of one of the carts on which the Wardian cases were carried. The remainder of these plants reached the Botanic Gardens on the 13th January 1862. On my return from Madras, I found that some seeds of *Chinchona Pahudiana*, sown during my absence, had germinated to the number of 548. In the report of last year, I mentioned the germination of seeds of species of chinchona brought by me from England. About 120 of these seeds had grown by the end of May 1861, but during the hot period between that time and the middle of October, many of the young plants died. On the approach of the cold weather, all the remaining seedlings, more or less, recovered; while four young plants of the red bark (*Chinchona succirubra*) grew rapidly. Of the chinchona plants raised in the Botanic Gardens, 31 plants remained on the 19th January 1862. The seeds I distributed in March 1861 germinated only at Ootacamund, and at Peradinia, the Botanic Garden of Ceylon. The following table shows the number of plants collected in the Botanic Gardens, Calcutta, on the 19th January 1862, as the commencement of the experiment in Bengal:—

TABLE showing the Number of each Species of Chinchona in the Botanic Gardens, Calcutta, on 19th January 1862.

——	From Ootacamund.	Raised in Botanic Gardens, Calcutta.	From Java.	TOTAL.
C. succirubra	87	4	- -	91
C. Calisaya	- -	- -	6	6
C. nitida	56	11	- -	67
C. micrantha	43	13	- -	56
C. Peruviana	4	1	- -	5
C. Pahudiana	- -	- -	59	59
C. species ignot	3	2	- -	5
GRAND TOTAL of Chinchona Plants in the Botanic Gardens, Calcutta, on 19th February 1862				289

On my return to Calcutta from Madras, I received permission to commence the cultivation of the chinchona near Darjeeling. I was, however, not able to leave Calcutta until the 25th March, being detained by my duties as Professor of Botany at the Medical College.

During this time, the chinchona plants suffered considerably, and a few died—in all, 34.

I engaged

I engaged the services of Mr. T. Stubbs, a European gardener in charge of the cultivation, and on the 25th March, I sent him to Darjeeling in charge of the following number of plants:—

Number and species of Plants of Chinchona sent from the Botanic Gardens, Calcutta, to Darjeeling, on 25 March 1862, in 13 Wardian Cases.

Names of Species.	Number of Species
C. succirubra - - - - - - - - -	84
C. Calisaya - - - - - - - - -	5
C. nitida - - - - - - - - -	56
C. micrantha - - - - - - - - -	42
C. Peruviana - - - - - - - - -	2
C. Pahudiana - - - - - - - - -	54
Seedlings of ditto - - - - - - - -	548
Species ignota - - - - - - - - -	6
Grand Total of Species sent to Darjeeling - -	797

Encouraged by the successful keeping of so many plants of chinchona in the climate of Calcutta for so many months, I was induced to test the effects of the climate on some of the species by a more prolonged trial. With this intention, I left two well-grown plants of *C. succirubra*, and four of *C. Pahudiana*, in the Botanic Gardens of Calcutta; and I gave directions that they should receive no more than the ordinary care bestowed on the other plants in the garden. Besides these plants, I was obliged to leave 14 cuttings of *C. succirubra*, three of *C. nitida*, and one of *C. micrantha* in the propagating beds of the Botanic Gardens.

The 13 Wardian cases containing chinchona plants were taken by railway to Sahebgunge, from whence, after a delay of two days, they were removed to Caragolah Ghaut in the small steamer. On the 29th March, the plants were transported by coolies to Purneah, but though the distance is only 24 miles, the difficulties attending the moving of such heavy cases were so great, that several of them were nearly 48 hours in arriving at Purneah, and they all suffered much from exposure to the sun. On the 1st April, the cases were still detained at Purneah for want of carriage.

— No. 115. —

Report on the Experimental Cultivation of the Quiniferous Chinchonæ in British Sikhim.

From *T. Anderson*, Esq., M.D., Officiating Superintendent, Botanic Gardens, Calcutta, to *H. Bell*, Esq., Under Secretary to the Government of Bengal.

Darjeeling, 6 August 1862.

Sir,

I have the honour to submit a report on the experiment of cultivating the Quiniferous Chinchonæ, in British Sikhim, from the 24th March until the 1st August. The report shows that the experiment was actually commenced on the 27th May, on which day there were 211 plants of the different species of chinchona, and that on the 1st August there were in all 1,611 plants in the nursery.

REPORT on the Cultivation of the Quiniferous Chinchonæ, in British Sikhim, from the 24th March to the 1st August 1862.

THE plants of cinchona which had been collected in the Botanic Gardens, Calcutta, from Java and Ootacamund, as well as those raised from seeds in the Botanic Gardens during the previous year, were sent by railway to Sahebgunge on the 24th March, in charge of Mr. Thomas Stubbs, a European gardener, accompanied by two Mallees from the Botanic Gardens. All the plants were contained in thirteen Wardian cases. Some of the plants were in earthen, others in Bamboo pots; almost all those of *Chinchona succirubra* were planted in the soil contained in the cases. The following table shows the number of plants of each species despatched from Calcutta on the above date:—

TABLE, No. I, showing the Number of Species of Chinchona sent to Darjeeling on 24th March 1862.

NAME of SPECIES.	No. of Plants.	No. of Seedlings.	Total of Plants and Seedlings.
Chinchona succirubra - - - - - -	84	–	84
" Calisaya - - - - - -	5	–	5
" nitida - - - - - - -	56	–	56
" micrantha - - - - - -	42	–	42
" Peruviana - - - - - -	2	–	2
" Pahudiana - - - - - -	54	548	602
" species ignota - - - - -	6	–	6
GRAND TOTAL - - -	249	548	797

No delay occurred at Sahebgunge; the plants were taken by the small ferry steamer across the Ganges to Caragolah Ghaut. They remained there until the afternoon of the 29th March. The distance from Caragolah Ghaut to Purneah, 24 miles, was performed very slowly. Some of the Wardian cases started from Caragolah on the afternoon of the 29th, not arriving at Purneah till noon on the 31st. This delay was caused by the inefficient coolies provided for the transport of the cases. Many of them were children of 12 and 14 years of age, who were not even tall enough to lift the cases from the ground. The result was that 18 hours after the plants had started from Caragolah Ghaut, I found two of the cases at distances of four and six miles from Caragolah Ghaut fully exposed to the burning heat of the sun, the coolies lying by them completely exhausted. Two carts were procured from a neighbouring village, but this means of conveyance was so slow that 20 hours more elapsed before the cases reached Purneah. The plants arrived flaccid and drooping from the effects of the exposure and the jolting; but, with a single exception, they all recovered before they left Purneah. At Purneah some delay occurrred, but this I did not regret, as Mr. Robinson availed himself of it to procure a party of strong Dhanga coolies, who most materially assisted in getting the cases over the next long stage of 40 miles to Kissengunge. The cases left Purneah on the 1st April, and arrived at Kissengunge on the evening of the 2nd. They reached Punkabarree, at the foot of the hills, on the 7th April, four days after leaving Kissengunge. After two days the plants were removed to Kursiong, which I had fixed on as the most suitable place for keeping them until arrangements could be made for their final disposal. The cases reached Kursiong on the 9th, and were at once placed in the square of the barracks used as rest houses for the European troops

troops proceeding to Darjeeling. These barracks are about 4,500 feet above the level of the sea. When the plants were carefully examined, on their arrival at Kursiong, eight were found to have perished since their departure from Calcutta. This is exclusive of casualties among the seedlings of *C. Pahudiana.* I look on this as a very small mortality, considering what the plants had undergone since leaving Calcutta. Mr. Stubbs deserves great credit for the unremitting attention he bestowed on the plants, and for the care with which he carried out my orders to give the plants as much air and as little water as possible. The exposure of the plants to air and light, and all changes of the weather was commenced soon after their arrival at Kursiong, and, after a few days' gradual inuring, they were left exposed night and day with great benefit to all the species.

While the chinchona plants were left at Kursiong, under the care of Mr. Stubbs, I was engaged in exploring the forests, in the neighbourhood of Darjeeling, for a suitable site for the permanent nursery. I hoped to procure land near enough to Darjeeling to allow of the permanent propagating house and a temporary dwelling for the European gardener being erected within two months. This I soon discovered was quite impossible, as all the land within several miles of Darjeeling had been purchased for the cultivation of tea, and that whatever piece of Government land I might select, a new road must be made to it before any buildings could be commenced. The nearest and most suitable tract of land I could obtain lay on the slopes of Sinchal, extending to the river Teesta, and which contained suitable land from heights of from 800 feet above the sea to 8,600, the summit of Sinchal. The nearest point of this tract which had not been acquired by private individuals was not less than 10 miles from Darjeeling, and was quite inaccessible from the dense forest with which it was covered. I was thus forced to seek for some temporary accommodation for the chinchona plants. After consulting with Captain Fitzgerald, the Executive Engineer, it was agreed that the best plan would be to convert one of the empty officers' quarters at Sinchal into a temporary propagating house, and to make over another as the dwelling-house of the European gardener. Two rooms were accordingly thrown into one, and a glazed roof substituted for the wooden one. A plan for heating the atmosphere of the house, and for affording bottom heat to the plants was contrived. This was done by blocking up the chimney of the room, and carrying the smoke and heated air through a horizontal flue of masonry, which, after passing through the room, ends in a short chimney outside. The plants were brought to Sinchal on the 5th May; they suffered more during the short journey of 20 miles from Kursiong to Sinchal than they did on the way from Calcutta to Kursiong. A serious accident occurred to the case containing the seedlings of *C. Pahudiana;* by the stumbling of one of the eight coolies carrying the case, it was upset, and all the plants were, more or less, uprooted. Although they were immediately replanted by Mr. Stubbs, and the case containing them was left for nine days near the spot where the accident happened under the care of an experienced native gardener, not one of them survived. On the 27th May the conservatory was completed, and the chinchona plants were at once moved into it from the room where they had been placed on their arrival at Sinchal. All had suffered greatly from the effects of their long journey, and the unavoidable delay in preparing proper accomodation for them. There is, however, a very marked difference in the loss between the plants from Java and those from Ootacamund. Out of 59 plants obtained from Java only one death occurred, while of the 170 plants from Ootacamund, no less than 30 were completely lost. This difference in the healthiness of the plants from the two places becomes more striking, when it is known that the plants from Java were brought by coolies from the mountains in the interior of that island to Batavia, and thence by steamer to Calcutta; while those from Ootacamund were transported in 12 hours by railway over most of the land journey, and the sea voyage only lasted three days. The plants from Java were, in addition, exposed for two months longer than the others, to the confinement of small pots and Wardian cases, as they arrived in Calcutta two months before them.

The following table shows the stock of chinchona plants on the 1st June, and the number of deaths in each species from the time of their leaving Calcutta:—

TABLE II, showing condition of Chinchona Plants from 24th March to 1st June.

NAME of SPECIES.	Loss of Plants.	Loss of Seedlings.	Total of Losses.	Plants Remaining.	Seedlings Remaining.	Total of Plants and Seedlings.
Cinchona succirubra -	10	–	10	74	–	74
" Calisaya* -	None	–	None	5	–	5
" nitida -	15	–	15	41	–	41
" micrantha -	9	–	9	33	–	33
" Peruviana -	None	–	None	2	–	2
" Pahudiana* -	1	548	549	53	None	53
" species ignota	3	–	3	3	–	3
GRAND TOTAL - -	38	548	586	211	None.	211

The plants of the species marked*, were obtained from Java. The seedlings of *C. Pahudiana* were raised in the Calcutta Botanic Gardens.

During the month of June, the propagation of all the species, except *C. Pahudiana*, was successfully prosecuted, and the number of deaths was reduced to seven. The process of layering was the only method followed, and by it, young well-rooted plants were procured in from 21 to 30 days, in the case *C. succirubra*, *C. nitida*, and *C. micrantha*. The plants of *C. Pahudiana* could easily have been artificially propagated, but as they were all finely formed plants raised from seed, I was unwilling to do anything that might interfere with their attaining their full development, the more so, as I had a large quantity of apparently good seed which I had sown in the end of May. The only seedlings among the other species, were the few plants raised in the Botanic Gardens, Calcutta, and of these, none were layered.

During June, a few of the seeds of *C. Pahudiana* germinated. On the 1st July, the return of the stock of all the species was as follows:—

TABLE III. showing the Number of Plants of Chinchona on 1st July 1862.

NAME of SPECIES.	Loss of Plants since 1st June.	Increase of Plants since 1st June.	Increase of Seedlings since 1st June.	Total Increase of Plants and Seedlings.	Total of Plants and Seedlings on 1st July
Cinchona succirubra - - -	3	36	–	36	107 .
" Calisaya - - -	None	1	–	1	6
" nitida - - - -	2	9	–	9	48
" micrantha - - -	2	7	–	7	38
" Peruviana - - -	None	No n	–	None	2
" Pahudiana - - -	"	"	486	486	539
" species ingota - -	"	"	–	None	3
GRAND TOTAL - - -	7	53	486	539	743

In the following month, July, the increase was much greater, both by layers and seed. All the plants made a considerable growth, and had acquired a much healthier appearance. On the 1st August, most of the seedlings of *C. Pahudiana* had their two pairs of leaves well developed, and a few had formed their third pair.

This last table is the return of the plants on the 1st August, drawn up in the same manner as table III. :—

TABLE IV., showing the Number of Chinchona Plants on 1st August.

NAME of SPECIES.	Remaining on 1st July.	Loss of Plants since 1st July.	Increase of Plants since 1st July.	Increase of Seedlings since 1st July.	Total Increase of Plants and Seedlings since 1st July.	Total of Plants and Seedlings on 1st August.
Cinchona succirubra -	107	1	32	–	32	138
,, Calisaya -	6	None	2	–	2	8
,, nitida -	48	,,	13	–	13	61
,, micrantha -	38	2	6	–	6	42
,, Peruviana -	2	None	2	–	2	4
,, Pahudiana -	539	,,	None	814	814	1,353
,, species ignota	3	,,	2	–	2	5
GRAND TOTAL - -	743	3	57	814	871	1,611

The rate of propagation will increase every month, as in periods varying from three to six weeks; the new plants are ready to be artificially propagated in their turn, while the many shoots made by the plants that have already yielded new plants, are likewise available for layers or cuttings.

On leaving Calcutta in March, I placed four plants of *C. Pahudiana*, and two of *C. succirubra* under the charge of Mr. Scott, head gardener, Botanic Gardens, with directions to treat them like any other tropical plant, but to keep them in a rather shaded part of the gardens. I was also obliged to leave 14 cuttings of *C. succirubra*, three of *C. nitida*, and one of *C. micrantha*, in the cutting beds of the Botanic Gardens. I received a report on the condition of all these plants on the 22d July. Up to that date, the losses had been two plants of *C. Pahudiana*, eight cuttings of *C. succirubra*, and the cutting of *C. micrantha*. The two plants of *C. succirubra* were in good health; one of them was then 18 inches in height, and the stem immediately above the ground, was one inch and six-tenths in thickness, while the leaves average six to ten inches in length, and from five to seven inches in breadth.

The climate of Calcutta does not seem to be too hot for this species, by far the most valuable of all the cinchonæ.

— No. 116. —

INFUSION of the Leaves of Chinchona succirubra used as a Febrifuge.

From *T. Anderson*, Esq., M.D., Officiating Superintendent, Botanic Gardens, Calcutta, to *H. Bell*, Esq., Under Secretary to the Government of Bengal (No. 13), dated 9 September 1862.

I HAVE the honour to report to you, for the information of the Lieutenant Governor, that I have succeeded in forming an infusion of the leaves of *Chinchona succirubra* from the plants of that species in the cinchona nursery, near Darjeeling. The leaves fell off spontaneously during the months of June and July.

 I sent

I sent the infusion to Dr. Collins, civil surgeon of Darjeeling, with a request that he would administer the infusion to some of the patients in the civil hospital.

He has just informed me that he had given the infusion in doses of one fluid ounce to the first four cases of intermittent fever that occurred, and that these patients had been cured without any other medicine whatever.

This result proves that the infusion of the leaves of *Chinchona succirubra* possesses some of the febrifuge properties of cinchona; the infusion is of a dark chocolate colour, and is intensely bitter. I hope to be able to submit an account of the chemical analysis of this infusion by Dr. Macnamara, chemical examiner to Government.

— No. 117. —

Bengal Revenue Proceedings, December 1862, No. 161.

EXTRACT from a Report from *C. B. Stewart*, Esq., on the Province of Cachar, to the Landholders and Commercial Association at Calcutta.

10 November 1862.

IN fulfilment of the promise made to the chairman of the association, I have now the pleasure to submit a report of my observations during my recent visit to Cachar and Sylhet.

* * * * *

Chinchona.—From what I have seen of the country, and from what I have read and heard regarding the culture of the cinchona, I feel assured that the plant would thrive well in the open air on the more elevated ranges of hills in Cachar and Assam; it would therefore be well if Government would either introduce it into those districts, or give small contributions of seeds and plants to a few well-known men who would willingly undertake the experiment.

— No. 118. —

From *J. Murray*, Esq., to *Herman Merivale*, Esq., C. B.

Sir, Foreign Office, January 1862.

WITH reference to your letter of the 30th April of last year, I am directed by Earl Russell to transmit to you, for the information of the Secretary of State for India in Council, the accompanying copy of a Despatch from Her Majesty's Consul General at Batavia, enclosing a report and memorandum respecting the cinchona plantations in Java. 22 January 1862.

I am, &c.
(signed) *James Murray.*

Herman Merivale, Esq., C.B.,
&c. &c. &c.

Enclosure 1, in No. 118.

From *A. Fraser*, Esq., to Earl *Russell.*

21, Clarendon-crescent, Edinburgh,
22 January 1862.

My Lord,

I HAVE the honour to wait upon your Lordship with information respecting the cultivation of the cinchona plant in Java, called for by the India Office by letter of 30th April 1861, copy of which was transmitted to me by your Lordship's Despatch of 8th May 1861.

The information embodied in the report enclosed is derived from the latest official returns kindly supplied to me by order of his Excellency the Netherlands Colonial Minister at the Hague, and the memorandum of instructions annexed to it is merely a translation made by me from the Dutch original. I have had both these documents printed for my own convenience, and forward with this letter several copies of each.

During

During my short stay in Calcutta in December 1860, I recommended to members of the Bengal Government interested in the subject, that a formal application should be made to the Governor General of Netherlands India for a supply of seeds and cuttings of the several kinds of the cinchona, being satisfied of the readiness of his Excellency to comply with a requisition of this kind; and I further suggested the mission of some scientific person from India to Java for the purpose of receiving the supply, and taking the required care of the seeds and cuttings in their carriage from Batavia to Calcutta.

I have been gratified to learn that both the recommendation and suggestion were acted upon, and that Dr. Anderson, superintendent of the Botanical Gardens, Calcutta, left Java about two months ago fully supplied with seeds and cuttings, and with every information regarding the cultivation of the cinchona in the power of the Java Government to give.

Had this information not been obtained by the Indian Government in the way described above, it was my intention to have accompanied the present report with translations of further documents of considerable length and detail, bearing on the cinchona plantations, which were also supplied to me from the Hague; and the leisure anticipated as necessary for this laborious work, taken in connexion with private engagements incident to my recent return to this country after an absence of many years, must be my apology for the delay which has occurred in submitting this report.

Trusting that the report as it stands, with the annex, may contain all the information desired by the India Office,

I am, &c.
(signed) *Alexander Fraser.*

The Earl Russell.

Enclosure 2, in No. 118.

REPORT of Mr. *Alexander Fraser*, Her Majesty's Consul at Batavia, respecting the present state and future prospects of the Cinchona Plantations in Java, and the Nature of the Organisation adopted by the Netherlands Government for the conduct of the experiment.

THE cultivation of the Cinchona plant in Java is still in a state of experiment, and still requiring scientific management, does not as yet belong to those branches of cultivation which are under the management of the Director of Cultures.

[These several branches of cultivation are fully treated of in a work entitled "Java, or how to manage a colony," by J. W. B. Money, published by Hurst & Blackett, London, 1861, vol. i. chapters 3, 4, and 5, to which reference is here made for the sake of brevity.]

THE conduct of the experiment has been entrusted to the care of Dr. D. F. Junghuhn, a scientific gentleman of considerable eminence, and it is the intention of the Government to leave it under his superintendence until the cultivation shall be considered as quite successful, *i. e.*, when the present trees are large and old enough to be barked, and the propagation no longer requires scientific supervision. The management will then be transferred to the Direction of Cultures.

Dr. Junghuhn is assisted in the management by Dr. J. E. de Vry, a chemist of some eminence, whose special duty it is to apply chemical tests from time to time to the barks of the cinchona to ascertain their intrinsic value.

To these officials is attached the following staff of overseers and labourers, whose duties, as well as those of Dr. Junghuhn, the superintendent, are laid down in a printed memorandum of instructions, translated from the Dutch, and forming the annex to this Report.

	Florins.		£.	
1 European Overseer, 1st Class, on	125	monthly	= 125	per annum
1 " " 2d "	100	"	= 100	"
6 " " 3d "	75	"	= 75	"
1 " " 3d "	50	"	= 50	"
1 Native " (Mandore)	6	"	= 6	"
15 " Labourers (Boedgangs)	5	"	= 5	"

The salary of the superintendent, Dr. Junghun, is 1,250 florins monthly, or 1,250*l.* per annum; that of Dr. de Vry, the chemical assistant, 1,000 florins monthly, or 1,000*l.* per annum; besides which they are entitled to a free house, or allowance for house rent, which may be taken at about 100*l.* each per annum. Thus the whole present permanent annual outlay may be stated as follows:—

	£.
Salary of superintendent - - - - - - - -	1,250
Salary of chemical assistant - - - - - - - -	1,000
Allowances for house rent - - - - - - - -	200
European overseers - - - - - - - -	725
Native overseers and labourers - - - - - - -	81
	£. 3,256

On

On the 31st December 1860, the state of the cinchona plantations in Java was as follows:

Calisaya:

Seeds in germination - - - - - - - - - -	264
Young plants in the beddings and germinating sheds - -	5,510
Plants and trees planted out - - - - - - - -	1,806

Lucumæfolia:

Seeds in stock - - - - - - - - - - -	700,000
Seeds in germination - - - - - - - - - -	533,396
Young plants in the beddings - - - - - - -	349,700
Plants and trees planted out - - - - - - -	56,686

Succirubra (Red Cinchona):

Young plants in the nursery shed - - - - - -	13
Young plants planted out - - - - - - - -	14

Lancifolia (Yellow Cinchona):

Young plants in the nursery shed - - - - - - -	38
Young plants planted out - - - - - - - -	42

Besides the above, there was then a supply in the nurseries of—

1,030	live cuttings of	Calisaya.
8	" "	Succirubra.
28	" "	Lancifolia.
10	" "	Lanceolata.

The extreme height attained by the trees at the same period (31st December 1860), was—

Calisaya,	15 feet	8 inches	English	measurement.
Lucumæfolia,	25 "	6 "	"	"
Succirubra,	8 "	8 "	"	"
Lancifolia,	15 "	2 "	"	"
Lanceolata,	13 "	0 "	"	"

The ultimate success of the cinchona experiment in Java would seem mainly to depend upon the question (which time only will solve) whether a sufficient supply of seed shall continue to be obtained from the *Calisaya* and *Succirubra*. The other sorts contain less quinine, and it is specially maintained that the *Lucumæfolia* is a species producing very little quinine.

Alex. Fraser,
Edinburgh, 21 January 1862. H. M. Consul.

ANNEX to REPORT on Cinchona Plantations in Java.

(Translation.)

MEMORANDUM of Instructions for the Official or Superintendent charged with the experiment of the cultivation of the Cinchona; for the Overseers employed in that culture, and the Rules of Administration to be observed therein.

Art. 1. The cultivation of the cinchona in Java is as yet considered as an experimental culture. The Governor General is to appoint the period at which the same shall come to be regarded as an ordinary Government culture (whether locally or generally), and when it shall therefore pass over to the ordinary management and direction of the chiefs of the provincial Government, under the Director of Cultures. So long as no declaration to this effect has been made this culture is to continue under the management and direction of a separate scientific functionary, appointed by the Governor General, whose income, official title, &c., are to be regulated on his appointment.

Art. 2. The success of the experiment of the cinchona cultivation, and, on its attainment, the preparation of the measures for its becoming one of the ordinary branches of the Government cultures, form the special duties of the superintendent. He is further, along with this, to make scientific and practical observations in respect of everything directly or indirectly connected with the cinchona culture.

Art. 3.

Art. 3. The superintendent of the cinchona culture will address to the Governor General all such proposals and reports as may appear to him to be advisable.

He will address to the Governor General:

a. At the end of every month, a report of the state of the experiment, of his own proceedings, and of the progress of the plantations, accompanied by a statement, showing the number and height of the cinchona trees in each plantation, and of the cuttings and young plants in the nurseries.

b. At the end of every year, a general report of the state of the experiment, and of the scientific and practical observations referred to in Art. 2.

The Report, and other returns before-mentioned, are to be addressed, under cover, to the Director of Cultures, who will send them forward to the Governor General, accompanied by his opinion upon them.

Art. 4. The superintendent will have the free use, without payment, of the Government post-horses, from the place of his own residence to the places where the cinchona experiment has been introduced, and the free use, at the expense of the Government, of the so-called district horses, and of other means of transport, where no posting establishment exists, and will visit these places as often as he shall consider advisable.

If he considers it necessary for the interests of the cinchona experiment to proceed elsewhere, he must apply for authority from the Governor-General, detailing his plans, and making known the nature of the assistance or co-operation on the part of the European and native Government servants which he expects to require.

The authority granted for this purpose by the Governor General will be considered, though not expressly mentioned, to extend to making use of steamers, or other opportunities by ship, of district horses, and other means of transport, at the public expense, and of the free use, without payment, of the Government post-horses.

Art. 5. The cinchona is not to be introduced into new districts without special authority to this effect from the Government. The decision pronounced on such proposal shall also regulate the outlay required for the first establishment, permanent staff, and necessary repairs.

Art. 6. The experimental cinchona culture, at the place where it is introduced, will be under the supervision of European overseers, who will be appointed to that office on the recommendation of the superintendent, and their income and further emoluments are to be regulated in the resolution by which they are appointed.

Art. 7. The European overseers are directly subordinate in the discharge of their duties to the superintendent, who has to furnish them with the necessary orders. They are responsible for the proper execution of these, and of all regulations published by the Government which have reference to the cinchona cultivation. Under their orders are placed the native overseers and labourers who are employed in the cinchona culture.

Art. 8. The experimental cinchona culture is to be carried on, if anyway possible, entirely by means of free labour.

To maintain and keep in repair the present establishments, nurseries and plantations, native overseers (mandores), and native labourers (boedgangs), are to be permanently employed on monthly allowances by the European overseers who shall, however, follow the orders of the superintendent regarding them.

For other extraordinary duties incident to the laying out of new plantations, such as the opening out of new ground, the clearing of the forest soil, the making of new fences, &c., extraordinary native overseers (mandores), and labourers (boedgangs) are to be employed.

The necessary materials should as much as possible, be procured by voluntary delivery or purchase from the population in the neighbourhood.

The monthly wages of the mandores and boedgangs, and the daily wages of the extraordinary mandores and coolies, are to be regulated according to the remuneration usually paid for free labour, regarding which the head local authority shall give a declaration to the superintendent, who, on his part, shall send in to the Government this declaration, along with his demand for authority for the outlay to be made, or approval of the outlay already made.

Art. 9. In case it should appear impossible to the European overseer to obtain free labourers, he shall give timely notice of this circumstance to the chief local authority, and apply for his interference to obtain them.

Should the chief local authority be also unable to obtain free labourers, he shall then proceed to call out the legal servitude of the native population. These forced labourers shall receive the same wages as are allowed to free labourers.

The chief local authority shall, in like manner, proceed to obtain the necessary materials from the population, paying them the prices already fixed for the same.

Art. 10. With a view to provide for such necessaries as cannot readily be obtained by the chief local authorities within their jurisdiction, and must therefore be imported from elsewhere, the superintendent shall make a demand in writing to the chief local authority once a year, about the month of September, of what he may expect to require during the following year, and, in that case, those necessaries shall be served out to the overseer at once, and he will then be responsible to the superintendent for the use of them. For articles to be ordered from Europe, the demand must be made at least a year beforehand.

 Art. 11.

Art. 11. The overseers must refrain frm arbitrary proceedings in the discharge of their duties in those cases which are provided for by the superintendent in general regulations or special orders.

They must strictly refrain from planting out young plants from the nurseries to the plantations in the forest, or from making changes in the existing plantations, without having received an express order to this effect from the superintendent.

Art. 12. The overseers have to take care that no forest trees are cut down or burnt in the vicinity of the cinchona plantations, and especially in parts or places indicated by the superintendent, and must immediately give notice thereof to the head of the local government and to the superintendent.

Art. 13. The overseers must try, by a considerate treatment of the natives with whom they come in contact, to incline them to provide voluntary labour and materials for behoof of the cinchona culture experiment.

Art. 14. The overseers, permanent mandores, and permanent boedgangs, must reside, as much as possible, in proximity to each other, at some place in the vicinity of the cinchona plantations which shall be pointed out by the superintendent. They must not absent themselves therefrom unnecessarily, to the prejudice of the interests entrusted to their care, and in no case at variance with orders received.

Art. 15. The overseers receive their salaries, and those of the permanent mandores and permanent boedgangs, once a month, at the end of the month, from the public treasury nearest to the place where they reside, on the presentation of a salary table made up by the overseer in duplicate.

If any part of the salary remain unpaid, in consequence of the discharge, or otherwise, of one of the native staff, this amount shall be deducted from the salary table of the following month, and so much less received.

Art. 16. The superintendent makes written demands, in duplicate, for extraordinary disbursements in the purchase of materials, which he sends to the overseer, and the local government can make advances successively on these demands, according to the requirements to be stated by the overseer, taking care, at the same time, not to exceed the amounts allotted by the Governor General for this purpose for each working year.

The superintendent takes care that this advance is adjusted once a year, in the account of disbursements made to labourers and for materials, which must be made up in duplicate by the overseer; and, after having been signed for, seen and approved, by the superintendent, shall be receivable at the public treasury.

Art. 17. The chief of the local governments will appoint a native official, who shall always be present at any labour performed by ordinary forced labourers, supplied by the government of that locality, and shall receive, at the charge of the account for extraordinary labour, the double day's wages of an extraordinary mandore. To this native official is entrusted the direction of the duties of the extraordinary labourers, according to the orders and directions of the overseer.

He requires to be always present at the daily payment of the extraordinary labourers, and of the materials delivered by order of the government, and to keep a note of them, which he shall send in at the end of each month, through the Regent, to the head of the local government.

The local government shall from time to time assure themselves of the proper financial administration of the overseers, by having their cash inspected, and balance in hand told, by a comptroller or other official, in connexion with the advances given in the above-mentioned monthly statements of payments made.

Art. 18. The overseers of the cinchona culture have to keep the following registers, according to forms to be fixed by the superintendent:—

1. A name payment-roll of the permanent mandores and boedgangs, in which must appear their names, the district or village in which they last resided, and where they come from, if they are married or single, the date of their entering into service, the date of their leaving service, the monthly wages paid, and the sum total; also the price of the victuals supplied.
2. A cash-book, in which all receipts and disbursements are stated.
3. An inventory-book, in which the implements in stock, received or written off, tools, utensils, or other materials; also nursery tubs, stores, cases, panes of glass, &c., are noted down.
4. A register of the cinchona plantations, in which the number and height of the cinchona trees in the plantations, and the number of the plants in the nurseries, are noted, the height of the plants being all measured on the 20th of each month, a measure for which will be supplied by the superintendent.

Art. 19. The overseer of the cinchona culture addresses to the superintendent, at the end of each month, according to the forms to be fixed by him:—

a. An extract from the cash-book.
b. A statement of the cinchona trees, and of the plants in the nurseries.
c. A report, regarding the state of the plantations and nurseries, of the principal duties performed, and other occurrences; and,
d. Every three months, an extract from the inventory-book.

—No. 119.—

CEYLON.—ROYAL BOTANIC GARDEN.

REPORT for 1861, by Mr. *Thwaites* (Director).

HORTICULTURAL DEPARTMENT.

CHINCHONA.—It gives me great pleasure to be able to report very satisfactorily upon the progress of the important experiment now being made in the island, in the cultivation of species of the valuable quinine-producing chinchonas. An experienced gardener has, as requested by the Government at my suggestion, been sent out by Sir William Hooker, from the establishment at Kew, and I have much reason to be satisfied with the zeal and intelligence shown by Mr. M'Nicoll in his charge of the plauts now under his care at the Hakgalle Garden near Newera Ellia.

The plants of chinchona which, in my last report, I mentioned as being expected from Bombay, arrived at the latter place in so unpromising a condition that it was thought best to have them all dispatched at once to the Neilgherries, instead of sending a portion, as was at first intended, for trial on our hills. Nearly all of these plants subsequently died. Another consignment of chinchona plants, collected by Mr. Spruce in South America, arrived some months afterwards at Bombay, in very good condition; but these were also all conveyed to Ootacamund, not any being reserved for Ceylon, as I was given to understand would be the case. As far, therefore, as regards Mr. Markham's mission to South America, we have received here no growing plants of chinchonas; but a parcel containing seeds of *Chinchona micrantha* and *Chinchona nitida*, collected by Mr. Pritchett, was sent to me in February last, from Mr. M'Ivor, through the Chief Secretary to Government, Fort St. George; and a parcel was received by me shortly afterwards from the Secretary of State's Office, which contained seeds of *Chinchona succirubra*, collected by Mr. Spruce. From these seeds more than 800 plants have been raised. (*C. succirubra*, 530; *C. micrantha*, 180; *C. Peruviana*, 25; *C. nitida*, 45; uncertain, 60;) which, although at present necessarily of small size, are nevertheless progressing very satisfactorily in the locality which has been selected for them.

From Mr. William Ferguson have been received a few chinchona seeds, which he obtained from a friend at Lima; but these have unfortunately not germinated, and they were probably not in a sufficiently fresh state for doing so.

To Sir William Hooker we have been indebted for the transmission to us, at different times, from the collection at Kew, of six plants of the very valuable *Chinchona Calisaya*: the greater number of these, however, suffered so much in their transit, that two only of those kindly taken charge of for me by Dr. Anderson of the Calcutta Botanic Gardens, arrived here in a healthy state. They are now planted out in the Hakgalle Garden, and are growing vigorously. Mr. M'Nicoll has, without risk of delaying the period of flowering, succeeded in obtaining from one of them eight cuttings, two of which have produced roots, and he has every reason to anticipate success with the remainder.

During the present month, I have received from Dr. J. Anderson, a portion of a supply of chinchona seeds, communicated by the Government of Java to that of India, but from what species they were collected has not been stated. These have been sown at the Hakgalle Garden, and a very few of them here; they have, however, not yet been in the ground sufficiently long a time to germinate.

From the experience we have had of the species of chinchona now growing in the island, I think it may be considered certain that *C. Calisaya* would not be likely to succeed at an elevation much below that of Hakgalle, and that it should be planted above 5,000 feet. *C. succirubra* grows extremely well at Hakgalle; but as it also grows tolerably well at Peradenia, with the appearance only of being a little too much forced by the heat, I think it might succeed probably at any elevation above 3,500 or 4,000 feet. *C. micrantha*, judging from one little plant we have retained at Peradenia, appears to thrive quite as well here, as at Hakgalle: it will, however, have to be ascertained bye-and-bye at what elevations

 respectively

respectively this and the other species will produce the largest relative quantity of quinine.

As I have reason to believe that many gentlemen engaged in coffee-planting would be glad to co-operate in trying experiments in the cultivation of the chinchonas at different elevations upon their estates, it may possibly be considered desirable to distribute, some short time hence, under conditions to be determined upon, a few plants of those raised at Hakgalle. This course of action might probably lead to a more extensive cultivation of chinchona in the island, than the Government would feel disposed itself to undertake, though it would be no doubt desirable for the present experiment to be carried on with every possible activity and carefulness, until the cultivation should be well understood, and it could be fairly given over to private speculation.

— No. 120. —

Royal Botanic Garden.

Report for 1862, by Mr. *Thwaites* (Director).

Horticultural Department.

Chinchona.—The experiment in the cultivation of some of the quinine-producing cinchonas is proceeding most favourably, and the progress made may be considered extremely satisfactory, taking into consideration the limited supply of seeds we received to commence with. Mr. M'Nicoll has been very successful in the management of the plants under his care at Hakgalle. Several of the larger ones have been planted in the forest, and are flourishing vigorously, and preparations are now being made for many more being put out. Open spaces of a moderate area are being cleared in the forest, in order that the plants may have plenty of light, and yet be sufficiently protected by the surrounding trees from too much wind, which the chinchona plants are not able to bear without injury, owing to the large size and not very firm texture of their leaves. Much care is required in these arrangements; for the chinchona plants become drawn up and weak when in dense shade; whilst, if exposed to plenty of light, with direct sun light upon them for a few hours during the day, they assume a most healthy and robust appearance, with stems of a deep red colour, and leaves of a much firmer texture. A certain number of the plants, placed in very favourable situations for shelter from the wind, are being allowed to grow up to their full height, with the view of their producing flowers and seed; but as it will probably be only after the expiration of some few years that this will occur, and as it is desirable, in order to be prepared for an early distribution, to increase the number of our plants as rapidly as possible, Mr. M'Nicoll is effecting the latter object by striking cuttings from a considerable number of plants which he has reserved for the purpose. Large cuttings of *C. succirubra* would appear to strike readily in the open ground; but of large cuttings we can of course get only a few at present, owing to our plants being all young. Smaller cuttings are struck in a hotbed, and roots are produced upon them in a fortnight or three weeks. After as many cuttings have been taken from the reserved plants as these will at one time yield, some interval must necessarily elapse before other shoots are produced of suitable size for removal for the next lot of cuttings. Mr. M'Nicoll will have, before many days, nearly 600 plants of *C. succirubra* struck from cuttings, and he anticipates that this number will be very considerably added to in a few weeks. Many of these plants will probably be sufficiently established in growth to bear removal in three or four months, should it be deemed desirable by Government to commence their distribution so soon—on a small scale, of course, at first. It may be thought advisable to allow applicants to have, at a price to be determined upon, a few, say, four or five plants, to enable them to ascertain the suitableness or otherwise of localities they may have selected for the cultivation of this valuable plant. Some plants of *C. succirubra* received from the establishment at Kew during the past year, and which arrived in not very strong condition, I have deemed it desirable

sirable to keep at Peradenia, for propagation from by cuttings. Of 150 which were despatched from Kew 110 survived, and are now growing well here. From these, and from a few plants we raised from seed, Mr. Cameron has, by means of a hot-bed he has constructed here, succeeded in striking a good many cuttings which will be useful by-and-by for distribution in districts contiguous to this.

Although the climate of Peradenia is not so favourable for *C. succirubra* as is that of Hakgalle, some plants of it growing in the open ground here are, nevertheless, doing very well; and we find that, even at this low elevation, they thrive best when well exposed to the light, with the sun upon them for an hour or two during the day. Exposure to the sun for the whole of the day is more than they can bear without injury.

Of *Chinchona Condaminea*, a small supply of most excellent seeds was received a few months ago from Mr. Clements R. Markham. From these a number of young plants have been raised by Mr. M'Nicoll, and are in a thriving condition at Hakgalle. The climate of Peradenia is much too hot for this valuable species.

C. Calisaya has not succeeded so well with us as have the other kinds we h av under cultivation, owing, I believe, to the plants, which were all received from Kew, having been injuriously affected by the long voyage from England. I am expecting a number of plants of this desirable kind from Java; Mr. Van Spall, of the Civil Service of that island, who visited Ceylon a short time ago, having kindly interested himself in the matter, and obtained the sanction of the Javan Government for the transmission of some plants of *C. Calisaya* to this establishment.

The following is a list of the chinchona plants under cultivation at Hakgalle:—

C. succirubra,	planted out in the forest - - - - - - - - - -	194
	The largest plant being just four feet high, with a stem $1\frac{1}{4}$ inches in diameter, and leaves 18 inches long by 12 inches wide.	
Ditto -	in pots, to be planted out as soon as spaces have been cleared in the forest for their reception - - - - - - - -	338
Ditto -	in pots, struck from cuttings - - - - - - - -	395
Ditto -	cuttings not yet quite rooted - - - - - - - -	200
C. Condaminea,	in pots - - - - - - - - - - - -	960
C. crispella,	in pots - - - - - - - - - - - -	24
C. Calisaya,	in pots - - - - - - - - - - - -	2
C Pahudiana,	in pots - - - - - - - - - - - -	4

The following plants, raised from seeds sent to me under the several names appended to them, are at present quite undistinguishable by their foliage:—

C. micrantha,	planted out in the forest - - - - - - - - -	43
Ditto -	in pots - - - - - - - - - - - - -	130
C. micrantha provinciana.	planted out in the forest - - - - - - - -	18
Ditto -	in pots - - - - - - - - - - - - -	6
C. nitida,	planted out in the forest - - - - - - - - -	15
Ditto -	in pots - - - - - - - - - - - - -	40
Cinchona sp.	planted out in the forest - - - - - - - - -	34
Ditto -	in pots - - - - - - - - - - - - -	31

The following is a list of the cinchona plants at Peradenia:—

C. succirubra,	planted out in the grounds - - - - - - - -	36
Ditto -	in pots (including the plants received from Kew) - - - - -	114
Ditto -	in pots, struck from cuttings - - - - - - - -	143
Ditto -	cuttings not yet quite rooted - - - - - - - - -	118

C. micrantha, which, when in a young state appeared to thrive well at Peradenia, put on subsequently an unhealthy weak appearance, and the few plants we had here have been sent to Hakgalle.

— No. 121. —

Sir, Foreign Office, 27 March 1862.

With reference to your letter of the 12th instant, I am directed by Earl Russell to transmit to you a copy of a letter which has been addressed to Her Majesty's Ambassador at Paris by Monsieur Thouvenel, stating that the Governor General of Algeria would be glad to be furnished with some chinchona plants, with

with the view of endeavouring to acclimatise them in that colony, and I am to request that, in laying this letter before Secretary Sir Charles Wood, you will move him to cause Lord Russell to be informed whether this request can be complied with.

I am, &c.
(signed) *E. Hammond.*

Herman Merivale, Esq.
&c. &c. &c.

Enclosure 1, in No. 121.

M. l'Ambassadeur, Paris, le 22 Mars, 1862.

J'ai eu l'honneur d'écrire à V. E. le 6 Février dernier et le 10 de ce mois pour l'informer que le Muséum d'Histoire Naturelle et la Société Impériale d'Acclimatation acceptaient avec empressement quelques uns des pieds de cinchona que l'India Office a bien voulu offrir de mettre à la disposition du Gouvernement de l'Empereur.

Le Gouverneur Général de l'Algérie, à qui j'avais également fait connaitre cette obligeante proposition, vient de m'informer que la culture du cinchona pourant être tentées avec quelques chances de succès sur plusieurs points de la Colonie, il recevrait avec reconnaissance un certain nombre d'exemplaires de ce végétal.

Je me plais à espérer, M. l'Ambassadeur, qu'il sera possible à l'India Office de satisfaire encore à cette nouvelle demande.

Agréez, &c.
(signé) *Thouvenel.*

S. E. le Comte Cowley.

Enclosure 2, in No. 121.

From *Herman Merivale*, Esq., C.B., to the Under Secretary of State for Foreign Affairs.

Sir, India Office, 29 March 1862.

I am directed by the Secretary of State for India in Council to acquaint you that, in compliance with the request from M. Thouvenel, forwarded with your letter of the 27th instant, Sir William Hooker has been instructed to reserve 200 or 300 plants of the chinchona for transmission to Algeria, at a proper season. I am also to inform you that as the arrangements with the authorities at the Royal Botanical Gardens at Kew terminate this day, Sir William Hooker has been referred to your department with regard to any expense incurred on account of these plants after the 31st instant.

I have, &c.
(signed) *Herman Merivale.*

Enclosure 3, in No. 121.

From *Herman Merivale*, Esq., C.B., to Sir *William Hooker*.

Sir, India Office, 28 March 1862.

The Secretary of State for India in Council having received an application through Earl Russell from the French Government, for a supply of chinchona plants for transmission to Algeria, I am to request that you will reserve 200 or 300 plants for transmission to that destination. You will be informed in a few days with whom you should communicate on this subject, and I am to refer you to the Foreign Office for the liquidation of any expenses which may arise under this head.

I am also directed to inform you that it has been resolved by the Secretary of State in Council, in consequence of the success which has attended the cultivation of the chinchona plant in the Government gardens at Ootacamund, to discontinue the auxiliary establishment under your charge in the Royal Gardens at Kew, and that the time has arrived when your account with this office may be closed. It will therefore rest with you to determine respecting the disposal of the plants under your charge, after having allotted those required for the French Government.

I am to take this opportunity of expressing the thanks of the Secretary of State for India in Council for the ready and able assistance which has been afforded by yourself and your subordinates on every occasion when it was required to promote the success of this important experiment, which has now been initiated in several quarters of Her Majesty's dominions.

I have, &c.
(signed) *Herman Merivale.*

CPSIA information can be obtained
at www.ICGtesting.com
Printed in the USA
LVHW100444110522
718424LV00003B/220

9 783375 006518